THE ACCIDENTAL WIFE

A novel by

Shayla Hart

"THE COURSE OF TRUE LOVE NEVER DID RUN SMOOTH."

-William Shakespeare.

COPYRIGHT

ISBN: 9798577065010

ACKNOWLEDGEMENTS & DEDICATIONS

I want to say a big thank you to my family first, my kids, especially for sacrificing their time with me so I could finish working on this book. Then I would like to thank my supporters and friends for all the love and encouragement they showed me and this book. Thank you for believing in me; you mean the world to me.

A very special thank you to ***Sylwia Umelo*** for all her help editing this book.

I love you!

I want to dedicate this book to all my supporters, you all helped make this book happen, and I appreciate each, and every one of you.

Lots of love,

Shayla Hart x

Chapter One

SHAYLA

"Miss Hart?"

I blink and lift my gaze to the elder man sitting in front of me, staring at me, patiently waiting for me to answer his question. I study his appearance, grey hair, but not completely white. He has streaks of a darker shade running through the strands—his eyes a startling green, cool and glorious. For an older gentleman, he was handsome. He's sporting a stubble of a greying beard. He was a silver fox in every sense of the word. I shift in my seat and cross my legs, sitting upright, hopeful this will give him the impression that I am confident and accomplished.

"I believe my greatest quality is that I'm headstrong. While some may consider this a flaw, it just means I never give up. However difficult the task at hand may be. Once I put my mind to something, I won't stop until I achieve it." I say confidently, looking him directly in the eyes. He nods slowly, holding my gaze for a beat before he leans forward, and his full lips quirk ever so slightly.

"I like that answer. All I have heard all day is that they are confident, ambitious, and trustworthy." He says and leans back in his chair, dropping his pen on his desk. "I like you, Miss Hart. Are you able to start Monday?"

I resist the urge to squeal and press my lips together. I smile politely. You can freak out when you leave Shay. Keep it together! "Yes, sir."

"Excellent. Come in on Monday morning at nine o'clock sharp, and Heather will show you around and get you on the system." He says, rising from his chair and holding out his hand. I stand and take his offered hand, squeezing it gently.

"Thank you so much. I appreciate this opportunity, Mr Hoult." I tell him, picking up my handbag. He escorts me to the glass door to his office.

"Welcome to the team, Miss Hart." I smile up at him politely, thank him and leave his office. Once outside, I heave a sigh of relief. I got the job. I will be working for the most prestigious architectural firms in the world. Granted, as an executive assistant to the CEO, but still. I will work my arse off, learn everything I can from him, and finish my degree. One day, I can show them I have the talent and skill to be an architect at one of their firms.

After a crappy couple of months, things are finally starting to look up for me. Having to drop out of university, unable to afford the tuition fees and provide for my brother and mother has been challenging. I had to put my career on the back burner and take care of my family. We lost my father just after my sixteenth birthday to a traffic accident eleven years ago now, and I have been the sole provider for them since. I have an older brother, Sam, but he's unable to hold down a job for longer than a couple of months due to his ADHD and anger management. He does try, but he's unable to concentrate for long, which often results in poor performance. My mother hasn't left the house since my father died. He was the love of her life, and when we lost him, we lost a massive part of my mother too. She's terrified to leave the house and hasn't been able to face the world without him.

I have a good feeling. My life was finally about to get a little easier.

I rush up the stairs to the apartment that I share with my two best friends Jo Sinclair and Aimee O'Connor. They're my lifeline, and I'm so happy I have them in my life. The moment I slide the key into the lock, the door is practically ripped open, and they both stand there, hair in messy buns on top of their heads, both in oversized sweatshirts staring at me expectantly with wide eyes.

"Well?" They say in unison.

"What?" I question, looking between them. I know they've been dying to find out how my interview went if the fifteen voicemails and fifty texts I got earlier was any indication.

"Bitch, how did the interview go?" Aimee utters after she swallows her mouthful of lucky charms.

"It went well," I reply, trying to walk in, but they both block my way.

"More…" Jo drawls, narrowing her honey-coloured orbs at me in scrutiny. I huff and shrug my shoulders.

"Well, he seemed interested, but there were so many more suitable applicants there with more experience, so…" I watch as both their faces fall, and I fight the urge to smile.

"Oh, well, it's their loss because you're amazing, bish," Jo says, wrapping an arm around my shoulder and guiding me into our apartment. "Something else will come up. I know it." She adds positively, like the good friend she is. I look around our cosy apartment. Three decent sized bedrooms. An open plan lounge, with a small kitchen to the left, and a decent-sized bathroom with a walk-in shower. Our apartment, conveniently based in the city of London, wasn't flashy by any means, but near enough everywhere was ten-fifteen minutes away by train. I loved it, and I love living with my girls. If I didn't get this job, I would have had to move back home with my mother and brother, and I didn't want that. My mother and brother are the only family I have. My parents brought me up in a strict household. They were very proud people, they valued traditions, respect, and culture above anything else, and they instilled those qualities into Sammy and me growing up.

"Yeah. I guess you won't have to find another tenant to move into my room after all." I tell them as I take my jacket off and drop it on the sofa.

"Don't talk like that. Something will come—wait, did you say *won't* have to?" Aimee mumbles, setting her bowl down. I smile, and their eyes go wide like saucers. "You got it. You got—YOU GOT THE JOB?!" I nod, they both scream and launch themselves at me, and we all tumble onto the sofa in a heap of arms and legs.

"I got the job! You're stuck with me bitches!" I laugh when they both poke my sides tickling me until I'm crying with laughter.

Jo hops up onto her feet, "We're going out tonight to celebrate. I don't want to hear excuses. We're going!" She says, running down the corridor toward her bedroom with her sock-clad feet sliding along the wooden floor. Aimee follows her, and I stay lying on the sofa, staring up at the plain white ceiling. The knot I have had in my stomach for months finally vanished.

"Bish, get your juicy arse off that sofa. We're going to get smashed!" I hear Jo call out from her bedroom. Laughing, I get up from the sofa and come face to face with Aimee, who steps out of her bedroom. We both look at the bathroom door and back at each other before we make a run to it. I bump Aimee out of my way with my hip before I slide into the bathroom and close the door swiftly. I laugh when I hear her curse on the other side of the door.

"Every fucking time!"

"I do have longer legs than you, Aimes." I tease while I strip off for the shower.

"Yes, and I hate you for it. Hurry up, and don't forget to shave your hooch. You never know what the night might bring." She sniggers, and I roll my eyes and grin as I step in the shower. "It's about time you dust off those cobwebs and get some action, girl."

"You know damn well that my hooch is waxed clean, and I'm quite content with my 'cobwebs' thank you very much." I pick up an empty shampoo bottle and throw it against the door when I hear her cackling on the other side. "Get lost. Let me shower in peace."

Many hours, three bottles of prosecco later, we roll into a bar called 'Luxe' in central London. The girls forced me into wearing a red mini dress that hugs my natural curves nicely. My long dark hair curled loosely and left out. Jo and Aimee were also in dresses. Aimee chose a silver sequin dress that showed off her natural d-cup breasts, while Jo was in a strapless white bodycon dress. The atmosphere was something else, music playing at a loud volume, the bass of the song playing was vibrating through my entire body. We head over to the bar and order a round of tequila shots, and then another, followed by four more rounds of pornstar martinis. Jo kept her promise of getting us smashed for sure.

While I'm dancing with Jo, my eyes caught a pair of attractive yet startlingly vivid green eyes watching me. Damn. He was the most beautiful man I have ever seen. His gaze on me was intense while he sips the amber liquid in his glass. He and his friend had girls swarming around them. I see a leggy blonde sitting beside him lean over and whisper something in his ear, his eyes narrow however they were still on me. Tearing my eyes away from his, I turn and continue dancing with Jo.

Aimee came over to us with three shots of green apple sours. "Drink up, Bish!" We clink our glasses and take the shots. I wince when the liquid burns my inside. Justin Bieber's 'Despacito' starts thundering through the speakers. I laughed hard at Jo whispering something in my ear when I back up against something warm and firm. Jo's eyes went wide when she saw whoever it was behind me. I give her a wary look, and she presses her lips together and smiles, backing away.

"Dance with me." I hear a deep voice burr in my ear. I look back and see it was the guy watching me from the VIP section. My god, he's even more beautiful up close, and his eyes are so green, clever and curious, glittering like two emeralds, like every hue of the forest. Their brightness reminded me of summertime. I turn and face him, craning my neck to look up at him. He's tall, well over six-foot, light brown hair, cut short on the sides and longer on the top, styled perfectly. My fingers itched to reach out and touch it to see if it was as soft as it seemed. His features were strong, chiselled, and so very masculine.

"Was that a demand or a request?" I reply, narrowing my eyes at him. His soft, full lips curl up into a smirk.

He licks his lips slowly, "Whichever one gets you to dance with me." He drawls confidently. Someone was trying to pass by him, so he takes a step closer to me.

I lift my eyes and smile at the handsome stranger whose strong arms lock around my waist, drawing me against him. We sway together to the music. His movement matched mine, and we move together smoothly. He could dance. I liked that. He bows his head, and his lips brush against the shell of my ear as he speaks lowly, and I visibly quiver at the roguish tone of his voice.

"What's your name, sweetheart?"

"Shayla. Yours?" I ask, and I could swear a look of surprise flashed across his handsome face before he grins sexily, and two deep dimples form on his cheeks making me swoon.

He has dimples! Two of them!

"Cole." I smile up at him, and he drags his tongue along his bottom lip and squints his eyes a little while he looks over my face. We dance together, heatedly, for a while. Grinding, hands exploring. The heat between us was immense, the way his hands wander over my body, squeezing, caressing. Everything else fizzles away like it was just the two of us. His eyes were staring into mine fixedly.

"Hungry?"

I laugh and nod, "Starving." He smiles and brushes a strand of my hair stuck to my sweaty face and tucks it delicately behind my ear.

"How about we go someplace and get something to eat?" I nod without hesitation, and he grins, taking my hand in his larger one, he pulls me through the crowd of people. I manage to catch Jo on my way out and gesture to her that I was leaving. She waves me off with a thumbs up. The girl was more smashed than I was.

We finally walk outside, and my head spins when fresh air hits me. Cole wraps his arm around my waist, steadying me. I follow him as we both stumble toward a Silver Rolls Royce Phantom. A driver, an older gentleman, opens the door, and Cole places his hand on the small of my back and guides me in. I sink into the plush white leather seats once I slide over as Cole gets in beside me. "Wow. This car is bigger than my apartment." I state with a drunken giggle as Cole pours us two glasses of champagne.

"What's your stance on sushi? I know a great place." I blink up at him, and he smiles at me charmingly.

"Sushi?" I wrinkle my nose in distaste. "Who in their right mind eats sushi when they're drunk?" Cole laughs heartily. "Listen, I love sushi as much as the next person, but I'm not one of those girls who eat pretentious crap like caviar and sips Cristal. I can't think of anything worse, *especially* right now." I lean over and tap the driver on his shoulder. He glances back at me through his rear-view mirror. "Take us to Old Street, please, good sir." He chuckles and nods his head.

"Yes, ma'am."

I giggle, "Ma'am?" What am I fifty?

Cole tugs me back and shifts so he could face me properly. "What's in Old Street?" I grin at him impishly and finish off my drink.

"The best food ever! No offence, but you strike me as one of those stuffy rich kids that think a good night out is sipping on Don Perignon and chewing on fish babies. I'm going to show you a night you'll remember when you're sitting in your rocking chair at eighty years old, Mr Cole."

Cole chuckles and bites his lip, his green eyes alight with glee. "Oh? And will you be sitting beside me in that rocking chair?" He drawls, brushing his thumb along my jaw.

"That depends..." I whisper, smiling as he runs his fingers through my hair.

"On what?" He whispers back, his eyes flickering down to my lips before they meet mine again.

"You'll have to marry me to find out." I tease, and he laughs before he draws my lips to his and kisses me softly. I moan when his tongue runs along my bottom lip silently requesting access, which I joyfully grant him, parting my lips, he seeks out my tongue and expertly deepens the kiss. If my mind was hazy before, it's turned to complete mush after his kiss. As far as first kisses go, this was by far the top of my list.

We spent the better half of the car journey kissing until his driver alerted us that we had arrived at our destination. "What is this place?" He asks as I pull him to the entrance of 'The Breakfast Bar.'

"Oh, you poor, poor child. You haven't lived until you've had their pancakes." I say as we sit down, and he looks at the menu. I pluck the menu out of his hands, and he looks at me bemused. "You don't need that," I tell him, and he smiles and shakes his head. "We'll have the sharers stack of pancakes, please, and two salted caramel lattes," I order, and the girl smiles before taking the menus and disappearing.

Twenty minutes later, Cole licks his fork clean and slumps back in his chair with a delightful groan. "My god, that was heaven on a plate." I nod triumphally, chewing on my last bite of pancakes.

"Mm, I know, right." I moan, licking the cream off my finger. "You can thank me later," I say with a wink, and Cole grins, reaching over he takes my right hand in his and gazes into my eyes for a long moment.

"You are the polar opposite to what I'm used to, but I don't remember having this much fun with someone I just met. Ever." He affirms, stroking his fingers over my knuckles gently. I feel my cheeks burn under his gaze and avert my eyes to my cup of coffee.

The rest of the night went by in a blur. We had a couple more cocktails with shots before we somehow wound up on a private airstrip. We clamber out of a private jet, laughing hard. We'd been playing a drinking game the entire flight, which wasn't a good idea. "Vegas, baby!" I slur, throwing my hands up in the air and almost toppling over. I look around the dark airstrip and pout. "Wait. There's no chapel here?"

I hear Cole laugh behind me before he wraps his arm around my neck from behind and kisses my cheek. "We can't land in the middle of the Vegas strip, sweetheart," He murmurs drunkenly. "We need to drive there."

I giggle, "Hokay! Driver! Take us to Evlis to be wed." Cole and I fall into the back of the black limo, and we head to the Las Vegas strip. I think we gambled for a while, drank delicious cocktails, and the last thing I remember was Cole carrying me out of a chapel, kissing like two lust-crazed adolescents.

~

MANY HOURS LATER, I stir in my sleep with the blinding sunlight shining in my face. I groan and roll over, burying my face in the plush pillows. 'Mm so soft' I snuggle into the pillows further until I suddenly remember I don't have plush soft pillows. My pillow is hard and lumpy. I peel my eyes open and groan at the sudden ache in my head.

'Ow, water…I need water and possibly a new brain.'

I force my eyes open and blink, looking up to the ceiling, I frown when I see a reflection of myself staring back at me in the bed, naked, wrapped in the sheets.

'What on God's green earth…' I sit up in the bed when I take in my surroundings, and it finally hits me. I'm not in my bedroom. I'm naked in a strange place with a hangover I'm sure is about to put me into an early grave. I lift the bedsheet and stare down at my very naked body under it. *'Yep, definitely naked.'* I groan and cover my face with my hand and

freeze when I feel something cold and hard pressed against my nose. I pull my hand back slowly and stare at the enormous diamond ring sitting on my finger.

'What the fuck...' I wrap the sheet around my body as I clamber out of bed and take in the clothes scattered haphazardly all over the room. "Oh my god, where the hell am I?" I pick up the black shirt off the floor and look at it before dropping it again. I walk over to the window and look out at the view shielding my eyes from the brightness of the early sun. "This isn't London."

"Good Morning." I squeal and spin around when I hear a deep voice behind me. I look at the half-naked man standing before me in a pair of Dior boxers. I wrap the sheet around me tighter as I throw myself back up against the window. "You're finally up."

"Who are you?" I ask him warily, and he winces, rubbing his forehead. He looks as rough as I felt, although a beautiful man. Amidst my mini panic attack, I was trying desperately not to think about how God awful I must look to him right now. My hair was a tousled mess, and my make up from the night before smeared, eyes rimmed red, lips still tinted red from the lipstick I wore.

"I'm Cole."

"Where the hell are we?"

"Vegas, I believe..."

Chapter Two

COLE

Oh, sweet Jesus.

The ache in my head rouses me from my very peaceful slumber—that and the smell of coconut and something rather exotic. What is that? Passion fruit? I shift to roll onto my side and frown when I feel a heaviness on my chest. I force my eyes open and wince from the sheer brightness of the sun beaming on my face. I glance down at the head of silky brown hair and get another waft of the coconut, passion fruit concoction. It's her. I shift my head to the side and study the face of the girl currently sprawled across my chest. Not bad. I've woken up with worse. Her lips soft and pink, long dark lashes, perfectly shaped eyebrows.

What the hell happened last night? I can't remember a damn thing. Who is this girl? I peel her arm away from my chest gently, detangle our legs, and she moans as I roll her off me, and she snuggles into the pillow with a sigh. I let my eyes wander over her naked body, half wrapped in the sheets while she's sprawled out on her front, her long dark hair splayed out on the pillow. I take a closer look at her face and frown. Nope, don't remember a fucking thing. Complete blackout. I look around the room. Our clothes littered haphazardly on the marble floor. Where the fuck are we? I pull my boxers on and walk over to the window. Why does the view look so familiar? Wait. Am I in fucking

Vegas? I rub my hands over my face and look at the scenery ahead once again. Oh yeah, I'm in Vegas all right. I pick up my jeans off the floor and stuff my hands in the pockets, hoping I'll find some clue of what the hell went down. I pull out a piece of paper from my back pocket along with my passport and unfold it. It's damp— come to think of it, so are my jeans.

'Marriage Certificate.'

I stare at the words blankly for a long moment. *No fucking way*. I did not go and get married to a random girl. I read the rest of the document and curse. *Oh fuck.*

'Marriage of Tristan Cole Hoult and Shayla Hart.'

If the certificate wasn't enough proof, I had a gold wedding band on my finger. I lean closer and look at the girl in the bed, and she's also wearing a diamond ring on her finger. We got married. We flew to Vegas and got *married.*

"Fuck." I find my phone on the table by the bed and walk out of the room. I have to call my lawyer. I'm hoping—no *praying*—that this marriage wasn't legal.

"Mr Hoult? How can I help you?" Franc—my lawyer's sleepy voice came from the other end. Of course, time difference, it's probably early hours there.

"Franc, apologies for waking you. Is a drunken marriage in Vegas legally binding?"

"Do you have a wedding certificate?" He responds. I snap a photo of the certificate and send it to him.

"I've just sent you a photo. Take a look."

I hear him fumble with his phone on the other end. "Yes. It's legal, Mr Hoult." He confirms. My heart sinks to the pit of my stomach. I stare at the certificate in my hand and sigh.

"Jesus Christ. I don't remember a damn thing. We were so drunk. Surely there is a legal loophole to get me out of this?"

"I'll look into it. We'll get the marriage annulled on the grounds of you both being intoxicated." He says, and I nod, pacing back and forth.

"Great. Keep me updated." I respond and end the call. What the fuck were you thinking marrying a girl you don't even know, you absolute idiot. This is so unlike me. I don't drink this much. Ever. Hell, I don't even go out. My life is all about work, and when I do have time to blow off some steam, I have a couple of glasses of scotch, then leave with whatever girl catches my attention that night. No, this is reckless and irresponsible, two things I most definitely am not. I've never gotten so intoxicated that I blackout and have no memory.

I turn around when I hear footsteps in the other room. I see Shayla wandering around the penthouse's dining area, with a sheet wrapped around her body. A look of horror on her face as she tries to work out her surroundings. The first thing I notice about her was her eyes—a darker shade than my own. Almost olive green, lined with long dark lashes, not the fake kind girls wear, no, hers were natural. Her hair shiny and long, cascading down her back in loose beach waves, albeit tousled from a night of wild sex.

I come up behind her and lean against the doorframe as she looks out the floor to ceiling window. "Good morning." I greet, and she jumps startled, lets out an adorable little squeak, and turns to face me. Her eyes wide and confused, they rake over my topless torso and back up to my face again. "You're finally awake."

"Who are you?" She asks, backing up against the window. I sip my coffee and lick my lips. My head was still thumping unpleasantly and judging by the way she was rubbing her head. I'm going to assume she wasn't feeling much better.

"I'm Cole." I introduce myself, and she blinks up at me when I walk over to her. She averts her gaze from mine, wrapping her arms around herself as if to shield away from my prying eyes, her fingers gripping the sheet tightly.

"Um, where are we?" She questions, glancing around the penthouse.

"Vegas, I believe."

Shayla's eyes go wide as she stares at me, unblinking for a good minute. She shakes her head and frowns deeply.

"Vegas?" She intones incredulously, and I nod my head in response. "How the hell did we end up in Vegas?"

I shrug, "Beats me. I can't recall a damn thing about last night. The only thing I remember was leaving the club with a girl. After that, it's a blank. Do you remember anything?"

Shayla shakes her head, "No, I don't remember a thing. I was ludicrously drunk. I don't recall ever meeting you." She explains, chewing her lip nervously. She drops her gaze from mine and brushes her slender fingers through her soft hair. "Um, why am I wearing a ring?"

I rub the back of my neck, and I hold up my hand and show her the wedding band on my finger. Her face falls. She looks down at the ring on her finger and then up at me again. "Tell me we didn't. Did we get *married*? How the hell did this happen? How did we go from a club in central London to getting married in Las Vegas?!"

I groan when my head suddenly aches at the loud tone of her voice. "Easy with the volume, sweetheart. My head is still thumping." I sigh, massaging my temples. "I don't know how this happened, okay? I didn't exactly plan to get in a drunken stupor and marry some stranger I met in a club."

Shayla scowls at me, "Oh, and I did? No offence, but you're not exactly my type." It was my turn to glare at her. Is this girl for real? She doesn't have any idea who I am. I've not met a girl whose type I've not been.

"Oh, is that right? I sure as hell seemed like your type last night." I point out, and her eyes narrow to slits, and she takes a step toward me.

"You…you said you didn't remember anything." She says, pointing a finger in my face. I look at her finger and back at her again and roll my eyes.

"I don't. But the state of the room when I woke up this morning was a clear indication of a good night," I take a step closer to her, and she cranes her neck to look up at me. "There was a trail of clothes from the door to the bed, which means we were completely lost in our passion to not give a damn about anyone's type," I state matter-of-factly and wink at her. "Not to mention you're sporting my signature 'fucked out' look."

Shayla's green eyes grow wide. She huffs and takes a big step back, putting some space between us while raking her fingers through her hair, clearly frustrated.

"Wow. I'm not even going to dignify that remark with a response." She sighs, stops pacing, and looks at me again. "What are we doing to do? Is this marriage even legal?"

"I'm afraid so." Her shoulders slump, and she shakes her head.

"Surely they can't marry us when we were that drunk?" She questions, glaring at me. I shrug and set my cup of coffee down, and take the marriage certificate off the table.

"Anything can happen in Vegas. Here, I found this in my pocket this morning." She takes the paper from me and unfolds it.

"What is this?"

"Our marriage certificate. Signed by us both *haphazardly* but still signed nonetheless." I tell her, and she reads through the document before she looks at me.

"Oh my God, we're *actually* married." She mumbles, leaning against the dining table. I sigh and rub the back of my neck awkwardly. She looks distraught, just staring at the floor, and I don't do well with consoling girls who are upset. I get uncomfortable and clam up.

"Hey, look, it's not the end of the world. We'll get an annulment or a divorce, and we'll go on with our lives like this never happened." I assure her. She lifts her gaze to look at me, and I swear the sadness in her eyes sent a tremor through me.

She nods eventually and straightens, "Yeah, I suppose you're right," She sighs and looks around the room in bewilderment, then frowns a little, scratching her head awkwardly. "Uh," She chews her bottom lip a little. "I can't find my dress…" I let my eyes roam around the room. "I also need to figure out how the hell I'm going to get back home."

"Oh, I've sorted that. Our flight to London leaves in two hours." I inform her, and she nods. "I've also arranged some clothes to be delivered for both of us. You look about a size ten. Coffee?" I offer. She stares at me, her mouth agape, and nods before she sits on a chair at the dining table. I pour her a black coffee and set it down on the table in front of her.

She continues to stare at me, her brows knitted together. "Thank you. You didn't have to do that. Please let me know how much I owe you, and

I'll pay you back." She lifts the mug to her lips and takes a long sip, closes her eyes, and sighs. Yeah, that first sip of coffee when you're hungover is like heaven. I hadn't noticed I was staring at her until she looks up at me and frowns.

I shake my head and shrug. "Don't worry about it. It's no problem. I'm sure you'd like to shower and freshen up. I didn't order breakfast because I wasn't sure what you would like to eat." I tell her and disappear into the bathroom. "Why don't you go ahead and order us some room service?" I suggest while she blinks and hesitantly nods.

AFTER A LONG, well-needed shower, and a couple of business calls, Shayla and I ate breakfast to soak up the alcohol we consumed the night before. My stomach felt queasy, and the avocado toast I had helped settle it. Shayla showered and dressed in the clothes I had arranged for her. She came out of the bathroom looking refreshed in a pair of tight-fit light blue jeans and a low-cut black tee. We left the hotel and made our way to the airport. Shayla gets out of the car as we pull up at my private jet and stares up at it bewildered. "This is yours?" She questions as we walk over to it.

"Sure is, sweetheart," I tell her and gesture for her to walk up the steps. I honestly cannot wait to get back home. I feel rough, and I have so much work I need to catch up on. I slide into a seat on the plane and watch as Shayla wanders around. She seems apprehensive, and I find myself wondering if she's a nervous flyer. "Do you plan on standing there the entire ten hours of the flight? Take a seat. I won't bite unless you ask." I tease, and she shakes her head, mumbling something under her breath while she hesitantly slides into the seat next to me, staring out of the window, her fingers fumbling in her lap while she nervously chews on her bottom lip.

I wish I could read her mind right now. There is something about this woman. I couldn't put my finger on it, but she's very different compared to the women I go for usually, and this is by far the longest I have spent with any girl I've slept with ever. I don't even stay the night with them. I usually leave right after we get done doing the deed.

Like my best friend Josh says, *'You fuck and duck out.'* Sounds awful, I know, but I don't have time for relationships. Between my workload and the travelling that I do, there is simply no time for a girlfriend or a social life of any sort. After my last relationship of three years crashed and burned almost a year ago, I've made work my priority.

I stir out of my sleep when I hear the captain's voice over the intercom. I must have fallen asleep while reading. Shayla's sleeping with her head on my shoulder, her arm wrapped around my bicep, and I had my head resting on hers. I brush a strand of her hair out of her face gently. She's stunning, even without makeup.

As the wheels of the plane touch down on the tarmac, Shayla suddenly jolts awake and slowly lifts those olive coloured eyes, and looks up at me. I smirk at her, and she blinks. It takes her a moment to realise her head was on my shoulder, and she jerks away and sits upright, brushing her fingers through her hair, and she clears her throat, looking around uneasily. "How long have I been sleeping?"

"A good few hours." She looks at me and frowns a little before leaning over and pulling her shoes on.

"Oh. I'm so sorry. You should have woken me." I smile and shake my head, watching her as she straightens, rubbing her neck.

"Don't sweat it. I was asleep, too. We must have been more tired than we realised." Shayla nods with a sigh as she walks through the plane toward the exit.

"Tell me about it. It's been a hell of a weekend." She says as we make our way down the steps of the plane. She stops suddenly and looks at the car and then back at me. "Did we use this car last night?"

I nod, and she blinks and looks at the car again. "We left the club in this last night."

"Huh, I remember the car but nothing else." She replies and looks at the driver, and frowns. "Actually. I remember him, too." Gerald smiles and nods curtly at her before he opens the door for her to get in.

"Evening, Miss." Shayla eyes him sceptically before she gets in the car. An hour later, we pull up at the address she gave Gerald. She steps out of the car, and I follow her out and walk around the vehicle.

“Well, this is me.” She announces, looking up at her building and back at me again. "Thank you for getting me back home."

“Don't mention it. Here, this is my card. My lawyer has already started drawing up the divorce papers. We’ll meet up in a few days, and you can sign it. Sound good?”

Shayla takes my card and looks at it before looking at me and frowns. “Tristan? I thought your name was Cole?” She questions.

“It is. I prefer to be called Cole outside of work,” She nods, satisfied with my answer, and tucks the card in her pocket. Wow, she genuinely doesn’t know who I am. That actually makes a nice change.

“Well. I guess I’ll wait to hear from you. I will text you my number,” I nod, and we look at each other awkwardly for a moment, unsure of what to say or how to act. Do we shake hands? Do we hug? What is the appropriate etiquette here? Shayla turns to walk away but stops suddenly, takes the ring off her finger, and hands it to me. “We’ve never met before, right?” She questions, looking over my face, her eyes narrowed.

I shake my head and shrug. “I don’t think so. I would have definitely remembered meeting you.” I answer with a smirk, and she blinks up at me, surprised, her cheeks turning pink. Oh *fuck*. If that isn’t the sexiest thing ever.

Shayla clears her throat and nods, "Thanks again."

I smile at her, “Thank you for an eventful weekend, Shayla Hart.” Shayla nods, mumbles a goodbye and turns to walk away. “I guess I’ll be seeing you in a few days…*wifey*.” She stops, turns, and glares at me unamused.

“Don’t call me that.” I chuckle and watch her disappear into her apartment building. What an eventful forty-two hours.

Chapter Three

SHAYLA

I START from my sleep when I hear my alarm chirping away on the bedside table next to me. I reach over and feel around for my phone; eyes still closed, I managed to find it and snooze the alarm. Ahh silence. Just as I'm about to doze off again, I remember it's my first day at my new job, and I jump out of bed excited. It was seven-forty-five, and I had to be there at nine o'clock. Satisfied I had enough time, I drag myself to the bathroom to shower and get ready.

Staring at my reflection in the mirror while I brush my teeth. Eyes bloodshot from lack of sleep and a weekend of heavy drinking had me looking like something out of the night of the living dead. Honestly felt like my brain was about to fall out of my arse. After a steaming hot shower and two mugs of strong coffee, I was feeling a little better. I was trying to convince myself the fluttering around in my stomach wasn't nerves. Why would I be nervous? I can do this job in my sleep. Ugh, butterflies explode in my stomach again at the thought of it.

I was applying my mascara when my bedroom door suddenly bursts open, and Jo walks in with Aimee in tow. I jump at the intrusion and get mascara all over my eyelid, ruining my eyeshadow I spent a good ten minutes blending.

"Where in the seven kingdoms of *HELL* have you been?!" Jo hollers, glaring, her eyes wide and wild and hair tousled from sleep.

"Shayla, we've been worried sick! We thought something awful happened to you!" Aimee chastises me.

"Jesus Christ, you scared the bloody shit out of me. And you ruined my mascara!" I grumble, annoyed, picking up a cue tip to remove the black blob on my eyelid.

"Stuff the mascara! Where the fuck have you been all weekend? We thought you brought that hot guy you left with back to the apartment, but you weren't home." Aimee explains, walking over to sit on my bed. "Then we figured maybe you went back to his, and you'd be back Saturday, but you didn't show up, and your phone was off."

"Do you have any idea how scared we were, that you were face down in a ditch somewhere," Jo adds, placing her hands on her hips to illustrate her annoyance.

"You should have thought about that before you let me go off with a stranger. What the hell were you thinking, letting me go off with some rando?"

"You seemed really into each other, and he was hot, so we thought you'd gone to get a little nookie," Aimee explains with a shrug and smirks. "Speaking of, how was the nookie? Must have been good if he didn't let you leave all weekend."

"Oh my god!" I pick up a brush and throw it at her, which she dodges skilfully, and grins quite pleased with herself. "You know why I wasn't back Saturday. Let me tell you why— because I was in *Vegas*."

"Vegas?" They say in unison, and I nod. "As in *Las Vegas*…"

"Yes! Vegas, as in Nevada, Las Vegas!" Jo looks over at Aimee, who stares at me, her mouth agape. "I can't remember a damn thing. I was so drunk I somehow ended up on a *private jet* flying to the fucking states."

"With *that* guy?" Jo questions, a dumbfounded look on her face.

"Yes, with *that* guy," I say, pulling my lacy black top on. "That's not even the worst part, oh no, it gets better. Get this. We got married by Elvis. Like legally married."

Silence.

They gape at me. "You…you got *married*?" Jo sputters, shaking her head. I nod and apply my lipstick.

"So, wait, let me see if I got this right. You met a hot guy at a club who flew you in his private jet to Las Vegas and *married* you?" I nod, and she chuckles in response and scratches her nose. "Tell me you at least put out?"

"Aimee!" I exclaim, rolling my eyes and hurl a bottle of primer at her; she falls on the bed and laughs heartily.

"Shayla. Who is this guy?" Jo asks, and I shrug. I pick up his card from the table and hand it to her.

"I don't know who he is. All I know is his name. Tristan Cole… something."

Jo stares at the card, and her eyes grow wide. "Oh, my God. Shayla…" Jo gasps, staring at the card in her hand, and looks at me. "Tristan Cole Hoult! That's who you're married to?"

"No fucking way! Let me see." Aimee howls, jumping to her feet, and snatches the card from Jo. "I knew I recognised him! Oh my god. Shay, do you have any idea who this guy is?"

I shrug and shake my head, staring at the both of them in bemusement. "No, am I supposed to?"

"Um, yes!" They both shout together, startling me.

"*You* of all people should know, Shayla! He's a renowned architect, and the man is also a billionaire! He's the hottest and most sought after CEO in the country. Look, this is him, right?" She shows me a photo on her phone, and I nod.

I frown and look between them. My head was starting to hurt again. That's why he looked familiar to me. I've seen him in magazines. Oh shit. "Yes, that's him."

"Oh my god, you lucky bitch!" Aimee hops up on my bed. "Not only did you sleep with him, but you're also married to a billionaire, Shayla!" I roll my eyes and pick up my jacket. "I can't believe it."

"Oh, Jesus. I can't deal with you two. Let's not make a big deal about this. It was a stupid mistake. Now, I have to go to work. I don't want to be late on my first day."

"Don't go. You're rich now." Aimee sings, jumping on my bed and dancing.

"Aimee, get the hell off my bed! I just made it up." I grab her leg, pull it, and she tumbles over and rolls off the bed.

Aimee pouts, "Ouch. I think you broke my arse." She grumbles, rubbing her behind gingerly.

"I have to go. I'm already running late. Fix my damn bed." I say, throwing my pillow at her head and walking out of the bedroom.

"Yes, Mrs Hoult," Aimee calls out and giggles when I flip her off as I walk to the front door. I can't even think about the whole Tristan Cole fiasco right now. My head is a scrambled mess, and I'm pretty sure I'm still a little drunk. I need to focus on my career if I ever want to make it as an architect. I can barely remember how to spell my name at the moment. I am never drinking again.

I MAKE it to work with five minutes to spare. Please don't ask me how fast I was driving to make it on time because I expect a fair few speeding tickets in the post.

"Shayla." I spin when I hear my name and see the girl that greeted me the last time I came in. Heather, I think her name was.

"I'm Heather. If you're ready, let me show you around first, and then we can go through Mr Hoult's schedule for the day."

"Yes, of course. Sounds good." I follow her through the glass doors, and we walk through an open plan office with several fancy cubicles, high-tech computers with two monitors that are for drawing your designs.

"So, this is your desk, and you already know where his office is." I nod, smiling, my eyes taking in the office, as she continues to go on and on about his schedule. "He's very peculiar and likes things a certain way. For example, he has his coffee black, with skimmed milk on the side, on his desk at seven-forty-five. He has a sesame bagel with smoked salmon and fat-free cream cheese at eight o'clock every morning, religiously."

"Got it."

"Excellent. A little helpful advice. He works a lot, like around the clock. So, he's often quite grumpy because he's tired. If you see him loosening his tie and rub his temples, it means he's angry; steer clear unless he calls for you. If he does— do not speak. I found nodding helps. Do not enter his office without knocking; wait for him to gesture you in. Understand?"

I look over at the empty office and gulp. Oh boy, this man sounds like a real head-case. It sure is going to be a hoot working for him. I follow Heather back to the open office. "Well, I think you've pretty much got the gist of the job. I'm sure you two will get along great. He should be out of his meeting shortly, and we can head over and introduce you to him." Heather explains as we walk over to the kitchen area where the coffee machines and fridges are stocked up with drinks and shelves filled with snacks. At least they look after their employees.

I was enjoying my caramel latte and people watching when Heather came bouncing along. "He is out of his meeting. Let's go and get you acquainted." I nod and follow her toward the CEO's office. I was real baffled every time she said the words 'introduce you' like I hadn't met him at the interview. Maybe she forgot.

We walk into the office I had my interview with the silver fox. The painting on the wall caught my eye, and I was admiring it when I just about noticed Heather say my name. "Mr Hoult, this your new executive assistant, Shayla." I spin and look at him. Our eyes meet first. I let my gaze wander the length of him, and my heart slowly sinks to the pit of my stomach.

"You."

"You?" I shake my head and look over at Heather and back at the six-foot-something man standing in front of me. "No. No, my boss was an older gentleman…you're not...*old*."

Cole blinks and nods slowly. "You must have met my Father—Tony Hoult. He was interviewing for me while I was out of town on business."

I stare at Cole and curse the fate that keeps screwing with me. "So, *you're* my boss? I'm going to be working for *you*?"

Cole nods and fiddles with his cufflinks, his brows fused tightly. "It sure looks that way, Miss Hart."

"You've already met each other?"

"Heather, leave us." He commands, his eyes on mine, and Heather scampers out of the office, leaving us alone.

What the hell is going on?

"This is a joke, right? Because this can't be happening," I mutter, pacing back and forth. "It can't be."

Cole rubs the back of his neck, watching me pace frantically, mumbling incoherently to myself like a lunatic. "Shayla, why don't we sit?" He offers, and I shake my head.

"No. I can't sit." I reply, brushing my fingers through my hair in frustration. "I feel as though I'm trapped in a nightmare I can't seem to wake up from." I stop pacing and look at him. "What the hell is this? Are you like…stalking me?"

Cole laughs—and I don't just mean a chuckle— I mean a full-on belly laugh. "Stalking *you*?" He says in between breaths as I stand and watch him unimpressed. "I should be asking you that question, sweetheart. You're the one that keeps showing up everywhere. It can't be a coincidence."

I scowl at him and slap the folder in my hand on his desk somewhat hard. "Excuse me? Are you insinuating that I'm some psychotic fan girl or something?" I ask, taking a step toward him, and he watches me closely. "I think you will find that it was *you* who approached me at the club," I say, poking his chest, and he smirks and arches a brow. "And it was also your idea to leave the club together," I add, poking him again, and his smile grows into a grin. "It was also *you* that kissed *me*, so please, explain how I come off as the stalker here?" I finish, placing my hands at my hips and stare up at him expectantly.

Cole licks his lips and shrugs, "I was just kidding, but it's nice to see you have a feisty side, sweetheart. I adore that in a wife." I sigh and roll my eyes. I'm going to kill this boy.

"I'm not your wife and you'll see feisty when I beat you over the head with my folder." I grouse heatedly and he smirks. "Actually, you know what? I'm not your assistant either. I quit." I tell him and turn to leave, but Cole grabs my arm and stops me.

"Shayla. I'm only teasing you. We can work this out, come and sit for a minute, will you, please?" I tug my arm out of his hold, walk over to his desk, and sit on one of the cream chairs opposite. Cole comes and stands in front of me, leaning on his desk. He crosses his arms over his chest and regards me seriously. "You don't have to quit. We're both adults. We can still work together."

"How? How can we possibly work together after everything that has happened? We got married, remember?" Cole shrugs.

"Yeah. So? Who here knows we're married, but the two of us? You're overreacting. Besides, my father hired you for a reason, so you must be good at what you do, and I trust his judgement." I sigh heavily and shake my head.

"Overreacting? I got drunk and married my boss. I went from being an assistant to the office slut who has slept with the CEO." Cole straightens from his leaning position and runs his fingers through his hair. "Oh my god, people are going to think that's why I was hired." I utter pressing my fingers to my forehead.

"Shayla, you're no such thing. You're honestly overthinking this. No one will find out what happened between us, I promise you." Cole assures me and he seems genuine, but the nagging feeling I have in the pit of my stomach is making me feel uneasy.

"Fine," I give in with a sigh. I narrow my eyes at him. "You must have thought I was a right dimwit for not knowing who you were. Why didn't you say something?"

"I thought no such thing," Cole smiles warmly. "If anything, it felt good to be treated like a normal human being rather than a—"

"—notorious playboy billionaire?" I finish, and he chuckles a little while lowering his gaze to the black Louboutin leather shoes on his feet. "I go just a touch deeper than that, but yes. I may have liked that you didn't seem fazed by the fact that I was wealthy."

"Why would I be? Just because you have money doesn't make you better than anyone else. When cut, you still bleed red like the rest of us mere mortals."

Our eyes meet, and we stare at one another for a long moment. Cole smiles and shakes his head, seemingly pleased by my response. He walks around his desk and sits in his chair. "It's almost lunchtime. Would you like to go out for lunch?"

"Lunch?" I intone, and he nods, leaning back in his chair.

"Yeah, we can go to the breakfast bar." I groan and stand up. "We can share some pancakes." He sniggers.

"I hate you," I utter and turn to walk to the door. I hear Cole laugh behind me.

"Hey, what happens in Vegas..."

"Shut up." I walk out of his office and look back to see him watching me with a grin on his face while shaking his head. The girls are going to have a fit when they hear about this.

I walk to the bathroom and dial Aimee's number. She answers after two rings. "Yo ho, what's up?"

"What's up? Let me tell you what's up. Remember that billionaire I accidentally married?"

"The hot billionaire, yes."

"Well, that 'hot billionaire' is not only my dear husband…he's also my new boss," I tell her and hear her coughing and sputtering on the other end, clearly choking on something. "You dead?"

"I'm good. I'm okay. What do you mean he's your boss?" She questions, clearing her throat.

"He's my boss. The man that interviewed me was his Dad--Tony Hoult. How did I not connect the dots here, Aimes? For fucksake. I'm a smart girl—at least I thought I was. I held his card in my hand, and it didn't click. He probably thinks I'm a fucking idiot. Jesus, I'm mortified." I mumble, closing the lid of the toilet and sitting on it.

"A lot has happened in the space of four days. My mind can't cope with all this; I don't know how you're dealing with everything so calmly." She says in an attempt to make me feel better.

"Calmly? I'm freaking out Aimee. I can't work here. It's too awkward working with him side by side day in, day out. I can't do it. I'm going to quit."

"Shayla, no. Don't forget that you need this job. Remember how excited you were to finally be in a job that is in a field you're interested in. This job will open all sorts of doors for you in the future. Just focus on your work, and I promise you, in the end, when you're a kick-arse architect, it will all be worth it." I nod and sigh. She was right. As much as the situation sucks, I need to stick it out as long as possible. "So what if you slept with him? He's slept with dozens of girls. He clearly doesn't care. Why should you?"

"Yeah, you're right. I mean, he did promise what happened will stay between us." I tell her.

"There you go. Just chill and enjoy your first day. It's all going to be okay." I sure hope she was right because I honestly can't take much more. Knowing my luck, he'll end up being my long-lost brother or something, on top of everything else. I shudder at the mere thought of it.

Heaven forbid.

Chapter Four

COLE

"TRISTAN, we've had this conversation before. I've had it with your philandering ways. If you want me and your grandfather to take you seriously and pass on our shares to you, you need to prove you're responsible enough to run a multi-million corporation on your own. You'll be thirty soon. The time for you to settle down has come and is passing. I let you have your fun and sow your wild oats so that you'll get it out of your system before you settle down and the time has come." My father scolds me while cutting into his fillet mignon steak. "Hollie comes from a respectable family who has been our dearest friends for generations. She's a beautiful young lady, and she shares the same passion for architecture as you do. What more could you ask for in a life partner?" He adds, lifting his green eyes to look at me.

I clench and unclench my fist under the table. I feel my annoyance grow more by the minute. "Well, I would like to be attracted to my future wife, for starters. I also want to marry someone I love, Dad. I have zero interest in Hollie. She's not my type, and we have absolutely nothing in common other than our careers. Why would you want me to marry someone I don't even love?" I ask, and he sets his fork down and wipes his mouth before speaking.

"Son, love doesn't just happen overnight. You need to work at it, and it grows as you get to know the other person. You loved Sophie and look how that turned out? She left you devastated. You've not been the same since she broke your heart." I feel my insides recoil at the mention of my ex. "I don't want to see you hurt like that again. Do you think your mother and I were in love when we married? No, we weren't, but we grew to love each other, and now I couldn't imagine my life with anyone else." He explains, looking at my mother, who smiles at him lovingly and takes his hand when he holds it out for her.

"Dad, I've known Hollie since we were kids, and I don't see myself loving her…ever," I tell him earnestly, but he shakes his head and holds his hands up.

"Enough, Tristan. I've said my piece. If you want our shares, you'll marry Hollie as planned, and that's final. The arrangements are in place." He says and goes back to eating his food. I look over at my mother, who shrugs and smiles apologetically at me. This is ridiculous. This marriage fiasco started when Grandpop was diagnosed with motor neuron disease and was given less than a year to live. Guess what his dying wish was? To see his first-born, favourite grandson married before he dies. His shares will not transfer over to me until I am married, and if I don't, it goes to my idiot cousin Harry who will run the company I have spent years building up into the ground quicker than I can blink. It's times like these that I wish I had a sibling. My Dad wants to retire early but won't give me full control of Cult Designs until I'm married and settled down.

"Excuse me," I mutter, dropping my napkin on the table and stand up.

"Honey, you've not touched your food." My mother says, looking up at me. I shake my head and rub the back of my neck tiredly.

"I'm not hungry," I tell her. "I'm going to take off. I have a ton of work to do for the presentation tomorrow."

"Hollie and her parents are coming over the day after tomorrow for dinner. I expect you to be here. We'll discuss the details of your engagement." My father states as I walk off out of the dining room. I wave them off without so much as a glance and leave the house.

I feel like I'm suffocating. I jump in my Audi R8 and speed out of the gates. They've got me cornered with this marriage bullshit, and I can't seem to find a way out of it. I've been fighting them for weeks. I don't want to be stuck marrying a girl I don't love or even find the least bit interesting. She's a beautiful girl, yes. She's smart and accomplished. Any other guy would give their right leg to marry a girl like that, but not me. She's not for me. If I get forced into marrying her, I know I'll struggle to stay loyal, and I am not the kind of guy that cheats.

~

AFTER AN HOUR of driving around mindlessly, I find myself at my best friend Josh's house. I'm currently sprawled out on his sofa, sipping on my fifth bottle of beer, staring up at his plain white ceiling miserably.

"How the fuck am I going to get out of this?"

Josh sighs, leaning back on the sofa, and sips his beer. "Well, you're not. You'll have to marry Hollie, my brother. We both know how stubborn your Dad is. He's not letting this go."

I close my eyes and nod. Josh was right; my Dad will not let this go. Especially if it means losing the company he has worked so hard to build to his brother-in-law's son. "Damn it. Please, tell me there's a better solution, anything but this." I frown when I feel my phone vibrate in my pocket. I pull it out and see a text from Shayla.

I open the message and read it.

Shayla:

'I'm going to be late for the meeting tomorrow morning. Some idiot stole all four of the tyres off my car.'

I sit up and frown, and despite my bad mood, I laugh. This girl has the worst luck in the world. I type a message back to her.

Me:

'Ouch. I'm sorry to hear that. I can have someone over within the hour to replace the tyres for you.'

I send the text, and a reply comes right away. I open the message.

Shayla:

No. That's okay. I'll sort it. I can find somebody to fit new ones tomorrow. Just tell your lawyer I'll be a little late.'

I smile and shake my head. She's so stubborn it's infuriating.

Me:

'I'll pick you up on my way. We can go to the office together after.'

I set my phone down and look at Josh, who was watching me with a smile on his face. "What?" I ask cagily, sipping my beer.

"Your mood just drastically changed. Who are you texting?" He asks and swipes my phone off the table when it vibrates. "Shayla?" I reach over and try to take my phone, but he moves it out of reach. "Hang on, is that the hottie from the club you disappeared with." I nod and grab my phone from him.

"Yes, that's her," I say and read her text. Of course, she's saying no. I text her back quickly, telling her I will pick her up at nine and that I wouldn't take no for an answer.

"Why are you going to the lawyers with her?" Josh questions raising a curious brow at me. I was too distracted arguing with Shayla over text.

"Uh, to sign some papers for a divorce," I answer distractedly with a shrug, and he kicks my knee. I scowl at him.

"Divorce?" He sits upright and stares at me in bewilderment, and I realise I just let our secret slip out. "When did you fucking marry her to get a divorce?!"

"When we flew to Vegas…" I trail off, and his eyes widen as he waits for me to continue explaining. I sigh, "This is all your fault. You forced me to go out and got me stinking drunk. After we left the club, we kept drinking and ended up on my private jet flying to Vegas to get married."

"Holy— you got married? Like legally married?" Josh questions getting to his feet. He throws his head back and laughs when I nod.

"Yes, Josh. I'm legally married. And like that wasn't bad enough, she shows up at my office as my new executive assistant. My Dad hired her while I was in Paris. What are the fucking odds of that, tell me, please?" Josh covers his mouth with his hand and shakes his head.

"Odds? Bro, this girl is either one psychotic stalker and planned this, or fate's just dropped a motherload of an opportunity in your lap." I watch Josh as he moves around the room.

"Josh, she didn't even know who I was. And she tried to quit the moment she saw I was her boss. She's not a stalker, and she certainly didn't plan any of this." I explain, running my fingers through my hair.

"Cole, are you an idiot, bro?" I scowl at him hard. "Do you not realise all your prayers have been answered. This whole Hollie debacle is solved." I lean forward and rest my elbows on my knees and watch him closely.

"How so?"

"You're married, you idiot!" He shouts, throwing his hands up in the air. "You can't marry Hollie if you're already married. Take Shayla to your grandfather, introduce her as your wife, problem solved."

Oh. Why didn't I think of this? I am married.

I frown. "You mean, we stay married?" Josh nods, widening his blue eyes. "She wouldn't agree. Why would she want to stay married?"

Josh throws a cushion at me. "Because you're Tristan Cole Hoult, that's why. You're the most sought-after bachelor in the country—after me, of course." He says in jest, and I throw the cushion back at him.

I roll my eyes, exasperated. "Fuck you, arsehole." Josh catches the cushion and rests his elbow on it, grinning. "She doesn't care about any of that. She's nothing like the rest; my fame and money didn't deter her one bit."

"Sound chick. Just tell her the truth, maybe you'll appeal to her good nature, and she'll pity you and agree to help. If that fails, offer her a pay-out, a couple of mill, like a bearding service."

I rub my hands over my face with a heavy sigh. "That sounds rather crude."

"Would you rather marry Hollie?" I shake my head and fall back against the sofa.

"Fuck no." I curse, looking at the beer bottle in my hand. "At least Shayla's fun to be around. I'd much rather be stuck married to her."

"Just ask her." He states, taking a swig of his beer. "Worse case, she'll say no."

"Oh, she will absolutely say no. She's feisty and stubborn as hell." I mutter, tapping the neck of the bottle thoughtfully. It can't hurt to ask. Like Josh said, maybe she will feel sorry for me and help me. Perhaps I could give her a raise? And I'd prefer to be married to Shayla than Hollie. At least she's amusing to be around. She cracks me up throughout the day.

"Feisty, huh?" Josh intones, raising his brows with intrigue. "Good in the sack?"

I bite my bottom lip, recalling our passionate night together. "Oh, definitely," I murmur.

I sigh, feeling relieved. I hadn't realised how much this marriage arrangement was weighing me down.

I leave Josh's place and head home. I had a big day ahead of me the following day, and I needed to get my shit together before the presentation.

THE NEXT MORNING, I sat waiting for Shayla outside her apartment building. I'd been waiting fifteen minutes, and she's yet to come down. Women. I will never understand why they take a year to get ready for everything. I honk my horn impatiently, just as she pushes the door open and walks toward the car. I let my eyes wander over as she approaches me. That tight, black pencil skirt and red satin blouse she's wearing are hugging her in all the right places. Her dark tresses cascading down her back in beach waves, just like the night we met.

"Jesus, keep your hair on. You'll wake the neighbours." She grumbles, getting into the car. I'm not proud of this, but my eyes instantly drift to her skirt, which rides up to her mid-thigh when she sits, and I find myself checking out her shapely legs. I have a sudden flashback of our night together in Vegas, those legs wrapped around me as she drew me deeper into her.

"Cole."

I blink, snapping out of my thoughts, and look at her through my shades. "Yes?"

She looks at me with a frown, "Are we going or are we just going to sit here? You were just rushing me a moment ago?"

"Yes, we're going," I say, pulling away into traffic. "How are you? Did you manage to sort out your tyres?"

Shayla glances at me and shrugs, "Yes. Someone will be coming to fit new ones later this evening." She explains, and I nod. "Thank you for offering to help. I was in a sour mood. I hope I didn't come off rude." She looks over at me, apologetically, and I shake my head.

"Not at all," I wave off her apology. "Honestly, it would have pissed me off too if someone stole all the tyres off my car. Did you report it?" Shayla shakes her head. I frown, "Why not?"

She sighs, looking out the window, "What's the point? It's hardly the crime of the year, is it? It's inconvenient sure, but I think the police have much bigger cases that require their attention than my stolen tyres." I smile, shaking my head.

"That's one way to look at it."

Shayla sighs, brushing her hair away from her pretty face, "Nothing seems to be going right for me at the moment. It truly is bizarre."

I smile and glance at her before I look at the road again. "Oh, I've been there. But you should always try and stay positive because you never know when your luck might change." Shayla looks at me briefly. "Might be sooner than you think."

"I doubt that." She utters, her voice an octave over a whisper. The rest of the twenty-five-minute journey to the lawyer's office, we spent reviewing my work schedule.

"Your two-thirty meeting got pushed back by fifteen minutes. Mr Cohen's flight got delayed from Belgium; his driver dropped me an email earlier." I nod as we walk into the office, and Franc— our lawyer, greets us.

"Morning, Mr Hoult, Mrs Hoult," I observe Shayla's reaction when Franc called her by her married name. She smiles tightly and takes his offered hand, and sits at the table. "Okay, Mr Hoult I have drawn up the papers for the divorce. All I need are your signatures, and I can get it processed." Shayla nods and picks up her pen, and signs the papers. She holds the pen out to me, and I take it and stare at the paperwork in front of me.

"Cole?" I lift my gaze and look at Shayla. "Sign the papers."

"Franc, will you leave us a moment, please?" Shayla watches as he stands up and leaves the room before she looks at me again.

"What's wrong?" She questions, eyeing me warily.

"Shayla. I have a proposition for you."

Her frown deepens, "A proposition?"

I nod slowly and hold her gaze, "Yes, a proposition."

"Okay…"

"What if we don't get a divorce?" I suggest, and she stares at me blankly, then laughs suddenly.

"Hilarious, Cole. Stop screwing around and sign the papers so we can get out of here." When I make no move to sign the papers, her smile fades slowly. "You're not—wait, are you serious?!"

"Very."

"Very? Very what, Cole? We agreed to get a divorce. What are you talking about?" She exclaims, rising up from her seat.

I sigh and put the pen down, and watch her as she glares daggers at me. "I'm only suggesting we stay married for a little while longer."

Shayla stops pacing and looks down at me angrily, "And I'm suggesting we get a divorce—right now."

"Shayla, just listen to me for a second. I'm stuck in an impossible situation, and I need your help." I explain, and her gaze softens a little. "My Dad, he's forcing me to marry someone I don't love in exchange for his and my grandfather's shares to the company." I sigh and stand up. "My grandfather has a terminal illness and doesn't have long to live. His dying wish is to see his firstborn grandchild married before he dies. If I don't, he will give his shares to my cousin Harry who is an absolute goon and will fuck up everything I've worked so hard to achieve at the company."

Shayla shakes her head. "Cole, have you lost your mind? You're talking about lying to your family. To a dying man. Absolutely not."

"I can't marry Hollie. She's just not the type of girl I see myself settling down with. She's not for me." I explain, and she shrugs indifferently.

"How is that any different to what we did? We don't exactly get along either. Just marry her, get your shares, then divorce her." I sigh and shake my head, feeling frustrated.

"Shayla, you don't get it. This girl has been obsessed with me since we were ten years old. Do you think she's going to divorce me after waiting years to tie me down? No fucking chance,"

"Cole, listen to what you're asking of me? You're asking me to stay married to you, to lie and scheme. I don't even know you." She declares, pacing again. I grab hold of her arm and draw her toward me.

"I'll pay you." I blurt out.

Shayla's green eyes grow wide, and if looks could kill, I'd be dead and buried right about now. "You'll what?" She grits annoyance evident in her tone. "If you think just because I slept with you, I now owe you something; you're sorely mistaken. Screw you and your job, you arrogant pig." She hisses vehemently and rips her arm from my hold.

"No! Christ, Shayla, it's not like that. Think of it as a business arrangement. Name your price; money is no object." Shayla steps back with an appalled look on her face. A glimpse of hurt flickers in her eyes before it's replaced with anger again.

"Who the hell do you think you are?! I'm sorry to disappoint you, Mr Hoult, but I am not for sale! Your money can get you a lot, it seems, but not me." She tries to sidestep me, but I block her path. "Get out of my way." She spits furiously.

"Jesus, Shayla, please just listen to me. I'm not trying to buy you, and the last thing I'd ever want to do is insult you." I explain and sigh dejectedly. "I wouldn't ask if I wasn't desperate. You're my only hope out of this arranged marriage." I say pleadingly, and she licks her lips and brushes her fingers through her hair, still fuming. "I know you need the money. You've got outstanding debts on your student loans." She spins and glares at me. "It came up in your background check. You can pay those off and finish your degree. Let me help you."

"I don't want your help! There are a million girls out there who would marry you without a second thought, so go pick one of them." She claims while snatching up her blazer and purse.

"I don't want them." Shayla rolls her eyes and tries to push past me to leave, but I stop her. "I trust you." She lifts her gaze slowly, and our eyes meet.

"Tristan?" We both jump apart when I hear my name. I turn and see my Dad standing there. Fuck.

"Dad?"

"What is going on here?" He questions, looking between Shayla and me sceptically. "What's with all the shouting?" Shayla looks at me and straightens her skirt. "What are you both doing here?" I look over at Shayla, and I'm not sure what came over me, but I wrap an arm around her waist and pull her up against me.

"Dad, I'd like you to officially meet my wife…Shayla."

Chapter Five

SHAYLA

'God? What the hell did I do in my past life for you to be punishing me like this?'

Looking at Coles father, I stand there—utterly humiliated—might I add while he's just staring back at me confused. "Your wife?" He repeats, averting his gaze to his son. "I don't understand."

I open my mouth to speak but Cole pipes in, "We're married. What's not to understand." I look up at him, and he pulls me closer against him, and I have the sudden urge to punch the kid in his throat.

"I should give you both some privacy," I say and turn to leave the room.

"Stay right there, young lady!" He shouts, and I jump, startled at his sudden outburst. I nod and hang my head in silence, shrinking back beside Cole. "Tristan, I hired this girl a few days ago to be your assistant. What do you mean you're married?" He questions, his green eyes, identical to Coles, darting between us, waiting for an answer. "What? Did it just slip your mind that you're married to the CEO of the company?" He asks me, and I gape at him, my mouth opening and closing, probably resembling a fish out of water.

"I, uh, we—" I stammer pathetically, looking up at Cole, who stares back at me.

"I told her not to say anything." He answers for me. "She didn't want anyone to think she got the job because she was married to me. She wanted to earn it herself." I stare at the floor. I can feel my cheeks burning with embarrassment. I'm going to kill him, revive him, and kill him again!

"Is that true?" I lift my gaze and after a glance at Cole, his eyes pleading with mine, I sigh and nod.

"Y-yes, sir," I answer nervously. I feel Cole's fingers lace with mine, and I dig my nails into his skin. He flinches, squeezing my hand tighter in return.

"We're not done discussing this. I have a meeting I must attend right now. You're both coming to dinner this evening. You've got some serious explaining to do!" He glares at us both before he storms out of the office.

I let out a breath I hadn't even noticed I was holding. Ripping my hand out of Cole's, I look up at him. "What the hell did you just do?"

Cole shrugs sheepishly, "I'm so sorry. I panicked when he asked what we were doing here. I just blurted it out." I turn to face him while I watch his father walk away, and when see's the rage in my eyes, he takes a step back as I walk toward him.

"You panicked?" I utter through clenched teeth as I advance toward him. I lift my arms and hit him anywhere I can reach.

"Ouch, hey! Stop hitting me!" Cole says, grabbing my arms. "I'm sorry, okay. He was about to find out we were getting a divorce. If I hadn't distracted him, he would have found out anyway." I glower at him and shake my head in disbelief.

"Oh, bull! You saw an opportunity, and you jumped at it. I can't believe you. I told you I didn't want any part of your stupid ploy to trick your family, but you completely disregarded my wishes and did what you wanted anyway." I argue and we glare at each other heatedly, so much so that I didn't even notice he was still holding my arms with me pressed against his hard chest. My senses come hurrying back to me, and I shove him away from me, grab my bag and storm out.

"Shayla, wait," I hear Cole call out as he follows me out of the office. "Shayla, will you just stop and listen to me? I'm telling you I didn't mean to just blurt it out like that." He explains, but I ignore him and continue walking, rather briskly toward the exit, trying to convince myself my feet aren't throbbing in these stupid stilettos I decided to wear. Just as I reach the rotating doors, Cole slides in with me, pushes his foot against the side of the door, and it stops spinning, trapping me with him.

Clever bastard.

I spin, not realising how confined the space between the doors were and our faces are mere inches apart. Usually, I'm about a good seven inches shorter than Cole, but I was wearing heels, and we were practically nose to nose— well, nose to lips, he's still taller.

"What are you doing? Move your foot." I demand, and he shakes his head.

"No, not until you listen to what I have to say." I sigh, roll my eyes just as an alarm starts ringing.

"Cole, people are looking at us," I say, looking around at the people waiting to either enter or exit the building.

"I don't give a fuck, let them look." He bites out, his eyes never leaving mine. I peer up at him, growing more and more annoyed by the second. Cole breaks eye contact when a security guard knocks on the door and asks if we were okay and Cole glares at him and gestures to him with his head, the security guard nods in response, and people begin dispersing.

"Wow. You see, this is your problem. You're so used to having control over everything and everyone around you that you seem to think it's acceptable behaviour to act out when you don't get your way. I have news for you; you can't control me, Cole, you can't buy me."

"You know what. You're right. I am used to getting my way, and to this day, no one, not one person has ever challenged me and said no to me. Nobody but *you*. Do you have any idea how suffocating it is to have people around you that are constantly expecting something from you?" I watch him closely as he speaks, his gaze locked on mine. "Do you know how many times I have asked someone for help in my life?" He questions, and when I only blink up at him, he snorts and shakes his head. "Zero." He finishes. "When I say I trust you, know that I mean it because I don't trust people easily, and I've never met anyone like you, Shayla. You're so unfazed by my lifestyle, the money, the cars, all of it. That's why I asked you, not because I'm trying to buy you off, but because I can't imagine a person more deserving of a break than you. And I know you won't try and screw me over."

I stare up at him, completely stunned. I had no idea what to say back to him after that. I've known this man for less than a week. "Now we can go." He says and removes his foot from the door. The alarm stops, and the doors start moving again. We walk to his car in silence. Once we get in, we drive back to the office. I couldn't stop thinking about what he'd just said.

I sigh and watch him as he drives, eyes fixed on the road, a frown on his handsome face causing a deep vee to form between his brows. He looks so unhappy and stressed. I felt a pang in my chest. Goddamn it. "Fine. I'll do it."

Cole looks over at me briefly and back at the road again. "You will?" He replies, surprised. I nod and stare at the road ahead.

"Yes." I sigh and look at him. "I don't like it, but you did make up that whole spiel about trusting me, so…" He smiles brightly and shakes his head.

"That was all true." He assures.

I nod. "If you say so," Cole takes my hand in his and brushes a gentle kiss over my knuckles. My stomach tightens.

"Thank you, Shayla. You have no idea how much this means to me. Honestly." I nod and pull my hand back.

"Well, nobody should be forced to marry someone they don't love. Even entitled rich boys like yourself ought to have a happily ever after." I tease, and he scoffs and pokes my side.

"I am not an entitled rich boy." He defends, feigning annoyance, but I see the corner of his lips curl. "I work *really* hard, okay." He says and chuckles when I give him a pointed look. "Ok fine, I work hard."

"Whatever you say champ. Can we please discuss what we are going to tell your parents because I'm kind of terrified here?" I question, and he nods.

"We just need to get our stories straight. My parents know me very well, especially my mother, so if we are going to convince them that we are in love, we have to act the part." I shake my head and hold my hand up.

"Hold up. Define '*in love'* because, if by that you mean you're going to be shoving your tongue down my throat, you can think again. That is not going to happen," I inform him matter-of-factly, and he smirks at me in return.

"Why? Are you afraid you might enjoy it too much like last time?" I punch him in the ribs, and he groans.

"Ow! Fucking hell." He guffaws, rubbing his side. "You punch like a dude!"

It was my turn to smirk, "Perks of having a crazy protective older brother. Touch me without my consent, and I will make those sunglasses a permanent fixture on your pretty face." I threaten him, and he chuckles, amused.

"You think my face is pretty?" He asks, raising his brow, clearly intrigued. I lift my hand to hit him again, and he flinches. "Whoa, hey! I'm kidding. I'm kidding." He laughs, "Put your fist away, Balboa, before you hurt yourself."

"I'm going to wind up in jail before this is over, I swear to God. You're going to make me kill you."

Cole chuckles and we continue to bicker back and forth until we got to the office.

"We have to make sure we go through everything step by step before we get in that room. Kyle Turner is very fussy, and if we miss something, he will walk with this project." He explains as we walk through the open-plan office. I look around and notice people staring at us as we walk by toward Cole's office.

"Hey, is it me, or is everyone staring at us?" I whisper, and Cole doesn't even look up from his phone.

"It's you." He mutters distantly and walks into his office with me in tow. I look back and see the team on the floor, watching us and whispering to one another. I frown and tap Cole's shoulder, and he mumbles a 'hmm' while typing away on his phone.

"Cole, I'm serious. People are staring at us. You don't think your father told anyone we're married?"

"Hmm." I look over at Cole and notice he's not even listening to me. I roll my eyes and resist the urge to smack him upside the head. Maybe I was paranoid. I force it out of my mind and focus on the presentation with Cole.

"Mr Hoult?" Heather knocks on the door and enters when Cole waves her in. "You need to see this." She hands Cole the tablet in her hand and gives me a startled look before dropping her gaze. Weird.

"Oh shit." Cole curses and shoots up from his seat, looking at the tablet, his green eyes wide.

"What is it?" I ask, looking from him to Heather, who shakes her head and averts her gaze from mine. "Cole?"

He lifts his gaze and meets mine. The usual soft green eyes I'm used to now stormy and dark. He's angry— scratch that, he's livid. "Get Lucy here now!" He barks. Heather starts at his tone and nods before scampering off.

I watch as he paces the office, stroking his jaw, evidently irritated by whatever was on that tablet. He swipes his hand over the lamp on his desk, which goes flying and smashes on the floor. "Cole, what's going on?" I ask again, and he closes his eyes for a second and holds the tablet out to me. When I take it, he continues pacing back and forth.

I look down at the tablet, and my blood runs cold in my veins. There, in a big block of letters, were the words...

'HEARTTHROB BILLIONAIRE, TRISTAN HOULT ELOPES WITH MYSTERIOUS BRUNETTE IN PASSIONATE LAS VEGAS WEDDING! SORRY LADIES, THIS BACHELOR IS OFF THE MARKET!'

There is a picture of me in his arms bridal style, both of us laughing. There are other images of us kissing as he carries me toward the hotel that we spent the night, "Oh my God," I whisper, staring at the article. This can't be happening. I look up from the tablet and notice all eyes in the office watching us. The sheer panic that was creeping up inside of me left me breathless. “No, no, no. My God. This can’t— this can’t be happening.” My fingers were trembling, and the tablet slips and falls smashing on the marble tiles.

“Shayla,” Cole comes over to me and lifts my gaze to his. “Hey, look at me. It’s going to be okay.”

I blink up at him, “How?” I whisper. “How is this going to be okay? Everyone knows, that’s why they were all staring at us, cause they…” I cover my hand with my mouth. “Oh my God, how am I going to face these people again.”

Cole walks over to his desk, pushes a button and the windows looking into his office frosts to give us some privacy. He reaches out to take my hands and I pull away, shaking my head. “Don’t.” I step a couple of paces away from him, and Cole watches me as I retreat.

“Shayla...”

“Don’t!” I shout. “Don’t tell me it's going to be okay because it’s not! How the hell did this happen, Cole?”

“Someone must have seen us going into the chapel and wanted to make a quick dime. I’m going to find the person responsible and make them pay for this.” He explains, and I shrug.

“What good is that going to do now? Is it going to change the fact that our faces are plastered all over the internet? No. Call whoever it is you need to call and make them kill the damn story!”

“I can’t do that, Shayla. Over three million people have seen it in one hour. Besides, it’s not like they sold a fake story. It’s the truth, we *are* married. I can’t sue them for selling factual news.” He explains calmly, and I feel all the air leave my lungs at the thought of my family seeing this.

“Cole, you don’t understand. My family can’t find out about this. This will crush them. This whole thing has blown way out of proportion. I don’t need this shit!”

“Oh, and I do?” Cole replies, holding his arms out and glaring at me. “Quit blaming everything on me. We were both at that chapel, we both said, ‘I do’ so the both of us need to take responsibility.”

“This was a mistake! And it was supposed to stay between us. How am I going to explain this to my family Cole? Do you have any idea how disappointed they will be with me when they see those pictures of us? My family isn't like yours. My brother's going to kill you and then kill me." I explain, pacing frantically.

"Shayla, just calm down. We'll figure this out together. If I have to go to your family and convince them that we're in love, I will. You had my back, and now I have yours." He assures me and catches my arm as I continue to pace and draws me close to him. I look up, and he wipes the tear that rolls down my cheek with his thumb. "Please don't cry. We'll deal with this together." He adds after a beat, his tone calm and eyes back to the usual startling green I'm accustomed to.

I close my eyes and relax when his fingers brush through my hair gently. I allow him to slowly tug me closer against him. Cole's free hand comes up to my waist, and he presses his forehead to mine while my hands rest on his well-defined chest. I can feel every thud of his heart under my palm, and it's oddly soothing to me.

The warmth of his breath on my lips sends a mass of tingles cascading down my spine.

Chapter Six

COLE

I WISH I had the option just to hit pause and stay in this moment for a little while longer. I let my eyes roam over Shayla's face, her eyes closed, soft lips faintly parted just begging to be kissed, but I know that's not what she needs right now, and If I tried, she would probably punch me. When a knock sounds on my door, Shayla's eyes flicker open, she looks up at me and quickly pulls herself away, putting a couple of feet between us. Her gaze drops to the floor, and I would give my left nut to be able to read her mind. Was she waiting for me to kiss her? I wonder if she felt as disappointed as I did when she pulled away?

"Tristan?" I look over at Lucy— my publicist— when she pokes her head through the door. I wave her in. "I've just seen the article. My phone hasn't stopped ringing." She says, walking toward us.

"How do we fix this?" I ask her, and she sets the tablet in her hand on my desk and sighs.

She looks over at Shayla and back at me again. "I need you to tell me how you want me to spin this Tristan. In the interview you had a couple of weeks ago, you told them you were enjoying being single and not looking to settle down anytime soon, and now you're suddenly married. There is a lot of speculation out there that doesn't make either of you look good."

Lucy explains. Shayla looks at me and a worried look descends upon her face.

"What does that mean?"

Lucy sighs, "They're speculating that you got pregnant, and that's why Tristan married you in such a rush."

"What?" Shayla and I say at the same time.

"That's not true at all. I'm not pregnant." She declares stonily, and Lucy nods and looks over at me. "We were just—"

I wrap my arm around Shayla's shoulder and draw her close to me. "—In love. I wanted her out of the public eye for as long as possible; we didn't want a big fuss with a wedding, so we eloped. That's it."

"Tristan, this article can hurt your reputation as an esteemed businessman. You've continually said that your loyalty and integrity toward your clients played a major factor in your success as an architect. If they suspect anything otherwise, this will tarnish that reputation, and investors might start to pull out if they suspect you're irresponsible. So, we need to act fast, and the public must see that this marriage is legit and you two genuinely are in love with one another. Your supporters can be a little excessive, as you are well aware." I roll my eyes and nod. Excessive isn't the word I'd use for sending used underwear to my apartment or breaking in and waiting naked in my car. That's downright psychotic.

I look down at Shayla, and she lifts her gaze to meet mine, "I don't care what they say about me, but you protect Shayla and her privacy at all cost." I declare and look over at Lucy again. "You hear me? One thing reported out of context, and I will hold you personally responsible." She nods and picks up her tablet before walking out of my office.

Shayla pulls away from me and leans against my desk. "Cole, this is insane. This whole thing is getting out of hand. We've gone from only lying to our parents to the whole damn world. You heard her, if they figure out that we're lying, it will hurt your career, and I'm going to lose my family." I move closer to her and shake my head.

"No one will figure out anything if we both play our part. We'll stay married a while until this all blows over, then we'll get divorced quietly." I explain and she exhales, closing her eyes.

"Cole, I can't lie to save my life." She admits sorrowfully, lowering her head. I smile. "I don't want to be the reason you lose everything." My smile fell as quickly as it appeared.

I take her face into my hands and lift her gaze to mine. "And I don't want to be the reason you lose yours. We'll figure this out together as we go, okay?" I assure her, and she nods in response. "But first, we need to get through this presentation, so please be a good little wife and get your husband a coffee." I tease to lighten the mood, and she glares at me unamused.

"Cole..."

I chuckle and shrug, "What? Get used to me calling you that. You'll be hearing it a lot more sweetheart."

Shayla rolls her eyes exasperated and straightens from leaning against my desk. She strolls over to me and fixes me with a sultry look, and I feel all the blood in my brain rush down to my cock. "You might want to stop annoying me, Mr Hoult, because I notice people love to talk in this place. How unfortunate would it be if someone starts telling people you can't—oh I don't know, *perform* well in the bedroom."

I look down into her upturned face and step closer. "You can certainly try. They will not believe you though." I speak softly as I slowly lean in closer.

"Oh?" She replies, narrowing her eyes challengingly, "And what makes you so sure?"

I deliberately lick my lips and smirk as I back her up toward my desk; her step falters so I wrap my arm around her waist and pull her against me. "It's clear you know nothing about me or my past, sweetheart. My reputation speaks for itself. I recommend you do your homework." I brush a strand of her hair away from her face and stare into her eyes. "I don't recall hearing you complain about my performance that night." I lick my lips slowly, "In fact, it's quite the opposite. You were pretty darn vocal while you were coming wildly, squeezing and milking my cock."

Her lips part, and she stares at me before her eyes narrow, "Maybe I'm just good at faking it." She responds, pulling her face away from my hand.

I look over her face and grin, "You're right," I tilt her head up so our lips are aligned perfectly. "You can't lie for shit," I whisper and drop a kiss on her cheek, and she pulls away again.

"What are you doing, Cole?" I pull my head back and grin.

"Playing my part," I say and step away from her. She frowns, and I gesture with my head to the crowd of employees that just watched our entire exchange. "It seems I was too into fondling my wife that I hadn't noticed I 'accidentally' unfrosted the glass." She looks around and swallows hard before she turns her stony gaze to me.

"Oh, you son of a—," I wink at her and walk around my desk.

"Ah, ah, ah, you love me, remember?" She huffs, spins on her heels, and walks off toward the door. "Don't forget my coffee."

I hear her mutter profanities under her breath as she stalks off, and I watch her disappear out of sight. Ten minutes later, she comes back with a coffee and bagel, sets it on my desk and turns to leave.

"Shayla?"

She turns and looks at me over her shoulder. "Yes?"

"Sit." I point to the seat next to mine at the conference table. For once, she doesn't argue and obeys. "So, I was thinking. If we want this whole thing to work, we should put some ground rules in place. We should have a contract or some form of an agreement, so we both know where we stand. What do you think?"

Shayla looks at me blankly for a long moment but shrugs and nods in agreement. "That's probably wise."

"Great, after dinner at my parents, we can go to my place and discuss the terms of the contract," I explain, and she nods again.

"Fine,"

"Good. Now, let's take one last look at this presentation." Shayla groans and drops her pen.

"Cole, we've been over it fifteen times. It's great. Besides, they're here." She informs me, gesturing to the group of men escorted to the conference room by Heather. I nod, gather up my laptop and files I need, and stand from my chair.

"I guess it's showtime," I say, and Shayla follows me as we walk out of my office toward the conference room to greet Mr Turner and his associates. "Mr Turner, it's so nice to see you again. Welcome." I greet and gesture for them to take a seat. “Okay, without further ado, let me present to you the design for your new eco-friendly hotel.” I watch the men's faces in the room as I explain the in’s and out’s of the project. From the corner of my eye, I can see Shayla watching me as I walk around the room. I try to avoid looking at her the entire time I was talking because I knew one look at her, and I would lose all train of thought.

“As stated, all of the materials used to build your hotel will be economically friendly.” I finish and click the screen off.

“That is just incredible, Tristan. It’s like you’ve just plucked the image from my brain. It’s just as I imagined my hotel would be. I love it.” Kyle Turner says, standing from his seat. “Send over the contract, I’ll sign it, and we can start the project.” I smile and shake his hand. He takes one last look at the building and mumbles “Incredible” before he walks out, leaving Shayla and me alone in the conference room. After weeks and weeks of stress and hard work, I finally felt my shoulders relax. I look over at Shayla, who smiles up at me prettily, her green eyes alight with excitement.

“We did it,” I whisper, and she nods; standing from the chair, she crosses her arms over her chest and leans against the table. “We won the project.”

“*You* did it.” She corrects. “You’ve worked your arse off for weeks to get this project done, and it’s beautiful, Cole. Why aren’t you more excited?!” She exclaims. I grin, and without a second thought, I wrap my arms around her, lift her off her feet and hug her tight.

Shayla squeaks in surprise but laughs and hugs me back. “Thank you for keeping me on track; you’ve been incredible these last couple of days,” I declare, pulling back and looking into her eyes. She smiles at me warmly and shrugs.

“You were a royal pain in my arse, but it was worth it. Seeing your face light up when he told you that you got the project certainly made up for the late nights and early mornings we’ve pulled the last couple of days.”

“I was pretty awful, wasn’t I?” I wince, and she nods again with a dramatic sigh.

“The things I put up with for this job…” She adds sarcastically, and I laugh. "Speaking of…" She smacks my head with a sweet little frown on her face. "Put me down."

I set her down and ruffle her hair, and her arms flail, trying to hit me. I grab my laptop and power walk out of the conference room, laughing while she follows me, grumbling about me messing up her hair.

~

AN HOUR LATER, we were standing outside my parents house. I look over at her. She's chewing her lip anxiously. "Here, you'll need to wear this." I pull out the diamond ring and hand it to her. Her nose wrinkles in distaste, but she takes it and slides it on her finger. I swear she is the only woman I know that turns her nose up to diamonds. "You ready?"

"Ready as I'll ever be." I hold out my hand, and she looks down at it and back up at me again. "We need to act the part, remember?" I remind her, and she sighs and laces her fingers with mine. "Cole, I'm begging you, please don't do anything to make me uncomfortable in there." I nod and give her hand a little squeeze before I push the door open, and we walk in.

"I'm hoping Hollie and her parents aren't here for dinner," I whisper to her as we walk through the foyer.

"What? Hollie? Isn't that the girl your supposed to marry?" She whispers back, and I nod.

"Yeah, they were supposed to be here to talk about our engagement arrangements. If they are, please don't freak out. Just stick to the plan." I tell her and pull her toward the living room. "Mum. Dad." I greet my parents, who stand when they see us.

"Tristan," My father greets me and nods at Shayla, she smiles kindly at him. "Shayla, welcome dear."

She flushes. "Good evening, sir."

"Mum, this is my wife, Shayla. Honey, this is my mother, Elaine Hoult." I introduce. Shayla smiles and holds her hand out to shake my mother's hand, who stares at it expressionlessly.

"It's lovely to meet you, Mrs Hoult," Shayla says, dropping her hand and shifting back, the smile on her face faltering a little.

"Mother," I warn sternly, and she looks at me and then back at Shayla.

"It's nice to meet you too, Shelly." I open my mouth to correct her, but Shayla squeezes my hand and shakes her head a little, silently telling me to let it go. "Dinner is served. Let's eat." My mother says and walks toward the dining room. We all follow her and take a seat at the dining table.

"Your home is beautiful, Mrs Hoult," Shayla smiles, laying her napkin in her lap.

"I know." My mother responds curtly, and I bite back the urge to snap at her when I see the saddened look in Shayla's eyes at the terse remarks my mother keeps throwing at her.

My father feeling the tension thicken in the room, clears his throat and sparks up a conversation. "How was the presentation, son?"

I take a sip of my water and nod. "It went very well. Mr Turner was incredibly pleased with the design." I look at Shayla and she smiles at me warmly as she did at the office earlier. "We got the project." My father reaches over and pats my shoulder proudly.

"Well done, son. I didn't doubt you for a second, and I'm pleased I was right. I say that's worth a toast, no?" He holds up his wine glass, and we all follow suit. "To you and your success, son."

"Actually, I didn't do it alone." I turn my gaze to Shayla, lift her hand, and kiss her knuckles gently. "My beautiful wife played a big part in keeping me on track with everything. When I got so stressed, I didn't believe I could do it; she was right there to pick me up and kept urging me forward. I honestly wouldn't have finished this project without her."

Shayla's cheeks go bright pink, and she smiles, shaking her head, "I didn't do anything, Cole. It was all you. You put your heart into your work, and it clearly showed."

"Well done, Tristan, but what I would like to understand is how your assistant became your wife?" My mother questions, arching her perfectly shaped brow inquisitively.

"I've known Shayla for a while. We've been friends for some time. What you think you never wanted turns out to be everything you've needed all along." I express, turning to face Shayla, who holds my gaze steadily. "I fell in love with her without even knowing it."

"Why didn't you tell us about her before? Why on earth would you go off and elope in Vegas of all places. That is so unlike you, and the photos all over the internet, my goodness like you're some commoner." My mother grumbles, glaring at Shayla and then at me.

I sigh, growing irritated, "I did want to tell you, but everything happened so fast. It's my fault. I was being selfish and wasn't ready to share Shayla with the world yet. Besides, you were both, so hell-bent on me marrying Hollie even though I was so against it. I just felt like this was the only way you would listen. Our relationship was still relatively new, but I didn't want to spend another day without her by my side as my wife." I look over at her, she's watching me. I turn my gaze back to my parents. "We just wanted to enjoy our time together before we went public, but someone, unfortunately, snapped photos and videos of us in Vegas, and well... here we are," I explain. My mother drops her fork and shakes her head, disappointment radiating in her eyes. I did feel guilty lying to them like this. However, if they didn't give a shit about my happiness, I had no choice but to be selfish and look out for myself.

"Shayla, what does your family do?" My father questions while chewing on his seabass.

"My family?" Shayla clears her throat and pats her mouth with the napkin. "Well, my father passed away when I was sixteen years old, so it's just my mother and my older brother Sam."

"Oh. I'm so sorry to hear that, dear. Must have been awful losing your father at such a young age." My father says. Shayla shrugs and pushes the food around on her plate. Her eyes glaze over for a couple of seconds as she recalls, I'm assuming the moment she lost her Dad. I reach over and rub the nape of her neck supportively, she closes her eyes, sighing slowly.

"It was a real shock to all of us. My mother especially, she's never quite been the same since he died. My father was the love of her life, and they were so happy together. She's so different now, absolutely terrified of leaving the house." She explains sullenly, her eyes welling up.

"If she doesn't leave the house, what does she do for money?" My mother questions, and I glare at her, which she completely ignores.

"I provide for them. After Dad died, I got a job as a waitress at a café near our house, and I worked there and continued to go to school." Shayla explains, putting her fork down carefully on the plate.

"That's very honourable of you, dear." My father praises, but Shayla shrugs it off.

"Thank you, Mr Hoult, but they're my family. Of course I will provide for them." Shayla looks around the table briefly and bites her bottom lip. "Could I use your restroom, please?"

"Of course, Hayley will show you the way." My mother gestures for one of the housekeepers, and she smiles politely at Shayla and shows her the way. I wait for her to be out of earshot when I turn my attention to my mother.

"Mother, what do you think you're doing? Stop being so rude. Why are you interrogating her?" I snap, and she presses her lips together and nods. I drop my napkin on the table to go check on her, but my mother stops me.

"You're right, sweetie. I'll go and apologise to her." She says and leaves the room. I sit back down and run my fingers through my hair in frustration. I knew this would be tough, but I will not let anyone— especially my mother make Shayla feel bad about herself.

I check the time and notice they've both been gone for about ten minutes. How long does it take to say sorry? "Excuse me, Dad, I'm going to go check on them," I tell my father, he nods and waves me off. I make my way up the grand stairs case and stop when I hear voices.

"...you will divorce him. He already has the perfect girl waiting to marry him." I hear my mother say, and I slowly walk up the rest of the steps.

"Oh, you mean the one he's *adamantly* refusing to marry. What kind of a mother forces her child to marry someone he doesn't even love?" I hear Shayla retort, and my mother scoffs in distaste.

"One that knows what is best for him, and I'm sorry to burst your bubble honey, that is not nor will it ever be *you*." My mother responds, "You don't belong in our world. Tristan will see you're worthless just as I do, and you'll be left where you belong." She adds, and I feel hot rage boil up inside of me. How dare she speak on my behalf, especially in such a manner.

"Maybe he married me because he didn't want to end up in a loveless marriage, stuck with a bitter woman like his mother." I stop dead in my tracks when I see my mother slap Shayla hard across the cheek. The sound of her hand meeting her cheek hangs in the air for a second.

"You insolent little—"

"MOTHER!

Chapter Seven

SHAYLA

"Are you okay?" I blink up at Cole, he cups my face cautiously in his big hands, his green eyes scanning over my face. I wasn't okay, not one little bit. My cheek was throbbing, and my ear was ringing. I nod despite the rage brewing inside of me to punch the face-off of the snooty bitch for laying a finger on me.

"I'm fine," I assure him, pulling my face away from his hold and hiss when he brushes his thumb over the cheek his mother just bitch slapped. "I'm okay, honestly. I'm fine."

"Stay here." He demands and storms off, leaving me standing there.

"Where are you going? Cole?" I call out after him, but he ignores me and disappears down the stairs. Oh, Christ. How did everything get so damn messed up? I head downstairs, and I can hear Cole's angry voice echoing through the house.

"How dare you lay a finger on her!" He shouts. I follow his voice and stop just outside the living room. "She's my wife, mother!"

"And I am your mother, Tristan. You didn't hear what she said to me up there!" She argues back.

"Oh, I heard all right. I heard everything you said to her first. What the hell gives you the right to treat someone like that, especially the woman I love, mother."

"I don't trust her. I can spot a girl with an agenda from a mile away, and that girl is only after one thing, and that's your money, Tristan. She doesn't love you. She loves the idea of the life you can provide for her. Was I the only one that was listening at that table? She's had a hard life—of course, she's going to latch onto you. You didn't even sign a prenup. She can you to the cleaners." His mother claims.

"Oh my God, you're unbelievable! You're wrong. You don't even fucking know her! And enough with the damn prenup! I couldn't care less whether you trust her. I do, and that's all that matters to me. How dare you stand there and judge her without even attempting to get to know her!" Cole exclaims firmly. I couldn't take much more, so I decided to walk into the living room. His mother notices me first, and she rolls her eyes.

"Tristan, that is enough!" His father barks. "Remember you're talking to your mother!" Cole was about to argue but stops when he hears my voice behind him.

"Mrs Hoult, I understand your reasons for not trusting me, I do. I've just been thrust into your lives out of the blue, and you're entitled to your own opinion and judgment of me. I'm happy to sign whatever papers you need me to. It isn't about money for me; it has never been. I promise you both I have no agenda." I explain, and the look of surprise on both his parent's faces was all I needed to see.

I look over at Cole, and he shakes his head, "Sweetheart, you don't have to sign a damn thing. I—"

"—I love your son," I blurt out, cutting off whatever Cole was about to say. He stares at me, surprised, for a moment. Cole's jaw clenches tight, and he takes two long strides toward me, and for a brief second, I thought he was going to kiss me. I released the breath I was holding when he wraps his arm around my waist and draws me against him. I look up at him, and he smiles warmly at me. "You've raised a wonderful man," I tell both his parents. His father stood from his seat.

"That's nice of you to say, Shayla. Understandably, we're still both very shocked by all of this. As you can imagine, it's every parent's dream to see their child get married and happy with a family of their own. If Tristan has chosen you to spend the rest of his life with, then we have no other choice but to trust his judgement. Are we happy about it? No, we are not, but as his parents, we must respect that he's grown enough to make his own choices." He explains. Cole and I nod silently. I avoided eye contact with his mother, glaring at me, and I fix my eyes on the marble floor. My cheek was still aching, I can feel a dull headache coming on.

Thankfully, Cole notices me shifting uneasily and makes up an excuse to leave. "Go to the car. I'll be out in a second, sweetheart." He says, handing me the keys to his Audi. I nod and walk out of the house. He probably wants to have a private talk with them. Once outside, I lean against the hood of the car and look up at the star-filled sky and exhale.

I can't seem to catch a damn break. I'm exhausted. Is it ever going to get better for me, or am I just doomed to suffer for the rest of my life? Lost deep in thought, I didn't even notice Cole was standing in front of me, watching me gaze up at the sky.

"Hey, you okay?" I jump, startled when I hear his voice and look at him. He's smiling at me sheepishly. He's holding an ice pack in his hand, and he moves closer to me. "You need to ice your cheek, or you'll bruise."

"I'm fine. There's no nee—ow." I hiss at the sudden jolt of pain when he presses the ice pack to my cheek. I close my eyes when it throbs unpleasantly.

"I'm so sorry, Shay." He whispers, brushing my hair out of my face and tucking it behind my ear. I open my eyes and look up at him; he looks so sad that it made my insides ache.

"Don't be. I deserved it. I shouldn't have said what I did. I should have just kept quiet and let your Mum say her piece. She's your mother, Cole. I've been raised not to disrespect my elders. I should have known better." Cole shakes his head and frowns.

"No, Shayla, you didn't deserve any of that. She was wrong, and she had no right to lay a finger on you." He tells me sullenly, and I shrug, closing my eyes. "I feel responsible for getting you hurt, and I—"

"—Cole," I place my hand over his, holding the icepack on my cheek. "Please, it's not even an issue. I'm honestly fine." He sighs, nodding, pulls the ice pack away from my face, and examines my cheek.

"Does it feel any better?" He asks. I nod. It didn't, but I couldn't stand to see the guilty look in his eyes any longer.

"It does, thank you." I smile and wince a little, and he chuckles.

"Getting the hang of lying, I see." He teases.

"I am?"

He snorts, "No. You're still pretty awful at it." I pout and nudge him away from me so I can stand up straight.

"You know what. I've had enough of you today. Take me home." I sulk, shoving the icepack at him, and walk around the car to the passenger side while he just howls with laughter while I glare at him.

"You're adorable, sweetheart." He chuckles, opening his car door, and we both get in.

"Oh, bite me," I grumble, crossing my arms over my chest and looking out my window.

"Just say where baby," He drawls leaning closer. I cover his face with my hand and push him back. He licks my palm, and I yank my hand back and wipe it on his shirt.

"Ew! Oh my God, you did not just lick my hand!" I exclaim, and he giggles like a girl as he pulls out of his parents' driveway.

"I couldn't bite you, so I improvised." He claims with a shrug, squinting at me sideways with a mischievous grin on his stupidly handsome face. I hate him. I swear to God, these antics of his drive me up the wall. I sneak a look at him, and he looks at me at the same time. I couldn't contain the smile any longer. We laugh. On the journey home, we had the top down to the car, music up loud, and singing along to the songs on my playlist. I find Chicago – 'If you leave me now' and crank up the volume. Cole looks at me puzzled when I start to sing the song to him while he fights the urge to laugh. His lips curl into a smile, his eyes darting from the road then back to me as I sing the lyrics dramatically.

"If you leave me now, you'll take away the biggest part of me. Ooh, no, baby, please don't go!" I sing pleadingly, grabbing his hard bicep, and he cracks up laughing.

"A love like ours is love that's hard to find." We sang together, leaning into each other when he stopped at a light and burst out laughing and didn't stop till we pull up outside my apartment building.

Grinning, Cole kills the engine and turns in his seat to look at me. "Do you want me to pick you up tomorrow morning?" He asks. I shake my head and fish out my keys from my handbag.

"No, my car is sorted. I'll just see you at the office. Thank you for offering, though." I reply and could have sworn I saw a little disappointment on his face, but it vanished as quickly as it appeared.

"Of course. We still need to work on the contract. Tomorrow?" I nod and smile before I push the door open.

"Tomorrow. I'll see you in the morning." I get out of the car and close the door. Just as I get to the door, I hear him call my name. I look back and see him jog over to me.

I look up at him, and he holds out the icepack. "Here, you'll need this. Make sure you ice it every twenty minutes for at least an hour." I take the icepack from him and nod. He reaches up and brushes his thumb over my cheek tenderly.

I lose my breath at his touch. "I will, thanks." Our eyes meet again, and my heart does that weird thing where it flickers a little when he smiles at me.

"Thank you for introducing me to 'caraoke.' That's most definitely the most fun I've had while driving." He expresses with a little laugh, and I chuckle nodding in response.

I was thankful it was dark out, so he couldn't see the blush on my cheeks. "You're very welcome." I smile, biting my bottom lip. "Goodnight, Tristan Cole Hoult," I say, and he licks his lips and looks down at his feet before he looks at me again.

"Goodnight, Shayla Hart." I pull the door open and glance back at him one last time; he looks back as he walks toward his car and waves. I wave back and walk into the building. I lean against the wall by the door and close my eyes, willing my heart to stop fluttering wildly in my chest.

Stop it Shayla.

I groan and walk up to my apartment. What I need is a hot shower, a good movie, and my girls. Speaking of the girls, as soon as I walk into the apartment, Jo and Aimee fly to the door and greet me with broad smiles on their faces. They've seen the article.

"Oh my God, Shayla! We've been trying to call you for hours, where the hell have you been? What on earth is going on? You're literally on every magazine cover?" Aimee asks in a flurry.

I drop my keys in a bowl that we keep by the front door and sigh,

"Girls. I have had a hell of a day. I will answer all of your questions, I promise, but please just let me take these shoes off and shower first." I say tiredly and they both nod in response.

"Okay, fine, but hurry up! We've been dying to find out the deets!" I wave them off as I kick my shoes off and walk toward the bathroom. I don't even know where to begin explaining the whirlwind that has become my life.

I run the shower and look at the mirror at my reflection and notice the bruise forming on my cheek just under my eye where her giant wedding ring caught me. I reach up and brush my finger over it gently. I close my eyes, and the image of Cole brushing his fingers over it and the concerned look in his eyes flashes through my mind.

I try to shake off all thoughts relating to Cole Hoult and try to enjoy my shower, but of course, I fail miserably, and my mind wanders off to him again. I wonder if he was thinking about me too.

Ugh. Get a grip, Shayla. Of course he's not, you idiot!

~

AFTER MY SHOWER, I get into my pj's, the girls and I order pizza, and we open a bottle of wine while I fill them in with everything that's happened. "I'm relieved you're not pregnant, obviously, but what are you going to do about your family Shay? Sam called me twice today." Aimee says, pulling her knees to her chest.

I sigh and shrug, "I don't know girls, he's called me a dozen times too, but I keep ignoring it. I'm terrified to answer because I don't know what to tell them. I might go and see them tomorrow." I take a sip of my wine and stare into my glass. "I'm all tangled up in this giant web of lies, and I don't know how I'm going to get myself out of it."

"Can you imagine you guys play the roles of being in love so well that you end up falling in love? How romantic would that be? Just like a movie." Aimee gushes, and I roll my eyes.

"That only happens in rom-coms Aimes, let's get real, Cole and I are just too different ever be anything serious. We're complete opposites and not even each other's types at all." I utter picking off pieces of my pizza slice.

Aimee looks at her tablet and holds it up for me to see, "I'm so sorry, but this doesn't look like two people who aren't each other's types. If I saw this and didn't know either of you, I would say you guys are genuinely in love."

"Aimee's right Shay, we haven't seen you that happy in a long time." I shake my head and run my finger along the rim of my glass.

"Girls, I was drunk. What you see in that photo are two people too hammered out of their minds to know what the hell they're doing. The only time I ever try a one-night stand and I end up marrying the guy and make the fucking tabloids." I say with a bitter laugh. "Never again. In fact, I'm going to take a vow of celibacy. Right now."

Aimee chokes on her wine and coughs while Jo pats her on the back. "Easy Aimes, she said her, not you." While the girls were bickering, my eyes drift to the photos of Cole and me on Aimee's tablet. I remember pieces of that night, its slowly starting to come back to me, despite me telling Cole I didn't remember any of the night we spent together, I did.

I remember Cole, and I stumble into the elevator, laughing hysterically at something. A couple of other people stepped into the car with us, and Cole couldn't keep his hands to himself. His fingers kept trailing up my bare spine, grazing the side of my breast, his lips on my ear whispering the things he wanted to do to me. "I can't wait to taste you, baby." He breathes, his voice was deep and husky. I press my thighs together and bite back the moan that was about to escape me when he nips at my ear gently. "I'm going to drive you wild."

Once we hit the tenth floor, the elevator emptied, and it was just us. As soon as the doors slid shut, Cole spun me to face him and had me pressed up against the wall, his mouth on mine hot and needy, kissing me hungrily. I moan and kiss him back just as eagerly, tongues duelling. Cole scoops me up with one arm and lifts me into his arms, pinning me against the wall while he rocks his hips into me. I feel his erection pressed against me, hard and throbbing. "I want you so fuckin' bad." He groans, biting and tugging my bottom lip with his teeth.

The elevator finally dings, and the doors open to the penthouse suite he booked for us. With me still in his arms, he walks out of the elevator. His fingers find the zipper to my dress, and he slides it down while I unbutton his shirt, he kisses my neck, biting and sucking a trail down to my breasts, I slide my arms out of the straps.

Cole kicks a chair away from a table in the middle of the suite and lays me down on top of it. I look up at him standing there in front of me, shirt unbuttoned, hair messy where I'd been running my fingers through it a moment ago. He looked gorgeous. The man was carved by the Gods. "Fuck. You're *so* hot." I swoon, watching him as he peels his shirt off his broad shoulders, his muscles flexing with every movement. I sit up, reach over, and hook my finger at the hem of his jeans. I pull him to me and kiss him deeply while I run my hands over his lean, rock hard abs to undo his buttons and pull them down.

I grin against his lips when I rake my nails down his taut chest, and he responds with a throaty moan. "Mm, so hard and perfect." He watches me intently, lifts his hand and brushes my hair away from my face, his eyes lock with mine. I sigh when he drags his thumb over my bottom lip, down to my throat, where he grips gently laying me down on the table again, his knee pushing my thighs apart. His fingers eagerly push my dress up around my waist, revealing the black lace panties I was wearing. I mentally thank Aimee for making me wear them. Those jewel green eyes darken with desire, and he slides them down my legs slowly, his eyes on my most sacred part, taking in every inch as he takes my underwear off and discards it on the floor along with the growing pile of clothes.

The last thing I saw was the devilish grin he gave me before his head disappeared between my legs. I gasp when he licks up my slit, slow and deliberate. I rock up against his mouth, and he grips my waist holding me in place. "Uhh! Cole." I moan when his tongue flicks against the hidden bundle of nerves. My fingers curl in his hair, and I arch up when he continues to suck and lick my clit. "Ohh! God, yes, right there." I grip the edges of the table when I feel that delicious warmth building and building with every flick of his tongue. I writhe and moan his name over and over as I near my release. When he slides a finger inside me and sucks my clit hard, I arch up and come with a shuddering cry. Cole moans as he continues to lick up my juices.

"Holy shit," I pant, falling back on the table a quivering mess. Cole kisses up my stomach, stopping to take a rosy nipple into his mouth, he nips at the hard and tight nub, and I moan.

"I was right," He whispers, brushing his lips over mine. "You taste fucking incredible."

I grin, "Mm, let me see." I curl my fingers at his neck and kiss him. Tasting myself on his tongue turned me on even more than I already was, which I didn't think was possible. He groans when I suck his tongue hungrily.

Cole pulls away from the kiss panting. "I have to be inside you. I can't wait anymore, I'm losing my mind baby. I want that tight, slick pussy around my cock." He breathes, pressing his forehead to mine.

"Shayla?!" I jump and look over to see Aimee and Jo both staring at me.

I blink, "Huh?"

"You zoned out on us, you okay, you look flushed?" Jo questions and I swallow hard and shift in my seat, suddenly feeling extremely hot.

"I'm, uh, I think the wines just got to me," I tell them, and thankfully they believe me and go right back to talking about something that happened to one of Jo's colleagues. I knock back the rest of my wine and sigh.

It's going to be a long night.

Damn you, Tristan Cole Hoult.

Chapter Eight

COLE

"COLE?" I blink when I hear my name being called and look over at Josh, who is waving his hand in my face.

"What?"

Josh frowns and eyes me warily, "You all right, bud? You've been off in your own world since the match started." I rub my hands over my face and nod.

"I'm good. I'm just thinking about work." I lie. Josh smirks and shoves a forkful of chow-mein in his mouth. I wasn't thinking about work. In fact, for a change, work was the last thing on my mind. I have one thing on my mind tonight. *Shayla.* I have never been so anxious to get to work only because I get to see her.

I've been staring at the television absent-mindedly for over forty-five minutes. I heave a sigh, grabbing my bottle of beer, and get up off the sofa. Josh looks up at me and frowns. "Where are you going?"

I shrug, "I need some air." I tell him and walk outside onto my terrace. I pull my phone out of my pocket, and the moment I unlock it, the article of Shayla and I pops up on my screen. I zoom into the photo of us kissing and I feel my stomach tighten just like it did that night.

I can't remember the last time I felt so free and happy than I did that night with her. Or earlier in my car, singing along to songs.

It's just a game, Cole. She's doing you a favour by helping you out. That is it. She would divorce you in a heartbeat if she could. She doesn't want you, so get your shit together and do not allow yourself to get too close to her.

"Fuck," I exhale, looking up at the glimmering stars. Why do I miss her? I barely even know this girl. I've known her what, a week for God's sake. Today is the seventh day. This time last week I was at the club, watching her dancing sensually, laughing with her friends. Completely mesmerised. The funny thing is, I can't remember what my life was like before her anymore. How pathetic is that?

I shake my head and groan. Maybe I should text her? I mean, it is our one-week anniversary. I could use it as an excuse to tease her a little. I unlock my phone and type out a text.

'Happy one-week anniversary, Wifey.'

I hit send and chuckle. I can just picture her face when she reads the message. I take a seat on the sofa and gaze out at the view when my phone vibrates. I open the message and see she sent me three emojis, a coffin, a skull, and a middle finger. I laugh out loud and shake my head. She's so adorable. I press the call button, and she answers after a ring.

"What?" She grumbles, trying to sound annoyed, but I can hear the smile in her voice.

"That's what I get for being a thoughtful husband? A death threat." She laughs softly, and I hear her shuffle on the other end.

"I want it to be known on record that I did try to warn you *before* I killed you." She says. I smile and bite my lip.

"I was only being a dutiful husband and wishing my beautiful wife a happy anniversary. I'll cancel the ten dozen roses and the giant bear then, shall I?" I tease and bite back the laughter when she groans.

"What?" She croaks. "Cole, I swear to God, if you've done that, I will literally come over there and feed you every single rose, and I promise you, you'll be shitting out potpourri for a month straight." She threatens, and I throw my head back and laugh heartily.

"Mmm, that sounds rather intriguing. You're highly creative. I like that." I reply, swirling the beer in the bottle.

"I'm thrilled I can please you. Now, seen as you have fulfilled your daily dose of annoying me, was there anything else you need? Because I have work in the morning and my boss is a real headcase." She scorns me playfully, and I grin.

"Headcase, huh? I'll remember that."

"You do that." She retorts with a yawn.

"Get some sleep. I'll see you in the morning. Good night, Shayla Hart."

"Mmm, good night Tristan Cole Hoult." She replies, her voice sleepy. We end the call, and I sigh, grinning at the phone. Annoying her has become my favourite pass time.

"YES!" I jump when I hear Josh shout from inside. "And that's how we make a comeback baby," He yelps jumping on my sofa dancing. "Cole, get in here. You have to see the last-minute goal they just scored. What a finish!" I roll my eyes, walk back inside, and tell Josh off for jumping on my white sofa.

Once I send Josh home, I have a shower and go to bed. I've had the hardest time sleeping lately. Come to think of it, the last couple of nights, I haven't had a decent night's sleep. My mind just refuses to shut off; add sexual frustration to that mix, and you've got a very frustrated man on your hands. Before this whole marriage debacle, I would get laid at least four days out of the week. I stare up at my plain white ceiling and bite my lip thoughtfully. I can't sleep with anyone else while I'm married to Shayla, and obviously, sex with her is out of the question. What the hell is a man to do? We don't even know how long this game is going to last. I'll die of blue balls, and jerking off only gives you so much. A man needs a woman's touch!

With an exasperated groan, I roll over onto my stomach, and hug my pillow, willing my brain to shut off, so I can get some sleep. I toss and turn for over an hour and finally gave up trying to force it. I was wide awake—and rocking an aching hard-on. I senselessly let my mind wander off to the night I spent with Shayla and got myself all worked up. Every time I close my eyes, I see her sprawled out on that bed, body glistening with a sheen of sweat, those gorgeous green eyes gazing up at me full of want.

Fuck it. I grip my throbbing cock and stroke the length slow and steady. I remember that remarkable feeling when I slid inside her hot and wet pussy. Fuck. My head went dizzy from the tight grip of her around me, and I still as I fed my cock deep inside her. The sound of her gasp as I pushed deeper still echoes in my mind—especially the way she moans—my god, her moans made it almost impossible to fight the urge not to pound into her till she was screaming my name. But I couldn't bear the thought of it ending too soon and not being inside her. No, her pussy felt too good for that. I wanted to take my sweet time feeling her out, drawing it out as long as I could.

I thrust into her slow and deep, gathering her arms up and pinning them above her head. I kiss her ardently, swiping my tongue over hers as we move together. She mewls and rocks her hips up against mine, matching my rhythm—the bed squeaks as I thrust deeper, building up momentum. Shayla's moans get louder as she nears her orgasm. I feel her walls fluttering, closing down on me—she's ready to come. I press deeper into her, grinding harder, deeper and she arches up, panting as she goes over, my name on her lips, her body trembling as I fuck her through every ripple of her orgasm. I still for a couple of seconds, kissing and biting her neck while her body calms before I start thrusting again.

"You're going to come with me this time baby," I whisper into her ear, and she moans, raking her nails down my back. "I want you to come with me." She nods and tugs me down, soldering our lips in a fiery kiss as we move together again. I feel that tension as it builds with every hard thrust. My balls tighten, and the moment I feel her clamping down around me again, I thrust deeper, and we climax together. "Ohhh! fuck, fuck yes, Shayla," I moan, pressing my forehead to hers as I spill my load inside the condom. I collapse on top of her breathless, both damp with sweat, and truly spent. "You're fucking incredible," I whisper, making no move to get off of her—instead, we lay as we were, kissing ardently until we fell asleep.

The next morning the chirping of my alarm woke me. I turn the alarm off and notice I fell asleep naked. I must have dozed off after I climaxed. I can't even tell you when I had. I was so lost in the memory that I only remember the intense pleasure of my orgasm and whispering her name repeatedly while I spill my seed all over my stomach.

I have got to get a handle on this ridiculous attraction I have for her. I'm hoping it's only temporary, and I'll get over it soon because I don't know how long I can keep going like this.

After a long cold shower, I make my way to the office. I check the time as I pull up at the underground car park. 07:30 am. I grab my briefcase and walk to the elevator from the car park to the main building, checking my emails as I enter the foyer.

"Good Morning, Mr Hoult." The concierge greets me as I walk over to the elevators. I nod and smile as I walk past them. The elevator dings, and I walk in typing an email. I push the button to the thirtieth floor and lean against the wall.

"Hold the elevator."

I step forward to hold the door open just as someone comes running in, we crash into each other, and the two cups of coffee in her hand spills over both of us. "Shit, that's hot!" I grumble. We both pull our coffee-soaked shirts away from our skin and look at each other at the same time.

"Oh, my God! I'm so sorr—*Cole*?"

"Shayla?" We say together. Shayla rolls her eyes and shakes her head.

"Oh, come on. Of course it's you. I'm not even surprised anymore." She utters using a napkin to wipe the coffee off her hands.

I frown, shaking the coffee off my hands. "What is that supposed to mean?"

She sighs, irritated, "I mean, of all the people in this building, of course, I would crash into you. It's beyond a joke at this point."

"Clearly, our fates are aligned. What can I say? I'm a catch." I tease her, and she glowers at me. "Hey, don't look at me like that, you came crashing into me. This is on you." I say, gesturing to our soiled shirts.

The elevator doors start to close with her standing in between, so I quickly grab her wrist and pull her toward me before she gets sandwiched between them. We slip and fall in a heap on the floor. Shayla lands on top of me as the elevator starts ascending. I groan and look up at her as she stares down at me, eyes wide, lips parted. She was so close I could feel her breath on my face. "You know, it's a good thing we're married, or you'd get me into a lot of trouble with H.R if people saw me straddled by my assistant in the elevator." I joke, and she flushes a nice shade of pink and shifts off me. I groan when she pushes down on my stomach and stands up.

"Why on earth would you pull me like that?" She mutters, dusting off her skirt. I get up off the floor and pick up my briefcase and phone.

"You were about to get crushed by the doors. Would you rather I let you get hurt?" I ask. Shayla huffs and mutters something under her breath. The elevator doors open into our office, and thankfully it was too early for anyone else to be around to see the state of us.

"Ugh. I'm all sticky and smell like coffee. What the hell am I going to do now? I'll never make it home to shower and make it back in time for the first meeting." She complains as we walk toward my office.

"You can use the shower in my office. I have some spare shirts, you can wear one for the day. No one will be here for at least another hour, so we can get cleaned up before they all get here." I tell her, and she sets her bag and laptop on her desk and nods.

"Sounds good." I follow her into my office and close the door behind us. I unbutton my shirt, take it off and set it on the side. The smell of coffee was starting to give me a headache. Luckily, I always keep spare shirts at the office in case of emergencies.

Walking over to the bathroom, I run the shower for her and walk back out. "There are fresh towels under the sink."

"Thanks," Shayla walks into the bathroom, stops, looks around, and walks back out again.

"Uh, there's no door." She states, pointing toward the bathroom. I look over at her and nod.

"I know,"

She frowns, "Why do you not have a door on your bathroom?" She questions while crossing her arms over her chest.

"Well, because it's my bathroom and no one else uses it, and putting a door there would ruin the whole feel of the room," I explain, and she looks back at the bathroom and back at me again bemused.

"Well, that's stupid. What if someone walks in while you're showering or using the toilet?" I smile and rub the back of my neck.

"Sweetheart, no one walks into my office without announcing themselves first. You know yourself, I'm very firm with that rule." I explain, walking over to her. Shayla's eyes wander over my torso as I near her. She blinks averting her gaze.

Too late, baby, I've already seen you checking me out.

"You expect me to shower with no door?" She asks sardonically while I watch her with a cocky grin, "And with you hovering in the room. No chance."

I take a step closer to her and lick my lips, "Shayla, you forget that we've already had sex. I've seen you naked," I smirk and close the space between us, staring down into her upturned face. "I've tasted every bit of your body. I can see you naked whenever I want. All I have to do is close my eyes." I whisper, closing my eyes and bite my lip. "Mmm, there you are." I groan when she jabs her elbow into my ribs, and I laugh when I open my eyes to see her face is beet red.

"I'll hold onto that image if I were you," She chides, scowling at me. "Because you will never see it again." With that, she spins on her heels and walks to the bathroom.

"Hey, never say never," I call out after her

"EVER!" She looks back at me once more before she disappears into the bathroom. "You better not peek." I walk over to my desk grinning wickedly. She's so easy to wind up. I love it.

"Activate cameras!" I shout after a couple of minutes, just loud enough so she could hear me.

"What?! Cole, I swear to God, you better be joking!" She hollers from the bathroom, and I crack up laughing, picturing her covering herself up and looking around for any cameras.

"Come on, no need to cover up baby…let me see you."

"God damn it COLE!" I snicker and lean back against my chair at my desk.

"I'm kidding, relax, there are no cameras. What the hell do you take me for?" I ask, and she mutters something in return, but I couldn't make it out from the sound of the shower running.

Ten minutes later, I see her hand sticking out from the door. "Shirt?" I chuckle and get up from my chair and walk over to her. I pick up the pale blue Prada shirt and hand it to her. "Thank you."

I turn my back to the door to give her some privacy, and when I hear her footsteps behind me, I turn to face her. The shirt was three sizes too big for her, so she rolled the sleeves up and tied a knot at the bottom half around her midriff, showing her smooth tan stomach. She catches me watching her and looks down at herself and back at me again. "What? Does it look bad?"

I shake my head and smile, "No. Not at all. It looks better on you than it ever did on me." She smiles a little and blushes. "One thing…" I step closer to her and fix the collar of the shirt. "There, much better."

"Thank you. I'm done in there if you want to shower. I'll towel dry my hair a little and get out of your way." I nod and rub the back of my neck.

"No problem." I brush past her and walk to the bathroom. By the time I finish showering, she had already left my office and was at her desk typing away on her keyboard. I didn't see her much for the rest of the day unless I was in a meeting and needed her to take minutes. I'd catch glimpses of her as she walks past my office with files in her arms.

I was so busy working that I hadn't even noticed the time had gone past six, and the office was near enough empty. I look over at Shayla's desk and see her focussed on something in front of her, a pen cap in her mouth, her eyes narrowing as she concentrates on whatever she was working on.

I lean over and push the intercom and watch as she starts when it buzzes on her end. She looks over at me before she reaches over and pushes the speak button. "Yes."

"I'm all done for the day. Are we still going to mine to go over the contract?" I ask, and she nods back at me.

"Yes, unless you have other plans, in which case we can always rearrange." I shake my head and loosen my tie.

"No. I just wanted to check you were still up for it."

"Sure," She replies, "Best we get it out of the way, right?"

"Exactly. You ready to go then?" I ask, and she nods and begins gathering her things, straightening her desk. I pick up my briefcase and pull my suit jacket on before I walk out of the office.

"Ready?"

"Yes, but my car is here." She states with a shrug.

"You can leave the car here, and I'll drop you off home and pick you up tomorrow morning," I explain as we walk over to the elevators.

"Are you sure that's not too much trouble for you?" I smile and shake my head as we step into the elevator, and I push the button to the car park.

"Of course not. It's no problem at all." I assure her leaning against the side. Shayla tucks a loose strand of her hair behind her ear and looks at me sideways before nodding.

"If you're sure."

"I am."

We step out of the elevator and walk to my car. "There they are!" Shayla and I both jump when we hear a group of people with cameras rushing toward us.

"Oh shit." I curse, and Shayla looks up at me worriedly. "Paparazzi. Keep your head down." I tell her, and she shifts behind me, shielding herself from the cameras. I lace my fingers with hers and pull her hurriedly toward my car.

"Tristan! Tristan, is that your wife? Is it true she's pregnant with your first child?"

"Tristan, can we please get a quote? Why did you lie about being married?"

I open the door, so Shayla could get in, and I walk around the car. "Guys, you're trespassing on private property. Please leave."

"Can you please confirm the pregnancy?"

I sigh and roll my eyes, "She's not pregnant. I wasn't forced into marrying her. I married her because I'm in love with her. There's your quote. I urge you to stop printing false stories and respect our privacy." I tell them and open the driver side door and get in. They push the cameras against the tinted windows and keep snapping photos of us as I pull out of the parking space. I speed away and out of the car park. "You all right?" I ask, glancing over at Shayla, who sighs and nods while looking out of her window.

"I'll never get used to having cameras shoved in my face and people screaming at me like that. I don't know how you do it."

I shrug, "You get used to it after a while. It's overwhelming the first few times, but eventually, it just becomes the norm."

"If you say so." She mumbles, looking at me briefly before averting her gaze out of the window again. We didn't exchange any more words until we got back to my place.

Shayla looks around my apartment as we walk in. "You live here alone?"

I nod, tugging my tie off and folding it up neatly. "Yes, why?"

"It's pretty big for just one person. Don't you ever feel lonely in this big apartment?" I smile and shake my head.

"Not really. I barely spend time here, to be honest. I'm out of the house early, and I get home pretty late from work, so it's pretty much used as a crash pad now." I explain, setting my briefcase on the white marble countertop, unlock it, and pull out the contract I had my lawyer draw up. "I don't know about you, but after today I could use some wine," I say, walking over to the kitchen to grab two glasses and a bottle of wine.

"Sounds good." I open the bottle of white wine and watch as Shayla wanders around the apartment. She walks over to the bi-fold doors to the terrace and looks out at the view. "Wow, that view is gorgeous."

I walk over to her with two glasses and the bottle of wine in my hand. "I know. It's why I bought this place. I fell in love with the view instantly. Would you like to sit outside? The sunset is stunning from up here." I ask, and she nods beaming. I hand her the bottle of wine and pull the big bi-fold doors open. "Take a seat, and I'll grab the contract."

Shayla walks over to the white sofa outside and places the bottle and the glasses on the table. I grab the contract and walk over to her, taking a seat beside her. I pull the paperwork out of the envelope while she pours the wine. "Shall we?"

"Sure," She picks up her copy and flips the first page, her eyes skimming over the front page. "Miss Hart may not speak of nor share the contractual agreements with any third parties?" She reads and lifts her eyes to look at me. "In doing so, a penalty of £500,000 will be imposed."

I nod, "I mean, I know you wouldn't, but just in case you take this agreement and sell it off to the tabloids. It's a discretion agreement. It's just a clause to protect myself and my family. You understand."

Shayla chuckles but nods. "Right, because if had that much money laying around I'd be working for you." I give her a mega-watt smile and she rolls her eyes before she turns the page and reads the first line. "Whoa, hold on, we have to stay married a year?" She looks at me again and shakes her head. "No, absolutely not."

I frown, "What do you mean absolutely not? A year is a sufficient amount of time for people to believe we tried to make it work." I explain, and she shakes her head again.

"A year is an exceptionally long time, Cole. Six months." She says, and I shake my head this time.

"Too short, nine months."

"No, three months."

I sigh, and we glare at each other, "Fine, six months." I concede striking out the clause and amending it to the new timeline. "You're so stubborn."

Shayla smiles and takes a sip of her wine. "I know, it's a gift." She looks at the next line, and her eyes go wide. "Wait. What? This clause says I have to move in with you?"

"Yes, that's correct."

She shakes her head swiftly. "No, no bloody way. I am not living with you." She claims, dropping her pen and crossing her arms over her chest while glowering at me.

I rub my forehead in frustration, "Shayla, we're married. It's expected of us to be living together. If you keep saying no to everything we will never get anywhere."

Shayla stares at the papers apprehensively and looks at me again sulking. "Fine." She agrees, picking up her glass of wine and knocks it back.

"Thank you. Okay, moving on."

"Neither participants must engage in any other sexual activities or relationships with any other persons for the duration of the marriage." She reads and chuckles. "Oh good, a no cheating clause, the pillar of every good marriage." She drawls sardonically, and I smirk into my glass.

"Doesn't hurt to be clear. If we want this to be believable, then we need to be careful and if that means we can't see other people, then so be it." Shayla watches me for a long moment and drops her gaze to the papers in front of her.

"Well, I've been single for two years and in no rush to jump into another relationship anytime soon, so you're safe on my account." She clarifies and leans over to read through the rest of the contract. I caught a little bitterness in her tone, and I couldn't help but wonder why her relationship ended. Did someone cheat on her? Is that why she has issues trusting men? I poke her side with my pen and smile at her when she looks at me with a scowl fixed on her pretty face.

"What kind of fool would ever dream of breaking your heart?" I ask. Shayla licks her lips, and she looks ahead.

"The kind that didn't think I was good enough to be with him. He chose to believe his family when they filled his head with all sorts of shit, and he broke up with me. After I gave him almost three years of my life, he dropped me like I didn't even matter. Arsehole." She explains resentfully, and I felt my gut clench at the sorrow in her voice.

I reach over and rub the nape of her neck gently. She looks over at me, and I brush a strand of her hair out of her face so I could see those beautiful green eyes. "What an absolute arsehole indeed. One would have to be completely dense to ever let a girl like you go," I tell her earnestly, and she stares at me surprised, her eyes searching mine for sincerity. I force myself to keep my eyes on hers and not look down at her lips because if I so much as glance at them, even for a second, I'll lose the battle within me and kiss her. Her face was glowing under the late afternoon sun, catching her eyes perfectly. I never noticed that her eyes have flecks of hazel in them.

"Cole." She says softly.

"Yeah,"

She licks her lips slowly and leans in close, and I feel my heart rate accelerate, "You've put a clause that I get a settlement figure of two million pounds when we divorce." She whispers. I must be honest. I didn't hear a single word she was saying at this point. I was too lost in her eyes and the sweet smell of her perfume.

"Mhm."

"Strike it out." I blink, and when she averts her eyes, my senses come rushing back to me.

"What?" I utter confused, while she taps her pen on the papers in her lap.

"I already told you I don't want your money." She states openly, and I frown. Is this girl for fucking real?

"Shayla, that clause will stay. You need to get something out of this; otherwise, what is the point." I explain, and she shrugs her shoulders in a blasé manner.

"I'm not doing this expecting to get anything out of it. Besides, you're helping me too, with my family. That's more than enough." I sigh and pinch the bridge of my nose.

"No, don't be ridiculous. The clause stays, and that's final." She glares at me hard.

"Are you not listening to me? I don't want it." She argues back.

"I don't care," I contend sternly. "You'll get the settlement, and I don't want to hear any more about it, understood?" Shayla juts her chin out defiantly and rolls her eyes, shaking her head, clearly displeased with me. She can be angry all she wants. She's getting that money whether she likes it or not.

We went through the rest of the contract and continued bickering for another hour. "Shayla, you're my *wife.* I have to be able to touch you in public! Jesus, I'm not going to maul you in front of everyone. Relax."

"Minimal contact! Change it. Right now."

"Shayla, you're being very irrational. How are we supposed to convince people we are in love if I can't even touch you? I don't have a problem with you touching me." I try to reason with her, but she shakes her head stubbornly crossing her arms over her chest.

"I said minimal Cole,"

I throw my hands up in frustration. "Define minimal?"

"Hand-holding. *One* arm around the shoulder—"

"—waist."

"Shoulder."

"Waist."

"Shoulder!"

"Waist!"

"Argh! You're so infuriating!"

"Right back at you sweetheart!"

"I really don't like you!"

"Oh yeah? I'm not so crazy about you either!"

There we stood. Nose to nose, in the middle of my terrace as the sun sets around us. Our lips a mere breath apart, staring angrily at one another, and all I could think about is devouring her beautiful mouth.

Chapter Nine

SHAYLA

"Don't go."

I look over at Aimee, who picks up my neatly folded clothes out of my suitcase and tosses them haphazardly on the floor.

I sigh, "Aimee. You think if I had a choice, I wouldn't choose to stay here?" I tell her while picking up the clothes and tossing them back in the suitcase for the third time. "Cole will be here to pick me up any minute. Will you just help me pack, please." I pout and give her my best puppy eyes, and she sighs in response.

Jo walks in with another empty box. "Here, I found this in my closet." I smile gratefully and take it from her and start packing up my perfumes and makeup. "Still can't believe you're moving out."

I nod sadly and look up at the girls, "It's only for six months, and I'll be right back with you guys. I'm still paying my share of the rent, so don't go letting my room out to anyone."

"Of course we won't. Don't be silly." I fasten up the zipper on the suitcase and tape the box. I look around my bedroom one last time and bite my lip.

"I think I have everything I need. I'm leaving some of my things here, so I'll be back and forth to pick up stuff as and when I need them." I tell the girls, and they sit on my bed and nod while watching me gather my belongings.

A sound of a horn comes from outside. I walk over and look out the window. Cole pulls up with his black Range Rover Sport. He climbs out of the car, looking like he just stepped out of a magazine shoot, and my mouth waters. He's wearing a tight black tee-shirt, a pair of light blue, tight-fit ripped jeans that hug his muscular thighs nicely, finished with a pair of black boots. His hair styled perfectly as usual, and a pair of aviator sunglasses shielding away those mesmerising eyes of his.

"My God, he is so fucking gorgeous." Aimee groans, awe-struck. Cole looks up at my window, and he lowers his sunglasses to the bridge of his nose and grins, showing those gorgeous dimples on both his cheeks. I gesture for him to come up, and he nods and walks to the front entrance of the building. "Is he coming up?! Oh, my fuck, I look like shit." Aimee squeals, running to her bedroom to doll herself up, no doubt. "Tristan Hoult is going to be in our apartment. Holy fucking shit!"

Jo and I laugh at her antics. "Aimee, will you please calm down. He's just a guy."

"Excuse me, the hottest guy in the country!" I roll my eyes and walk over to the door when I hear a knock. I can smell his aftershave before I even get to the door. I take a deep breath and open it. He smiles at me and takes his sunglasses off.

"Hey," I greet him.

"Hey you." I gesture for him to come in, and he steps into the apartment and drops a kiss on my cheek before he straightens and looks around. "Nice place." He claims, tucking his sunglasses into the collar of his shirt. I give him a pointed look, and he chuckles. "What, *it is*."

"Mhm." I shake my head and lead him to my bedroom. "I'm almost packed, just have a few things I need to sort out first, then we can go," I tell him, and he intones a sure in response. When I walk into the bedroom, I see Jo and Aimee sitting on my bed. "Cole, these two are my roommates and my two best friends, that's Jo," I introduce, pointing to her, and she gives him a little wave, mumbling a timid 'hi' in response. "And that's Aimee," I finish, gesturing to Aimee sitting with her legs crossed rather seductively. She smiles up at him sweetly and wags her fingers at him while openly giving him a once over.

"Nice to meet you both girls," Cole says with a charming smile. I give Aimee a 'what are you doing' look from behind Cole, and she shrugs. Good lord, this girl is hopeless.

"Uh, we'll get out of your way so you can finish packing," Jo says, pulling Aimee up by the arm. "It was nice meeting you, Cole. Please look after our girl." She adds as they pass by him.

Cole smiles, nodding his head, "I will, I promise." The girls leave the room, and as I close the door behind them, I hear Cole laughing while he walks over to my bed and sits down.

"What's funny?" I ask, picking up various items from around the room and dropping them in the box.

"Your friend Aimee, she's uh…very full-on." He expresses, watching me as I move around the room.

I snicker, "Oh yeah, she sure is. She's our resident man-eater. She means well though. I wouldn't change her for the world." Cole grabs my pillow and lays back on my bed. "I think she's got a little crush on you. Actually—scrap little, she has a *very* big crush on you," I explain.

Cole smirks, "You're the only one that doesn't, sweetheart." He says playfully, kicking my bum when I bend over to pick up my shoe.

"And you wonder why," I reply, slapping his foot away and throwing my stuffed bear at him. "I'm not into egomaniacs."

Cole scoffs, lifts himself on his elbows on the bed, and gapes at me. "I am not an egomaniac." He claims affronted. "There's a very big difference between arrogance and confidence." Ahh, I hit a nerve. Let's keep poking.

I frown and shake my head, "And what dare I ask might that difference be?" I say tauntingly, raising my brow. While I smirk at him, Cole narrows his eyes at me and bites into his bottom lip. I shouldn't have goaded him. I gasp when he catches my wrist and yanks me down on the bed with him. Before I even realised what was happening, he had me pinned down beneath him.

"I'll happily show the difference." He burrs, looking into my eyes deeply. I place my hands on his chest to push him off me, but he gathers my arms and pins them above my head. There's a daring glint in his eyes, and I feel my stomach tie itself into knots as I lay trapped under him. He leans down close to my ear and whispers. "Relax. I'm not going to touch you."

The heat of his breath against the shell of my ear sent quivers down my spine. My heart was hammering against my ribcage so hard, making it difficult to catch my breath. Cole sweeps his nose along my jawline and back up to my ear again. "I bet I can make you come without even touching you."

"Cole…" I tried my best to keep my voice firm, but instead, it came out as a breathy whisper.

"Are you brave enough, sweetheart?" He speaks softly, ghosting his lips over mine. I open my eyes and look up at him.

"The girls can walk in and—."

Cole smirks, and his gaze drift down to my lips, "Let them." He murmurs, his voice deep and smooth. "Answer my question, yes or no."

Say no, say no!

I curse the stupid, stubborn girl inside of me that refuses to give him the satisfaction of being right. "Yes," I say before I can stop myself. *Fuck*

Cole smiles lazily and licks his lips, his eyes on mine. "That's my girl." He mouths, shifting so he was directly on top of me. He pushes my legs apart using his right knee and laces our fingers before pressing his forehead to mine. His thigh comes up in between my legs. I swallow hard, and my mouth suddenly goes dry when I feel his breath on my throat, "Do you remember the night we spent together in Vegas, sweetheart?"

"Yes,"

"Do you remember what I whispered in your ear in the elevator?" He groans in my ear, and I feel an unnatural heat rush through me at the tone of his voice. I nod silently, closing my eyes. "Tell me."

"I can't wait to taste you, baby." I breathe, and he moans, brushing his lips over the shell of my ear lightly.

"What if I told you that I can still remember just the way you taste and would give anything to taste you again." He whispers. "Would you let me taste your honey, baby? Would you let me run my tongue over your clit and suck it, just a little?" I felt an ache in between my legs and moan. My hips rock on impulse, and when my sex makes contact with his thigh, I shudder. "What if I told you that I wish I could bury myself deep inside your tight, wet pussy right now, just to feel you choking my cock as you come hard for me. Would you want me to, baby?" He groans while gently nipping at my ear. I feel the hard length of him pressing against my hip and bite my lip hard, willing myself to keep still, but my body defies me, and I rock against him urgently. He hisses, and every hair on my body stands on end. I tighten my fingers around his own, and he raises his thigh higher, so I could rub myself against him harder.

"What if I told you that I was dying to kiss you right now." He closes his eyes, pressing his forehead to mine. "Would you let me, baby?" He whispers, his lips a breath away from mine. I couldn't think straight. Every nerve in my entire body was tingling. I want him so bad, and I honestly thought I would die if he didn't touch me.

"Cole." I whimper, arching up when I feel that familiar heat building up inside me and rushing straight down to my core. "Christ, Cole…I …oh god, I'm going to come."

"Come for me, Shayla. Let me watch you come apart for me." I rock my hips once, twice, and I bite my lip hard to stop from screaming as I climax. I shudder in his arms as I hit the peak of my orgasm, and he covers my mouth with his hand to smother my cries of pleasure. Cole presses his lips to my temple, smiling as my body begins to settle down. I peel my eyes open and look up at him panting, and I feel my cheeks burn. Did that really just happen?

"How did you—I can't believe I just—oh, Christ." I stammer, closing my eyes. My face aflame, I try to look away from his intense gaze, but he stops me and gently turns my head, so I could look at him.

"The difference between confidence and arrogance is empathy, Shayla. A man that is confident within himself doesn't need to brag or seek assurance from others around him because he already has an awareness of his abilities and qualities." He says, brushing his thumb along my jaw. "Don't you ever be ashamed of your desires because that was so incredibly sexy."

I sigh and lick my lips, "That's easy for you to say. You're not the one being defied by your own body." Cole chuckles and bites his lip.

"Oh, please. I get defied by my own body at least four times a day."

He says and looks down at the very visible bulge in his jeans. "Case and point."

I chew my bottom lip gingerly, wondering if the girls heard anything, and as if on cue, I hear their voices approaching. I shove Cole off me and quickly sit up, fixing my shirt just as the door opens and Aimee walks in.

"Oh. You're still here. I thought you would have left already." She says, looking at me and then at Cole, sprawled out on the bed, his back against the wall and my pillow on his lap.

"Uh, yes, we were just talking about um…work stuff," I answer, looking over at Cole, smiling at me knowingly, and nods. Aimee frowns a little and gives us a very wary look before she picks up my maroon jacket from the back of the door.

"Right. Well, I just came to get this, so you guys can go back to your 'talking' about 'work stuff.'" She drawls, making air quotes with her fingers as she walks out of the room with a grin on her face. The door closes, and I slap Cole's leg when he starts to laugh.

"Ow, why are you hitting me." He grumbles, rubbing his thigh.

"You could have been a little more helpful instead of sitting there smirking like an idiot. Now she thinks we were up to no good in here," I say in a huff, and Cole laughs again.

"Well, she would be right because we were up to no good. Besides, your face is all flustered, and your hair is a mess. So, at the very least, she's going to think she interrupted a very steamy makeout sesh." He says with an amused smirk. I pull the pillow from his hold and hit him with it.

"Oh my God, I really wish the ground would open up and swallow me whole right now." I feel Cole shift on the bed and sit beside me.

"Shayla, I am your husband. It is only natural for people to assume we get it on when the doors are closed. We're not doing anything out of the ordinary—as far as others are concerned anyway." He explains, bumping his shoulder with mine.

"Cole, they're my best friends. They know this whole thing is a sham. I told them."

He nods, "Ah, I see."

"Ugh. Come on, let's go already before I change my mind, unpack my stuff, and stay here," I say, picking up my suitcase. Cole nods, picks up the box before he takes the suitcase from me, and walks out of the room.

"Go say bye to your girls. I'll wait for you in the car." I sigh and look around my bedroom one last time before I walk out and close the door. I stroll over to the living room where Jo and Aimee were stood waving at Cole as he leaves the apartment.

"Well, I guess I'll see you guys soon," I pout, and we all hug.

"I'm going to miss you, Bish," Jo says, tightening her arms around me.

"I'm going to miss you too, both of you." We pull apart, and Aimee sulks, watching me as I walk to the door. "I'll come and see you guys all the time. It will be like I never left." They nod and wave when I blow them a kiss.

I leave the apartment and make my way down the stairs. Suddenly it feels like everything in my life is changing, and I don't like it. I've never lived with a man before. I'm quite nervous, and after what just happened in my bedroom, I can't trust myself around him. I just have to find a way to avoid getting into situations like that.

As I walk out of the building, I see Cole leaning against his car, shades on, arms crossed. When he sees me, he straightens and walks over to me. "You okay?" He asks, wiping away a tear that I hadn't even noticed rolled down my cheek.

I nod, "Yeah. I'm going to miss my girls, that's all." Cole smiles and wraps an arm around my shoulder, and pulls me against him as we walk over to his car.

"Sweetheart, I'm not locking you up and throwing away the key. You can come and see your friends whenever you want, or they can come and see you at our place." I look up at him as he opens the door for me to get in. *Our place.* He didn't say my place; he said *our* place.

"Really? They can come whenever they want?" I ask, and he smiles and nods, tweaking my nose.

"Whenever they want." I slap his hand away from my nose, and he grins down at me. He helps me up into the car as I was a little too short, and the steps to the range rover was a little on the high side. I look up at the girls who were at the window watching us. I wave up at them as Cole gets in and starts the car. They wave back and blow kisses at me as we drive away.

I sigh and sink back into the plush leather seats. “By the way, we’ve got to go and see my family tomorrow. I can’t avoid them anymore.” I tell him, and he looks over at me and nods.

“Sure, we can go tomorrow. It’s the weekend, so we can have some breakfast and go see them around lunchtime? That work for you?” I nod silently and look out the window. I miss my family so much, but I am terrified of what awaits me. It feels like I’ve not seen them in so long when it's only been a week.

I watch Cole as he drives, and I wonder what he usually does on weekends. I bet he has a schedule that he sticks to religiously. “What do you usually do on weekends?”

Cole smiles and licks his lips, “I play golf most weekends.” When I look at him blankly, he laughs and glances at me sideways. “What?”

“I’m starting to realise why God has put me in your life,” I respond dryly, and Cole cackles.

“Oh yeah, and why is that?” He questions, amused.

“Because your life is depressing as hell. Golfing on weekends? What are you sixty years old?” I retort, shaking my head. “No, I am convinced now more than ever that I have been chosen to bring some colour to your life.”

“Hey, I happen to really enjoy golfing, and I do other fun activities.” He says, put out, and I roll my eyes.

“Please, do enlighten me.” I urge, crossing my arms over my chest and stare at him expectantly.

“I shoot skeet.”

I roll my eyes. “Bore. Next.”

“I enjoy horseback riding.”

I shrug, “Okay, I like horses. Go on.”

“I go sailing.” He adds.

“Oh, cool. You have a boat?” He nods and looks over at me.

“I have many boats. Have you ever been sailing before?”

“Of course you do, and no, I’ve never been on a boat. Come to think of it, I've never gone horseback riding either. I always wanted to go as a little girl, but my parents were always too scared to let me get on a horse."

Cole smiles, "Maybe I can teach you one day. Would you like that?" I look over at him, surprised.

"You would do that?" I question and he nods.

"Yes, of course. I tell you what, every weekend we do one thing and experience what the other person enjoys. What do you say?" I muse over his idea and nod.

"Okay, but I swear, you try and take me antiquing or some shit, and I'm out of there," I warn him, and he laughs.

"Antiquing? What am I sixty years old?" He drawls, using my own words on me, and cheekily smiles when I poke my tongue out at him.

"That is still up for debate, my darling," I say as we pull up at his apartment complex. Cole parks up, and we get out of the car. He helps me carry my suitcase and boxes up to his apartment.

There I stood, in his five-million-pound apartment, completely clueless as to what was awaiting me.

Chapter Ten

COLE

"Ow, shit!"

I jump out of bed and rush over to Shayla's bedroom when I hear a crash and her shout.

"Shayla? You okay?" I call out, knocking on the door. I listen out for her, and when I don't hear an answer, I open the door and walk inside. I find her sitting on the floor in the dark, holding her foot surrounded by glass. She looks up at me and blinks, surprised when I turn the light on. "What have you done? Are you hurt?"

She takes her Airpod out of her ear. "Huh?"

"I asked if you were okay?" She bites her lip and nods, glancing at the broken lamp on the floor.

"Oh, uh, I'm okay. I broke your lamp, though. I'm still trying to get used to my surroundings. I'm so sorry." She hisses and looks down at her foot. "I'll replace it." I roll my eyes and walk into her bedroom, careful not to step on any broken glass.

"Jesus, Shayla. Fuck the lamp. Is your foot okay?" I ask her, and she shrugs and moves her hand, and her fingers are covered in blood. "You're bleeding."

"No. No, Cole, there's glass everywhere. You'll cut yourself too." I ignore her protests and step over the broken glass till I can reach her.

"Can you stand up?" She nods and takes my hand when I hold it out to her. I sweep her into my arms bridal style, and she gasps when she's unexpectedly lifted off the ground, and her arms instinctively wrap around my neck.

I carry her to the ensuite bathroom in my bedroom. I keep a first aid kit in there, so I could clean up her foot. "Cole, I can walk. You don't have to carry me." She sighs, looking at me, and I smile as I carry her to the bathroom and sit her on the counter by the sink.

"You're bleeding, Shayla. You could get your foot infected if you step on the floor. Now, spread your legs." I say, tapping her bare thighs, and she looks at me wide-eyed.

"Pardon?" She snaps, scowling at me. I chuckle and rub the back of my neck.

"The first aid box is in the draw between your legs. You need to move them, so I can get it out." I explain, and her frown softens a little. She spreads her legs, and I open the drawer to get the box out. I close the drawer with my hip and open the box to retrieve the antibacterial wipes and bandages.

"Cole, I can clean it up myself. Give me the box." She says, reaching for it, but I pull it away from her reach and shake my head.

"How are you supposed to see if there's any glass in your foot from your angle?" I ask as I kneel in front of her and she looks down at me.

"It's my foot. I'm sure I can feel it if there were." She replies, holding the edge of the counter when I brush my fingers down the back of her calf, lifting her leg so I can look at her foot.

"Stop being stubborn and let me clean you up," I tell her with a stern look, and she sighs, relenting, and leans back against the mirror. I hadn't noticed when I walked into the room what little she had on. A pair of black fitted shorts and a pale pink crop top with no bra. I simply cannot explain the turmoil inside my head right now. I fix my gaze to her foot and keep it there, not daring to look up. "This might sting," I warn her as I rip open a packet of sterile wipes to clean up her cut. It wasn't big or deep, luckily. I hear her hiss when I press the wipe to her cut, and she instinctively tries to pull her foot away, but I hold her ankle to keep her still.

I raise her foot and blow on the cut to ease the stinging and lift my gaze to her. She had her eyes closed. Head tilted back against the mirror, with her bottom lip between her teeth. Fuck my life, how will I live with this girl for six months and control myself?

I clean her up and put a band-aid on her foot as quickly as I could before I did something stupid. I can already feel myself getting hard. I stand up and clear my throat. "All done," I say, cleaning the wrappers off the floor and dropping them in the trash under the sink. I look everywhere but at her and rub my jaw. "Uh, you can stay in my room tonight. We can clean up the glass tomorrow morning when we can see it better."

Shayla shakes her head and slides off the counter, and hops on one foot to avoid standing on her wound. "No, it's okay. I'll just jump over it or something. I'll be fine."

I stare at her. "Jump? With an injured foot? No. Absolutely not. You're staying in here, and I'll sleep on the sofa for the night."

"Cole, no. You sleep in your room, and I'll sleep on the sofa—ahh, hey!" She yelps when I pick her up and throw her over my shoulder. She wriggles in my hold and slaps my back as I carry her to the bed. "Cole, you put me down right this second!" She grumbles hotly. I walk over to the bed, place one knee on it, and throw her down on her back. She tries to sit up, but I crawl up over her, and she lays back down and stares up at me, her green eyes broad as I stare down at her.

"You're staying in here."

"I am not."

I smile. "Yes, you are, and if you keep arguing with me, I'll be forced to lock us both in here."

She frowns, "You wouldn't."

I lick my lips and narrow my eyes at her. "Wouldn't I?" She looks at me sceptically but shakes her head. I chuckle, "You underestimate the lengths I will go to just to get my way, Shayla Hart."

"Because I know you're bluffing, Tristan Cole Hoult." She retorts, arching up a brow impudently.

She wants to play. I'll bite. I lean down close, my eyes fixed on hers. "Activate locks," I say aloud, and on my command, all locks in the house enable. Shayla looks around the bedroom when she hears the windows and doors clicking as they lock.

"What the hell?"

"Security feature designed by yours truly." I grin smugly at her, and she gapes at me. "In case of an emergency and someone tries breaking in all doors and windows lock and won't unlock until I deactivate them."

Shayla sighs, "Okay, fine, I'll stay, just unlock the doors." I shake my head and shrug before I roll off her onto my back on the bed.

"No can do. Must wait two hours before I can deactivate it. You should have listened and not provoked me; now we're both stuck in here." I say with a grin while she sits up and glares at me.

"I don't believe you. What kind of a stupid emergency system deadlocks and doesn't open for two hours? What if there's an emergency and you need to get out?" She questions, and I sigh, resting my head on my forearm.

"There's an override system, but it's too much effort to activate right now. Go to sleep." I reach up and cover her face with my hand, and she slaps it away.

"Sleep?" She utters, sitting up on her knees. "Sleep where? I am not sharing a bed with you." I smile and grab my pillow to lay on it, but Shayla yanks it from under my head and hits me with it. "Well, you're stuffed then, aren't you? Because I am not sleeping on the floor. I offered to take the sofa, and you decided to be difficult." I tell her, grabbing the pillow and pulling on it.

"Well, you're going to have to sleep on the floor because I am not sleeping in the same bed as you." She groans, trying to push me off the bed, which resulted in a play fight.

I laugh, "Shayla, I am stronger than you; you're going to get hurt." I warn her, but she continues to try and shove me off the bed.

"I have an older brother who is bigger and stronger than you." She grumbles as she changes tactics, places her foot on my back, and kicks me off the bed. I roll off and land on the floor with a thud. I groan and look up at her when she leans over the bed grinning at me with pure joy. "Nighty night."

I smile up at her, reach up, I catch her wrist, and pull her off the bed. She squeals and lands on top of me, our heads colliding as she does so. I swear I have not met a girl as accident-prone as her. Amazingly, she's made it to her twenties. I shake off the blow to my head and look up at her rubbing her own with a pout. "See, I told you you'd get hurt."

Shayla presses her forehead to my chest and groans. "You win, you imbecile." She mumbles, and I smile, rubbing the back of her head gently.

"I always win, sweetheart," I state matter-of-factly and hiss when she pinches the skin on my arm. "Ahh fuck," I rub my arm as she rolls off me onto her back on the floor beside me and sighs. "You're so aggressive for such a small thing."

She looks up at the ceiling licking her lips, "Shut up."

"By the way, you've got a spider crawling on your head." I tease, and Shayla screams and jumps off the floor, and starts shaking her head vigorously.

"Oh my god, get it off, get it off!" I throw my head back and laugh heartily, watching her try and get the spider out of her hair. When she sees me sniggering, she stops, puts her hands on her hips, and glowers at me, with her hair a mess.

"You…ugh, there is a special place in *hell* for people like you." She grouses, getting on the bed. She picks up the pillow and throws it at me. "That wasn't funny. I'm really scared of spiders." She sulks adorably.

I crawl up on the bed behind her and poke her side. "I'm sorry." She jumps but turns her head away from me, so I couldn't see her face. "Come on, don't be like that, sweetheart. I was only kidding." She ignores me and continues to give me the cold shoulder. I smile and come up behind her. I wrap my arms around her and bury my face in her neck. "I'm sorry, please forgive me." I plead, and she attempts to shrug me off, but I hold tighter.

"No, get off me."

"Forgive me," I mumble, nuzzling her neck. "I'm not letting go until you do." I see her lips curl a little, and I continue to nuzzle her neck until I hear her giggle a little. "If you leave me now, you'll take away the very heart of me." I sing to her quietly and Shayla giggles.

"Okay! Okay, I forgive you, stop it." She says, and I grin and kiss her cheek before I begrudgingly release my hold on her. "Can I please go to sleep now?" She sighs tiredly, and I nod, pulling the covers back so we can get into bed. She looks at me as she climbs into bed. "You better stay on your side, or you'll end up right back on the floor." She forewarns, and I nod and hold my hands up in mock surrender.

"Scouts honour," I promise. Satisfied, Shayla lays down and turns her back to me. I turn the lights off and find myself staring at her back. I can just about make out her silhouette in the dark with the help of the moonlight shining through the window. I envisage how good it would feel to just scoot over, gather her in my arms, and fall asleep with my nose buried in her hair. I drift off into a peaceful slumber not long after.

THE NEXT MORNING comes all too soon for my liking. I forget to close the blackout blinds the night before, and I wake up to the sun beaming in my face. Peeling my eyes open, I blink, allowing my eyes to adjust to the brightness of the room, and the first thing I see is Shayla, still peacefully asleep, curled up against me. Our legs tangled together, and I had my arm thrown over her waist, keeping her close to me.

I brush a strand of loose hair away from her face and tuck it delicately behind her ear. She moans and snuggles into me, burying her face into the crook of my neck. I press my nose into her hair and close my eyes, dozing off again. The next time I opened my eyes, I was alone in the bed. Shayla nowhere to be seen. I sit up and rub my eyes; the bathroom door was open, so she wasn't in there. Looking over at the bedroom door I see it's ajar and figured she'd snuck out at some point and gone to her own bedroom.

I roll out of bed and go to the bathroom, but I stop when a waft of something delicious tickles my senses, and my stomach growls. Susan, my chef, is off today, so who is cooking. I follow the smell to the kitchen and see Shayla whisking something in a bowl, her back to me. She had music playing quietly in the background as she sways to it sensually while she pours some batter on to the pan on the stove.

While Shayla sings along to the song playing, I grin and walk over to her. "Good morning," I murmur lowly in her ear, and she jumps frightened, not expecting me to be behind her. I laugh and pull away when she bumps me away with her hip, her cheeks a nice shade of pink.

"You scared the shit out of me. Stop creeping up on me like that." I pour myself a glass of water and sip it.

"I couldn't help it, you looked so adorable singing and dancing away," I admit smiling charmingly at her when she gives me a dubious look.

"Mhm, you better go get ready. We overslept. We're leaving in an hour to see my family. Breakfast will be ready in ten minutes." She tells me, pouring the batter in the pan and swirling it.

"Yes, dear." I mock, grabbing an apple. I kiss her temple as I walk past her back to the bedroom to get ready. After a quick shower, I was dressed and sitting at the table, thoroughly enjoying my pancakes. "These pancakes are incredible!" I call out to Shayla, who was currently getting ready in her bedroom.

"Glad you like them!" She shouts back. "Still prefer the breakfast bar ones, though." I moan at the mere thought of those fluffy pancakes. They really were to die for. Ten minutes later, Shayla comes out dressed and ready to go. "Wow, that was fast."

"What do you mean?" She questions, looking at me confused while sliding her phone into the back pocket of her jeans.

"I mean, you took ten minutes to get ready. I've never known any female ever to take less than an hour to get ready for anything." I explain as we walk to the front door of the apartment.

"Cole, I have never taken an hour to get ready for anything in my life." She says with a shrug while we wait for the elevator side by side.

"Sweetheart, you truly are a rare breed." I compliment her, and she responds with a toothy grin. I reach over and tweak her nose, and she bats my hand away.

"What is it with you and touching my nose?" She grumbles, walking into the elevator.

"I like it. It's small, like a cute button." I chuckle when she touches her nose and looks at me.

"It is not."

"You're adorable."

"Shut up."

Chapter Eleven

SHAYLA

"SHAYLA?" I stare at the front door to the house I grew up in, my heart beating up in my throat. "Shayla." I blink and look over at Cole, who was standing beside me, watching me with a frown. "It's going to be okay." He assures me, and I inhale a deep breath to calm my nerves. He turns me so I could face him, and he brushes his hands down my arms supportively. "I'll be right there if you need me, okay?" I nod and turn to face the door. I slide my key in the lock and hesitate until I feel Cole's fingers lace with mine and his soft lips on my temple. I glance up at him, and he nods encouragingly. Unlocking the door, I walk into my childhood home with Cole behind me. It's quiet, but I can hear the TV's faint sound coming from the living room.

I close the door, and I walk through the corridor toward the living room. "Mum? Sam?" I call out when I see the living room was empty, but the tv was on.

"Well, well, well," I hear my older brother's voice behind me. I turn and see him standing in the doorway with a kitchen cloth in his hand. "Look who finally decided to grace us with her presence." He says sardonically, his chocolate-colored eyes avert to Cole, and I see the anger flare up almost instantly. "Finally remembered you have a family, did you?"

"Sam, I—"

"You what, Shay? Were you too busy with your new life that you forgot we existed, or are you just embarrassed someone will see you associated with us poor folk now you're married to a billionaire?" He claims snidely, and I shake my head.

"Don't be ridiculous, Sam." I snap, and he throws the cloth in his hand over his shoulder and walks over to me. "You know me better than that. It's not like that at all. I've just had a lot going on."

"I bet you have." He replies smarmily and glares darkly at Cole, who stares right back. I can't lie, I'm terrified of my brother, picture Vin Diesel but taller and more muscular. He would crush Coles head like a ripe tomato with his bicep. I was raised in a very strict, traditional, and cultural household where respect and honour mean everything.

"Let's talk." I feel the tension thicken in the room, and I slide my hand out of Cole's hold and step closer to my brother, and we walk into the kitchen. Cole stays back, giving us some privacy to talk. "Where's mum?"

"Locked herself in her room," He says, looking at me. "I haven't seen her this devastated since Dad died. He's probably turning in his grave too." I shake my head and swallow the lump forming in my throat.

"Don't say that. I didn't mean—"

"Didn't mean to what?! Have your pictures plastered all over the papers kissing some bloke?" He shouts angrily. "You're supposed to be the responsible one, Shay! What the hell was going through your head, running off and marrying some fucking rich playboy who will drop you like a bad habit when he's bored!" He exclaims. I drop my gaze to my feet and bite my lip.

"Sam, you don't even know him. He's not like that at all," I argue, looking up at my brother again, who tosses the cloth in his hand on the table furiously.

"Know him? I don't have to his reputation speaks for itself. Notorious playboy billionaire! He's a fucking player, Shayla!"

I scowl at him, "Oh, and you're not?! How many hearts have you broken, Sam? How many girls have walked out of this house crying over the years because you broke their heart?" I retort, and he glares at me hard. "Oh, but it's okay for you, isn't it, Sam? Because you're not a billionaire, so it doesn't matter who you've hurt. I'm sorry, but I don't judge someone based on their past. Cole has been nothing but good to me."

"Why are we only just finding out about him, then? Why did we find out you're married from the fucking internet?!" He shouts, glowering at me. "Why didn't you come and tell us you were seeing someone? It was only two weeks ago you were single and had no intention of seeing anyone. That's what you said. I don't trust any man after what Adam did to me. That's what you stood there and said to me!"

"Sam, I was afraid to tell you. I never meant for you guys to find out like this, I swear." I explain, and he shakes his head and rubs his hand over his scalp agitated.

He walks over to me and grabs my upper arms and looks down into my face. "Shayla, this isn't you. You don't do shit like this. Tell me the truth. Has he forced you or pressured you into marrying him? Is that why you were scared to tell me?" I drop my gaze, and he shakes me, squeezing my arms. "Look at me when I'm talking to you!" He bellows in my face.

"Hey, let go of her." I hear Cole's voice behind me, and I'm suddenly pulled from my brother's hold and shielded behind him.

Sam eyes Cole and smirks darkly. "You've got some balls showing up here after you disrespect my family, kid."

"I am not a kid, and I assure you I meant no disrespect to you or your family, but Shayla's my wife, and if you have a problem, you handle it with me. You don't touch her," Cole tells him bluntly, and Sam nods, taking a step toward him.

"Sam…" I warn, stepping out from behind Cole when I see that dangerous glint in my brother's eyes.

"Oh, I have a very big problem, *kid*." My brother growls.

"Well, here I am. Let's deal with it." Cole provokes him.

"Cole, stop it," I plead, but he doesn't even acknowledge me. His eyes are fixed on my brothers. "Sam, no," I press when I see his hand fist at his side.

"Fucking lets," Sam growls, pushing me aside when I grab his arm. He swings for Cole and punches him in the face hard.

"SAM! No! Stop it!" I yell as he leans over, pulls Cole up by the shirt, and punches him again. “STOP!” I push him away from Cole. “What are you doing?!”

“Teaching him a fucking lesson!” Sam barks down at Cole, who wipes the blood off his busted lip and shakes his head. I lean down in front of Cole and lift his head so I could see his face.

“You’re lucky you’re Shay’s brother.” He hisses gravely, and my brother snorts and takes a step toward him again.

“Richie Rich has got some big brass balls. Come on then, don’t hold back on that account, kid!” I jump up and hold Sam back.

“No! Stop it, Sam!” I shout, pushing him back. I kneel beside Cole again, my stony gaze on my brother.

“My God. Are you okay?” I ask Cole, and he nods

“I’m fine, sweetheart.”

“Cole, you’re bleeding.” I tilt his head up and take a closer look at his busted lip.

“I’m okay.” He assures me with a smile. I stand up and look over at Sam.

“Have you completely lost your mind?!” I scold him. Sam glares down at Cole and then back at me.

“No, but he fucking has! I don’t give a fuck how rich you are! You think you can come in and disrespect me in my own home?”

“He’s my husband, Sam!” I shout, and he walks over to me.

“And I’m your fucking brother! I’m your blood!” He shouts back, grasping my arm.

“Grow up Sam!” I rip my arm out of his hold. “You had no right to hit him. You’re pissed off with me, I get it, but you don’t fucking touch him. What the hell is wrong with you?!”

“Enough! Both of you.” Sam and I stop shouting when we hear my mother’s voice behind us. I turn and look at her standing in the doorway of the kitchen, glaring at both of us penetratingly, just like she used to when we were younger and got into trouble.

“Mum...” I say, and she looks at me and shakes her head sullenly.

“No. You don’t get to call me that anymore.” She says, looking over at Cole and back at me again.

I feel my heart clench painfully when her green eyes fill with tears. "Mum. I'm sorry—"

"You're sorry? You think a simple sorry will fix the damage and embarrassment you have caused this family?" She states, staring at me with such disappointment. "Do you have any idea how appalled I was to see my daughter, my Shayla, all over magazines in the arms of some boy, kissing like an adolescent teenager? Not only did you disgrace this family, but you broke our trust."

I drop my gaze to the ground and try to blink back the tears, but they spill over my cheeks. "Is this how I raised you? To disrespect your family's honour and bring shame upon your father's name?" She berates me. "I never thought I would live to see the day I would be ashamed to call you my daughter. I'm just thankful your father isn't around to see this." I bite my lip hard to keep the sob from escaping. "Is it true? What they're saying, did he get you pregnant? Is that why you got married so fast and in secret?"

I shake my head and wipe away the endless tears that kept rolling down my face. "No! No, mum, I'm not pregnant. I'm not, I swear."

My mother looks over at Cole, "This is him? The boy you chewed your family over?" She asks, her voice breaking ever so slightly as she tries to keep her emotions inside. "They're calling you a gold-digger, Shayla. My daughter, a *gold-digger*."

"Mum, I would never do something like that. People are just speculating. It's not true. You and Sam mean the world to me, you know that." I plead, and she looks up at the ceiling shaking her head.

"But you did Shayla! You chose to run off and marry this boy without consulting us first. I had to hear that my daughter was married by our neighbours. You didn't even have the decency to call us and explain. You leave it over a week later to show your face. Well, I'm afraid it's too late for apologies now."

I shake my head and walk over to my mum and take her hands in mine, but she pulls them away and folds her arms over her chest. "Mum, please, please forgive me. I'm so sorry. I was going to tell you, I swear. I was." I sob helplessly, and she averts her gaze from mine and stares at the wall, her eyes drowned in tears.

"Mrs Hart," I hear Cole's voice from behind me. "I assure you we never intended to hurt you or Sam or for everything to blow up like this. We had every intention of coming here and telling you both about our marriage, but somehow our photos got leaked to the press before we had a chance." Cole explains earnestly, and my mother looks over at him. "I know you have no reason to believe me, but I love your daughter very much."

"You love her?" She repeats and shakes her head, disappointed. "If you had an ounce of respect for my daughter, you would have come over here like a man and told us about your intentions and asked for our blessing first. Instead, you fly her off to another country and marry her in that joke of a chapel without her family present, without a priest. Is that the value and worth of your love for my daughter?" She explains, her tone wounded. "Do you have any idea what you've taken from me? My only daughter and I didn't get to see her in a white dress. I didn't get to see her brother walk her down the aisle. I didn't get to share the happiest day of her life because you…" She jabs her finger at his chest. "…stole that dream from me. You stole her from me." She sobs wretchedly. I clamp my hand over my mouth and whimper. "Now take your wife and get out of my house. As far as I'm concerned, you're no longer a part of this family." She adds, looking at me one last time before she turns to leave.

"No!" I go after her and fall to my knees in front of her, wrapping myself at her legs. "Mum, please, please, I'm so sorry. Please forgive me, don't do this." I sob. "I didn't mean to hurt you. I swear, I didn't." I look up at her helplessly. "I love him."

My mother looks down at me, tears streaming down her face. Cole comes and kneels beside me and looks up at my mother. "Mrs Hart, I'm terribly sorry for everything, and I swear to you, I will make this right. You're right, I stole something so very precious to you, but it wasn't intentional. I'll do whatever it takes to fix this. If it's a wedding, that can easily be arranged, but please don't punish her like this. She's been torn up about letting you both down as it is." He says, rubbing my back soothingly as I sob on the floor.

My mother looks at Cole, "You want to make this right young man. You do things properly. Bring your parents here to meet us, maybe then;

I'll consider forgiving you both." I look over at Cole, and he meets my gaze before he nods.

"Consider it done," Cole says and helps me up to my feet as I watch my mother disappear out of sight. I take one last look at my brother, who watches me with eyes full of sorrow.

"Sam," I whisper, tears running down my face. He shakes his head, drops his gaze before he turns, and storms out the back door, slamming it shut behind him. I bow my head and cry. Cole steps in front of me; he cups my face in his hands and wipes my tears away before pressing his lips to my forehead. "I'm so sorry," He whispers woefully. "I'm going to do everything I can to fix this, I swear."

I close my eyes and whimper. "They're never going to forgive me." I cry.

"Hey, look at me." He lifts my head so I could look up at him. "They will. I will do everything in my power to make that happen. I'll throw the biggest fucking wedding this world has ever seen if that's what it takes." He declares, pulling me against him. "I'll lay my entire fortune at their feet if I have to. It killed me watching you fall to your knees at your mother's feet like that." He says, pressing his forehead to mine.

I sniffle, "I can't lose my family; they're all I have." Cole brushes his fingers through my hair and pulls back to look at me.

"You're not going to. Trust me." He whispers, gazing into my eyes.

I nod, "I do." I look at his lip and notice it's still bleeding, and I reach up and brush my thumb over it gently, and he closes his eyes. "Your lip, it's swollen."

"I'll live." He says and smiles a little. "Maybe you can kiss it better later?" He suggests wagging his brows suggestively at me. This boy is something else.

I decide to tease him a little. I look at his lips, then back up at his eyes. "Maybe I will," I whisper and see the surprise on his face at my response. He stares at my lips for a drawn-out moment before they flicker to my eyes. "Really?"

I nod, "Really." Before the word even left my mouth, Cole took my hand and pulled me to the front door. "Cole, where are you taking me?"

"Home."

"Home?" I intone, and he nods, opening the door and pulling me out with him toward his car.

"Yes, home. My lip really hurts. I need some lip therapy." I chuckle when he opens the door and all but stuffs me into the passenger seat and closes the door. I watch him as he walks around the car to the driver's side and gets in. I felt so bad teasing him like that. He's as excited as a child in a toy store. Would it be so bad if I did kiss him a little? It's not like we haven't kissed before. Oh God, now I'm all nervous and tingly all over. Maybe this is a bad idea. What if it doesn't stop at a kiss? After what happened in my bedroom a few days ago, it's clear I can't control myself around this boy. I mean, just last night, I fell asleep on the other end of the bed, and I somehow woke up in his arms this morning. I remember opening my eyes, and the first thing I saw was his handsome face peacefully asleep. He had his arm thrown over my waist, securing me against him, and our legs were tangled together like a pretzel, making it almost impossible to tell where he ended and I began.

~

I HADN'T REALISED I was lost in a daze until we pull up outside our apartment building. We make our way up to the apartment, a comfortable silence between us. We walk in, and I go over to the sofa in the living room and set my handbag down before turning to watch Cole, placing his keys and wallet on the counter in the kitchen.

I stroll over to him and take his hand in mine. He looks back at me questioningly when I pull him toward his bedroom. We walk into his bedroom, and I lead him to the bathroom. "Sit," I say, pointing to the toilet seat. He obeys and sits down, watching me closely as I move around the bathroom, gathering supplies to clean the wound on his lip. I step between his legs and tilt his head up so I could see a little better. I tear open a sterile wipe and clean the dried blood from the corner of his lip. I wipe his gash gently, and he winces a little when it stings. I lean in close and blow on it just like he did for my foot the night before.

His eyes close, and I see his Adam's apple jump up in his throat. I admire his face for a second, and my heart flutters. Cole opens his eyes, and our eyes meet. There's something in the way this boy looks at me that makes me forget to breathe. I brush my fingers down his neck, and he tilts his head back, closing his eyes again as I unbutton his white dress shirt, which had blood stains on it. I slide his shirt off his muscular shoulders, and he looks up at me with hooded eyes as he takes the rest off and drops it on the floor.

"Thank you for being there for me today," I whisper letting my hands fall to my sides from his shoulders. Cole smiles kindly and places his large hands at my waist, and licks his lips.

"Don't mention it." He whispers back and smiles. "Do I get my kiss now?" He asks with a cheeky grin.

I laugh, "You're unbelievable, your lip is busted and bleeding, and you're thinking about kissing?"

He nods, his green eyes glittering mischievously. "But it hurts, and you promised." He says with a playful pout.

"Okay, I'll give you a kiss," I say and tilt his head up. I lean in close, and just as his eyes slid shut, I kiss him gently on his jaw and pull back. "There you go."

Cole opens his eyes and blinks up at me. "Wha— that's it? That's not what we agreed. You said you'd kiss my lips better."

I shrug and try to pull away, but he draws me back again. "I held my end of the deal."

"No, no, you most definitely did not." He groans and presses his forehead to my stomach.

"Cole, your lip is swollen and seeping blood. Be reasonable. How am I supposed to kiss you without hurting you?" I ask, placing my hands at the back of his head.

"It's worth the pain," He mumbles against my stomach and then pulls his head back and looks up at me again. "Fine, but you owe me a kiss."

I smile and nod as I pull away, "Mhm." I turn and walk out of the bathroom.

"I'll be coming for that kiss, Shayla Hart." He calls out after me, and I grin as I walk to my bedroom.

"Keep dreaming, Cole Hoult."

Chapter Twelve

COLE

"SHAYLA. Will you please come over here?" I ask for the umpteenth time and watch as she stubbornly shakes her head, arms crossed over her chest. "There is nothing to be afraid of, I promise," I assure her, but she still shakes her head, eyeing Casper— my all-white stallion sceptically.

"No. I can't. I'm scared." She mutters with a shrug.

"Honey, it's just for a photoshoot. I'll be right there with you." I assure, walking over to her. She lifts her gaze to mine and scowls. "People are looking. Come on," I urge quietly, and she rolls her eyes.

"Why do we have to do this photoshoot anyway?" She huffs, brushing away a strand of loose hair that fell into her face with her fingers.

"Because people are curious and want to know who I married. If we don't put something out there, they will just keep digging and chasing us around. Is that what you want? To be hounded by the paparazzi all the damn time?" Shayla looks at me and shakes her head.

"No," She sighs. "But this is a bit extreme, isn't it?" She claims, glancing down at herself. She looks gorgeous dressed in a simple white flowy dress, her brown hair curled and styled in half-up, half-down fashion with a braid around her head like a band. She looks like an absolute Goddess.

"Not at all. You look like an angel. We just need to pose for a couple of pictures looking all happy and loved up." I explain, brushing that same strand of her hair away with my fingers. She bites her lip and nods.

"Okay, fine." She agrees and walks toward the horse but jumps back, startled when Casper makes a sudden movement. I chuckle and go over to her.

"Come here." I place my hands at her waist and move her toward him. "Horses can pick up on your nerves. I promise you he's not going to hurt you. Here, give me your hand." I say, moving behind her. I lift her hand and move closer to Casper. "Just relax," I whisper in her ear as I lift her hand, guiding her fingers over Casper's soft fur. "There you go, nice and easy. The last thing you want to do is spook him. If he doesn't feel connected with you or doesn't trust you, he will refuse to let you on, and you'll get hurt. Casper likes to be petted on the head or his face." I tell her, and when I feel her relax, I let go of her hand, and she strokes his face gently. "Hey buddy, there you go."

"He's so beautiful." Shayla smiles as she confidently strokes his shoulder, and Casper groans and turns his face against hers. She grins, touching his face.

"He likes you," I whisper in her ear, and she smiles, brushing her fingers through his hair.

"Please don't kill me," She pleads sweetly, and I step back and let her interact with him on her own for a couple of minutes while I watch.

"Are you ready to mount him?" I ask after a while, and she looks back at me and nods. I step forward and place my hands at her waist. "I'm going to lift you, and you'll need to put your foot in the stirrup, throw your leg over and sit on the saddle, okay?" She nods, and I easily lift her off the ground. She follows my instructions and mounts him like a pro. "Good job. Okay, now, hold the reins, but don't pull it and don't make any sudden movements. I'm going to climb up behind you."

Shayla looks down at me and nods. "Tristan, can we get a photo of you just as you are. If you can, just look up at Shayla. The sun is catching you both perfectly right now. Shayla, reach over and place your hand on Tristan's cheek gazing down at him.

"Uh, okay." I look up at Shayla, and she gazes down at me placing her hand on my cheek. We stare at each other while they take the shots, and I can see the corners of her lips twitch ever so slightly as she tries to fight the urge to smile.

"Excellent. That's just stunning." The photographer says, looking at the image on her camera. "Okay, Tristan, you can climb up on the horse now." I nod and mount Casper placing myself behind Shayla. I reach around and take the reins from her.

"You okay?" I ask, leaning into her ear, and she nods. "Squeeze your thighs and hold onto the reins with me.

"What? Why?" She questions.

"We're going to go for a ride," I whisper in her ear. She turns to look back at me.

"Right now?" I nod and click my tongue, and Casper starts moving forward.

"Do you trust me?" I ask. She presses her back against my chest and nods.

"Yes." When I whistle, Casper moves at a canter. Shayla shrieks and closes her eyes. "Oh my gosh!"

I laugh as we canter through the trail, and Shayla keeps her eyes squeezed shut the whole time. "Open your eyes." She shakes her head.

"No. I feel like we're going to crash into something. Oh my God, he's so fast!" She squeals, and I smile, biting my lip.

"This isn't him at full speed. You should see him gallop. Open your eyes, sweetheart." She peels her eyes open and gasps, her fingers tightening around the reins so tight her knuckles go white. I pull the reins, and Casper slows a little. "Trust him. I'm going to let go of the reins, and you're going to be in control."

"Cole no—"

"You got this." I let go of the reins and wrap my arms around her waist. "Pull the reins back gently, and he will slow down," I instruct, she does as I tell her, and Casper slows to a trot. I feel Shayla relax in my arms when he slows down, and she sighs. I brush her hair over to the other side and rest my chin on her shoulder.

"My heart is racing. That was insane." I chuckle, nuzzling her ear gently.

"You did great." She smiles and shakes her head before she cranes her neck and looks back at me.

"I should have known you were up to no good." She chides, elbowing me gently in the ribs. "That was mean."

I chuckle and pull my head to look at her. "Exciting though, no?" Shayla rolls her eyes and leans forward, petting Casper gently.

"Hey Casper, the next time your owner rides you, do me a favour and throw his arse off. Like buckeroo his butt to Timbuctoo, okay? Can you do that for me?" She says, smiling while brushing her fingers through his hair.

I laugh, poking her sides, and she jumps sniggering. "Stop corrupting my stallion, you little minx."

She grins at me playfully, slapping my hands away when I try and tickle her, "He's *my* stallion now."

'Oh, baby, your stallion is right here.' I have the urge to whisper in her ear. Instead, I bury my nose into her hair and inhale her exotic scent. "Steady girl. You have a lot to learn still before you can ride him solo." She pouts and continues to pet him. "We better get back to the shoot. I promised them we'd be back in fifteen minutes." I explain, and she nods, disappointed. "Hold on tight." She grips the reins and leans back against me. I whistle, and Casper takes off again, galloping through the trail back to where we left the photographers.

"Hooo," I say, pulling the reins, and Casper slows as we reach the set for the shoot. I look over at Veronica, the Editor-in-Chief of the magazine. "Are we done with the horse?" I ask, and she shakes her head before she calls the photographer over.

"Not yet. I have a couple more shots in mind now you're both up there. Shayla, can you turn and face Tristan." She instructs. Shayla looks at her, then back at me, and shifts to face me. "No, sweetie, I want you to fully face him. In fact, why don't you go ahead and straddle him."

"Pardon?" Shayla asks startled. Veronica looks at me bemused as if she said something wrong. I turn my gaze to Shayla and give her a knowing look. She rolls her eyes. "I swear to God, if I fall off this horse, I'm going for her." She mumbles to me, and I laugh while holding onto her as she shifts awkwardly, throwing her leg over, she turns and faces me, resting her legs over mine. I wrap my arm around her and pull her into my lap, so she was straddling me. "This is so stupid. Who sits on a horse like this? It's so dangerous. What if he bucks us off?" She grumbles, casting an annoyed look at Veronica, who was instructing the photographer.

"He won't. Casper is a calm stallion unless he's provoked. You're safe, don't worry." I assure her, and she nods with a sigh.

"Looking a little stiff over there you two, let's try relaxing a little," Veronica says, coming over to us. She reaches up and tugs Shayla's dress up, exposing her leg. "Tristan, I want you to hold her thigh…" I nod and brush my fingers up her smooth thigh, and she shifts a little, closing her eyes for the briefest second. "Good. Now, I want you to gaze into each other's eyes. Bring your faces closer…" We lean in close and stare into each other's eyes. "Shayla, wrap your arm around his neck, your fingers just at the nape of his neck as if you're about to kiss him. Tristan, head up a tiny bit. Yes, right there."

As I gaze into Shayla's green eyes, everything around me fizzles away. The only thing I can concentrate on was the warmth of her breath on my lips and the way her fingers were gently rubbing the nape of my neck, causing every hair on my body to stand on end.

"Great. Now, let's get a shot of you kissing." Veronica says, and I bite back the grin and the urge to jump off the horse and hug her. Fuck yes! Shayla looks at me and then at Veronica. Her green eyes widen, and I smile and shrug while she glares back at me.

"Pucker up, princess," I whisper, and she sighs and shakes her head, licking her lips. She narrows her eyes briefly while she leans in close. The excitement I felt at that moment was inexplicable. I close my eyes, and our lips merely touch when a phone rings, interrupting the moment.

"Oh, that's me," Shayla announces, pulling back, looking around for her phone.

"Leave it," I say, pulling her close again, but she places her hands on my shoulders and pulls back.

"But *Honey*, it could be important." She declares and waves one of the assistants over to help her off the horse. She smirks at me and winks before she slides off and rushes over to her phone and answers it in a flurry.

I curse my damn luck and whoever it was on that phone inwardly and jump off of Casper. "Okay, guys, that's a wrap. I think we have all we need. I'll send over the photos for approval, and if you can forward me the answers to the questions I gave you?" I nod and shake Veronica's hand.

"Sure. Thank you for everything. We look forward to reading the article." I see Shayla over Veronica's shoulder. She's watching while she's on the phone, clearly not listening to whoever was on the other end. "It was nice seeing you again, Veronica," I say and drop a kiss on her knuckles, and she blushes smiling, tucking her hair behind her ear.

"It's always nice to see you, Tristan." She replies coquettishly, swiping her tongue over her lips in a sultry manner—good lord, too easy. I refrain from rolling my eyes and drop her hand just as Shayla walks over to us.

"Honey, can we go? Something has come up." She states, giving Veronica a side-eyed stare.

"Sure, baby," I say, lacing my fingers with hers, and we both utter a goodbye to Veronica before we walk towards the car. "So, what's come up? Everything okay?" I question starting the car, and Shayla nods.

"Yes, everything is fine. I just said that so we can leave." She admits with a guilty smile, and I chuckle, shaking my head. "A minute longer of hearing that woman's annoying voice and I would have throttled her." She complains, brushing her hair away from her face with a sigh. "I don't know about you, but I am drained and starving."

I nod and smile, looking at the road. "You literally took the words right out of my mouth. Shall we order in? What would you like to eat?" I ask and glance over at her. Shayla chews on her lip thoughtfully and shakes her head.

"No. I'm tired of eating out." She looks at me with her brows raised. "I'll cook something."

I smile, "Yeah?"

"Yes. In fact, you're going to cook with me." She adds with a grin, reaching over and squeezes my cheek. I laugh and pull her hand away from my face and place it on my thigh, covering it with my own to keep it there.

"I mean, I can't cook to save my life. However, I'll be happy to learn if you teach me?" I reply, and Shayla smiles brightly.

"What?! Lord Hoult doesn't know how to cook and wants me to teach him?" She drawls mockingly. "No way." She places her hand over her heart and fans herself dramatically. "Oh, be still my heart."

I laugh jovially, reach over, and squeeze her face till her lips pucker up. "*You* are going to be the death of me." I tease, and Shayla smacks my hand away while grinning back at me.

"The weather is wonderful. How do you put the top down?" She says, looking around for the button to put the roof down to the car.

"It's the blue button. Aren't you worried about your hair getting messed up?" I question and she laughs, shaking her head.

"No! Are you kidding me? What better feeling is there than having the wind in your hair on a hot summer afternoon."

"Air con," I utter dryly while she pushes the button, and the top to my Maserati convertible opens.

"Loosen up and live a little, Hoult!" I watch Shayla as she lifts her arms, eyes closed, the most wonderful smile on her face while the wind blows her wavy dark hair back. I'm fascinated with her energy.

"Oh! I love this song!" I grin and shake my head when she turns the sound system up and starts dancing and singing the lyrics to me. "We fight, and we argue you'll soon love me blind." I laugh when she gives me a pointed look. "If we don't fuck this whole thing up guaranteed, I can blow your mind. Mwah!" Shayla sings and leans over, grabs my face, and playfully smacks an audible kiss on my cheek. I can't even begin to explain the feeling of peace and contentment that spreads within me whenever I am with this girl. You'd think we've been in each other's lives for years when it's only been three weeks. "Hey grandma, put your foot on it." She heckles, gesturing for me to drive faster. I was currently cruising at eighty miles per hour. "Show me what this bad boy can do!"

I grin at her, "Oh baby, buckle your sweet arse up." I drawl and put my foot down, and the car goes from eighty to a hundred and twenty in a matter of seconds.

After an hour-long drive back to the city, we finally get back home. I unbutton the top three buttons to my shirt and fall back on the sofa with an exhausted sigh—what a long day.

Shayla makes a beeline to the kitchen, and I can hear her humming to herself as she opens the fridge. I scroll through my phone, checking my emails, when it's suddenly plucked from my hands. I tilt my head back and see Shayla peering down at me with a playful scowl on her face.

"No work today, Hoult." She scolds, waving my phone at me. I stand up and look at her. She grins and retreats when I walk toward her.

"I need to check my emails really quick," I say, reaching for it, but she shakes her head, pulling it away. I smile.

"It's a Saturday. No emails, no business calls, nothing work-related—hey, eyes on me." She says when I look over at my phone.

"Five minutes, then I'm with you." I try to bargain, but she shakes her head and stuffs the phone down her top. I throw my head back and laugh out loud. "Do you think I won't go in there and get it back?" I ask, and she shakes her head, taking a giant step back. "I will, and I'll have a hell of a time doing it too. I promise you."

"You dare," She contests, and I bite my lip as I advance toward her. Shayla backs away slowly, her eyes trained on me, watching my every move as I walk toward her. I notice she's about to back up against the refrigerator, and I grin. The moment she backs up against the surface of the fridge. I close in on her and place my arms on either side of her caging her in.

"Rookie mistake," I mutter, and Shayla looks at my arms and then up at me. I bow my head, so we are at eye level and slowly lick my lips. "You should know better than to provoke me by now, Shayla. If I say I'm going to do something, I'll do it." I drop my gaze to her lips and back up again.

Shayla observes me closely when I reach up and drag my finger up and over her stomach, over the flowy white dress she was wearing. "Unlike you, I keep my promises," I add, brushing my finger up the path between her breasts. I was silently wishing the dress she's wearing was one of those that was low cut but instead, it was the type that tied at the neck.

She frowns, "What's that supposed to mean?" She asks, affronted, and I smirk, dragging my finger along her collarbone.

"I believe you promised me a kiss, Miss Hart." I remind her, and she licks her lips and smiles a little.

"And I kissed you, Mr Hoult." She replies, mimicking my tone. I shake my head and bite my lip while brushing my fingers up her throat and to the back of her neck, where I gently pull the string to her dress, untying it.

"No, you chickened out. You made a promise, and you couldn't keep it." I tell her, my tone gruff as I brush the back of my fingers along her rosy cheek.

"I did not chicken out." She claims, narrowing her eyes at me. "Your lip was cut and bleeding. I didn't want to hurt you."

"Well, I told you I was coming for that kiss. My lip is all healed now. Will you make good on your promise, or will you make an excuse and run again?" I question, gazing into her eyes.

"Why do you want to kiss me so badly, Cole?" She questions while her eyes search mine, and I smile.

"Because…" I whisper, staring at her lips while I lift my hand and brush my fingers over her bottom lip lightly. "I vaguely remember kissing you while I was drunk, and it was intense. I'm curious to see if it would feel the same or if my inebriated mind had just amplified it." I explain, and Shayla blinks. "Aren't you the slightest bit curious too?" She clears her throat.

"One kiss."

"One kiss," I whisper, tilting her head up. I brush my fingers through her silky hair and draw her mouth close to mine.

Chapter Thirteen

SHAYLA

One kiss.

Just one kiss. That's it. It's no big deal; you've kissed before. Just breathe Shayla.

I look into Cole's eyes as he tilts my head up gently. He brushes his fingers through my hair and steps closer. I instinctively lick my lips as he leans in. In reality, those soft, luscious lips linger upon mine for less than a second. At that moment, however, it felt like an eternity till they brush over mine. My eyes slid shut, and I fight the urge to moan when he presses his lips to mine with the subtlest pressure before his tongue trails along my bottom lip—wordlessly requesting access—which I grant him by parting my lips. Cole's fingers curl into my hair, drawing my mouth against his a little firmer, deepening the kiss, his tongue expertly seeking out my own. When I brush my tongue over his— he moans, a deep throaty moan that hums through me—and he sucks my tongue gently. It was my turn to sigh lustfully. Butterflies explode in my stomach when he pulls back and sucks my bottom lip, tugging on it ever so slightly before he melds our lips together again, kissing me meltingly sensual.

I should have put a stop to it, but for the life of me, I couldn't. It felt so good, I couldn't think straight. He's intoxicating. I felt as though I would drop dead if he stopped kissing me for one damn second. Who kisses this good, my God. I push up on my toes and wrap my arms around his neck as our kiss gets hot and more desperate. Moaning and panting, Cole wraps his arm around me and lifts me into his arms as he walks us over to the island in the middle of the kitchen. Our lips still locked, not parting even for a second, neither of us giving a damn if our lungs were burning from lack of oxygen. Cole sits me on the island, one hand on my hip keeping me pressed against him, the other tangled in my hair while my fingers were trailing down his neck toward his smooth chest where he had unbuttoned his shirt.

My mind was in a complete haze. Cole's lips felt incredible. I inadvertently whimper when he stops kissing me and brushes his lips along my jaw and down my neck. He nips at my skin before lapping at it gently. I grip the counter tight when he nips at my ear, rocking against him shamelessly when he presses himself upon me intimately so I could feel his erection hot and rock hard. I bite my lip, tilting my head back to give him more room as he licks up my throat in a way that made me shudder and whisper his name in a breathy moan.

When I rake my nails gently over his chest and abs, feeling every ripple of hard muscle, Cole groans. "I love the way you touch me," He burrs, brushing his lips over mine, "Don't ever stop baby." He whispers.

"Cole." I pant when his hand disappears under my dress. "We should s-stop…" I stammer breathlessly. "We said one kiss."

Cole moans, "This is one kiss," He breathes, nibbling my bottom lip. "One, long, fucking insatiable kiss." He drawls, drawing me in for another feverous kiss, which I respond too readily.

I was gone. Cole Hoult managed to suck me into his sexual vortex, and my mind and body just wouldn't listen to reason. He was touching me in all the right places. Whispering all the right things, and I had no fight left in me. With my dress around my waist, Cole plucks his phone out from where I had hidden it in my bra and grins at me sexily before he tosses it aside and kisses me again. His shirt was off and thrown on the floor, his trousers unbuttoned, he had me laid out on the island, his lips on my stomach when the chime of the doorbell suddenly echos in the apartment.

My eyes flutter open, and I look down at Cole, who curses and presses his forehead to my stomach and groans. "Ignore it." He growls.

And just like that, the moment was gone. My senses come rushing back to me, and I sit up, pulling my dress up to cover myself. The doorbell chimes again, and Cole buttons up his trousers and snatches his shirt off the floor. He walks to the door to answer it, a very peeved look on his handsome face. He yanks the door open with a scowl and clears his throat when he sees his mother standing at the door.

I quickly tie my dress back up and straighten myself before she sees me. "Tristan, did I come at a bad time?" She questions, casting me a look before she turns her gaze to Cole, half-dressed, his hair dishevelled, both our lips were swollen and our faces flushed.

'Well, this is bloody embarrassing.'

"No, mother. Shayla and I were just about to make dinner. Come on in." He says, gesturing for her to enter. He looks over at me when she walks in and rolls his eyes.

"Hi, Mrs Hoult." I greet her, and she nods and utters a half-arsed hello back, and I resist the urge to roll my eyes.

"Actually, Mum, I'm glad you came," Cole states, walking over to me; he wraps his arm around my waist and pulls me against him, so my back was pressed against his chest. I look up at him questioningly and get my answer when I feel something hard pressed against my bum. I feel my cheeks go hot. "I did have something I have to tell you." He adds, and his mother's shoulders drop.

"Oh, good heavens, go on, tell me she's pregnant and let me faint right here." She utters dramatically, placing her hand on her forehead.

I choke on my own saliva and start coughing hysterically. Cole pats my back. "You okay, babe?" I nod and wave him off, walking to the kitchen to get some water.

"No, mum, she's not pregnant…" He frowns. "Right, baby?"

"Hell no!" I reply after swallowing my water. He smiles and nods.

"No baby, sorry to disappoint." He says with a smirk, "The thing I wanted to discuss with you was, uh, well, Shayla's family would like to meet you and Dad. Her mother was terribly upset that we eloped. She feels she got robbed of seeing her daughter get married with the wedding and the white dress, which is understandable, of course."

Elaine Hoult looks at her son, unimpressed with a deadpan look on her face. "Why yes, Tristan, I completely understand where her mother is coming from because I also feel very robbed of seeing my only son get married."

"So, you'll meet them then?" He asks hopeful, and I just watch them while wolfing down a couple of doughnuts.

Elaine sighs, "Yes, we will meet them. On one condition." She leans over and looks at me, stuffing my face with doughnuts, and wrinkles her nose in distaste. "Are you sure she's not pregnant? That's the second doughnut she's consumed in sixty seconds."

"Mother!" Cole scolds her, and she holds her hands up.

"What? Okay." She grumbles, flicking a strand of her mahogany hair out of her face. "The condition is, we will throw a post-wedding party for you. I mean, if you're adamant about going through with this marriage, then we need to announce this properly and introduce your…*wife* to our society." She says, putting a little too much emphasis on wife like the word scalded her mouth or something. Ugh, witch!

"Uh," Cole looks back at me, and I shake my head slowly. "You got yourself a deal."

I groan and glare at the back of Cole's head. What the hell? I'm going to kill him. I don't want a bloody wedding. I'm trying to get out of this stupid arrangement, not get sucked in deeper.

"Very well. Where is your chef, sweetie?" She asks, looking at the kitchen. I sigh, readying myself for the insults as I wash some vegetables.

"She's right over there, mother," Cole points at me, grinning toothily. "My beautiful wife is cooking."

"Would you like to stay for dinner, Mrs Hoult?" I offer with a sugary smile, and she shakes her head.

"No dear, I'll be having dinner with my husband at home." She sneers, and I nod, plastering a fake smile on my face.

"Next time then." Trust me to get the monster-in-law from hell.

"Yes. We shall see." She mutters, turning her attention back to her son again. "I better go, Honey. I'll be in touch with the arrangements for the party." Cole nods and drops a kiss on his mother's cheek.

"Okay, I will let you and Dad know once Shayla and I arrange a date for you to meet her family." He tells her, walking her to the front door. I busy myself in the kitchen while he's seeing his mother out. I'm hoping— no, *desperately* praying— it won't be awkward after our heated make-out session moments ago. What the hell was I thinking? I instinctually touch my lips when images of us kissing flash through my mind. The man can kiss a corpse back to life.

"What are you thinking about so deeply?" I start jumping out of my lucid thoughts when I heard the deep tone of his voice in my ear.

"Nothing," I reply quickly, picking up the pepper and slicing it in half. Cole smiles, placing his arms on either side of me. I feel the warmth radiating off him against my back and suck in a deep breath.

"You sure? You're looking mighty flushed, sweetheart." He drawls, playing with my hair. *Bastard.* He knows exactly what he's doing. He's going straight to my weak spot. I resist the urge to shiver visibly, but goosebumps break out all over my body when Cole dips his head and presses a kiss on my bare shoulder. *Oh, damn those lips...*

"It's just warm in here," I reply, clearing my throat, and Cole chuckles, running his fingertips over my arms.

"I think it's about to get a lot warmer." He whispers in my ear, his lips brushing against the shell of my ear. My knees go weak, and I bite my lip, contemplating cutting my finger to stop these stupid urges I'm having to turn around and kiss him till my lungs cave in.

Bloody hell, Shayla!

"I thought I was teaching you how to cook?" I ask, tilting my head back and looking up at him—another stupid move. Cole smiles down at me, cups my face before he lowers his lips to mine with an upside-down kiss, sucking my bottom lip softly and making me melt.

Awe shit. Here we go again.

I drop the knife I had in my hand when Cole spins me around, breaking the kiss for a second before fusing our lips together again. I place my hands at his chest and pull back a little.

"Cole, what are you doing?" I just about get out before he pulls me back and kisses me again.

"Nothing." He moans, brushing his tongue over my bottom lip, skilfully coaxing my own. I lose my bearings again. Everything got hot amazingly fast, especially when he runs his tongue in the dip of my collarbone. Oh damn. My weak spot.

"Cole," I whimper, breathless when he lifts me into his arms. I wrap my legs around him, and he walks us over to the sofa, kissing as if our lives depended on it. "Cole, we have to stop." I breathe, and he lays me down on the large L-shaped sofa.

"We will." He groans, crawling over me, pressing his forehead to mine while his large hand glides up my thigh, pushing my dress up to my waist. "I need to taste you..." He whispers, kissing me softly whilst dragging his finger enticingly across my slit over my lacy underwear. I couldn't help it. I rock my hips up against his touch and gasp when he flicks his thumb against my clit. "Fuck, you're so wet, sweetheart." He groans huskily. "Let me bury my tongue deep inside you, baby. I'm dying for a taste of your sweet honey."

"Ahh God, Cole…" I pant when I feel his fingers slide into my underwear, and he rubs them in teasing circles over my clit. "Oh…my…God, yes."

"Shayla?" My eyes pop open, and I see Cole leaning against the island in the kitchen watching me, his green eyes narrowed slightly.

I look around and notice I was still in the kitchen, lent over the island, green pepper in one hand and my head resting in the other, lost in a steamy daze. "Huh?" I utter, straightening, and clearing my throat. Cole smiles a little bemused. Someone kill me.

"What are you thinking about so deeply over there?"

I avoid looking at him and stare down at the peppers on my chopping board. "Food. I was thinking about food," I say quickly, and Cole moves around the island and stands next to me. My heart rate accelerates when his shoulder brushes mine. When did I become so damn pathetic? I keep my head down, so my hair falls around me like a curtain in an attempt to hide my flushed face.

"Okay, Chef, what can I do to help?" He asks, smiling charmingly. I hand him an onion, and he looks at it, then at me bewildered. "What do I do with this?" He questions adorably.

I laugh, "Well, you can start by peeling it." I instruct him, and he smiles sheepishly. Reaching over, he takes a knife from the block next to me. Thankfully, he didn't mention anything about our heavy petting session earlier. If he was thinking about it, he didn't show it.

"What are we cooking anyway?" He asks, attempting to peel the onion, a frown on his face.

"A pasta dish my mother used to make my Dad." I smile when he looks over at me and bites his lip. I turn the Bluetooth on my phone and play my music through the speaker system in his house. "This is literally my favourite thing about this place. And the view, of course." I tell him as I pull my hair up into a messy bun.

Cole smiles, chopping the onion, "Do I not make that list then?" I laugh and shrug my shoulders.

"Why yes, you're at the very bottom of the list." I joke, feeding him a piece of cheese. He laughs and bumps my hip with his playfully.

"Still not getting any better at this lying thing, babe." He says and sniffles, his eyes watering as he chops the onion.

"Well, if you're going to cry about it. Fine, I'll place you after the view. You're not so bad to look at, I suppose." I tease with an exaggerated eye roll. He throws his head back and laughs while sniffling.

"My fucking eyes are on fire! What kind of devil vegetable is this?" I laugh and lean over him to wipe the tears that roll down his face. He drops a quick kiss on my nose, and I glare at him mischievously. We spent the rest of the hour and a half dancing around the kitchen to various songs, feeding each other food, and flirtatiously touching as we pass by each other.

Cole was currently chasing me around the kitchen with a lobster he found in the fridge. "Cole, don't! I swear to God I will hurt you!" I yelp, running around the island as he chases me.

"Oh, come on, this little guy needs love too. It's just adorable, look." He grins, waving it at me.

"Stop it!" I squeal and pick up a plastic spoon off the counter and hold it up. "Put that damn thing away."

"Just give it a little kiss." He chuckles, pushing it toward my face, and I jump away, disgusted. "It's so smooth."

"Kiss it? You must be joking. I wouldn't put that thing anywhere near my mouth." I grumble with a shudder, and Cole laughs heartily.

"Just touch it then. Here, give me your hand." I shake my head and back away, wrinkling my nose, I hit his hand with the spoon when he reaches for me, and he laughs.

"Nope. Cole, please put it away. You're creeping me out. I feel like it's staring at me!" I pout, and he sniggers, finally giving up and putting it back in the fridge.

"You know if anyone overheard that conversation, you'd come off a little prudish." I send him a withering look as I serve the food onto plates.

"Bite me, Hoult."

"Oh yeah? Where do you want me to bite you?" He drawls, grabbing my hand and spinning me till I was pressed up against him, his dark brows twitching suggestively.

I look up at him impishly and smile, "Mmm, wouldn't you like to know."

Cole stares into my eyes deeply, "Don't provoke me. You know I will make good on it."

I chuckle and pick up the plates of food after I pull away from him. "Don't I just. Grab the wine, stud muffin." I say, walking out onto the terrace. It was such a beautiful night, the sky was clear, and there was a nice summer night breeze. I place the plates on the table, and Cole follows with the bottle of white wine and glasses.

We settle on the sofa and eat while gazing out at the view and talking about random things. "This is amazing." Cole moans after swallowing his mouthful. I smile and nod, chewing on a delicious piece of prawn. "This was your father's favourite dish?" He asks, shifting so he could face me. I nod, looking down at my plate.

"Sure is, once a week, my mum would make this for him. He'd eat it and be like, my dove, I don't know how you do it, but it just gets more delicious every time I eat it." I tell him, smiling at the fond memories I had of my Dad. I set my plate on the table and pick up my glass of white wine.

"They sound like they were very happy," Cole says, mimicking my actions. He leans back, sipping his wine and watching me.

"They really were," I tell him. "God, they were so in love with one another. I'd sit at the top of the stairs and watch them dancing in the living room, wrapped up in one another like they were the only two people in the world. He'd find little ways to touch her all the time." I explain, my eyes watering. "I want a love like that. I want to *be* loved like that." I sigh, laying my head on the cushion of the sofa and looking at Cole while he watches me intently. He shifts nearer to me and brushes his fingers through my hair. "Can I ask you something?" He nods, playing with my hair. "Why me?"

"What do you mean?" He frowns.

"Of all the girls in the club that night, why did you choose me?" I ask and he drops his gaze to his wine glass.

"I don't really know. I was surrounded by girls that night, but you caught my eye. There was something about you, the way you were laughing. That's the first thing I noticed, your smile. Possibly one of the most genuine and heartwarming smiles I've ever seen. You were dancing with your friends, and I was just drawn to you." He explains while he softly brushes my hair away from my face. "Your turn. Why did you choose to leave with me that night? You had plenty of other guys interested?"

I smile and gaze up at him. "Honestly, I don't know either. I was really drunk, and I just remember thinking God, his eyes are so beautiful, and I really want to stick my tongue in his dimples." Cole laughs out loud.

"You wanted to stick your tongue in my dimples?" He gushes, poking my sides, making me blush.

"Shut up. I was really stupid drunk, and your dimples really are adorable when you smile," I say, reaching up and sticking my finger in one.

Cole chuckles and wraps his slender fingers around my wrist, and pulls me closer to him. "I'm intrigued. Come here. I need to know how it feels to have your tongue in my dimple. Do it." I laugh and shake my head.

"What? No! I am not sticking my tongue in your dimples." Cole chuckles and pulls my hands away when I try covering my face to hide my blush.

"Come on, just a little." He sniggers. "Get over here, and tongue fuck my dimple."

I tilt my head back, and we laugh uncontrollably. "Oh my god, you're something else."

"We may have invented a new kink here." He adds with a grin. "We're doing this. Come here." I allow him to pull me closer, so I was pressed against him, and he looks into my eyes. "Choose your dimple." He says with a snigger, and I reach up and turn his head to the side a little.

"I cannot believe we're doing this." I giggle and lean in close to his cheek and lick his dimple with the tip of my tongue. I can feel Cole's shoulders shaking as he tries to contain his laughter.

"Oh yes, baby, go deeper." He says with a chuckle, and I press my forehead to his temple laughing hysterically. Chuckling, Cole turns his head and presses his forehead to mine, our noses touching, he brushes his thumb along my jaw. Rubbing his nose over mine, I close my eyes when I feel his lips press against mine ever so lightly.

Chapter Fourteen

COLE

You know that feeling when you're just about to drift off to sleep, where your mind and body are in a completely peaceful state. That's how I feel right now—in this very moment with Shayla. I couldn't focus on anything but her. Her intoxicating smell, the way she was nibbling on her bottom lip, the way the wind was gently blowing her dark hair back. She's galvanising, and the more time I spend and get to know her, the more I'm finding myself attracted to her.

I'm not even going to get into our kiss earlier. If we weren't interrupted, I can almost guarantee that we would have had sex on that kitchen island. There was no way I would have found the strength to stop myself —not when it comes to Shayla. My body acts on its own might. I can't stop touching her. I keep telling myself to stop looking for excuses to touch her or hug her, but I can't do it. She's like this magnet that keeps drawing me to her. Like right now, for example. We've had such an amazing time together today, laughing and flirting, but right now, all I can think about is kissing her again. I want to take her to my bed and make her come in every way I possibly can till the sun comes up.

I chuckle as she dips her tongue in my dimple, another excuse to get her close to me. "Oh yes, baby, go deeper," I say with a snigger, and she bursts into fits of laughter. When she presses her forehead to my temple, I turn my head so we were nose to nose. Our laughter subsides when I brush my thumb along her jaw, her eyes close when I press my lips to hers softly. I was praying she wouldn't pull away and lets me kiss her.

She does.

She parts her soft lips for me, and I kiss her slow, brushing my fingers through her silky tresses. I deepen the kiss when she flicks her tongue against mine. I moan when she sucks my bottom lip and tugs it gently before she pulls back and looks at me. I open my eyes and meet her gaze.

"That's the last kiss you get, Cole Hoult." She tells me while licking those delectable lips.

I groan, looking at them longingly, "I say we get a free pass for kissing today. You know, to get it out of our systems. We should kiss more," I whisper, leaning in closer.

Shayla smiles and takes hold of my jaw, and gazes into my eyes. "We can't do that."

"But why?" I whine. "We've already kissed twice, what's another couple more times?" I add, and she laughs.

"Because it doesn't just stop at kissing. Your sticky little fingers start to wander, and before you know it, I'm half-naked, and…" She trails off, swallowing hard, and I smile lazily at her.

"And…?" I urge waiting for her to finish her sentence, but she just shrugs and averts her gaze.

"And nothing."

I grin and turn her gaze to mine again. "And what, sweetheart. Tell me?" I ask, brushing my thumb over her bottom lip.

"And you've got your fingers all up in my lady bits." She sighs, her cheeks turning a pretty shade of pink.

I chuckle and lean in close to her ear, "If the doorbell didn't ring interrupting us, it would have been my *tongue* all up in your lady bits." I groan, deepening my voice, and I feel her quiver ever so slightly.

"Exactly." She sighs while I brush my lips down her neck.

"What if I promise to behave? Would you let me kiss you then?" I ask, sucking the base of her throat.

Shayla's head tilts back, and she bites her lip. "Like you're behaving right now?" I smile against her throat and hold my hand up when it was trailing up her thigh.

"See behaving." I retort with a pout, and she looks at me shaking her head.

"You, Cole Hoult, can charm the panties off a nun." She states, those olive-green eyes looking over my face. I grin and drop soft kisses to her jaw.

"The only panties I want off right now are yours, sweetheart," I whisper. "I bet they're soaking wet too." Shayla releases quivering breaths while I drag my nose along her jaw. "Are you wet for me, Gorgeous girl?"

"Cole," Shayla whispers, biting down on her bottom lip as I trail my fingertips over her thigh and between her legs.

"Open up, sweetheart, let me feel how wet you are." I plead, inching my fingers closer to her pussy. Shayla stills for a moment, and her thighs quiver under my touch, but she parts her legs for me a little. I can feel the heat between her legs, and my cock pulses and throbs hungrily against my jeans. I hiss, closing my eyes when I feel the dampness of her panties. I press my forehead to her temple and moan, "Fuck Shay, you're so fucking wet it's dripping down to your thighs." I growl lowly, and just as I'm about to sink my fingers into her underwear, she stops me.

"Cole," She breathes. "We can't. You asked for a kiss, and I gave you two. Playtime is over. Let's not forget why we are doing this." She tells me, pulling away. I groan and watch her pick up the plates and walk inside to the kitchen. I look up at the star-filled sky and sigh while readjusting myself in my jeans. She's right. It is just an arrangement, after all. We need to keep in mind that this agreement has an expiration date.

I pick up the glasses and the empty bottle of wine and walk to the kitchen. I see Shayla washing the plates and loading them into the dishwasher. She must be the only person in the world who washes the plate *and then* puts it in the dishwasher. I smile and walk over. I lean over her, purposefully pressing my chest against her back as I put the two wine glasses in the sink.

"You know sweetheart, the dishwasher does clean the dishes. You don't need to wash the dishes before you load them." I say poking her sides. She jumps and flicks water in my face.

"I know, but I like to make sure dishes are cleaned properly. Plus, you get all the food bits in your machine, and that's just gross." She explains, loading the glasses.

"Why are you cleaning anyway? That's why I have Maggie. Leave it." I say, leaning back against the island while she wipes down the counters. She rolls her eyes and gives me a disapproving look.

"Cole, I'm not letting someone else clean up after my mess. I'm perfectly capable of cleaning up after myself." I smile and roll my eyes. That sounds about right. The rest of the night we spent making idle conversation, Shayla made sure we always had more than two meters between us.

WE RETIRED to our respective bedrooms. I had a long cold shower to ease the pent-up sexual frustration I was currently feeling. I'm so fucking horny. By far, this is the longest I have gone without having sex, and we are only in week three. No wonder I can't keep my hands off her. She should count her blessings that I'm not humping her every second of the day. I stare over at the wall between our bedrooms and suddenly wished I had x-ray vision so I could see what she was doing. Was she asleep? It's only eleven o'clock, surely not. I strain my ear for any noise coming from her bedroom but hear nothing. A little while later, I was engrossed in reading a book when I hear a scream coming from her bedroom. I toss the book aside, jump out of bed, and rip my bedroom door open. I run to her bedroom and open the door and hear her scream again.

"What, what is it? What's wrong, Shayla?" I look around the bedroom, thinking someone had broken in or was hurting her, but there was no one around. It's just her sitting in bed, her bed covers pulled over her head. I look at her tv and see she's watching a horror movie. I finally let myself sigh in relief and glared at her when she peeks over the blanket.

"Cole?"

"Jesus, what the fuck Shayla? I thought something happened to you." I scold her, and she blinks up at me.

"I'm sorry. I didn't expect this movie to be so.... gruesome." I cross my arms over my chest, look at the tv, and back at her again.

"If you're scared, why are you watching it?" I question, and she shrugs, eyeing the tv nervously.

"It's a good movie." She mumbles, and I turn to leave her room.

"Cole, wait." I stop and look back at her over my shoulder. She fumbles with the corner of her duvet, chewing her lip anxiously. "Will you, uh, will you stay and watch it with me?" She asks, her eyes wide and pleading.

I smile and lick my lips, "Scoot over." I close the door and walk over to the bed. She pulls the covers back for me while I get in beside her and lay back. "Fill me in. What's it about?"

Shayla shifts and leans back against the headboard next to me. "Okay, so this group of friends go on a road trip to this cabin in the middle of nowhere, and on the night that they get there, the main guy's girlfriend goes missing." I watch her as she explains the movie to me. "So, they go looking for her, but then this fugly looking man shows up and drags them off, one by one, and tortures them."

I chuckle, "That's it? That's why you were screaming?" She smacks my shoulder playfully and rolls her eyes.

"You haven't seen him yet, watch and then judge. Oh God, look, that's him, that's him." She groans, covering her eyes with an adorable squeal.

"Oh, he really is fugly." I agree, wrinkling my nose at the half-man/half creature on the screen.

"See!" She peeks at the screen and yelps when the killer guts the woman, her intestines falling out on the floor. "Oh my God, I can't." She shifts, turning her head and pressing her forehead to my shoulder, eyes closed. I smile and shift, lifting my arm and wrapping it around her shoulder so she could nestle her face into my neck more comfortably. "I'm going to kill Aimee. This was her suggestion." I hear her muffled voice and grin, brushing my fingers up and down her back.

"It is pretty graphic." I feel her nod, and she looks at the screen again. Halfway through the movie, I feel my eyes growing heavy, and I hadn't heard a peep out of Shayla either. I glance down and see she had fallen asleep, her head resting on my chest.

I shift a little trying to get out of bed, and she stirs in her sleep, snuggling further into me. "Mm, don't go." She whispers drowsily. I smile and press my lips to her forehead and continue to brush my fingers through her long, silky hair. The smell of passion fruit and coconuts, taking me back to Vegas when I first smelt her shampoo. I lay there with her in my arms, and it suddenly hit me, soon I'll have to let her go. She'll walk out of my life just as quickly as she came.

One hundred and fifty-two days. That's how long we have left.

THE NEXT MORNING, we woke up bright and early to get ready for work. We woke up as we usually do, completely wrapped up in each other. Only this time, Shayla was on her side while I was spooning her from behind. Shayla's alarm jolted us both awake from our peaceful slumber. She reaches over and hits the snooze button, closing her eyes again briefly.

"Cole."

"Mmm."

"That better be the remote pressed up against my butt." She mumbles, making me chuckle.

"Why don't you have a feel around, see for yourself," I express, nuzzling her neck and groan when she kicks my shin. "Ow, Jesus," I grumble, rolling onto my back with a yawn. "It's scientifically proven that morning sex is a healthy way to start your day. A little morning loving would have been nice."

Shayla rubs her eyes and sits up watching me as I stretch myself out. "Feel free to give yourself some 'morning loving' in your own room." She tells me, pushing the covers back and getting out of bed. "I'm not going to ask how we even ended up in bed together again. I'm just thankful I woke up with my clothes on." I lean up and watch her as she stretches. The loose shorts she's wearing rises when she lifts her arms, giving me a nice view of the curve of her shapely bum. My mouth waters, and I feel my cock strain against the material of my boxers. Christ, if only she'd let me, I'd fuck her ten ways till Sunday tirelessly.

With a frustrated groan, I get out of bed and leave her bedroom. Time for another cold shower and some one on one time with my left hand. I'm going to lose my fucking mind and my cock to frostbite at this rate.

I was just about through jerking off when I hear a pounding on the bathroom door. My cock was still pulsing in my hand. "Cole! Get out of the bathroom, you've been in there forever. What on earth is taking you so long?" I hear Shayla's annoyed voice on the other side of the door.

"I'd tell you, sweetheart, but you'll only blush!" I holler back, lazily grinning when I hear her muttering on the other side as I step out of the shower. Wrapping a towel loosely around my waist, I walk over to the door and open it. Shayla turns and looks at me, her eyes skimming over my wet torso and lingering on the bulge under the towel for a drawn-out second.

"Like what you see, sweetheart?" I drawl, eyeing her right back fixedly. Shayla blinks and clears her throat looking everywhere but at me.

"You have your own bathroom. Why do you insist on using this one every morning?" She questions, crossing her arms over her chest. I lean against the doorway and smile charmingly at her.

"Because it's got the power shower and many, many, fun functions," I declare, taking a step toward her. "You should try the pulsing one. You can thank me later, Gorgeous girl," I murmur in her ear, pull back, and wink with a knowing smirk as I deliberately brush past her. Shayla watches me as I walk to my bedroom, her mouth agape.

And thus, began the heavy flirting and teasing. If she thinks I'll be the only one suffering from sexual frustration, she's sorely mistaken. Two can play at this game. I'm going to drive her fucking wild. After Shayla's shower, she was in the bathroom doing her make-up while I style my hair. I step behind her and place my hand at her waist as I reach over and pick up my hair wax. "Excuse me." I breathe in her ear as I lean to pick it up. She closes her eyes for a second before she goes back to applying her make-up. I watch through the mirror as she brushes her fingers through her hair, messing it up a little and sweeping it to one side, all the while biting her lip. I had a sudden vision of us fucking on the countertop, with my fingers curled all up in her hair, messing it up all over again.

I smirk when I 'accidentally' drop my wax, and it rolls between her legs. I kneel and brush my fingertips up her calf. She gasps and looks down at me. I stare up at her and reach over, picking up my wax and standing again, towering over her while she gazes up at me and blinks, snapping out of her stupor.

We are both completely aware of what the other is doing, but I'm just as stubborn as she is. I'm going to continue to tease her until she cracks, and she will. She will be mine.

"Are you ready to go?" I ask, readjusting my tie before I spray my cologne. Shayla nods, applying her red lipstick.

"Yes, I'm ready. Let's go." She says, looking in the mirror one last time before she strolls out of the bathroom. I watch her avidly as she walks, swaying her hips in that tight checkered mini skirt she's wearing. She's such a cock tease. How the fuck am I supposed to focus on work with her walking around in that skirt and not fantasise about bending her over my desk, fucking her raw while she fights the urge to scream while she comes hard. I groan inwardly and tried to put it out of my mind, but it was exceedingly difficult—especially in the car where the skirt rose and exposed her upper thighs. Fuck my life. I was already sporting a hard-on, and it's not even been one hour since I relieved myself.

It's going to be a long day.

Shayla and I get to work just before seven forty-five. She grabs my coffee and bagel, and we go through my schedule for the day.

"You have an hour free after your one o'clock meeting with the Frasier brothers. Would you like me to arrange lunch for you then?" Shayla asks, typing away on her iPad.

"Sure, book a table for two at that Italian restaurant I like," I tell her, and she nods briefly before lifting her eyes and looking at me.

"For two?" She questions bemused.

I nod, "Yes, two. You're coming with me."

"I am?" She asks again, frowning a little. "Since when do you have lunch with your assistant?" She adds.

I smirk, "Since my assistant also became my wife. It's only natural for a husband to take his wife out to dinner, no?" Shayla stares at me blankly. "Besides, it will be good for us to be seen together."

She nods. "Ah, okay," She says, licking her lips and dropping her gaze to her tablet again. "Table for two booked. I'm done here." She says, standing up and walking to the door, sashaying her hips, knowing full well I'm watching.

"Can you get me the files for the Marina proj—"

"--It's already on your desk." She finishes opening the door and walking out. I look down at my desk, and sure enough, there were the files with a sticky note on it saying 'I need a raise' with a smiley face.

The day dragged on with meeting after meeting, and I was really feeling rather burnt out. I'm currently staring at the marina's design in Spain when I hear a knock on my door, and someone waltzes in before I announced them. I look up with a scowl, ready to chew out whoever it was that had the gull to just stroll into my office like that.

I frown, "Sophie..."

Chapter Fifteen

SHAYLA

"Ugh," I grumble, deleting the sentence I just typed out for this email for the hundredth time. I need to reapply for my grant to go back to university and get my degree, but I can't seem to get the wording right on this stupid email. I look up when I hear the distinct sound of heels clicking on the marble floor approaching. I see a leggy blonde walking toward me, dressed in couture from head to toe, her silky curls bouncing with every step she took. She looks like she just stepped off a catwalk, for god sake.

"Can I help you?" I ask as she strolls by me, walking toward Cole's office as if I wasn't sitting there. She looks back at me, her icy blue eyes raking over me before she smirks.

"I'm here to see Tristan." She declares, turning and walking toward his office again. I get up and follow her.

"Excuse me, do you have an appointment? You can't just walk into his office. He's busy." I say, irritated, and she spins and faces me, brushing a loose curl out of her face with a perfectly manicured nail.

"Oh, sweetie, I don't need an appointment. I need a soy latte, so why don't you be a dear and fetch me one. Thanks." She chirps, knocks on the door once, and proceeds to walk in. I watch Cole through the glass. He lifts his head, a scowl on his face, which softens to a frown when he sees the blonde in his office. His eyes dart over to me for a second, and I shrug, holding up my hands, and he looks back at the blonde.

I observe as she saunters over to him when he stands from his desk. Who the hell is she? I stand behind the wall where they can't see me watching them. Cole leans against his desk, and this blonde sits on the chair in front of him, giving him a nice view of those stilts she calls legs when she crosses them.

"What are you doing?" I start when I hear a voice in my ear. I turn and see Josh— Cole's best friend and head of security, watching me with a smile.

"Jesus, Josh, you scared the shit out of me," I mutter, looking back at Coles office.

"Are we spying on the boss?" He asks, leaning over to see what I was looking at. I press my finger to his forehead and push it back. He laughs.

"Uh, no, I was just waiting to get a report I need from him, but he seems busy," I tell him, and he gives me a dubious look and nods.

"Uh-huh, sure. So, you're not even the tiniest bit curious what he's talking about with his ex-girlfriend?" Josh says with a knowing smirk, and I look at him.

"Ex-girlfriend?"

Josh nods, "Mhm, that's Sophie Turner. He hasn't told you about her?" I shake my head and look over at them again. "They dated for about three years, and she just up and dumped him like eight months ago."

"Wait, she dumped him?" I ask surprised, and he nods. "Why?"

Josh shrugs, "I'm not sure. He never really said why they broke up, only said they wanted different things at the time. He never showed it, but she hurt him bad. He was crazy about her." He explains, and I'm not sure why, but I felt my stomach drop at his words.

"Right. Well, she asked for a coffee. I better do my job and get that for her." I excuse myself and walk off to the kitchen to get her coffee from the machine and had Heather take the coffee into his office. I couldn't bring myself to see him in the same room as his ex. It was almost lunchtime, Cole and I had a table booked, so I could use that as an excuse and tell him we had to leave.

I'm currently sitting at my desk, chewing my nail anxiously, repeatedly telling myself not to look at them, but every so often, my eyes take a sneak peek. I was dying to know what they were talking about. Cole had a profoundly serious look on his face while listening to whatever she's yapping on about.

I had enough of waiting around. I walk to the door and knock; Cole lifts his head and looks at me before he nods his head for me to enter. "Hi, sorry to interrupt, we need to leave if we're going to make the lunch reservation." I remind him, and he opens his mouth to speak, but Sophie interrupts whatever he was going to say.

"Actually, I've made lunch arrangements for us already." She smiles at Cole, who looks at me then back at Sophie again. She gives him a meaningful look, and he sighs.

"Looks like I'm sorted. You go ahead, sweetheart." He tells me stiffly, and I nod curtly before walking out of his office without another word. Why do I feel so butt hurt like he just rejected me and chose her? I ignore the gnawing feeling of jealousy in the pit of my stomach and go off to get some lunch for myself.

As I sit by the river eating my sandwich, all alone, I try to make sense of this boy's actions. He said it made sense for us to be seen together to make this stupid ruse more believable, yet he's out with his ex-girlfriend. How is that going to look if he gets caught by the paparazzi or something? I sigh, closing my eyes, not having an appetite anymore; I feed the rest of my sandwich to the seagulls.

He was crazy about her...

I keep hearing Josh's words in my head. Why am I so bothered by this? I shouldn't care, it's just a stupid game, and in one hundred and fifty-one days, I'll be free of him.

You're starting to like him. I shake off that annoying little voice in my head, trying to convince me that I have feelings for him because I don't. It's just a crush, that's it. He's an extremely good-looking guy, and I see him half-naked all the time. We live together. It's only natural for me to develop an innocent crush on him. I just need to keep it at that and not let it develop into anything more.

Yes, that's the plan. Keep it professional.

With that in mind, I return to the office and notice Cole wasn't back yet. I groan when I felt that little pinch in my heart. I picked up a smoothie for myself and got one for Cole, too, because I know he loves it. I even had them write the word 'Stud' on it—the nickname I call him. I place it on his desk and go back to mine, busying myself to not let my mind wander off to him. What if they're in a hotel somewhere having raw post-break-up sex? The thought alone made my stomach hurt.

~

TWO HOURS LATER, Cole strolls into the office. I see him approaching from the corner of my eye and keep my eyes glued to the paperwork in front of me. He marches past my desk and walks into his office without a word. I watch him as he takes his suit jacket off and tosses it on the sofa. He looks royally pissed off and loosens his tie while he walks over to his desk. Cole stops when he sees his smoothie. He picks it up and looks at it, reads the writing on the cup, and smiles. I feel a warmth engulf my heart whenever he smiles. Before he sees me watching him, I turn my attention back to my work and bite back the urge to smile myself.

I jump when my intercom buzzes. I look over at him and push the button. "Yes, Mr Hoult?"

He licks his lips and holds his smoothie up. "Thank you."

"Just doing my job," I tell him and go back to work. I successfully manage to avoid him the rest of the day until the office empties, and it's just us two. Being his assistant, I can't leave until he does. He's also my ride, which means I was stuck loitering while he caught up on his work after taking a long lunch.

The intercom buzzes again, and I reach over and push the button. "Yes?"

"Come here." He demands, not even bothering to look up. With a sigh, I get up and walk into his office.

"What do you need?" I ask, crossing my arms over my chest. Cole looks up and narrows his green eyes at me.

"What's up with you?"

I shake my head and shrug, "What do you mean? Nothing is up with me." Cole leans back in his chair, rocking a little while he observes me, his expression stoic.

"You've been unusually quiet today. Something is off. What's wrong?" I sigh and rub my forehead.

"Cole, nothing is wrong. I've just had a busy day, that's all." I explain, exasperated. Cole shakes his head, gets up, and walks over to me.

"You've been avoiding me all day, Shayla. You're usually in and out of my office all day. I've barely seen you."

I scoff, "How would you know? You were gone most of the afternoon." I retort bitterly and regret it instantly. I mentally kick myself when Cole nods in understanding and smirks.

"You're angry with me for this afternoon."

Frowning, "Why would I be angry?" I ask derisively. Cole rubs his jaw and sighs. "I honestly don't care. What you do on your lunch break is your business." I say and turn to leave, but Cole grabs my arm, stopping me.

"Whoa, come back here. Why are you saying it like you're accusing me of something? Do you think I went off and had an afternoon shag with Sophie?" He snaps hotly while scowling at me. "Is that what you think?"

I pull my arm out of his hold and laugh. "Cole, I didn't say anything. I don't know where you're getting this from. I honestly couldn't care less what you did with this...*Sophie*." I say her name with more venom than I had intended and curse myself when Cole's eyebrow goes up.

He smirks, "Well, I don't believe you."

I peer up at him and narrow my eyes, "Well, that's your problem." I answer and spin on my heel to leave, but he catches my wrist and yanks me back to him again. I glare up at him and take a step back, putting some space between us so I wasn't pressed up against him so intimately.

"You're jealous." He states, taking a step toward me. I shake my head and retreat.

"What? Why, why would I be jealous?" I stammer with a nervous chuckle—Jesus, what is wrong with me.

Cole takes another step toward me and looks down into my upturned face. "You tell me? Why *would you* be jealous?"

I take a step back and gasp when my back is pressed against the glass window. Cole takes this as an opportunity and cages me in, so I can't escape. "I am not jealous."

He steps closer. "Mm, are you sure about that, sweetheart?" He drawls, leaning so close that our noses touch.

"Yes," I whisper, and my mouth suddenly goes bone dry. Come on, Shayla, get it together. He's goading you, don't fall for it. Who the hell does he think he is? I fix my gaze to his and lick my lips. Let's turn this around on him. "You look disappointed, Cole," I breathe, brushing my nose over his. "Did you want me to be jealous?"

Cole smiles knowingly, biting his lip, "Maybe a little."

I smile back and raise a brow, "Well, I'm sorry to disappoint you, but I'm not in the least bit jealous. You can spend as much time with Sophie as your heart desires." Cole looks into my eyes, and a slow smile appears on his face.

"So, you wouldn't care, even a little If I had her like this…" He drawls while he gathers my arms up over my head as he presses me up against the wall, his hard, muscular body covering my own robustly. Our foreheads pressed together, we stare into one another's eyes.

"No," I answer, desperately trying to keep the tremor from my voice. Cole's lips hover over mine teasingly.

"What if I did this," He whispers, dipping his head and running his velvet tongue over my pulse point. I gasp involuntarily, and I feel my legs wobble in the heels I was wearing. My eyes close, I bite down on my lip to keep from moaning when he sucks my flesh, making my head swirl. *Oh damn.* "Would you care then?" He breathes huskily in my ear.

"No," I answer breathily and force my eyes open when I feel him pulling away to look at me. His gaze was hot and hungry, and it took every last bit of control I had to not give in to him and have him bend me over his damn desk. He laces his fingers with my own and pushes his forehead to mine, his bottom lip between his teeth.

"I can do this all night, baby."

I smile defiantly and deliberately lick my lips while he watches. "So can I. You can have her sprawled out on that desk and pound into her till she sees God himself, and I still…" I whisper, brushing my lips over his.

“Wouldn't care.” I finish, his eyes lift to mine, and he just looks at me for a long time before he smiles.

“Oh? But what I’m hearing from here…” He whispers, dragging his thumb along my bottom lip, “Doesn’t match what I’m seeing in your eyes.” He adds, trailing his index finger down the side of my face. “You’re looking at me with tempestuous eyes, baby.”

“Maybe that’s because you’re making me angry with your silly assumptions,” I utter, slapping his hand away from my face. “You’re free to do whatever you want with whomever you want. You don’t owe me an explanation. You’ll be the one branded a cheat, not me.” I smile, ducking under his arm and making a beeline for the door before he catches me again.

“This isn’t over!” He calls out after me as I walk away, and I laugh out loud.

“Get over yourself, Hoult,” I call back, picking up my handbag and jacket while he gathers his own belongings. We leave the office and make our way back home. The car ride was quiet. Cole didn’t say much, and I wasn’t up to talking either. The music plays in the background, and I stare out the window, my mind full of questions I would probably never get the answers to because I’m too proud to ask. The main one being—is he still in love with Sophie. Why did he come back so annoyed? What the hell did they do for three hours?

Once we got home, I went straight to my room and locked myself away the rest of the night. I tried reading, but my mind wasn’t taking anything in. I put my music on and just stared at the ceiling pondering over what Cole was doing. Was he itching to come in here as I was to go to his room? I left the room to go to the bathroom and saw the door to his bedroom was shut, and a dim light was shining under it. He was still awake.

~

THREE IN THE MORNING. I sigh and toss in bed for the umpteenth time before I gave up and snuck out of my room and tiptoed to the kitchen. It was a stuffy night, and I figured some ice cream might help cool me down.

I take out a tub of cookie dough ice cream quietly and pop it in the microwave for a couple of seconds before I hop up on the kitchen island with my spoon ready to dig in. That first spoonful of ice cream was like heaven on my tongue. I moan and close my eyes, sucking the spoon clean and lick my lips. Who needs sex when you have a tub of Ben and Jerry's? I groan. Me, that's who. It's been an excruciating month without any sort of relief. I was all hot and bothered. I couldn't even get myself off because it feels weird, and I feel like I'm being naughty in someone else's bed. Not to mention I'm terrified Cole will hear me. God, I miss my bed. I also miss having sex—which is odd because I've gone almost a year without getting any, but lately, I've been feeling friskier than usual. I mean, that's partly Cole's fault for looking like he does. Actually, no, it's his fault…entirely, for touching me, kissing me, and looking at me the way he does.

I groan and shove another spoonful of ice cream in my mouth. Would it really be so bad if we had a little sex? Just a tiny bit?

Yes, it will. You don't want to go there. I roll my eyes at the neurotic voice in my head. "Killjoy," I grumble to myself, sulking like a brat that has her favourite toy taken from her. Cole is like rich chocolate-covered strawberries sitting in front of me that I can't touch or lick. Maybe just a little nibble?

"What do you want to nibble on?" I jump and squeak when I open my eyes and see Cole standing in front of me in the dark— in nothing but his boxers *again*. Crap, did I say that aloud.

"Shit," I utter, holding my hand over my chest. "Do you get some kind of kick out of scaring me half to death?" Cole smiles handsomely.

"Not my fault you're so easily startled, sweetheart. You were so lost in whatever you were thinking about nibbling on." I roll my eyes and scoop up another spoonful of ice cream. "So, what was it?"

I look at him, thoughtfully, "Chocolate covered strawberries." I slide the spoon into my mouth while he watches, deliberately sucking it slowly, closing my eyes.

"Strawberries, huh?" He swallows hard. I nod, opening my eyes and meeting his gaze. "I can think of something so much better I would love to nibble on." He drawls, takes a step toward me, a hungry look in his eyes, but I lift my foot and press it against his chest, stopping him.

"Ah-ah," I utter with a teasing smile, which he returns with a bite of his lip. Cole wraps his fingers around my ankle, lifts my leg on his shoulder, and yanks me swiftly, so my hips were pressed against his. I fall back against the island, and the ice cream tips over, spilling all over my chest. I gasp audibly, closing my eyes when the coldness of the melted ice cream suddenly catches my breath. "Shit," I breathe as the ice cream trickles toward my neck.

"Oops." Cole tuts with a devious smirk. He brushes his lips up to my inner thigh while he lowers my leg and leans over me, placing his large hands at my hips. "Let me help you clean that up." He whispers, pulling me up so I was sitting upright again, the cream leaking from my throat down to the path between my breasts. I hiss when I feel his hot tongue lick up my throat. *Oh, sweet heavens.* Cole moans when he sucks the melted ice cream off my neck. I quake when he bites and sucks my collarbone hard.

"Cole," I gasp, raking my nails down his back. He groans in response and licks down my chest. His fingers find the clasp at the front of my top, he flicks it, and it pops open, freeing my breasts.

"Fuck," He burrs huskily, sliding the straps to my top off my shoulders and down my arms. I throw my head back when he cups both my breasts in his hands, squeezing appreciatively while running his tongue over the valley between my breast, licking up the ice cream.

I open my eyes and look at him, biting my lip. "I think you got it all," I whisper, and he shakes his head.

"No, I missed a bit." He whispers back, scooping a handful of ice cream and smearing it over my breasts and stomach. I whimper and shiver against the cool feeling of the ice cream. My nipples got hard and tight.

"Ahh, Cole!" I cry out, biting my lip hard when his mouth captures one of my nipples and sucks it hard. "Jesus, Cole, what are we doing?" I pant, rocking against the hard length of him.

"Cooling off." He mumbles, licking ice cream off my stomach.

"I'm not feeling any cooler." I moan, arching up and gripping the side of the counter when I feel Cole grind himself against me. It was quite the opposite. My entire body felt like it was on fire.

"Just wait…"

"For what— uhhh Christ!"

Chapter Sixteen

COLE

I THINK I've just died and gone to heaven. I want to slap myself to make sure I'm not dreaming, but that requires having to let go of her beautiful breasts, and that wasn't about to happen. I flick my tongue over a rosy nipple and suck it into my mouth. Shayla arches up and moans, rocking her hips, grinding against my erection. If ever I had a chance to sleep with her again, this was it, she's clearly as horny as I am, and there is no chance of interruption. She's mine tonight.

"Jesus, Cole, what are we doing." She whispers in a breathy tone. I greedily lick up the melted ice cream off her stomach.

"Cooling off," I mumble, nipping at her hip and sucking hard enough to leave a nice mark. She moans, arching up and gripping the counter when I grind my dick against her pussy.

"I'm not feeling any cooler." She sighs, biting her lip.

"Just wait…" I whisper, sliding her shorts down her gorgeous legs. I'm pleased to see she's not wearing any underwear. Oh, fuck, her pussy is to die for. Waxed clean, plump, and pink, glistening with her juices just begging to be eaten. My dick twitches with excitement. Oh, come to Daddy.

"For what—" She lifts her head to look at me, and my tongue only just touches her clit when the fucking fire alarm starts going off. Her eyes flicker open, and she looks around the kitchen. "Oh, god! Is that the fire alarm?"

I wanted to scream in frustration and put my fist through the counter. I groan, "Yes. Ignore it. It's probably nothing." I mumble, going for the lick, but she puts her hands on my head and pushes back while sitting up.

"Ignore it? Cole, there could be a fire in the building." She says, looking around for her clothes. She picks up her top, trying to put it on, and I take it from her and toss it over my shoulder.

"Fuck it, let's just burn," I growl, pressing my forehead to hers. I tilt her head up and lick up her throat. "I need you desperately, and I know you want me just as bad. I can't take it anymore, baby. I have to have you."

Shayla moans, biting her lip, but she pulls back and looks at me. "Cole, come on, be serious. I'm not risking our lives to have sex in a burning building." She hops off the counter and disappears to her bedroom.

I bite my knuckle furiously, "Son of a bitch. I swear to God if it's a false alarm, I'm going to kill someone." I grumble, walking to my bedroom to grab some clothes. We get dressed and walk out of the apartment. I smirk when I see Shayla wiping her neck with a wet wipe, she's probably feeling real sticky right now. Oh fuck, I was so close, so fucking close to having her.

I see my neighbour come out at the same time as us. "Sup man." He greets me, and I nod back. He's a model/actor. A real arrogant knobhead, I can't stand the little prick. He looks over at Shayla and smiles at her as we walk down the corridor to the stairs. "Hi, I've seen you around the building. I'm Seb. You must be—." He introduces himself, and Shayla nods, smiling politely. I glare at the back of Seb's head.

"Married," I say through gritted teeth, wrapping my arm around Shayla's waist and tug her against me. "She's my wife."

Shayla looks up at me and back at Seb again, "Nice to meet you, Seb. I'm Shayla."

Seb smiles and nods, "See you around, Shayla." He winks and walks on ahead of us.

I glare at Seb as he walks away, and Shayla clears her throat. I can tell she's fighting the urge to smile, but the corner of her lips twitch. "Now, who's the jealous one?"

I look down at her, and she grins as we continue to walk down the stairs. "That wasn't jealousy. I was just making it clear you're spoken for, so he doesn't waste his time trying to pursue you." Shayla chuckles and shakes her head.

"So, to summarize, you're jealous." I roll my eyes and shake my head.

"About as jealous as you were about Sophie, baby." I retort, and Shayla sighs.

"Bite me."

"Not enough. I'm going to devour you.." I wink and grin at her smugly as we exit the building. Once we got to the assembly point, I look up at the building and see no sign of a fire. "I fucking knew it! It's a false alarm," I grumble, annoyed, running my fingers through my tousled hair.

Shayla chuckles, "Maybe it's God's way of telling us not to have sex. That's twice we got interrupted. What are the odds of that."

"Or maybe it was us that set the alarm off," I suggest, and she lifts a brow at me.

"How so?"

"Our burning loins." I grin, leaning close. "Our red-hot passion and this fiery need for one another may have triggered off the alarm. Just saying, shit was about to get really hot up there." I explain, holding my hands up teasingly, and Shayla laughs.

"You're something else, you know that." She mocks, and I draw her against me.

"Oh, baby, you haven't seen nothing yet," I murmur lowly in her ear. I look down at her and see she's still got a little ice cream on the back of her neck. I smile and brush her hair away before I lean in, run my tongue over it slowly and suck. Shayla gasps, surprised.

"What are you doing, Cole?" She questions, her eyes darting around to the people around us.

"You still have some ice cream on your neck. I thought I'd be a gentleman and clean it up for you," I whisper in her ear, and she sighs, tilting her head back, giving me more room to kiss and lick her neck teasingly. "Fight me all you want, but one of these days, I'm going to have you," I murmur in her ear and feel her shiver a little. "I'm going to give you a fuck you'll never forget."

Shayla bites her lip, "Cole, we had this conversation. We can't have sex. It will only complicate things between us." She sighs, turning around to look at me. "Whatever this thing is between us has to stop. We can't be anything more than just friends. Because, when this is all over, you'll still be my boss, and we'll have to continue to work together." She explains sullenly, and I nod. She has a point. I know she did, but I couldn't just be her friend. I just fucking can't—I'm too attracted to her for just a friendship-based relationship.

"Shay, I hear you, I do, but when two people have this amount of sexual tension between them, it makes it impossible to be 'just friends' I can't be around you and not want to touch you. I can't look at you and not get a hard-on. It's ridiculous. Do you know how rare it is for me to get an erection just by standing next to someone? Very. It takes a lot to get me this hot and bothered, and I can't even remember the last time I was this affected by any woman, let alone one I've already slept with." I tell her, and she smiles, averting her gaze. She's flushed again, and I can feel myself getting hard.

"Cole, you're just sexually frustrated, that's it. Put any other girl in my position, and you'd still feel the same because it's only sexual. I don't possess a magical vagina that gets men all captivated with me." She explains with a smile when I groan.

"Could have fooled me," I say, pulling her close and pressing my forehead to hers, closing my eyes. I lick my lips. "If what you're saying is true, then, say we have sex again, it should diffuse the tension between us. *If* you claim it's just sexual frustration, then there's really only one way to test your theory."

Shayla's eyes narrow. "And what if we have sex and it diffuses nothing. Then what?" She questions, peering up at me inquiringly. I smile and look into her eyes, brushing my fingers through her hair, I cup her jaw.

"I mean," I grin, licking my lips slowly. "I'm not opposed to keeping at it till it does," I say sincerely, and Shayla laughs.

"I'll tell you what," She peers up at me, her eyes gleaming, and rests her hands on my chest. "Let's not put too much pressure on ourselves by forcing it. If it happens, it happens. Deal?" She states with a sincere smile.

"Can I still touch you?" I ask, and she blinks up at me, narrowing her eyes.

"Define *touch…*"

I smile, "You know as I have been. Can I still do this…" I say, brushing my fingers through her hair, and her eyes close at my touch.

"Yes,"

"What about this…" I whisper, dragging my nose gently over hers. She smiles and nods.

"And this…" I wrap my arms around her waist and pull her up against me, our lips a breath apart. I feel my heart rate spike the closer my lips get to hers.

"Yes," Shayla whispers, parting her lips.

"This…" I breathe, closing my eyes. I brush my lips over hers.

"Ladies and gentlemen, can I please have your attention!" A shrill voice comes over a megaphone causing Shayla and me to jump apart. My shoulders slump, disappointed, and I lift my gaze to the sky. Give me a bloody break. Why are we always getting interrupted in such amazing moments? "Fortunately, there is no fire. It was a false alarm, so you can all please retire to your homes." We hear the maintenance manager announce over the megaphone.

I lean into Shayla's ear when she turns her back to me, "See, I told you. We could have been on round two by now if you'd listened to me." I grumble in her ear, and she chuckles, her shoulders shaking.

"Round two?" She asks as we walk toward the building. "That's rather promising."

"Oh baby, let me take you upstairs and show you what *this* bad boy can do," I growl, squeezing her bum appreciatively. Shayla gasps and shoves me away playfully.

"Behave yourself. People are watching." She scolds me, her green eyes scanning the area, and people really were staring and whispering.

"So, let them. You *are* my wife."

Shayla rolls her eyes. "Fake wife."

"The marriage certificate in my drawer states otherwise, my mini muffin." I tease, wrapping my arm around her shoulder and pulling her against me.

"Oh my God, please don't call me that. I think I prefer sweetheart." I grin and press a kiss to her temple as we walk toward the elevators.

"Mmm, nope, I'm digging it. It stays." Shayla sighs, tugging on her shirt with a grimace.

"I need to shower. I'm all sticky thanks to you." She grumbles, eyeing me with her nose scrunched up. I reach over and tweak her nose, and she slaps my hand away.

"How about I make it up to you?" I suggest leaning against the wall in the elevator, and she pushes the button eyeing me sceptically.

"Why do I get the feeling I'm not going to like this?" She asks, raising her brow. I shrug, smirking at her suggestively, and she shakes her head.

"I don't even want to know." She sighs, brushing her fingers through her hair, and groans when she finds a spot soaked with ice cream.

We make it to the apartment. Shayla and I both stop when we see the mess we left on top of the counter in the midst of our passion. I felt a tingle cascade down my spine when images of what we did flashes before my eyes.

Shayla must have had the same reaction because she was staring at the island, a faraway look in her eyes, lips parted, her breathing slow and shallow. We look at each other simultaneously, her cheeks flushed. She clears her throat, moves over to the island, and proceeds to clean up. I know one thing for sure, tonight we'll both be struggling to get to sleep.

I leave her with an inward groan and go to my bedroom, taking off the jeans and t-shirt I was wearing. I fall back on the bed. Moments later, I hear the shower running, and I let my mind wander off to her naked and wet in that shower and all the things I would do to her in there. I wonder if she's thinking about me and touching herself? I'd give anything to be in there right now.

~

THE NEXT DAY WAS FRIDAY, and as we had a late-night, we got into the office after ten in the morning. Shayla slumps down on her chair and yawns tiredly, both of us only getting four hours sleep I wasn't feeling much better. I had a total of four coffees just to wake myself up a little after I almost dozed off in the middle of a meeting. If it weren't for Shayla kicking my shin under the table, I would have fallen asleep listening to the client drone on and on about their ideas.

We walk out of the conference room laughing. "Did you see that guy's face when you jumped awake?" Shayla cackles hysterically.

"Hey, that was your fault. I saw your eyes grow heavy too, so naturally, of course, I would fall asleep." I defend myself, and Shayla smacks my arm playfully.

"Oh, yes, blame me. You almost fall asleep in the middle of a meeting, and I get the blame. Typical."

"Yes, it is absolutely your fault. You kept me up most of the night with all your shenanigans." I tease with a grin, and she narrows her eyes at me.

"My shenanigans? Who told you to smother me in ice cream?"

I laugh, "Well…"

She holds up her finger and scowls at me. "Don't you dare say it!" She knows me too well.

"All right, all right, put your finger away before you hurt yourself." I tease and walk into my office, still laughing. I look over at her as I sit at my desk, and she's grinning too, shaking her head.

I just adore her.

The rest of the day, I buried my head into work. I've been really distracted lately, so I put my air pods in and drown out the rest of the world. I frown when I realise it's not my music playing. I look at my phone and discover it's Shay's playlist. She synced it with my phone, so we could listen to it in the car. I glance over at her desk and watch her for a couple of minutes while she works. She's so freaking beautiful. I could watch her forever and never get bored.

With a drawn-out sigh, I try to focus on working for the remainder of the day. I seem to find my flow, and the next time I look up was when I hear a knock on my door. I was expecting it to be Shayla, but to my surprise, it was Sophie at the door. She doesn't wait for me to give her permission to enter, and she walks right in and closes the door before she saunters over to my desk. Twice in one week, what does she want now?

"Sophie?" I greet, leaning back against my leather chair. Sophie walks over and drops her handbag on my desk before she sits on the chair opposite me.

"Hey sweetie." She sighs, flipping her hair over her shoulder.

"What are you doing here?" I ask, and she presses her glossy lips together before she lifts her blue eyes to mine.

"I wanted to talk to you. I didn't like the way we left things the other day at lunch." She explains, and I sigh, rubbing my jaw.

"What is there to talk about? I think we said everything we had to say, right?" Sophie shakes her head and crosses her legs leaning back in the chair, regarding me seriously.

"No, Tristan, we didn't." She retorts snidely. I roll my eyes. It grates me when she calls me that. I've told her I want to be called Cole outside of work for years, but she incessantly calls me Tristan because it sounds better than Cole.

"What else is there to say, Soph? You said you and Derrick are engaged to be married, and I told you my opinion on the matter. You're making a mistake jumping into a marriage blind with this guy." I explain, scowling at her.

"Oh, you mean like the mistake you made marrying that assistant girl, Tristan?" She snaps back hotly. I lean forward, placing my forearms on the desk, and I glare at her hard.

"Who said I made a mistake? I love her." Sophie throws her head back and laughs.

"You *love* her?" She croons. "Come on, Tris, you and I both know that girl is the farthest from your type. You like your girls classy and sophisticated, and she is neither of those things. She's a simpleton. A nobody."

I pinch the bridge of my nose. "Watch your mouth Sophie, that's my wife you're talking about," I growl through gritted teeth.

"Your wife?" She tuts, standing up and walking over to me. "Give me a break, Tris. I know you too well. Why don't you just admit that you married her to spite me? You cannot honestly stand there and tell me you're really into this girl."

I frown up at her and shake my head before I stand up also. "Why do you even care, Soph? You're the one that walked out on me, remember?!"

"Yes, because you didn't care about our future! You wouldn't marry me, but you'll go and marry a worthless nobody who you wouldn't look at twice if she walked past you on the street. I spent three years of my life with you. I know you well enough to know you couldn't possibly be interested in a girl like that. You're using her to hurt me, aren't you?"

I laugh bitterly and walk toward her. "Hurt you? You mean the way you hurt me when you just up and took off because you didn't get your own fucking way?! I loved you!" I bark angrily, and she glares at me, her icy blue eyes watering.

"No! You loved your work. I gave you a choice, Tristan! You chose your job over me every time. Your life is all about your job; that's how it's always been. Ever since you took over the company, you made me less of a priority in your life. You didn't see how much you hurt me by pushing me aside like I didn't matter. I didn't want to be second best—not to you!" She shouts, pushing at my chest.

"Do you have any idea how I felt when I saw those pictures of you in the papers with *that* girl? Or the ones all over the internet this morning. That guy is not the Tristan I know. You hate public displays of affection; you wouldn't even hold my hand, but with her, you'll do this." She says, tossing her phone at my chest. I catch it and look at the photos of us from last night. Someone snapped pictures of us while we were outside. It was the moment our noses were pressed together, eyes closed, and I was asking if I could touch her.

I look at Sophie, who wipes a tear that rolls down her cheek. "Sophie I—"

She shakes her head, "Three years, and all I ever wanted was for you to look at me like that. So, tell me, either you never really loved me or that in that photo and all the rest of it is a show."

I lick my lips and hand her phone back to her. "Of course I loved you, Sophie, a part of me will always love you," I admit, and she stares at me for a long moment before she steps closer and presses her lips to mine.

Chapter Seventeen

SHAYLA

I STARE at my reflection in the bathroom mirror as I wash my hands and couldn't help but feel giddy. Our moment in the kitchen last night keeps replaying in my mind. I'm trying so hard to keep things professional between us, but it doesn't seem to work. I mean, let's be honest, if you were in my shoes, would you be able to resist him? I think not.

I feel the butterflies explode in my stomach just at the thought of seeing him. I fluff up my hair and freshen my makeup before I leave the bathroom. He should be finished by now. I'm freaking starving, and the office is near enough, empty other than the cleaners. I walk through the office toward my desk. I can hear voices coming from Cole's office. I stop in my tracks when I see Sophie in there with him. They're arguing heatedly about something.

The light on my intercom is flashing, which means the button was pressed. I reach over, push the button, and hear Sophie's voice.

"Your wife?" She says, standing up and walking over to Cole. "Give me a break, Tris. I know you too well. Why don't you just admit that you married her to spite me? You cannot honestly stand there and tell me you're really into this girl."

I frown, "Why do you even care, Soph? You're the one that walked out on me, remember?!" Cole shouts, getting up to his feet from his chair.

"Yes, because you wouldn't commit! You wouldn't marry me, but you'll go and marry a worthless nobody who you wouldn't look at twice if she walked past you on the street! I spent three years of my life with you. I know you well enough to know you couldn't possibly be interested in a girl like that. You're using her to hurt me, aren't you?!"

Cole laughs angrily and steps closer to her. "Hurt you? You mean the way you hurt me when you just up and took off because you didn't get your fucking way?! I loved you!" He shouts angrily.

"No! You loved your work. I gave you a choice, Tristan! You chose your work over me every time. Your life is all about your job; that's how it's always been. Ever since you took over the company, you made me less of a priority in your life. You didn't see how much you hurt me by pushing me aside like I didn't matter. I didn't want to be second best—not to you!" She shouts, pushing at his chest.

"Do you have any idea how I felt when I saw those pictures of you in the papers with *that* girl? Or the ones all over the internet this morning. That guy is not the Tristan I know. You hate public displays of affection. You wouldn't even hold my hand, but with *her*, you'll do this." She says, tossing her phone at him. Cole catches it and looks at it before he looks at Sophie again. What photos is she talking about? I press myself behind the wall so they couldn't see me watching them.

Cole sighs when he sees Sophie angrily brush a tear away, "Sophie I—"

She shakes her head, "Three years, and all I ever wanted was for you to look at me like that. So, tell me, either you never really loved me, or that in that photo and all the rest of it is nothing but a show."

Cole hands her phone back to her, a sullen look on his face. "Of course I loved you, Sophie, a part of me, will always love you." He tells her earnestly, and I watch as they stare at each other for a long moment before Sophie steps closer, cups his face, and kisses him.

I couldn't breathe. The enormous lump forming in my throat felt like it was choking me. I feel hot tears burn the back of my eyelids. I grab my handbag and jacket and run out of there as fast as my trembling legs would take me. My entire body was shaking as I stood waiting for the elevator. I was angry and hurt that he would use me like that. But then, what the fuck did I expect? She was right. If he weren't drunk that night, a guy like Tristan Cole Hoult would never notice me. He's been lying to me from the beginning, using me to make his ex-girlfriend jealous. God, I feel like such an idiot for thinking he could like me.

I stare at my reflection in the mirror of the elevator. You're a damn fool, Shayla. I hastily wipe away the tears and bite my lip hard. At least now I see him for who he really is…a liar, just like the rest of them. After my ex wrecked me, I made a promise that I would never let another man make me feel worthless ever again. I walk out of the building and jump into a cab. There's only one place I need to be right now. I need to clear my head and avoid seeing him for a couple of days—at least till I can see him again without having the urge to rip his stupid face off. To think I was going to sleep with him again.

As I sat in the back of the taxi, I scroll through my phone and find the photos Sophie was talking about. It's all over Twitter and Instagram. A picture of us from last night while we were standing outside. The caption at the top,

Love is in the air – Newlyweds Tristan & Shayla can't keep their hands off one another.

He almost had me. Hot tears roll down my cheeks as I stare at the photo. I hate him for lying to me and breaking my trust. But most of all, I hate him for toying with my emotions. Why couldn't he just tell me what his agenda was from the beginning? Why did he have to use me like that?

As I stare out of the window, I feel my phone vibrate. Cole's calling me. Probably noticed I had left. Surprised, he came up for air long enough while kissing Sophie to even notice I was gone. *Bastard.* I decline the call, and a few seconds later, he calls again. I stare at his name flashing on my screen, and a part of me just wants to answer it and tell him to go fuck himself, but the other side of me, the proud part, doesn't want to give him the satisfaction of knowing he could hurt me. I won't give him that power over me.

Cole sends a text when I don't answer the three times he called.

Cole:
"Where are you? Have you gone home?"
Me:
"No. I'm spending a couple of nights with the girls.
Cole:
"Oh. Okay, why aren't you answering my calls? What's wrong?"
Me:
"Nothing. I just miss my girls. I need to spend time with them. I'll see you Monday."

I ignore the rest of the texts he sends me as I walk up to my apartment. I unlock the door and walk-in. As soon as the door clicks shut, Jo and Aimee come running over to me.

"Shay Shay!" Aimee squeals hurling herself at me. I wrap my arms around her and blink back the tears that gather in my eyes. "We missed you so much."

I smile sadly, "I missed you girls, too." I tell them, wrapping my arms around Jo, who pulls back and looks at me.

"Whoa, hold on. Something is wrong. Have you been crying?" Jo asks, brushing my hair out of my face. I shake my head, but my eyes water giving away my lie.

"Wow, if ever there was a competition for the world's worst liar, you would win it hands down," Aimee says with a soft frown, and I half chuckle, half sob. "What happened, babe? Not that we're complaining, but why are you here? Shouldn't you be at Cole's place?"

I sigh and shake my head, "I'm staying here for a few days." I tell them, and they exchange looks before they turn their gaze to me again.

"BHT?" They both say in harmony.

I nod sadly, "BHT." Aimee and Jo wrap their arms around me as we walk over to the sofa. BHT is our code for Broken Heart Therapy, consisting of take-out food, lots of wine, and gallons of ice cream while we talk about the situation until we either get too drunk or pass out from a food coma.

Once I had a shower and changed out of my work clothes, our Chinese arrived, and we settled on the floor by the fireplace, and I fill them in with everything that's happened from the contract to my family and Sophie.

"So, you saw them kissing in his office?" Jo asks, her brown eyes almost bulging. I nod in response, pushing my food around my plate.

"Yeah, after she told him he would never look twice at a worthless nobody like me even if I walked past him in the street," I utter with a scoff and shake my head. "He always said I wasn't his type, and if you see her, she's just perfect from head to toe."

Aimee scoffs, "I've seen her. She's always in the tabloids, but she sounds like a royal bitch. I'm sorry, but you can be the most beautiful woman in the world, but if you have a shit personality and an ugly heart, then what have you really got going for you?" She angrily utters while taking a sip of her wine.

"Aimee's right, Shay, don't let an entitled snob like her put you down. Who the fuck is she? You're beautiful both inside and out. She's obviously threatened by you. Besides, you heard her yourself. She said he's never looked at her the way he looks at you or touched her as he does you. Surely that's got to count for something?" Jo explains, reaching over and taking my hand.

I sigh and shake my head, "It could all just be a show to get a reaction out of her—which it did because she's back in his life as he wanted." I explain sullenly.

Aimee sighs, looking at her phone, "I don't know, Shay, it just doesn't add up. I mean, until you told us about this contract, I genuinely thought you two were into each other. When he was here that day, the way he was looking at you and I'm not even going to get into the state of you both when I walked in on you doing god only knows what." She states with a knowing smile. I smile a little, remembering that day.

"I don't know what you're talking about." I deny averting my gaze, and Aimee cackles, slapping my thigh.

"Sure, there was some major petting going on in that room judging by the flustered state of you and the smug smirk on his face. He was incredibly pleased with himself for whatever he did to you." I chuckle and feel my cheeks grow hot.

"Oh my God, shut up." Jo and Aimee both laugh and awe.

"You've been living with him for two months now. Have you had sex again?" Jo questions, and I shake my head.

"No, we didn't have sex. We did kiss a few times, and last night things got a little hot and heavy, but we got interrupted, so." I shrug indifferently and sigh, "I'm just so confused girls, he keeps touching me, and kissing me, and he tells me he has to have me when we're alone, and the sexual chemistry between us is just so intense." I close my eyes and press my head back against the wall.

"Well, there you go. If it were all for a show, he wouldn't do those things in private. He's telling you he has to have you, Shay. I think he really likes you. I mean, look at this photo of you both. You can't fake moments like this. It's like nothing else around you exist, but the two of you." Aimee explains, holding up her phone with the picture of us from last night.

"Yeah, because he was talking about giving me a fuck I'd never forget. He's just horny Aimee. He can't sleep with anyone else while he's married to me, because of the contract, of course, he's going to say he wants me. He's got no other choice. Six months is a long time for a guy to go without any sort of sex." I say and shake my head. "That's why he's so adamant about sleeping with me, not because he wants me, but because he has no other choice. I feel so stupid for trusting him. I thought he wanted me, and I almost convinced myself to sleep with him. I'm such an idiot!"

Aimee sighs, "That does make sense. He is a guy, after all, he might just be biding his time, and he's clearly thinking with his knob."

"Shayla, you don't know that," Jo Interjects, throwing a side glare at Aimee, who shrugs.

"He said he will always love her, Jo, right before she kissed him. How much clearer does it have to be? I heard him." I explain, pulling my knees to my chest.

"Shayla, have you fallen for him?" Aimee asks. I look at her and shake my head.

"No, I haven't fallen for him. I was developing a little crush, maybe, but no, I don't love him. I'm just angry that he would lie and use me like that." I grumble and stand up, picking up the bottle of wine, not even bothering with the glass anymore. “Can I even be angry? He’s not mine. Not really, so what right do I have to be mad at him for kissing her? As she said, I’m a nobody.” I utter bitterly, pacing the living room, and taking a long gulp of the wine.

Aimee and Jo exchanged glances before they turn their gazes to me, pacing furiously. “You are not, a nobody Shay. Don’t let that bitch get into your head. You’re perfect the way you are. You’re kind and compassionate to everyone around you, and that’s a beautiful thing. With all the shit you’ve had to go through in your life, you’re still one of the strongest people I know.” Aimee says, watching me. I sigh and shake my head, taking another long sip of the bottle of wine.

“Ugh, you know what, I don’t even want to talk about this anymore. I just want to spend the next two days free of anything and everything to do with Cole Hoult.” I say, slumping down on the sofa with a huff.

“Uh,” Aimee holds my phone up. “He’s calling you.” I roll my eyes and sigh. I take the phone off her and stare at his name screen.

“Why are you calling me?! What do you want?! What?!” I shout at the phone before I decline the call. “In fact,” I snap, turning the phone off completely. “Eat that, you rotten bastard,” I utter icily and toss my phone aside before gulping down the rest of the wine. “I hate men!”

"Oh-kay then,” Aimee utters, looking at us both. “Shall we go out?”

I look at the time on the watch on my wrist, “It's eleven o’clock.”

Aimee shrugs, “So? Its Friday. All good bars open after ten anyway.” I muse over her words and nod. Fuck it, anything beats sitting around sulking over a guy.

“Yes! I want to dance. Let’s do it,” I say and they both nod and clamber up to their feet. “Hold it! If I end up in Vegas and wake up married to some stranger again, I will literally throttle the both of you,” I warn, pointing at them both, and they laugh. “Do not let me out of your sight—not for one second, and don’t let me drink tequila either. Tequila makes me stupid, and stupid is no good for me.” I throw over my shoulder while walking to my bedroom.

“What are the odds of that happening twice?” Aimee laughs.

I shrug. “This is me we are talking about. If it happens to anyone, you bet your arse it will be me.” Jo laughs as she walks to her bedroom.

"Fair enough. Don't worry boo, we got you." Aimee chimes in from her bedroom. I look through my closet for an outfit and pick out a black mini dress. I match the dress with a pair of red stilettos and straighten my hair. Nobody, my foot. You can kiss my naturally curvy arse, you bulimic bitch.

Nobody tells me I'm not good enough.

"You ready?" Jo asks, standing in my doorway as I apply my red lipstick to match my heels. I nod and take one last look at myself before we leave. I did my best to try and put Cole out of my mind, but he kept sneaking in when I would see a couple dancing or kissing on the dance floor.

"Did we really have to come back here out of all the clubs in London?" I ask the girls while sipping my mojito, and Jo shrugs.

"It's the best club around, plus the DJ is lush." She utters, swaying to the music and eyeing up, said DJ, who winks at her.

"I'm going to go talk to him." She says and saunters over to the DJ booth. Aimee and I laugh, shaking our heads. Aimee and I scan the club while we sip our drinks.

"This song goes out to Shayla and her girls." The DJ announces over the microphone, I look over at Jo when our song starts thundering through the speakers, and she blows me a kiss.

"I love that bitch! Let's dance." Aimee exclaims, dragging me out on the dance floor to the throng of people already dancing. I close my eyes and let the music take over as I dance with my best friend. No matter how bad things may get, I'm thankful I always have them to help pick me up.

"Shayla?!" I turn and look when I hear my name being called. I see Josh, Cole's best friend, behind me. My eyes immediately scan the area for Cole, thinking he might be here with Josh, but I couldn't see him around.

"Josh!" I smile, "Hey, fancy seeing you here."

He smiles, nodding, and steps closer to speak into my ear, "Same. I didn't think I'd see you here. Is Cole with you, too?" He asks, and I shake my head.

"Oh. Uh, no, he's not. I don't know where he is. I'm here with my girls." I tell him, and he studies my face for a second before nodding.

"Oh, all right. Well, if you need anything, I'm around okay. Come find me." I smile gratefully, he winks before he disappears into the crowd.

"Who the fuck is that hottie?! Aimee shrieks in my ear, almost bursting my eardrum, watching Josh's retreating back.

"That's Josh, Cole's best friend and head of security," I tell her, and she smirks, swaying to the music.

"Interesting. Single?"

I nod, smiling, "I believe so. Big player. I don't really quiz him about his love life, ya know."

"Bitch, you're surrounded by all these hot men all day. How you get any work done baffles me." I laugh while she pulls me with her to dance again.

An hour and four cocktails later, I was buzzing, and my feet were aching. Jo was still with the DJ flirting away, and Aimee's flirting shamelessly with some guy she was dancing with.

"Hey gorgeous." A deep voice burs in my ear from behind. I turn and look up at the tall brunette standing in front of me. "Can I buy you a drink?"

I hold my glass up to him, "Already have one. Thank you."

"How about a dance then?" He asks, stepping close, so close I can smell the bourbon on his breath. I shake my head and pull my head away.

"No, thanks. I'm going to go sit." I turn to walk when he grabs my arm and stops me. I look up at him and back down at his hand on my arm.

"Come on, don't be a tease, babe." I yank my hand out of his and glare at him.

"I'm not being a tease. I just said no. I'm not interested. Take the hint." I jeer, narrowing my eyes at him, and he licks his lips.

"What you got a boyfriend or something?" He questions, rubbing his jaw while openly checking me out.

"No, she has a husband, though." I turn around when I see Cole standing behind me, his eyes fixed angrily on the guy leering at me.

"Oh, my bad, I didn't see no ring." He says, looking at Cole, who lifts my hand, looks at the diamond ring on my finger, and back at the guy.

"Can't really miss it, mate." He hisses darkly. "Leave." The brunette holds his hands up and walks away. Cole spins me around so I could look at him.

"What are you doing here?" I ask him with a frown, and he narrows his eyes at me, licking his lips.

"Looking for my wife." He replies, his tone serious.

I roll my eyes and take a step back from him. "Your wife? How did you find me? Did Josh tell you where I was?"

He nods, "Yes, he did. He said you've had quite a few cocktails, and your phone is off. I wanted to make sure you were okay."

I shrug, "Josh needs to mind his own business. I'm fine, as you can see. You can be on your way now." I say and turn to walk away, but he grabs my arm and pulls me back again.

"He's doing his job. When your safety is in question, it most definitely is his business," Cole explains gravely while staring into my eyes. "Why are you ignoring my calls and messages? Have I done something to upset you?"

I laugh resentfully and a little drunkenly. "I don't know, Cole, have you?"

Cole continues to stare at me, "Shayla..."

I pull my arm out of his hold and stagger a little, "What? Shayla, what, Cole?" I brush my fingers through my hair. I sigh, annoyed, trying my best to avoid his gaze.

"What is up with you?" He snaps hotly, taking hold of my shoulders, lifting my gaze to his.

I pull my face out of his grasp, "Nothing!"

"Bullshit, don't fucking lie to me!" He bellows over the loud music. We glare at each other in the middle of the dance floor, other couples around us dancing heatedly with one another. "We're leaving." He states, lacing his fingers with mine. I shake my head and pull my hand back. He looks down at his hand and back up at me again, scowling.

"No, let's stay! Come on, dance with me." I yank him closer. "Maybe you can give me that fuck you promised me in a dark corner, hm? What do you say, baby? You need me, right?" I purr seductively, taunting him while running my hands over his chest. Cole bites his lip, staring at me furiously before he wraps his fingers around my wrists and grips them tight. I lean up close, so my lips brush over him as I speak. "Come on, you promised me a fuck I'd never forget, right?" I whisper hotly, and he lifts his head, his green eyes looking around the club, his jaw clenching tight before he looks at me again.

"Shayla, stop it. What has gotten into you?" He glowers at me. I shrug and pull away from him.

"I'm giving you what you want, Cole," I tell him simply, and he frowns, his eyes looking over my face questioningly.

"And what's that, Shay?"

"A fuck!" I shout angrily, and he looks around when people dancing next to us hear my outburst. He glares at them, and they look away. I laugh bitterly.

"Christ, Shay." He hisses, turning his hot gaze to mine again. "You're drunk. We're going home."

"No. I'm not going anywhere with you." Cole closes his eyes, shoving his fingers through his hair irritated. I gasp when he wraps his arm around my waist and pulls me up against him.

"You have two choices, sweetheart, you either walk out of this club with me like a good girl, or I will throw you over my shoulder, and fucking carry you out. One way or the other, you're coming home with me. Do you understand?" Cole growls angrily.

"You don't tell me what to do! Why the fuck would I go anywhere with you?" I question stormily while scowling up at him, and he bites his lip.

"Why? Because you're clearly upset about something and we're going to talk about it," He answers, pulling me through the crowd. I see Aimee, who watches me as Cole guides me through the club. I roll my eyes, shrugging, and she makes a heart shape with her fingers and gives me an encouraging nod. We walk out of the club toward Cole's car. I pull my hand out of his and cross them over my chest. Cole stops and looks at me. "Shayla, get in the car."

I stare ahead and shake my head. Childish, I know, but I really didn't want to go anywhere with him. "You're wasting your time. There is nothing to talk about."

Cole walks over to me; he looks around and pinches the bridge of his nose before he lifts his gaze to me again.

"Shayla, it's clear you're pissed off about something. Now, are you going to be that mature girl I know and talk about it, or are you going to keep acting like a petulant child?" He glowers at me, and I chuckle, averting my gaze so he wouldn't notice the anger in my eyes. He holds my jaw and turns my face to his again. "What did I do?"

"I already told you. Nothing."

"I'm not going to argue with you in the middle of the fucking street!" He shouts angrily.

"Then don't!" I shout back. "Go bother Sophie and leave me the fuck alone!" I add, pushing him away and walking off down the street. I regretted it the minute I said it, but it just flew right out of my mouth.

Cole walks after me, grabs my arm, and pulls me into a dark alleyway hidden from prying eyes. He presses me up against a wall and cages me in so I couldn't walk off. "What the hell are you talking about?"

I heave a sigh to try and calm down, "What do you want from me, Cole?"

He looks at me, "I want to know what your problem is."

"You want to know what my problem is? All right. I want to know why you lied to me?" I question, and Cole frowns, confused.

"When did I lie to you? About what?"

"The real reason you're pretending to be 'happily married' to me. It's not entirely about wanting your father and grandfathers' shares, is it? It's about Sophie. You're still hurt that she left you, so you're using me to get her back because you're still in love with her." Cole blinks and shakes his head.

"Shayla, what on earth are you talking about? Using you? I would never do that. Where are you getting all this from?"

I look away from his gaze and bite the inside of my cheek to keep the tears at bay. I will not cry. "Don't stand there and lie to my face. I heard you arguing in your office earlier."

Cole sighs, closing his eyes, "Christ. Shayla, listen—"

"I did, Cole. I listened to your ex go on and on about me being a worthless nobody who you wouldn't look at twice. But you know what, that's not what hurt me, because I couldn't give a toss about her opinions of me." I sigh and shake my head. "I trusted you and chose to help you because you seemed so genuine to me. Little did I know, you were lying to my face the whole time about your real agenda."

Cole licks his lips, "Shayla, I didn't lie to you! Sophie has nothing to do with any of this, I swear to you."

"You're still lying! I heard you, Cole, you stood there and told her you love her, and you kissed."

"Shayla, you've got this all wrong." He says, trying to touch my face, but I push him away from me.

"Don't touch me. The only thing I got all wrong was you. But you know what, it's my fault. I was an idiot for trusting you in the first place. I'm done." I say and brush past him, but he pulls me back.

"Shayla, listen to me," He looks down into my face. "She kissed me, and it was only for a second."

I roll my eyes and glare up at him, "Did you kiss her back?" I question, and he stares at me for a second and drops his gaze, his jaw set tight.

I shake my head. "I'm done. Screw you and your fucking arrangement." I push past him to walk off, but he catches me by the wrist again.

"The hell you are!" He glares at me. "Even if this had something to do with Sophie— which it doesn't, what difference would it make to you? What we have isn't real, right?" He probes, looking into my eyes. "Right?!"

"Right!" I shout back.

"Then why do you care if Sophie and I kissed? Were you or were you not the one who stood in my office yesterday telling me you wouldn't care if I fucked her on my desk?" He asks, taking hold of my shoulders and staring into my eyes furiously. I stare up at him, shaking my head. "Were you just full of it?"

I shove him away from me, "This has nothing to do with jealousy and everything to do with you using me to hurt your ex-girlfriend! I'm not your fucking toy!" I argue while Cole glowers at me, his eyes narrowed while he watches me.

"My toy?! I didn't use you, Shayla!" He declares frantically. "If I wanted Sophie back, I would have gone after her a long time ago! Why the hell would I need you?"

I cross my arms over my chest and shrug. "I don't know, Cole. Maybe your ego was bruised that she left you, and you wanted to hurt her back!" Cole pinches the bridge of his nose and sighs. "It doesn't even matter anymore because I'm done with you and this whole fucking arrangement," I tell him before I turn to walk away, but Cole steps in front of me, blocking my path.

"You can't just walk away!"

I stare up at him, and he stares back heatedly. "Watch me!"

"What the fuck do you want, Shayla?! Tell me, so I know, because I'm tired of spinning in circles around you!"

"You know what I want, Cole? I just want to be myself again because this entire time, I have never been made to feel so worthless in my life than I do when I'm with you!" I declare hotly. We stare at each other for a long moment before I brush past him and walk away.

Chapter Eighteen

COLE

What the fuck is happening?

That was all I could think as I stood in that dark alley watching Shayla storm off. Did she just say she feels worthless when she's with me? I've never done anything to make her feel worthless. My rational side is telling me to let her go and give her time, but something inside of me refuses to let her be. I stare at her retreating back and shake my head before I go after her.

I was worried that something was wrong when she disappeared earlier because it's not like her to leave without a word. Even the text messages she sent me were frosty and direct. I can only imagine what she must have thought overhearing that conversation with Sophie, but she really did get it all wrong. Was a small part of me hoping to get a reaction out of Sophie when she found out I was married? Yes it did. I loved her with all my heart, and she broke me when she just up and left me. I didn't do this to get her back or get one over on her. It just went in that direction through no fault of my own. I can't lie though, it did please me a little to see her so worked up over Shayla.

When she kissed me, I was shocked, to say the least. Did I kiss her back? Maybe a little, but only out of habit. I spent three years with Sophie. Her lips, smell, and kiss brought so many memories and feelings back for me. I do miss her. She is essentially the perfect girl for me. The brief conversation we had after the kiss has got me all confused.

I pull away from the kiss before it got too deep and took a step back from her. Sophie watches me confused, her blue eyes looking at me forlornly.

"Soph," I sigh and rub the back of my neck, "You shouldn't have done that. I'm happily married, and you're engaged to Derrick."

Sophie sighs and tucks a loose strand of hair behind her ear, "Tristan, I had to see if there's still something there between us, and there is. You kissed me back, which means you're not over me either." She explains, taking a step toward me, and I shake my head and retreat, putting my space between us.

"Soph, stop. That kiss was a mistake. I'm happy with Shayla—"

"You're lying. If you were genuinely happy and in love with her, you wouldn't have kissed me back, but you did. I'm the one you want, Tristan. I'm the girl for you. I always have been, not *her*. Just like you're the guy for me. Your marriage is a sham. You're not only lying to yourself, but you're lying to that poor girl too, and one day you'll realise that you made a mistake and you're going to break her heart." Sophie explains, taking a step toward me. "Deep down, you know as well as I do that, we're meant to be together." I watch her as she leans up and kisses my cheek before pulling back and gazing into my eyes. "I still love you, Tris."

I swallow hard, unable to look away from her eyes. She reaches up and rubs my jaw affectionately, drops a chaste kiss on my lips before pulling away and walking out of my office. I sigh and close my eyes. "Fuck."

Oh shit. Shayla!

My eyes open, and I look at her desk. She wasn't there. I walk out of the office and look for her bag and jacket, not there either. She was gone. I feel my stomach tie itself into knots, and I pray she didn't see what just happened in my office. I grab my keys and walk through the empty office, my eyes darting around for any sign of her. Maybe she was waiting by my car in the parking lot.

I rush out of the elevator as soon as I hit the ground floor and walk over to my car. She's not there either. She might have gotten bored with waiting and went home. But she would have said something before she left, surely. I get in the car and dial her number, it rings three times, and it goes straight to voicemail. She declined the call. Fuck.

I dial again, and it rings—No answer. I punch the steering wheel. I send a text and wait anxiously for a reply. My phone vibrates, and I feel my heart race when I see her name appear on my screen. I read the text, she's not coming home, she's staying with her friends. We text back and forth, and I can tell something is off. She's being cold, or am I just being paranoid?

She won't be back the whole weekend, she tells me. I was tempted to drive to her place and see her, but she would think I'm some fixated idiot if there really is nothing wrong. I go home and figure I'd leave her with her girls for a few days. I could use some time alone too.

I had an awful feeling in the pit of my stomach. I don't know if it was guilt or what, but I couldn't shake it. I just wanted to see her. The apartment was quiet without Shayla, and I felt a little ache in my chest. I take my tie off and unbutton my shirt as I walk to the kitchen, open the fridge, taking out a bottle of beer. I unscrew the top and toss it on the kitchen island before I walk out onto the terrace. My mind was reeling. I'm confused, and I don't know what to make of my feelings.

On the one hand, there's Sophie, with who I've been in love for over three years, despite the fact she broke my heart. I'm clearly still not over her. And the other hand, I've got Shayla, with who I've got this undeniable connection. She's the opposite of everything I want in a partner, but she just makes me feel some type of way when I'm with her. I call her again, and she turns her phone off. Something was wrong.

I sat outside on the terrace, staring out at the city before me as the sky grew darker and darker, trying to discern the chaos in my head. I check my phone for the millionth time and disappointedly sigh when I don't hear from her. An hour later, my phone rings. I snatch it off the sofa, thinking it was Shayla, and groan when I see it was Josh.

"Josh, I'm really not in the mood. Can we talk later?" I mutter and take a sip of my beer.

"Mate, I'm at Luxe. Shayla's here with her friends." I sit up when I hear her name.

"She is?"

"Yeah, she's had a bit to drink. I'm keeping an eye on her, but I thought you would want to know." He says, and I bite my lip hard. "She's looking fire though, bro. Guys are swarming around them."

"Don't take your eyes off her. I'll be there soon." I tell him and end the call before I go to my room to get changed into a pair of black jeans and a white button-down shirt. She's perfectly fucking fine, out having a blast by the looks of it. The thought of other guys buzzing around her annoyed the shit out of me.

IT TOOK me less than an hour to get to the club, the one where we first met. Walking in there brought that night back to me. I scan the club and finally find Josh standing by the VIP area, arms crossed, his eyes narrowed and glued to the dance floor watching something intently. I walk over to him, and he looks at me and juts his jaw to the dance floor. I follow his gaze and see a tall, burly brunette with Shayla, his hand clasped around her arm, and she's glaring at him. *Ah, hell no...*

I make my way through the crowd and step behind Shayla just as she pulls her arm out of his hold and tells him she's not interested. His eyes leer at her openly, and I fist my hands at my side.

"What you got a boyfriend or something?"

"No, she's got a husband, though," I say, glaring at him hard. Shayla looks back and up at me. I couldn't see her reaction because I was glaring daggers at the fucker who dare put his hand on my wife.

"Oh, my bad, I didn't see no ring." He claims. I nod and lift her hand, look at the diamond ring on her wedding finger, and look at him.

"Can't really miss it, *mate*." I hiss, putting a little emphasis on the mate. "Leave." I growl and watch as he holds his hands up and backs away. As soon as he leaves, I spin Shayla around and look down at her. Her usual bright green eyes go dark the moment our eyes meet.

She was pissed.

So, here I am, at one in the morning, chasing her down the street. I grab her hand before she could get too far and pull her back to me. "Shayla, will you please just get in the car and let's talk?"

She sighs and stares at the ground. “There is nothing to talk about. Go home, Cole.” She tries to pull her hand out of my grasp and looks up at me when I tighten my grip, not letting her go.

“We’re going to talk about this, and you’re going to hear me out. Get in the car.” I retort, and we glare at each other. “Please.”

Shayla finally relents, “Fine.” We walk over to the car. I open the door for her to get in. We drive back to my apartment in silence. I glance over at her while she’s staring out of the window. Her entire body was turned away from me, almost as if she couldn’t even bear to be around me.

I pull up behind my apartment complex, in front of a beautiful waterfront. Thought it would be a nice place for us to talk. I take my seatbelt off and turn to face her in my seat. She doesn’t look at me, just stares ahead silently. “Shayla, look at me,” I say, and she ignores me and keeps staring ahead.

“You said you wanted me to hear you out. I’m listening. Talk, or I’m leaving.” She utters icily.

I sigh and lick my lips, “Shayla, I can see why you’re angry. I get it, I do, but I didn’t lie to you.” I explain and watch her reaction. “What I told you from the very beginning is the sole reason I asked for your help. It had nothing to do with Sophie, not really. I mean, did a very small part of me hope to get a reaction out of her? Yes it did.” I add, and she continues to stare ahead. “I would have hoped that you, of all people, would understand the feeling of wanting some closure after having your heartbroken. If your ex—the one that hurt you, came back into your life suddenly, can you honestly tell me you wouldn’t get some sort of satisfaction out of watching him squirm after he hurt you?” I ask, and Shayla sighs. “You would, wouldn’t you?”

When she doesn’t answer, I reach for her hand, but just as my fingers brush hers, she pulls it away. “Are you still in love with her?” She asks, her voice barely over a whisper. I wanted to say no, but it felt like my mouth was glued shut. Shayla turns her head and looks at me, her eyes searching mine before they look away again. She nods, “What do you want from me, Cole?” She whispers.

Again, my mouth suddenly feels heavy, like even if I tried to speak, I couldn’t get the words out. I could only look at her. “If you’re still in love with her, why don't you just divorce me and tell her how you feel? She obviously feels the same, or she wouldn't have bothered coming back into your life."

I lick my lips, shaking my head, "Honestly? I'm not so sure what she wants. I can't tell if she's back because she genuinely still loves me or if she's threatened by you and just wants to sabotage my life out of spite."

Shayla wraps her arms around herself and chews her bottom lip. "You're afraid of getting hurt again." She states, and I nod, spinning the ring on my finger. "If she comes back, would you give it another go?"

I shrug, "I don't know. I honestly don't know, and until this week, I thought I was over her. Then she told me she was marrying Derrick, and I just blew up at her." I explain, scratching my forehead. "I'm just…" I trail off and look at Shayla, who was twirling her diamond ring on her finger. Her hair fell around her face like a curtain, and I wanted to reach out and brush it back so I could see her face, but I couldn't find the nerve to touch her.

"Cole, if you genuinely love this girl, just tell her and find a way to make it work. There's no point in hanging onto this arrangement we have for another three and a half months." Shayla explains, looking ahead. "We'll divorce like we originally planned, and you can get your shares the right way without lying to your family."

I frown, "You want to end our arrangement?"

She nods and looks down at her hands placed in her lap. "Yes. It's the right thing to do, and deep down, you know that too. This whole thing was a mistake from the beginning."

I shake my head and feel my gut twist at her words, "What about you? Your family?" She shrugs.

"Don't worry about me. I'll figure something out, I always do." She says with a faint smile and reaches for the door handle. I curl my fingers around her wrist and stop her. She looks back at me, our eyes meet, and even in the dark, I can see the sadness she's trying to conceal in her eyes.

"Shayla…"

"Cole, please, *let me go*." She whispers pleadingly. There was something so final in her words and the way she said 'let me go' that made my heart clench. I loosen my hold on her, and she opens the door and steps out of the car. I watch her as she closes the door and walks along the waterfront. The wind blowing her hair back, she wraps her arms around herself while she looks out at the water.

I get out of the car, shrug my jacket off and walk over to her. I place my coat on her shoulders, draw her back against me and press my forehead to the top of her head, my hands rubbing her arms slowly to warm her up. When she doesn't make any movements nor pushes me away, I wrap my arms around her shoulders and press a kiss to her temple. "Don't hit me with the goodbye…not yet," I whisper in her ear, and I feel her heave a sigh. "You promised to be the light in my life, remember?"

"You don't need me, Cole."

I close my eyes, "Yes, I do. We have a signed agreement, and I gave you and your mother my word, and I'm not about to go back on that promise," I turn her around to face me, and she looks up at me. "We're going to see this thing through as we planned, and when the six months is up, then I'll let you go. Not a minute sooner."

Shayla sighs and licks her lips, "And what about Sophie?"

I shrug with a sigh, "She's getting married soon, and I don't really know if I'm ready to open up that particular can of worms just yet."

Shayla bites her bottom lip, "It's obvious there's still something there between you. I think she's using this Derrick guy to get a reaction out of you."

"You think so?" She nods.

"Yeah, I really do, or she wouldn't be kicking off one second and kissing you the next," Shayla explains, averting her gaze to the water. "The moment you give her the green light, she'll be yours. I promise you."

"It's not that simple though, I can't just forget the fact that she walked out on me." I tilt my head back and groan, "I want her to feel just a fraction of what she put me through. Maybe then, I'll consider giving us another chance."

Shayla shakes her head and fixes me with a look I couldn't quite decipher. "Eye for an eye, you say?"

I nod, "Exactly."

"Have you never heard the saying 'An Eye for an eye leaves the world blind' Cole Hoult?"

"Ahh yes, my good friend, Gandhi," I say as I wrap my arm around her shoulder, and we walk to the apartment complex.

"Good friend?" Shayla asks peering up at me as we walk.

I smile, "Why yes, he was a good buddy of mine."

Shayla snorts, "Cole, you weren't even thought of when he was killed."

I chuckle, "In a former lifetime, mini muffin."

"You're incorrigible." She mutters and pushes me away from her.

"You love me."

"Don't push your luck, Hoult."

Chapter Nineteen

SHAYLA

HAVE you ever had that feeling where you feel as though you're slowly suffocating like someone has their hands around your lungs? And they're just squeezing every bit of air out of you. That's the only way I could explain the way I was feeling at that very moment when I asked Cole if he was still in love with Sophie, and he couldn't answer me. I felt all the oxygen leave my lungs, and it hurt. When I turned and looked at him, I got my answer. He's still in love with her, even if he can't admit it to himself. I had to get out of that car. I was in desperate need of air, and I was terrified he would see the tears that I was fighting to keep at bay.

As I walk along the waterfront, I keep telling myself that I'm being stupid. It's just an arrangement, a ploy from the very beginning. I have no right to be upset with him. He can love whoever he wants. He doesn't owe me a damn thing. As far as he's concerned, he's holding his side of the deal, and now I have to hold mine. Whatever these feelings are, I have to bury them and keep reminding myself that it's not real.

I bite the inside of my cheek when I feel him wrap his jacket around me and rest his head against mine. The smell of his aftershave makes me dizzy. He always smells so good. My eyes close when he wraps his arms around my shoulder and kisses my temple. On the outside, I was quiet but inside, I was screaming.

'Don't you dare cry, Shayla, keep it together, keep it together.'

It wasn't until we got to the apartment, and I went straight to my bedroom, closed the door, leaned against it, and finally let that dam within me break. I silently cried and cried until I had nothing left inside me. Nothing from this day on would ever be the same between us. I made a promise to myself that I would close the doors to my heart and chain them shut. I had to keep Cole out at all cost because if I didn't, I'd get hurt, and I couldn't bear the thought of going through another heartbreak. He wants Sophie. They're perfect for one another, so I'll play my part in this agreement as planned and walk out of his life like I was always supposed too.

THE NEXT COUPLE of weeks dragged on both at home and work. I put the barriers up between Cole and me, much to his dismay, but he didn't mention anything if it did bother him. I did see his face fall a couple of times when he would try and touch me flirtatiously, and I would back away, finding any excuse I could to get away. I spent less time at his apartment and more time with the girls back at our place. We're at the end of our three months and coming up to the fourth month now. I did miss him terribly, but I have to stay away for the sake of my own heart.

I was currently sitting with the girls out on our terrace, my knees pulled to my chest, staring at my phone, wondering why he wasn't calling or texting me. Was he with Sophie?

Aimee sighs and looks over at me, "Shayla, you've been staring at the phone for the last three hours. A watched phone doesn't ring, babe."

I lift my gaze to her and shrug, "I wasn't."

Jo chuckles, "Right, you're obviously wondering what he's up to. Just text him." I shake my head and look ahead. "Better yet. Why don't you just tell him you like him and stop torturing yourself by pretending you don't." She adds, looking at me pointedly.

I sigh, "I can't."

"Why?" Aimee asks, taking a bite out of an apple and chewing gingerly. "You've gone cold turkey on the boy. He's probably confused why you're pulling away from him, and he's likely respecting your need for time apart by trying to give you space."

I close my eyes and rest my chin on my knee, "Aimee. I don't like him. Even if I did, how can I just go and tell him while he's still in love with his ex-girlfriend? Would you do it? Be honest, would you go and tell a guy who is in love with someone else you have feelings for him, especially when he's given you zero indication that he might like you back?" I ask, irritated, and Aimee looks at me blankly, her eyes wide.

"I mean, when you put it like that, no, I wouldn't. But zero indication? Come on, Shay, you can't be that unwitting, surely. We all saw the way he dragged you out of that club that night. Why would he bother coming after you if he didn't like you? Are you certain he doesn't feel anything for you?"

"Yes!" I snap angrily, and both girls jump, startled. "I saw it in his eyes. I saw it on his face when she kissed him. Stop filling my head with all this shit, okay. He doesn't want me. I know where I stand. I know my place, and I'm going to do my bit in getting him his shares and in eight weeks, I'm done. To hell with him and all of this bullshit. I just want my damn life back." I declare bitterly, standing up. I grab my jacket and handbag and walk out of the apartment. I needed to get some air and clear my head before I went back to Cole's place.

I walk out of the building and pull my jacket on. As I walk down the steps, I stop when I see a black Audi R8 pull up. Cole's car. He gets out of the car and walks over to me.

"Hey," He greets, shoving his hands in his pockets. I nod, wrapping my arms around myself.

"Hi, what are you doing here?" I question, and he looks around before he looks at me again, eyes narrowed.

"I, uh, went out for a drive and wondered what you were up to? I've barely seen you in the last couple of weeks." He tells me, and I look down at my feet, plaster a fake smile on my face.

"Why, Lord Hoult, is that your way of telling me you miss me?" I ask with a smirk, and he smiles and rubs the back of his neck.

"If I say yes, would you judge me?" I look at him, and the sincerity in his eyes makes me ache deeply.

I shrug and hold up my thumb and forefinger, "Maybe a little."

He chuckles. "Then, yes, I miss you." I smile, and he reaches out and pokes my side gently. When I don't slap his hand away like he's used to, he drops his hand to his side, a little frown on his face. Cole sighs a moment later and runs his fingers through his hair. "I'm really burnt out, and you're always so good at distracting me, so I thought we could do something?"

I frown, "Do what?"

"Something fun." He suggests with a shrug, and I bite my lip. I have been avoiding him lately, maybe doing something fun together might be good for us both.

"Uh, sure. What do you have in mind?" I question as we walk toward his car. Cole winks and smiles at me mischievously.

"You'll see." I nod, and we get into the car. We made small talk on the journey to wherever he was taking me. "Oh, by the way, don't be mad, but we have to go to my parent's place this weekend," Cole says, glancing at me sideways.

I frown, looking at him, "Why?"

"Remember that party she was going to throw us?" I nod, and he smiles sheepishly. "That's this Saturday. My mother has arranged it in their back garden."

"What? Cole, that's in three days? Why didn't they give us more notice?" I question, glaring at him. He shrugs.

"I think she mentioned it to me two weeks ago, and I completely forgot to tell you—Ow hey!" I punch his arm, and he chuckles, scowling at me while rubbing his arm. "I'm sorry. We've been really busy at work, and you've not been around lately, so it completely slipped out of my mind."

"Do we have to go?" I complain with a pout, and he looks at me rather amused.

"Well yes, it is a party for *us*, so I assume we may have to make an appearance."

I roll my eyes at his sarcastic tone, and he grins back at me.

"Great, so I'll have to go shopping for a dress and stuff." I groan, closing my eyes.

"Actually, my mother has arranged everything. All you have to do is show up at four." I open my eyes and look at him.

"I swear to God if your mother tries dressing me up like some preppy malibu barbie, I will walk right out of there," I warn, and Cole laughs as he parks up the car.

"Shayla, you two really need to stop butting heads. It's one-night sweetheart, just go with it and keep her happy. This socialite crap really means a lot to her." Cole explains, looking at me once he finishes parking the car.

"You couldn't have married someone else, could you? No, you had to pick me." I grumble, and Cole laughs again, turning in his seat to look at me.

"Sweetheart, you're just as guilty. The last time I checked, I wasn't holding a gun to your head. We both skipped down that aisle and said yes at that altar." I sigh with a groan and smack his hand away when he squeezes my cheek.

"Fine, but if she tries digging me out in front of her rich friends, don't expect me to sit there and take it," I inform him while taking my seatbelt off, and Cole smiles at me warmly.

"I wouldn't dream of it. Come on." He says and gets out of the car. I follow him out and look around.

"Golf?" I say incredulously, watching Cole, who smiles, walking around the car. "Oh man, you have not learnt a thing about me."

"Crazy golf." He corrects, taking hold of my hand, and pulls me along with him. When I try to pry my hand from his, he tightens his fingers around mine and smiles. "It's a lot more fun than golf, I promise." He adds, pulling me through the gates.

"If you say so," I utter as we collect our clubs. I look around and see other couples laughing and flirting with one another. *Great.*

We make our way through to the first course, "Have you ever been crazy golf before?" Cole questions as we wait for the couple in front of us to take their turn. I shake my head, averting my eyes from his, and pretend to look at my club.

"Nope, never been," I reply, watching the couple before us flirtatiously touch one another. It's definitely their first date. I miss feeling that excitement of a new relationship. “Shay?”

I blink and look at Cole, who is watching me his brows raised slightly, “Huh?”

He smiles, “It’s our go.” I nod and step forward. I drop my ball on the fake grass and look at my club. How the hell do you hold this thing. I recall it from one of the movies I watched with the girls recently, but I was drawing a blank. I wrap my fingers at the top of the club and step to the side. “You’re holding the club wrong, here.” Cole steps behind me and presses his chest against my back.

He reaches over me, and I close my eyes when I feel his warm breath on the shell of my ear while his fingers close around mine. “Okay, the object of the game is to get the ball in the hole with one shot. This one is fairly simple. It’s a straight line so pull the putter back like this…” He whispers, drawing my arms back.

“Now, tap the ball but not with too much force.” He lets go of my hands and places them at my waist instead. I take a deep breath and try not to think about the warmth of his fingers against my skin. I tap the ball, and it rolls slowly and drops in the hole.

“Ah! I did it!” I squeal and jump excitedly. Cole laughs and drops a kiss on my head before he steps back.

“That’s my girl, hole in one on your first go.” I smile up at him and step aside while he takes his shot. I watch as he expertly hits the ball, and it lands perfectly in the hole. He grins smugly at me, wags his brows lifting his club over his shoulder, and moves to the next course.

“Hey, wait a minute. How is this fair? You’re a golfer that puts me at a disadvantage here.” I pout as he takes his shot on the second course, and it lands in the hole perfectly. Cole looks over his shoulder and grins at me.

“I helped you, didn’t I?” He asks, feigning innocence. I give him a suspicious look as I prepare to take my shot. I draw my putter back, and just as I’m about to hit the ball, Cole coughs in my ear, causing me to mess up my shot. I watch as the ball rolls off and falls into the water. I gape at him, and he laughs heartily.

“Oh, okay, so that’s how we’re playing, you little cheat!” I exclaim, shoving him, and he grins ruffling up my hair.

"I am no such thing!" He retorts as he jogs over to the next course with me hot on his heel.

"Oh, it's so on." I declare, narrowing my eyes at him. "You just declared war, Hoult. Your arse is going down."

Cole smiles and nods, "Is that right? Care to make it interesting?"

I peer up at him and nod with a shrug, "Let's."

Cole places his club over his shoulder and rubs his chin, "Okay, name your terms?"

I look at him thoughtfully and bite my lip, "If I win, we end the agreement end of this month." Cole throws his head back and laughs.

"Why did I know you were going to say that." He tells me arrogantly, and I arch my brow at him challengingly. "Okay deal. If you win, you can back out of the agreement early." He licks his lips with a boyish smile.

"Great, your terms."

Cole rubs his jaw, his eyes on mine for a long moment. "If I win, I get to kiss you whenever I want for a whole week."

I stare at him, and he stares back. I shake my head. "Cole, no."

"Why not?" He questions, smirking at me daringly. "I'm agreeing to let you break our agreement earlier than planned, and all I'm asking for is a kiss."

I scoff and shake my head, "No, you're asking for trouble. And you're not asking for just *a* kiss. You're asking for a week of kisses." I huff, and he shrugs his shoulders.

"It's a fair trade, in my opinion. However, if you're too much of a wuss, we can just forget the bet and carry on as we were." He suggests swinging his club while looking at me, a little smile on his face. He was goading me, and I knew it. My mother always told me that my stubbornness and competitiveness would get me into trouble one day. I wish I would have listened.

"You're on," I agree, and Cole grins and nods in response. He holds his hand out to me, and I take it. We shake on it and carry on with our game. I could do this. I watch as Cole steps up to take his turn. I slide my jacket off and drop it on the floor. If he wants to play dirty— so will I. Lifting my arms, I stretch with an audible moan. I was in a white, low-cut crop top and a pair of faded low-rise jeans, so when I stretched my top rises to give him a glimpse of my lacy white bra. I can see him watching me from the corner of my eye, so I bite my lip and roll my neck.

I hear Cole clear his throat, and I open my eyes and watch as he takes his shot, and it just misses the hole and rolls into a bush. "Oh dear, looks like you missed. You should keep your eyes on the ball." I tease and saunter past him to fish out my ball from the water.

He grins, watching me. "I prefer to keep my eyes on the prize." He replies charmingly—smooth bastard.

I resist the urge to smile and drop my ball and line up my shot. I glance over at Cole, watching me intently. He puckers up his lips and blows me a kiss. With a roll of my eyes, I turn my attention back to my ball. I hit it and watch as it rolls and bounces off the wall and rolls toward the hole. I hold my breath as it gets closer and closer and finally drops into the hole. "Yes!" I cheer, jumping up and down. I wave at him as I move to the next course. Cole smiles, licking his lips. He shakes his head and fishes his ball out of the bushes before he hits it and drops it perfectly in the hole.

"That was a good shot," I smirk at him as he walks over to me, and I turn to watch the couple in front of us take their shots to see if there's a special technique involved that I could use. I drop my ball on the floor and line up the shot.

"What can I say? I'm exceptionally good when it comes to playing with balls." I smile suggestively, and Cole's smile grows into a full-on grin while he looks at me. I meet his gaze, and he bursts into a fit of laughter. I giggle and hit him with my club while he leans over, hands on his knees, laughing with gusto.

"Oh," He straightens, still chuckling, "I have so many good remarks to that comment, but I'll let you off this time, sweetheart." I roll my eyes and take my position to line up my shot. "Mm, this one looks tricky. Don't miss." He leans over and whispers near my ear. I nudge him away with my shoulder and take my shot.

I miss.

I look over my shoulder when I hear Cole laugh. I watch as he hits the ball effortlessly, and it lands in the hole. He looks at me, licks his forefinger, holds it up, and points at himself.

Arrogant little shit.

It went like this for a while, he would distract me, I'd miss, I would distract him, he'd miss. We are currently at the last two courses going head to head. Cole steps up to take his shot while I eat my ice cream cone. He lifts his gaze to look at me while I seductively lick the ice cream, deliberately getting it all over my lip so I could wipe it off with my finger and suck it while looking into his eyes.

Cole watches me intently. His Adam's apple jumps up in his throat when he swallows. I wink at him, and he shakes his head, smiling knowingly, and takes his shot. It lands in the hole. As he walks over to me, I watch him take my hand holding the ice cream, he brings it to his mouth and licks, his eyes locked with mine. "Mm, not bad, but I think I prefer my ice cream *melted* as a topping on *you*." It was my turn to swallow hard. *Damn him.*

I slide my hand out of his, leaving him with the ice cream, and walk over to take my shot. *Come on, Shayla, you got this. Focus!* I avoid looking at him while I concentrate on lining up my shot. I hit it and watch as it goes under the rock and rolls toward the hole. *Come on...come on...* It drops in the hole. "YES!" I yelp and dance around.

Cole smiles and bites his lip as we pick up our balls and walk to the next course. "Final hole." He says and drops his ball on the floor. I look at the course and frown.

"Wait, is the hole in that weird roulette thing?" I ask, looking at Cole, and he shakes his head.

"No, it's a final score, so you hit the ball, and it goes into that roulette spinner, and whatever number you land on gets added to your final point."

"Oh." I frown and nod. "Well, that sounds easy enough. What's the score so far?" I ask, looking at the scorecard in his hand.

"Fifty-forty-eight." He says and smiles. "Close game, this is where we leave it up to fate."

I nod and sigh, suddenly feeling incredibly nervous, "Okay, I'll go first." I drop my ball and exhale slowly. I say a quick prayer in my head and hit the ball. Cole and I watch the ball spin and spin and spin till it finally lands on number five. "I got five. That puts me up to fifty-three." Cole nods as I step aside, and he prepares to take his shot. I watch the look on his face. He stares at his ball for a drawn-out second and finally hits it.

We both lean over and watch the ball spin around and around. I hold my breath as we watch the ball slow and finally drop…

Chapter Twenty

COLE

'COME ON…COME on. Please, please let me win.'

Shayla and I both stood still, watching the ball go round and round and round before it drops. We lean over and stare at the number before we look at each other. "Yes!" I exclaim, holding my club up over my head. Shayla stares at the number for a long moment before she looks at me. I reach over and take hold of her chin and tilt her head up. "Pucker up, baby, because these lips are mine for the week," I say, gazing into her green eyes, and she pulls her head back, moping.

"Cole, come on, you can't be serious about this." She says, crossing her arms over her chest. I laugh and nod rather animated.

"Oh, but I am. If the shoe were on the other foot and you won, you would have made me end the agreement, wouldn't you?" I ask smugly, smirking at her. She rolls her eyes and exhales audibly.

"Fine, no tongue."

I frown, "No. No, no, it's too late for negotiations. We shook on it. If you had any qualms, you should have made them known at the time." I retort, and she glares at me, snatches up her jacket, and storms off. I laugh, following her. "Hey! Where are you going? I want my prize for winning!" I chase after her, wrap my arm around her waist, and pull her against me. Shayla looks up at me, her eyes wide. I brush her hair out of her face and trail my finger along her jaw gently. "No point in sulking sweetheart, you held your own, but I won fair and square."

Shayla rubs her forehead and sighs, "You're going to take the piss with this now, aren't you?" She questions, pouting adorably, and I smile.

"Maybe a little, but let's not act like you don't enjoy kissing me," I tell her haughtily, and she looks at me blankly in return. I throw my arm around her shoulder, and we walk to the exit.

"Whatever. I'm hungry, and you're buying me food." She grumbles as we walk to the car together. I grin and drop a kiss on her temple before she pulls away from me.

"Of course, anything you want, my mini muffin." I chuckle when she glares darkly at me in the middle of putting her seatbelt on.

"All right then, little sausage." I pull out of the parking spot and frown at her.

"Little sausage?" I intone, and she nods, smiling toothily back at me.

"Yes, if you insist on calling me a mini muffin, I will call you little sausage." She explains, grinning, looking rather chuffed with herself.

"What? No, my nickname is cute and loving, whereas yours indicates that I have a small dick. *Wait*, is that what you're trying to imply? That I'm small?" I retort, glancing over at her as I drive, and she smirks while looking ahead.

"Yours implies that I'm short and fat, so..." She trails off with a nonchalant shrug.

I gawk at her, "No, it doesn't! It implies that you're short and cute." I say, reaching over, I poke her side, and she jumps away.

"Well, mine implies that you're a little sausage. Besides, I'm not short. I'm five foot six. You're just too tall." Shayla claims, slapping my hand away when I ruffle her hair.

I chuckle, amused, "I don't remember you complaining at the time about my size. Actually, if I remember accurately, you were very much satisfied after the three orgasms my little sausage gave you." Shayla turns her head to look out of the window, and I could tell she's laughing because her shoulders are shaking. I bite my lip, fighting the urge to laugh myself. "Hey, I'm talking to you!"

"What?"

"You have ten seconds to take back your little sausage remark or so help me God, I will pull over and whip it out and prove to you in this car that my sausage is well and truly jumbo," I threaten with a snigger, and Shayla laughs out loud.

"If you stop calling me your mini muffin, then I will stop calling you a little sausage." She replies with a satisfied smirk.

"But I like calling you mini muffin!"

"And I like your sausage!" She yells and freezes, her eyes wide like saucers when she realises what she just said.

I slam my foot on the break, thankful it was a red light, and no one else was on the road behind us. I smirk, "What?" Shayla clamps her hand over her mouth and closes her eyes. "Did you just admit you like my sausage? I knew it!"

Shayla shakes her head quickly. "No! That's not what I meant at all; it came out all wrong." She groans, her cheeks bright pink. "I meant to say I like *calling* you little sausage."

I laugh and shake my head, "Nope, no backtracking. I heard what I heard, and you said it full of zest too."

Shayla grimaces and shakes her head, avoiding my gaze. "Oh my God, Cole, just drive before I throttle you." I laugh and reach over, poking her relentlessly. She bites back her laugh and shoves me away, cheeks red like a tomato.

She's fucking adorable!

"I think I'm going to throw myself off the bridge now. It was nice knowing you. Tell my family I love them." She mutters, going to open the door, but I grab her wrist and pull her toward me. Cupping her jaw I press my lips to hers. She stills instantly when I brush my tongue along her bottom lip, silently coaxing her to part her lips for me, but just as she was about to a car horn from behind interrupts us, and we jump apart. I chuckle and rub my jaw when she sinks back in her seat, eyes looking at anything but me. I'll finish that kiss the next chance I get.

"What do you want to eat?" I ask her. Shayla clears her throat and bites her lip thoughtfully.

"Uh, there's this place by the river, they have amazing street food, let's go there."

I frown, "Street food?" She glances at me and nods. "You sure that's what you want? We can go to a nice restaurant?" I suggest, but Shayla smiles and shakes her head.

"You've never had street food, have you?" She asks with a wayward grin, and I shake my head looking ahead. "Oh boy, you really have been raised with a silver spoon in your mouth, time to widen that horizon, Lord Hoult." She says, putting the address in my satellite navigation. "Drive."

"Fine, but if I get food poisoning, you've been warned I'm going to throw up all over you." I threaten her jokingly, and she grins while flicking through the songs on the stereo.

"You'll be fine, Richie Rich." She says, winking at me when I smile at her. She reaches over, pushing her finger into my dimple.

"If you're getting the urge to tongue fuck my dimple again, baby, go right ahead." I tease, and she giggles, smacking my arm. We spent the rest of the drive joking around about various things and rapping along to songs on the stereo.

~

THE TIME WAS JUST after nine 'o clock at night when we pull up at the place Shayla suggested. It was bustling with people, everyone eating food while walking around, music playing in the background, twinkling lights. It was a nice setting. It felt cosy and welcoming. Shayla and I make our way through the crowd of people. I lace my fingers with hers and smile when she doesn't pull away. She tugs me along to one of the carts. "So, what I usually do when I come here, is get little bits of food from different carts because there are too many good choices to just pick one. You up for that?" She inquires, looking up at me curiously, and I smile, nodding my head while I look around.

"Sure, let's do it," I reply, and she pulls me to a Mexican cart first.

"Hola Guapa!" The guy in the cart greets her when he sees her. Shayla laughs when he takes her hand and kisses her knuckles.

"Federico! Cómo estás?" Shayla asks. I watch her in awe as she converses with the guy in Spanish.

"What can I get you, beautiful?" Federico asks, smiling and greeting me with a nod, which I politely return. "The Shayla special?" Shayla nods with a beautiful grin and holds up two fingers, indicating she wants two of whatever her special is. While Federico is busy preparing the food, I pull her against me and kiss her forehead.

"I didn't know you spoke Spanish," I murmur in her ear, and she smiles with a shrug peering up at me.

"There's a lot you don't know about me, Cole. I'm just full of surprises." I brush my fingers through her hair as we wait for the food to cook.

"You really are, and I'm hoping to know more," I tell her earnestly while I gaze into those endless green eyes of hers.

"You do?" She questions curiously, and I nod, looking over her angelic face.

"You simply fascinate me, Shayla, and I can't wait to know more about you," I admit brushing my fingers lightly along her jaw while she watches me.

"What's so fascinating about me? I'm just like any other girl." She replies, her brows knitted together a little, and I shake my head, my eyes on hers.

"You're absolutely not," I declare, my thumb gently dragging along her bottom lip. "You're unlike any girl I've ever met." Shayla smiles and turns to speak to Federico again. I can't even begin to explain how awful it's felt the last few weeks. It's been so awkward since our fight over Sophie. Shayla did a complete one-eighty on me and was avoiding me like I was the plague. Thank God we work together, or I'd never see her the way she's been with me lately. I've missed her terribly. I was so lost in thought that I hadn't even realised I had my nose buried in her hair until she moved to take the food Federico was handing her.

I take my wallet to pay, but Federico waves it off and winks at Shayla, who beams at him. "Federico, te amo." She coos, blowing kisses at him.

"Love you too, Princesa, now shoo, go have fun." He grins, waving us off. I thank him, and he gives me a thumbs-up before we walk off. Shayla hands me the makeshift plate of food. I take it, and the smell alone made my stomach growl in appreciation.

"What is this?" I ask, taking a forkful of the rice.

Shayla looks at me sideways, chewing her food with a little frown on her face. "It's a paella." She answers after swallowing her food and smiles when I scoop up another forkful and moan. "Federico makes it special for me whenever I stop by." She explains as we walk, and I notice she's waving near enough to everyone she passes by.

"Wow, you're popular here, huh?" I say, watching her as she converses with the people around her. I have never witnessed anything like it. She's like this magnet that people flock to. So, it's not just me— she has this effect on everyone around her.

"I've been coming here for years. These people are like my family now. Usually, I'm here every other Sunday. The atmosphere is magical, isn't it?" She says with a content smile, her eyes sparkling like emeralds under the twinkling lights. Once we finished our paellas, Shayla took me to another cart that was serving Indian food. We got two giant lamb samosas and ate them as we continued to walk. I must have bitten into a chilli or something because my mouth was on fire. Shayla laughs and hands me a bottle of water, which I gulp down. "You okay?" She asks, smiling up at me. I cough and nod, drinking more water to wash down the burning in my stomach.

"That was lethal, fuck." I chuckle when she laughs, shaking her head, she takes my hand, and we walk to the next cart.

"The next one isn't going to be spicy. I promise." She assures me as we walk over to another cart. Again, the guy at the cart greets her in a foreign language, and she responds with a bright smile. Ah, kebabs— Turkish food. This one, I know.

Shayla ordered two kebab rolls for us and made sure to tell the guy not to add any chilies to mine. I can usually handle my spice, but that was insane. We take our food, and Shayla takes my hand and pulls me through the crowd. "Why are we rushing?" I ask, trying not to drop my food.

"Because I don't want to miss it." She says in a flurry swerving through the crowd. We come to a halt suddenly and join a crowd of people gathered around. We eat our food while we stood around.

"What's going on?" I ask, confused and Shayla smiles back at me.

"Shh, just watch." I frown, standing behind her, and music starts playing from a boombox, and a couple steps into the middle of the crowd. The music gets louder, and they start dancing the Bachata. I recognise the dance from the dance lessons my mother insisted I took when I was a kid. I look down at Shayla, who is watching them with a gorgeous smile on her face as she gently sways to the music singing along to the song.

I place my hands at her hips and pull her back to me while she rests her head back against my chest. We sway together to the music while we watch the couple dance beautifully together. I wrap my arms around her waist and press a kiss to her temple; her eyes close, and she tilts her head against my lips, smiling. It was such a simple gesture, except that something deep inside of me came apart. It felt like we were in our own little bubble; we stayed that way, just swaying together, everything around us fizzled away, leaving only us.

But of course, as our luck would have it, we couldn't just have one fucking uninterrupted moment. No, Shayla is suddenly ripped from my arms. I hear her gasp, and by the time I open my eyes, ready to beat the life out of whoever it was that laid a finger on her, I see the male dancer had her in the center, and they were dancing.

Shayla looks over at me and shrugs as they dance together. I exhale slowly to suppress the annoyance I was feeling watching this man grinding up against her. It was no surprise that Shayla was a great dancer. I see her dancing in the kitchen or around our apartment. However, watching her swaying so sensually with this guy while they whisper to one another smiling, bothered me more than I would have liked to admit.

Thankfully, other couples joined in the dance, so I walk over to the guy dancing with Shayla and tap his shoulder. He looks back at me, and when I gesture to Shayla, he smiles in understanding and steps away. He winks at Shayla and blows her a kiss before he disappears. Shayla peers up at me, and I wrap my arm around her waist and drawing her against me. "I swear to god the next person to interrupt us will find themselves buried alive six feet under," I whisper in her ear, and Shayla tilts her head back and laughs. I smile and tug her closer to me, she wraps her arms around my neck, and we dance the bachata together.

"I didn't know you could dance the bachata," Shayla says, surprised as I spin her and pull her back to me, and our hips sway together rhythmically.

I press my forehead to hers and smile, "What can I say? I'm just full of surprises." I answer, using her own words on her, and she grins, shaking her head. "I dated a couple of Spanish girls back in the day, and they taught me," I admit pressing my forehead to hers as we sway together, the thumb of my hand placed at the small of her waist, gently stroking her silky smooth skin. "How about you? Where did you learn to dance like this?"

Shayla smiles fondly, "My mother. She was a dancer before she got married to my father. She taught me when I was a little girl because I was always fascinated with the way she would dance and discovered I loved it too."

"I've noticed. You're a hell of a dancer yourself." Shayla smiles, and much to my dismay, the song comes to an end the crowd disperses. Shayla pulls away, brushing her fingers through her hair, and looks up at me.

"So, we have one last thing we have to do, then we can go." She says while I follow her navigating through the crowd. We walk over to another cart, and I groan. I'm honestly so full I can't eat anymore.

"More food?" I ask her, and she smiles up at me as we queue up.

"This is dessert, and you won't be sorry after you eat it, I promise." I nod, and she steps up and tells the girl at the stand her order. She's given a cup full of something I couldn't even tell you what, drizzled with some sort of syrup. "Come on." I follow her again, and we walk over to the banks overlooking the river. She sits down and pulls me down next to her, that excited smile lighting up her face beautifully.

"What on earth is that?" I question warily, and she looks at me blankly for a moment and shakes her head.

"Seriously? You've never had churros before?" She sputters, her green eyes wide and disbelieving. I shake my head in response, scratching my temple. She blinks at me and picks up a churro, and holds it up to my lips. "Prepare yourself to fall in love." She purrs, looking into my eyes.

I look down at the churro between her fingers before I gaze into her eyes and take a bite. She watches me intently as I chew and lick my lips, eagerly waiting for my reaction. Mm, fucking sensational. "Wow," I mumble and stop to swallow before I continue. "That's incredible."

Shayla grins, nodding enthusiastically before she takes a bite herself and chews, moaning delightfully. I continue to ogle her lips as she licks the caramel syrup off her bottom lip with a swipe of her tongue. Shayla feeds me more of the churros as we sit, and she tells me about the times she's come here with her brother or the girls. I watch her with a smile while she talks, my fingers idly brushing through her glossy dark hair. I love her hair. I could play with it forever tirelessly. Actually, I could listen to her talking and never get bored. It's impossible to be bored around her. I can't think of a single moment since I've known her that I've been remotely uninterested.

I notice she has a little cinnamon sugar on her lip, and I've been dying to just lean in and suck it off. Shayla looks at me and blinks, probably noticing I'm staring at her lips like some perv. Biting my lip, I move my hand from her hair and brush it along her jaw toward her chin. "You've got some sugar on your lip," I whisper while leaning in and suck it off her bottom lip gently. Shayla's eyes close when I brush my lips over hers as I did earlier, only this time she parts her lips for me, and I kiss her slow and deep as I've been dying too, and my God, it felt good.

I hear her soft moan when our tongues touch, and it spurs me to deepen the kiss. We sat there kissing rather passionately until I feel her shivering in my arms from the chill of the wind by the water. We pull away, panting, ending the spine-tingling kiss. I press my forehead to hers and bite my lip.

"Shall we go back to the car?" I whisper to her, and she nods in response. I stand up and pull her up with me wrapping my arms around her to shield her from the cold. She nestles herself into my hold as we leisurely walk back to the car. There was barely anyone else around as it was quite late, and the stands were all cleaning down as they close for the night.

Shayla smiles, waves at Federico, and he waves back as we stroll past his cart. "Hey Muchacho, you take good care of my princess, okay?" He calls out to me, and I chuckle, nodding.

"Always Federico, I'll be back again for the Shayla special real soon," I call out, and he cackles with a nod.

"Anytime brother." Shayla grins up at me as we walk toward the car.

I look down into her upturned face. "What?" I ask, smiling myself.

“He likes you.” She replies and closes her eyes when I press my lips to her forehead.

“He seems like a good man,” I say, unlocking the car, and Shayla nods in response and shivers again. “You’re freezing, sweetheart. I hope you don’t get sick.”

“I’m fine. You’re actually quite warm.” She sighs when I hug her tighter. I open the car door for her, and she gets in rubbing her arms to get warm. I rush around the driver's side so I can start the car and turn the heating on for her.

The air blows out cold, and I hear Shayla hiss when it hits her. “The air will be cold till the car warms up. Come here,” I say, holding my hand out to her, she takes it, and I pull her into my lap. Luckily, she’s quite small, and I’m tall enough that I have my seat all the way back, so we have a little room. I wrap my arms around her, and she curls up against me, still shivering. “You okay?” I ask, glancing down at her. She opens her eyes, looks up at me, and smiles warmly.

“Yeah,” She whispers back sweetly.

I brush my thumb along her jaw, my eyes on hers, I lean in and drop soft little pecks on her lips, and she sighs faintly. “Shall we go home, sweetheart?” I whisper when she finally stops shivering, and she’s not cold to the touch. Shayla nods, and I help her shift into the passenger seat again. She was quiet on the drive back home. I glance over and see she’s asleep. I reach over and take her hand in mine gently and drop a kiss on her palm before I place it on my thigh and rub her knuckles gently as I drive.

~

Once we got back to the apartment, I walk around the car and shake her awake. She opens her eyes and blinks up at me. “We’re home, babe.” She yawns as I help her out of the car. I notice her eyes drift shut as we walk to the building's entrance, so I stop and lift her into my arms. Shayla lays her head on my chest and moans as I carry her up to our apartment. I type in the code to our place, and the door clicks open. It’s times like these, I am thankful I chose the keyless entry system. I carry Shayla toward her bedroom and walk over to her bed, gently laying her down on it. I look down at her and brush her hair out of her face. She stirs and opens her eyes, smiling up at me drowsily. "Good night, Gorgeous girl," I whisper and shift to pull away, but Shayla holds my wrist to stop me.

"Stay," She whispers, peering up at me almost pleadingly. I nod and crawl up on the bed next to her. Gathering her into my arms, I press my lips to her forehead while she snuggles up against me. As I was lying there with her, it suddenly hit me that in less than eight weeks, she would walk out of my life, and that thought did not sit well with me. Not one little bit.

Chapter Twenty-One

SHAYLA

"COOOOOOLE?!"

"Yeeeees?"

I bite my lip and curse myself for leaving my towel on my bed. I stood in the bathroom for over ten minutes, wondering what the hell I'm going to do. I can't walk out naked without Cole seeing me, and I'm bloody freezing.

"Uh, I left my towel on my bed. Can you please bring it to me?" I call out and hear his footsteps as he walks past the bathroom.

"Aren't there any in the drawer?" I hear him ask.

"I wouldn't ask you if there was, now would I?" I retort, shivering. I hear him chuckle on the other side of the door.

"Fair enough, unlock the door then." I tiptoe over to the door and unlock it before opening it wide enough to get the towel. When he doesn't let go of the towel, I frown, and he smirks at me roguishly as I stare up at him inquisitively.

"Cole, let go of the towel," I say, tugging on it, and he pulls it back again playfully.

"Not until I get my reward for fetching your towel." He claims coolly with a shrug, and I arch a brow.

"What are you, a puppy? Okay," I let go of the towel and pat his head a couple of times. “Who’s a good boy.” I coo, and he scowls at me in return, looking less than amused. “Would you like a belly rub too?” I add sardonically, and he glares at me while I bite back the laughter bubbling up inside of me.

“You’re not getting the towel now.” He grumbles yanking it back out of my reach.

“Cole, come on, I’m freezing here.” I pout, but he shakes his head.

“Nope, not until you thank me properly.” I exhale and contemplate just walking out of there naked.

“Fine, what do you want?” I ask, exasperated while he grins at me, puckering up his lips. I roll my eyes and heave a sigh. “Can you not wait till I’m dressed at least?” I question, and he shakes his head slowly. “Fine, come here then.” I poke my head out of the door, and he brushes his lips over mine. While he was distracted, I take the towel from him, pull away and slam the door shut in his face.

“Hey!” I laugh out loud and wrap the towel around me while he mutters behind the door. “I’m going to get that kiss, Shayla Hart!”

“Don’t hold your breath, Cole Hoult!” I retort with a grin while brushing my hair. Once I was finished in the bathroom, I open the door and walk out. Using a smaller towel to dry my hair as I was walking to my bedroom, completely unaware that Cole was hiding behind the door. I yelp when I kick the door shut, and he grabs me from behind, picks me up, and walks over to the bed. “Jesus, Cole! Put me down right now!” I demand, holding the towel around my body tightly as he carries me. He tosses me down on the bed like I weigh nothing at all. I stare up at him dumbfounded while he smirks at me darkly, a naughty glint in his green eyes. “Cole…” I eye him warily as he places one knee on the bed and crawls up, looking at me hungrily like a predator does its prey. I try to back away, but he grabs my ankle and pulls me down the bed with no effort at all. My heart was hammering against my ribcage as I watch him get closer.

“You shouldn’t toy with a hungry man, Miss Hart.” He drawls huskily, his eyes on me as he leans closer, licking his lips. I squeak when he curls his fingers at my jaw and tilts my head up before his lips come crashing down on mine hard. He groans throatily, bites my bottom lip, and tugs it gently. When I say he stole every bit of air from my lungs with that kiss, I am not exaggerating. My mind was in a haze like I had just come off those teacup rides at the fairgrounds. By the time my head stopped spinning and I open my eyes panting, he was already out the door. He left me staring at the door he just walked out of, utterly stupefied

I sigh, frustrated, and fall back on the bed with a whimper covering my face with my pillow. I wanted to scream till my lungs exploded. As much as I love being kissed by Cole, it's not helping me fight off this stupid crush I have on him. I was feeling more confused than ever about why he wants to kiss me when he's in love with Sophie. Why can't he just go and kiss her and let me be? Ugh, five more days and this stupid bet will be done with.

We have this dumb post-wedding party tonight at his parent's place, and I have to be there in less than two hours. I'm not even going to get into how it went with the parent's meeting because that was a bloody disaster in itself. His snooty mother and my proud one clashed and sniped at one another all night. Every time his mother made a snide remark about our traditions and my upbringing, my mother would retort with a scathing answer leaving Cole and I staring at each other completely horrified.

"Shayla, we have to go!" I hear Cole call out to me. I sigh and finish getting dressed in a simple pair of ripped jeans and a white tee. My hair was still wet, and I didn't bother with much make-up because I'm sure there was a whole team waiting at the Hoult's mansion to barbie me up, so I look worthy of their precious family. I grab my phone and walk out of the bedroom toward Cole, who stood waiting for me by the front door, looking every bit as delectable as he always does. He's wearing a casual grey shirt with the top three buttons undone, showing his smooth, tan, well-defined chest, and a pair of black jeans. Oh, how I would love to just jump his bones right here and now.

"Are you checking me out?" He asks with a smirk, lowering his shades down to the bridge of his nose while looking at me pointedly.

I blink and let my eyes glide down the length of him as I pass by. "No, your flies are undone," I say, opening the door. I grin when he looks down and shakes his head, following me.

"Such a tease." He mumbles, closing the door and following me to the elevator. I lean against the wall as we wait for it to arrive. Cole stands beside me, and I can feel his gaze on me as I stare up at the numbers showing what floor the elevator was on. I really hate this stupid magnetic pull I have to this man. I tell my brain one thing, and it does the complete opposite. I kept telling myself not to look at him because I know if I do, and our eyes meet, he's going to know he's having an effect on me. Damn my brain to hell because I look up at him, and he smiles, licking his full lips. He's so beautiful I want to cry. Our eyes linger on one another until the elevator dings, and I avert my gaze and straighten, waiting for the doors to open so I can walk in.

I stand at the back of the elevator. Cole walks in after me and pushes the button to the underground car park. He leans on the wall beside me, his hands in his pockets, his arm brushes mine, and I feel goosebumps break out all over my body the moment his skin touches mine. I chew on my bottom lip, suddenly feeling very anxious as I stare up at the numbers again. I feel Cole shift beside me, and he leans in close to my ear. "You're making me crazy. Stop biting your lip like that." He burrs huskily. The warmth of his breath made me quiver visibly.

I turn my head and lift my gaze slowly to his lips, then up to his eyes. He was so close to me that our noses touch when I look up at him. Butterflies explode in my stomach when he drags his nose over mine. *Oh damn.*

I lick my lips instinctively, and my eyes close when I feel his lips ghosting along my jaw. "Tell me something, Shayla. Why have I never craved anything in my life the way I crave your lips?" He whispers, brushing his lips over mine sensually. "Tell me, sweetheart, why I can't seem to get enough of you."

I moan, biting my lip when I feel his fingers sneak up under my shirt, and his thumb brushes over my already hardened nipple through the lace of my bra. "Cole…"

"I want you, Shayla. I want you so fucking bad baby, look at what you're doing to me." He groans, taking my hand, and he presses it to his crotch so I could feel his rock-hard erection. When I rake my fingers over his hard length through the thick fabric of his denim jeans, he moans. "Shayla," He growls, pressing his forehead to mine. "Don't," He pleads with a harsh breath. "I'm on edge, and if you touch me like that, I'll sod this party off, take you back home and fuck you relentlessly right through the weekend."

Oh, my fucking God!

If only I could find the words to describe the tension between us at that moment, there are simply no words. My vagina was literally throbbing. My clit was pulsing, and he hasn't even touched me yet. I was about ready to lose my mind. Cole drags his thumb along my bottom lip, and his eyes close for a second when I suck his thumb. "Fuck." He hisses, watching me intently while biting his lip hard. Cole gathers my arms and pins them above my head while he presses his hard body against mine, his lips hot on mine. "Do you have any idea what I want to do to you right now?"

My mind couldn't form any words at that moment. I could only mewl and writhe helplessly as he continues to whisper all the right things to me. "My mouth is watering just thinking about burying my tongue deep and fucking your pussy, baby." He groans, nipping at my bottom lip.

"Cole, please…" I pant breathless, and Cole unbuttons my jeans and slides the zipper down slowly.

"Shayla…" He breathes, trailing his lips up to my throat. "For the love of God tell me to stop. I'm about to lose my mind, please baby, tell me to stop." He pleads desperately, and I moan, biting my lip hard.

"I can't," I whimper when I feel his fingers slide into my underwear, and just as his fingers brush my clit, the elevator pings. I open my eyes and see we've reached the car park.

"Fuck, you're so wet." Cole moans, pulling back to look into my eyes. "Come on." Before my hazy mind could figure out what was happening, Cole's hand disappeared from inside my jeans and was pulling me out of the elevator. We walk briskly toward his range rover sport, and he unlocks it, but before he opens the door, one arm wraps around me, and the other hand curls at my throat while he presses me back against the door and kisses me hard and dirty.

All the frustration we were feeling was poured into that kiss. It was hot, wet, angry, and rough all at the same time. We were both pretty worked up and had one thing on our minds— sex. I pull away from the kiss, panting, my lungs burning from lack of oxygen, and my heart racing from exhilaration. "Get in before I drag you to the backseat and ravish you." Cole pants, dropping a chaste kiss on my lips before he steps away. I watch him as he walks around the car, and he watches me back, his eyes radiating such desire my stomach did a little flip.

I get into the car, and Cole tears out of the car park. The entire journey, he wouldn't stop touching me. His hand was resting on my upper thigh, squeezing and caressing it gently as he drove. We didn't say one word—we didn't need to because our actions spoke volumes, and that's all we needed. We stop at a red light, and Cole leans over and kisses me slow and deep till it goes green. He did this at every light we stopped at, and I was praying we'd get stopped at every single one we approach just so he could kiss me again.

~

AFTER A THIRTY-MINUTE DRIVE, we pull up at his parent's place. He opens the door for me, and as I shift to get out, he stops me, steps between my legs, and kisses me again, his hands on my thighs slowly trailing up to my hips where he squeezes and yanks me closer, grinding his erection against me. We moan in unanimity into each other's mouths, our hips rocking and grinding intimately, the friction only fuelling our desire for one another. Cole pulls away, and I groan, disgruntled. Cole presses his forehead to mine and licks his lips. "Later, sweetheart, later. I'm going to take care of every single one of your needs one by one." He whispers, brushing his fingers through my hair. We stare at each other longingly for a while till we hear his mothers' voice.

"There you are," Elaine huffs, walking over to us. "We have just over an hour to get you ready young lady." She scolds me as Cole helps me out of the car. Elaine takes my arm and starts pulling me toward the house while I look back at Cole, watching me fixedly as his mother drags me away. The last thing I saw before I get pulled into the house was his sexy smile and wink. Goddamn, this stupid party, all I wanted right now was to run back to Cole and kiss him some more. Instead, I'm shoved into a room full of people and racks of dresses and shoes. "Here she is. Do your magic. I want this duckling turned into a swan or as close to one as you can manage." Elaine tells the team of people in the room before she saunters off. I gape at her retreating back. Did she just blatantly call me ugly?

"Oh my, you're mighty flushed sweetie pie." The man says, waving his hands in my face in an attempt to fan me so I can cool off. You suck faces with Cole Hoult and see if you'll be able to keep cool. The more they try to cool me down, the hotter I felt thinking about what just happened between Cole and me. "Oh honey, you're all flustered. I can't do your make up like this." He complains, whipping out a fan out of nowhere and waving it in my face. "Take some nice deep breaths for me."

"Maybe just open some windows. It's hot in here," I suggest, and he laughs.

"The windows are already open, you silly goose. Now, let me take a look at you, see what we can do." I sigh, feeling extremely uncomfortable with some random man in my face and another messing around with my hair, even if they were both evidently gay. I'm not used to being fussed over.

"What shall we do with your hair, sweet?" The other guy asks, brushing his fingers through my hair.

I shrug and bite my lip. "I don't know. I'm leaving my duckling self in your capable hands," I mumble with a pout, and both men chuckle at my candor, clearly amused.

"Oh honey, don't pay any mind to Elaine. You're stunning already." The one doing my makeup says, smiling at me assuringly.

"Thank you, that's very kind of you to say." Okay, maybe they're not so bad after all. We spent the rest of the hour making idle chit chat, and they were both gushing about how handsome Cole is and how lucky I was to be married to such a hottie.

"I'd be all over that twenty-four-seven, honey." The guy that was doing my hair groans while he curls my hair with a curling iron. I giggle when the other makes a grunting sound in agreement.

I look at myself in the mirror in front of me. My make-up was done flawlessly, but it was all-natural tones, and I was thankful Marcus didn't cake my face with make-up. My hair pulled into a ponytail, the top slightly raised with loose curls at the ends.

"What do you think?" Marcus, the one that did my make up asks, watching me through the mirror.

"I love it. It's not too over the top. It's like you read my mind." I smile at him, and he nods grinning.

"Honey, you're a natural beauty. Your skin is flawless. You don't ruin a masterpiece by painting over it." He gushes, touching my chin gently.

Henry sprays my hair with hairspray and smiles when I cough a little. "I keep telling him he's going to kill someone with the amount of hairspray he uses, but he never listens." Marcus scolds him. I giggle.

"Okay, come on, come on, let's pick out a dress for you." I nod, and we walk over to the racks of dresses. The boys hold out various dresses for me, but I shake my head. They were not my style at all, too frilly or covered in sequins or patterns.

"Sweetie, I think this one will look amazing on you," Henry says, holding up a long silver, backless silk dress with diamantes for straps. "You have that gorgeous hourglass figure, and this will hug all your curves beautifully." I nod and take the dress from him, and walk to the next room to change.

I slip the dress on and look at myself in the full-length mirror. Henry was right. The dress was perfect. Plain and simple, just like me. I notice the room went quiet, and I could no longer hear the boys bickering. I smile and look down at myself again before I raise my gaze and gasp when I see Cole behind me through the mirror. He was looking *insane* in his black suit and black silk shirt. His hair styled perfectly, and he kept his stubble. I *love* the way he looks with a beard. He was standing there, hands in his pockets his eyes slowly gliding down my body.

I felt that nervous pull at the pit of my stomach as we watch one another. Cole walks over to me slow, licking his lips. He stands behind me and looks at me through the mirror. I suck in a quick breath, close my eyes when I feel his finger slowly trail down my spine. "You look, sensational sweetheart." He whispers in my ear, never taking his eyes off me. "How am I supposed to keep my hands to myself tonight when you look *this* good." He murmurs, dropping a kiss on the base of my neck, "Your scent makes my head spin gorgeous." He whispers, brushing his nose along the length of my throat.

"Cole, please…" I bite my lip a little, "I only just managed to cool myself down from before." I breathe as he brushes his lips along my bare shoulder. He smiles a little and lifts his eyes and stares at me while he rakes his fingers up my thigh through the high slit of the dress. I whimper when his fingers sink into my underwear, and he groans, brushing his fingers over my sex.

"No, you haven't." He moans, sliding a finger inside me. My head falls back against his shoulder, my knees buckle, and I fall back against him. Cole wraps his other arm around me, steadying me. "You're still soaking wet." He breathes, closing his eyes, sliding his finger out again, and bringing it up to his lips, he sucks it, and his eyes roll to the back of his head. I watch him with bated breath while he sucks his finger clean and groans throatily. "Christ, Shay. It's taking everything in me to not spread you out on this bed right now and feast on your sweet pussy till you come again and again." I squeeze my thighs together and sigh longingly.

I was moments away from spreading myself on that bed, like an all you can eat buffet and begging him to devour me. I was on the brink of insanity. I have never—ever in my entire life yearned for anything as much as I did for this man. At that moment, I didn't care about later.

All that I cared about was giving myself up to him completely. Even if it was just for one night, I wanted to be his.

Chapter Twenty-Two

COLE

GODDAMN. I was on the verge of losing my mind. When I walked into that bedroom and saw Shayla all dressed up in that sexy silver dress, I felt like my soul was on fire.

I was worried they would overdo everything and turn her into one of those girls who slapped the make-up on as if their lives depended on it, but they didn't. She had the bare minimum on, and I was thankful because, damn, she's naturally so beautiful, she would outshine every woman in the room without a drop of make-up on.

And the dress, a simple yet classy, backless silver satin gown, hugs her natural curves flawlessly. I went for girls that had long legs, blonde hair, and a slender frame all my life. That was my type until I met *her*.

I have a severe case of tunnel vision. I can't see anything but Shayla—I'm fixated. I don't know how I'll make it through this party without dragging her off to one of the bedrooms, slipping her out of that silk dress, and making her mine.

The chemistry and tension between us have increased tenfold, and I know she wants me as much as I do her.

THE PARTY WAS in full swing and my mother kept dragging her away from me throughout the party, her socialite friends intrigued about the girl her son eloped with.

I keep my eye on Shayla as she moves around the room and converses with people politely. I'm anxious and worried my mother's friends will make stupid digs at her, and even though Shayla can hold her own, I won't tolerate anyone upsetting her. She turns her head, her green eyes scanning the room until they find me. Our eyes meet across the room, and I smile, observing her, not even caring who would see us giving each other the 'fuck me' eyes.

"Tristan?" I turn when I hear my name being called. Hollie. I groan inwardly and resist the urge to roll my eyes.

"Hollie." I greet her distantly while glancing over at Shayla, watching us with a little frown on her face.

"Just wanted to come over and congratulate you on your nuptials." She says with a smile and hands me a champagne flute. I take the offered drink and smile politely.

"Thank you, Hollie." I nod, taking a sip of my drink and looking over at Shayla again, who was talking to my little cousin Louise.

"I haven't had a chance to meet your wife yet, but she seems…*nice*. She's vastly different from the women we're used to seeing you with." Hollie utters, taking a sip of her own drink, her blue eyes following my gaze to Shayla.

"She is different, which is why I married *her* and not the other girls you're 'used to' seeing me with," I tell her curtly, and Hollie brushes a strand of her bleach blonde hair out of her face and looks at me again.

"Still, I can't say I'm not disappointed. That should have been me up there working the room as your wife." She sighs, licking her overly glossed lips and running her finger down the length of my arm. "We would have been good together, Tristan." I scoff and pull my arm away from her touch.

"No, we wouldn't have. No offence Hollie, but I was never going to marry you," I tell her coolly and scan the room, searching for Shayla, who disappeared.

"Honey," I smile when I feel Shayla's hand on my back. I look at her, and she smiles up at me, her beautiful green eyes alight with glee.

"Hey, Gorgeous girl," I greet, pressing my lips to her jaw and letting them linger for a couple of seconds while I wrap my arm around her waist and bring her close. Shayla looks at Hollie and smiles warmly.

"I'm sorry to disturb you," She looks up at me again, "Can I steal you away for a little bit?" I kiss her temple and smile.

"You can steal me away forever, sweetheart," I murmur, and she grins and looks at Hollie again, watching Shayla enviously.

"Excuse us. I hope you don't mind. I need a little one on one time with *my husband*, you know, newlyweds and all," Shayla tells Hollie with a wink, laces her fingers with mine, and pulls me away.

I chuckle and rub her knuckles with my thumb, "Jesus, if looks could kill, you'd be dead and buried right now." Shayla laughs softly and shrugs.

"You looked very uncomfortable, so I thought I should play my part as the dutiful wife and save you." She tells me as we walk through the crowd of people in the garden. "Besides, your mother has arranged a first dance and wanted me to come find you."

I nod and sigh, "Course she did." We walked over to my mother, standing with my Dad, and talking to my aunt and uncle.

"Oh, there you are, it's time for your first dance. Do you have a special song between you that you would like to dance to?" Shayla and I look at each other, and she shakes her head.

"I'll be right back." I pull away from her and walk to the band and tell them to play a song, and they nod. The band announces that it was time for a dance from the newlyweds, so I take Shayla's hand, and we walk into the center where my mother arranged a dance floor. I pull her against me as the song starts to play, and Shayla frowns a little and looks at me.

"Oh my God, this is…"

I nod, "The song your parents would dance to every night, I know." Shayla's eyes water a little as we begin to sway together. "I don't know if you remember, but this song was actually playing in the chapel while we were getting married," I tell her, and she blinks up at me.

"It was?" She questions, her eyes filling with tears, and I nod, pulling her closer against me.

"I remembered it not long after you told me about this being your parent's song. Maybe it's nothing, but I'd like to think it was a sign that your father was there watching over you." I tell her, reaching up and wipe the tear that rolls down her cheek. Her eyes close, and she leans into my touch. The moment is interrupted by the sound of glasses clinking.

"What's going on?" She asks, opening her eyes and looking around. I smile and lick my lips.

"They want us to kiss," I tell her, and she peers up at me a little startled, her cheeks turning pink.

"In front of everyone?" I nod, gazing into her eyes.

"May I?" I ask, and she hesitates for a moment but nods. I smile and brush my fingers along her jaw before I curl my fingers at her neck and draw her in for a slow sensual kiss while we continue to sway. Shayla reaches up and strokes my jaw as she kisses me back, and I swear to everything holy that her touch sent electric shocks through me. That's the first time she's actually touched me on her own account since Vegas, without me coercing her, and it felt incredible.

We pull back from the kiss when everyone around us applauds. I press my forehead to hers as we continue to dance till the song came to an end. "Tristan, your grandpa would like to see you both." My father tells me as he walks past us. I nod and look at Shayla, who pulls away averting her gaze.

"He probably wants to meet you. Come on." I take Shayla's hand, guiding her through the crowd of people in the garden to where my grandfather sat under the patio. He smiles when he sees me walking toward him. "Hey, Grandpop," I greet him with a smile, and he nods.

"Ahh, Tristan, come here, my boy." He holds his arms open, and I hug him. My grandfather gave the best hugs growing up, and it still hasn't changed.

"Grandpop, I want you to meet my wife, Shayla." I place my hand at the small of her back, and Shayla kneels beside his wheelchair and takes his trembling hand in hers, smiling warmly up at him.

"It's so nice to meet you, Grandpa Joe." She says tenderly, "I've been looking forward to meeting you. I now see where Cole gets his good looks from." My grandfather chuckles and lifts his hand; his trembling fingers touch her cheek affectionately, and Shayla leans into his touch, closing her eyes.

"You remind me of my late wife, Maisie, when we first met." He tells her, and Shayla looks up at him. "I was a dashing young man just like my grandson, and my goodness, she had me chasing her all around town before I finally got to court her." He explains. Shayla grins and looks up at me. I watch them both interact with one another, and I felt my insides go warm. She's always surprising me.

"Tristan, despite your galavanting, you've managed to catch a good girl. Keep hold of this one because she'll change your whole world just like my Maisie did mine." He pats Shayla on her head gently, and she sits like a five-year-old girl would by her grandfather's knee, listening to him eagerly while he tells her about his youth with my grandmother. I chuckle and shake my head—she's even got my Grandpop twisted in her love web.

I take out my phone and discreetly snap a photo of them both. It was such a beautiful moment I wanted to remember it forever. I took one of Shayla too because the look on her face, the warmth in her eyes, while she listened to my grandfather talk, was something that rendered me speechless. "Now, dear, would you be so kind as to let me have a little talk with my handsome grandson?" He asks Shayla and kisses her knuckles. Shayla nods and stands up, leaning over, and drops a kiss on his cheek.

"I'm so happy I met you. I want to hear more about Grandma Maisie. I'll come to see you soon, you can finish your story, and I'll read you that book as I promised." She tells him, and my grandfather nods, smiling up at her, his green eyes watching her fondly as she walks away. Our eyes meet as she passes by me; she smiles as she walks off toward the crowd of people.

"Tristan," I tear my eyes away from Shayla and look at my grandfather who motions me to sit next to him. "Thank you, son, you've made a dying old man incredibly happy. I only wish your grandmother were alive to meet your beautiful bride. She would have adored her." I smile sadly at the mention of my grandma. She died ten years ago of a stroke. "Son, there's an expression, I don't know if you've heard it. When a person's heart is pure and beautiful, that beauty radiates to that person's face, and they glow brighter than anything you've ever seen. Nothing is more beautiful than a person with a pure heart, just like that young lady right there." He explains, taking my hand into his trembling ones and pats it gently.

"Grandpop, you just met her. How could you possibly tell?" I question curiously, and he chuckles.

"I've been around a long-time, son. That girl's soul is that of an angel. Take the advice of a man who was lucky enough to endure a great love some could have only wished for. Hold onto her for dear life, and don't let go." I feel my heart swell at his words.

"It means a lot to me that you approve of her Grandpop. She's incredibly special to me." I affirm, and my grandfather smiles with a sigh.

"You're very special to her too. I could sense the connection you both share from where I was sitting, watching you dance like you were the only two people in the world." I bite my lip and look over at Shayla dancing with my cousin. "A bond that strong is hard to come by, son, don't take it for granted."

I sigh, "I won't, Grandpop."

"Good lad. I wanted to tell you that I will sign my shares over to you in the morning. I'm immensely proud of you, you and your father took the little company I started and made it what it is today, and I couldn't possibly thank you enough. Hopefully, one day, you will have a son of your own who will make you just as proud as your parents and I are of you."

I sigh and force myself to smile, trying to ignore the knot in my stomach, tightening from the guilt I felt lying to everyone around me. I swallow thickly. "Thank you, Grandpop."

"Go on, go back to your blushing bride." He says, patting my back lovingly. I smile and drop a kiss on his cheek before I walk off toward Shayla.

I'm done with this party now. I'm mingled out. As I reach Shayla, I take her hand, and she looks up at me bemused. "You all right?" She questions, following me closely.

I nod, licking my lips, "Yeah, I'm just anxious to get out of here." I smile at her, and she bites her lip and drops her gaze, a nice blush touching her cheeks. God, I'm going to ravish you.

"Tristan, where do you think you're going?" My mother asks in a flurry catching us as we walk through the foyer of the house.

"Uh, we're going to go home. Thank you for the party mother, it was incredibly special, and we appreciate it." I say, dropping a kiss on her cheek, and she looks at me with a scowl.

"You can't leave. It's so late, plus you've been drinking, so you shouldn't drive. Spend the night here. I've had the girls prepare your old room for you both." I frown and look at Shayla, who stares at my mother, her eyes wide and unblinking.

"Mum, I've had a couple of glasses of champagne. I'm perfectly fine to drive, okay, don't worry," I assure her and notice her face drops and her shoulders slump in disappointment.

"Oh, I thought it would have been nice to have you spend the night, and we could have had breakfast together tomorrow morning as we used to every Sunday before you moved out." She sighs dejectedly. I feel Shayla squeeze my hand, and I look down at her; she's peering up at me with those big green eyes, all sad. Fucking hell!

"Of course we'll stay, Mrs Hoult." She says before I could stop her, and my mother's face lights up like a Christmas tree.

"Oh, excellent! I'm so pleased." She exclaims, kissing my cheek, and rushes off in a flurry. I look over at Shayla, smiling at me sheepishly.

"What did you do that for?" I groan and Shayla shrugs, biting her lip.

"What? Didn't you see her face? She looked so sad when you said no, I couldn't help it." She claims with an adorable little pout. I pull her against me and gaze into her gorgeous green eyes.

"But I want to take you home." I moan, leaning in to kiss her, and just as our lips touch, I get slapped on the back causing us to jump apart.

"Congrats my man!" I glare at my cousin Harry who grins at Shayla and me, wagging his brows.

"Thanks Harry." I grit out through clenched teeth, and he chuckles and scampers off with whatever girl he rolled up with. "Come on," I sigh, lacing my fingers with hers and pull her upstairs with me.

"Cole, where are we going?" She asks in a flurry, following me as I pull her along like an errant puppy. I tug her to my old bedroom, which my mother had prepared for us for the night, and close the door before I press her into it all in one motion. Shayla gasps and looks up at me as I place my hands on either side of her caging her in.

"Alone at last," I murmur, staring at her lips, which she licks alluringly.

"Cole, I am not sleeping with you in your parents house. Especially with all these people roaming around the place," Shayla mumbles, watching me closely as I inch closer to her lips.

"Shayla, I was more than happy to take you home, but you went and accepted my mother's invitation for a sleepover." I remind her, licking my lips as I stare into her eyes. "There is only one person I give a shit about right now, and she's standing right in front of me looking delectable, and I'm *hungry* baby." I burr huskily, brushing my nose over hers.

"What if someone hears us?" She whispers back.

"It's our post-wedding night. It would be weird if we didn't have sex," I say, and she chuckles a little and moans when I dip my head and kiss her collarbone.

"Cole, this is so bad." She breathes while I slowly run my tongue up her throat, my fingers find the straps to her dress, and I slide them down her shoulders.

"Then let's be bad, baby, let's be *really* bad." I moan, nipping at her ear gently, my fingers gliding the straps down her arms. "I've been picturing the moment I get to slip you out of this dress all night, visualising the silk just gliding down your beautiful body," I step away from her a little, and she opens her eyes and looks at me. "Do it," I whisper.

Shayla swallows hard and pushes herself off the door, licks her lip a little before she bites her bottom lip, and slides her arms out of the straps to her dress. My eyes eagerly watch her as she reaches back and slides the zipper down to her dress. I inhale a sharp breath when the dress glides down her body and pools around her feet. There she stood in nothing but her heels. Fuck! When did she take off her underwear?

All the blood from my brain rushes to my cock as I stood, taking her in inch by inch. "*Fuck*," I growl and walk over to her. I curl my fingers at her neck and pull her mouth to mine hungrily.

I lift her up into my arms and slam her hard against the door. Shayla moans and kisses me back just as fervently. I feel her fingers unbuttoning my shirt while we continue to kiss, and I walk her back toward the bed. In the end, she got frustrated with the buttons and tore it open with a groan. Shayla pulls my shirt off my shoulders while our tongues continue to duel heatedly. I tilt my head back when Shayla kisses down my throat, stopping to suck and bite at my pulse point hard enough to leave a mark.

I lay her down on the bed, and she leans up on her elbows, looking at me through her lashes while I take my shirt off. She lifts her foot, still in her heels, and presses it to my chest, stopping me as I was about to crawl over her. She sits up and scoots closer to me.

Our eyes locked, she reaches up, unbuckles my belt, and tugs it off, tossing it aside before brushing her finger up the length of my cock tantalizingly slow. I hiss and close my eyes, tilting my head back when my cock aches under her touch. Such a simple motion, but it sent shockwaves of pleasure pulsing through me. "Shayla." I moan, biting my lip as she continues to touch me teasingly.

I watch her closely while she unbuttons my trousers and tugs my zipper down before she leans in and licks up my stomach, her tongue trailing along the outline of my abs. "Oh, baby." I brush my fingers along the nape of her neck, and she slides my trousers down my legs, her nails raking up the back of my thighs, causing goosebumps to rise all over my body.

"This right here…" She breathes, brushing her fingers along the abdominal V-line muscle, also known as the Adonis belt. "Make's me go stupid." She finishes, leaning in tracing the lines with her tongue. I make a mental note to walk around shirtless more often.

"God *damn*, baby." I moan. I was at my wit's end. I was going to implode if I didn't have her soon. While Shayla's mouth was on my stomach, her fingers slide into the elastic of my boxers, and she tugs them off, pulling back to look at my cock spring free from its confines, all nine inches throbbing and aching to be inside her.

I kick my boxers and trousers to the side watch as Shayla's eyes glide over my dick, licking her lips eagerly. It's all yours for the taking, baby. I gasp when she wraps her fingers around my cock; her eyes lift to mine, watching my reaction while she strokes me slow and steady. “Fuck, Shayla.” I groan, biting my lip hard when she wraps her lips around the crown and sucks gently.

My head went dizzy. I curl my fingers around the base of her ponytail and moan throatily when she slides my cock deeper into her mouth. “Ah, baby.” I pant heavily, thrusting my hips as she continues to suck me rhythmically. I felt that all too familiar stir, and I wasn’t about to blow it all in her mouth. Oh no. “Shayla, stop baby, stop, you’ll make me come.” I pant, looking down into her eyes. Shayla moans in response and gives me one last hard suck before she releases me. I growl, wrap my fingers around her throat, and pin her down on the bed.

“Naughty girl.” I breathe, leaning down I bruise her lips with another passionate kiss. Shayla moans when I flick my tongue over hers and suck. I gather her arms and pin them over her head, lacing our fingers together as I rock my hips against hers, brushing my cock against her wet pussy lips. As much as I was dying to bury myself balls deep inside her, I didn’t want to rush. I’m going to taste every inch of her first.

I let my hands explore her body while my mouth finds a hardened rosy nipple. I suck it a little and smile when she hisses, arching up against my mouth, silently pleading for more. I love it when she does that. I mimic the same on the other nipple, and she bites her lip hard, whimpering when I tug it gently between my teeth. My wandering hands find themselves at her pussy. I brush my fingers through the slit and watch in delight as she cries out when my thumb flicks the bundle of nerves just at the top. Mm, my mouth waters at the thought of tasting her again.

“Uhh, Cole...” I push her legs apart and settle myself between them. Using my fingers, I spread her pussy lips apart, exposing her clit. I smile excitedly, oh baby I’m about to turn your world upside down. I brush the tip of my index finger over her nub gently, and her thighs quiver. I play with her clit teasingly, flicking, brushing, and pinching gently. “Cole, please, uhh fuck.”

“Please, what baby, tell me what you want?” I drawl, “Is it this…” I whisper, brushing the tip of my tongue over her clit with the barest of pressure, and she fists the bed covers, her hips rocking up.

“Mmm, yes, more.” She whimpers breathless. I grin and flick my tongue over her clit again and again with soft kittenish licks. Shayla thrusts her hips up again, yearning for more contact than I was giving her, wordlessly telling me what she needs. I could keep teasing her, but my patience was wearing thin.

I finally give in and suck her clit into my mouth hard, and she bites her lip to keep from screaming. “Fuuuuuck.” She groans, grinding her hips up against my mouth as my tongue flicks over her clit quicker. Her breathing becomes laboured, and her clit pulses under my tongue, and I know she’s close, so I slide my finger inside her and rub her g-spot. I moan against her while sucking her clit, and she climaxes with a shudder, her pussy clamps my fingers and clenches with every delicious spasm of her orgasm. With a breathless whimper, she collapses onto the bed while I drink up her honey.

I place little kisses on her stomach, her breasts while I slowly crawl up over her. She peels her eyes open, still panting, she curls her fingers at my neck and pulls me down for a deep and hungry kiss. “Mm, Cole, I need you, please baby.” She pleads breathily, brushing her lips over mine. Oh Jesus, the way she called me baby had my heart racing.

“Oh baby, I need you too so fucking bad,” I whisper, kissing her softly before I pull away and pick up my trousers and pull out a condom from my wallet and roll it on. Shayla pulls me back down and kisses me avidly. After dreaming about this moment for so long, I finally push myself into her slowly, savouring every sensation as I feed myself deeper into her hot, insanely tight pussy.

We moan in harmony as I start to thrust slow and steadily into her. Shayla wraps her legs around me and rocks her hips up, meeting my thrusts. I made love to her as I had been longing to for so long, and doing it sober was even more spectacular. I made sure every kiss, every moan, every sensation was burned into my memory.

Shayla Hart has well and truly left her mark on my soul.

Chapter Twenty-Three

SHAYLA

I MOAN and stretch out in the super king-size bed, peel my eyes open, blinking out the early morning sunshine. The birds were melodiously chirping as I snuggle into the soft goose feather pillows and sigh in content. Then, like a tsunami, everything that happened between us the night before hits me all at once, and I realise I'm naked in bed...*alone* again, Cole nowhere to be seen.

I roll onto my back and stare up at the ceiling, all sorts going through my mind. Was he having regrets about us sleeping together last night? What if the reality of us having sex didn't hold up to the expectation he had built up in his mind? I mean, he seemed really into it, the way he kept whispering how good I felt and the sounds he was making while he climaxed. Oh, shit what if it's awkward now.

Oh, Shayla, you idiot. What were you thinking, sleeping with him!

I lean up and look at his side of the bed and notice a note on his pillow with a white rose. I pick it up and read it.

"Waking up beside you and starting the day with your intoxicating scent is the most beautiful feeling in the world."

I smile, press the note to my chest, and squeal like a giddy teenage girl.

Where is he though? Why did he just leave me here to wake up alone?

I press the rose against my nose and smell it with a smile. My heart was thrashing around like crazy in my chest. I wrap the sheet around myself and walk over to the huge window overlooking the beautiful garden at his parent's place.

I notice my hair was still up in a messy ponytail, I was too caught up in our passion, I completely forgot to let my hair out. I slide the pins out of my hair, one by one and pull out the band holding up my ponytail. I shake my hair loose, and it falls across my back. I hadn't realised how tight the ponytail was till I brush my fingers through my hair and moan.

"Good morning, sweetheart." I gasp, startled when I hear Cole's voice in my ear suddenly. He wraps his arms around my waist and kisses the nape of my neck.

"Good morning." I greet back, closing my eyes as he trails his lips along my neck. He spins me around and presses me back against the window, his forehead against mine, and bites his bottom lip.

I smile shyly, my cheeks feeling hot all of a sudden. "Sleep well?" He whispers, combing his fingers through my hair.

I nod, "Like a baby." Cole tilts my head up so I could meet his gaze, his eyes a startling green, brighter than I've ever seen them. "Where did you go?" I ask him, and he smiles a little.

"Something urgent came up that needed my attention. Believe me, if it wasn't important, there is no force strong enough to make me leave you alone and naked in my bed." He explains, brushing his thumb along my jaw. "You were sleeping so peacefully that I couldn't bear to wake you." Cole adds, making me smile bashfully.

"Well, did you sort it?" He nods again, slowly leaning in, he brushes his lips over mine.

"I did." He kisses me softly. "I was disappointed, though, that I didn't get to wake you up as I had hoped."

I smile and kiss him back, "Oh? And how did you hope to wake me up?"

Cole grins darkly and wraps his fingers around my wrists, and pulls them away from the sheet I was currently holding against me. The sheet drops to the floor around our feet, and Cole wraps his arms around my naked body and lifts me into his arms, his lips snatching mine and drawing me in for a passionate kiss. Cole walks me over to the bed and lays me down on it gently, his body covering mine as we continue to kiss ardently. I groan when he pulls away, breaking the kiss and looking down into my face.

"I was hoping to wake you up in the best possible way, my tongue gliding over your clit gently like this..." He burrs, brushing his tongue over my clit ever so lightly. I hiss and curl my fingers in his hair.

"Ohhh, Cole..." I moan as he continues to tease me with gentle licks, flicks, and swirling of his tongue in lazy circles till I was a quivering mess begging him to make me come. He kept me on edge, licking until I feel that delicious build-up to climax, when every nerve in your body tingles, and just as I'm about to go over, he stops for a second and starts over again. I whimper, frustrated, "Cole, I can't take anymore, please..."

Cole smiles devilishly, watching me in delight, "Uh ah, you see this feeling right here, where you want something so desperately but can't have it. That's how I felt every time I was near you." He mumbles huskily, sucking my clit lightly.

"Ohhhnnn God, yes." I was so close, so damn close to climaxing, when we hear a knock on the door. Cole's head pops up from between my legs, and I open my eyes and look at the door.

"Um, Mr and Mrs Hoult...uh Mr and Mrs Hoult senior are waiting on you for breakfast." Cole and I look at each other at the same time, and we burst out laughing.

"Thank you, Hayley. We'll be down shortly," Cole replies with a chuckle while I cover my face with my hands.

"Oh my god, I think she heard me moaning." I groan, utterly mortified, while Cole leans up and pulls my hands away from my flushed face.

"I think she did." He chuckles, dropping a kiss on my lips. "Don't be embarrassed, what did she expect to hear knocking on a newlywed couple's door?"

I sigh, "You're a very bad man, Cole Hoult." I say, pushing him off me and getting up while Cole leans up on his elbow, watching me as I move around the room. Suddenly feeling very exposed and coy, I wrap the sheet around my body again. "What the hell am I supposed to wear? Where are my clothes?" I ask looking around the bedroom for the outfit I arrived in, but it was nowhere to be seen.

"I had the girls pick some clothes up for you. It's in that white bag over there," Cole tells me. I look back at him and down at the bag.

"Oh, well thanks," I utter, picking up the bag. Whoever these girls were, they had great taste in clothes. They picked out a cute cream co-ord short skirt and a crop top. "Remind me to thank them before I leave and let me know how much it cost so I can pay you back," I say, and Cole frowns.

"Don't be silly. You don't have to pay me back." He replies, and I stop before I walk into the bathroom and look at him with my eyes narrowed.

"Cole…" I press, and he sighs, watching me closely.

"Shayla." He retorts in the same manner, getting up from the bed and strolling over to me. "It's a gift. You don't have to pay me back for something that was bought for you as a gift." I look up at him when he cups my face in his large hands. "Just kiss me, and that will suffice." He drawls with a handsome smile while gazing into my eyes.

"How about I kiss you and still pay you back?" I suggest impishly, and he grins.

"I'll eagerly accept the kiss but not your money." He whispers leaning in. I wrap my arms around his neck, draw his lips to mine for a soft, lingering peck on his lips. I pull back a little and look up at him, and he smiles, eyes still closed. "Mm more." He groans, sealing our lips again and kissing me with so much passion my toes curl.

"You're spoiling me."

Cole grins. "Good. You deserve it."

I'm in so much trouble with this boy. After a few minutes of kissing, I walk into the ensuite bathroom to have a quick shower and get dressed.

~

TWENTY MINUTES LATER, Cole and I joined his parents at the dining table for breakfast. "Good morning." I greet before taking my seat beside Cole.

"Good morning dear. Did you sleep well?" Coles father asks, folding up the newspaper he was reading and setting it on the side.

Cole and I share a little look, and he smile's nodding. "We slept very well."

"Have you seen the photos of the two of you in the papers this morning? Everyone is talking about the party." Elaine says, delighted, scrolling through her tablet. I sigh inwardly. I really hate being in all these magazines and tabloids.

I take a sip of my coffee and pick at bits of the food they had on the table. You could feed an entire town with the amount of food they had spread out in front of them. How much can four people eat? I tune out the idle chit chat they were having amongst themselves. "Actually, Shayla and I are going to take a little trip." He lifts my hand to his lips and kisses my knuckles softly.

"We are?" I ask him, surprised, and he nods, smiling at me charmingly.

"We sure are, sweetheart." I frown and bite my lip. What is he up to? I'm actually quite nervous all of a sudden. "We better make a move. Thank you again for the party last night, and breakfast was amazing," Cole says, pushing his chair back and standing.

"Thank you for everything, Mr and Mrs Hoult." I manage to say before Cole laces his fingers with mine and pulls me toward the front door and out of the house.

"Where are we going?" I question as we walk to the car, and Cole's smirking at me happily. He opens the car door for me and kisses me before I got in. He's so darn hot.

"You'll see." He beams at me and closes the door walking around to the driver's side. "I figured we needed some time to get away from work, family, and the press." He tells me as he drives out of the gates.

It was such a beautiful day, and I honestly couldn't feel happier. We drove to wherever Cole had planned for us, laughing and flirting, unable to keep our hands off one another. The top was down to his car, the sun beating down on us as we speed down the empty coastal roads. I reach over and take Coles sunglasses and slide them on. He grins at me and lifts his arm, rubbing the nape of my neck as he drove. It's the last week of summer, so the weather was that much sweeter, the warm breeze blowing my hair back. Everything dare I say, was perfect.

~

AN HOUR later we pull up at the airstrip, I look at Coles private jet, and he smiles at me. "What? Where are we going?" I ask grinning, he shrugs, tapping his nose. I give him a pointed look and narrow my eyes at him. "You're not taking me Vegas again, are you? I am not marrying you again!"

Cole throws his head back and laughs. "No, no, we're going somewhere a little closer." He says, opening my door and holding his hand out to me, which I take, and he pulls me out of the car.

I smile when I see Gerald, the driver I met on our first trip. "Hi Gerald." I greet him, and he chuckles nodding.

"Morning, Miss." Cole snickers and pats his shoulder before handing the keys to his Maserati over to him. "We'll be back Monday evening or early Tuesday." He tells Gerald, and he nods and utters a 'very well, sir' before getting into the car.

Cole takes my hand and leads me to his private jet. "Boy, this brings back so many memories," I say as we walk into the plane. Cole laughs and drops a kiss on my temple.

"Mhm, it sure does." I turn and face him, meeting his gaze. He brushes my hair away from my face.

"Where are we going? Don't you have that important meeting tomorrow morning?" I ask again, and he slowly walks me back further into the jet.

"We're going to France—well, Nice to be precise— and no, I had the meeting this morning, so I could clear up our schedule for the next two days. I went by the apartment and picked up our passports. We're good to go." He grins, holding up said passports.

I blink up at him. "Wow, really?" He nods, sitting in a chair and pulling me into his lap.

"Mhm, really. Two days. No interruptions. No work, nothing but you, me, and the French Riviera." He explains, brushing my hair over my shoulder and dropping a kiss on it, his green eyes looking into mine.

I smile, an overwhelming feeling I couldn't quite decipher fills my body from head to toe. I cup his jaw and kiss him. He moans and draws me closer, kissing me deeper. The flight to Nice was just an hour. We spent the entire flight making out heatedly like two horny teenagers encountering sex for the first time. The plane touched down in Nice fifty minutes after we took off. I was so excited to see Nice. It's on my bucket list of places to visit. Cole led me to another car once we step off the plane. This one was a classic car, a red 1960 Ferrari. Absolutely stunning car.

"Oh my God, this car is incredible. My father had a picture up of this car in their bedroom." I say while brushing my fingers along the interior. "It was his dream car." I smile sadly, remembering how excited he would get talking about it.

Cole smiles and holds the keys out to me. "Well, then it's only fair you drive." He replies, smiling handsomely at me.

I look at the keys in his hand and back at him. "Cole, no, it's such an expensive car. I'm happy just sitting in it, believe me." Cole laughs and hands the keys to me.

"Then do it for your Dad." He insists and gets out of the car. I jump out of the car and walk around to the driver's side while Cole gets in the passenger seat. "Take it away, baby." He grins, sliding his shades on, his hand on my thigh.

I was honestly buzzing. As I drive, Cole teases me like an errant teen unable to keep his hands and lips to himself. "You sure know how to handle a gear stick." He whispers in my ear, grinning, his fingers slowly disappearing up my skirt.

I half laugh, half moan when his fingers brush against me intimately. "Cole, you're going to make me drive off this mountain and kill us both." I groan when he sucks at my pulse point.

"Then pull over, I want you. *Now*." He growls wantonly in my ear.

"Now?"

"Yes. Now." He sucks my pulse hard.

"Christ." I moan, pulling the car over the first chance I get. I pull his face to mine and kiss him hard and deep. We were currently driving in the mountains, so there weren't many people around. Cole pulls me on top of him, so I straddled him in the passenger seat while kissing like two crazed animals. His large hands slide under my skirt, squeezing my bum appreciatively while he rocks his hips up against me. Before my sexed-up mind could comprehend what was happening, Cole was inside me, and we were having hot, mind-blowing sex right there in the 1960's Ferrari, somewhere in Nice in the middle of the mountains, the French Riviera stretched out before us.

Our foreheads pressed together, panting, Cole looks into my eyes, his slender fingers brushing my hair back away from my face, and licks his lips. "What have you done to me, Shayla Hart."

I smile, meeting his adoring gaze, "The same as you've done to me, Cole Hoult." I pant, and he kisses me deeply, sucking my bottom lip gently before he pulls away. Sweet Jesus, this man's kisses drive me insane.

AFTER WE CLEAN OURSELVES UP, we continue with our drive to the heart of Nice and start our day with a stroll along the Promenade des Anglais. Cole had his arm around my shoulder, and I had one of mine tucked in the back pocket of his jeans and the other laced with his as he told me stories around the architecture of the buildings we pass by, and I listen with fascination.

"The coffee here is amazing. Come on." He says, guiding me to this adorable little café by the Riviera where we sat and had the most incredible coffee, and I ordered the best coconut cream cake I have ever eaten in my life.

I moan, licking my lips, "Oh my God, Cole, you have to try this." I hold the cake to his lips, and he smiles, takes a bite, and moans in appreciation, sucking the cream off my fingers. "Doesn't it just melt on your tongue?"

"Mm, it is very good, but I prefer something else that melts on my tongue." He drawls, biting his bottom lip while leaning across the table, staring deeply into my eyes.

"Oh yeah, and what might that be?" I whisper, leaning in also, holding his gaze with a teasing smile.

Cole brushes his nose over mine, grinning like a Cheshire cat. "Chocolate." He says po-faced, and I laugh, pressing my finger to his forehead and pushing it away when he tries to kiss me. He takes hold of my wrist and laces his fingers with mine before he drops a kiss on my knuckles, those mesmerising eyes never leaving mine.

It was afternoon when we got to the Marina where Coles yacht 'Freedom' was waiting for us. "Oh wow," I utter, looking up at the big boat as I walk onboard. "I could live on this boat and never get tired. It's stunning." I say in awe, looking around.

"She is a beauty. Freedom is my first love." Cole explains, taking my hand and leading me up to the top deck. "I promised myself, the first hundred million I made on my own, I would buy myself a yacht, and I bought her." He claims proudly, and I give his hand a gentle squeeze.

"There's no feeling like working hard to accomplish your goals and having something to show that your hard work paid off. Whether it be a pencil or a yacht, an achievement is an achievement." I express to him, and he smiles down at me and nods.

"I couldn't agree with you more."

I smile, looking around, "So, where are we setting sail to, captain?" Cole chuckles, wrapping his arms around me from behind and nuzzling my neck lovingly.

"Someplace very special I know you're going to love." I close my eyes and sink back against him as the yacht begins to pull away from the marina. Cole led me down to the bottom deck where the bedroom was, and we spent a good hour making soul-shattering, uninterrupted love to one another. God help me. I couldn't get enough of him. Cole has unleashed this insatiable side to me that I never knew existed. He's taken the good girl I was and turned me into a sex-crazed vixen. It seems I had the same effect on him if his actions were anything to go by. I try to push away the emotional predicament that will surely follow after all this comes to an end. Right now, I want to enjoy every moment I had with him.

The yacht came to a stop, and Cole holds up a white bikini he'd had purchased for me. "Put that on and meet me up on the top deck." He instructs with a wink and disappears upstairs.

I smile and shake my head. I won't be wearing this bikini for long because he will undoubtedly take it off me. I make my way up the stairs to the top deck blinking out the bright sunlight. I stop and look around, eyes wide, mouth agape. The scene before me was something you only see in movies. Clear azure water, overhanging ferns providing shade from the baking sun, and smooth rockslides drop into perfect little bathing pools and a stunning waterfall. "Oh, my God."

"You like it?" Cole murmurs in my ear coming up behind me; his muscular arms wound around my waist. I look back at him and nod, still awestruck.

"Like? Cole, I love it. This place is mesmerising." I whisper, and Cole grins, kissing my temple.

"Shall we swim before the sun sets?" I nod, and he leads me to the back of the boat, where we dive into the warm, clear blue water. I come up to the surface, and Cole follows me up a moment later. He reaches for me, but I swim away from him, retreating slowly as he advances toward me with a hungry look in his eyes. "Where do you think you're going?"

"I think I've made it too easy for you, Mr Hoult." I drawl with a teasing smile as I swim away from him. "You want me. You're going to have to earn me."

Cole grins sexily at me and bites his lip, "Oh sweetheart, I have earned you. I've waited four agonizing months to have you. Please don't torture me anymore." He groans impatiently, gazing into my eyes, "Come here baby."

I shake my head with a wicked smile and dive under the water, swimming toward the waterfall. I swim and stop under the stream. I close my eyes and tilt my head back, letting the cool water cascade over me. I feel Cole's warm hands on my hips as he comes up in front of me, joining me under the stream.

I wrap my arms around his neck and kiss him slow and deep. Cole's arms coil around me, and he moans, kissing me back just as ardently. Just as I had predicted, the bikini came off, and so did his shorts. He guides us behind the caves, hidden away from any wandering eyes. No one was around but us and the captain on the yacht. We step behind the stream of the waterfall, his lips on my throat as he lifts me on a flat rock of some sort before he crawls up over me, laying me back, his eyes staring into mine as if he wanted to see into my soul.

Of all the moments I have had with Cole, this was by far the one I would remember and cherish forever. His gentle touch, the sweet taste of his lips on mine, the deep timbres of his voice whispering my name as he pushes himself into me while we rock slow and steady till we climax together.

It was a moment I would never forget, simply because it was at that moment, I realised I was falling in love with him.

Chapter Twenty-Four

COLE

"TRISTAN COLE HOULT, are you trying to get me drunk?" Shayla giggles as I pour us another glass of white wine.

I shake my head chuckling, "No, not at all." I declare, feigning innocence, and she narrows her eyes at me sceptically. "Besides, a couple of bottles of wine isn't going to get us that drunk. I don't think anything will top how drunk we were the night we met."

Shayla groans with a smile shaking her head, "Oh my god, don't remind me. I was hungover for three days straight. I will never drink that much ever again." She declares, putting her glass down and lays back, staring up at the star-filled sky with a sigh. I couldn't even tell you what time it was. We've been sitting up on the top deck of the yacht just talking and drinking wine and eating a cheese board. I lay down beside Shayla, and we gaze up at the stars together. She looks over at me when I feed her a grape and smiles. "Tell me a secret about yourself?"

I look at her and frown, "A secret?" I ask, and she nods, watching me.

"Yes, something no one else knows about you."

I lick my lips and mull over her question, "Well, I don't know if this counts as a secret, but I can sing." I confess to her, and she lifts her head and looks at me, surprised.

"You can?" Shayla questions and I nod, rolling onto my side. I rest my head in my hand and watch her. She does the same and holds my gaze. "Will you sing for me?"

I smile and rub her jaw gently, "Sure, I'll sing for you someday."

She beams at me, "You're a man of many talents, Lord Hoult. You continue to surprise me every day." She claims, leaning into my touch. "Thank you for arranging this getaway. I've honestly had such an incredible time." I look into her eyes, smiling, and drag my thumb along her bottom lip.

"So have I, sweetheart. I'm so disappointed we have to go back." I admit studying her angelic face.

I wish we had more time.

Shayla smiles prettily, kissing my thumb. Arranging this mini getaway with her was the best idea I have ever had. I've never felt so relaxed and at peace than I am when I'm with her. She does something to me, something I simply can't explain. It's like that feeling you get when you eat something so good that you just want to take your time and savour every bite and not finish it because you're scared you'll never find it anywhere again. She's my coconut cream cake, and now I've had a taste of her, I can't imagine giving her up or not having her in my life.

"Cole?" I blink, snapping out of my thoughts when I hear Shayla call my name. "You okay? What are you thinking about so deeply?"

I sigh, "Shayla, I—"

"Mr Hoult, we need to head back to the marina. There's a storm headed this way." The captain alerts us, and I nod.

"Thank you, Captain, we can head back," I tell him, and he nods and walks off. I look back at Shayla, and she shrugs with an adorable smile.

"Guess the boat party for two is over," She states, getting up to her feet. She walks to the front of the boat and looks out at the ocean. The night was so clear you could see the full moon perfectly, the stars twinkling in the sky like diamonds. I watch her as she stood there, the wind in her hair, a faraway look in her eyes, and I wish more than anything I could read her mind right now.

With a sigh, I get up and walk over to her. I wrap my arms around her and pull her against me holding her tight. Shayla smiles and wraps her arms over mine, and sinks back into me. “What’s on your mind?” I ask, pressing my forehead to her temple and feel her sigh.

“Nothing, just letting this moment sink in.” She replies, tilting her head back to look up at me. “Today is the seventh day of the bet.”

I look down into her eyes and stroke her jaw softly. “Oh, wow. I forgot all about that. So, I can’t kiss you anymore after tonight?” I ask, leaning in closer, and she doesn’t answer, just looks at my lips and back up to my eyes.

“That is what we agreed,” She whispers, leaning in also.

“What if I forget and kiss you…” I whisper back, my lips a breath away from hers. Shayla’s eyes close when I brush my lips over hers. “Would you pull away?”

“Mhm,”

I look down into her face and fight the urge to smile. “Then pull away now.” I breathe, trailing my finger down her throat. Shayla moans and lifts her arm, curls her fingers at my neck, and pulls my head in, closing the gap between our lips. I rub her jaw and kiss her softly before I spin her around so she was facing me. She drapes her arms around my neck, and I envelop mine around her waist, pulling her up against me. I kiss her slowly and thoroughly as if my life depended on it. How am I supposed to be around her and not kiss her when she kisses like this? I felt the first drop of rain on my head before it started absolutely chucking it down.

Shayla gasps, and we pull apart and look up. The skies that were clear moments ago were now engulfed with dark clouds. “Come on, let's go inside,” I say, pulling her, but she shakes her head laughing and tugs me back to her.

“No, stay…” I look at her with a frown, and she pulls me in for another kiss.

“We’ll get sick, sweetheart,” I whisper between kisses, and she cups my face in her hands and smiles.

“I don’t care.” She whispers, kissing me back avidly. There we stood in the pouring rain, completely soaked, kissing passionately without a care in the world about anything else but each other. That moment was definitely worth catching pneumonia for. The flash of lightning, followed by a loud rumble of thunder, interrupts our moment. We jump apart, and I take her hand, pulling her inside to the bottom deck just as the boat pulls up to the marina.

"You're shivering," I say, rubbing her arms, and she shakes her head, smiling up at me.

"So are you." She breathes, panting. I watch her closely as she lifts my t-shirt up and over my head, dropping it on the floor before her cold, trembling fingers rake down my chest and stomach. I press my forehead to hers while she unbuttons my jeans and pushes them down. I moan when I feel her soft lips kissing along my chest. I kick off my wet jeans, cup her face, and kiss her softly. I lift her arms, breaking the kiss for a second. I tug her top off before sealing our lips together again.

The yacht rocks a little against the waves, raindrops, and thunder, the only sounds other than our breathing and soft moans. The frequent lightning was the only form of lighting we had, giving us glimpses of one another in the darkness of the room. I undress Shayla, lift her into my arms bridal style, and carry her to the bed, still kissing fervidly. I lay her down on the bed and crawl up over her. Shayla opens her eyes and looks up at me, eyes so bright and pure it took my breath away. I could honestly stare at her all my life and never get tired. We stare into each other's eyes, penetratingly for a long moment, and I feel my heart rate accelerate.

"Cole," Shayla whispers, reaching up, she trails her fingers along my cheek while I brush mine through her hair, my thumbs stroking her temples softly.

"You're so beautiful, sweetheart," I whisper, sweeping my nose over hers lightly. Shayla smiles, a gorgeous pink touching her cheeks, and skims her finger over my lips before she takes hold of my white gold chain and tugs me down for a spine-tingling kiss.

"Make me yours, one last time I want to be yours." She breathes, and my stomach clenches at her words. *One last time...* Of course, whatever this was between us was only temporary. I keep forgetting that she's going to walk out of my life in thirty-six days.

I shove aside the gut-wrenching disappointment and focus on appreciating this moment with her. I push into her slowly, and we moan into each other's mouths amid our kissing. Our fingers lace and I thrust into her slow and deep, taking my sweet time. If this were the last time I could have her, I was going to make damn sure it lasts for as long as possible. And it did— until our once freezing bodies were hot and dripping in sweat. The storm had passed by the time we were done. Only the gentle tap of the rain on the window remained. I've never made love to anyone like this before: hair-raising, rip-roaring, and all-consuming. I've had my share of women, but Shayla—she's intoxicating.

We were both spent. Shortly after we climax, we kiss for a little bit, and she dozes off to sleep in my arms. I lay there staring at the ceiling for a while, my mind full of questions I can't seem to find answers to. Eventually, I manage to fall asleep, and the next morning I woke up alone. I lean up and look around the room. Where has she snuck off too?

I get out of bed and pull my jeans on from last night; thankfully, they were dry. I wander around the yacht and finally find Shayla on the top deck sitting with her knees pulled to her chest, gazing out at the ocean, watching other boats as they leave the marina. I rub my hands over my face and walk over to her. "Morning." I greet her, leaning over, I drop a kiss on top of her head.

Shayla smiles up at me though it doesn't quite reach her eyes. "Morning."

I frown and crouch down next to her, "What's the matter?" I question, brushing a strand of hair out of her face, and she shakes her head.

"Nothing," She smiles. "I was just enjoying the sun. It's beautiful out today. You wouldn't think there was a storm last night."

I nod and glance around. It really was a nice day. "Shall we get some breakfast before we leave?" I suggest and watch as she nods.

"Sounds good. I'm starving." She says, getting up to her feet. We get dressed and take a stroll to a café by the Riviera.

~

AS WE SAT CHATTING, something, or should I say *someone* caught my eye behind Shayla. Sophie. She was sitting a couple of tables away with her fiancé Derrick. As if on cue, she lifts her eyes, and they lock with mine. What the hell is she doing here? We stare at one another till she looks away when Derrick strokes her face. I clench and unclench my jaw as I watch them from afar. Sophie kept looking at me and averting her gaze. I was feeling irritated all of a sudden. This is the first time I'd physically seen them together, and it made my stomach tighten painfully. "Cole?" I tear my eyes away from Sophie and look at Shayla, who was watching me perplexed. "You okay? You look really upset, is something wrong?" I blink and glance over at Sophie again, who was watching us.

"No. I'm fine, I'm fine," I mutter, shaking my head and rubbing my jaw agitatedly. My eyes would involuntarily glance over to Sophie despite me telling my stupid brain not to. Shayla glances back when she catches me staring at something behind her and sees Sophie.

She licks her lips and smiles faintly, "Wow, talk about a coincidence." She mutters, dropping her gaze to her coffee cup.

I sigh and lean over, taking her hands in mine. I press a kiss to her knuckles. "We can go if you're uncomfortable."

She shakes her head smiling and looks at me, "I'm not the one that's bothered. You shouldn't show her she's gotten to you, or you'll give her the satisfaction she's clearly craving." She tells me blankly, and I frown.

"Shayla, I honestly don't—"

She shakes her head, "Don't lie to yourself, Cole. You do care. You're practically seething. If you want her to feel even a little of what you are right now, you need to act like she doesn't exist, or you're just proving her right." Shayla explains, resting her head in her hand and stirring her coffee.

"I wish it were that easy to up and forget when someone wrecks you. I can't believe she's here. I hadn't seen her once in eight months, now she keeps popping up everywhere." I express bitterly with a shrug taking a sip of my coffee. Shayla pinches the bridge of her nose and sighs.

"Look, this is the first time she's seeing us out together, so far you're doing nothing but proving her right about your marriage being nothing but a sham. From where she's sitting, she can see how annoyed you are by their presence." Shayla explains, leaning closer.

"Hard not to be." I sigh, setting my cup down. "I can't just magically forget she exists."

Shayla bites her lip and nods, "Yes, you can, just focus on me." She whispers, looking into my eyes. I lick my lips and reach over to brush my thumb along her jaw. “You get one last kiss. Make it count.” She states, looking at me, but the warmth she usually has in her eyes when she looks at me has disappeared, and she stares at me vacantly.

“I’m not going to waste a kiss from you on the likes of her,” I declare, pressing my lips to the corner of her mouth. “Let’s get out of here,” I whisper and drop a kiss on her forehead. Shayla nods, and we stand up. I drop some cash on the table, wrap my arm around Shayla’s shoulder, and we leave the café. I can feel Sophie's glare as I pass by her without so much as a glance, focussing all my attention on the one girl who actually deserves it.

Just when things were going so great for us, we took a giant step back, and things have been strained between us since we got back. It’s like she hit the reset button and forgot everything that happened between us the last couple of days. She’s not home again, gone off to spend time with her family.

Two weeks pass since our trip, and I’ve barely had time to see Shayla as I’ve been hammered with work. I had to fly to New York for three days for a conference. I asked her to join me, but she refused and said her mother wasn’t feeling great, so she’s been staying there to look after her. I did a stupid thing and met up with Sophie when she called me a couple of nights ago, and now I’m more confused than ever before.

She’s due to be wed to another man and she said she’s having doubts and can’t stop thinking about us. She told me she loves me and never got over me. She wants us to give it another go. If I was willing to walk away from Shayla, she would do the same and we could be together.

So, here I am, sitting in my living room with Josh trying to get my head straight. “Cole, you need to make a decision. You only have two weeks left with Shayla before you lose her for good and Sophie isn’t going to wait around for you forever.”

I sigh rubbing my forehead, “I know Josh, but it's not that easy. On the one hand, I’ve got Shayla who is incredible, and we have so much fun together, and I like her so fucking much. We have such an amazing connection, but she’s the complete opposite of me. How well do we really know each other? We’re constantly butting heads, and I’m worried once the sexual chemistry and attraction wear off, we'll end up resenting each other." I explain, twirling the ring on my finger. "And then there's Sophie, who I've been in love with for years, she's the perfect girl for me in every way. She's familiar and uncomplicated. She's the logical choice in every way." I justify staring at the floor.

"But.." Josh presses.

I sigh, closing my eyes, "She's not Shayla."

Josh groans, "Oh my God, Cole, we're going round and round in circles. Look, if they both stood in front of you right now asking you to make a choice, who would your heart tell you to pick?" Josh asks, sitting forward and picking up his bottle of beer. I mull over his words silently for a while.

"My heart says, Sophie," I admit with a defeated sigh. "Deep down, it's always been, Sophie."

"Well, there you go. I think you're confusing your attraction and sexual chemistry with Shayla with having actual feelings for her." Josh says, taking a sip of his beer, and I frown.

"What do you mean? I do have feelings for her, Josh. I'm just not in love with her."

At least, I don't think I am.

"Look, what I mean is, Shayla is the 'meantime girl' like a rebound—if you will. She's the girl you have some fun with but never commit to. She's a good distraction to help you nurse your broken heart." Josh explains with a shrug, and I stare at him. "And she has helped take your mind off Sophie the last couple of months. You've been happier and a lot more pleasant to be around."

"I don't know, Josh, this thing with Shay has been an emotional rollercoaster. Besides, she always made it abundantly clear that she would walk away once the agreement was done. I think, no, *I know* she's counting down the days till she'll be free of me and can go back to her own life, where she can be herself again. She told me she feels worthless when she's with me, and I care about her enough to understand that she doesn't want to be a part of my lifestyle. It's simply hard to face the fact that I have to let her go." I swallow the lump forming in my throat and sigh. "I really like having her in my life."

"Are you going to talk to Sophie and see if you guys can work things out?" Josh questions leaning back against the sofa.

I nod, "Yeah, I'll talk to her in the next couple of days. I just need to sort my head out before I go over there and tell her that she's the one and I'm still in love with her." I tell him, chugging back the rest of my beer. I pick up the divorce papers from the table and look at them.

"Are you going to sign it?" Josh asks, gesturing to the divorce papers I'm holding. I sigh and stare at Shayla's signature at the bottom, where she signed it months ago. I nod, picking up the pen and ignoring the pull in my heart and sign the papers and drop them on the table.

There, it's done.

I hear the front door click shut and sit forward. Josh and I exchange looks. "Was that the front door?" I ask, and Josh shrugs, pursing his lips.

"Sounded like it."

I get up and walk toward the entryway, thinking Shayla had come home, but no one was around. Maybe Josh forgot to shut it when he came over. I sigh and push aside the disappointment of hoping Shayla was back so I could see her and throw myself back on the sofa with a frustrated groan.

Chapter Twenty-Five

SHAYLA

"Mum, are you sure you feel okay? I can stay longer if you need me?" I argue with my mother, but she shakes her head and waves me off.

"No, honey, I feel fine now, honestly. You've run yourself ragged looking after me as well as working this past week. Go home to your husband." She says while I pull the blanket over her so she stays warm.

"But Mum—"

"Shayla, I'm okay now. Beside's, I have Sammy to look after me too. *Go home*." I look over at Sam, who nods his head, agreeing with her.

"Anything changes, or she starts to feel worse you call me? You understand?" I tell my older brother, and he nods again with a little smile.

"I will, I promise. Mum's right, you look exhausted Shay, go and get some rest before you get sick too." He says, ruffling my hair like I was a six-year-old. I slap his hand away and punch his shoulder, scowling at him, and he chuckles.

"Ouch, still got that right hook on you, kid." He groans, rubbing his arm playfully.

"I was taught by the best." I shrug and pick up my bag. "Seriously though, Sammy, you call me if anything happens, *anything*, I mean it," I demand, and he nods his head.

"I will, Sis, go and get some rest." I sigh and walk to the front door. I look back at my mother one last time, and I blow a kiss at her.

"I'll come to see you soon, mama," She waves at me, smiling tiredly. I walk out of my childhood home and sigh. I worry so much about her when she gets sick. She's asthmatic, and when she catches the flu or any chest infections, she struggles to breathe on her own without a ventilator.

The doctor did say she was out of the woods, but I can't help but worry about her. I've missed being home with them so much. With everything that's happened with Cole lately, I needed to get away and clear my head. Since we got back from Nice, things have been weird between us, and I think I'm partly to blame for that. After I saw the way he was looking at Sophie that day and his reaction to seeing her with her fiancé, the love he still holds in his heart for her slapped me back to reality again.

I'm really dreading going back to his apartment and seeing him. It's come to the point where I'm really struggling to not make my feelings evident to him. Neither of us has spoken about where we stand after we slept together. He didn't bring it up, and neither did I. I just slap a fake smile on my face and keep telling myself I'm okay just to get through the day, and it's exhausting. Two more weeks and this nightmare will be over.

~

As I make my way to the apartment I wonder if he's home. I type the code in and push the door open. I hear voices and my name and stop where I was. Was that Josh's voice? I quietly closed the door and moved to hide behind a pillar where I could see Cole sitting on the sofa talking with Josh.

"Are you going to talk to Sophie and see if you guys can work things out?" Josh questions.

Cole nods, "Yeah, I'll talk to her in the next couple of days. I just need to sort my head out before I go over there and tell her she's the one and that I'm still in love with her." He says and picks up the envelope with our divorce papers. I cover my mouth with my hand to keep quiet.

"Are you going to sign it?" Josh asks, and Cole nods, picking up the pen, he signs it without hesitation before tossing them back on the table.

I back away quietly toward the front door and open it as quietly as I could, and run as fast as my legs would take me. I couldn't breathe. I walk into the elevator and push the button furiously, panting, trying to catch my breath. I press myself against the wall as the doors slid shut, and you know that moment when your silent sobs just build and build to a point where you can't catch your breath, and you stop breathing for a second until that painful whimper just rips out of you, and all your emotions hit you all at once. The last time I cried like that was when I found out my Dad had died.

Oh, God, what have I done?

I thought I had prepared myself for this moment, but a part of me, a small part, wanted to believe he would choose *me*— however silly and baseless as it may have been. I thought he felt something for me too. I can't blame him, though. It's my fault. I did this to myself by allowing him to get close enough to hurt me. I got caught up in the emotions and let myself fall in love with him knowing deep down he's in love with Sophie. Of course, he's going to end up with her. Cole had his fun with me and got it out of his system, but she's the girl that gets the guy at the end of the story, and I'm just the girl who helped him get her.

I get into my car and drive to the one person I know who would listen and not ask me any questions. As I drive, I get flashbacks of our moments over the last six months. The night we first met, our first kiss, the day we cooked together in his apartment and laughed ourselves stupid over my dimple fantasy, the night we got locked in his bedroom, everything that happened in Nice, all these stupid moments we shared just hit me all at once.

~

I PARK up the car and walk in the dark till I see him. I stop and bite my bottom lip. "Hi Daddy," I whisper, an endless stream of tears rolling down my cheek as I kneel by his grave. "It's been a couple of weeks since I last came and saw you, I know, I'm so sorry." I bite my bottom lip and wipe away the tears that just kept falling down my face.

"I just, I didn't know where else to go," I whine and press my hand to the gravestone with his photo on it. "If I had one wish right now, it would be to have you back, so I could lay my head on your knee and have you stroke my hair till all the pain goes away— because it hurts Daddy, it hurts *so* much." I sob uncontrollably.

"I know what you're going to say, you did this to yourself Peanut, and you're right, I did. But I couldn't help it, Daddy. I tried to stop myself, but he somehow wormed his way into my heart." I sniffle and press my forehead to his cold gravestone. "What do I do, Daddy? Please tell me what to do, because right now I just want to disappear. How am I supposed to go and face the man I love knowing he's in love with someone else and pretend it's not killing me?" I sob. "Help me please…"

I brush my fingers over his face printed on the gravestone, "Am I really so unlovable? What is wrong with me? Why does everyone find it so easy to just toss me aside and walk away from me? Why can't I ever be *the* girl?" I hiccup, shaking my head.

"I'm so mad at myself because I knew this would happen, but I didn't expect it to hurt this much." I laugh bitterly and wipe away my tears. "I deserve this. I deserve to feel this way because I'm stupid. I should have walked away from him that day, but I couldn't. I should walk away now, but I can't because my heart and my pride won't let me." I whimper, dejectedly closing my eyes. "Oh, Daddy, what am I going to do?" I felt a chill run down my spine when I lay my head on the dirt and sob until I was all cried out. "I miss you so much," I admit, my voice breaking. "Thank you for listening to me, and I know you're probably very disappointed in me and what a mess I've made of myself, but near you is the only place I find any sort of comfort."

I sigh and dry my eyes, "It's weird, but I can almost hear your voice scolding me as you did when that Danny kid broke my heart when I was fourteen. You raised my head and said, 'Hey, whose daughter are you? Didn't I teach you that however hard you may fall, you never let your head drop for anyone—especially over a boy who doesn't deserve you.' I live by those words, and I promise you, Dad, I'll find a way to get through this with my head held high, just like you taught me." I say, and kiss my fingers before I press them to his gravestone. "I love you, I'll be back soon, good night, Dad." With a sigh, I get up and walk back to my car. I didn't know how I would get through the next two weeks, but I had to somehow. I couldn't face seeing Cole, not tonight, so I went back to my apartment after driving around and sitting by the river, blankly staring at the city lights before me.

I SNUCK INTO THE APARTMENT, not wanting to wake the girls because I couldn't face anyone or answer any questions without breaking down. I didn't sleep a wink. I tried so hard, just to get a moment of solace where my heart didn't clench painfully at the thought of Cole. I just sat in the dark, knees pulled to my chest, tears falling down my face, rocking back and forth, desperately trying to pick up and put together the pieces to my heart. I sat watching the sun come up out my window, and I felt so utterly drained, mentally and physically.

I left the apartment before the girls woke up and drove back to Coles. I sat in the car staring up at the building for a while, dreading seeing him again. I had to find the strength somehow and pretend like I'm okay in front of him. Just walking into the apartment made my eyes water. I had to take a couple of deep breaths and count to ten to calm myself down.

I tiptoe to my bedroom, and just as I reach it, I hear Coles door open and his voice behind me. "Shayla?"

I bite back the tears and hold my breath so he couldn't see my shoulders rising and falling. I feel his hand on my arm, and the touch that I once loved now hurt me.

"I'm fine," I say, keeping the emotion out of my voice, but it quivers a little, and I shake his hold off my arm and walk to my bedroom, not daring to look at him because my eyes were drowned in tears.

"Sweetheart, what's wrong?" He presses following me, he grabs my arm and stops me, and I wince.

"Don't!" I snap hotly before I could stop myself, my shoulders rising and falling quickly. I honestly felt as though my emotions were suffocating me. "Don't," I whisper and walk to my bedroom. I close the door behind me and lock it before I slid to the floor and sob into my hand silently.

"Shayla, what's going on? Did something happen?" I hear his voice from the other side of the door. "Shayla, come on sweetheart, unlock the door. Talk to me."

I wipe my tears and press my head against the door. "Cole, I'm fine,"

"No, you're not. Did something happen to your mum? Is she okay?" He asks, concern evident in his voice. "Shay? Talk to me please, what's happened?"

"My mums fine Cole. We just had an argument, and I'm a little upset, that's all. Please just leave me alone for a bit, okay." I lie, burying my head in my hands. "Please just go." I whimper.

"Shay…" I hear him sigh and could picture him standing there with his head pressed against the door.

"Cole, please, let me be." I sigh and hear him shuffling on the other side of the door.

"Okay, I'm here when you want to talk." I hear him say, and I shake my head as I hear his footsteps retreat. Shit, shit, shit! I was supposed to keep it together, but I fell apart the moment I'm around him. I recall the promise I made my Dad. I'll bury my emotions and slap a smile on my face—no one but me will know that I'm slowly dying inside. He'll never know how much he's wrecked me.

After figuratively shoving my emotions into a box and locking it away, I had a long shower and got ready for work. Cole was already dressed and waiting for me, pacing back and forth while rubbing his neck. When I walk out of my bedroom, he stops and looks at me. Our eyes meet, and I feel my insides quiver, but I force it back down and walk toward him. "Are you okay?" He questions, thinning his eyes in scrutiny.

I lick my lips and force myself to hold his gaze, "I'm okay." He frowns a little. He doesn't believe me. I wouldn't believe me either if I stood there looking at myself. Drained, eyes were swollen and rimmed red. "Um, you can go. I have something I have to take care of before I make my way to the office." I tell him as I walk past him. Cole watches me before he catches my hand and pulls me back.

"I'll drive you wherever you need to go." I shake my head and look up at him.

"No, that's okay. I'll drive myself. I'm not going to be very long. I'll see you at the office, okay?" I say and smile at him. He looks into my face and blinks. I pull my hand out of his and walk to the front door. I open it and walk out of the apartment. I heave a sigh when he doesn't follow me and rush to the car to leave as quickly as possible. I don't even wait for the elevator; I take the stairs.

Thirty minutes later, I was sat waiting for Franc at his office. "Miss Hart, Mr Clement, will see you now." I nod and smile politely at the young receptionist and walk to his office. Franc stands and moves over to me when I walk in and shakes my hand.

"Miss Hart, welcome. Please, take a seat." He greets, gesturing to the leather chairs opposite his marble desk. "How can I help you?"

I sigh and lick my lips, "Before I tell you the reason I'm here, I need to know if the client/lawyer confidentiality applies to me too? I know Cole is your client technically, but does it apply to me as well?"

Franc frowns and leans forward, placing his arms on his desk regarding me seriously, "Yes, it applies to you too. Is everything okay? Are you in some sort of trouble, Shayla?"

I shake my head and tuck my hair behind my ear, "No, nothing like that. Uh, as you know, our divorce date is in less than two weeks, and I… I want to sign away my rights to a settlement. There's a clause in our agreement that I will get a figure of two million after the divorce."

I say, and Franc frowns deeply.

"Shayla, as your lawyer, I strongly urge you to rethink this decision. If you sign away your rights to a settlement, you won't get a single cent."

I sigh, "I know Franc, I don't want anything. I just want to get the divorce out of the way as quickly as possible." I explain, and Franc nods, rubbing his jaw thoughtfully.

"All right, if you're sure this is what you want?" He probes, and I nod in response. "Very well, I'll get the papers, and you can sign them."

"There's one more thing." I say, and Franc nods, looking at me questioningly, "Cole can't know about this."

Franc nods and laces his fingers together, "He will find out on the day because the judge will announce that there's no settlement before he grants your divorce." He explains, and I nod in understanding.

"That's fine. If you can get the papers, I'll sign them now." I tell him. Franc nods and walks out of the office. I sat there staring at the diamond ring on my finger until Franc walks back in moments later with papers in his hand.

"Here we are. If you could sign the dotted lines on both pages, I'll have them processed." I nod and took the pen he held out to me, sign the papers, and hand it back to him. "Great, that's all done." He smiles a little, and I sigh getting up to my feet. We shake hands before I turn to walk out of his office.

"Shayla?" I stop and look back at him. "I've met many couples going through a divorce in my twenty-five years of being a lawyer, but you're the first person I've come across to reject a large settlement figure. Usually, it's the opposite; they always want more. Would you think me rude if I ask why?"

I drop my gaze and sigh, "Because I've seen how hard Cole works to earn his living, and believe me when I say he pours his heart into his work." I shrug, "I was raised to only take what's earned, and I didn't earn that money. He did, along with his father and grandfathers' hard work. It's never been about the money for me. It wasn't then, and it certainly isn't now." I tell him earnestly, and he stares at me for a long moment and smiles a little. "Thank you for your help."

"Of course, I'll see you in two weeks for the hearing." I nod, opening the door, I utter a goodbye and walk out of his office. At least that's out of the way. Now, for the next part.

Four days pass by painstakingly slow. I've been trying so hard to keep myself together while I'm around Cole, and as hard as it is, I think I'm managing...*somehow*. We have ten days left till our hearing. The signed papers have been sent back to Franc, all that's left for us to do is wait for the date.

I fold up the piece of paper in my hand and stand up, my legs trembling a little as I walk to Coles office. I knock on his door, and he looks up and gestures for me to enter. I inhale a deep breath and walk into his office. "Sorry to disturb you. Do you have a second?" I ask him, and he nods, dropping his pen, he regards me curiously.

"Of course, what's up?" I sigh and step closer, drop the paper in my hand on his desk and step back a little. Cole looks at the paper on his desk and up at me again before picking it up. "What's this?" He questions, unfolding it, his eyes never leaving mine.

"My two weeks' notice," I reply fighting to keep the quiver from my voice. Cole frowns, looking at the paper, his eyes scanning the words before he looks at me again.

"What?" He drops the paper and stands up. "You're leaving? Why?"

I lick my lips and shrug, "I've gotten a job offer as a junior architect. It's a really good opportunity for me to get my foot into the industry." Cole walks around his desk and steps closer to me.

"Shayla, what are you talking about? No, you don't have to leave. You're already in the industry. I'll make you an architect here." He says, taking hold of my arms. I wince and pull back, closing my eyes.

"Cole, working here has been good for me. It's given me opportunities I could have only ever dreamed of, and I've learnt so much from you, which I'm so grateful for," I tell him. "But I have to take this job," I explain, swallowing the giant lump in my throat as I will myself not to cry when I saw the melancholy look in his green eyes.

"Shay…" He whispers, and I force myself to smile at him.

"We both knew this day would come, right? I wasn't going to be your assistant forever, Cole. I've fulfilled everything I had to do here." I tell him, lacing my fingers together. "And now, it's time to move on and make my dream a reality." I chuckle a little, "You've been a great boss, Lord Hoult."

Cole looks at me wordlessly, his jaw clenching and unclenching as he stares at me. "I knew this day would come, but I never thought letting you go would be so hard." He says, looking at me sadly. I felt my stomach tighten, and that box with all my emotions was starting to unfold. "What am I going to do without you?" He whispers, stepping closer to me. He looks into my eyes and brushes my hair away from my face.

I stare at my feet, not having the nerve to hold his gaze, "You're going to be fine." I assure him and look around the office. "It's been a hell of an adventure."

"Shayla…"

"Don't," I whisper, lifting my eyes to his. "I'll remember you fondly, Tristan Cole Hoult," I whisper with a smile. I turn my back to him before he saw the tears roll down my cheeks and walk out of his office.

Chapter Twenty-Six

COLE

"TRISTAN?"

I lift my eyes from the cup of coffee I've been staring at for the past twenty minutes. I look at Sophie, who waves in my face. "Hm?"

"I've been talking for the last twenty minutes, and you've not even been listening to me." She huffs, slumping back in her chair and crossing her arms over her chest, seemingly annoyed with me.

I shake my head, "I'm sorry, babe, I've just got a lot on my mind." I sigh and reach over. I take her hand in mine and rub her knuckles gently. "I'm listening,"

Sophie smiles and places her hand over mine. "I was saying now you're getting divorced tomorrow we can arrange a dinner and get our families together to announce that we're back together again. Wouldn't that be nice?"

I rub my forehead and smile, "Soph, that's a great idea, but let's do it in a couple of months when my divorce is done and out the way. I just need some time to get my head together, plus the press is all over Shayla and me at the moment. I don't want to disrespect Shayla or her family by being seen with you too soon after the divorce."

Sophie pulls her hand away and sighs, "Disrespect her and her family? Are you kidding me? I just walked out on my fiancé a week before our wedding for *you*, and you're sitting there talking about disrespecting a girl you've barely had a relationship with? Give me a break." I rub my temples tiredly and sigh.

"Sophie, however short it may have been, Shayla was my wife, and I won't let anyone disrespect her, not you, not the press, not anyone. She deserves better than that. We've waited this long to be together. What's a couple of weeks or months." I explain, and Sophie shakes her head, averting her gaze.

"Sounds to me like you still care an awful lot about her." She mutters cuttingly, and I lean closer, scowling at her.

"Of course, I care about her. Shayla's been nothing but good to me. Our marriage may not have worked out, but her friendship means a lot to me, Soph." I utter, dropping some cash on the table. I push my chair back and stand up. "I have work to do," I utter and walk off, leaving her sitting there, her mouth agape as she watches my retreating back.

I have way too much on my mind to sit there and listen to her insistently slating Shayla. I will not rub my relationship with Sophie in her family's face so soon after our divorce. Even if our marriage was staged, our families don't know that, and how will it look when I'm seen with another girl so soon after we divorce? That wouldn't only put Shayla in an awkward situation, but it would ruin my integrity too. *Fuck that.* As pleased as I am to be back with Sophie again, I'd like to enjoy us being with one another before we get hounded by the media again. I don't understand why she's in such a rush to go public.

I DRIVE BACK to the office and sit in my car, looking up at the building for a long moment. It's Shayla's last day at the office today, and I can't face going up there and watch her packing her desk up. When she handed me her notice, I was devastated she was leaving. Even after we divorced, I just assumed she would be there, and I'd still see her about at work— but now she's quit, and after tomorrow she's walking out of my life for good. I won't see her ever again. That was a hard pill to swallow.

The past two weeks have been weird, to say the least. Shayla's been cold and distant. Where's the girl that made my heart race with her smile. When I told her that I'd worked things out with Sophie and we were going to give it another go, she just gave me a tight-lipped smile, said she was thrilled for us, and went back to reading her book. That's the reaction I got. I was hoping for a conversation of some sort. After everything, I didn't expect her to be so blasé about it. She clearly didn't care, and as she said, she was ready to move on with her life.

I walk out of the elevator toward my office and stop when I see the flowers I arranged to be sent to her had just arrived—a bouquet of rare blue lilies— her favourite. I remember how excited she got one day when she came across one. I watch her as she looks at the flowers, leans in, and smells them before she smiles sadly. She picks up the card and opens the little envelope just as I walk up behind her. As she reads the note, I lean into her ear and whisper, "You'll always be my mini muffin." She jumps, startled but doesn't move or look at me. I press my nose into her hair.

Shayla heaves a sigh and steps away from me, taking her scent with her. She turns and looks at me, her eyes watering. "And you'll always be my little sausage." I chuckle sadly, and we stare at each other for a long moment.

"Come here." I pull her into my arms, and we hug. I bury my face into her neck and inhale, filling my lungs with her scent. I close my eyes, "Don't go." I whisper in her ear, and I feel her tremble in my arms.

"Cole."

"Please stay," I mumble into her neck. "I'm so used to you being around, I don't know how I'm going to function without you. You're my best friend." Shayla sighs and pulls away from me, shaking her head.

"You're going to be fine. You have everything you've always wanted. The company is now yours, and you're back with the girl you love. Your life is just as it should be." Shayla explains, looking down at her feet.

"Will I ever see you again?" I ask, and she shrugs with a little smile. "I'd like to see you."

"Who knows, maybe our paths might cross one day, and if it doesn't, then it's not meant to be Tristan Cole Hoult." I sigh and bite my lip. "Thank you for the flowers. They're beautiful." She adds, looking around her desk. "I better get my desk packed up and head out. I'll see you tomorrow at the courthouse?"

I frown, "Wait, are you not coming back home?" I question and she shakes her head and rubs her forehead.

"No, uh, I have a couple of things I have to do, and I'm going to stay at my apartment. No point in dragging it out. I've already packed up my things at your place, I just have a few more things, and I can do that tomorrow after the courthouse." She explains, and I push aside the disappointment and nod.

"I was hoping I could take you out to dinner, or we could do something together," I tell her, and she licks her lips and shakes her head.

"I can't. I promised the girls we'd go out for some drinks. Besides, aren't you sick of me yet? You just reconciled with your girlfriend, go and spend time with her. I'm sure you two have plenty to catch up on." She says with a smile and nudges me with her shoulder. *'I don't want to spend time with her. I want to spend time with you!'* I have all the damn time in the world to spend with Sophie. Fucking hell Cole, stop pushing her, she clearly doesn't want to be around you.

I sigh dejectedly, "I suppose you're right. I'll leave you to pack up your things. I'll see you tomorrow." Shayla nods and starts packing up her desk.

"You sure will." I glance at her one last time before I walk into my office. I take my jacket off and set it aside before I sit at my desk and watch her. Shayla leaving is hitting me harder than I ever thought it would. It's like someone's just taken my security blanket away from me and kicked my arse out into the cold. I have to avoid going home for a few days until her scent and all traces of her disappear out of my apartment, but then I don't want it to.

Ah, I want to scream, why won't my mind just shut the hell up! I exhale and shake my head, forcing myself to focus on the work in front of me, but my eyes lift to her again. She's packed up her desk and is now hugging everyone. Heather is crying, never seen her cry in all the years she's worked here. This office is going to be so depressing once she's gone.

Shayla turns and looks at me through the window. Our eyes meet, and when I see tears roll down her cheeks, everything in my being hurt so fucking much.

I clench my jaw tight. My fingers were trembling, so I fist them to stop myself from walking over there and holding onto her for dear life. Shayla kisses her index and middle fingers and presses them over her heart. I kiss mine and press it to mine, and we nod. My eyes burn as I blink back the tears. That was a gesture we did when we were in Nice while we were making love. Shayla had taken my fingers, kissed them, and placed them over her heart. It was so sweet and so meaningful that I kissed her till I hadn't a breath left in me. It was just a silent way of us telling each other that we cared deeply for one another.

Shayla will forever hold a special place in my heart.

I bite the inside of my cheek when she picks up her box and flowers and walks away. I sit up and almost went after her to at least walk her to her car, but I couldn't. I honestly couldn't handle saying goodbye to her again. Once she disappeared, I push the button, frosting the glass looking into my office. I rush over to the bathroom in my office. I grip the side of the basin and look at myself in the mirror. "Let her go," I whisper through clenched teeth. "Let her go." I close my eyes and finally let the tears fall free. Was this it? Was it over just like that?

I shake my head and go after her. I can't leave it like this, I can't. Not with her. I race out of the office, not even caring if my employees watched me, and looked up at the numbers at the top of the elevator. She's on the 20th floor. I can still make it if I hurry. I run to the stairs and take them two at a time till I get to the car park. I see her standing by her car. She's talking to someone on the phone, her voice echoing in the parking lot.

"I'm done Aimee, this nightmare is finally over. After our divorce tomorrow I'm finally free. I can be myself again. Do you have any idea how hard it's been for me the last six months? Taking shit left and right from his family and the media. I just kept burying that crap and pretending like I was okay when I wasn't. I did what was expected of me. I kept my promise. That weight I've been carrying on my shoulders has finally lifted, and I feel like I can breathe again. After tomorrow, I'm free of him." I hear her say, and I close my eyes.

I knew she was miserable. I just knew it. The façade she had put on would slip from time to time, and I could see the sadness in her eyes for being stuck in this situation, but I chose to ignore it for my own selfish reasons. As much as I care deeply for her, she doesn't want to be in my life and couldn't wait to get away from me, and I have to respect that. I sigh and stand behind a pillar and watch her as she gets in the car and drives off. I close my eyes and press my head back against the pillar swallowing the lump forming in my throat.

It's over.

I SAT AT MY DESK, staring at her empty one. So many memories flash through my mind's eye. There was one day where I was annoying her constantly by pushing the buzzer until she got so angry she pulled the plug off the wall and flipped me off. Or the day she spilled coffee all over us, and we had to shower in my office before anyone got here. I have so many memories with her, and I'll carry every single one in my heart forever.

I couldn't breathe in that office. I drove around the city aimlessly for a while, not wanting to go home yet. Sophie is blowing up my phone with calls and texts— a habit of hers I absolutely loathe. If I don't answer, it means I'm busy or don't want to talk. Which right now, it's the latter. I just want to be alone. I put my phone on airplane mode and drove—a million thoughts on my mind. I find a quiet little venue and sit at the bar. "Scotch," I utter stonily. "Leave the bottle." I sigh and pour myself a double and sip it. That first sip felt like heaven. I don't want to feel anything tonight. Halfway through the bottle, I sense someone sidle up beside me.

"Hi," I don't even look up from the glass I'm currently staring into. "You look as though you could use a drinking partner there, darling."

"I'm managing perfectly fine on my own, thank you," I speak frostily. I lift my gaze and look at the young woman sitting beside me, and I sigh, licking my lips. "Does this look like the face of someone who wants to be bothered?" I scowl at her, and she scoffs and scampers off, muttering under her breath. I finish off the bottle and walk to my car. I can't drive like this. I curse and unlock my phone and while I fumble to find Josh's number. I accidentally pull up a photo of Shayla and me and stare at it. She's grinning at the camera, and I'm laughing with my forehead pressed to her temple.

She had made some stupid joke just before she took the picture that made me laugh till I was crying.

I sit on the curb flicking through photos on my phone of her, of us, and my insides ache. I hadn't realised how attached I became to her over the six months. I send a text to Josh with my location and ask him to pick me up. Whilst I was waiting for him to arrive, I stare at Shay's number, wondering if I should call her just to hear her voice. I miss her so fucking much.

"Cole? What the hell, man? What are you doing out in the damn sticks?" He asks, perching down in front of me. I blink up at him from my reclined position on the floor.

"I was driving and driving, and then I was here. Shall we have a drink? Come on, lemme buy you a drink." I slur, and Josh helps me up to my feet.

"I think you've had enough to drink for the both of us, mate. What were you thinking, getting yourself in this state?" He scolds me while dragging me to his mustang. I fall into the passenger seat, and Josh shakes his head.

"I wanted to not feel." I smile at him, and he frowns. "It didn't work. I still feel everything."

Josh gets into his car, and we drive. "Not feel what? Did you and Sophie break up again or something?" I scoff and shake my head.

"No. No, we're good," I mumble, waving my hand and chuckle.

"So, what's got you in this state bro? Shouldn't you be with her right now?" Josh asks, giving me a side glance before looking ahead again.

"Nah, bro. Sophie is awesome, and I love her so fucking much, but she's just…" I sigh longingly and shake my head and lift my phone and look at the photo of Shayla. "She's not her."

Josh rolls his eyes, shaking his head, "Jesus, Cole. I thought you decided you were letting this Shayla thing go man?"

"I am!" I shout angrily. "She fucking left. She left work, she's left home, she's leaving me tomorrow!" I groan and turn my head to look at Josh. "Will you take me to her?"

Josh laughs, shaking his head. "No. You show up at her door like this, she's going to think you're a moron. The only place you're going right now is to bed, my friend. You need to sleep it off. You're going to see her tomorrow anyway. You can tell her whatever you need to tell her there." He explains, and I groan, staring out of his window up at the black sky.

An hour later, Josh carries, half drags me through my apartment to my bedroom. "No, no, no," I mumble, pointing at Shayla's bedroom. "In there." Josh nods and carries me over to her bed, and drops me down on it. The whole room still smelt like her, and it made my heart clench hard, especially when I hug her pillow and sniff it. Coconut and passion fruit. "Mmm Shay." I moan before I drift off to sleep.

~

THE NEXT MORNING, I woke up to a dry mouth and thumping headache. I roll onto my back and peel my eyes open. I blink and stare up at the ceiling. It took a long moment for my memory to come flooding back from last night. I sit up when I remember the divorce hearing was today. I lean over and look at the time. Shit, I had less than an hour to get ready and make my way down to the courthouse. I force myself up off the bed, my head was thumping terribly, so I took a couple of pain killers and had a hot shower. I still felt like shit, but at least the headache was down to a dull ache and more tolerable.

I slide on my shades as I walk into the courthouse and find Franc inside, waiting by the entrance. "Oh, Mr Hoult, there you are. I thought you weren't going to show up." Franc tells me, and I nod, looking around.

"I was running a little late. Is Shayla here already?" I ask my eyes scanning the area, but she was nowhere to be seen.

"Yes, she is here. She's gone to get a coffee." My stomach drops in disappointment. A small part of me was wishing she hadn't shown up. I sit on the leather chairs and close my eyes. I hear the clinking of heels, and I open my eyes and see Shayla walking toward us, two cups of coffee in her hand. Ahh damn, she's so fucking beautiful it hurts. She was in a plain black formal dress, her hair straightened and neat.

"Morning." She greets me with a small smile. She looks tired, like she hadn't slept much last night. She must have had a good night out, celebrating her freedom.

"Morning," I reply with a nod. Shayla drops her gaze briefly and holds out a steaming cup of coffee to me.

"Here, I got this for you." I push the shades down my nose and look at her, then the cup of coffee in her hand. "You don't wake up till you've had your second cup of coffee."

I smile gratefully and take the cup from her hand. "Thank you."

"Mr Tristan and Mrs Shayla Hoult?" Shayla and I both look at one another then back at the lady calling our names. I rub my forehead, and Franc gestures for us to follow him. Shayla and I walk side by side into the courtroom. I glance at her through my shades and notice she's chewing her bottom lip anxiously. She's probably itching to get this over with already.

We take our places, and the judge walks in and takes his seat. Shayla and I sat opposite each other while Franc stands in the middle of the room, speaking to the judge.

"All right, this looks like a nice and easy divorce." The judge says, flicking through the paperwork. "Grounds of divorce, cultural differences." He closes the papers and sighs, looking at Shayla first, then at me for a moment. "The paperwork is all in order, but I am obliged to ask one last time, are you both sure you would like to go through with the divorce?"

I stare at the table hard, and Shay's words from yesterday replay in my mind over and over again. "Yes, your honour." I force myself to say and lift my gaze and see Shayla staring at the wall opposite.

"And you, Mrs Hoult?"

She clears her throat and nods, "Yes, your honour." I bite the inside of my cheek, and we stare at one another.

"Very well. Seen as you both agree and there's nothing to settle, I am granting your divorce." I look at the judge and shake my head with a frown.

"Wait, there must have been some mistake. There is a settlement of two million." I tell him, and the judge looks at the paper in front of him and back at me again, bewildered.

"Not according to the paper your wife has signed relinquishing any rights to a settlement, Mr Hoult." The judge says, and I look over at Shayla, who keeps her gaze on the floor. "Has there been a mistake, Mrs Hoult?"

She shakes her head and looks at him. "No, your honour, that is correct."

"Excellent. Then I hereby announce that you are divorced. You're free to go." He declares, getting up and walking off.

I walk around the table I was sitting at and catch Shayla's arm as she tries to walk off. "What the fuck Shayla?! Why would you do that? I thought we settled this already?" Shayla looks at her arm and back at me before she pulls it out of my hold, sighing.

"Cole, I was never going to take that money. You refused to listen when I told you I didn't want it. I don't need it." She explains, licking her lips. "You gave me no other choice but to go behind your back and sign the papers." I frown and shake my head in disbelief.

"So, you did all of this for nothing. What the hell did you get out of this then, Shayla?" I question, irritated, gesturing between us, and she shrugs and stares at my tie for a long moment before she lifts her gaze to me again.

"Who said it was for nothing? I gave you my word, and I kept it. That might not mean anything to you, Cole, but to me, it means everything." She tells me, her sincerity radiating in her green eyes. "Look, I'm sorry I had to go behind your back. I didn't do it to hurt you or get one over on you. I honestly don't want it Cole, I don't. If you really want to do something, take that money, and give it to those who really need it. Be the guy who leaves his mark by making a difference in the world. However, big or small that difference may be." I stare into her eyes, and she smiles, but it doesn't reach her eyes. "I have to go." She whispers, and I reach out and take her hand in mine.

"Can I drive you anywhere?" I offer, but she shakes her head.

"No. I drove here, so I'm good." She replies, looking into my eyes, and I can see them watering. She reaches up and brushes her fingers along my jaw. "You were a good fake husband." She smiles. I wrap my fingers around her wrist as she's about to pull it away and kiss her fingers before I press them over my heart. Shayla's bottom lip quivers, and tears spill from her eyes and roll down her cheeks.

"Cole." She whispers, and I press my forehead to hers, closing my eyes.

"Shayla." I breathe, brushing my nose over hers as I used to.

"I've got to go." She sighs, pulling away and looks at me one last time. "I'm glad I met you, Tristan Cole Hoult." She whispers, walking back, and I squeeze her hand, shaking my head.

"I'm glad I met you too, Shayla Hart." She pulls her hand back and whispers goodbye, and walks away from me for the last time. I watch as she disappears out the front entrance, and I sigh, closing my eyes, my heart slowly sinking to the pit of my stomach. "Goodbye"

I feel someone squeeze my shoulder, and I look back and see it was Franc. "That is one remarkable woman." He says, and I nod, staring at the door, silently wishing she would come back. She didn't. She came into my life like a whirlwind and left in the same manner.

When I went back home later that day, it felt empty and hollow as my chest did. I walk to her bedroom and look around. All traces of her are gone. I walk over to her dresser, where she left her diamond engagement ring sitting in the box. I pick it up and stare at it for a long time before I hurl it across the room and watch as it hits the wall and falls to the floor.

I was aching in places I didn't even know was possible.

Later that evening, while I sat out on my terrace, staring absent-mindedly out at the view, my phone rings. I snatch it up, thinking it was her, but it wasn't. It was my mother.

"Mum, can I call you tomorrow? I—"

"Sweetie, it's Grandpop. He's not doing so well." She sniffles. "They just called me from the hospital. They're saying he won't make it through the night."

Oh, no, no. I can't handle another loss today.

"I'm on my way."

Ten minutes later, I was rushing through the hospital toward his private room and stop dead in my tracks when I see Shayla sitting there by his bedside. She's reading a book to him while he listens to her, hooked up to a ventilator and heart monitor. What was she doing here?

"Excuse me? Are you a relative of Joe's?" An older nurse questions when she saw me lurking in the doorway.

"Yes, I'm his grandson," I answer, not taking my eyes off Shayla as she continues to read to him.

"Ah, you must be Shayla's husband, Cole. Joe speaks very fondly of you and your wife. She's such a sweetheart. She's been coming here three times a week; she sits and reads to him." I turn my gaze to the nurse.

"How long has she been coming to read to him?"

The nurse looks thoughtful for a moment, "Um, just over a month now."

"Tristan?" I hear my mother's voice approaching. I press my fingers to my lips, telling her to be quiet. "What is it?" She looks into the room and frowns. "Is that Shayla? What is she doing here, didn't you get divorced today?" She questions in a flurry drying her eyes.

"Apparently, she's been coming here and reading to him a couple of times a week." My mother looks at her and back up at me.

"His memory is very intermittent, sometimes he knows who she is, and other times he thinks she's his late wife." The nurse explains as she watches on sadly. "Bless her. She just goes along with it to keep him happy."

"My goodness. I can't even believe that after the way I've treated her, she could be so…selfless."

I nod, keeping my eyes on Shayla, and I feel my heart swell. "That's Shayla for you, always putting others before herself," I whisper and watch while she wipes away a tear that rolls down her cheeks. I walk into the room, and she looks up and stops reading when she sees my parents and me in the room.

"Maisie, why did you stop, dear?" My grandfather croaks, looking adoringly at Shayla, who looks at me and shrugs, her eyes watering. I walk over to her and press a lingering kiss to her forehead.

"Grandpop, that's not Grandma. It's Shayla. You remember, Shayla, my wife." I say, perching down by his bedside, but he shakes his head smiling.

"No, no, that's my Maisie. I would never forget her angelic face. Look dear, our little Tristan is here to see us." My grandfather says, reaching out, he takes Shayla's hand into his.

"Hallucinations are usually common when it's time for them to pass." The nurse explains, and I hear my mother sobbing in the back.

"Let's go home Maisie, I'm ready to come home." I look up at Shayla, her lip quivers, and she nods.

"Okay, we'll go home together, and I'll finish reading to you." She tells him, her voice quivering.

"My beautiful Maise…" He whispers, and the machines beep, and the monitor shows a flatline. My mother's scream of despair at watching her father die and Shayla's sobbing was enough to wreck me. The doctors come in, call the time of death and begin unhooking him from all the machines. No matter how much you prepare yourself for this moment, it still hits like a wrecking ball to the gut. When the doctors tried to pry his hand away from Shayla's, I broke down because, in his mind, he was holding onto his wife's hand, who he loved with every bit of his heart.

My head fell into Shayla's lap while I sobbed uncontrollably, and she cradles me in her arms, mourning the death of my grandfather with me.

At that moment, the only person I wanted by my side was her. She's all I needed.

Chapter Twenty-Seven

SHAYLA

IS THERE a pain worse than watching the man you're in love with break down in your arms after losing someone he loves dearly?

This was the man he looked up to growing up, and he just watched him die right in front of his eyes. The way his head fell into my lap and his heartfelt sobs would haunt me for an awfully long time. Grandpa Joe held my hand so tight they hand to pry his fingers from mine. I couldn't suppress the whimper that escaped me, especially when I heard Elaine's screams of despair over losing her father. I know that feeling all too well. Grandpa Joe died surrounded by his children and grandchildren; even if he didn't recognise any of them, in the end, he died in peace with the image of the love of his life before his eyes.

Someone once told me that right before you die, the angel of death appears to you as the person you love the most, and to Grandpa Joe, that was Grandma Maisie. I may have only met him a couple of months ago, but I grew to love him just as I did my own grandfather.

I rub the back of Cole's neck while his body shook with hoarse sobs, and it honestly broke my already wrecked heart. I brush my fingers through his hair soothingly, and his arms tighten around me. I lean over and whisper in his ear. "They're going to take him away soon. Say your goodbye." He shook his head, sobbing.

"I can't,"

"You'll regret it if you don't," I tell him, lifting his head so I could look into his face. I brush his tears away, but more just followed.

"He's gone, Shay. He can't even hear me." He whispers woefully, and I shake my head.

"You don't know that. I'm sure he can hear you." I tell him earnestly, and he looks over at his grandfather. "I'll give you and your family some privacy," I say and try to get up, but he shakes his head.

"No, please don't go. Let's say goodbye together." I nod, and he laces his fingers with mine and turns to face his grandfather. He takes his hand into his and inhales a deep breath. "Grandpop, you were and will always be my idol. You taught me everything I know, and I'll cherish all those times I spent with you and Grandma for as long as I live. I'll continue to make you proud. I promise. I love you." He says and presses a kiss to his hand. "Tell Grandma I love her too. I'll miss you, Grandpop."

I rub Coles back soothingly and lean in close so I could say goodbye to him too, "I wish I knew you sooner, Grandpa Joe. I'm glad I met you and got to spend some quality time with you. Even if it was short, I'm going to miss our time together. We never got to finish our book, and who's going to sing Frank Sinatra to me now?" I sniffle, brushing my fingers over his soft cheek. I sigh. "You're an incredible man, and you'll live on in our hearts forever. And don't you forget your promise to me, okay, you tell Grandma Maisie I want to meet her someday." I smile sadly, and Cole takes my hand and places it with his over Grandpa Joe's hand, "Until we meet again, Grandpa." I whisper, and I play the song he requested when he did pass. 'My Way by Frank Sinatra' Cole presses his forehead to Grandpa Joe's hand and sobs along with the rest of the family.

I look up when I see Elaine come up beside Cole, and I slip away when she hugs him and let them grieve privately, together as a family. I stood in the doorway and watched them say their goodbye. It was so heart wrenching to watch, and a little voice in my head kept telling me I didn't belong there, but my heart wouldn't allow me to leave Cole when he was hurting. I pushed aside my own woes and was there for him, not because I had to be, but because I wanted to be.

I walk to the vending machine at the end of the corridor to get something to drink, but I just stood there staring at it blankly. "Shayla?" I blink and jump out of my trance. I look back and see Elaine standing behind me.

"Mrs Hoult, I'm so sorry for your loss. I know all too well how it feels to lose your father." She sighs and dabs a tissue to the endless tears that fell from her eyes.

"Thank you, dear, and you can call me Elaine." She says, and I stare at her, surprised, and sigh. "Would you spare me a couple of minutes to talk?" I nod and gesture to the seats by the vending machine, and we sit together. "First of all, I want to apologise to you for the way I treated you throughout your marriage to my son. You turned out to be the complete opposite of everything I thought you'd be. I honestly thought you were using my son for a quick pay-out, but I watched you with Tristan, and I realised that I might have been wrong. My suspicions were confirmed when I got a call from Franc, and he told me you signed away any rights to a settlement and walked away without a penny." She bites her lip and sighs.

"He also explained that when he asked you why, you said you would never take money you didn't earn, and that money rightfully belonged to him through all the hard work he and my husband put into the company." I nod and look down when she places her hands over mine and squeezes them. "I misjudged you, and for that, I'm terribly sorry, Shayla. My son adores you, and so did my father. I really hope you can find it in your heart to forgive me?"

I lift my gaze to hers and nod, "Of course. I appreciate the apology. My marriage to your son may not have lasted, but you were right. We're too different, and I don’t fit into his world, but I do care for him deeply and wish him nothing but happiness in whatever he chooses to do next." I explain, blinking back the tears that I feel burning the back of my eyelids. “Cole is a wonderful man.”

Elaine smiles sadly and pats my hand, "You're an incredibly unique girl Shayla Hart, and the love and respect you've shown my father in his last moments will forever have a special place in my heart." She sighs, wiping away her tears. "You'll come to the funeral, right?"

"I'd like to if that's okay with you?" I ask bashfully, biting my bottom lip, and she smiles.

"Of course, you will be there. I would have it no other way." I smile a little and nod gratefully. "Would you mind if I give you a hug?" I look at her, surprised, and shook my head. She wraps her arms around me and hugs me tight, her hands brushing my hair. "Good luck with your future, and if you ever need anything, you can reach out to my family or me, always. And thank you for being here for both my father and my son today." She declares sweetly, pulling back and looking at me.

I wipe away the tears the spillover my cheeks and nod. "Thank you, Elaine," I watch her as she gets up and walks off down the corridor.

~

AFTER I ATTEMPT to pull myself together, I go back to where everyone else was standing, and I look around for Cole but don't see him. I wonder if he's left as I walk through the corridor and find him around the corner, his arms around Sophie, who is consoling him. Watching him with her, I honestly didn't think my heart could break any more than it already has. My vision blurs with tears that pool in my eyes when she kisses him. I slip away before anyone sees me, and I walk away, my insides bleeding. The only way I could describe how I was feeling at that moment was wanting to scream; my lungs felt like they were on fire as I hurry out of the hospital to get oxygen. I was slowly suffocating like someone was siphoning the life right out of me.

I throw myself into the car and drive off, away from the hospital, away from him.

As I park up my car at my apartment, my phone rings.' ***Cole calling…'*** flashes across my screen. I pick up the phone and stare at his name, and hot tears roll down my already pale cheeks. "Let me go." I whimper sobbing. "Please, Cole, let me go." I'm so tired of hurting. He's with his girlfriend. What does he still want from me? I don't understand. Can he not see how hard all of this is for me?

I turn my phone off and walk up to my apartment. I walk in and collapse onto the sofa, utterly drained. "Shay?" I open my eyes and look over at Jo, who frowns and walks over to me. "What's wrong?"

I sigh and shake my head, "Cole's grandfather just passed away right in front of me." I explain. Jo takes my hand and sits next to me.

"The one you've been reading too. Oh no, that's so sad." She says, brushing my hair away from my face. "Was Cole there?" I nod.

"He was. It was awful, Jo, the way he collapsed into my arms and cried, I just…it broke me." I cry, reliving his pain. "His grandfather thought I was his wife, and his hand, held onto mine so tight the moment he passed away, they had to rip his hand off mine." I sob, and Jo covers her mouth with her hand, her eyes filling with tears. "I just keep replaying that moment over and over again, the way Cole's body shook, his anguished sobs, it all hit me so hard."

"Oh, babe, come here." Jo pulls me so I could lay my head in her lap. She brushes her fingers through my hair while I cry, explaining everything that happened with his mother and Sophie showing up.

"I went looking for him to make sure he was okay, and there he was in *her* arms while she consoled him, and I just stood there like an idiot, frozen, unable to move, while I watch her kissing him." I sigh dejectedly and close my eyes. "Knowing they're together is one thing, but seeing it right in front of you, that hurt more than I could have ever imagined." I sob helplessly.

"Shayla, in all our years of friendship, I have never seen you so utterly broken. Even after Adam broke your heart, you weren't this bad." She says, looking down at me. "You're in love with him, aren't you?" I stay silent, and she sighs, "Shay, don't keep your feelings bottled up. Just admit to it, and maybe that ache inside of you will lessen a little. You don't have to go through this on your own. Aimee and I are here for you all the way."

"Damn right we are," Aimee confirms, stepping into the living room and walks over to us. She kneels in front of me and takes my hand in hers, her blue eyes watching me sadly. "Jo's right Shayla, just admit it out loud, and maybe you can start to heal."

I sniffle and sigh, closing my eyes, "I am in love with him, but I don't want to be. I don't regret a single moment I had with him, but I don't want to love him. I don't want to hurt anymore. I just want to forget about him."

"Shayla, I think he—" Aimee stops when she hears a knock at the door. "Who the hell is that at this time?" She asks, getting up to her feet and walking to the door to answer it. She pulls the door open, and Jo and I hear her utter an 'oh'. "Uh…Shayla." I sit up and wipe the tears from my cheeks and walk over to the door.

There he stood.

All six-foot-four of him, looking just as wrecked as I was feeling. Our eyes meet, and he looks at me and shrugs before he walks in and pulls me into his arms, burying his face into my neck. "I can't breathe. I feel like everything is closing in around me." He cries. "Can I stay with you tonight?" I look over at Aimee, who places her hand on her chest, her eyes filling with tears.

"Of course," I whisper, wrapping my arms around his neck, and he squeezes me tightly. Why does he keep doing this to me, and why do I keep letting him? Why can't he just let me go? We pull apart, and I close the door once he walks into my apartment. He greets the girls with a nod, and they both walk over and hug him, which he returns.

"We're so sorry for your loss Cole," Jo says when they pull away from the hug. Cole nods and shrugs.

"Thanks, girls, and I'm sorry to show up like this. I just couldn't bear being alone tonight." Aimee and Jo both nod in understanding.

"Of course, you can stay as long as you need to," Aimee tells him, and he smiles gratefully and looks over at me.

"Shall we go to my room?" I suggest, and he nods silently. I walk down the corridor to my bedroom, and he follows me closely. We walk in, and he strolls over to my bed and sits down, leans over, and puts his head in his hands as I close the door behind me and lean against it looking at him. I was unsure of what to do at that moment. My instincts tell me to walk over and hold him, but I can't. He has a girlfriend now. Something that came so naturally to us was now so strenuous, and that hurt.

Cole lifts his head and looks at me, his green eyes rimmed red and woeful. "You left." He whispers, his voice hoarse after hours of crying.

I sigh and drop my gaze to conceal the tears I felt coming, "I thought I'd give you and your family some time to grieve in private." I lie and bite my bottom lip. "Also, you had Sophie there with you. I didn't want her to see me there and give you a load of grief on top of what you're dealing with," I explain with a shrug, and Cole nods and drops his gaze also. "Shouldn't you be with *her* right now?"

Cole shrugs, licking his lips, "After we left the hospital, she told me to go back to hers, but I just wanted to be on my own. I love the girl, but she wouldn't know grief if it slapped her in the face. She just kept telling me that I'll be fine, that Grandpa lived a full life, and he would hate to see me so miserable," He explains, massaging his forehead agitatedly. "It wasn't making me feel better at all. It's not what I needed to hear, plus Grandpa never warmed to her. They never got along, so she couldn't even relate to what I was going through." I nod, and he lifts his eyes to mine, and he sighs. "I was driving home and somehow found myself here. I sat outside your building for over an hour, debating whether I should come up or not, then I found myself at your door." He clarifies.

"It's stupid, I know, but the longer I was alone, the harder it was to breathe, and the only place I knew I could find any peace was with you."

I shake my head and watch as his head falls, "It's not stupid at all." I say, shuffling over to him. I stand in front of him and lift his head so he could look at me. "In the short time we've known each other, we've been through quite a lot together, plus I was there with you when he passed away, so I know how you feel," I explain, brushing his tears away as they roll down his cheeks.

Cole reaches up, places his hands at my hips, and pulls me closer, so I stand between his legs. "In one day, I lost you and my Grandpa, the two people who meant a lot to me." He utters sorrowfully, his voice breaking. I close my eyes when he wraps his arms around my waist and presses his forehead to my stomach. I circle my arms around his head and cradle it against me.

"Cole, don't talk like that," I whisper, and he pulls his head back and looks up at me.

"It's true, though. After tonight I'll probably never see you again." He sighs, nibbling his bottom lip.

"Cole," I plead with him, and his shoulders fall. "Listen to me, my presence in your life was always going to be temporary," I explain with a sigh. "You're only struggling because we spent so much time together at work and home, but give it a week or so, and you'll go back to your old life before you know it, and I'll just be someone you used to know," I tell him, and he looks up into my eyes, shaking his head.

"That's not true at all. You're not just 'someone' Shayla, not to me." He sighs dejectedly, and when I stay quiet, he bites his lip. "Why do you have to go? Why can't we just be friends? I don't want to lose you completely." He questions sadly, and I feel my stomach tighten at the word 'friends.'

"Cole, being friends with me won't help your relationship with Sophie, trust me. And too much has happened between us for that even to be a possibility."

Cole sighs, "You mean us sleeping together."

I nod, "Exactly, you said it yourself. We can't be just friends, Cole." He tries to interject, but I press my fingers to his lips, and he watches me. "Look at us, is this how two friends hold each other," I whisper, and he shakes his head, his eyes never leaving mine.

I brush my fingers along his jaw. "Is this how two friends look at one another." He shakes his head again, those green eyes flicker down to my lips and back up to my eyes again. "Is it still a friendship if we can still remember just the way the other tastes." Cole stares at my lips and swallows hard. I curl my fingers at the nape of his neck and press my forehead to his. "How could you think I'd be your friend," I whisper to him, closing my eyes. I bite back the tears, just itching to fall. "You have to let me go, Cole, *please*," I beg him miserably.

"I'm trying, Shay, believe me, *I'm trying."* He breathes, sweeping his nose over mine. "It's just so hard. I think I have feel—"

I shake my head and cover his mouth with my hand. "No. Don't. Please don't." I sigh, looking at him pleadingly, and he pulls my hand away from his mouth. "You're upset and looking for comfort, that's all. I'm just comfort for you. We've done this Cole, we both know how it's going to end. Sophie loves you, she up and left her fiancé for you because you told her you're still in love with her, now you owe it to her to give it a real go." I explain, taking a step back from him, but he grabs my arm and pulls me down into his lap, encircling his arm around my waist, securing me.

"I wish we could go back to the day we were in here packing you up to move in with me." He expresses, combing his fingers through my hair while I look at him. "This isn't me. I have no idea when I became this guy. I'm stuck between both of you, and I don't know what to do." He explains with a heavy sigh. "I love her with all my heart, I do. But I want you too." I drop my gaze from his and shake my head.

"You said it yourself, Cole, you love her with all your heart. I was always the interim girl, not *the* girl. You're confusing yourself by over-thinking what we had. It was just attraction, sexual chemistry, it was new and exciting, but all those feelings fade eventually. What you have with Sophie is real, okay, you made the right choice. You and I, we don't make any sense." I tell him and break out of his hold before standing up, putting some space between us. "This is why we can't be friends because it's confusing for both of us. So, after tonight when you walk out of that door, you leave me behind you, and you walk away… for good."

"Shayla—" Cole stands and steps closer to me, and I back away, shaking my head.

"—I don't want to see you anymore, Cole," I tell him coldly, keeping the emotion out of my voice hoping he finally understands that I'm serious. We stare at one another, and he shakes his head.

"You're a shitty liar." He states, taking a step toward me.

"I mean it."

"No, you don't." He replies, taking another step.

"Yes, I do," I whisper craning my neck to look up at him as he towers over me.

"Then why wait till tomorrow. I'll walk out of your life right now then, shall I?" He suggests, and I keep my eyes on his and shrug.

"Do whatever makes you happy."

Cole nods, licking his lips, "Fine."

"Fine." I gasp when Cole grabs my face with one hand and pulls me to him, fusing our lips. I moan when his tongue glides over mine, deepening the kiss. It took a couple of minutes before my hazy mind realised what was happening, and I pull away breathless and look at him. "What the hell did you do that for?" I breathe, and he looks at me and shrugs.

"You said, do whatever makes you happy. That makes me happy." He justifies, and I gape at him before I shove him away from me.

"That's not what I meant Cole. You have a girlfriend now. You can't kiss me whenever you feel like it." I scold him shaking my head, and Cole sits back down on the bed.

"She kissed me when we were married, think of this as payback." I roll my eyes and glare at him.

"Payback? Do you think this is a bloody game? I'm not Sophie. I don't make a habit of kissing other girl's boyfriends."

"But you did." He tells me matter-of-factly, "You kissed me back, and don't you even try and deny it. I heard you moan."

"Oh my God, this is exactly what I meant by us not being able to be around each other, Cole." I groan, leaning back against the door. "You have to go."

Cole looks at me sadly and shakes his head. "No, you said tomorrow. I'm not walking away a minute sooner." I close my eyes and heave a sigh. This boy is going to drive me insane. I swear to God. "Shayla, come here." I shake my head, and he gets up, lifts me off the floor, and tosses me on the bed. He kicks his shoes off and gets on the bed with me. "I'm sorry I kissed you, that was way out of line, and you're right, you're nothing like Sophie. You would never do anything like that."

"No, I wouldn't, because I wouldn't want it done to me," I tell him, and he nods, biting his bottom lip looking remorseful.

"I know, I'm clearly not thinking straight. I'm sorry." He whispers, brushing my hair out of my face as we lay on my bed facing one another.

I sigh, licking my lips, "It's fine. It's done now."

"Will you do something for me?" He asks while his thumb massages my wrist. I nod, and his eyes search my face for a long moment before he speaks. "Will you read to me?"

I look at him, surprised but nod. "Sure, what would you like me to read to you?"

Tears gather in Cole's eyes, and he swallows hard, "The book you were reading Grandpop. Will you finish it off with me?" I nod and sit up. I reach over and pick up the book off my nightstand before opening it to where I left the bookmark. Cole lays his head in my lap, and I inhale deeply before I start reading to him, my fingers brushing through his hair as I read the remaining story of Tristan and Isolde.

"And Tristan answered, thank you, friend; this is my prayer: take this ring, it is a sign between her and me; and when you come to her land pass yourself at court for a merchant, and show her silk and stuffs, but make so that she sees the ring, for then she will find some ruse by which to speak to you in secret…."

Chapter Twenty-Eight

COLE

TWO WEEKS.

That's how long it's been since I walked away from Shayla after that night I spent with her. The last time I saw her was at Grandpop's funeral a week later. I didn't know she'd be there, so when I saw her, the emotions I'd been suppressing bubbles up again. She sat two rows behind me on the other side at the church. I kept looking back at her, and her eyes would find mine, and we'd stare at one another until she breaks eye contact and looks ahead. Sophie was stuck to my side the entire time, so I couldn't even speak to her properly, which fucked me off royally. After the burial, she disappeared without a word, and I still remember my gut twisting in disappointment. I made her a promise that I would let her be, and I'm trying to keep my word, but it's just so hard.

~

THAT MORNING I woke up in her arms. I must have fallen asleep while she read to me. I can see why Grandpop loved it when she read to him. Something is soothing about the way she reads that calms your mind and body. I stir awake, and the first thing I see is her angelic face. I can't even tell you how we ended up in this position with my face nuzzled in her neck, while her arms were wrapped around my head, her fingers curled in my hair. I lay as still as I could, just watching her sleep for a while.

How the fuck am I going to walk away from you for good.

Shayla eventually stirs in her sleep and opens her eyes. I close mine feigning sleep. I wasn't ready to say goodbye, not yet, and a part of me was curious to see if she would wake me or let me sleep as I had her. Even with my eyes closed, I can feel her watching me, she brushes her fingers through my hair, and I resist the urge to shiver. When she presses her lips to my forehead, it made me ache significantly. I open my eyes and wrap my arm around her waist, drawing her closer against me, and she tightens hers around me with a sigh. "Cole, your phone is vibrating." She tells me, and I shrug in response.

"So, let it," I mumble, nuzzling her neck. Fuck how is it possible to smell this good all the damn time? It's a mixture of laundry detergent, her sweet vanilla perfume, and her shampoo. If I could package that smell and take it with me, I honestly would.

"It could be important, Cole." I shake my head. Nothing is more important than being in her arms right now.

"It's not," I sigh, rubbing her hip with my thumb. When she gives me a pointed look, I groan and reach for my phone and see Sophie's name flashing across the screen. I curse my fate when Shayla sees her name and pulls herself away from me.

"You can get it if you want. I'll leave the room." She offers, shifting off the bed, but I sit up and catch her arm before she can get up completely.

"It can wait, Shay. I'll call her later." I say, and Shayla stares at me with a forlorn look on her face.

"Cole, this isn't right." She utters, pulling her arm out of my hold and shoving her fingers through her hair.

I blink up at her, confused, "What isn't?"

"This…*us*," She answers. "Sharing a bed. Waking up the way we did, the kiss, everything. It's not fair to Sophie. If my boyfriend spent the night and was waking up wrapped in his ex-wife's arms, I'd be devastated." I watch her as she paces up and down the room, then she stops and looks at me. "Cole, you've got to go."

I stand up and walk over to her, but she backs away, shaking her head, "You're kicking me out?" I question.

Shayla sighs, shutting her eyes, "Deep down, you know this isn't right too. You should be with her. You should be waking up with her, not me. The media are all over us at the moment. All it takes is one photo to get leaked, and how will you explain it to her, Cole? To everyone?" She questions, and all I could do was look at her. She was right. But I just can't control myself around her. Shayla opens her bedroom door; her eyes cast down. "You should go." She whispers.

I was hurt that she would kick me out like that. Is this how we're going to say goodbye? I nod and walk out of her bedroom. Shayla follows me to the front door, but I don't even look back. I open the door and step out without a word, and pull the door shut hard behind me. I lean back against it and close my eyes, biting my lip hard. Thirty seconds later, I turn around and knock on the door. Shayla opens it not even a second later. We stood still for a moment looking at one another, before I take a giant step toward her and wrap my arms around her waist, pulling her in for a hug at the same time as Shayla wraps her arms around my neck, and I lift her off the ground, burying my face into her neck. We hold each other tightly, neither of us wanting to pull apart.

Shayla pulls her head back while I lift mine and press my forehead to hers. "I'll never be sorry," I whisper to her, and she shakes her head.

"Me either." She whispers, and I kiss her forehead before I set her back down to her feet. "Goodbye, Tristan Cole Hoult." She whispers gazing up at me.

I bite my lip, "I'll see you, Shayla Hart." We share one last look before I turn and keep my promise to her. With a heavy heart, I walk away and leave her behind me. I cried the whole drive home. The heaviness in my chest grew the further away I got from her.

Adjusting to life without her has been challenging. I threw myself into work much like I did before I met her. I took on project after project, flew all around the world to keep myself distracted so that I wouldn't think about her.

I put all my energy into my relationship with Sophie, and it was going well. Day's drug on, nights even longer when I lay in bed with Sophie and

Shayla's face creeps into my mind, or I dream about her. I wonder what she's doing at least a hundred times a day. I miss her terribly, her laugh, her voice, her smell, the way she would glare at me when I annoyed her, and I wonder if she misses me too or if she even thinks about me. I want to call her. I get tempted, and my finger hovers over her name on my phone before I toss it aside and groan.

One month goes by, then two, then three, but the gaping hole Shayla has left in my life doesn't seem to be disappearing.

"Baby?" I look over at Sophie, who smiles at me lovingly. "What are you thinking about. You look as though your miles away." She questions and I shake my head. I reach over and take her hand, kissing her knuckles.

"Nothing, babe, I was just thinking how beautiful the day was." I lie with a smile, and she returns my smile and rubs her thumb over mine. 'If you leave me now' by Chicago comes on the radio, and I lean over and turn the volume up. I get flashes of the day Shayla and I were singing the lyrics to one another. We'd belt this out together whenever it came on in the car. I smile fondly at the memory.

"If you leave me now, you'll take away the very heart of me." I sing along quietly.

Sophie looks over at me before leaning over and turning the volume down to the song. "My God, what is this stupid song you're listening to." I watch her as she pulls down the visor and attempts to fix her hair. I turn the music off with a sigh. "Oh sweetie, there's this yacht party Saturday. We're going, right?" I stare at the road ahead, and I nod mutely. I tune her out when she starts babbling on about the people attending this party.

~

AN HOUR LATER, I'm sitting at the dinner table at Sophie's parent's house, and I'm listening to her Dad drone on and on about how well his business is doing. I never met a more tedious and self-centered man in my life, he talks, and I literally fall asleep with my eyes open. I mastered that technique when I was dating Sophie previously.

After the slowest dinner ever, Sophie and I drove back to my place. I'm currently stood out on my terrace, looking out at the city before me, sipping on a scotch. I don't usually drink much, but lately, a couple of glasses of scotch a night seems to help take the edge off, and I can get some sleep. I start out of my thoughts when I feel Sophie's arms wrap around me from behind. I turn around and look at her, her beautiful blue eyes gazing up at me lovingly. She was dressed in sexy lingerie, a red lacy number that shows off her slender figure.

"Hi," She breathes, wrapping her arms around my neck.

"Hey." I greet, brushing her shoulder-length blonde hair off her shoulder before I wrap my arms around her, drawing her against me. "You look beautiful."

Sophie smiles up at me, sultrily, "Oh yeah, maybe you should take me to bed then, stud." She whispers, leaning in to kiss me, but I freeze when she calls me 'stud.' That's what Shayla used to call me. I shake off the thoughts of her and meet Sophies waiting lips. She moans when I swipe my tongue along her bottom lip before I dip my tongue into her mouth seeking out her own.

My brain does this weird thing where it flickers, and I taste Shayla's lips and hear her breathy moans. "Cole..." Wait. Sophie doesn't call me that. *Shayla.* I groan and toss the glass in my hand aside, and bruise her lips with an ardent kiss. I lift her into my arms, lips still locked, and walk to my bedroom. I lay her down on my bed and look down at her with heavy-lidded eyes, her gorgeous green eyes watching me. Her fingers begin unbuttoning my shirt, and she pushes it off my shoulders before she leans up and brushes her luscious lips over mine.

"Fuck, baby, I've missed you like crazy." I breathe into her mouth, and she moans, flicking her tongue over mine teasingly while her hands trail down my back, leaving a trail of fire behind. I pull back a little panting, and she whimpers in protest when I stop kissing her. My fingers find the clips holding her outfit together, and I tear it open with a growl. She grins up at me, panting. I let my eyes roam over her natural breasts and lean down, taking a hardened nipple into my mouth and sucking it hard just like she loves. She arches up into my mouth and cries out, her slender fingers curling into my hair as I leave open-mouthed kisses down her stomach, to my most favourite part. I keep my eyes on her as I spread her legs open.

She lifts her head and looks down at me, her chest rising and falling with every quick breath she took. I run my tongue torturously slow up her slit relishing in her taste. I moan throatily and hold her hips as she rocks her pussy against my tongue, seeking more contact.

"Colee…" She whimpers, rolling her hips up, rubbing herself against my mouth. "Yes, baby, yes," I tease her clit with the tip of my tongue before I suck it hard, and she screams in pleasure as she climaxes. I moan against her when I feel her clit pulsing against my tongue with every wave of her orgasm. She collapses on the bed breathless while I drink up her tasty girl come. Once her body stops quivering, she grabs my head and yanks me up, kissing me hard and deep, moaning when she tastes herself on my tongue. "You're incredible, baby." She breathes, biting, and tugging my bottom lip before she rolls me over and straddles me.

I don't take my eyes off her, not for a damn second while she kisses down my chest, her fingers tug open the buttons to my jeans and pull them down my legs along with my boxers. She licks her lips avidly, her eyes skimming over my fully erect member.

I hiss when she wraps her fingers around the base and strokes up the length. "Oh baby, yes, fuck, you have no idea how much I've missed your touch." I exhale, biting my lip, looking at her while she wraps her lips around me. "Oh god…" I moan, closing my eyes when I feel her hot mouth around my cock. Swirling her velvet tongue before she flicks and sucks me hard and deep. I curl my fingers in her hair and watch lustfully as my cock disappears into her mouth. After a couple of minutes, I was ready to explode. I pull her up and kiss her hard, hungry, and dirty.

It was my turn to groan in disappointment when she breaks the kiss and sits up, her dark hair falls around her like a curtain as she positions herself, pressing my cock against her entrance. Our eyes lock, and she slides down the length of me slow. Her mouth falls open as I stretch her out while I push deeper.

Once I'm fully immersed inside her, we moan together, and she starts to rock her hips back and forth slowly. "Oh, fuck sweetheart, you're so fucking perfect." I burr huskily, holding her hips and grinding mine up, meeting her thrusts. “I want to watch you come for me. Fuck me, baby.” Once she finds her rhythm, she picks up the momentum, rocking harder and faster until she clamps down on me hard, and I follow her over the edge. I thrust my hips up hard and explode deep inside her. "Ohhhnn baby fuck, fuck, uhhhh." We collapse on the bed, breathless.

"Oh my gosh, I think that was the best sex we have ever had, baby." Panting, I open my eyes and look over and see Sophie staring back at me in the dim lighting of my bedroom. Ahh, fuck me. Did I just fantasise that whole thing? The level of disappointment I felt at that moment was gut-wrenching. I force a smile on my face and kiss Sophie's forehead before I sit up and rub my hands over my face, regally annoyed with myself. "What got into you suddenly? I've never seen you so worked up and passionate before." She pants, grinning at me.

Maybe not with you.

Sophie wraps her arms around my neck from behind and kisses along my shoulder. “It seems you missed me just as much as I did you, sweetie.” I close my eyes and wince before I stand up.

"I'm going to have a shower," I utter and walk into the bathroom.

"Want some company?" I hear Sophie call out as I run the water.

"I'm not going to be very long," I inform her and close the door, locking it behind me just in case she gets any ideas and comes to join me. I stand under the spray and place my hands on the wall; my head hangs low as the water beats down on me. I feel a sudden surge of infuriation, and I punch the wall with a growl. What the fuck is wrong with me? I just had sex with my girlfriend and fantasised about Shayla. Sophie is good in bed; she really is, but as she said, we never really had that intense passion like Shayla, and I had. My connection with Shay was just something else. I've never experienced anything like it in my life. She's like a drug I can't seem to quit. I'm just so tired of missing her.

Fucking hell, what am I doing?

~

THE FOLLOWING week I was sitting at my desk, completely lost in my work, when I hear voices outside my office. I lift my gaze and see Ben;

our tech guy was at Shay's desk, well, it's now Jess—my new assistant's desk. I frown when Ben waves me over to him. I sigh, get up and walk over to them.

"What is it, Ben?" I question with a scowl.

"There's an issue with Jess's computer, and we need to restore it completely." He informs me, and I shrug, annoyed that he would call me over for something this stupid.

"So, restore it then, what are you telling me for?" I snap at him and turn to leave.

"Mr Hoult, I just wanted to make sure you have a copy of this design before it gets erased from the computer." I stop and look at him with an exasperated sigh.

"What design?" I ask with a frown, and he points at the screen. I walk around the desk and look at the design of a building on display. "Where did you find this?" I question, looking over at him and back at the screen again.

"Uh, Jess found it when she was fiddling with the software." He answers, scrolling down. "The initials on the design are, S.H. Isn't that—"

"Shayla," I whisper, staring at the screen. "Email this to me. Right now!" I bark and rush into my office. The email arrives just as I log into my computer; I open the file and study the design closely for a while. "Fucking hell." It was incredible. The attention to detail was just fantastic. I slump back in my chair and stare at it for a good thirty minutes before I grab the tablet and walk toward my Dad's at the other end of the office. I knock, and he lifts his head, looks at me, and waves me in. I walk into his office and close the door behind me before I stride over to his desk.

"Tristan? What can I do for you son?"

"Take a look at this," I say, handing him the tablet. He takes it and slides his glasses on; his eyes scan the design, and he looks up at me.

"Tristan, this design is remarkable. The detail on the building is just—"

"Incredible, I know." I finish for him.

"This is fantastic." He smiles, looking up at me, and I shake my head.

"It's not mine. It's Shayla's." I tell him, and he gapes at me, pulling his glasses off and frowns, looking just as bewildered as I did.

"Your ex-wife Shayla? The girl we hired as your assistant. That Shayla?" I nod, pacing his office. "Why on earth did she apply for an assistant role if she can create designs like this?" He questions, looking at the design again. She designed a sixty-two-floor skyscraper.

"I don't know, maybe because she never got to finish her degree, or maybe she doesn't believe in herself. Who knows?" I shrug with a sigh and rub my jaw. "I'm going to put that design-forward for that super hotel they want to build in the United Arab Emirates."

My Dad nods in agreement. "That sounds great, but you can't use her design without her consent. She doesn't work for us anymore, remember."

"Dad, I'm going to ask her to come back and work alongside me on that project," I say, shoving my fingers through my hair as I continue to pace in his office. My father watches me and laces his fingers together.

"Are you sure that's wise? Working alongside your ex-wife? What will Sophie say?" He questions, his brows fused. I shrug and shake my head.

"It's work, she'll understand," I explain, and my father nods and leans back against his chair.

"Son, you don't need my permission. This company is yours, do what you think is right. I trust you'll make the right call." He tells me with a supportive smile holding the tablet out to me. I nod and take it from him before I thank him and rush out of his office.

"Heather?!" I bark as I walk past her desk to my office. She jumps, startled, and flies out of her chair, following me.

"Yes, Mr Hoult.”

"When Shayla left, did we provide her job with a reference?" I ask sitting at my desk, and Heather nods.

"Um, yes, I'm assuming we did." She answers in a flurry.

"Good, call H.R and get the address to where she works and bring it to me," I demand, and she nods, smiling, but doesn't move. "NOW!" I shout, and she jumps again and rushes out of my office. I felt a bubble of excitement erupt inside of me at the notion of seeing her again. I lean back in my chair, bite my lip, and heave a sigh of relief.

Now, I just need to convince her to come back and work here.

Chapter Twenty-Nine

SHAYLA

I GROAN when I hear the annoying and incessant buzzing of my alarm—not bothering to lift my head from where it's buried under my pillow. I lift my arm and feel around my nightstand for it. I hit the snooze button and sigh when silence falls upon the room again. I lift my head and roll onto my back, staring up at the plain white ceiling. I honestly don't have the energy to move a muscle.

I've not been sleeping very well the last couple of months; this new job is wearing me to the bone. That and I'm still trying to pick up the pieces of my broken heart. It's been months— three to be exact. When is it going to stop hurting? I thought I would have gotten over him by now, but no, I just miss him, and I'm sick of it. I'm sick of thinking about him when I wake up. I'm even sicker of thinking about him when I go to bed, when I shower, try to eat. I have emotional surges at work. One second, I'll be fine and the next, I get all emotional, and I lock myself away in the bathroom and cry.

Cole Hoult has well and truly turned my life upside down. Why do I feel like I'm going through a breakup when he was never mine to begin with? Ah, crap, here come the tears.

For fucksake Shayla, pull yourself together. He's probably balls deep in his girlfriend right now. You're nothing but a distant memory to him while you're here torturing yourself.

With a shake of my head, I force myself out of bed and have a shower before I have to get to the office. I promised myself that I wouldn't allow myself to think about Cole in any way. Today was going to be a Cole-free day. Yes, I was determined.

~

IT WAS JUST BEFORE nine when I stroll into the office drinking my second latte in an attempt to wake myself up for this meeting that we have in forty-five minutes. "Morning Shayla." Bella greets me, chirpy as always, when I walk past her desk and set my coffee on my own desk opposite hers.

"Morning freckles," I grumble, taking my jacket off and draping it over the back of my chair. Bella is also a junior architect, just like me. She's a sweet girl with fiery red hair, amber eyes, and adorable freckles over her nose. I call her freckles because I'm obsessed with them. I think they're super cute. She hates it, though, and playfully flips me off when I do. Hence why she's currently holding up her middle finger at me. I smirk at her.

"You look exhausted, Shayla. Tough time sleeping again?" She questions, pulling her hair up in a bun and using a pencil to secure it. I taught her that. It's a habit of mine when I need to focus.

I sigh and sit in my chair. "Sadly, but it's fine though; sleep is overrated. I'll just sleep when I'm dead." I utter bitterly and sip my coffee before I fire up my computer. "Do you have any idea what this meeting is about first thing in the morning?" I ask with a yawn, and Bella smiles at me, shaking her head.

"Not a clue. It must be a big deal, though, because the big boss is in." She gestures over to where the CEO of the company is currently having a meeting with the managers and H.R. I yawn again and lose interest, turning my attention to my work.

"Shayla?" I jump when a pencil hits my chest and falls on the floor. I take my AirPods out and look at Bella with a scowl.

"What?" I hiss annoyed. I was finally concentrating on my work, and she just distracted me again.

"Meeting?" She reminds me, and I curse and look at the time. Shit. I grab my notepad and pen and walk to the conference room with the rest of the employees. I slide into a leather chair on the glass table and doodle absentmindedly on my notepad while we all wait for the meeting to start.

"Good morning, everyone. Thank you so much to all of you for attending this meeting." Emma, one of the company's head architects and partner, greets us all as she walks to the front of the room. "We have some exciting news to share with you all. Another company has bought us out, and we will work in partnership with them moving forward. This means more budgets, bigger projects for you all." She says, and I sigh, not bothering to lift my gaze until the light of the projector shines on my face, almost blinding me.

"Our first project with this new company will be a super hotel they are planning to build in the UAE." I lift my gaze and look at the projector screen and almost swallow my tongue. I drop my pen and sit forward, gawking at the design— *my design*—on display.

"Excuse me, Emma. Where did you get that?" I ask, interrupting her, and she smiles and looks at the design and back at me again.

"It was sent over by our new owners. Isn't it fantastic? This is the design they're thinking about for the hotel." She replies, and I gape at her and shake my head.

"What owners? That's my design." I tell her, and Emma blinks at me bemused and looks around the room before she chuckles.

"Your design? Shayla, come on, you don't seriously expect me to believe a junior architect designed *that*, do you?" She jeers, and everyone in the room snickers.

"Actually, Miss Clarke, that is her design." I freeze when I hear that voice behind me. The same voice that has been haunting me for the past three months. I force the lump forming in my throat down and will my heart to stop thrashing around in my chest.

Please let it be my imagination again, and don't let him be standing there when I turn around. I suck in a lungful of air and turn my head slowly to look back and see him standing there. Oh damn. I forgot how beautiful he was. Our eyes meet after months, I stare at him, and he stares back. The room falls silent—everyone's eyes on the infamous Tristan Cole Hoult. Everything and everyone in the room just fizzles away, leaving only the two of us. I don't know how long we stood there just looking at one another, but it couldn't have been that long, surely.

"Shayla." Cole drawls, standing there in a crisp blue suit, hands in his pockets looking sinfully good as he watches me intently. I notice his stubble is gone, and I hate that. I bet Sophie made him shave it off. Witch.

"Cole," I reply, and he averts his gaze to everyone else in the room.

"Leave us." He commands, looking at me again. The room clears, and I stand leaning against the glass desk with my arms crossed over my chest. Cole walks over to me, licking his lips. He tilts his head to the side, frowning while he looks me over. "You look thinner. Have you lost weight?"

I stare at my feet, not wanting to look at him and nod. "Yeah, it happens when you're working all hours and studying too." I sigh and force myself to look at him. "Your beard is gone."

Cole smiles a little and nods, rubbing the back of his neck. "Yeah, it happens when you work all hours of the day and don't have time to maintain one."

"What are you doing here, Cole?" I inquire, and he takes a step closer.

"Jumping straight to the point huh? What, no hello, how have you been? Or a hug even?" I exhale slowly and glare at him. Cole chuckles, shaking his head.

"Are you going to explain what the hell is going on, or shall I just walk out of here?" I snap agitated, uncrossing my arms and placing them on my hips.

"I bought out the company. As of this morning, I own Starlight." I gape at him and shake my head.

"You did…you did *what*?" I utter scowling at him. He did not just say he bought out the company I work for, did he?

"I bought—"

"I heard you!" I shout, and he frowns, throwing his hands up in the air.

"Then why ask?!"

I pinch the bridge of my nose and count to ten to calm myself down before I smack him over the head with my shoe. "Cole, please, *please* tell me this doesn't make you my boss again. Tell me you're just a silent investor or something?" I question, peering up at him, and he raises his brows and purses his lips.

"Well…"

"Oh my God!" I shout at him and start pacing the room frantically. "Of all the companies you could have bought, you come and buy the one I work at? Are you fucking serious? Why, Cole?!"

Cole shakes his head and shrugs. "It's a good investment; they were struggling financially, so I stepped in and bought it. I've been wanting to expand Cult Designs for some time now. I saw an opportunity, and I took it. Starlight and Cult Designs are now linked, so technically speaking, I'm your bosses, bosses boss which effectively makes me—" He explains calmly, and I glare at him furiously.

"—An arsehole." I finish for him, and he stares at me unamused. "You could have bought any company. I refuse to believe this was another coincidence. There's just no fucking way! I cannot be this unlucky surely." I snipe, running my fingers through my hair as I continue to pace. I'm going to lose my mind— this boy is going to make me lose my mind at the tender age of twenty-seven.

"Actually, it wasn't a coincidence. I knew you worked here. I asked Heather to track you down." He confesses, and I stop pacing and look at him incredulously.

"Why? Why, Cole, why would you do this? I don't understand. We agreed to walk away from one another. You promised me you would let me go." I state, not bothering to mask the annoyance in my tone as we stood staring at one another.

"I did!" He shouts, taking another step toward me. "I kept my promise. I walked away and left you alone, didn't I?!"

"For good. I said for good, Cole, not just a couple of months! What the hell do you want from me? Huh? What?" I question desperately while looking into his eyes, and he licks his lips holding my gaze.

"I want you back at Cul—."

"No."

"Will you just listen to me before you outright refuse?!" He yells angrily, and I shake my head.

"I'm not coming back, and if you keep pushing me, I will quit this job and disappear for good. Do you understand me?!" I scream back and take a sidestep to walk past him, but he grabs my arm and jerks me back, his angry eyes looking over my face.

"Shayla, this is strictly professional, I swear to you. It's got nothing to do with us. You belong at Cult, not here. I want you to come back as an architect and the head of the hotel project in Dubai. Let's make your dream a reality." He says, and I watch him dubiously for a couple of seconds.

I bite my lip and shake my head, "*My* dream Cole," I say, placing my hand on my chest. "It's my dream, which means I wanted to do it MY way, not through yours or anybody else's handouts or pity."

Cole's brows fuse as he glowers at me. "Pity? You think I came looking for you because I pity you? You're talented, Shayla, more than you're clearly aware of. Why won't you let me help you achieve your goals?" He cups my face in his hand, and I pull my face away.

"Maybe I don't want your help, Cole. I want to do it on my own. That way, when I make it one day, and I will make it, no one can tell me I got to where I did because of you," I answer earnestly, and Cole exhales glances around the empty conference room before he looks at me.

"Shayla, nobody gets that more than me. I get it, sweetheart. All I'm asking here is a chance to help you up that first step because that's the hardest, after that, I know you'll fly."

"Cole, you have helped me. Do you think I don't know that I got this job because I was married to you? Or that I worked for you? I would have never been considered for an opportunity to work as an architect *anywhere* if it wasn't for you," I explain, and Cole watches me, his eyes searching mine. "I have to do this my way, without you, however hard it may be. At least that way, I know I earned it, and it wasn't just handed to me because your name was involved."

Cole remains silent for a moment and shakes his head before he steps up close to me and looks down into my upturned face. "Shayla, listen to me. I have never met anyone more deserving of this opportunity than you. You didn't get to where you are because of me. You got there because you fought for it tooth and nail, and you still are. Even when life threw every obstacle your way— when most would—you never gave up on your dream, and I fucking love that about you. Your passion to achieve your dream is what got you here, maybe my name helped open that door, but you walked through it." He tells me, his hands on my arms while his green eyes intently stare into mine. "All I'm asking is to mentor you. That's all."

"And what about Sophie?" I ask him, and Cole shrugs. "Won't she mind that you're working with me again?"

"Sophie is mature enough to understand it's just business. We need your talent at Cult, and I can arrange for your tuition at Uni to be covered by the company." He assures me and probably foresaw I would push back when I open my mouth, so he holds his hand up. "Which you can pay back once you get your degree," He adds with a little smirk.

"Cole, I don't know," I whisper, looking down at my feet, and he slides his fingers under my chin and lifts my gaze to his.

"Tell me you'll think about it."

"I'll think about it," I whisper.

"I've got a flight to Dubai tomorrow afternoon to present your design to them. If you decide to take up my offer, meet me on the tarmac at two o'clock." I nod.

Cole keeps his eyes on mine, "Why didn't you show me this design?" He asks, pointing to the screen. I drop my gaze and shrug.

"Because I didn't think it was good enough. I was just messing around trying to familiarise myself with the software, Cole." I explain, and Cole looks at the screen and back at me again with a frown.

"Messing around? You produced that by simply messing around on the software?" He questions. When I nod, looking at him blankly, he laughs, shaking his head.

"Shayla, that design is exquisite! When I saw it, I was in awe, and so was my Dad. You have so much talent, and I can't believe you wouldn't share it with me or come to me for guidance. Even if it was bad— which it isn't, if you want to learn and grow as an architect, you have to believe in yourself and your work first and foremost." He says earnestly.

I rub my forehead and sigh, "Cole, just having you acknowledge and recognise that I have talent means more to me than you know. Especially coming from you, you're one of the world's most renowned architects. You're my idol. That up there may be 'exquisite' to you, but when I look at it, all I see is mistakes and errors, and that's why I trashed it because I wasn't ready to share it with anybody." I explain, averting my gaze.

"Come here," Cole takes my arm and turns me around, so I was facing the screen, his hands on my arms. "Show me the mistakes." He speaks quietly in my ear. I force away the giddy feeling at the pit of my stomach when I feel his chest pressed up against my back and look at the screen.

"The tunnel in the middle, it's all wrong," I explain, pointing at it. Cole nods.

"If you move it slightly to the left, right here, it will flow better, see." He explains, pointing at it. "What else?"

I sigh, "The windows, they don't look right to me."

"The windows are perfect. I wouldn't change a thing. It will give the building an airy feel." He says, squeezing my arms gently. "Shayla, you think the designs I do are without mistakes or flaws? Believe me, I have to correct myself constantly, but what makes an excellent architect is not to be ashamed of the imperfections or mistakes, and more importantly being able to recognise and improve them." He explains. "And you have that ability, sweetheart." He whispers in my ear.

Turning, I look up at him with a sigh, "I'm glad you think so." Cole's green eyes search my face, and he looks as though he wants to say something but then decides against it. "I should go back to work."

Cole nods and takes a step back, allowing me to step away from him and walk to the door. "Shayla?" I look back at him when he calls my name. "I really hope I see you on that tarmac tomorrow." I bite the inside of my cheek, and without a word, I turn and walk out of the conference room.

I slump down on the chair at my desk and watch as Cole walks out of the room and speaks to Emma as they walk through the office. Our eyes meet across the room, and he holds it till he disappears out of sight. "Shit," I whisper, closing my eyes. What the hell am I supposed to do? Cole is giving me an opportunity of a lifetime; my design will be built in Dubai. *Freaking Dubai!* I still couldn't believe it.

I should be jumping at this chance, but working alongside him every day, I only just started clawing my way out of that dark place he left me in. Do I really want to put myself through that again?

THAT EVENING I WENT HOME, and I couldn't focus on anything else for the life of me. I tried, I really did, but my mind would just turn and turn. I walk in through the front door, and the girls look at me as I drop my bag on the floor with a thump.

"Uh-Oh." They mutter, sitting upright, and they share a look.

"So, he's back then?" Aimee questions stuffing her mouth with crisps and chewing loudly while her wide blue eyes look at me with interest.

"He's back." I sigh, letting my head fall back on the sofa.

"Oh lord, here we go again," Jo mumbles, handing me the tub of ice cream and a spoon before she sits on the sofa beside me. "So, what are you going to do, Shay? Are you going to accept his offer?" She asks, and I shrug.

"Of course she is!" Aimee exclaims after she swallows her mouthful. "Shayla, the boy is offering you your dream on a plate. You'd be an idiot not to accept it." She states, crumpling up the empty packet in her hand. "Your design, yours, will be built in one of the most iconic places in the world. *Dubai* Shayla, you're always so selfless you deserve this break, babe, and I know Cole knows this too that's why he wants to help you achieve your dreams. It's okay to accept help, Shayla." Aimee explains, and I close my eyes and exhale slowly. "I know you hate hearing this, Bish, but that boy is in love with you, he just doesn't know it yet." She adds and shrugs at me when I lift my head and glare at her.

"I agree with Aimee. I don't know what you've done to that boy with your golden vagina, but he is hooked on you girl. He couldn't go more than a couple of months without you and even bought the company you work for, Shayla." Jo says and laughs when I pick up a cushion off the sofa and hit her with it.

"Shut up. Cole isn't hooked on me. If he 'loved' me or was 'hooked' on me, why didn't he choose me? He told me he loves her with all his heart but only *wants* me. He's thinking with his knob and nothing else. He's probably bored with Sophie already and is looking for a thrill. That's all I bloody am to him, a good time." I utter bitterly scooping up some ice cream and eating it. "I'm a good time girl," I mumble miserably into my tub of ice cream.

"Oh, please, if anyone's the meantime girl it's that witch Sophie. Mark my words, that boy will be yours. She's just keeping that seat warm for you, baby girl," Aimee claims with a laugh when I throw a glare her way and sits forward, clapping her hands. "Now! Let's get you packed for Dubai because you are going." She declares, jumping over my legs and pulling my arm to get me up. I groan and shake my head. "Move your fat arse off the sofa, you little ho."

"Yes, come on, get up. We'd be the worse friends in the world if we let you pass up an opportunity this good. Get up, Bish!" I squeal when they manage to pull me off the sofa, but we lose our footing, and all go tumbling, landing on top of one another.

"Ahhh my face!" Aimee exclaims when the entire tub of cookie dough ice cream empties on her face. Jo and I roll on the floor, laughing hysterically. "My fucking eyeballs are frozen!" She sits up and scoops up the ice cream off her face, and throws it at Jo and me. "If I go blind, I expect an eyeball from each of you hoe bags." She grumbles, wiping the ice cream off her face with her shirt. "Oh, sweet Jesus, I've gone blind! I can't see shit! Help me wash my face instead of laughing, you bitches!" She scolds while reaching for us.

"Ohhh God, I haven't laughed that hard in a long time," I chuckle, wiping away my tears, Jo and I still giggling.

"I'm so glad you're fucking amused at the prospect of me going blind. I hate you both!" Aimee grumbles and squeals when Jo and I haul ourselves at her.

"You lie!" I exclaim laughing while I sit on her, bouncing on her stomach and she groans laughing.

"Get your fat arse off me, you sexy bitch!"

"You're the sexy bitch." Jo laughs, tickling her relentlessly while she squirms.

"I second that," I say with a smile, and we all scramble up to our feet. Maybe the girls are right. As hard as it's going to be, I shouldn't pass up an opportunity this big. It will be really tough working with him again, but at least I'll kick start my career, and all this grief wouldn't have all been in vain.

Jo and I go to my bedroom to pack up a bag for me while Aimee showers and joins us after. "All right, ladies, this is an epic moment for us. We have to do this right." She says, walking in with a bottle of prosecco and three glasses. The music goes up, and we sing at the top of our lungs while we pack my bag for the trip.

"Shayla, if I were you, I would look smoking on this trip, show that boy what he's missing. I guarantee you, he will crack, and you two will have angry I-need-to-have- you-now sex." Aimee grins, popping the cork of the prosecco and filling our glasses.

"Oh, hell yeah. Aimee's right. You don't have to sleep with him, but you can make him regret his choice a little. We already know his attraction to you is off the charts, so it shouldn't be so hard." Jo says, folding my clothes with a suggestive grin. "Or maybe it will be…hard…eh?" She adds, wagging her brows.

I roll my eyes, grinning, "What am I fifteen? I'm not playing these stupid games with him. That's just asking for trouble. He has a girlfriend, and I'm certainly not the type of girl to seduce another girl's boyfriend. No, thank you. We can't control ourselves around each other as it is, add all of that shit into the mix, and as Aimes said, we'll end up fucking each other's brains out. I'm only in this for my career, and I would like to achieve it with my dignity intact."

"That's my bitch right there!" Jo chirps, and we clink our glasses. After we pack my bag, I went to bed. I couldn't sleep again. I was feeling comprehensive about my decision. Was I doing the right thing? By the time I fell asleep, it was gone past four in the morning. I woke up the next morning with a headache and was simply exhausted. I still had doubts, but I pushed them aside and convinced myself this was the right thing to do for my future. As the cab pulls up at the airstrip where Cole's jet was waiting, I feel my stomach clench. After I pay the cab driver, I take my bag and walk up to the plane. Cole appears at the door, and I look up at him. He smiles handsomely.

"We really doing this?" I call out over the loudness of the engine, and he nods.

"We're really doing this." He says back. I sigh and walk up the steps where he's waiting; he holds his hand out to me. I look at it and hang my bag's strap on it and walk past him. I hear Cole chuckle, and he follows me through the jet. I sit in the leather seat, and he takes the one opposite me. Our eyes meet, and I feel that familiar pull in the pit of my stomach.

Please don't let me regret this decision.

Chapter Thirty

COLE

SHE CAME.

When I saw that cab pull up from the window and Shayla stepped out, my heart skipped a beat from excitement. I cannot lie; I was worried she would not show. It was ten minutes to two, and she had not arrived. I had lost all hope till I saw that cab. Now here she is, sitting in front of me, curled up in the leather seat reading a book. We took off four hours ago, and Dubai is eight hours from London. I keep sneaking little peeks at her over my laptop on the table. She's either too engrossed in what she's reading or is good at faking distraction. I lean back in my chair, bite my lip, and look out of the window, watching the clear blue sky and the clouds down below.

I let my mind drift off to the last time she and I were in this jet flying to Nice. I'd give anything to go back to that day and relive that whole getaway with her again. I did something a little senseless, and I don't know if or how to tell Shayla about it without ruining this entire trip for us. Last night, when I went back home, Sophie came over, and I explained to her that Shayla would be working at Cult again. When I said she would be mature and understanding, I was wrong, so very wrong. She flipped out on me and accused me of still being in love with Shayla simply because I tracked her down and begged her to come back to work for me. I sigh, recalling the argument we had late last night.

"Sophie, you're overreacting! It's just business, babe. I need her for this project, it's her design. Why can't you understand that?!" I shout angrily and duck when Sophie hurls another glass toward me. "Christ, will you stop throwing shit at me!"

"You're a rotten bastard, Tristan!" She screams, picking up another glass. "Why her? You have a million other architects you can work with. Why her Tristan?!" She hollers, her blue eyes icy and glaring at me angrily.

"Because she's talented!" I retort, trying to reason with her, but she shakes her head.

"Bullshit!" Sophie shrieks, throwing another glass, and it hits the wall beside my head and smashes. "Just admit it, you're still in love with her, aren't you?" She cries, and I sigh and shake my head.

"If I were in love with her, why would I divorce her and get back together with you, Soph? I would have never let her walk out of my life, would I, if that were the case, but it's not. I love you!" I tell her earnestly, and she drops her gaze.

"Do you, Tristan? Because we are right back to where we were a year ago. You're disengaged again, and you're working all hours of the day and night. You don't talk to me. I barely even see you. And now you're standing there telling me your *ex-wife* is back in your life, and you'll be working 'closely' with her, and that you're flying off to Dubai together." She utters, wiping away the tears that roll down her cheeks. "Can you honestly, hand on your heart, tell me I have nothing to worry about here?" I rub the back of my neck tiredly and shake my head.

"What Shayla and I had is over Soph. This is strictly a professional relationship, babe," I explain for the umpteenth time. "I have never given you a reason not to trust me. I've always been faithful to you. If anyone should have trust issues in this relationship, it's me with you, because as I remember it, you were the one that slammed the door shut when you walked away from me, not the other way around." I add, and she looks at me wistfully. "I chose you. What more can I do, Sophie?"

Sophie sighs and pulls out a little blue box and holds it up to me. "Did you buy this for me? Were you going to propose before I left?" I clench my jaw tight and drop my gaze.

"You went through my things?"

"Answer the question. Was this ring bought for me?"

"Yes!" I snap hotly annoyed she would go through my belongings. "I was going to propose that weekend. I had everything planned out, but you took off and left me." I answer, kicking a shard of glass lying on the floor.

"Well, I'm here now." She whispers, and I lift my gaze and look at her. *Oh shit.* When I don't say anything, she holds up the box and shrugs. "You want to know how you can prove to me that I'm the one, you have your answer."

"Sophie, we've only just got back together. We're not ready for marriage." I sputter, and her eyes water.

"It's me, isn't it?" She sobs. "You're never going to marry me." I look at her while she cries, and I sigh. "I'm tired of waiting, Tristan."

"Right here? Like this? This is how you want your proposal?" I question, and she shakes her head, wiping away the tears.

"I've waited three years for a proposal. At this point, I'll take what I can get as long as it ends with me putting this ring on and being your fiancée." She explains, and I press my lips together and fist my hands by my side before I nod and walk over to her, stepping over the broken glass all over the floor.

"I'm not getting down on one knee with all this broken glass," I say firmly, and she giggles tearfully, nodding. I grab the box and take the ring out. "Sophie, will you—"

"Yes," She answers in a flurry, and I blink and look at her. I didn't even get the fucking question out yet. I shake my head and slide the diamond ring on her finger. She cries and hauls herself at me, pressing her lips to mine. I kiss her back for a couple of seconds, and she wraps her arms around my neck, hugging me. I rest my arms around her small waist and stare at the wall ahead numbly. Did I just get engaged?

"Mr Hoult?" I blink and look up at the flight attendant who was holding out some food to me. I take it and smile, thanking her. I look over at Shayla, who shakes her head when offered the food. "You can leave it here. She'll have it," I tell her, and Shayla looks at me and scowls.

"I'm not hungry." She sighs and looks down at her book again. I sigh and close my laptop before I lean over and pluck the book from her hands.

"Hey!"

"You're eating, and that's final," I tell her firmly, and she sits up and glares at me narrowing her eyes slightly.

"I will not. I said I'm not hungry." She argues, sitting back, her arms crossed over her chest.

"Oh, no? But I've had it specially delivered for you." I tell her, raising my brows, and she looks at me and then at the covered dish in front of us, intrigued.

"What is it?" She asks, lifting the silver cover. Those jade eyes grow wide, and she slowly licks her lips.

"Rico sends his love," I say with a wink, and she smiles beautifully, just like she used to. It's been a while since I've seen that smile, and I miss it. I miss the way it warms my insides like hot chocolate on a cold winter's day.

"Oh my God, I can't believe you got the Shayla Special. Cole, this is so sweet of you. I honestly haven't had the time to go recently." She gushes, picking up her fork, and leans over to smell the food, her eyes closing. I watch her with a smile. It's so easy to make her happy. I have never met anyone so easy to please in my life. That's my favourite trait of hers. She has many good characteristics, but that one is for sure the best thing about her.

We eat the 'Shayla Special' and reminisce about the day we went to that place by the river. It's been a while since we talked like this. It hit me once more how much I missed her or just being around her. We sat leaning on the table between us once our food was finished, our heads in our hands, enjoying a bottle of white wine while laughing and talking.

You know, in those cheesy rom-com movies, you see the guy just watching the girl while she talks, smiling in slow motion; that's literally how I felt in that very moment. I was enthralled with this girl; she does something to me.

"Why are you looking at me like that?" She asks, smiling, a beautiful blush forming on her cheeks.

I grin, watching her, "Like what?"

Shayla laughs, "Like that." She points to me. "With your eyes all wide like a puppy staring at its owner waiting to be petted." She giggles, looking into my face. "Cole, stop it."

"Why? Do you think I'm cute?" I smile, looking at her a little more intently, and she grins, shaking her head.

"I'm not going to feed your ego, Cole Hoult." I chuckle at her remark and tweak her nose. She slaps my hand away, but I catch her hand and rub her fingers with my thumb. I look down at her hand and brush my thumb over her finger she once wore the diamond ring I gave her. The mood quickly goes glum between us. I lift my gaze to hers, and she does the same, likely thinking the same thing I was.

"I've missed you," I declare, those green eyes I adore search mine for a second before she bites her bottom lip.

"I've missed you, too." She whispers, looking down, her finger also brushing along mine where I once wore the gold wedding band. My stomach does that weird twitchy thing when she touches me.

Fuck, I want to kiss her so bad. She's so close I can smell her intoxicating scent whenever she moves. I need to find out what perfume and shampoo she uses and buy gallons of it. With my free hand, I reach up and brush my fingers through her soft, long hair. I love the way my fingers just glide through her silky strands.

Shayla's eyes flicker up to mine, her tongue swipes across her bottom lip, and I watch avidly, fighting the urge to pull her in and kiss her like I've been longing to. Five hours in, and I'm already struggling; if I don't control myself and make a move on her, she will freak out and walk away again. "So, um, how long are we in Dubai for?" Shayla questions clearing her throat a little.

"A couple of days," I reply, dropping my hand from her hair and leaning back into my chair, drawing back the hand I was rubbing her fingers with. "It will be just after ten o 'clock at night local time when we land, so we can either rest if you're tired or we can go and explore a little," I suggest, and she shrugs, leaning back in her chair also.

"I've never been to Dubai, so I'm definitely up for exploring if you are." She answers with a smile, fiddling with the cork to the wine.

"Sounds good to me. Seen as you've never been, you should know there are strict rules in the U.A.E." I explain, and she frowns, looking at me questioningly.

"Rules?" I nod, leaning against the table again, and she does the same, listening intently.

"Yes, public displays of affection are prohibited when you're out and about. If you're married, you can get away with holding hands, but that's it. Two people who are not wed aren't allowed to touch in public or share a hotel room. If you're caught breaking the rules, you get arrested, and it's up to a year jail time." I explain, and Shayla's eyes grow wide.

"A year? That's a little extreme." She mutters, shaking her head. "Sucks for those coming as an unwed couple. Imagine having to stay in separate rooms while on holiday." She smirks.

I smile, nodding, "Dubai isn't as bad as Abu Dhabi. It's more laid back. They don't care as long as you're not having sex in public. You can do what you want in the privacy of your hotel room." I explain, and Shayla nods, chewing on her bottom lip, a little smile on her face. "What?" I ask, and she shakes her head, her smile growing into a grin.

"Nothing." She mumbles quickly, averting her gaze, her cheeks turning pink.

I chuckle, "What are you thinking about? You've gone all red." Shayla touches her cheeks, her green eyes wide.

"Nothing. No, I haven't." I laugh, reaching over. I poke her, and she giggles, shaking her head.

"Liar. You're thinking about something naughty I know that look. Tell me." I laugh when she goes even redder, "Oh my God, it must be good look how red you've gone." I tease her.

Shayla covers her face with her hands shaking her head, embarrassed. "Cole, shut up!" She chuckles, mortified, turning her head so I wouldn't see her face. "Why is it so hot in here." I snicker, taking hold of her wrists. I pull her hands away from her face and look at her grinning.

"You were picturing us having hot sex in a country where it's forbidden, weren't you? Admit it." I drawl teasingly, and Shayla shakes her head.

"I don't know what you're talking about." She denies still smiling. I narrow my eyes at her and lean in close, my thumbs rubbing the pulse point on her wrist as I gaze into her olive-green eyes. "Sex is forbidden to us full stop Cole not just in Dubai."

I look over her face, "Maybe the act itself is, but no one can stop us from thinking about it, can they?" I reply, letting my eyes drift down to her plump, soft lips, "Or talking about it." I add with a breathy whisper.

"What's there to talk about?"

I lick and bite my bottom lip, "You can tell me what you were thinking about, for example." I question, trailing my fingers down the length of her arms slowly. "Where were we?"

"Cole," She sighs, her eyes closing, and I watch her closely.

"Tell me," I whisper.

"At the beach."

"What were we doing at the beach?" I ask, looking at her face. Shayla's lips part, and her breathing go shallow.

"Walking barefoot along the shore at night. We're all alone, just the two of us, the sound of the waves washing up on the shore soaking our feet as we walk under the moonlight." She explains while I play with her fingers.

"Mhm, and then…" I breathe, gazing at her as she bites her lip.

"Our hands brush as we walk, and you intertwine your fingers with mine," I smile a little and lace my fingers with hers.

"Like this?" She nods, wetting her lips. "Do I brush my thumb over yours like this?" I say, rubbing her knuckle, and she nods again. "Then what?"

"We stop walking, you pull me close and brush your fingers through my hair, sweeping it away from my face while you look into my eyes." I close my eyes and use my free hand and brush my fingers through her hair.

"And then…" I whisper, trailing my thumb along her jaw, and she leans into my touch and moans breathily. I bite my lip so hard I taste blood.

"You lean in close and ghost your lips over mine for just a second before you brush them softly over mine and kiss me." I swallow hard and press my forehead to hers, my thumb caressing her lips, which she parts, her breath hot against my thumb.

"How do I kiss you Shay..." I groan, and she exhales a little. "Is it slow and deep when I tease your tongue with mine, and you moan quietly into my mouth in that way that drives me crazy, or hard and urgent where I suck your tongue, bite your bottom lip, and you whimper a little?"

"Slow and deep." She breathes with a moan, and my head spins. *Fuck.* I swallow hard and rub my nose over hers. Shayla's hand comes up, and she brushes her fingers along my jaw. I sigh.

"Shayla," I whisper urgently, my lips inching closer to hers. "What are you doing to me, sweetheart." I breathe against her lips.

"Cole..." She moans, her voice a breathy whisper full of so much desire. Tell me how I'm supposed to resist kissing her when she says my name like that.

"Fuck, Shay, if you don't pull away right now, I'm going to kiss you," I murmur, my voice laced with the desperate need I have for her.

"You can't." She sighs, her fingertips lightly graze over my lips.

"Then pull away." I groan, kissing her fingers, and she shakes her head.

"I can't," She whispers, whimpering a little. I swear to the seven kingdoms of heaven, she is the only woman in the world who has ever made me feel like this. If I could only find the words to explain the way I was feeling at that moment, I would, but there are honestly no words—not a single one.

My heart was thumping wildly in my chest, and my stomach tied into knots with anticipation. It feels as though the blood in my veins was boiling. You know when you have two magnets, and you try to pull them apart, but that force between them keeps drawing them together again. That's the only way I could describe what I feel when I'm around this girl. It's like everything around me disappears, and she's all I see, she's all I want. I've never felt anything like this.

Am I in lust with her, or is it love? I've been in love, but it was never like this. What the hell is this? I'm driving myself crazy, trying to figure out what I feel for her.

Chapter Thirty-One

SHAYLA

OH, what the hell am I doing?

It's moments like this where I really question my integrity when I'm around this boy. I do things I would never usually do, and it's entirely out of my control. My body just acts on its own accord, and even if my head is screaming at me to stop, something deep inside me doesn't listen to reason. Like right now, I should pull away, even getting this close to him is wrong. It's so immoral because he belongs to someone else now. Not that he was ever mine, to begin with, but he was at least single, and whatever we did, we weren't hurting anyone. I just wish I could find a way to resist him, but it's just so hard because it doesn't feel wrong; it feels so right, being this close to him, it feels like it's the most natural thing in the world.

God, please help me find the strength to put an end to this before I do something stupid and let him kiss me.

"Fuck, Shay, if you don't pull away right now, I'm going to kiss you." I hear him murmur. I feel the warmth of his breath on my lips, and I ache to kiss him just a little.

"You can't," I sigh disappointedly, lifting my hand I brush my fingers over his lips.

"Then pull away," He groans, kissing my fingers softly. I honestly want to cry. I want him so much it hurts.

I tried. I swear I tried, but I couldn't move. "I can't." I whimper, and at this point, his lips were touching mine. I was ready to cave in, to hell with it all. The plane suddenly shook, and we jerk apart. I open my eyes and look around, my breathing heavy and back at Cole, who closes his eyes, his jaw clenched so tight it was twitching. He exhales slowly and opens his eyes. Our eyes meet, and we hold our gaze for a moment till we hear the pilot announce that we are preparing for landing shortly. Cole and I tear our eyes away from one another and buckle our seatbelts. I look out of the window, and as we approach Dubai, you could see the lights.

Do we just ignore what happened? I sneak a look at Cole, who is staring out the window, his brows knitted together tightly, lost in his own thoughts. Was he feeling guilty, or was he disappointed we didn't get to kiss? I'd give everything just to be able to read his mind right now.

The plane touched down in Dubai, and we step off the plane. It was warm and humid at ten o'clock at night; Aimee did say the climate here is hotter than back home. I didn't even see what Aimee and Jo packed for me; they distracted me with the alcohol and dancing. I'm honestly quite nervous about what I'm going to find in there.

We step off the plane and walk over to a white rolls Royce waiting for us. "Mr Hoult, Welcome back to Dubai. Please..." A young man dressed in a traditional white robe greets us and opens the door for us to get in.

"Thank you." I smile politely as he takes mine and Cole's bags and gestures for us to get in the car. Cole gets in, texting someone, a scowl on his face. More than likely texting his girlfriend telling her we've landed. I sigh and look out the window as we drive. I can't believe I'm in Dubai. I feel like I'm dreaming. I sit forward and roll the window down and watch the buildings whiz past us.

"If you're feeling hot, I can turn the AC on, Miss?" I hear the driver say, and I shake my head smiling.

"No, I prefer the fresh air, thank you," I tell him and close my eyes when the warm air hits my face.

"First time in Dubai?" The driver asks again, glancing back at me through the rear-view mirror, and I nod smiling.

"Yes, I'm really excited to be here. I've heard so many great things about Dubai." I tell him, resting my head on the side and looking up at all the lights. "I'm mostly excited about the food," I add, and the driver chuckles. "I find the Arabic culture so fascinating, the music especially. What is this one you're listening to? It sounds so beautiful. My Arabic isn't so good."

"It's an old song. The title is 'wahashtiny'; it means I'm missing you. He's singing about a girl he met and fell in love with upon seeing her for the first time. They break up. Years pass by, and he still misses her terribly and is telling her he still dreams of holding her, and he's not alive unless she's with him again." I swallow thickly and turn my head and look at Cole, who was watching me. I force myself to look away from him and look out of the window again. Sounds a little too familiar.

We pull up at the hotel a little while later. I look up at the giant building in front of us. Wow. We're staying at the iconic Burj al Arab. We get out of the car, and I stare up at the building in awe. "Wow."

"Beautiful, isn't it?" Cole says, coming to stand beside me. I nod wordlessly. "Yours will be just as stunning, if not more so." I look over at Cole and smile at him. He gestures for us to walk into the hotel, and my jaw almost hits the floor when I look around the interior. When I say the pictures don't do it justice, I mean it. While Cole went to get the keys to our suite, I explore the lobby. I stare up at the ceiling as Cole walks over to me. He looks up at the ceiling then back at me. "What are you staring at?"

"Is it just me, or does that design on the ceiling look like a..." I look around and lean in a little closer. "...a vagina," I whisper to him. Cole's lips quirk, and he looks up and starts cracking up laughing.

"Oh, wow. I never noticed it until you mentioned it." He chuckles, shaking his head. "I am never going to unsee it now. Come on, trouble." I smirk sheepishly and look at the design as we walk toward the elevator. \

Who in their right mind came up with that design? I muse, shaking my head. Cole arranged for us to have the presidential suite, the largest hotel suite, which had two bedrooms. The suite was insane. As you walk through the double doors, right in front of you is a grand staircase to the second floor. There were butlers holding cocktails, greeting us as we walk in. The room itself was stunning. From the design to the décor, it felt like I was in an Arabian dream. However, I was feeling really overwhelmed suddenly. This was way, way out of my comfort zone.

Cole tips the bell boy, and he bows his head and leaves us. I walk around the suite and frown when I wander to one of the bedrooms. I push the bed, and it spins. I press my lips together and stifle the bubble of laughter at the images I got of people having sex on this bed. It's a carousel bed. I giggle at the thought and jump when I hear Cole's voice in my ear.

"Imagine having sex on that thing. I think I would either pass out or throw up. Possibly both." I laugh.

"You can have the carousel bed. I know you. You'll wake up early and spin me awake." I say, walking over to the window, and I hear Cole chuckle behind me.

"You know me too well, sweetheart." He utters, walking to stand beside me. "Some view, huh?"

I nod, gazing out at the view of the ocean and the palm island. "It's gorgeous. I can't wait to see it in the morning. I can stare at that view all day and never get bored," I sigh, and Cole nods, looking over at me.

"I know that feeling." I turn my head and look up at him. I feel my cheeks grow hot under his gaze and look away before he teases me again.

"Are you tired?" I ask him, and he shakes his head.

"Not at all. Do you want to go out for a bit?" He suggests, and I nod, smiling at him. Cole returns my smile and nods also. "Okay, why don't we get changed and go explore a little. There's someplace I want to take you."

"Okay, sure." I walk to the second bedroom and set my bag on the bed, and look through it. I'm going to hurt those girls when I get back. They've packed me all revealing outfits: shorts, crop tops, skirts, and dresses. If I end up arrested, I'll literally kill them. Although Cole did say they are more laid back here than the 'old' Dubai. I pick out a long fire-truck red skirt that had high slits up both legs. I match it with a white crop top and sandals. I let my hair loose from the messy bun I put it in after the flight and do some light make up. I smile when I remember the girls telling me I should tease him a little to show him what he was missing. Even though I don't want to play games with him, a small part inside was intrigued. I look in the mirror and smile. I pick up the black eyeliner and line my eyes to stand out, and put some matte red lipstick to match the skirt.

Satisfied I got the look I was going for, I spray my fruity perfume and walk out of the bedroom the same time as Cole walks out of his at the suite's opposite side. He was in a white linen shirt with the top two buttons undone, slowing his well-defined, smooth chest and a pair of baby blue shorts. He stops walking when he sees me, his emerald eyes rake over me, and he licks his lips slowly. I feel a tingle cascade down my spine when his eyes meet mine.

"Ready to go?" I ask, he nods, and we leave the suite.

Cole clears his throat when he pushes the button to the elevator. "You look gorgeous." I smile at him and hold his gaze.

"Thank you, right back at you," I say and step into the glass elevator. "Where are we going?"

Cole slides his hands in his pockets and looks at me. "It's a surprise." He informs me, grinning mischievously. "I need to make sure I don't let you out of my sight tonight."

I look at him puzzled, and he licks his lips. "You're every Arab man's dream right now." I smile and give him a tart look.

"Only Arabs?" I ask, and a look of surprise crosses his features at my flirty response before it disappears, and he grins handsomely at me.

"You already know the answer to that." He answers knowingly, his eyes flickering down to my lips before they lift to mine again.

"Do I?" Cole nods slowly, staring into my eyes. "And what if I need reminding?"

"That can be arranged."

I raise my brow in response, "And what might that *involve* exactly?" I question, and he only smiles wantonly. We observe one another intently until the elevator doors open.

We leave the hotel and get into one of the Rolls Royce's the hotel provided for us. Two men open the doors for us to get in. Cole tells the driver where we need to go before he slides in beside me, and the driver nods and runs around the car to get in the driver's seat.

Cole leans in close to my ear and whispers, "Have I told you that I love the way you look in red." I close my eyes and resist the urge to shiver when I feel his lips brush against the shell of my ear. I turn my head toward him and lift my eyes to his, smiling sensually.

"Once or twice," I reply softly, gazing into his eyes. "Wouldn't mind hearing it again, though."

"I love the way you look in red." He whispers, his eyes lingering on my lips as he speaks. I deliberately lick my lips slow and bite my bottom lip while he watches avidly. He groans and closes his eyes; his Adam's apple jumps in his throat. "You have no idea how badly I want to ruin that lipstick you've got on right now." He breathes, and I watch him for a beat.

"It truly is a shame that you can't," I tell him and pull my face away from his and look out of the window, my lips curling into a satisfied smirk when I hear him sighing in frustration.

A while later, the car rolls to a stop, and I look around. We're by a marina surrounded by lit-up buildings in the middle of the city. "Come on," Cole says, placing his hand at the small of my back he guides me toward a lit-up dhow boat.

I take his hand, and he helps me up into the boat. "Oh, wow." I breathe, looking around. The boat had two floors; the bottom was filled with tables for diners, but it was empty. "Where is everybody?" I ask as we walk up the steps to the top floor.

"It's a private tour, so it's just us," Cole tells me as he leads me up the steps. I nod in understanding and see a table for two on the top deck. "I hope you're hungry."

I'm starving." I smile and take a seat when he pulls the chair out for me. "Thank you." I look around the boat. It was so beautiful and romantic. The boat starts to pull away from the marina, and while we wait for the food, we drink wine, and I listen to Cole talk about the buildings as we pass by them. I love how passionate he is about his work. It's honestly so endearing.

Cole stops talking when he notices me watching him, "Now who's looking at whom like a puppy that wants to be petted?" I smile and shrug.

"I love listening to you talk about architecture. You speak so passionately about it you can't help but feel engrossed." I tell him earnestly, and he smiles warmly at me and takes my hand in his, his thumb gently brushing over my knuckles.

"That's really nice to hear because there isn't a lot of people I can share the love and passion I have for my work with." He explains, "Only someone who feels the same excitement for architecture would understand." He adds, giving me a pointed look, and I nod, smiling.

"I completely agree." The starters arrive, and we ate the delicious fig salad with spiced chicken while discussing the presentation we had the next day. The mains arrived shortly after we finished the starters, Cole chose two Lamb shanks for us, and it was delightful; the meat just fell off the bone and melted on your tongue.

For dessert, I chose the chocolate souffle, while Cole chose a creamy strawberry cheesecake. I moan in delight when I taste the first spoonful of the warm souffle. Cole watches me as I suck on the spoon. "Good?"

I nod slowly and look at him. "So good." I moan, licking the chocolate off my finger. Cole shifts in his seat and clears his throat, looking down at his own dessert.

"Never thought I'd be so envious of a dessert." He mumbles under his breath. I resist the urge to smile, pretending I didn't hear him. I continue to make sexy little noises while I ate each spoonful, and he watches me with hooded eyes, sucking on his bottom lip.

I scoop up a piece and hold it to his lips, "You have to try this. It's to die for." I say, he opens his mouth, and I feed him the souffle making sure I smear a little chocolate on his bottom lip with the spoon. Cole moans appreciatively. "Isn't it sensational?"

He nods, swallowing, "It really is." I smile and set the spoon down on the plate before I lean close to him. Cole watches me closely, his green eyes darting from my eyes to my lips.

"You have some chocolate on your lip," I tell him softly, brushing my finger along his bottom lip where I had smeared the chocolate before I bring my finger to my mouth and suck the chocolate off while he watches me avidly. "Got it," I whisper, and Cole licks his lips and picks up his fork and scoops up a piece of his cheesecake, and holds it to my lips.

"Try this cheesecake. It's so rich and creamy." He drawls, smiling a little. I know what he's up to, but I play along. I open my mouth, and he smears the strawberry sauce all over my lip before he feeds it to me. "Oops. I better get that." He burrs, taking hold of my chin, and pulls my face close to his own, eyes staring raptly at my lips while he sweeps his thumb along them, smearing the sauce over his finger. He was about to pull his finger to his mouth, but I part my lips and run my tongue over his thumb before I suck it a little, cleaning the strawberry sauce off with a breathy moan. Cole's eyes close, and he inhales deeply. "Christ…" He breathes, gulping hard. He opens his eyes and stares into mine longingly. "Shayla, you're not playing fair. That was my taste."

I smile and shrug. "You should have been quicker then," I retort impishly and pull away, leaning back in my chair. Cole groans and tilts his head back, exhaling.

"You'll be the death of me." Cole sighs, closing his eyes; he bites his lip. I bite back the smile and stand up. I stroll over to the front of the boat and look out at the buildings ahead and the lights glistening on the surface of the water. I close my eyes, enjoying the warm night breeze in my hair, on my face, and the slow, beautiful Arabic song playing in the background.

I open my eyes when I feel Cole's chest pressed up against my back and the warmth of his breath on my ear. "Dance with me." He whispers, trailing his fingers down my arms. I allow him to take my hand and spin me, so I was facing him. Cole pulls me against him and wraps his arms around my waist while I circle mine around his neck. Cole presses his forehead to mine, and we sway together slowly.

How is it possible to fall deeper in love with someone you're already madly in love with? How do I tell my heart to give up and move on when it's not even beating for me anymore. It's solely beating for him. I wish more than anything I were selfish enough to tell him how I really feel about him. But I can't. I need to bury him deep in my heart and continue to love him silently.

Cole's arms tighten around me, and I feel hot tears trail down my cheeks. A quivering breath escapes me when he presses his lips to my forehead. His lips brush soft kisses along the side of my face until he feels the wetness of my tears on his lips, and he pulls back. Cole's large hands come up and cup my face lifting it so I would look up at him. I slowly lift my gaze to his, and almost instantly, my eyes pool with tears that spill over and roll down my cheeks. Cole's green eyes search mine for a long time, and I was terrified of what he saw in them because his eyes glisten, and he closes them and pulls my head to his chest, holding me so tight against him. I nestle my face into his chest, and he strokes my hair as we sway together.

Chapter Thirty-Two

COLE

NOTHING WRECKS me more than watching a tear fall from this beautiful girl's eyes. Each one is like a knife plunged into my heart. When I pull back and look into her eyes that are swimming in tears, it's like a curtain fell for one fleeting minute, and she allowed me to see into her soul. I saw such sorrow and something deep in my chest hurt, so much so that it caught my breath. I feel tears burn the back of my eyelids. I'm an idiot. How could I not see it?

I'm *in love* with her. It's always been her.

I close my eyes tightly and lay her head on my chest, and we continue to sway slowly together. I wrap my arms around her tight, and I feel her relax in my hold. "Shayla…" I whisper in her ear. "I think I'm in love with you," I confess.

Shayla stills and slowly lifts her head off my chest and looks at me. "What?" She whispers, her bottom lip quivers a little, her eyes filling with fresh tears.

"I'm in love with you," I confess, not being able to hold it any longer. Tears spill over her cheeks, and I reach up and brush them away with my thumbs. "I'm an idiot. I can't believe it's taken me this long to figure it out. I always knew I had feelings for you, but it didn't hit me how in love with you I am until right now." I tell her, and more tears stream down her face. "All the signs were there, but I ignored them. I don't know when or how, but I love you, Shayla." I admit, brushing my fingers through her hair, my eyes gazing into hers. "So much." Shayla's eyes close, and she sighs her breath quivering as she exhales. "Please say something."

"I'm in love with you, too." She whispers, opening her eyes and looking at me. My breath hitches in my throat when I see the love concealed in the depths of those endless green eyes. "I've been in love with you for so long." She tells me sincerely, and I close my eyes and bite my lip.

"Why didn't you tell me?" I question, pressing my forehead to hers. Shayla shakes her head and shrugs.

"I couldn't. You said you were in love with Sophie. How could I possibly tell you I loved you when you're telling me you're in love with another girl. I thought she was the one you wanted, and I didn't want to confuse you, so I buried my feelings and pretended like it wasn't killing me." She explains sorrowfully, and I shake my head, my gut clenching tight.

"Sweetheart, I wish you would have told me. Maybe then I would have stopped kidding myself, and we could have saved ourselves so much heartache," I sigh, kissing her forehead. "Oh Shay, I'm so sorry for hurting you. I had no idea how you felt until you just looked at me the way you did before, I saw the sorrow in your eyes, and it hit me."

Shayla gazes up at me, "What about Sophie? Do you love her too?" She questions, her eyes watering, and I sigh.

"I honestly thought I did, but I've been miserable, Shayla. You're all I thought about the last couple of months. I hadn't even noticed that you've taken over my heart. There's no room for anyone else in there, baby. You've consumed my mind, my heart, and my soul." I whisper, sweeping my nose over hers. "I love you so much. My God, it feels so good to say it finally." I breathe, trailing my lips along her face. "Tell me you love me, baby."

"I love you, Cole." She whispers to me, closing her eyes.

"Say it again."

"I love you so much."

"I love you," I sigh, brushing my lips over hers. I comb my fingers through Shay's hair while I part her lips with my own and kiss her slow and deep. And, my God, what a kiss it was. I honestly thought my heart would rip out of my chest; it was beating so fast and hard. Shayla moans when I tease her tongue with my own, her fingers curl at the nape of my neck, and she draws my mouth closer, kissing me deeper.

~

IT WAS past midnight when we got back to the hotel, not wanting the night to end we take a stroll hand in hand to the hotels' private beach. Fire torches lit the path, and it was just the two of us. Shoes in our hands, we walk along the shore, the water washing over our feet. Shayla looks up at me, and I smile; wrapping my arm around her shoulder, I pull her closer and kiss her temple. I don't think it was possible to feel happier than I was at that moment. It feels like a weight has been lifted, and I was walking on clouds. "I wish we could stay longer. I'm not ready to go back home yet," Shayla says, looking at me, her startling green eyes twinkling like jewels.

I smile at her, "We still have another two days, baby." I tell her, and she smiles lovingly up at me. I chuckle. "What?"

"I love it when you call me baby." She whispers, gazing into my eyes. I grin down at her.

"I love that you are *mine*, baby." I drawl and stop walking before I pull her close, wrap my arms around her waist, I lean down and kiss her slow and deliberate. Shayla moans, pushing up on her toes so she could reach me better. Her arms circle around my neck, and she kisses me back affectionately. One of my hands comes up behind her head, and the other brushes her hair away from her face while we continue to kiss achingly sensual.

After we pull back from our kiss, we sit on the sand, Shayla sitting in between my legs, my arms around her, lips dropping soft, loving kisses along the side of her face. She's smiling, her eyes closed while her fingers play with mine. "I wish I had realised how I felt about you sooner," I admit pressing my lips to her temple. "What I feel for you is something so new to me, Shayla," I add, and her eyes open, she lifts her gaze to look at me.

"You said you were in love before." She states, her eyes searching mine. I shake my head and brush a strand of her hair away from her face.

"This feels different." I express, gazing into her eyes. "Either what I felt before wasn't lovc or what I feel for you is something more intense and much deeper than love," I explain, and Shayla smiles. "Being apart from you all those months was unbearable for me. I felt like one half of me was missing. I suffocate when I'm not near you, baby."

"I feel the same," She affirms, lifting her fingers to my jaw and stroking it devotedly. "I've never felt this way about anyone ever." I curl my fingers around her wrist, kiss her fingers, and press them over my heart beating wildly in my chest.

"This is what you do to my heart. It only beats like this when I'm around you." I assert. Shayla's eyes close, and she exhales slowly. She lifts my hand, kisses my fingers, and places it over her chest, and I feel her heart thumping hard against my palm. I didn't need her to say anything because I saw all I needed in her eyes. I cup her face and kiss her devotedly until the very last breath left my lungs, and I had no choice but to pull away.

"I want to make love to you till the sun comes up, baby." I groan lustfully against her ear, and she quivers, nodding.

"You better hurry up then because the sun rises early here." She smiles when I chuckle while nuzzling her neck.

I grin and nip at her ear. "Shall we go upstairs to our carousel bed?" I whisper, and Shayla grins.

"Yes, make me dizzy with your loving Mr Hoult." I laugh and lift her to her feet.

"You make me dizzy with your love, Miss Hart," I admit kissing her deeply once more before we walk back to the hotel. It was so hard keeping my hands to myself until we got to the suite. I let the butlers have the rest of the night off, tipping them five-hundred pounds each, telling them we no longer required their assistance for the night.

The doors click shut, and I look at Shayla, who stood watching me. I walk over to her and gather her in my arms and press my forehead to hers. "Shall we have a shower first, get the seawater off our skin," I ask, and she smiles, closing her eyes when I trail soft kisses along her jaw.

"Mhm," She lustfully sighs when I graze my nails lightly down her back. Something I figured out she loved a while ago. I take her hand and lead her to the bathroom with the walk-in shower.

We undress one another unhurriedly, lips a breath apart, eyes interlocked, hands caressing one another. I pull her under the spray with me, cupping her face in my hands, and kiss her till we're both breathless. Shayla's hands run down my chest while she kisses me back. I walk her backwards, till she's up against the wall. She gasps when the cold tiles touches her back, goosebumps break out all over her body. I smile against her lips when she shivers a little, and she opens her eyes and looks up at me, her fingers caressing my face. "Please let your beard grow back." She whispers.

"You prefer me with a beard?" I ask, and she nods, smiling beautifully.

"You look good clean-shaven too, but you just look even sexier with a beard." She explains, peppering kisses along my jaw.

"Miss Hart, you think I'm sexy?" I tease her with a grin, and she blushes and bites her bottom lip looking up at me through her lashes.

"So *damn* sexy," She whispers against my lips, kissing me softly.

I groan and squeeze her hips gently as I gaze into her eyes, "You're the sexy one. Your beauty is dazzling, baby." Shayla smiles and kisses my pulse point. I close my eyes and moan, tilting my head back, giving her more room while she leisurely licks up my throat. "Goddamn baby."

I lift her into my arms, and she wraps her legs around my waist as I press her into the wall and like two magnets, our lips fuse, and we kiss passionately; our tongues brush, and we moan. I can honestly kiss this girl forever and never get enough. Is it even possible to feel someone's love through a kiss? She kisses with such devotion it takes my breath away and warms my heart. I'm genuinely obsessed with her.

I make love to her in the shower, and I watch in delight as she climaxes, my name on her lips. I carry her to the bedroom and lay her on the bed before I cover her body with my own, and we continue making love for hours, in every position we could get into without losing contact for a second, tending to one another's needs. I thought the night we spent together in Nice during the storm was the best moment we've shared, but having her gaze into my eyes and hearing her whisper that she loves me while we make love was something else altogether.

I brush my lips over hers and lace our fingers as we rock together slow, “God, Shay, I love you so much,” I pant. “Come with me baby.” I plead huskily, pushing deeper into her, and she whimpers, rocking her hips up. I feel her tighten around me before she goes over and takes me with her. Her walls flutter and clamp down on me hard, milking me with every sinfully delicious spasm of her orgasm. “Ohhh yes, yes, Shayla,” I gasp, and she kisses me deeply as I explode deep inside her. I still when my own orgasm rips through me, and I spill my hot cum into her. Shayla rocks her hips up, drawing out every pulse, every wave of my blissful climax. “Fuck.” I pant.

I collapse on top of her breathless, kissing her neck while she caresses my back, panting herself. I can feel her heart hammering against my chest as I’m sure she could feel mine on hers. We lay there for a while till our breathing shallowed, just whispering to one another.

I look down into her eyes, my fingers stroking her hair. “I don’t know how I’ve survived as long as I have without your love, baby,” I tell her, and she holds my gaze for a long moment.

“Me either.” She confesses. I smile and kiss her nose gently.

“I’m never letting you go again.” I declare, and Shayla sighs heavily, closing her eyes. “What is it, baby?”

She opens her eyes and peers up at me, “I was afraid we’d end up in bed together at some point on this trip; I didn’t expect it to happen like this but, we should have waited to sleep together. You’re still in a relationship with another girl Cole. Whether you love her or not, you’ve just cheated on her, and I’ve become the other girl.”

“Shayla, you’re not the other girl. You’re *the girl*, the *only* girl. I’m going to speak to Sophie and end it as soon as we’re back home. You’re all I want, Shayla. I don’t want to think about anything but us for the rest of this trip. I want to enjoy every second I have alone with you. Can we just put a pin in all other problems till we get back to London?” I say, and she looks uncertain but exhales slowly and nods.

“Okay, yeah, I guess we can.” I smile and kiss her softly. I trail my fingers down her sides, and she giggles, squirming. “Stop that.” She mumbles against my lips, and I grin, gathering her arms up, I pin them above her head and lean down and brush my lips along her ribs where she's ticklish, she half moans half laughs.

"Ahhh, Cole!" She squirms chuckling. "Stop, baby, stop." She laughs hysterically.

"It's going to cost you. Say you love me, then I'll stop."

She laughs, "I love you! I love you so much! Please, ah!" I chuckle and look down at her, and she pulls her hands free from my hold, and she picks up the pillow and slams it in my face. "You're evil."

I laugh and pull the pillow off my face and look at her. "Hey, no abusing the boyfriend." I tease, and Shayla looks at me.

"Boyfriend? Where? I can't see him?" She says, looking around the room. I scowl at her, and she smirks cheekily. "Oh, you meant *you*. You're my boyfriend now, are you?"

I sit up and pull her up into my arms, so she was straddling me. "Damn right, I am," I whisper just before I kiss her hard and possessive.

"Isn't it strange that you went from being my ex-husband to my boyfriend?" Shayla wraps her arms around my neck and kisses me while I laugh.

"We're anything but traditional honey." I burr against her lips, and Shayla nods.

"You may be right, Lord Hoult."

I cackle at the nickname. "Never thought I'd be so happy to hear that nickname, my mini muffin." Shayla gasps when I spank her bum and rolls her eyes.

"Oh god, is that back?" She groans, and I laugh, nodding and roll her over onto her back and kiss her hard.

THE NEXT MORNING, I woke up alone in bed. I look around and lean up on my elbow; I see Shayla standing in front of the window wearing my shirt and nothing else. It was so big on her; it was hanging off one shoulder. I slip out of bed and stroll over to her. I wrap my arms around her from behind and nuzzle her neck. "Good morning, sweetheart."

Shayla smiles, wrapping her arms over mine and rests her head on mine. "Good morning, baby."

"Why are you up so early?" I mumble, kissing along her jaw, and she sighs, closing her eyes.

"I couldn't sleep." She bites her lip, looking ahead again. "I feel like I'm in a dream, and I'm terrified I'm going to wake up at any moment, and things will be back to how they were." She whispers sadly, and I turn her around to face me.

I cup her face with my hands and gaze into her beautiful eyes, "It's not a dream, baby. I'm still madly in love with you." I assure her, and she smiles.

"Something happens to my heart when you say that." She sighs contently, placing her hands on my chest. I reach down and lift her hand off my chest and bring her fingers to my lips. I kiss them and press them over my heart.

I press my forehead to hers, "You're locked away in my heart, baby; there's no getting you out of there now." I tell her solemnly.

"And you're locked away in mine." She replies, pushing up on her tiptoes; she kisses me softly. Goddamn, I don't think it's possible to feel happier than I do right now.

"As much as I'd love to take you back to bed and make love to you all over again, we have to prepare for the meeting," I murmur against her lips, and she smiles.

"Mmk." She sighs, snaking her arms around my neck and kissing me deeply. I moan and pull her against me, my fingers already unbuttoning the shirt she had on while we kiss heatedly.

"Mm, maybe a quick one then." I groan and lift her into my arms, carrying her over to the bed and lay her down on it before I crawl up, and she pulls me down by my chain and kisses me hot and hungry. The quick sex session ended up lasting for forty-five minutes, however hard I tried too we just couldn't stop, and we got utterly lost in one another and had to rush to get ready for the meeting. Luckily, the Arabs were running late, and we had time to catch up before the meeting. "They might request more floors, so I thought we could go wider here. What do you think?" I suggest, and Shayla looks at the tablet, her eyes narrowed.

She nods thoughtfully.

“That will work, we could add a shaft right here, and that should improve the stability.” She replies, nibbling on her pencil. I watch her, and she lifts her gaze to mine and smirks. “What?”

“I love you,” I whisper, leaning to kiss her, but she presses the pencil to my forehead and pushes my head back.

“I love you, but we can’t do that here.” She says, looking around to make sure no one was watching. I groan, displeased, and lean back in my chair while she continues to work. Ten minutes later, the Arabs arrived, and we started the meeting. I was right in assuming they would want more floors, so we agreed to seventy-nine levels, and they were happy.

“Excellent, where do we sign?” I look at Shayla, who was gaping at them, eyes wide and her lips parted.

“My lawyers have drawn up the papers with all the changes initially requested by yourselves. If you sign right here,” I hand him the pen, and he signs each page. I sign it also and hold the pen to Shayla. Our eyes meet, and I nod at her, silently assuring her it’s okay. She inhales deeply and signs the contract for her first billion-dollar project. We shake hands, and they leave happy.

“I can’t believe it. This is really happening, isn’t it?” She asks, stunned, and I nod, leaning on the table beside her. I discreetly brush my fingers over hers.

“It sure his, sweetheart. This one is just the first of many projects we’re going to build together.” I tell her, and she smiles up at me, her eyes alight with delight, I wanted to kiss her so bad, but we’d get ourselves arrested if someone reports us.

“So, are we done with work?” Shayla asks, and I nod, closing my laptop.

“We sure are, now we go out and celebrate your achievement,” I tell her as we walk out of the conference room. “What do you want to do?”

Shayla looks at me with a wicked grin, “We are going to make the best of Dubai, baby. Come on.” She chirps excitedly and pulls me along with her.

~

The first place we went after we changed our formal wear into more comfortable clothes was the desert. "Sand dunning?" I ask incredulously, and she pulls her shades down and looks at me with a grin.

"Cole, plcasc don't tell me you've come to Dubai on many occasions and haven't explored the fun things you can do here?" She questions and I shrug, shaking my head.

"I didn't have time. I was only here for work; I flew back right away." I explain, looking around the desert. It was so hot out I was sweating.

"Oh honey, allow me to rectify that." She says, climbing into the open-top jeep and motioning me to get in. I jump in beside her, and the jeep speeds off. I didn't think driving in a hot desert over dunes would be that fun, but once again, Shayla proved me wrong. Shayla holds onto the metal bar and stands up as the jeep speeds down the desert. I watch her as she lifts her arms in the air, eyes closed, her head tilted back, the biggest smile on her face while the wind blows her hair backward. "Baby, come up here." She calls out to me. I pull myself up and wrap my arms around her waist as we drive through the desert. After that, I convinced her to ride a camel with me, and she was indecisive at first but agreed and ended up loving it.

"I thought Casper smelt bad." She mumbles, wrinkling her nose. I laugh and shake my head.

"Hey, you leave my baby alone. He doesn't smell at all." I scold her playfully, and she shrugs, resting her chin on my shoulder.

"Would the lovely couple like a photo for memories?" The guy leading the camel asks when he saw us all loved up with one another. I nod and hand him my phone, Shayla lays her head on mine, and we smile for the photo. "You're a wonderful couple, very in love." He says, handing the phone back to me, and I smile, kissing her knuckles.

"Hu Hayati," Shayla tells him, and the man puts his hand over his chest and nods.

"Tsttye alqawl." He replies. Shayla bites her lip and shrugs. I look at her with a frown, and the older man must have caught on that I didn't understand, and he chuckles, amused.

"She says you are her life." He interprets with a warm smile. "And I say, you can tell." I look back at her and press my forehead to hers, pressing her hand over my heart.

"She's my life, too." The older man sighs, smiling, and continues leading the camel, mumbling to himself in Arabic.

After the camel ride, Shayla drags me to the dune buggies, and we ride those around for a while. I say ride, but we were racing through the desert. I laughed heartily when Shayla's buggy got stuck in the sand, and she couldn't move. "What happened, babe?!" I ask, circling her while she flips me off. "See what happens when you get all cocky." I chuckle and hold my hand out to her. "Come here, baby." I shift back and pull her in front of me on my buggy while I wrap my arms around her waist and kiss her pulse as she drives. The sun was setting as we ride around the desert. Shayla stops at the top of a dune, and we watch the sunset.

I rub her bare thighs, softly trailing my lips along her neck, and she moans, tilting her head back to give me more room to continue my ministration. "I really don't want to go back home." She breathes, closing her eyes. "Let's just move here."

"I'd quite happily stay here with you forever," I whisper in her ear, and she smiles prettily. As it got darker, the stars filled the sky. Shayla and I lay on the sand, looking up at the stars.

"I've never seen so many stars in the sky before. It's incredible." She sighs, smiling up at the sky, absolutely mesmerised. How can someone be so beautiful inside and out? I remember something my grandfather told me at our post-wedding party when he first met her. *"Keep hold of this one. She'll change your whole world just like my Maisie did mine. Hold onto her for dear life, and don't let go."* My heart aches a little when I remember him. He knew I was in love with her before I ever did. I wish I had listened to him; we'd still been married right now if I did.

While we were stargazing, the tour-guide comes to tell us the desert party had begun. Shayla hops up excitedly and squeals. "Come on, lover." She pulls me toward the jeep, and they take us to where the party is held. Upbeat Arabic music was thumping through the speakers, people dancing and eating delicious food from a barbeque they had going. "Oh, my God! Now, this is Shay's kind of party." I laugh while she pulls me along to where they serve the buffet. We sat on a blanket with all those huge floor cushions while eating our food, watching the belly dancers. Shayla was singing and dancing along to the music, her eyes glittering under the lights.

One of thc belly dancers comes sashaying over to me, and I watch her wide-eyed while she shakes and rolls her hips right in front of me. Shayla giggles watching me amusedly while the belly dancer leans over and brushes her hand over my cheek. Shayla smiles at the beautiful girl touching my face and slides money into her outfit. Before I could blink, the dancer had Shayla up and in the middle with her. I watch in awe as they dance together.

Another thing I didn't know about Shay, she could belly dance. My God, did I hit the motherload. I watch avidly the way her hips shake and sway to the song perfectly. Others started to join the dance, and Shayla motions for me to join her and begrudgingly get up and walk over to her. There is no way in hell I can dance to this type of music. I take her hand and spin her before I pull her to me.

"Excuse me, but why am I only just finding out that you can belly dance?" I scold her playfully, and she grins up at me and shrugs impishly.

"Some things are best kept a secret." She replies with a grin, and I wrap my arms around her waist.

"Nah uh, not this, absolutely not. First thing tomorrow, I'm buying you an outfit, and you're going to dance for me just like you did up there." I state, looking down into her upturned face while she laughs, swaying in my arms.

"Oh, am I now?" She purrs flirtatiously. "Are you going to slide cash in my panties too?"

I grin and lift her into my arms, "I'm going to slide something better than cash into your panties if you shake your sexy bum at me like that." I declare, pressing my forehead to hers, and she grins. "I'm going to explode If I don't kiss you soon," I mumble, and she pouts with a nod.

"Me too. Shall we go find an obscure corner and make out for a bit." She suggests with a wicked smile. I pull my head back to look at her and gasp.

"You mean, break the rules?" I smirk, and she nods, slowly licking her lips. "You're trouble, Shayla Hart." I follow her as she pulls me through the crowd of people dancing, and we find a secluded spot away from the party and prying eyes. I pull her to me and draw her lips to mine. We moan in unity the moment our lips touch. I've been dying to kiss her all damn day, and it seems she's been feeling the same frustration. We continue to kiss heatedly for a while, hands caressing over one another leisurely.

"Mm, take me back to the suite and make me yours, Cole Hoult." I groan and brush my lips over hers softly.

"Yes, my Arabian princess."

And I did—all night long. Unfortunately, our trip had come to an end. It was a trip I would never forget for many, many reasons. The plane touched down in London and if only I knew what was waiting for me and what it would cost me— I would have never come back.

Shayla and I walk out of the jet laughing at some ridiculous joke she was telling me. We stopped dead in our tracks when we come face to face with a group of photographers.

"He's out!" One shouts, and Shayla looks around wide-eyed.

"Tristan, over here, can you confirm your engagement to Sophie Turner?!" My blood ran cold in my veins when I heard that very question, and it completely froze when Shayla turns her gaze up to look at me.

"Shayla, over here! How are you feeling about the news of Tristan and Sophie's sudden engagement?"

Shayla held such hurt in her eyes; it wrecked me. No. God, no, no, please no. Tears fill her eyes instantly. I didn't even get to open my mouth before she hastily took off running.

Chapter Thirty-Three

SHAYLA

ENGAGEMENT? Oh, my God. He's engaged to…*her*.

While I stood there, frozen, looking into the apologetic eyes of the man I love, something inside of me died. I wanted to hit the floor. My knees threateningly shook as if they were about to give away on me. My vision blurs as I stare into his eyes before I shake my head and hurry down the steps of the plane and run away as fast as I could. How many times am I going to keep letting him hurt me before I finally give up?

"Shayla?!" I hear him shouting my name from behind me, but I ignore him and keep running till I feel his hand wrap around my wrist, and he pulls me back against his chest. "Shay, please, let me explain." He pants, pushing his forehead to the back of my head. I pull away, jerking my hand out of his hold as if his touch burned me before I turn to face him.

"Explain what? Huh? What are you going to explain Cole? How you *conveniently* forgot to tell me you're *engaged* to Sophie while you were declaring your supposed 'love' for me? Is that what you're going to explain?" I question, and he shakes his head, taking hold of my shoulders. He looks into my eyes.

"I didn't forget Shayla. I was going to tell you. I *wanted* to tell you so many times, but there wasn't a right time, and things were going so great between us, I didn't want anything to jeopardize that." He explains, stepping close to me. I shake out of his hold and drop my gaze.

"No right time?" I whisper. "We had three whole fucking days together where you could have told me, but you chose not to! Your poor fiancée was so happy she told the whole damn world, but *you* couldn't tell me?!" I shout, shoving him away from me when he tried to touch me. "Don't fucking touch me." I hiss angrily.

"Baby, I'm so sorry. I swear to you. I was going to speak to her and call off the whole thing. I lov—"

"Don't!" I shout, shaking my head. My vision blurs as I fight back the tears when I look into his eyes. "Don't you dare say that to me," I say with a sob and angrily wipe away the tears that roll down my cheeks, "Don't bother calling anything off. You two deserve each other," I tell him and turn to leave, but he wraps his arms around me from behind, stopping me.

"Shayla please…" He pleads, his voice breaking. "Don't walk away from me, from us, please baby, not again." I close my eyes and bite the inside of my cheek.

"I don't have anything left in me anymore, Cole. I'm beaten down and exhausted." I turn and face him. "I'm done," I whisper before I turn and walk away from him. I felt so numb. So utterly numb. I didn't understand why I couldn't feel anything. I felt dead inside. Was there a limit to how many times someone could get hurt before they just stop feeling? Or was I simply in shock? I just kept walking and walking; the rain was beating down on me. I could hear Cole's voice calling out to me, but I keep going.

"Shayla, get in the car. You're going to get sick. Please, baby, get in, and let me take you home." He begs, following me and getting soaked himself. "Shayla?!" He shouts over the rain; he grabs my arm and pulls me back to him. "I'm not leaving you like this. Please get in the car, and I will take you home. You don't have to talk or even look at me, please, sweetheart."

I lift my gaze to him and blink, "How could you do this to me, Cole?" I whimper, fisting my hands in his shirt while I look up at him. "After I poured my heart out to you, how could you do this to me?! What are you trying to do to me?!" I scream at him and push at his chest. "Why do you keep hurting me? What have I ever done to you?" I helplessly sob while gazing up at him. Cole's eyes well up as he lifts his hands and cups my face.

"Shayla hurting you is the last thing I ever want to do. I made a mistake by keeping it from you. I should have told you, I know, I'm so sorry I didn't. I was going to end it as soon as I got back home baby." I pull my face out of his hands and push him away from me.

I wipe the tears away with the back of my hand and look at him, "It's too late for apologies now, you had every opportunity to tell me, but you chose to lie to my face again and again."

"I didn't lie to you!"

"You didn't tell me, though, did you?! You're *engaged,* Cole, and you were having sex with me! Telling me you're in love with me! All the while, you've made a promise to share your life with another girl. How dare you put me in that position!" I shout hotly. "You're not the man I thought you were."

Cole shakes his head, shoving his fingers through his hair. "This was all before I knew how you felt about me, Shayla— before I even knew how I felt myself. I made a mistake by not telling you. It's not like I planned to propose to her. It just fucking happened the night I came looking for you, I haven't even had time to process it myself yet, Shay." He explains, reaching out for me, but I swat his hand away.

"It's a hell of a mistake, Cole. Whether it was planned or not doesn't change the fact that you're engaged." I shake my head. "It's not entirely your fault. I made a mistake by trusting you and allowing myself to open up to you. I should never have come back. I should have known you'd only wreck me again." I tell him firmly. "I'm done," I brush past him as I walk down the road.

"Shayla, please don't walk away." He pleads, watching me as I go. I stop and look back at him one last time. The rain was coming down hard, and I was shivering, but weirdly I didn't feel cold despite being completely soaked.

"I have no reason to stay," I tell him weakly before I turn and walk away from him—utterly wrecked.

It wasn't until I got to my apartment and the door clicked shut behind me that I fell in a heap on the floor. My entire body was shaking, my teeth chattering, I couldn't catch my breath.

"Oh my God, Shayla.." Jo came rushing over to me when she saw me on the floor. "Shayla? Shayla, look at me. Fucking hell, you're freezing. Aimee!" She shouts out, and her brown eyes look down at me again. "Shay, what's wrong? Shayla!" She yells, shaking me.

"What? What is it?" Aimee comes rushing out of her room and stops when she sees the state of me. "Jesus…"

"Aimee, she's freezing," Jo tells her worriedly, and Aimee comes beside me and pushes my wet hair off my face. "What do we do?!" She shouts at Aimee, who was looking around the apartment.

"I don't fucking know! What the fuck happened to her?" She retorts, and Jo shakes her head, shrugging.

"I don't know. I just saw her like this. She hasn't said a word. She's not even responding to me." Jo explains, looking at me worriedly. It was such a weird feeling; they were so close to me, but I could barely hear them through the chaos in my head.

"Of course, she's not going to respond to you Jo, she's fucking frozen like an ice pop!" Aimee scolds her. "We need to get her body temperature back up. Let's get her into a warm shower or something. Help me get her up."

"Shayla, come on, babe," Jo mumbles as they help me up to my feet and carry me to the bathroom. "I swear to God, if that idiot Cole has hurt her again, I'm going to go over there and castrate him," Jo growls as they sit me on the toilet seat while they undress me. "Shayla, come on, babe, say something please." Jo pleads, wiping away the endless tears that fell from my eyes.

"He's getting married," I whisper, staring at the wall ahead. I still couldn't believe it, a couple of hours ago I was the happiest I've ever been.

"Oh, fuck." Aimee sighs, wincing. "I fucking knew this would happen when I saw the news on the internet this morning."

"He told me he's in love with me…and I believed him." I look at Jo. "I *believed* him," I whisper, my voice quivering.

"Oh, Shayla." Jo sighs sadly, brushing her fingers through my wet hair, she cups my face in her hands, and I close my eyes. The emotions I hadn't felt before all come crashing down all at once—the hurt, the betrayal, and the devastation, all of it. The girls help me get in the shower, and I cry out when the hot water burns my skin as it hits me. "Shay…"

I sit on the floor in the shower, the water falling over me, feeling more broken than I ever have in my life. "What have I ever done to him?" I ask them frantically, placing my hand on my chest. "Other than love him more than anything, tell me, WHAT DID I EVER DO TO HIM?!" I scream in frustration, curling my fingers in my hair sobbing uncontrollably. Jo clamps her hand over her mouth, her eyes pooling with tears as she watches me fall apart in front of them. Aimee comes and sits in the shower with me, and Jo follows her, both wrapping their arms around me while I cry. "Why does he keep doing this to me." I whimper, burying my face into my arms. "Why…why….WHY?!"

Aimee strokes my hair, "Because you let him, Shayla. We've never seen you this like this before. He's clearly no good for you. Look at what he's doing to you, babe. You need to put this to bed now. Enough is enough." She explains, running her fingers through my wet hair in an attempt to soothe me.

I lift my head and look at her, "How?" I whimper helplessly. "Tell me how, and I'll do it." I sob, shaking my head. "I don't understand how he can look me in the eyes and tell me he's in love with me when all the while he's engaged to another girl." I sob shaking my head. "I thought he was different."

"Did you tell him how you felt?" Jo asks, tucking a wet strand of my hair behind my ear. I nod, closing my eyes.

"I did. I told him I was so in love with him and have been for a while, then we spent the most incredible three days together, but then we come back, and I hear from the paparazzi waiting for him at the airstrip that he's engaged to Sophie. He didn't even have the decency to tell me himself!" I sob.

Aimee shakes her head and presses her forehead to my temple. "No wonder you're a wreck. What a fucking idiot."

"Shay, do you think Sophie sent the paparazzi there?" Aimee questions, and I look at her miserably.

"Does it matter who sent them? *He* was supposed to tell me, not keep it from me the entire trip, all the while making love to me and telling me I'm the one he wants. It was bad enough sleeping with him when I thought he had a girlfriend, but to find out she's his fiancée." I cry, shaking my head, feeling repulsed with myself. "I hate myself and what 'I've become because of him."

"Shayla, you didn't know babe, you were just acting on your feelings. I'm assuming he told you he was going to finish it with her?" I nod woefully. "Well, that's on him, not you."

"That doesn't make me feel any better," I whisper hoarsely, closing my eyes. A knock sounds at the front door, and I open my eyes, and the girls look at me.

"How much do you want to bet that's him," Aimee says, getting up to her feet.

If it is, I'm not here." I tell her pleadingly, and she nods, walking out of the bathroom soaking wet to answer the door. Jo keeps her arm around me as I rock back and forth.

"Is Shayla here?" I hear Cole's voice, and I bury my head in my arms.

"No, she's not."

"Aimee, don't lie to me. I just want to talk to her." He says pleadingly, and I feel my heart ache.

"She's not here!" Aimee snaps hotly, and I can imagine her glaring at him menacingly.

"You're lying, her bags right there. Shayla?!"

"Haven't you done enough?!" Aimee shouts angrily. "I have never in all my years of friendship with that girl seen her this broken!"

"Aimee, I love her."

"Then let her go, Cole. If you genuinely love her, like you say you do, let her go because you're no good for her. She's a fucking wreck, and I don't even know where or how we're going to help her pick up the pieces this time."

"Please, let me see her, just for a second." He begs wretchedly, and I whimper, unable to control the sob that escapes me.

"You hear that? That's what loving you is doing to her." There's a moment of silence, and the only sound in the apartment was my weeping echoing in the bathroom. "She's the last person in the world to deserve this. Do yourself and her a big favour and let her go before you drive her away for good."

"Shayla, I'm so sorry! Please, baby, I love you so much!" I hear Cole say, his voice breaking. "I'm sorry." Jo wraps her arms around me tightly as I sob into her chest. "Let me see her, please, just for a second, let me see her." He requests, crying himself.

"Cole, she doesn't want to see you. All you're doing is hurting her more. Just go. The sooner you walk out of her life, the better it will be for her." Aimee tells him.

"I just want to say goodbye."

"Do you want to see him?" Jo whispers to me while she helps me out of the shower and hands me my robe. I shake my head. I did want to see him, of course, I did, but nothing good would come of it. I needed to hate him. I walk out of the bathroom, still shivering; my body just wasn't warming up. Aimee was about to close the door when I see him, our eyes meet, and he puts his hand on the door, obstructing it before it closed.

"Shayla…" My eyes burn with tears when I hear the despair in his voice and see the tears in his eyes. "I fucked up. I know. But everything I told you at the beach is true. If you can't believe anything, at the very least believe that."

I wipe away the tears that stream down my cheeks, "I do, but it's just not enough to fix the damage you've done." I tell him honestly, and he closes his eyes, biting his bottom lip.

"Shay, you're the one I want. Let's just talk, please?"

I shake my head. "I wish that there was more to say, but there isn't. I've got nothing left for you anymore."

"Please don't say I've lost you." He exhales woefully, and I shake my head.

"You can't lose something you never had," I whisper and tear my eyes from his and walk to my bedroom, ignoring his calls out to me. I close the door and lean on it, sobbing pathetically. I was so tired of feeling the way I did. Deep down, I knew it was too good to be true, I had a feeling in my gut that something would happen, and it did. I lived a dream for a few days, but I've woken to the reality of my pathetic existence yet again.

~

ONE WEEK PASSES by since I've seen or heard from Cole. It hasn't gotten any easier, but I'm learning to cope with the constant ache in my chest. On the tenth day, I was ready to face the world again. Something Aimee said hit me really hard. "I know you're hurting Shayla, but you're a lot stronger than you know. No girl should ever pin all her hopes and dreams on a man. You hold your head up, and you walk back into that office, and you work your arse off for that dream you were building long before Cole Hoult walked into your life."

So, I did. I buried my feelings for him yet again and put all my energy into my work. Seeing him for the first time after our break up was the most challenging part, but I somehow found the strength to face him.

When I knock on his office door, he lifts his stormy gaze to look at me, and he blinks surprised, getting up to his feet as I walk into his office. "Shayla."

"Hi, can we talk for a second?" I say, and he nods slowly.

"Of course, come on in." He answers, taking a step closer to me. I lick my lips and suck in a deep breath to calm my nerves before I raise my gaze off the floor to meet his steadily.

"My initial instinct was to quit this project and disappear for a while, but over the last ten days, I've had time to think about it, and I've decided to stay and see this project through," I explain, and his eyes light up instantly which throws me off a little. I rub my forehead, "Uh, I want us to forget everything that happened in Dubai and just focus on working on this project together like we initially planned."

"And if I can't forget?"

"Then I'll walk out right now."

"Shayla, that's not fair. You can't just expect me to forget everything that's happened between us and carry on like I'm not in love—"

"Cole, stop." I cut him off, closing my eyes. "That ship has sailed and sunk. If you're willing to work together *professionally*, I'm more than happy to do that, but that is as far as it will ever go between us." Cole's shoulders slump, and he looks down at the floor.

"If working together is the only way I can keep you in my life, I will gladly do that than not have you in it at all." He tells me earnestly. I force down the sudden urge to cry and nod.

"Great," I utter, looking at him. "I'll be at my desk then."

"Good." He replies, staring at me intently. I tear my eyes away from his before I turn and walk out of his office. The next few weeks, I was required to work long days and nights alongside Cole on this hotel project. I sigh, dropping my pen in frustration. I rub my temples tiredly. Cole lifts his eyes off his sketch and looks at me with a little frown. "What's the matter?"

"I've tried multiple times to get this bit right, but it's not working." I groan, closing my eyes. Cole gets up and walks around the desk to stand over me from behind.

"Show me." He says, placing one hand on the table and leaning over me so he could see my sketch.

"Here." I tap my pen on the part I was struggling with. While he studies my sketch, Cole's eyes narrow, he bites his lip, and his hand covers mine holding the pen.

"If you do it like this…" He speaks lowly beside my ear as his hand guides mine over the screen. I bite my lip, and my fingers tremble a little under him, but he tightens his hand around mine, steadying it as he draws expertly. "It should work." He murmurs in my ear.

"Thank you."

"You're welcome." I swallow hard when I feel his breath on my ear for a lingering moment before he pulls away and walks back to his seat, his eyes on mine till he smirks a little and looks down at his tablet again.

"I think I'm done for the day. I'm going to head out." I tell him, and he looks at me, nodding his head slowly. "Do you need anything from me before I go?"

He smiles, "I wouldn't say no to a back rub." He states boldly, raising his brows at me suggestively.

"But I would." I retort, smiling sweetly at him, and he chuckles, amused with a shake of his head.

"Killjoy," He pouts, throwing a balled-up paper at me, which I pick up and throw back at him.

"Bite me."

"Oh? Is that an invitation?" He questions, grinning handsomely, tossing it back at me again.

"Only in your dreams, darling." I throw the balled-up paper at his head and turn to leave his office.

"Only every night, baby." He retorts teasingly, throwing the paper and watches with glee as it hits my bum and falls on the floor. "Right on target." He smirks, winking at me while leaning back in his chair as I glare at him.

"Good night, Cole." I bite out before I turn and walk out of his office. I sigh tiredly as I stroll toward the elevator. It's been the longest day ever, and I couldn't wait to get home and get into my pj's and fall asleep to a good movie. I frown when I hear the clicking of heels on the tiled floor approaching me, I look up from my phone and resist the urge to roll my eyes when I see Sophie walking toward me.

"Well, well, well, if it isn't the little *ex*-wife. Why am I not surprised to see you here so late?" She greets snidely, raising her perfectly shaped brow at me, and I lick my lips, pushing the button to the elevator repeatedly. Give me a fucking break.

"Could it be because I actually work here, *unlike* yourself?" I retort back sardonically, staring at the numbers at the top of the elevator to avoid looking at the bitch.

Sophie chuckles, tossing her bleach blonde hair over her shoulder as she lets her icy blue eyes rake over me. "I'm the boss's soon-to-be *wife*; it would do you a world of good to get yourself used to the idea of seeing me around here more often." I ignore the pull at my heart and look at her with a sugary smile.

"Why is that? Are you planning on working here? Because the last time I checked, we design *buildings* here, sweetie, not *clothes*?" I tell her with a smirk, and she glares at me.

"You just can't help yourself, can you? Just when I let myself believe you're finally gone for good, you pop back up like a bad rash." She retorts stonily. "Don't think for one second that I don't know why you agreed to come back here, Shayla. You're wasting your time if you think you can worm your way back with Tristan." She scoffs, "Then again, I shouldn't be so surprised. What else did I expect from a girl who lacks any form of self-respect? After all, he did leave you to be with me." She says, crossing her arms over her chest, and I smile.

"Pardon? First of all, Cole didn't leave *me* for *you*. The decision to divorce was agreed upon mutually for reasons that, A… had nothing to do with you, and B… is and never will be any of your damn business. Secondly, where was this self-respect of yours when you were in here kissing *my* husband while you were engaged to another guy? Oh, that's right, non-existent, that's where." I respond cuttingly and watch in delight while her face goes all red with humiliation. "You clearly have issues in your relationship if you're coming by your fiancé's office to check up on him at this time of night. I don't know what you were expecting to find, sweetie, but going around deliberately kissing other girl's husbands is more your forte, not mine." I add with a wink and turn to walk into the elevator but stop and look at her again.

"And hey, at least whenever I kissed Cole or when we made love, I never, not once, had to worry if he was thinking about you because those beautiful green eyes were always on mine until the very last second. The next time he has sex with you, if those eyes are looking into yours, you have nothing to worry about, but if they're closed…well, I'll let you think about that one. Ciao." I drawl, waving at her as the elevator door closes.

I exhale deeply, closing my eyes. I hate that woman with every fibre in my body.

Chapter Thirty-Four

COLE

It's been over a week since Shayla and I parted ways *again*. I thought walking away from her before was hard, it's even harder now I've realised I'm in love with her. I can't believe what a mess I've made of everything. I've lost her. Every single night I jump out of my sleep to the sound of her anguished sobs. Watching her shed a tear was always tough for me, but hearing such despair and suffering in her cry still haunts me. I don't know what I was thinking, keeping the engagement from her. If I just told her from the beginning, she would be with me right now, but I was worried about her reaction, and instead, she got blindsided entirely and thought I was lying to her—which I wasn't. Christ, I'm a mess, and I've never felt so low in my life.

As hard as it is to admit to myself, Aimee was right with what she said. After hearing Shayla sobbing and the look of defeat in her eyes, when I saw her that day in her apartment, I made a promise to myself to leave her alone. What right do I have to keep hurting her? Even though it was killing me and I wanted to be with her, I had to do what was right and let her be free. She deserves so much better, and she's the last person in the world I would ever want to hurt intentionally.

I remember coming home after leaving her apartment that day. Sophie was at my place, and she'd had a romantic candlelit dinner prepared to celebrate our engagement. "Hi baby, welcome ho—" She stops when she sees the state of me. Completely soaked, eyes rimmed red from crying and angry. "Tristan? What on earth is this state of you? What happened?" I threw my bag on the floor and glared at her.

"Did you go public with our engagement?" I question, glaring at her. Sophie looks at me and shrugs.

"Well, yeah, I only posted a photo of my ring on Instagram, and it blew up." I close my eyes and clench my jaw tight to keep calm.

"And the photographers at the airstrip? Did you tell them where to find me?" I ask again, and Sophie looks at me.

"No. I—"

"Don't lie to me!" I bark, and she jumps startled and drops her gaze. "Of course, you fucking sent them. Otherwise, how would they know where and what time I would be arriving, right?" I hiss, pacing back and forth. I rub my jaw in agitation.

"Tris, what's the big deal? So what if people know we're engaged?" She questions, watching me pace and forth in the living room.

"What's the big deal?! We got engaged not even four days ago, Sophie! I haven't even had time to adjust to it, and you go and tell the fucking world!" I roar angrily, swiping the wine glass off the table, and it smashes on the floor. "What is it with you and your obsession with telling the whole fucking world our business Sophie?! Why can't we have one fucking private moment for us, just fucking one!" I shout angrily, kicking the chair.

"Baby, I didn't think—"

"No! You didn't think, and that's the problem Sophie, you don't think about anyone but yourself! What was the fucking need to go and post about our private life on your social media? I've told you a million times I want my private life to stay private, and our engagement was supposed to be *private,* for just us!" I scream at her, not even caring that her eyes well up.

"Tristan, I'm so sorry if I had known you'd be this angry, I would have never—"

I shake my head, "Yes, you would have because that's you all over, isn't it, Soph. You don't give a toss about what I think or how I feel as long your socialite friends have juicy gossip to fucking feast on." I retort, irritated. "You didn't even have the decency to warn me, so I'd be prepared, no you just completely blindsided me. Shayla was with me for fucksake; the poor girl didn't know what to do with herself with all the cameras flashing in her face!" I add, taking off my jacket and throwing it on the floor.

"Shayla? Are you standing there chewing me out over your ex-wife? Who cares about her!"

"I DO!" I roar livid. "I fucking care about her! I hadn't even told her about the engagement yet, and she finds out from the paparazzi. How do you think she felt standing there as my ex-wife hearing that I was engaged to another woman three months after we get divorced?! She was humiliated, and so was I! Are you seriously that dense, Sophie? Do you not have an ounce of empathy as a woman yourself to how she would have felt, Jesus Christ!"

"Why would I care how she feels? She wouldn't give a toss if the shoe were on the other foot and she was marrying you." She argues back, placing her hands on her hips and scowling at me.

"She was married to me! How many fucking times did you see her share anything about our private life on her social media? Never! You know why because she understands that somethings are supposed to be private, and she had some sense and enough respect for me and our relationship to keep shit out of the public and not go screaming about everything we did."

"I'm not Shayla, Tristan!"

"No, you aren't!" I shout hotly, taking my wet shirt off and walking to my bedroom. "Did you even stop for a second to think what the papers would write when they see Shayla, and I walk out of the plane together or did your brain not consider that little detail? She doesn't want to be in the public eye Sophie, and I was doing everything in my power to make sure it stays that way."

"Oh, my God. I am so sick of hearing about her! What about me, Tristan?! I'm your fiancée. Me! I've prepared a surprise meal for you so we could celebrate our engagement, and you haven't even acknowledged it." She argues, following me into my bedroom.

"When you do something worth acknowledging, I will. I'm not in the mood to celebrate shit with you right now. In fact, you're the last person I want to see Sophie, just go home." I hiss bleakly, not even bothering to look at her.

"Are you serious? You are kicking me out. For what?" She questions, gaping at me, and I rub the back of my neck.

"For what?! Have you not been listening to a fucking word I've been saying to you?!" I turn and bellow in her face. She looks at me; her blue eyes pooled with tears. "You know what, fuck this whole thing. I can't do this."

"Can't do what, Tristan?"

"This. *Us*. I can't do it," I admit and watch as tears stream down her cheeks. "I thought this was what I wanted, but it's not Sophie. It's just not the same."

"You're breaking up with me for sharing my happiness over us getting engaged? Are you serious?" She cries, and I sigh, closing my eyes. She's just not fucking getting it.

"No, Sophie, we're breaking up because of your complete disregard for my privacy and your lack of empathy for the people around you. Thanks to you, I'll be hounded by the press for months now about when we're getting married, and I don't need that shit on top of all the pressure I'm already under at work." I explain bitingly.

"Tristan, you're blowing this way out of proportion. This can't just be about me going public." She sniffles, raising her distraught gaze to mine. "You're using this press thing as an excuse to back out of the engagement, aren't you?"

I exhale and rub the back of my neck, agitated. "No, it's not just that, Sophie. I thought we could get back what we once had but we can't because I realised that what I want has changed. *I've* changed. All the yacht parties, and you and all your fake socialite friends pretending to like one each other, when secretly you're competing with one another. Who has the best clothing line, who will get married first, who has a bigger engagement ring? It's shallow and materialistic bullshit, and I'm over it. I want to be able to come home after a long day and relax with my girl-friend— but I can't do that with you, because you always want to do something, you always want to be somewhere. It's exhausting. Your whole lifestyle is gruelling to me now." I clarify openly. I wasn't lying. I was honestly so tired of all of it.

Sophie stares at me for a long moment. She nods and wipes her tears away before she pulls something out of her purse, which was on the bed. "I was going to give you this after we had our dinner as a surprise, but I guess now's a good time as any." I take the little card and look at her before I open it and frown. I glance at her and back down at the card again. *Oh shit*

"Wait. Is this what I think it is?"

"I"m pregnant, Tristan." I stare down at the picture of a sonogram in my hand, and I feel my heart rate decelerate drastically. I felt like someone had dropped a bucket of hot boiling water over my head.

"How did this happen? I used protection every time we…" I trail off, shaking my head. I used a rubber every fucking time. How could this happen?

"I don't know. I was just as shocked when I found out a week ago, but condoms aren't always a hundred per cent effective." She says, watching me as I sink on the bed staring at the picture between my trembling fingers. I know it may seem stupid, but at that moment, all I saw was Shayla and her cries of despair. I don't want to hurt her again. Fuck, this is going to destroy her. "Tristan, please say something."

"How far along are you?" I ask, my voice barely over a whisper.

"Eleven weeks." She replies, chewing on her bottom lip. I lean over, placing my forearms on my knees before I hang my head and put my hands ontop. That's around the time we got back together. *Fuck!*

"Have you told anyone?" I sigh, staring at the floor, praying she hasn't gone, and announced this too.

"No, of course I haven't. I wanted to tell you first." She states, stepping closer and sitting beside me. "I was so happy when I found out I was carrying your baby. I couldn't wait for you to come back from Dubai so I could tell you. Clearly, I wasn't expecting you to come back and dump me. I thought you would be just as happy as I was about having a baby. Why do you think I wanted to get engaged so fast?" She shrugs her shoulder. "My parents are going to be livid when they find out I got pregnant before we're married. You know how much their reputation means to them." She cries, shaking her head. "What am I going to tell them, Tristan?"

I close my eyes and bite the inside of my cheek so hard I drew blood. There's only one thing I can do. I have to marry her, whether I like it or not. She's carrying my baby, and I won't turn my back on my child. "You're not going to tell them anything until we're married," I utter numbly as I stare at the floor biting back the tears. "You don't breathe a word to anyone until the time is right, do you understand me?" Sophie nods silently and lays her head on my shoulder. I sigh and get up, massaging my temples, my fingers still trembling. "Go home, Sophie. I need some space." I throw over my shoulder before I walk into the ensuite bathroom in my bedroom. I stare at myself in the mirror till I hear the front door click shut.

"You fucking idiot!" I growl and smash my fist hard into the mirror a couple of times till it shatters completely, and I couldn't see myself anymore. "Ahh!" I scream at the top of my lungs as I sink to the floor, blood seeping down my hand and onto the tiled floor, crying at the mess my life has become.

In a way, I was relieved Shayla wanted nothing to do with me because it meant I didn't have to tell her about the baby and break her heart all over again. As much as it's killing me to stay away, I have no choice.

I'm getting married in four weeks to a woman I thought I was in love with but now can't tolerate for shit, and she's having my baby to boot. Aimee was right. I bring nothing but misery and pain to her life, so she will be much happier without me in it.

That was until she walked into my office ten days later. The moment I saw her, I wanted to fall to my knees in front of her and beg her to hold me so that I could find a moment's peace from the constant ache in my chest. But I couldn't. I deserve to feel this way for everything I put her through. It's okay, though; I'd much rather take the hit and be miserable for the rest of my life than watch one single tear fall from her beautiful eyes.

I suppose that that's what love really is, and that's what loving *her* has taught me, being selfless, or at least I'm trying to be. She makes me a better person.

When I saw her that day, it hit me once again how much I love her.

Despite all the shit she's been through lately, she still had the courage and strength to walk into my office with her head held high and is prepared to work on accomplishing her dream of becoming an architect. That's why I fucking love her. Divorcing her was the biggest mistake I have ever made in my life.

"Cole?" I blink and look at her watching me with a little frown on her face.

"Hm?"

"Are you okay? You've been staring at me without blinking for like a minute straight." She questions, looking genuinely concerned, and I sigh, closing my eyes. "Somethings wrong, what is it?"

I shake my head. "Nothing. I'm fine."

"Cole..." She presses with a sigh. "Whatever it is you want to say, just say it. You've been trying to tell me something for days. What is it? Just spit it out."

"There is something I've wanted to tell you, but if I'm honest, I'm fucking terrified of your reaction, and I'm afraid to break your heart again," I admit, and Shayla looks at me warily, sitting forward in her seat.

"What is it, Cole?" I close my eyes and bite my lip hard, trying to find the courage to tell her about the baby.

"That day when you found out about the engagement…" I begin explaining, and Shayla looks at me and nods slowly. "When I got home, Sophie and I got into an argument, and I told her I didn't want to be with her and that it was over between us," I say and swallow thickly. My voice breaks when I raise my gaze to Shayla, watching me intently while patiently waiting for me to finish explaining.

I exhale slowly. "Sophie's pregnant."

The glass of water in Shayla's hand slips out of her grasp and hits the floor while she stares at me her green eyes wide.

Chapter Thirty-Five

SHAYLA

"SOPHIE'S PREGNANT."

I stare at Cole numbly while my fingers lose the grip I had on the glass, which slips and smashes on the tiled floor. Did he just say Sophie is pregnant? Did I really hear him, right? I don't even think I was blinking while I just sat there staring at him like some kind of an idiot. I think I was on the verge of a nervous breakdown.

"Oh. Wow. Congratulations. I should, uh, c-clean the glass..." I mutter pathetically while I kneel on the floor, attempting to pick up the shards of glass with my trembling fingers.

"Shayla, what are you doing?" I hear Cole say as he hurries toward me, kneeling in front of me while I pick up the broken pieces of glass.

"It just slipped out of my hand when you…uh, God, I'm so sorry." I apologise.

"Shayla, leave it. Stop, you're going to hurt yourself, just leave it." Cole frowns and reaches out to touch me, but I flinch, and he pulls his hand back. My entire body was trembling so much that I couldn't get a grip on the pieces of glass.

"No. I made a mess. I need to clean it up." I whisper, trying desperately to keep the quiver out of my voice while I pick up the shard of glass.

"Shayla, you're going to shred your fingers! Stop." Cole shouts, shaking me. He takes my face into his hands and lifts my watery gaze to meet his. I look into his eyes, unable to utter a single word or make a movement. "Baby, let go of the glass." I stare at him motionless while he takes my hand into his, and he pries my trembling fingers open where I had fisted them tightly around a shard of glass. "Christ, Shay. What have you done? JESS!" He shouts, and his assistant comes running into his office. "Get me the first aid kit now!" Jess nods and runs out of the office while Cole looks down at my bleeding hand. He pulls the shard of glass slowly out of my hand and winces. "Jesus, Shayla, you're bleeding so much." He says, looking around the office frantically. "Why did you do that, huh? Why?" He asks, looking at me worriedly, and I stare at my blood-soaked hand blankly.

"She's *pregnant*?" I lift my gaze to his and blink, looking into his green eyes that well up as he watches me.

"Shayla, I'm so sorry."

I shake my head and drop my gaze, "Why?" I whisper with a shrug.

Cole looks at me, forlornly, "For making a mess of everything, for hurting you all over again." He admits, and I shake my head.

"It really is incredible. Just when I let myself believe that this is the worse I will ever feel, something else happens that breaks me that little bit more." I tell him, and Cole shakes his head, reaching up; he wipes the tears that stream down my face just as Jess comes in with the first aid kit. Cole takes it off her, dismisses her, and she leaves the office.

"Shayla, I swear to you, I was careful. I don't understand how this could have happened." He explains, wrapping a cloth tightly around my hand and putting pressure on it to stop the bleeding.

Cole looks up into my face expecting me to show some form of reaction to the pain but frowns when I stare at him vacantly. "I may have slipped when I slept with her while I was thinking about you." He explains, and I close my eyes and wince at the thought of him having sex with her. "I was miserable and started drinking every night to ignore the ache deep inside me after you left and I—." He justifies, and I close my eyes, not wanting to hear anymore.

"—Stop," I whisper bleakly, shaking my head. "You don't owe me an explanation, Cole. You're having a baby. You should be happy."

"How can I be happy, Shay? That baby is tying me to a life I don't want. I don't want Sophie. I don't want the baby." He tells me, his tone strained with desperation.

"Cole, don't say things like that; that's your flesh and blood." He sighs sullenly. "It's an innocent little baby. Whether you want its mother or not, that child is a part of you, and that will never change."

Cole closes his eyes and bites his lip. "Shayla, I want *you*. I want *us*."

"There never was an *us,* Cole. We need to both accept that now and move on because I can't take much more. I'm tired of constantly picking up the pieces, only for them to fall apart all over again. I don't have the strength, nor do I have anything left for you to break. I've given all I have, and I've taken all I can take. Please, I'm *begging* you, just release me and let my heart rest, *please*." I sob defencelessly with my head hung. I didn't have the strength to even look at him any longer. Cole presses his forehead to mine, an endless stream of tears rolling down his cheeks.

"I'm so sorry," He whispers, brushing my tears away with his thumbs. "Please don't cry. I know this is so very selfish, but you have no idea how much I wish it were you that was pregnant instead of her." He admits, and I whimper, shaking my head. "I would have been so fucking happy, especially if it was a little girl with your eyes, your gorgeous smile, and a beautiful heart like yours." He sobs, burying his face into my neck. I wrap my arms around him, and he hugs me tightly. "How am I supposed to let you go, Shay. Tell me how?" I sigh, closing my eyes, and pull away from him.

"Cole, coming back here, it was a bad idea. I can't be here anymore. It's too hard being this close to you every day." I admit dropping my gaze, and Cole shakes his head.

"No, please no, don't you dare tell me you want to walk out of my life for good. I won't let you."

"Cole, I can't be around you. It hurts too much."

Cole looks into my eyes, his fingers combing through my hair, "Please don't go. I'd rather see you every day, and have it kill me. I'd rather love you quietly from afar than have you walk away and never see you again, please don't." He pleads sorrowfully. "I know I have no right to ask this of you. If you have to hate me, then hate me, I'll take it. I'll take you hating me any day over losing you completely."

"I wish I had it in me to hate you, Cole, it might have made this constant aching in my heart more tolerable, but I don't think I have the strength to watch you get married and have a baby with her," I sigh with a shrug. "I just can't."

Cole drops his gaze from mine to my bleeding hand and licks his lips, "I understand." He whispers woefully and frowns when he unwraps the cloth and sees more blood oozing from my hand. "The bleeding won't stop. Your cut is too deep. I'm taking you to the hospital." He says standing, and I shake my head with an exhausted sigh.

"I don't need to go to the hospital. I'm fine." I reply, wiping the tears away that kept rolling down my cheeks. I'm so fed up with crying. I don't want to cry anymore. I just want it all to stop. Cole leans over and lifts me to my feet by my arms.

"You'll bleed out if you don't get stitches, Shay." I look at him; he has my blood all over his hands, grey trousers, and his white shirt.

"Then let me bleed out, Cole." I exhale tiredly, and he looks at me with a scowl on his handsome face. Cole takes a step toward me, cups my face in his hands, and lifts my gaze to his again.

"Hey, look at me, don't you talk like that." He scolds me, looking into my eyes. "You think I'll live if anything ever happens to you. I *won't*, you hear me?" He tells me earnestly, and I blink back the tears that gather in my eyes again. "I'm taking you to the hospital." I didn't have the energy to argue with him, so I nod. I think I lost quite a bit of blood because I was feeling legless. My knees shook, and before I could hold onto something, I collapse into Cole's arms. "Shayla?" The last thing I hear was Cole shouting my name and the feeling of being lifted off the ground before everything fades to black.

~

I DON'T KNOW how long I was out for, but it felt so good. There was no pain; there was no sound; there was stillness; there was peace and… Cole.

I was with Cole in Dubai. I didn't want to wake up. Why couldn't they leave me here? I wanted to stay where I was forever. "Miss Hart?"

My eyes felt so heavy. My entire body felt weighty, like I was buried under bags and bags of sand. I peel my eyes open and wince at the sheer brightness of the room. I peer up at a man standing over me, smiling in scrubs— a doctor. "There she is. How are you feeling, Shayla?"

I blink up at him and shake my head. "Tired." I breathe, and he nods, smiling. "What happened? Where am I?" I ask disoriented, and see Cole sitting beside me, looking all kinds of worried.

"You're at the hospital. You severed a vein when you cut your hand and lost quite a bit of blood, which caused you to go into hypovolemic shock. Luckily, Tristan brought you in just in time so we could stitch you up before you lost much more." I look over at Cole, who takes my hand into his and kisses my knuckles. "You're also very malnourished, Shayla, which tells me you've not been taking very good care of yourself. Your iron levels are remarkably low, which is why you've been feeling fatigued. We've got you on a drip to replenish your vitamin B and iron levels. We're also giving you some blood, so you should be feeling better real soon." He explains, checking the drips hanging over my bed. "We'll keep you in tonight for observation, and we'll see how you're feeling tomorrow. Okay?" I nod, and he smiles. "I'll be over later to check on you." He says and walks out of the room, leaving Cole and me alone.

"Are you okay?" Cole asks worried, and I nod, looking at him. "You scared the life out of me when you collapsed like that." He sighs, pressing my wrist to his lips, his eyes closing. "I thought something happened to you."

"I'm fine. I'm sorry for scaring you," I whisper, and Cole opens his eyes, looking at me.

"You have nothing to be sorry for, Shayla. I'm the one that's sorry. This is all my fault. All of it." He states desolately, looking down at my hand, playing with my fingers, "Look at what I've done to you, and like the selfish prick that I am, I'm still trying to hold on." I close my eyes and shake my head. "Aimee's right. I'm no good for you."

"Cole, we're both to blame for all of this. Yes, you keep hurting me, but I keep letting you by constantly coming back into your life. I should have stayed away and never agreed to come back. I should never have put myself in this position and told you how I felt— but I can't seem to get my heart to listen to reason when it comes to you." I explain, and Cole nods sadly, his thumb gently brushing over my pulse point while he looks at me brokenly, which hurts me more than I can ever put into words. "It's just not meant to be."

"How much ever it may hurt me, I don't and will never regret falling in love with you. I want you to know that I'm going to bury my love for you deep in my heart and love you forever, Shayla." He admits leaning over and stroking my hair.

I whimper and nod, "Me too. I'm going to love you forever too, Cole." I sniffle with a sad smile. "You're going to be an incredible Dad."

He closes his eyes and shakes his head. "No, I'm not. I'm going to fuck it up like I have everything else. I'm so fucking terrified, Shay."

I lift my hand and stroke his jaw, "It's okay to be scared, but you've got this." I assure him, and he presses his lips to my forehead.

"How do you still have so much faith in me after everything I've done?" He questions, pulling back and looking into my eyes with such devotion it stole my breath.

"Because I love you, you stupid boy," I whisper, and he smiles a little, but it doesn't reach his eyes.

"And I love you, you silly girl." He whispers back and leans in, kissing me softly on the lips. I sigh when he pulls back, and his eyes search mine for a moment.

"You should go," I tell him, and he shakes his head quickly.

"No, I'm not leaving. I'm staying with you." He declares, retaking his seat, and I try to sit up ready to argue with him, but I forget about the cut on my hand and cry out when I press down on it hard, and a jolt of pain shoots up my arm. Cole jumps up and takes my bandaged hand into his and looks at me worriedly, then down at my hand when he sees blood seeping through the bandage.

"Shit. Hey! Someone get a doctor in here!" He shouts, and a nurse comes running into the room. "She's bleeding," Cole tells her, and she takes my hand starts to cut open the bandage to get a better look. The moment the bandage opens blood streams down my arm and all over the bed.

"You've torn your stitches." She says and pushes a red button wrapping my hand in a clean cloth and pressing down hard to stop the bleeding. I whimper and bury my face into Cole's neck, hissing.

"Hey, take it easy. You're hurting her!" He scolds her angrily as the doctor comes rushing in.

"What happened?" He asks, taking my hand into his and unwrapping the cloth to take a better look at it.

"She's torn her stitches." The nurse informs him, and he nods.

"All right, get me the cart. We'll have to restitch it again." The doctor tells the nurse, and she nods and walks out. "Am I going to have to tie you down to keep you still, young lady?" I shake my head with a muffled 'no' from where my face is buried in Cole's chest. He brushes his fingers through my hair soothingly as the doctor prepares to restitch my hand. "Shayla, this is going to hurt a little, but I'll be as quick as I can. You're bleeding too much for me to numb it. You're going to have to bear with the pain for a little bit, sweetheart." The doctor says, and I nod. "Might help if your boyfriend distracts you." He adds, and I look at Cole as the doctor wipes my hand with that foul anti-bacterial liquid that burnt so much it brought tears.

"Ow, ow, it hurts." I whimper, trying to pull my hand back, but the doctor gives me a firm look, and I sink back into Cole's arms. I close my eyes as the needle inches closer to my skin.

"Shayla, your hand is shaking. I can't stitch you up properly if you're moving, sweetheart." The doctor tells me, pushing his glasses up the bridge of his nose and giving Cole a pointed look, who nods and turns my head so he could look into my eyes. His thumb stroking along my jaw before he brushes his lips over mine, slowly parting my lips so he could deepen the kiss. I moan when I feel his velvet tongue caressing my own. I suck his tongue, eliciting a throaty moan from Cole, who curls his fingers at the nape of my neck, drawing my mouth closer to his so he could deepen the kiss more.

Everything dissolves around us while we kiss. "All right, we're all done." The doctor announces and looks at us kissing, wholly lost in one another. "I said we're done." He tries again and chuckles, shaking his head when neither of us acknowledges him, and we continue to kiss. The nurse sighs, watching us, and the doctor gestures with his head to leave the room.

"I wish someone would kiss me like that." She mumbles, glancing back one more time before she closes the door behind her. Cole and I were too engrossed in one another to notice they were gone. It wasn't until our lungs ran out of oxygen that we pull apart, panting. I moan when Cole sucks my bottom lip and nibbles on it gently. We open our eyes and look at one another. "Wow." I utter, and he licks his lips, those stunning green eyes studying my face. "I forgot how good you kiss," I whisper, and Cole stares at me for a drawn-out minute before he drops a kiss on my jaw.

"I wish I could remind you every moment of every day how much I love kissing you." He declares, sincerity radiating in the depths of his eyes as he looks at me.

I sigh and pull back. "As tempting as that sounds, we can't. You shouldn't have kissed me but thank you for distracting me." Cole nods, leaning back into his chair. "You really should go home, Cole. The last thing we need right now is someone recognising us and leaking another photo."

Cole sighs, rubbing his forehead, "Shayla. I'll only sit at home and worry about you if I go. Let me stay with you. The blinds are all closed, so no one can see us." It was the sadness in his eyes that made me nod and allow him to stay with me.

"Fine. Can you call the girls and tell them; they'll worry if I don't go home." I request, laying down and Cole nods, picking up my phone. He calls Aimee and tells her I'm in the hospital, and I hear her shout from the other end of the phone.

"You don't have to come. She's resting. What do you mean, why am I with her? I brought her in, Aimee. No, I won't leave her side. Yes, I promise. Okay, I'll tell her." He sighs, hanging up the phone, and looks at me. "They said they love you, and I should wait for my impending castration." I laugh heartily, and he watches me shaking his head; his own lips curl into a smile before he starts laughing too. "It's really not funny. Aimee is one scary chick when she's angry— though not as scary as you are." He adds with a sheepish smile, and I shrug passively.

"You've met my brother. Try growing up with him and not have anger issues." I tell him with a sigh. Cole smiles, he leans over and plays with my hair while I watch him.

"I wouldn't have you any other way." He whispers, dropping a kiss on my nose. I bite my lip a little and close my eyes.

"Cole?"

"Hm."

"Will you sing for me? Like you promised in Nice?" I ask, peeking up at him, and he smiles.

"Right now? Here?" I shrug and look up at him pleadingly, and he nods, licking his lips. "Okay, I'll sing for you." He picks up his phone and plays an instrumental version of Amazed by Lonestar. "Every time our eyes meet, this feeling inside me is almost more than I can take…baby, when you touch me, I can feel how much you love me, and it just blows me away." I watch as he sings to me, his eyes on mine. His voice is beautiful.

"I don't know how you do what you do; I'm so in love with you…" He sings, wiping away the tears that roll down my cheeks. "I want to spend the rest of my life, with you by my side, forever and ever." He sings, gazing into my eyes meaningfully, tears flowing down his cheeks. "Every little thing that you do, baby, I'm amazed by you." He gets all choked up and buries his head in my chest, crying. I cradle his head in my arms, holding him tight against me as we both sob to our ill-fated love.

Can somebody please, tell me how I'm supposed to survive this. How will I watch the man I love get married and have a baby with another girl?

Chapter Thirty-Six

COLE

I MOAN when I feel something softly comb through my hair. "Get up, you goof."

"No," I mutter, my voice muffled, my face currently pressed into my arms, which are resting on my desk.

"Cole, I need the blueprint, but your giant forehead is covering the part I need to see," Shayla complains and taps my head with her pencil a couple of times. I smile into my arms and peek up at her, not fully lifting my head.

"Excuse you, this forehead has expanded to capacitate the knowledge and wisdom my brain has accumulated over the years," I tell her. Shayla narrows her eyes at me and tilts her head to the side while her lips curl into a smile.

"Uh-huh, looks like a receding hairline to me, but whatever makes you feel better, big boy." She utters, pulling on the paper and glaring at me playfully when I don't move. "Let go."

I grin at her, and she blinks at me. "Big boy?"

Shayla's cheeks flush, and she looks away while licking her lips, and I grin, resisting the urge to grab her face and kiss her. "I… I didn't mean…" She tries to backtrack, and I just watch her with glee. She sighs, closing her eyes. "I really hate you. I hope you know that."

"No, you don't." I chuckle amusedly and groan when she hits my head with the pencil.

"Shut up and focus on work," I laugh and look down at the blueprint we've been working on at my apartment.

"Baby, I'm home." I groan and close my eyes when I hear the front door open, and Sophie's voice echoes in the apartment. Shayla rolls her eyes and mutters under her breath.

"You said she wasn't coming over." She whispers to me furiously, and I shrug, rolling my eyes.

"She wasn't supposed to be, but she knows we're working from here, so…"

"Of course she was going to show up." Shayla hisses frostily and looks down at the blueprint in front of her.

"Look who I ran into in the lobby. Oh. Shayla's here too. I thought you were working from here tomorrow night?" She questions, walking over to me and leans over to kiss me, but I turn my head, and she catches my cheek. I look over at Shayla, who is staring down at the papers in front of her pretending to work. I glance over Shayla's shoulder and frown when I see Josh walk into the study.

"I told you this morning we were working from here today because we need to finish this by the end of this week." I nod, greeting Josh, and he nods back.

"Hi, Shayla." Josh greets her, and she looks up and smiles at him warmly.

"Hi Josh, how are you?" Josh nods, returning her smile.

"I'm well, thanks. I've not seen you around the office much lately. How's the hand?" Shayla looks at her bandaged-up hand and shrugs.

"Healing slowly and very itchy." Josh chuckles, and they begin talking back and forth. Since when have these two been so chummy? Sophie wraps her arm around my shoulder, and I don't even acknowledge it. I fixed my gaze on Shayla and Josh, laughing about something.

"Josh, Shayla, would you like to join Tristan and me for dinner?" Sophie offers, and Shayla looks at me bewildered before she shakes her head.

"Uh, no. I can't. I've got plans already." She declines politely, and I frown.

"What plans? It's Sunday?" I blurt out before I could stop myself and Shayla frowns a little.

"Uh, well, it's *Sunday*, Cole. I usually go to that place by the river with the girls, remember?" She reminds me, and I nod. Of course, the place with the food and dancing.

"What place by the river?" Josh questions, intrigued, and Shayla explains where it was, and he nods in understanding.

"Oh, wait, is that the place with all the lights and street food and…"

"Dancing." They say together and laugh. "Yes, it's amazing. I go there every other Sunday. I took Cole there a while back, and he loved it. Didn't you?" She asks, and I nod, smiling fondly.

"I've always wanted to go but never really found anyone to go with. My friends don't like places like that, and I don't really want to go alone like a weirdo."

Shayla grins, shaking her head. "You need new friends."

Josh cackles, "Tell me about it. I'll be sure to post an open ad for some." He jokes, making Shayla laugh. "I'll look forward to receiving your application."

"Maybe you can go with Shayla?" Sophie chimes in, and I glare up at her. What the fuck? Has this woman lost her marbles? Shayla sneaks a look at me before she looks at Josh and smiles warmly.

"I mean, you can join me if you want?" She offers warmly, and I watch as Josh nods, his whole face lighting up.

"I'd love to join you if you're sure. I wouldn't want to impose." Shayla shakes her head and packs her things up.

"No imposition at all. You're going to love it. The atmosphere, the food, the people, it's honestly magical."

"I mean, if *Cole* loved it, I have absolutely no doubt I will too." Josh chuckles, and I scowl at him.

"What's that supposed to mean? 'If *Cole* likes it' like I'm some snob or something." I grumble bitingly, and Josh grins at me while Shayla presses her lips together, stifling her laughter at my annoyance.

"I mean, I did drag him there, but once he was there, he loved it," Shayla explains, smiling sweetly at me. I return her smile.

God, I love her.

"I'm excited to see this place. It honestly sounds awesome." Josh gushes while watching Shayla gather her things and grab her jacket. "I'm driving."

"We'll come too," I suddenly announce, standing. Sophie looks at me surprised and wrinkles her nose in distaste.

"We will? I thought we were going to eat Italian from that place we love?" She sulks, and I ignore her.

"We always eat from there. Besides, the food at this place is amazing, and I could do with some *Shayla special*." I answer, and Shayla looks at me stunned and casts a look at Sophie, who gives me a side glare, and Shayla discreetly smiles.

"Shayla special?" Sophie iterates bitingly while she and Josh look between Shayla and me as we share a knowing look.

"It's a special dish that one of the vendors makes for me when I go there." She explains, avoiding my gaze and looks at Josh, who smiles at her, and she smiles back. I don't like this. I don't like this one bit. Like *hell*, I'm going to let them go off alone.

"How about we take my car?" I offer, and Josh shrugs, I look at Shayla, and she seems hesitant but nods, agreeing. "Great, let's go." Sophie goes to get her bag while she complains about having to go out again after she just got in, and I watch Shayla and Josh walk toward the front door conversing.

Sophie is suddenly friendly to Shayla simply because she's trying to push her and Josh together in a pathetic attempt to get her out of my life. As if I would let that fucking happen. Josh isn't even her type. She would never go for him, not while she's in love with me.

~

WHILE WE DROVE, I kept glancing back at her through the rear-view mirror. She was looking out the window, completely lost in her thoughts.

I reach over and put the music on to drown out the silence in the car. I glance back at her through the mirror when a song we love comes on, and she looks at me briefly, her lips curling into a smile as I sing the lyrics along to the music.

Forty minutes and a lot of discreet, lingering stares later, we arrived at our destination. We walk through the crowd of people— it was more crowded this time than the last time we were here. Shayla was walking beside me with Josh on her left, and I had Sophie on my right. Sophie laces her fingers with mine, and my insides recoil, but I let her hold my hand. She is carrying my baby, after all. We weren't even there five minutes before Sophie was complaining.

"Oh, good grief. Like *hell*, I'm eating off those disgusting carts. This place is completely unhygienic. Baby, I can't eat anything from here. Our baby and I will wind-up getting sick." She utters in distaste while Shayla and I glare at her.

"I think you'll find these carts are a lot cleaner than some of those five-star restaurants you're accustomed to eating in. All the food they cook is fresh on-site, and they check temperatures and have all their certifications. The difference is these people cook on the street with their customers and have fun while doing it." Shayla tells her and walks off with Josh in tow, who muttered something in her ear, and she throws her head back and laughs.

"As if she's ever been to a five-star restaurant in her life," Sophie scoffs snidely, and I roll my eyes.

"Actually, she has, and she hates it. Jesus Sophie, will you stop acting like such a snob and open up your mind and those blue eyes of yours. Take a look around you, and maybe try something new for a change without complaining. You might be surprised and find you enjoy yourself if you remove that stick that's up your arse." I mutter, shaking my head. I follow Shayla and Josh as they walk through the crowd of people, leaving Sophie gaping after me.

"Hey! Muchacho!" I turn when I hear Federico call me by my nickname. "Where's my Princesa?" He asks, looking around for Shayla. I point to where she was walking in front of me talking to a group of people. He nods, smiling when he sees her. "Princesa! Ven aca!" He calls out to her, and Shayla looks around and grins when her eyes find him, waving her over to him. She blows him a kiss and nods.

"Ya voy. I'm coming. Two seconds!" She responds and goes back to talking to a group of people.

"I don't see what's so special about this place. It looks like a carnival, the way you both explained it, I was expecting something a little more upper-class." Sophie complains again. I grind my teeth and wonder fleetingly if anyone would notice if I just pushed her into the river. How the hell am I supposed to put up with this woman for the rest of my life? I just need to be near Shayla, and watching her walk so closely with Josh was beginning to bug me. We walk over to Federico's cart, and he greets us both.

"Princesa!"

"Rico!" Shayla laughs, and Federico looks at Shay's bandaged hand. His smile falls quickly and turns into a scowl.

"Princesa, tu mano," He gestures to her hand with his brows. "What happened to your hand?" He questions, concerned, and Shayla shakes her head.

"Oh, it's nothing. I just cut it on some glass." She explains, keeping the smile on her face, but Federico sees the sadness in her eyes and looks at me.

"Muchacho, what happened to her?" Shayla looks up at me pleadingly, and I force a smile on my face.

"She cut her hand, trying to pick up a shard of glass, and had to get stitches. You know Shayla, she's clumsy, brother."

Federico doesn't seem satisfied with my answer and looks between us. "Who is this bruja with you?" He questions scowling, and I look at Sophie, who was watching Shayla with a frosty glare. I look at Shayla scratching her nose, trying hard not to smile at the nickname 'witch' Federico just gave Sophie.

"Uh, she's—"

"Rico! I'm starving, enough with the third degree. We've come with guests to give them a taste of your magical Shayla special." Shayla tells him, and he eye's Sophie and Josh before he looks at Shayla again.

"Cuatro?"

Shayla nods and thanks him politely, "Si, por favor." She turns her eyes to me, and I nod, catching the 'he's going to kill us' look behind her gaze. While we wait around for the food, I watch Shayla and Josh, who are engrossed in a conversation about how Shay learned to speak Spanish. She explained that her mother was a teacher, and she used to teach languages before her father died.

"Here you go, Princesa, four Shayla specials. Bon appetite." We all take our food, and Rico once again doesn't take the cash I hold out to him. "Shayla's guests are my guests." He adds, and I shake his hand.

"Gracias hermano." I thank him, he nods, and I see him exchanging looks with Shayla. She shakes her head and speaks to him in Spanish.

"I'm not liking the state of you, Princesa. We're going to talk." He tells her firmly and turns his chocolate gaze to me. "Keep an eye on her, Muchacho." I nod and look at Shayla, who sighs, shaking her head.

"Always. Ella es mi vida." I assure him. Rico chuckles and tells me he's impressed with my Spanish. He seemed satisfied when I tell him she is my life. Shayla looks at me and discreetly smiles before she turns, and we walk while we eat our food.

"Oh my God, this is sensational. *What is this*?" Josh groans appreciatively, chewing on his paella. Shayla smiles proudly.

"It's a paella." She tells him after she swallows her mouthful. "I could honestly eat this for the rest of my life and never, ever get tired of it." She tells him blissfully. I watch her from behind as she walks, and just like last time, people would call out to her or just run up and hug her.

"Shayla!" I jump when I hear Aimee's voice shrieking behind me. Shayla spins, beaming, and waves the girls over. Aimee and Jo walk over to us, and Shayla introduces them officially to Josh and Sophie. Aimee eyes Sophie distastefully before she turns to Josh and smiles. "I remember you. You're Cole's head of security, right?" Josh nods, and they shake hands. Aimee turns her gaze to me, and they go icy instantly, and I sigh. "Cole."

"Aimee," I say back, holding her gaze steadily until she looks away. I nod and smile at Jo, who waves at me. Jo is lovely; she's a lot more laid back than Aimee. Although, I am happy she has loyal friends who love and care about her enough to protect her.

"Uh, excuse me." I look back when I feel someone tap my shoulder. I see a young redhead standing there, beaming up at me. She couldn't have been older than seventeen.

I smile. "Yes?"

"Um, you're Tristan Cole Hoult, right?" She asks timidly, and I nod. She grins, her face turning a deeper shade of pink the longer she stands before me. "I'm so sorry to bother you, but…" She holds up her phone. "Would you mind if I get a picture with you guys? I'm a huge fan of yours." I rub my neck awkwardly and nod. Sophie beams and pushes herself up against me, and the girl looks at her and shakes her head. "Actually… I meant with you and Shayla?" She utters coyly and glances over at Shayla, who meets my gaze and smiles uneasily, handing her food to Aimee before moving over to us.

Shayla stands beside me, and I wrap my arm around her waist and pull her against me. I curl my other arm around the fan, and we smile up to her phone while she takes a couple of selfies with us.

"Oh my gosh! Thank you. I cried for days when I found out you broke up. You guys were so happy and perfect together." She gushes, looking between Shayla and me while we pull apart and share a look.

"Obviously they weren't sweetie, or they wouldn't have broken up." Sophie sneers, curling her fingers possessively around my bicep and smiling coolly at the teenage girl before us. I give her a firm look when she turns her gaze up to me.

The young girl gives Sophie a disgruntled look before she looks at Shayla and smiles again. "I hope I find a boy someday who will look at me the way Tristan looks at you." She says admiringly, and Shayla blinks a couple times when her eyes well up and smiles at her warmly before she pulls her in for a hug.

"I have no doubt that you will, sweetheart," Shay assures her, and they pull apart. We wave at the girl when she thanks us and skips off to her friends.

Well, that got awkward fast. After that whole exchange, Shay avoided me and wouldn't even look at me. I sigh inwardly. I hate this. We continue to walk around and try various foods from different carts. "Oh baby, look, can you win me one of those cute bears," Sophie chirps, wrapping her hand around my arm, clinging to me.

I resist the urge to roll my eyes and nod, letting her drag me to the stall where you had to shoot down the targets to win the prize. "What do we have here," Josh drawls, picking up the gun next to me. What was this boy doing? Is he seriously flirting with Shayla right in front of me? I fight off the agitation and shoot down the targets, and Sophie squeals, wrapping her arms around my neck, and kisses me. I pull away instantly and sigh.

"That's *my* sexy man." She coos, pressing herself up against me. "This can be *our* baby's first stuffed toy." I look over at Shayla, who watches us with a saddened look in her eyes, which she tries to conceal with a smile when Josh walks over and gives her a stuffed monkey.

"For you, as a thank you for letting me join you." Shayla looks at him and takes the monkey while Josh smiles at her charmingly. I was raging. How could my best friend make a move on the girl I love? Has he lost his fucking mind?

~

AFTER WE HAVE some more food, Aimee and Jo pull Shayla toward the crowd of people dancing when the music starts playing loudly. "These churro thingies are delicious, I must admit." Sophie moans while eating. I ignore her and move over to the crowd with Josh, where we watch as Shayla and the girls dance to the upbeat Latin music playing. Shayla was dancing and singing along to the song. It took everything in me to not go over there and take her in my arms and dance with her like I did last time.

"Baby, come on, let's dance," Sophie coos taking my hand and pulling me into the crowd of dancing people. I watch as Josh walks over to Shayla, and the girls pull him in to dance with her. I couldn't fucking see shit, there were too many people around, and Sophie's damn head keeps getting in my way. I fist my hands in annoyance at my side as Sophie grinds her bony arse on my groin. I wrap my arm around her when she staggers a little in her heels, she's not as graceful as Shayla when it comes to dancing, and I didn't want her to fall over and hurt the baby as I slowly move toward Shayla. My eyes were glued to Josh and Shayla dancing together, laughing like they were having a blast. They were dancing in perfect rhythm with one another, and it made my insides burn with envy.

I'm going to knock that bastard into the middle of next week in a minute. I'm genuinely struggling to keep my rage in check. I finally manage to catch Shayla's eyes, and her smile falters as she looks at me, probably noticing the irritation in my eyes while I watch her dancing with my best friend. Josh spins her around, so her back was pressed to his chest as they sway together.

Mother fucker!

"Ow, baby, why are you squeezing my hip so hard?" Sophie complains, turning to face me with a frown. I look at her and shake my head, resisting the urge to look over at Shayla. I lick my lips.

"Sorry, I got caught up with the dancing." I lie, and Sophie grins, wrapping her arms around my neck, and starts kissing along my jaw.

I sigh and pull my head back. "Soph, stop." I hear her sigh and her shoulders drop when she pulls away and looks over at Josh and Shayla dancing together.

"Where did she learn to dance like that?" Sophie scoffs, looking over at Shayla dancing sensually; the acidity in her voice made me smirk.

"Her mother, she was a dancer when she was younger, before she met and got married to Shay's Dad. She taught Shayla when she was a little girl, and the rest she picked up by watching her mother dancing around the house." I explain, watching her intently. She looks so fucking hot, the way her hips sway to the rhythm of the music, her hair blowing back with the breeze, the way she smiles and bites her lip. I groan in frustration.

As pissed off as I was, I was *so* envious of Josh at that moment.

It suddenly starts to rain—a sudden downpour. It was absolutely chucking it down, and the crowd dancing all cheer and continue to dance, not even fazed in the slightest that they were getting soaked. I couldn't contain my smile when I see Shayla tilt her head back, eyes closed, the rain absolutely soaking her while she dances.

"Oh my God, my hair! Tristan, let's go! My clothes are getting ruined." Sophie shrieks covering her head with her arms while she runs to a cart for shelter from the rain. The song finally comes to an end, and they walk over to us laughing. Shayla avoids my gaze as she walks past me with Josh and the girls. The rain slows to a drizzle, and Josh shakes the water out of his hair, spraying Shayla, who chuckles, brushing her fingers through her wet hair.

"How has it taken me this long to find out about this place. I honestly haven't had this much fun in a very long time, and I'm constantly out on the town." He tells the girls, who grin at him.

"Oh, this is nothing, my friend. In a couple of weeks, they have The Bubble festival." Aimee tells Josh, who smirks excitedly. "Imagine this, but bigger in Hyde Park. Food, live bands, dancing, foam, and paint pits." Aimee explains and grins at Shayla, who shakes her head smiling.

"It's messy, but it's so much fun. You will love it," Shayla tells Josh, who nods.

"Oh, I'll be there. Maybe we can all go together?" Josh suggests while Shayla and the girls nod in agreement.

"Why not."

I clear my throat interrupting their conversation. "Are you ready to go?" I ask Shayla and Josh, who look at one another just as Sophie comes back when the rain stops.

"Actually, we're going to stay a little longer. I'm still dying to try out more food, and the girls want to drink some margaritas. They've kindly offered me a ride home, so I'll pick my car up from yours tomorrow," Josh informs me, and I nod, looking at Shayla, who holds my gaze for a moment.

"Girls, I'll be right back. I just need to go give Rico something." Shayla says, and I watch her as she walks off into the crowd.

"I should go say bye to Rico, Sophie, you go to the car. I'll be there in a bit." I say and hand her the car keys. Sophie begins complaining once again and asks Josh to walk her to the car as I follow Shayla.

I see her say something to Rico, and he nods, winking at her. Shayla smiles at him and blows him a kiss. When she turns around, she crashes into me. Shayla gasps and looks up at me, her green eyes wide as I curl my fingers around her wrist and wave to Rico, who gives me a thumbs up in return. I pull Shayla through the crowd of people until I find a private spot away from prying eyes behind a vendor's truck and press her up against the wall. "What are you doing?" She questions, looking up at me with a frown.

"What am I doing?" I hiss, scowling at her. "I was watching you flirting shamelessly with my best friend Shayla. What the hell do you think you're doing?"

Shayla's brow goes up as she glares at me. "I'm not flirting with him. I was just being nice and showing him around. What the hell is your problem?"

"Oh really, you call dancing heatedly with him being *nice*. His hands were all over you!" I growl, and she narrows her eyes at me with a snort.

"Oh, that's mighty rich coming from you. I can't have an innocent dance with Josh, but it's okay for me to watch Sophie's hands all over you and watch while you slobber all over each other?" She snaps hotly while glaring at me and tries to walk away, but I cage her in by placing my arms on either side of her on the wall.

I lick my lips and look down into her fiery gaze, and my stomach twists. "I didn't kiss her. She kissed me."

Shayla rolls her eyes. "Oh here we go. I couldn't care less who kissed whom, Cole. If you're so damn bothered about seeing me with Josh, why the hell did you come with us?" She questions hotly, and I bite my bottom lip.

"Maybe I fancied myself a Shayla special," I reply with a shrug, and she narrows her eyes at me while I stare at her lips.

"Oh bullshit," She retorts. "You were glaring daggers at us all evening Cole. You only came here tonight because you couldn't bear the thought of leaving me alone with Josh. Admit it."

"You're damn right I did." I hiss irritably while staring into her eyes. "Did you honestly expect me to be okay with you two going off alone together? Have you lost your damn mind?"

Shayla's brows knit together tightly, "No, but you clearly have if you think for one damn second, you get to tell me who I can and cannot spend my time with." She glares at me hard and pushes me away. "You have no control over me or my damn life, so get over yourself."

I roll my eyes and grab her arm before she could walk away, "Get over myself? Do you think it's easy for me to see you moving on with somebody else when it was just a couple of weeks ago that you were mine!"

Shayla exhales slowly. "First of all, I was never yours, Cole. Secondly, do you think I don't feel the same damn thing every goddamn day knowing you're in bed with *her*?"

We stare at one another, and Shayla's eyes fill with tears. "I'm not in bed with her," I tell her, my fingers trailing down her arm. I curl them around her wrist and pull her close to me. "I can't bear to touch her when you're all I want, Shayla," I whisper, pressing my forehead to her temple. "How could you think I'd ever touch another woman when I'm crazy about you, baby." Shayla's eyes close, and tears roll down her cheeks.

"Cole, stop it." She whispers, turning her head away, but I cup her face in my hands and lift her gaze to mine, my thumbs brushing away her tears.

"Tell me how, and I will." I declare miserably. "When your hands are still the last to touch my bare skin, just as mine is yours. Your beautiful bare body is still the last to be pressed against mine, just like mine is yours." I sigh, brushing my nose over hers. "Until today, your lips were the last to touch mine," I whisper, ghosting my lips over hers. "Make it *yours* again, baby," I murmur and press my lips to hers softly. She squeaks, surprised but doesn't push me away, which pleases me. I brush her lips apart with my own and sneak my tongue into her mouth, massaging it against her own teasingly. She kisses me back just for a minute before she pushes me off, panting.

"Cole," She breathes, her hands still on my chest. I lick my lips and stare into her eyes.

"You were always mine, and as long as I remain the last man to touch you, you will continue to be," I answer, dragging my thumb over her bottom lip. "Just as I am yours."

"You're not mine." She whispers and pulls away, taking her scent and warmth with her. "You belong with your fiancée and unborn child." She turns and walks away

"You and I both know that's not where I belong," I say, and she stops walking for a second before she exhales and hurries away, leaving me behind.

Chapter Thirty-Seven

SHAYLA

"How do you say it again?" Josh asks, squinting as he leans into me to hear me better over the loud music.

"Salud," I repeat with a snicker, and he nods and holds his Margherita glass up.

"SALUD!" He hollers, and the people around cheer and repeat it holding up their drinks. "Oh, my God. This place is just awesome. I can't remember the last time I had such fun." Josh laughs, clinking his glass with mine.

"Ah, all you really need for a good time is some decent company. Surround yourself with people who are on the same wavelength as you, and you're good to go." I say with a shrug and watch as Jo and Aimee dance with two guys they just met.

Josh leans forward and licks his lips. "You know I get it." I look at him with a smile and shake my head confused.

"Get what?"

"Why Cole is having such a hard time letting you go." I keep the smile on my face and drop my gaze, not wanting to show him how hurt I was over Cole. "I still remember the first time I saw you at Luxe the night you and Cole met." He explains, looking at me with a smile. I watch him, intrigued. "You were dancing with the girls, just like you were tonight, but there was something about you. Your whole aura was just magnetic. I made a mistake pointing you guys out to Cole. I honestly thought he would have gone for Aimee because she was more his type, but when I saw his eyes zero in on you, he was just as enthralled with you as I was." Josh explains, and I gape at him, stunned.

"Wait. You saw me first?" I question, and he nods, looking down at his glass.

"I did, and I was trying to pick up the courage to come and talk to you, but Cole got to you first. I'm not a shy guy at all. I'm quite confident, but with you, for some reason, I just lost my nerve." He sighs with a little smile, shaking his head. "If I had just walked over to you, instead of hesitating, I could have saved you both so much grief, and maybe you and I might have had a chance."

I sigh, "Yeah, maybe, I definitely wouldn't have ended up married, that's for sure," I mutter, shaking my head while running my finger along the rim of my glass. Josh smiles and turns to face me properly.

"I really like you, Shayla," He admits, and I lift my gaze to his, taken aback, my smile fading slowly. "Is it definitely over for you and Cole?"

I sigh and nod, "Yes, it's definitely over. How could it not be? He's getting married in a couple of weeks, and he's having a baby with her. I'm not the type of girl to break up a family." I explain, and Josh nods.

"So, would you think me a complete dickhead if I asked you out?" I look into Josh's blue eyes and chew on my bottom lip thoughtfully.

"No. Of course I wouldn't, Josh, but don't you think it would be weird? The last thing I ever want to do is come between two best friends. And I don't think Cole would like you dating me." I explain with a shrug, while Josh reaches out, taking my hand into his, and rubs his thumb over my knuckles.

Josh sighs slowly, "I know it's a shitty thing to do because he's like a brother to me, but Cole's getting married, Shayla. Eventually, you are going to meet someone. He can't expect you to be single forever, right? If it's not going to be me, it's going to be somebody else." He chuckles a little. "And to be honest with you, I don't want to miss my chance again because I didn't ask. So, this is me shooting my shot."

"Are you sure, Josh, because this is going to cause you a hell of a lot of grief? I know Cole, and he's going to hit the roof when he finds out." I ask, and Josh shrugs a little and smiles at me.

"I'll talk to Cole. Besides, something tells me you're worth it." I feel my cheeks go hot under his gaze, and he chuckles. "Ah, fucking hell." He smiles with a sigh while rubbing his forehead.

"What?"

"You just, you make me feel some type of way. I mean, who looks that adorable when they blush, for God's sake?" I bury my face into my hands and shake my head, blushing like a little girl.

"Oh Jesus, stop it," I mutter, embarrassed, and I hear Josh snigger.

"I prefer to be called Josh, but I do go by Jesus too, only on the weekends and after hours." He teases with a chuckle, and I push his shoulder playfully. "So, what do you say, you want to go out with me?"

This was such a bad idea, but I look over at the girls who were nodding enthusiastically. What's the use of holding onto what Cole and I had any longer, right? It's not like we have a future anymore. Any chance we did have is now gone. Josh seems like a nice guy, and we do get along. Maybe he's what I need to get over Cole.

"Okay, I'll go out with you," I say before I lose my nerve and Josh grins, biting his lip.

"How about dinner tomorrow night?" He suggests. I wince and shake my head before I turn to face him.

"Let me tell you something about me. You've already gathered that I'm not like most girls. I'm not into expensive meals or big romantic gestures. I like things that are fun, going on adventures, not sitting in a stuffy restaurant while we talk about mundane things." I explain, and Josh frowns a little but nods after a minute.

"Okay, let me rephrase. How about paint-balling tomorrow night?" My eyes go wide with excitement, and I nod with a grin.

"Yes." I chirp excitedly, and Josh laughs out loud.

"You're certainly right about one thing; you're unlike any girl I've ever met." He chuckles, holding up his glass, and I clink mine with his. "Here's to our first date and hopefully many more after that."

"Salud." I smile, and we finish our drinks.

AFTER A COUPLE MORE ROUNDS, Aimee and Jo invited Josh over to our place, much to my dismay. I just wanted to shower and curl up in bed with a book, but no, they decided they wanted to watch a movie. I was lying on the sofa trying hard not to doze off, Josh sitting on the floor in front of me, his head resting half on the cushion and half on my chest as we watch the movie. I frown when I feel my phone vibrate and see a message from Cole. My heart instantly starts racing, and I open the message and read it.

Cole:
'Did you get home okay?'
Me:
'Yes, Cole, I'm a big girl. I can take care of myself.'
Cole:
'I know you can, but I still worry. What are you up to?'
Me:
'Watching a movie with the girls and Josh.'

While I wait for his reply, my phone starts ringing with his name on the screen. I excuse myself and walk to my bedroom to answer the phone. "Why are you calling me at this time?" I whisper as I close my bedroom door.

"Why is Josh at yours?!" Cole barks and I close my eyes, sighing.

"I told you we're watching a movie. What's it got to do with you anyway?" I ask hotly, trying to keep my voice down, and I can hear Cole pacing on his end.

"Christ, Shayla, are you trying to make me crazy? Are you deliberately doing this to make me jealous to get a reaction out of me? because you're fucking succeeding!" I scowl pacing my room.

"What the hell are you talking about, Cole. Why would I do such a thing?" I retort, and I hear him growl on the other end. "Shouldn't you be in bed with your fiancée?"

"Shayla, don't start that shit with me again. I already told you, I don't sleep with her. Send him home." He hisses through clenched teeth, and I shake my head.

"No."

"Fine. I'm coming over. I'll fucking do it."

"No, you fucking aren't."

"Watch me."

"Cole—" The line goes dead. Son of a bitch! I call him back, but he declines it, and it goes to voicemail. My entire body was shaking with infuriation. What the hell am I supposed to do now? I've never seen this side of Cole before, this possessive and jealous side. I pace my room like a lunatic, trying to find an excuse to get Josh out without being rude before Cole shows up and they kill each other.

I poke my head out of my bedroom and wave at Aimee till she sees me and frowns. I press my finger to my lips and motion her to me. She looks around and gets up off the floor, and walks over to me, confused. "What are you doing, you nut?"

"Shhh, you have to help me." I pull her into my bedroom and close the door quietly. "We need to get rid of Josh," I whisper, and Aimee frowns, watching me with her brows knitted together.

"Why?"

"Cole is on his way over," I tell her, and Aimee blinks at me.

"Again...why?"

"I stupidly told him Josh was here, and he flipped out, and now he's coming over. Aimee, I don't want them to fight. Please help me get rid of him before Cole gets here." I plead, and Aimee sighs, pinching the bridge of her nose.

"Jesus, Shayla. What possessed you to tell him? Of course he will hit the roof. I swear to God, I'm going to kill that Cole one of these days." She mumbles agitatedly. Opening the door, she walks over to the electricity mains and opens it. Aimee smirks at me before she flicks the switch, and all the electricity in the apartment goes off, leaving us in absolute darkness.

"Oh, well done." I praise her sardonically. "Now we can't see fuck all, and Jo is going to shit herself," I whisper to her furiously, and she shushes me.

"Ahhh!! What the hell?!" Jo hollers from the living room.

"See." I roll my eyes, and Aimee sniggers a little as we walk to the living room carefully. Great time to cut the electricity when we were watching a horror movie.

"Is there a power cut?" I hear Josh as he gets up to his feet.

"What the fuck is going on!" Jo shouts, crashing into the coffee table. "Ow, shit!"

"Jo, calm down. The mains must have blown again," Aimee tells her with a sigh.

"Again? What do you mean again? It's never bloody blown!" She retorts, the fear apparent in her voice. I smile, shaking my head. She's such a sissy.

"If you show me where the mains are, I can take a look for you?" Josh offers, and I sigh, shaking my head as if he can even see me.

"Oh no, it's okay. We'll just get the maintenance guy to have a look at it in the morning. It's getting late now anyway. We should probably get to bed. We all have work in the morning." I say, faking a yawn.

"Oh, well okay then. I best get going."

"Why don't I give you a lift home?" Aimee offers, leaning over to pick up her shoes.

"Oh no, that's okay. I can catch an uber it's no problem."

"Don't be silly. We offered you a lift home. It's not like you live far. Let's go." She chirps, snatching up my keys off the table by the door. Aimee opens the door, and the light from the corridor shines into the apartment. I smile at Josh when he looks over at me, and he grins back handsomely. I walk him to the door, and he lingers for a minute, looking at me.

"So, I'll see you at the office tomorrow, and we can discuss the details of our date?" I nod and tuck a loose strand of my hair behind my ear.

"Sounds good." I smile, and he nods, winking at me before he and Aimee leave the apartment. I close the door and sigh in relief.

"Shayla?!" I jump, startled at Jo's sudden outburst. "You want to explain what the fuck is going on?" I roll my eyes and walk to the electricity mains and shine my phone's flashlight on it so I could turn it back on again. I flick the switch, and the lights in the apartment come on, and I hear Jo sigh in relief.

"There, now calm down, you little chicken." I tease her, and she glares at me, not so amused.

"I thought it blew?"

I smile sheepishly, "Yeah, no, we flipped the switch so we could get Josh out of here." I tell her, and Jo looks at me just as Aimee had. "I mentioned to Cole that Josh was over, and he flipped out on me and is currently on his way over." I explain, and Jo's brows go up, her mouth forms into an 'o'

A COUPLE OF MINUTES LATER, we both jump when a loud knock sounds on the door. "You might want to go to your room because there's about to be an argument. A big one." I warn her, and she nods and hurries to her room as I walk to the door and open it to a livid Cole. A shiver passes through me at the anger in his eyes while he stares at me.

"Where is he?" He growls, looking around while he steps in through the front door, and I move in front of him, placing my hands on his chest. Cole's angry green eyes meet mine, and we glare at one another.

"He left, Cole," I tell him angrily and push him back. "You can go too." Cole shakes his head and retakes a step toward me. I crane my neck to look up at him as he towers over me.

"What the hell was he doing here in the first place?" He demands, narrowing his eyes at me. I bite my bottom lip as I look up into his eyes.

"We were fucking," I whisper to him, and Cole's eyes go dark, his jaw clenches tight. "Would you like a play by play?" I add tauntingly, and he bites his bottom lip hard as he glowers at me fiercely.

"You better be fucking joking because if he's laid a finger on you, I will destroy him." He growls, and I smile at him spitefully.

"You don't get to decide who touches me," I tell him coldly, and Cole licks his lips and kicks the door shut with his foot before his hand curls at my throat, and he presses me firmly against the wall.

"Wanna bet." He burs darkly, pressing his forehead to mine. I swallow the gasp about to escape me and keep my eyes on him. My heart was thrashing around in my chest. "Did you not hear me earlier. You're mine." He states possessively, his thumb trailing along my jaw.

"Did you not hear me. I was never yours." I retort snidely, and Cole tilts my head up till our mouths were aligned.

"Is that right? Is that why you would whisper the words 'make me yours' before I made love to you all those times." He tells me, and I gulp, closing my eyes when his fingers brush down my throat. "I made you mine, countless times, again and again."

"Those were simply words uttered in moments of passion Cole. Empty promises we made to one another while we fucked. That's it." Cole's eyes blacken, and his gaze goes hard on mine.

"Honey, I don't make empty promises— especially to you and most definitely not when my cock is buried inside of you. Our sex was never just sex Shay, and you fucking know that, so don't waste your breath trying to convince yourself otherwise. All those whispered words meant something to us both." He drawls huskily, and I stare up at him.

"What is it going to take for you to leave me alone?" I hiss hotly, and he stares at me heatedly. "You're getting married in a couple of weeks, Cole. You're having a baby. What is it you want from me?!"

"I want you!"

"As what?! Your fucking mistress?!" I shout, pushing him away from me. "Your bit on the side? Your fuck buddy?" I ask furiously. "You want to fuck me on your desk in your office before you go home to your wife and kid. Is that what you want?"

"Jesus Shayla, of course not!" Cole howls taking a step toward me, and I back away.

"Then what do you want, Cole?!" I ask, holding my arms out and waiting for him to reply while he shoves his hand through his tousled hair in agitation. "You can stand there and tell me you want me till you're blue in the face but it's not going to change anything, is it? Because you're still getting married, aren't you."

"You think I have a fucking choice? And if I did, I wouldn't choose you?!" He shouts angrily, and I roll my eyes and turn away from him.

"Goddamn it! I don't want to hear this anymore, Cole! Just get out!" I shout back and walk off to my bedroom. Cole follows me and storms into my bedroom, pulls my arm, and draws me against him again.

"What do you want to hear? Tell me?! You want to hear that it drives me fucking crazy thinking about another man touching you. Because it does! I'm not a jealous man, but when it comes to you, all bets are off. I don't give a fuck who it is." He claims, gazing into my eyes.

"So what, Cole? You can't have me, so no one else can? Is that it?"

"That's it!" He barks back.

I laugh bitterly. "And who are you to tell me otherwise? Huh?" I hiss. "Are you my boyfriend? My husband? My keeper? What the fuck are you to me?" Cole watches me silently, and I scoff. "Exactly what I thought. We're nothing to each other. I'm your employee, and you're my boss. That's as far as it will ever go between us." I state and watch as his chest rises and falls quickly. I pull my arm out of his hold and turn away from him, blinking away the tears that gather in my eyes.

"Shayla..."

"Get out," I utter with a shake of my head. When he makes no move to leave, I turn around and shove him back. "I said. Get. Out." I grit out, and he grabs my arms and yanks me against his chest. "I'm going to move on Cole, I will, and the sooner you get used to that idea, the better it is for the both of us. Because I can't do this with you forever." I tell him stormily trying to break free from his grasp, but he tightens his hold on me not letting me go.

"Shayla, I'm crazy about you. How the fuck do you expect me to watch you move on with another man?"

"I'm just as crazy about you, Cole, but you'll do it, just as I'll be forced to watch you marry and have a child with Sophie. With every piece of my broken heart aching, with every fibre in my body aflame!" I shout, slamming my hands into his chest and pushing him away from me. "That's how!"

Cole and I glare at one another irately, both our chests rising and falling with every raucous breath we took. Cole takes a step toward me, cups my face in his hands, and looks deeply into my eyes.

"I can't stand the thought of you loving someone else. It makes me crazy just thinking about him kissing these lips." He states, brushing his lips over mine before he sucks my bottom lip, eliciting a moan from me while he backs me up against the door slowly. “Tasting your skin.” He whispers, running his tongue up my throat. I bite my lip, curling my fingers around his jacket. “Feeling your silky-smooth skin against his fingers…” He breathes, trailing his fingers down my sides, making me quiver. “Smelling your intoxicating scent...” He sighs, burying his face in my neck, inhaling deeply with a guttural moan. Cole lifts me into his arms and walks over to the bed and lays me down on it before he rips his jacket off and tosses it aside. I should have stopped him. And my mind was screaming at me at full throttle to stop, but sweet lord. I could not find a thread of strength to resist him. This man is the devil himself. I fell in love with the fucking devil, he’s got me under his spell, and I can’t escape him, however hard I try.

I watch him as he crawls up on the bed, his eyes on mine while his fingers slide into the elastic of my shorts, and he slides them down my legs, “I lose my mind picturing anyone spreading these legs and eating your perfect pussy…” I gasp and arch up when I feel his mouth on me, and he groans fastly, his large hands on my hips holding me down as he licks leisurely up my slit to the bundle of nerves.

“Cole…”

Chapter Thirty-Eight

COLE

"Uh, Christ, Cole. We have to stop."

I lift my eyes to look up at Shayla and suck her clit hard. "You sure baby?"

She gasps, her legs quivering every time I swipe my tongue over her clit. Her fingers curl in my hair, and she rocks her hips up against my mouth. I resist the urge to smile, her mouth may be saying no, but her body is just begging for me. "Ohh fuck." She moans breathily, biting her lip as I slowly bring her to orgasm. "Cole, oh fuck, I'm gonna…come." She pants, biting her lip hard to keep from screaming while she fists the covers tight as she climaxes. I groan readily while lapping up every little bit of her girl cream while she quivers and pulses against my tongue. "Oh my God.." She pants breathlessly as I kiss up her stomach, pushing her shirt up till I expose her natural c-cup breasts.

"Shayla? You up?" We both jump when we hear Aimee call out her name. Shayla's eyes snap open, and it seems her senses come rushing back to her because she kicks me off the bed in a panic, and I land on my back with a thud.

"Fuck." I groan, and she leans over and looks at me concerned while I rub my back.

"Shit, are you okay?" I nod, sitting up as Shayla tugs her top-down and pulls her shorts back on. "You have to go." She whispers irately, and I sigh, rolling my eyes. That Aimee is such a cock block.

"Shayla, we're not done talking about this."

"Yes, we are," She snipes back stubbornly, shoving my jacket at me. "You can't keep doing this shit to me." She utters, turning me around and pushing me toward the door.

"Honey, I wasn't doing anything you didn't already want me to," I tell her matter-of-factly, and she glares at me hard.

"I'm not your honey, and this shit stops now, do you hear me? That will never happen again." I look into her face and lick my lips. "Stop it. Stop looking at me like that."

"Want to see how good you taste?" I drawl huskily while leaning in, and her eyes flicker to my lips before she meets my gaze again.

"It's my pussy; I can taste it whenever I want." She utters, pushing me to the door, and I grin naughtily.

"While I'm envious of that fact, this is a taste of you and me mixed into a delicious concoction that's sweet and so fucking addictive." I burr, and she stares into my eyes, "Your cum on my tongue. All it's missing is the taste of your sugary lips." I feel an unnatural heat course it's way through me and groan when my lips snatch hers, and I kiss her hard and dirty.

Shayla sucks my tongue, and then her eyes fly open, and she pushes me away a couple of seconds later and hits my chest all flustered. "God-damn it, Cole." She exhales slowly, closing her eyes and pushing me toward the door again. "Get the hell out of here." She groans, pushing me out of the bedroom and to the front door. I wave at Aimee as we go past her, and she glares at me darkly.

Shayla opens the front door, looks at me expectantly, and gestures to the door with her eyebrows, silently telling me to go. "Josh says he's really excited for your date tomorrow night, Shay," Aimee says with a smirk, and I look at Shayla, glaring at Aimee, who shrugs passively.

"What date?" I grit out through clenched teeth, and Shayla sighs, rubbing her forehead. "He fucking asked you out?"

"You bet he did," Aimee answers for her and I scowl at her before I turn my gaze to look at Shayla staring at the floor.

"And you said yes?" I ask in disbelief, and she sighs. "I'll fucking kill him. Did you not listen to a word I said to you in there, Shayla?" I hiss seething, and Shayla shakes her head.

"No, you won't, Cole— and yes, I heard you, but hear me." She answers, looking up at me, her gaze angry and hurt at the same time. "You're going to go back to your fiancée and your unborn child, and you're going to let me get on with my life because deep down, you know that's the right thing to do. You can't be so selfish that you'll want me to be miserable for the rest of my life, right?" She explains, brushing her fingers through her hair. "I'm sorry that it has to be Josh, but I have to get over you. Please understand that and let me go."

We stand there looking at one another. She was right. I had no right holding onto her, but that doesn't make it any easier to let her go. "You're seriously going to date my best friend despite being in love with me?" I ask, not bothering to mask the hurt in my voice, and Shayla blinks back the tears that pool in her eyes and nods.

"Yes, I am. Just like you're getting married to Sophie despite being in love with me." She whispers, and my heart sinks to the bottom of my stomach. I nod, and without another word, I walk out and slam the door shut behind me. I was furious. With her, with Josh, but most of all with myself. This is all my fault. I'm paying for my own mistakes. We're paying the price for all the lies I've told, all the lies *we've* told. What did we expect to happen if we started our whole relationship based on a lie? I'm doomed to live a life of misery for the rest of my life. I've got nothing left. I lost the girl I love, and I've lost my best friend. I've got no one to talk to, and I feel like I'm suffocating.

I stand outside her apartment building and stare up at it. I'm so tired of this empty void deep inside of me. I can't bear the thought of Shayla loving someone else. It's selfish, I know, but I want her to love me and only me. My heart clenches when I see Shayla come out on her balcony. I look up, watching her as she closes her eyes and wipes her face with her fingers. She's crying again. When she looks down, she sees me standing by my car, looking up at her. I take my phone out and dial her number. She looks at her phone for a long moment and answers it.

"Cole, what are you doing?"

"Let's go somewhere." I sigh.

"What?"

"Let's just disappear, go somewhere far away from here where no one can find us. Just you and me." I plead, and she closes her eyes sighing.

"In an ideal world, I would have gone anywhere with you, but that's just not an option for us. We can't do that, Cole." She tells me, her voice quivering.

"Why, Shayla, why can't we?"

"Because I have my family and you have responsibilities you can't turn your back on Cole." She says plainly, and I sigh. "And if you did, you wouldn't be the man I fell in love with."

"But I want *you*. I want to be with *you*. I want *YOU*, Shayla!" I shout, and she shakes her head sobbing.

"Cole, you're making this so hard, please. It's done." She cries, and I look up at her miserably.

"I can't accept that it's over for us." I groan, and she looks down at me.

"You have too, we both do. We can't be together, Cole."

"Then I don't want to *be* Shayla.." I whisper and end the call. She frowns and looks at the phone then at me. "I love you," I whisper. I kiss my fingers, and I press them to my heart.

"Cole?!" Shayla calls out to me, and I shake my head, getting in my car. "COLE!" She screams after me, and I slam my foot on the accelerator and tear away from her street. I see her name flash on my phone and turn it off. I didn't want to speak to anyone. I just needed this constant feeling of failure to stop choking the life out of me. I wanted to vanish. I'm backed up into a corner, and I can't seem to find a way out. I just keep sinking deeper and deeper into this giant hole of emptiness, and I hate it. I don't want to pretend that I'm okay anymore. I don't want to watch the girl I'm crazy about fall in love with someone else, and most of all, I don't want to resent my child for the rest of its life for being the one keeping me from being with her—from being happy.

I contemplated ending it all by driving off the road, but I just kept seeing Shayla's face, and every time I press down harder on the accelerator, something stops me, and I ease off again.

~

I DIDN'T KNOW where I was going until I pull up at the graveyard Grandpop was buried. If there was ever a time I needed his advice, it was now, even if it was from beyond the grave. I walk through the eerie graveyard till I come to his headstone and hit my knees in front of it.

"Help me, Grandpop," I whisper, closing my eyes, tears streaming down my face. "Please help me. I'm in a dark place, and I'm so scared of what I might do. What do I do, tell me, what do I do?!" I bellow as loud as my lungs allow. "I'm so in love with her." I sob helplessly. "How do I let her go and continue to live when she's got my heart? How am I supposed to watch her fall in love with someone else? Please tell me how?" I whisper wiping my face with the back of my hand. "I'm holding onto her for dear life as you said, but she won't let me."

"Then you set her free son." I jump when I hear a voice behind me. I turn and look at the elder man standing there with his hands in his pockets, a kind smile on his face.

"Who are you?" I ask, and he shrugs and walks over to me.

"Just an old, wise man who also lost the love of his life." He says, looking at my grandfather's headstone and then back at me. "Only I lost mine to cancer last year."

I blink up at him and wipe my face. "I'm sorry to hear that. Why are you here at this time?"

"Oh, I come and talk to her every week, fill her in on everything that's happening. You know, just in case she can't keep up from where she is." He explains with a smile and opens his folded-up chair and sits on it beside me. "I heard your shouting before, and it sounded like it came from someplace real broken. Would you like to talk?" He offers, and I shrug silently, and he reaches over and pats my shoulder just like my Grandpop used to, and my eyes well up. "You'll feel better, I promise."

I nod and sit down on the floor with my back pressed against the stone around my grandfathers' grave. "I found the perfect girl, fallen out of my mind in love with her, then fucked it all up, and now I'm losing her to my best friend."

"Ouch, that's very unfortunate. Is she the one?"

I nod and bite my lip taking out the ring I gave her in Vegas and look at it. "She's the only one," I whisper. "I fell in love with her without even realising it. Her love just consumed me like nothing I've ever felt in my life. We got married by accident in Vegas…" I explain, and he listens while I tell him about our whirlwind love story. "And now, she wants to move on with him, and I don't even know how to even begin to let her go." I look at him, and he sighs, rubbing his palms over his thighs. "What do I do? How do I chose between the girl I love or my child?"

He sighs and leans forward, regarding me seriously. "You do the right thing and set her free because that's what love requires. Sacrifice. Have you never heard the expression, set what you love free, and if it returns, it was always meant for you, and if it doesn't, it was never meant to be?" He expresses, and I sigh.

"It's just easier said than done, though, Isn't it?"

"Son, there are two types of love, there's selfless and selfish. Love is not only for the good times you share with someone but more so about the hardship you share and doing what's best for the other person. For example, like your girl, she loves you so much she walked away and let you be with the one you thought you wanted to be with. That's selfless love and what you have is selfish love. You're only thinking about what *you* want, *your* pain, and you're not sparing a thought to what *she* needs. What you're feeling, she's feeling tenfold, but she's doing the right thing and letting you go and be the man you need to be for your child without resentment and blame." He explains, and I close my eyes and nod. He was right. "That's an extraordinary woman."

"How do I let her go?" I whisper, staring at the ring in my hand.

"I can't tell you how son, but I will tell you this— it's going to hurt more and more each day you watch her slipping further away from you. However, you're going to keep telling yourself that it's what's best for *her* because *she* deserves to be happy. You do whatever you need to do to push her away, and you're going to take that knife to your heart, and you're going to bleed, but one day, when you see her smiling happily, it will all be worth it because you helped her get there, even though it's killing you inside you'll smile *for* her."

I nod and look at him, tears stream down my face, and he smiles sadly. "Thank you," I whisper, and he pats my shoulder again.

"Count yourself, lucky son; you're living a love most would only ever dream of. The love you only ever see in old movies and read in great books."

"I don't feel very lucky right now if I'm honest with you," I admit with a sigh closing my eyes. "Lucky would be, having her in my arms where she belongs."

"Son, most people search and yearn for a love like yours and never find it. The fact you found yours in this day and age where people take love for granted is a beautiful thing, and you should treasure it." He explains eruditely, and I nod in agreement.

"I do, of course, I do. I'm going to love her forever." I say earnestly and close my eyes when I feel him squeeze my shoulder supportively.

"You absolutely will, and I promise you, she will bury her love for you in the deepest corner of her heart and love you secretly till her very last breath. You'll be the great love she will tell her grandchildren about." He assures me with a sigh, and I choke on a sob when I remember what she told me the first day we met, *"I'm going to show you a night you'll remember when you're sitting in your rocking chair at eighty years old, Mr Cole."* She not only showed me a night I would never forget, but she changed my life in ways I didn't know was possible. If I had one wish right now, it would be to go back to that very first day, marry her all over again and never let her go. Ever.

"The love of a good woman can make or break a man, my sweet boy." I nod and look at him, smiling sadly.

"She did both." I exhale and look up at him as he stands up and folds up his chair. "You're leaving?"

He nods with a small smile, "Yes, son, I've given you all the advice I have, the rest is up to you. I hope for both your sakes you'll one day find your way back to one another, but right now, I have no doubt you'll do the right thing." He says, leaning over, he pats my cheek, and I look up into his blue eyes. "Good luck son." He smiles and turns to walk away.

"Hey, what's your name?" I ask, and he turns and looks at me once more.

"Joe." He says with a smile and waves before he walks off, disappearing out of sight. I watch his retreating back and sob, pressing my hand against my grandfather's headstone.

"Thank you, Grandpop," I whisper before I get up and walk back to my car.

~

I COULDN'T FACE ANYONE, so I disappeared for a few days. No phone, no contact with anyone, just me in a log cabin by a beautiful lake far away from everything and alone with my thoughts and a couple of bottles of scotch to help ease the pain. Utterly oblivious to the chaos, I left behind me when I disappeared. When I walked into my apartment on the third day, I came face to face with my parents, Sophie and Josh, each looking more wrecked than the other.

"Tristan!" My mother shrieks sobbing when she sees me, and comes running at me. I groan and wrap my arms around my mother, who sobs hysterically. "Oh, thank heavens, you're okay. We've been out of our minds with worry." She cries, pulling back and looking me over. "Are you okay, sweetheart?"

I sigh, "I'm fine, Mum. I just wanted to clear my head for a few days." I assure her, and she sighs in relief.

"Where have you been son, your phones been off for days. No one has heard from you? We thought something terrible happened to you." He says, pulling me in for a hug. "When Josh called me, we thought.." I look over at Josh and see he's on the phone with someone.

"I'm fine guys. I'm sorry you all worried. I should have said something, but I just needed some time alone," I say and look at Sophie, who shakes her head, her eyes glimmering with tears. "I'm really sorry." I apologise, and she gets up and runs over to me, wrapping her arms around my neck.

"I was so worried, Tristan. Why didn't you say something to me? I woke up in the middle of the night, and you were gone." She cries, and I sigh, shrugging.

"I had no right making you all worry, but I've just been overwhelmed with everything, and I needed to escape," I tell them and wrap my arm around Sophie and kiss her forehead. "But I'm fine now, and I just want to shower and get back to work."

"Son, if you need to talk—"

I shake my head. "I'm fine Dad, honestly. I'm okay now." I smile assuringly, and he nods with a sigh.

"Very well, we'll get out of your hair and let you get back to work. Don't disappear like that again." He says, slapping my back affectionately, and I nod.

"Sophie, can you leave Josh and me alone. I'll come and see you later." I tell her, and she looks between Josh and me but doesn't argue and picks up her things and leaves the apartment. I walk over to the window and look out at the gloomy city before me.

"Bro, I'm thrilled you're okay, but what the fuck were you thinking going off on Shayla like that man?" Josh snaps angrily, and I clench my jaw tight. "Do you have the slightest clue what the fuck you've gone and put her through the past few days?" He yells hotly. "She thinks you went off to die, Cole!"

"I did!" I bellow, fisting my hands at my sides as I turn to look at him. Josh shakes his head, looking at me dumbfounded.

"What?"

"I did. But I couldn't do it because all I saw was her devastated face every time I tried," I tell him, dropping my gaze to the floor.

"Cole, what the fuck are you doing, bro? She was screaming on the phone. The girls couldn't calm her down. She's fucking devastated!" He screams, shoving me.

"SO AM I!" I roar, shoving him back. "I'm devastated that my best friend, the guy I consider a brother, would even contemplate going after the girl I'm out of my mind in love with!"

"Is this what you fucking do to the girl you're in love with?! If so, you don't fucking deserve her!" Josh yells his blue eyes were glaring into mine. I couldn't contain my anger. I lash out and punch him hard. Josh shakes off the blow and rubs his cheek biting his lip. "Yeah, that's right, hit me, hit me because you know it's fucking true. You've done nothing but turn that poor girl's life upside down from the moment you met her."

"You don't know what the hell you're talking about," I growl, and Josh chuckles bitterly wiping the blood off his lip.

"Don't I? The girls have told me what state she's been in since she met you and watching her fall apart after she thought you were fucking dead—I think I have a fairly good idea what I'm talking about." He states stormily. "Cole, I was going to talk to you, but you fucking disappeared."

"Oh, you mean *after* you already asked her out?" I question hotly, and he sighs. "How could you even consider going after Shayla? Huh? How Josh?! Can you not fucking see how I feel about her? How we feel about each other?"

"She's fucking single, Cole," Josh retorts, and I fist my hands tight when I feel hot rage bubble up inside me. "She wants to move on and put whatever you two had behind her. I genuinely like her, and I think she deserves a real chance at happiness after all the shit you've put her through. I can make her happy."

"She's in love with me!" I growl, grabbing him by the collars of his shirt and glaring at him menacingly.

"Not for long!" Josh hisses back, and I headbutt him in the nose, and he falls to the floor. "Fuck!" He shoots up to his feet and punches me in the jaw, and I groan, shaking it off. "If you love her so fucking much, why don't you go be with her? Huh?" Josh goads me spitting out blood on the floor. "I'll gladly step out of your way, go on, go be with her, bro!" He shouts, pointing at the door.

"Shut the fuck up!"

"Truth hurts, doesn't it, brother. You can't be with her because you're getting married and having a baby with your ex, that same ex you were using Shayla to get back at." He laughs sardonically. "You can be fucked off with me all you want, but YOU fucked this one up all on your own, bro."

"And you think you have what it takes to make her happy, do you?!"

Josh narrows his eyes, "Cole, she would have been mine right now if you hadn't swooped in that night. She would have been MY girl! She would have been in love with me! And yes, I fucking do." He hollers, squaring up to me. "She deserves better."

"You should have worked up the courage and asked her out then, you fucking dick!" I roar, fisting his shirt and bringing his face close to mine. "Shayla's off-limits to you!"

"ENOUGH!" I lift my gaze from Josh's and see a livid Shayla standing in the living room glaring at both of us.

Chapter Thirty-Nine

SHAYLA

IF SOMEONE ASKED me to describe the absolute worst moments of my life — I would have told them about the day I lost my Dad. It was a moment I never wanted to live ever again. That is, of course, until the man you're in love with tells you he doesn't want to live anymore in the middle of the night and races off in his sports car. The way my hands and legs shook as I watched him speed off madly down the road. I call him on his phone to tell him to come back, but he doesn't answer. Instead, he ends my call and turns his phone off. I drop to my knees, screaming in the middle of my living room, my head in my hands.

Aimee comes running out of her room when she heard me and kneels in front of me, followed by Jo. "Shayla! What happened?!"

"What the hell is going on?" Jo asks Aimee, who shrugs and shakes her head while she tries to calm me down. "Shay, shhh, shhh, what's the matter, babe?"

"Cole's going to do something stupid!" I sob hysterically into her chest.

"What?" Jo asks, looking at Aimee. "What do you mean?!"

"He's said he doesn't want to live anymore!" I scream wretchedly. "Do something! Find him, please!"

Jo wraps her arms around me as I continue to sob, "What do we do?!"

"I'm calling Josh," Aimee says, taking my phone and dialling his number. "If anyone will know what to do, it's him." Aimee shakes her head, waiting for him to answer. "Come on, Josh, pick up!" She calls again, and he answers. "Josh, it's Aimee, I'm sorry to call you so late, but we need your help. Cole and Shayla have had an argument, and he's told her he doesn't want to live anymore. Shay thinks he's gone off to do something stupid. No. She's hysterical. We don't know what to do. She won't calm down." Aimee cries.

I take the phone from Aimee, "Josh, find him please before he does something stupid."

"Shayla, calm down. Cole's a sensible guy; he's not going to hurt himself. I'm going to find him. Please calm down, okay."

"I can't! You didn't see the state he was in; please find him, Josh. If anything happens to him, I won't survive, I won't!" I cry, and I hear Josh sigh on the other end.

"Don't talk like that. Nothing is going to happen to him, I promise you. Just calm down; he's probably upset and said it out of anger."

I cry, shaking my head and hand the phone to Aimee, "Can you keep us updated," She asks and looks over me. "We'll try. Okay, we'll wait to hear from you." Aimee sighs and hangs up.

"Josh will find him, Shay, I'm sure he's fine," Jo assures me, and I shake my head sobbing into her chest.

"He's not. He's not fine at all. Neither of us is Aimee. I saw the look of defeat in his eyes." I whimper. "If anything happens to him, it will be my fault. I drove him to this; it's my fault!" I exclaim, and Jo holds me tighter.

"Shayla, shh, none of this is your fault babe, you did nothing wrong," Aimee assures me, and I shake my head.

"I did. I should never have agreed to come back into his life, he'd be okay if I just stayed away, but I didn't. I didn't!" Jo brushes her fingers through my hair. "God, please, please let him be okay. I swear I will disappear out of his life for good just let him be okay."

"Shayla, how many times did you walk away? He wouldn't let you go. You did the right thing and stepped aside how many times. You're the last person to take any blame from any of this."

"How can you say that? He's hurting because of me! Because I told him I'm dating Josh. How could I be so stupid?! I would have reacted the same if I watched him dating one of you two." I cry, burying my head in my arms. "What have I done?!"

"Shayla.."

"NO!" I shout. "It's my fault if something happens to him. How am I going to survive? I won't." I sob weakly. Aimee wipes the tears that roll down her cheeks and looks at Jo, who shrugs helplessly.

"Shay, don't talk like that. Cole's going to be fine, I promise you. Josh will find him, babe." She says, and all I could do was hope and pray that she was right. I will never forgive myself if anything happens to him. I wouldn't survive. Walking away from him is one thing, but losing him completely, I'd never recover. They would have to bury me with him. Oh God, just thinking about it hurts like hell. I felt like I was slowly suffocating. Hours went by without a word, and with each hour that passed, my hope was diminishing. I kept calling his phone, and it kept going to his voicemail. "Cole, please, please don't do anything stupid, don't do this to me, please I'm begging you, wherever you are, come back." I sob.

TWENTY-FOUR HOURS GO BY, and still no sign of Cole. I hear a knock at the door and race out of my room to the door, hoping it was Cole, I open it and see a tired and concerned Josh. I look up at him, hoping for some news, but he shakes his head sullenly. "No news yet." I cry, and he wraps his arms around me. "I've looked everywhere I can think of. I was with his parents and Sophie; they've reported it to the police. They're looking for him. They'll need to come by and speak to you soon because you were the last person to see him." He explains, pulling back and looking at me.

"Oh my God," I whimper and collapse into his arms. Josh catches me and holds me tight against him. "He's gone, isn't he?!" I shriek, and Josh sighs, shaking his head.

"No, Shayla, don't think the worse he could be anywhere, babe. I know Cole, and he would never do something stupid to hurt himself. He's probably gone off to clear his head or something."

"Why isn't he calling me?" I wail as Josh closes the door and walks us over to the sofa. He sits me down and kneels in front of me, sweeping my hair away from my face. "He always calls me," I whisper.

"He'll be back. The police are looking for him, and it's all over social media that he's missing. Someone will find him, Shayla. I promise."

"I don't want promises, Josh! I want him back alive!"

"He will be. Please just calm down." He assures me, and I shake my head.

"Stop telling me to calm down Josh. I can't sit here anymore. I want to be out there looking for him." I sniffle, and Josh shakes his head.

"He hasn't left the country. His jet, his yacht, his helicopter, they're all here, so it's only a matter of time before someone sees him and reports it. Is there anywhere that you two went together that he might have gone? I checked that place by the river. He wasn't there."

I shake my head, unable to think of a place we shared. "No, I don't think so," I confess, closing my eyes. "Josh, I'm so scared," I whisper, and he nods, taking my hands into his squeezing them supportively.

"He'll be back, you'll see." He assures me, and I nod, an endless stream of tears running down my face. "You should get some rest; you look exhausted." I shake my head, closing my eyes.

"I can't, not until I know he's okay." Josh nods and presses a kiss to my forehead, and hugs me. I lay my head on his shoulder and sob. Josh sat by my side the entire time the police came over to ask me questions. Another twenty-four hours go by, and the pain in my chest grows tenfold. Where was he? How could he do this to me? I wanted to be at his apartment if he came back, but I couldn't, because his parents and Sophie were there, and I didn't dare to face them. I was going out of my mind with worry, pacing the house, waiting and praying for some news that he's okay. But nothing came. The evening of the second night, there was a knock on the door, once again, I rush to the door thinking it was Cole, but I come face to face with a distraught Sophie. Oh God, have they heard something? Did they find him? Was he hurt?

"Sophie?" I whisper, and she glares at me with those icy blue eyes of hers.

"What did you do to him?" She rasps, walking into my apartment. I watch her and close the door. "For him to up and disappear like this, what did you do to him, Shayla?!" She shouts angrily, and I just look at her. "You were the last person to see him. He was with you before he vanished."

I drop my gaze shaking my head. "Sophie. I'm so sorry, I truly am. I —" I gasp when I feel her hand connect with my cheek.

"Hey! What the fuck do you think you're doing?!" Aimee comes rushing over, ready to fight her, and I hold my arm out to stop her.

"Aimee, don't!" I shout, keeping her back.

"Who the fuck do you think you are! How dare you lay a hand on her!" Aimee screams, fighting in my hold. Sophie backs away as I pull a livid Aimee away from her. "I'll fucking hurt you, bitch!"

"Aimee, stop! She's pregnant." I tell her looking at her pleadingly, and she simmers, glaring menacingly at Sophie.

"I don't give a shit! What the fuck do you both want from her, huh?! Haven't you both caused her enough pain? Just leave her alone!" Aimee shouts angrily, and I sob.

"Aimee, please, stop." I plead, sobbing, and she looks at me, her blue eyes softening.

"No, Shayla, I've had it with everyone thinking they can hurt you! You're not everyone's punching bag; you don't deserve this."

"She drove him away! Whatever she did to him, he took off without a word!" Sophie wails, and I turn to look at her.

"You know what I told him, Sophie? I told him to go home to you and your baby. I told him I didn't want to be with him, and I was dating Josh." I tell her, and Sophie sobs into her hand. "I didn't know he would react like this. I didn't!"

"Why can't you just leave us alone? What is it going to take for you to disappear for good? Can't you see what having you in his life is doing to him? We're getting married in less than a week, and my fiancé, the father of my child, is missing, probably dead in a ditch somewhere, and it's all your fault!"

I shake my head. "Don't say that; he's not dead!"

"Then where is he?!" She screams hotly, tears streaming down her pale cheeks. "If anything happens to him…"

"Don't say that," I whisper, backing up against a wall, shaking my head. "He's not dead."

"You need to leave him alone. I don't want you anywhere near my husband! We're having a baby Shayla! Get off of his back already!"

"I'm trying!" I scream at her. "I don't know what else I have to do, Sophie!"

"Leave! Get the hell out of our lives forever, so he can get back to his old self again and focus on his family. I don't know what the hell you've done to him because this isn't Tristan. He would never do something like this. Ever since he met you, his life has spiralled out of control." She explains, raking her fingers through her hair and pacing the living room. "You think I don't know that he's still in love with you? And that he's only marrying me because I'm pregnant with his child?" She cries, and I look at her woefully. "Do you have any idea how hard it is loving someone who is in love with someone else? He doesn't look at me the way he looks at you. He won't even touch me or let me touch him, but I'm trying to hold onto him for the sake of our child, but I can't do it if you're still in his life Shayla. He will never be happy if you don't let him go."

"Why does she have to fucking leave? Every time she has tried walking away, Cole found her and brought her back. He's the one chasing her, not the other way around!"

"I know that!" She cries, picking up my mother's vase and smashing it on the floor. "But I can't walk away. I love him!"

"So does she!" Aimee screams back. "It's even harder for them because they love each other, Sophie. If it's so fucking easy, why don't you back off and let them be happy? It's clear Cole is in love with Shayla and not you. Why are you holding on so tightly to someone who doesn't love you?"

"I'm having his baby!" Sophie cries, shaking her head. "I can't leave him. We're going to have a child together. We're going to be a family."

I sink to the floor, sobbing while they continue to argue. "Stop it, please just stop."

"Look at her! Take a good look at what Cole is doing to her. There's nothing left of her anymore. Just leave her the fuck alone. You think Cole is the only one suffering?! She's at breaking point! Are you trying to drive her to the point of insanity!" Aimee shouts angrily. "I hope for both your sakes that Cole is okay, but I will not allow you both to destroy my friend. She's been through enough, now get the fuck out!" Aimee exclaims, coming to my side as I rock back and forth on the floor with my head in my arms sobbing.

Sophie walks out of the apartment, slamming the door shut behind her. "Shayla." Aimee kneels next to me, wrapping her arms around me and pulling me into her chest. "Shhh, it's okay, she's gone, babe, she's gone."

"He's gone, and it's all my fault." I wail, and Aimee shakes her head tightening her hold on me.

"He's not gone. He'll be back, I know he will." She reassures me and helps me up to my feet. "Come on, the stupid bitch cut your cheek when she hit you; you're bleeding. Let's clean you up." I allow Aimee to help me to the bathroom. I was utterly defeated. I couldn't feel anything but the ache in my chest. The night just drags on as I sit by my window, staring out at the dark sky, silently pleading for him to hear my cries and come back.

"Please, Cole, wherever you are, please hear me and come back," I whisper, closing my eyes. I press the photo of us on my phone to my chest, sobbing desperately. I dial his number just to hear his voice on the voicemail. *'Hi, you've reached Tristan Hoult. I'm not available to take your call right now. If it's urgent, please leave me a message, and I'll come back to you when I'm available.'* I replayed that message over and over and over again, repeatedly hoping it would ease my pain, but it didn't. It made it worse. I hadn't slept in days, I couldn't stop crying. My head was throbbing, and my body trembling with trepidation.

~

THE NEXT MORNING I sat in the shower for an hour, the water just beating down on my exhausted body.

I was convinced he was gone forever; it's been three days and no sign of him. I was waiting for the bad news to come at any moment, mentally trying to prepare myself, but something inside me wouldn't let me believe it.

I got out of the shower and wrapped the towel around myself when I heard Aimee calling my name.

"Shayla?!" I open the door to the bathroom and look at her. She's on the phone with someone. "It's Josh, Cole's back." I gasp, and it felt as though an invisible force hit me. My knees shook and gave away. Aimee drops the phone and catches me as I fall to the floor panting, trying to catch my breath and choke on a strangled sob. "Jesus, Shay. He's okay, he's okay, shh babe."

"Where is he?" I ask, looking up at her, and she wipes my tears away, her own blue eyes pooled with tears.

"At his place." I clamber up to my feet and rush to my bedroom as Aimee watches me tear the towel off my body and throw on whatever clothes I could find, which was a pair of jeans and a plain white t-shirt. "Shayla, where are you going?"

"I have to see him," I say in a flurry as I grab my car keys and rush to the door.

"Shayla, let me drive you. You're in no state to drive." She tells me. I nod and toss her my keys, and we rush out of the apartment. My heart was hammering against my ribcage the whole way there, a million questions on my mind. I was relieved and hurt, and most of all, angry with him. How dare he put me through this. I didn't know what I was going to do when I saw him. Was I going to scream at him or throw myself into his arms and tell him I love him? My emotions were all over the place. He was alive, and that's all I cared about at that moment.

As we pull up to his apartment, I run out of the car toward the building, not even acknowledging the group of photographers gathered outside his apartment with his security team holding them back. *"There's Shayla! Shayla is Tristan back?! Is he well? Please give us some information!"* They call out to me, but it falls on deaf ears as I race through his building, pushing the button to the elevator a thousand times as I wait impatiently for it to descend to the ground floor. I was tempted to take the stairs, but he lives on the thirtieth floor. I'd collapse and die by the time I got up there. The elevator pings, and I rush in, pushing the button again till the doors close.

I was shaking like a leaf, and it felt like the slowest elevator journey ever, as I stare at the numbers at the top anxiously. "Come on, come on, come onnnn." I whimper and don't even wait till the door fully opens before I run out and down the corridor toward Cole's apartment. I push the code in with trembling fingers and wait for the light to go green before opening the door and walking inside. Almost immediately, I hear shouting. Cole and Josh were screaming at one another.

I walk in and watch as Josh punches Cole in the face. "If you love her so fucking much, why don't you go be with her? Huh?" Josh says and spits out blood on the floor. "I'll gladly step out of your way, go on, go be with her, bro!" He shouts, pointing at the door.

"Shut the fuck up!" Cole growls irately.

"Truth hurts, doesn't it, brother? You can't be with her because you're getting married and having a baby with your ex— the same ex you were in love with and using Shayla to get back at." He laughs bitterly. "You can be pissed off with me all you want, but YOU fucked this one up all on your own, bro."

"And you think you have what it takes to make her happy, do you?!" Cole questions walking toward Josh.

"Cole, she would have been mine right now if you hadn't swooped in that night, she would have been MY girl! She would have been in love with me! And yes, I fucking do." He hollers, stepping up to Cole.

"You should have worked up the courage and asked her out then, you fucking wimp! Shayla is off-limits to you!" Cole shouts, fisting Josh's shirt and bringing his face close to his. I couldn't watch anymore; my anger hit a whole other level.

"ENOUGH!" I scream, glaring at both of them, my chest rising and falling with every desperate breath I took. Cole lifts his gaze to me, and his eyes soften instantly when our eyes meet. He drops his hands from Josh's shirt and looks me over. "Josh, leave us," I tell him, my voice hoarse.

"Shayla…" he interjects.

I look at him. "Please..." He nods and stops when he sees the bruise and cut on my left cheek.

"Shayla, what happened to your face?" He questions, reaching out to touch me, but I move my face away.

"Leave us," I whisper pleadingly, and he nods and walks out of the apartment, leaving Cole and me alone. I stood there looking at him, tears streaming down my face while he stood staring at me apologetically.

"Shayla, what happened to you?" He questions, walking toward me. I reach up and slap him hard across the face. Cole lifts his eyes to mine—a look of hurt flashes in his eyes as they well up with tears.

"That's what happened to my face." I hiss angrily, and he frowns. "How could you do that to me?! I thought you were DEAD!" I scream sobbing, I shove him hard, and he stumbles back, swallowing thickly while he watches me. "Do you have any idea what you've put me through the past few days?!"

"I'm sorry." He apologises, taking a step toward me. I back away, sobbing.

"No," I shake my head. "No, you don't get to be sorry. You don't get to be sorry!" I scream at him. "How could you let me think you went off to die? Didn't you stop to think for one second how I would have felt if anything happened to you?!" I cry, and he watches me, tears flowing down his face. "I was convinced you weren't coming back, and I blamed myself for pushing you over the edge. I blamed my damn self, you son of a bitch!" I scream, and Cole shakes his head, reaches out and grabs my arm, he pulls me against him.

"No!" I whimper, pushing at his chest, but he wraps his arms around me tight, and I fight in his hold. "I thought you were gone." I cry and collapse into his arms. "I thought you left me here to live without you." I sob hoarsely into his chest, and Cole buries his face into my neck, sobbing with me.

"I wanted to. I tried, but I couldn't, Shayla. I thought about ending it all countless times, but every time I tried, I saw your face, and I couldn't do it." He states, pressing his lips to my forehead, his eyes closed. "I couldn't leave you." He pulls my head back and looks into my eyes, his thumbs wiping away the endless tears. "I was in a dark place, and I couldn't see a way out of it, but you saved me from doing something stupid," Cole explains, looking into my face.

"Why didn't you call me? I left you a thousand messages." I ask, and he presses his forehead to mine.

"I broke my phone. I didn't want to be found, Shayla. I wanted to disappear from everything and everyone. Especially you." He sighs, and I close my eyes.

"I would have never forgiven myself if anything happened to you." I cry, and Cole brushes his fingers through my hair. "I'm so sorry," I whisper, and Cole shakes his head slowly.

"Shayla, you're the last person who should apologise for anything. You're the only innocent one in this whole mess. It's my fault, not yours. Do you understand me?"

"Cole, what have we done?" I whisper, looking at him, and he sighs heavily. "Look at us, how did we get here?" I ask him, and he bites his split lip and winces. "When did things get so toxic between us?"

"I don't know." I look at his face, his cheek is starting to bruise, and his lips are busted and bleeding. I brush my fingers over his bruise, and his eyes close at my touch. I still couldn't believe he was alive and well. "I'm okay, sweetheart," Cole assures me as if reading my mind. He lifts my face and looks at the bruise and cut on my cheek. "Who did this to you?"

"Doesn't matter." I sigh, twisting my face away, and he frowns, turning it again so I could look at him.

"It matters to me. Who? Was it my mother again?" He questions, his tone hard, and I shake my head. "Who, Shayla?" I lift my gaze to him, and he sighs, closing his eyes. "Sophie."

"She was worried about you, and she lashed out at me. It's no big deal. Aimee told her off enough for the both of you, so please just let it go." I plead with him, and Cole exhales deeply.

"I hate myself for everything I've put you through." He admits earnestly, his thumb brushing over my cheek. "Please forgive me."

I close my eyes and wrap my arms around his neck, and he hugs me tightly. "I'm so relieved you're okay. Nothing else matters to me, Cole." I whisper. "I love you so much, please don't ever do that again."

"I love you too, sweetheart." He sighs, burying his face into my neck. I pull away from him and stare at the floor.

"Cole, I'm leaving," I tell him, licking my lips. "I can't do this anymore; the pain of being around you is just unbearable. I have to go before either one of us does something stupid." I add looking at him. "I made a promise to myself that if you came back safe and alive, I would go, and I'm going to keep my promise."

Cole's eyes fill with tears, and he nods. "I understand." He whispers sullenly, looking down at the floor. I was expecting him to refuse, but it seems he's finally given up fighting for us. It felt so final this time. "I'm never going to see you again, am I?"

I shake my head. "No, this is for the best for us both. Please, don't try and find me or come after me." I plead, and he nods slowly, staring at the floor. I walk over to him, lift his head, and kiss him one last time before I pull back, pressing my forehead to his. "Goodbye, Cole Hoult," I whisper, and I feel his hand tighten on my hips.

"Goodbye, Shayla Hart." He whispers back, his voice quivering. I pull away and turn to walk away, and Cole's hand that was holding mine squeezes it, and I still for a second, my eyes closed, I lost my breath, I felt that squeeze in my heart. I exhale slowly and force myself to walk away without looking back. Cole's grip loosens, and my fingers slip away from his—just as our fateful love has slipped from us.

The apartment door closed behind me, and I lean on it for support. I bite my lip hard and squeeze my eyes shut when I hear his stifled sob on the other side of the door. I turn and press my forehead and palm to the door. "I love you, you stupid boy," I whisper before I walk away down the corridor, heartbroken and beaten, and my life in ruins. I've walked away countless times, but this time was the hardest.

Because it was final, and we both knew it.

Chapter Forty

COLE

"TRISTAN?" I blink and look at my father, who was watching me expectantly. "How do you like this one, son?" He asks, gesturing to his black tailored Armani suit.

"Looks good, Dad," I tell him, staring at the mirror at my reflection as they tailor my suit for the wedding. I can't believe I'm getting married in two days. The closer the date got, the tougher it got to breathe. Sophie has us running around doing all this wedding stuff, and I'm really trying to pay attention, but I'm struggling. I keep thinking about *her*. I know I shouldn't, but I can't help it. Ninety-nine percent of my day is spent thinking about her. I was hoping to see her when she returned the papers signing her rights to her design entirely over to Cult Designs. I was left disappointed when I saw Jo walk in and hand the documents to Jess to give to me.

"Jo?" I call out to her while she was waiting by the elevator.

"Hi, Cole." She greets me with a small smile, her brown eyes looking me over, and she winces a little, but it disappears quickly.

"How is she?" I ask, dropping my gaze briefly. Jo sighs sadly and licks her lips tucking a strand of her mousy brown hair behind her ear.

"I'm not going to lie to you; she's broken, Cole. More broken than I have ever seen anyone in my life, but she's a fighter. She'll get through it." She tells me, and I close my eyes when I feel the pinch in my heart.

"She hasn't left yet?" Jo woefully shakes her head.

"No, not yet. She leaves in two days." She replies and sighs when the elevator arrives and the doors open. "Well, um, take care of yourself, Cole." She adds with a little wave, and I nod.

"You too," I reply and turn to walk back to my office.

"Hey, Cole?" Jo calls out to me, and I turn to look at her. "I'm terribly sorry for the way things ended for you and Shay. I was rooting for the two of you. Aimee and I both were." She tells me, and I sigh deeply.

"Not as sorry as I am, believe me," I reply, and she looks at me sorrowfully. "I'm glad she has you and Aimee to look out for her."

"I just wish I could find a way to make her stay. That apartment, our lives, nothing is going to be the same without her." She sighs sullenly, and I nod.

"No one understands that more than I do, trust me," I assure her, and Jo nods and waves once more before the doors close. My life is never going to be the same without her.

"Mr Hoult, your fiancée wanted me to remind you of the doctor's appointment you have in an hour." Jess reminds me, and I nod, thanking her.

~

"BABY, how exciting is this? I can't believe I'm starting to show." Sophie chirps excitedly, taking my hand and placing it on her tiny bump while we wait at the doctor's office. "Soon, you'll be able to feel it moving around in there." She sighs, elated, while I stare at the photo of a woman holding a new-born baby on the wall and blink a couple of times. She's got a striking resemblance to Shayla, or was my mind imagining it again. "What do you think the sex is of the baby? Would you prefer a boy or a little girl?"

"A girl," I whisper, staring at the photo of the woman.

"Mrs Hoult?" I look over at the midwife when she calls out my last name, and Sophie stands up and pulls me along with her. Is she seriously getting people to call her Mrs Hoult? We're not even married yet, for fuck-sake. I remember how much Shayla hated being called that and the death glare she would give me whenever I teased her about it. We walk into a dark room with one of those ultrasound machines, and I sit on the chair while Sophie lays back on the bed. I should be excited, right? I should feel something about seeing my baby for the first time, but I feel *nothing*. I stare at the screen numbly, and even when I hear the baby's heartbeat, I still feel nothing.

"Look, honey, that's our baby." Sophie coos holding her hand out to me. I stand up and take her hand and look at the screen. "Can you tell the sex of the baby yet?"

The sonographer smiles and looks at the screen. "Let's see." She says, moving the receiver over Sophie's stomach. "Oh, yes, it's a little boy. He gave us a quick flash. Is that what you were hoping for?"

"My husband was hoping for a little girl, but I'm thrilled it a boy," Sophie tells her, and I look at her blankly while she smiles lovingly at me. My stomach clenches when she calls me her husband. "My boy is going to be just as handsome as his father." I drop her hand and rub the back of my neck.

"Uh, I just remembered I have to make a quick call for work. I'll meet you outside, okay?" I tell her, and Sophie nods with a smile and looks at the screen again. I walk out of the room, loosen my tie as I lean against the door, and close my eyes. I genuinely feel like something is choking the life out of me.

After the doctor's appointment, Sophie kept going on and on about names for the baby, and I just had this overwhelming feeling to scream at her to shut the fuck up. As she continues to talk, I squeeze the steering wheel so tight my knuckles go white. I clench and unclench my jaw so much it was aching. I force myself to zone out and just nod or utter an 'mhm' now and then, pretending like I'm listening to a word she's saying. I wasn't. I couldn't.

I drop her off back at her apartment and make an excuse that I have things to do before the wedding and our honeymoon. I drive past Shayla's place every day, sometimes twice a day, rerouting my drive to work or home in hopes I'll see her outside or on her terrace, but I haven't yet. Soon

I won't even be able to do that because she's leaving the country, moving, to get away from me. I feel like a lost soul, just wandering around without a body or a home.

~

THE NEXT DAY was the rehearsal dinner. Another day, I have to act like the happy groom, excited to marry the woman he supposedly loves. Thank God for scotch, I was currently on my fifth glass, and it was taking the edge off somewhat. I've been drinking a lot. Lately, it's the only way I can sleep and ignore that big fat gaping hole inside of me. I can't even look at myself. I can't stand the sight of myself; it makes me sick to the stomach.

"Cole?" I lift my eyes and look at the therapist sitting opposite me. "Do you want to tell me why you're here?"

"You look like her," I tell her, and she frowns a little and licks her lips. She was a beautiful woman, with long dark hair, green eyes, but older. She bears a striking resemblance to Shayla, and I found comfort in that. Shayla was miles more beautiful, though, in every way.

"Cole, this is your third session, and we haven't discussed the real reason why you're here," Annabelle tells me, and I shrug indifferently. "Tell me about these dark thoughts you mentioned in our last session."

I shrug and bite my lip, "I'm stuck in an impossible situation. I'm getting married tomorrow to a woman who I once thought I loved, but I can no longer stand. How does that happen? How can you go from loving someone to completely loathing them and everything they do?" I ask, and Annabelle sighs and shifts in her seat regarding me seriously.

"Because we change Cole and the things we want tend to change as we grow older. We often turn a blind eye to the things we don't particularly like about our partners because we love them, but once that love is gone, those annoying habits or all the things we hate about them become more prominent and intolerable to us." She explains, and I nod. I suppose that made sense. "Name something you hated about Shayla?"

I shake my head, "Nothing. She's perfect."

Annabelle smiles, "There must be one thing that annoyed you about her."

I search my brain for something that I found annoying, but there wasn't anything. "Nothing. I love everything about Shayla. Her stubbornness, her clumsiness, her lack of spatial awareness. I can't think of a single thing I would ever hate about her." I tell her, earnestly.

"Why is it you decided to marry Sophie and leave Shayla? Can you not be a father to the child without marrying her?" She questions, tapping her pen on the notepad, and I sigh.

"I contemplated that, but in our circle, that's not an option. My father told me if you're man enough to have sex with a girl and father a child, you need to be man enough to step up and do the right thing and marry her. What child wants to grow up as a bastard, right? A pretty backward way of looking at things, especially in this day and age where people don't even want to get married and have kids left and right." I explain, rubbing my hands over my thighs. "But in our circle, that's unjust, and people love to talk, and it will tarnish the reputation I have built as a respected businessman."

"I understand, but it is still quite a sacrifice you're making. It's actually very endearing, Cole."

I roll my eyes, "Nothing endearing about it, trust me. It's simply cowardice."

"No, it's not. You're doing the right thing by your child and making a great sacrifice. That's what being a parent is all about." She voices, and I sigh and look around the room.

"I have nightmares that I won't love this baby. I don't feel anything, even when I saw him on that monitor, and they told us it's a boy—I felt nothing. I should feel something, anything, right?" I ask her, and she frowns a little. "I just feel empty and numb, and that darkness I told you about consumes me, and I get the sudden urge to throw myself off the terrace or drive into oncoming traffic," I explain, tears falling from my eyes.

"Cole, you're going through a difficult time with the break-up and feeling obligated to marry Sophie and have a baby. It's a lot for one person to take. That all-consuming darkness you speak of is your fear. Your fear of not loving your child, your fear of spending the rest of your life with a woman you don't love, the fear of never seeing Shayla again or ever feeling anything for anyone like you did her." I nod and bite my lip.

"I can only give you advice as a professional, but this route you're going down is clearly the wrong one. Your body, your mind is trying to tell you something, Cole. You're fighting to keep everyone else around you happy while you suffer the consequences. Why should you suffer, for other people's expectations and opinions of you? Their opinions won't be sleeping in your bed at night, Cole, but you know what will? Resentment, guilt, and despair."

"It's easier said than done." I sigh, shaking my head, wiping away the tears. "I'm just so tired of feeling…" I trail off, searching for the right word.

"Incomplete?" Annabelle finishes for me, and I close my eyes and sigh.

"Incomplete," I whisper sorrowfully, laying my head back against the chair. "I have never felt so utterly wrecked and powerless. I can feel my life slipping away from me. My soul is broken. I have everything I can dream of, money, career, cars, private jets, and boats. All those things I thought made me happy, just don't anymore. I would give it all up in a heartbeat for her without an ounce of regret."

"Now that's a sacrifice worth making," Annabelle tells me with a small smile. "*Listen* to your body Cole, listen to your heart because it never steers us wrong." I swallow the lump forming in my throat and nod. "That's all the time we have today. We can meet again after your honeymoon if you're still struggling."

I stand up and shake her hand. "Thank you for all your help." Annabelle nods and smiles warmly.

"Good luck, Cole." I nod, thanking her I walk out of her office. I was hoping to feel better, but I didn't. If anything, I was more confused than ever. What did she mean by listen to your body? What the fuck is my body trying to tell me?

I SPENT my last night as a bachelor drinking on my own in my regular bar. I don't bother looking up when I feel someone sit beside me.

"You gonna share or what?" I look to my side and see Josh sitting there. I look down into my glass again.

"The fuck do you want," I utter icily and hear him sigh and order a glass of scotch for himself.

"Thought you could use a friend." He says, taking a sip of his scotch.

I snort, "Yeah? Do you see one because I fucking don't?" I retort coldly and knock back my drink. Is this kid for real? How dare he call himself a friend after what he did—imprudent bastard.

"Cole, you're my best friend. Beyond that, you're my brother, man. We've known each other for years. If you're waiting for an apology, you're not going to get one." He tells me, and I glare at him darkly. "Maybe going after Shayla wasn't the best decision on my part, but she was single, and you're engaged to be married to another woman. I would think if you cared enough about this girl, you'd want her to be happy with someone you know would treat her right."

"You can tell you've never been in love." I sigh, pouring myself another drink and knocking it back. "Shayla wasn't *some girl* I was casually seeing. I love her deeply, more than I have loved anyone in my life. Of course, I would want her to be happy. No one deserves it more, but out of my sight, not having her happiness shoved in my face with my best friend kissing her and touching her as I used to." I tell him, staring into my glass.

"I didn't even think about it like that, man. I really liked her, and watching her fall apart when she thought something happened to you just made me realise how much she really loves you." Josh tells me, lifting his gaze from his glass to look at me.

"I know you liked her, and I can't blame you for that. She's truly something else, and I'm envious of the next guy that gets to have her, but that can't be you." I tell him blankly. "And if you choose to be with her, I can't be your friend, Josh, because every time I see you with her, I'm going to want to ram your head through a wall." I hear Josh chuckle beside me, and I look at him.

"If I were a selfish bastard, I would have. But looking at the state that girls love has left you in, and the state you have left her in, there's just too much damage there for me to even attempt to fix, as much as I think she's worth the agg—I don't want to be a substitute for you." Josh tells me earnestly, and I nod, looking down at my glass.

"She is definitely worth it."

"Not that it matters anymore. She's leaving for Canada in the morning." Josh sighs, picking up the bottle of scotch and pouring himself a drink. My head snaps up, and I look at him with a frown.

"Canada?" I ask in a flurry, and he nods, sipping his drink. He looks at me questioningly over the rim of his glass.

"She didn't tell you she was leaving?"

"She did. I just didn't think it would be as far as Canada." I utter sullenly, my shoulders slumping defeated. "She really is running as far away as she can to get away from me." I sigh, shaking my head.

"Can you honestly blame her?" Josh questions swirling the scotch in his glass. "I saw the state she was in. I was on the phone when Aimee told her you were back, and bro, when I tell you, my gut hurt listening to her screaming on the phone. Aimee said she hit the floor like someone took out her legs. I think she's reached her limit of how much she can take and wants to get away."

I chew on my bottom lip, tears filling my eyes. "Josh, how am I going to live without her man." I cry, and he sighs, squeezing my shoulder.

"You're going to take it one day at a time like you did when Sophie left." I shake my head.

"This is completely different. That break up was a joke compared to how broken I feel now." I admit wiping my tears with the back of my hand. "I'm beside myself and incomplete without her, and I will be forever." I sigh miserably, burying my face in my hands. "Fuck."

We sat there drinking and talking for hours, and a little part of me felt better having my best friend back. As angry as I still am with him, it hit me how much I need him in my life if I'm going to get through this mess. Josh spent the night at my house, and he stayed up with me the whole night.

~

"WELL, THIS IT, BRO." He sighs, coming to stand beside me as I attempt to do my tie but fail miserably. My fingers were shaking uncontrollably.

"What time is her flight?" I ask Josh, and he helps me with my tie.

"Uh, in like three hours, I think. Why?" He questions warily, and I shake my head.

"Just wondering if she's left yet," I tell him. I felt sick, my chest was all tight, and this stupid tie was choking the life out of me. I'll be married in less than an hour. I didn't feel right—I didn't feel right at all. My heart was racing. "Josh, can you give me a minute," I say, and he nods and leaves the room. I pick up my phone and scroll through it until I find her number and stare at it for a long time. I exhale slowly and press the call button and hold my breath waiting for it to ring. '

The number you're trying to reach has been disconnected,'

"No!" I ram my fist hard into the wall with a growl. I wanted to scream at the top of my lungs. I pace the little room at the church frantically.

I couldn't fucking breathe.

I turn around when the door opens, ready to scream at whoever it was that just walked in, but I freeze, staring at the person standing in the doorway.

"Hi."

Chapter Forty-One

SHAYLA

"SHAYLA HART, what is your sexy bum doing out here in the cold?" Jo asks, walking out on our terrace as I lay there on a pile of cushions looking up at the dark sky.

"Waiting for the sky to open up and swallow me whole?" I sardonically utter as Jo lays down beside me and looks up at the sky.

"Looks like you might be waiting a while on that one, Bish." She sighs, and I smile sadly, staring up at that one bright star in the sky.

"I can't believe I'm leaving in a few hours," I sigh and lace my fingers with Jo's as we stare up at the sky together.

"Oh, Shayla, I really wish you wouldn't. Can't you just pretend you left and let him think you've gone?" She suggests, and I close my eyes and shake my head.

"I can't, Jo," I tell her. "I can't be here anymore. Too much has happened. I have too many memories, I know it's stupid, but just breathing the same air as him, I honestly feel like I'm suffocating. His face his everywhere I go. He's in everything I do. I can't survive here anymore." I whisper, wiping the tears away. "Every time the door rings, I'll have that little bubble of hope wondering if it's him, or every time I go out, I'll search for his face in everyone that passes by me. It's just too hard."

"What's too hard? What are you two tartlets talking about without me, hm?" Aimee grumbles, coming over to lay on the cushions with Jo and me.

"Cole." We say in unison, and Aimee rolls her eyes and groans.

"Of course, what a silly question." She sighs heavily and looks up at the sky. "Catch me up."

"I was just telling her how sad we are that she has to leave and asked if she had to go," Jo says, brushing her thumb over mine.

"As wrecked as I am that you're leaving, a part of me is relieved for you because watching you fall apart, again and again, these past couple of months has been so hard, Shayla," Aimee confesses sadly, and I nod, lacing my other hand with hers.

"I honestly don't know how I would have survived without the two of you through all of this." I sniffle, closing my eyes. "I think I honestly would have done something stupid, it's a scary thought, but that's how close I've gotten to the edge."

Aimee squeezes my hand. "Don't talk like that, or I won't let you go anywhere."

Jo nods in agreement. "We'll lock you away in your room and wrap you up in bubble wrap till you get over him."

I smile sullenly. "Who would have thought last year that I'd be up and moving to the other end of the world to get away from a boy." I laugh bitterly, wiping away my tears. "Leaving my family and friends, my whole life behind." I cry.

"Shayla, we said no crying," Aimee cries with me, rolling onto her stomach to look at me.

"I've been crying since yesterday," Jo confesses, dabbing her eyes with a tissue and rolling over too, both of them looking down into my face while I sob.

"My mother was in bits when I told her everything. She's so heart-broken that I lied to her, I doubt she'll ever forgive me." I whimper, shaking my head. "And Sam, well, I had to beg him, to stop him from finding Cole and killing him when he saw the state I was in. What a fucking mess."

Aimee sighs, brushing her fingers through my hair. "What are we going to do without you, Shay? I honestly want to kill that Cole repeatedly. I fucking hate him for doing this to you." She murmurs irritated.

I shake my head. "No, girls, please don't hate him. Yes, he's burned me more than I have ever been in my life, but he's also taught me what it's like to love fiercely and to be loved just as intensely." I say sincerely. "He made his mistakes, and so did I, but despite everything, he's a good man and has such a good heart," I admit solemnly, closing my eyes. "I can say without a doubt he's the love of my life. It's just unfortunate that we weren't given the opportunity to be together."

"I didn't see it ending like this Shayla, you two were supposed to fall in love, stay married, and have cute babies and live happily forever." Jo sniffles wiping her eyes. "It's like I'm watching a really sad movie without a happy ending, and it's not fair." She wails into her tissue, setting me off, and Aimee hits Jo on the head with a cushion.

"Now look what you've done." She cries, pointing at me while sobbing herself. There we were, all three of us sobbing like three teenagers, just like when we watched The Notebook.

I stare down at my finger where I once wore a diamond ring and sigh. "He's getting married tomorrow." I sob wretchedly, and the girls wrap their arms around me and cry with me. "God girls, I love him so damn much," I whisper, and they nod.

"We know baby girl, and Cole loves you too. That's what makes this so fucking shit because you both love each other so much, and you can't be together. It's so heartbreaking." Jo cries, brushing her fingers through my hair comfortingly. How am I going to get over him? I had no idea how I was going to go on without him. I sigh and lay back, staring at the sky, remembering all our moments together. The first day we met, dancing in the club, our first kiss in the back of his car, the night we almost had sex at his apartment but got interrupted by the fire alarm, our moments in Nice and Dubai, we had so many. I felt like my heart was ablaze.

I miss him so much.

"Here," Aimee says, coming back with a bottle of tequila and three shot glasses. While I'm lost in my thoughts, I didn't realise she got up. "Let's get drunk because my emotions are running wild right now, and I want to scream." She claims, pouring us all shots. "I don't even want to imagine what you feel, so drink."

I sit up. "I'm not getting drunk. I have a flight tomorrow morning, and I don't fancy being hungover for an eight-hour journey," I tell them both and take the shot. I wince as the liquid burns my insides as it goes down.

"No more crying. This is our last night together. The three Amigas! So, we are going to drink, and we're going to dance and laugh, remembering our fun times we've had here over the years." Aimee says, pouring us another shot each. I nod and take the shot, shaking my head. I do my best to try and enjoy my last night with my girls, but the more I drank, the more I wanted to see Cole. "Drink Shayla!" Aimee shouts, handing me another shot. I wince and take it after clinking the glasses with them. Aimee gasps when Bitter by Fletcher starts playing and turns the music up, and we sing at the top of our lungs. "I know you think about me when you kiss her. I left a taste in your mouth. Can she taste me now… " I sing along to the song, tears of despair flowing from my eyes.

I want to scream.

"You bet your sexy bum he's thinking about you when he's with her!" Jo shouts, throwing her arms around me, and we topple over laughing. "Cayla foreveeeerrr!"

Aimee and I look at Jo, confused. "Who the hell is Cayla?"

Jo giggles, "Your portmanteau, silly! It's your names together. Cole and Shayla equal Cayla!" I laugh sadly, shaking my head.

I look at Aimee, who is laughing hysterically. "Don't let her drink anymore."

"Hey, it's better than Cophie! What kind of lame arse name is that?" Aimee hands me another shot, grinning, and I groan. I was already tipsy, and honestly, tequila makes me go stupid.

"She has a point." Aimee giggles, taking her shot. "Their names don't even sit right together. Should have let me punch the bitch square in her fake nose."

"Team hashtag Cayla!" Jo chirps, making a hash sign with her fingers and pressing it to her face. "Fuck Sophie."

I sigh, "What good would that have done? She's pregnant, Aimes; besides, I get where she's coming from. As much as I dislike her, I can relate to what she's going through as a woman. It's hard watching someone you love be in love with someone else."

"She had no right blowing up at you like that, though. You did the right thing and walked away. You're fucking leaving the country so he can be with her. You're a better woman than I am Shayla because I would have fought tooth and nail to be with the man I love, especially if he loves me too." Aimee says, pulling her knees to her chest.

"You think I haven't thought about that? If she wasn't pregnant, there's no force strong enough to keep us apart, I know that much, but she's having his baby. As hard as a pill it is to swallow, he's made the right choice." I explain sadly with a shrug, and Aimee groans, resting her chin on her knees again.

"Yes, but you still have to go. You're the innocent one in all of this, and you're the one paying the price."

"Love isn't love without consequences or sacrifices, Aimes. It's not always rainbows and butterflies; not everyone gets the happily ever after they want. This is the hand that fate dealt us, we've tried, but life has other plans in mind for us, I guess. Maybe there's something better out there for me. Maybe Cole was just a life lesson." I tell her, and she shakes her head sadly.

"Life sucks." She utters, handing me another shot.

"I'll drink to that." I sigh, tapping my glass to hers before taking the shot. "I'm done. I'm one shot away from running to Coles and begging him not to marry her." I groan, and Aimee chuckles, biting her lip while she watches me.

"I love you, Bish."

"I love *you*, Bish," I reply and look at Jo sleeping with her head on my lap. "I love you both so much." I sigh, stroking my fingers through her hair. I didn't sleep a wink that night. My heart was so full of emotion I honestly couldn't bear the thought of sleeping, so I packed my things up while the girls were asleep. I was tempted to call Cole, so I snapped my sim card in half so I wouldn't give in and call him.

THE MORNING CAME QUICKER than I would have liked. Jo and Aimee had work, so we said our goodbyes, broke down, and cried for over an hour until I kicked them out and told them to leave so I can pack the rest of my things before my flight. My flight was at eleven forty-five, and it was currently eight-thirty, so I had an hour or so before I had to leave for the airport.

I had a shower and had about four cups of coffee to avoid the hangover that I felt coming from a night of drinking tequila. I was not looking forward to the long flight ahead. I look around my bedroom one last time and pull my suitcases to the living room, waiting for my cab. I leave my keys to the apartment on the side with my car keys for Aimee. She wanted to get a car, so I left a note telling her to take good care of my baby.

I jump startled when the apartment door bursts open, and Aimee runs in panting breathlessly like she'd run a marathon. "Oh, thank God… you're still…here." She gasps while holding her chest.

"Aimee, why are you back? Shouldn't you be at work? What's wrong?" I ask, watching her while she shakes her head, leaning over, her hands on her knees, trying to catch her breath.

"Fuck work…Shayla, fuck, I can't breathe…" She wheezes breathlessly. "You remember Becky…the one from my office?" She asks, and I frown and nod. "Guess who her best friend is cousins with?" She explains, panting, and I shake my head with a shrug.

"Aimee, my cabs here. I'm going to miss my flight. What are you on about?" I question, bewildered, and she shakes her head.

"Her cousin is Derrick, Sophie's ex Derrick." She says in a flurry, and I blink, waiting for her to continue.

"Okay….so?"

"The baby is Derrick's!" She exclaims. "Not Cole's." My handbag slips from my hand and hits the floor as I stare at her unblinking. "I think I'm going to pass out. Did it just get really dark in here?"

"Aimee, what are you talking about? How do you know this?"

"Derrick told his cousin he and Sophie had sex after they broke up when she went to pick up her things, and she got pregnant because they didn't use protection! Derrick confronted her, and she admitted it to him, but then slapped him with a confidentiality agreement and a payout to keep his mouth shut and sign away his rights to the baby." She explains, and I gape at her in utter shock. "That stupid bitch Sophie's been lying to trap Cole and force him to marry her." I felt paralysed; my feet felt like led. "Shayla, what are you waiting for? GO TELL COLE!" She screams at me, and I pace back and forth. My hands and knees were shaking frantically.

"Oh, my God!" I shout my fingers in my hair. "What if I'm too late?!"

"You fucking will be if you keep standing there!" She shouts, and I look at her, still stunned. "GO!" She screams, making me jump, and I snatch up my keys and run to the door, not even bothering with the elevator. I race down the stairs, my heart up in my throat. I couldn't believe it. This whole time that bitch was lying to him. Oh God, please, please don't let me be too late. I jump into my car and drive as quickly as I could to the church.

"Move!" I beep frantically at the car that cuts in front of me as I swerve in and out of traffic like a lunatic. After what felt like the longest drive ever, I pull up at the church and run through the people scattered around and the paparazzi gathered outside the church.

"Look! There's Shayla!" One of them shouts, snapping photos as I run through the crowd. "Shayla, are you here to stop the wedding?!"

"YES! MOVE!" I shout as I barge past them and race up the steps. They applaud and whistle as I race into the church and push the doors open and run in panting. Everyone turns and looks at me. I glance at the altar and see no Cole or Sophie. Oh no, I was too late. My heart sinks to the pit of my stomach.

"Shayla?" I lift my gaze and look at Cole's mother. Tears spill down my cheeks, and she reaches up and wipes them away. "What are you doing here, sweetheart?"

"I'm too late," I whisper sullenly, and she smiles, lifting my head so I could look at her.

"No, you're not. Tristan left. He didn't marry Sophie. He ran off to find you to stop you from leaving." She tells me, and I blink, surprised, tears of joy streaming down my cheeks. "Go get him, honey." I give her a watery smile, and she hugs me before I turn and run out of the church.

God damn it, why did I break my sim card! I can't even call him. I run into Josh, and he smiles, shaking his head when he sees me.

"You two are fucking bat shit crazy."

"Where is he Josh, where did he go?" I ask in a flurry and Josh chuckles.

"He's gone to your apartment to stop you from leaving. He left like ten minutes ago." I nod and thank him before running out of the church again, ignoring the photographers screaming at me as I run to my car. He didn't do it. He didn't marry her. Oh God, I was feeling so many things I didn't know which one to focus on. I drive back to my apartment and race up the steps as fast as my already shaking and tired legs would take me. I burst through the door and look around frantically. I look at Aimee, stuffing her face with cereal, and she frowns.

"Where's Cole?!" I gasp breathlessly as I try to catch my breath.

"He left like five minutes ago to go back to the church to find you!" She shouts with a mouthful of cereal, sputtering milk everywhere.

"Son of a bitch!" I pant and run out of the apartment again. My mouth was dry, my heart was racing, and I was a sweaty mess running around the city trying to find him. Why wasn't he staying put? For God's sake, my heart was about to give out on me. I run back to the church again, and the same people as before watch, bewildered as I race past them once more. I look around the church and see no sign of him. Where the hell was he? My head was spinning, and I was starting to see spots.

Josh laughs when he sees me again. "What the fuck are you two doing?"

"Please… tell me… he's here." I wail, and Josh shakes his head, grinning.

"No, he just left like two minutes ago thinking you're waiting at your apartment." I heave a sigh and shake my head.

"I can't…I can't *breathe*. Call him. I can't run anymore. I can't."

"I would, but I've got his phone. He ran off in such a rush he left everything." Josh tells me, and I groan before leaving the church and running back to my car again.

"Shayla?!" I spin around when I hear Cole calling my name. I search for him and see him sprinting toward me down the street. I sigh, relieved, close my car door and run to him. I leap into his arms, and he catches me, winding his arms around me tight and burying his face into my neck. “Oh, baby.” He pants breathless

“Oh my God,” I sob hysterically. We hold one another in the middle of the street without a care in the world who was watching. I pull my head back and look into his eyes; he smiles at me. His green eyes pooled with tears. “Cole, the baby isn’t yours. It’s Derricks.”

Cole nods, pressing his forehead to mine. “I know,” He pants. “He came and told me everything. She’s been fucking lying to me this whole time.” I sigh, thankful. “It’s over now, baby. Nothing will keep me from you ever again.” He declares lovingly, his fingers curling at my nape; he draws my lips to his and kisses me slow and deep. I moan, kissing him back with every bit of love I held in my heart for him.

We pull apart, and he looks into my eyes, his eyes alight with such joy it made my heart soar. “Marry me, Shay. Let’s go back to where it all began in Vegas with everyone we love and marry me again.” He says, and I look into his eyes, tears of absolute joy spilling down my cheeks. “What do you say, baby? Do you want to do this, do you want to be my wife again? For real this time.”

I nod, “More than anything.” Cole grins handsomely and presses his lip to mine again. His strong arms wrapped tightly around me as we kiss in the middle of the street like two idiots undeniably and madly in love.

Chapter Forty-Two

COLE

"Hi," I frown while I look at Derrick standing in the doorway. "Can we talk?" He requests. I nod and gesture for him to come in, and he does, closing the door behind him.

"What are you doing here?" I question puzzled, leaning against the wall and watch as he paces the small room rubbing the back of his neck, seemingly troubled.

"Tristan, I should have done this a long time ago. I don't know what the fuck I was thinking keeping it from everyone this whole time." I straighten from my position leaning on the wall and look at him, baffled.

"Told me what, Derrick, spit it out?"

Derrick sighs, "That baby isn't yours. It's mine." He blurts out, and I stare at him, my hands fisted at my sides. "After Sophie broke it off with me, she came over to collect her things one night, and we got into an argument, things got pretty heated, and well, we had sex. I didn't use protection. I was too lost in the moment, and we both forgot."

I couldn't believe what I was hearing while I stood frozen, listening to him. My entire body was shaking with fury. "When I found out she was pregnant, I confronted her and asked her if it was mine, and she was adamant it was yours, but I kept pushing, and she admitted that it was mine." He explains. "I was freaking out, Tristan. I wasn't ready to be a father, and Sophie was so desperate to hold on to you that she offered me a payout to keep my mouth shut and made me sign a confidentiality agreement, and I did." I shake my head horrified. "It didn't feel right. I couldn't sit back and let her pretend my child was another mans. I'm so sorry, Tristan." I close my eyes, shaking my head.

"I can't fucking believe this. She's been deceiving me this whole time." I growl and look at him. "Thank you, Derrick. You just prevented me from making the biggest mistake of my life." I tell him, and he nods. I open the door and find Sophie's brother in the corridor.

"Where's Sophie?" I bark, and he jumps and points to the room down the hall. I was livid, no fuck that, I was beyond livid. Every time I thought of all the pain she's put Shayla and me through, I got even angrier. I open the door and walk into the bridal room, and Sophie turns and looks at me. Her bridesmaids and mother, and a team of people doing her hair and make-up in the room with her. "Everyone out." I hiss menacingly. They all look at one another only when Sophie nods, they all leave the room. Sophie stands up and walks over to me.

"Baby, what's the matter?" She questions her blue eyes, searching mine.

"What's the matter?" I growl, taking a step toward her. "I just had a surprise visit from Derrick." Sophie's face drops, and she backs away when I walk toward her.

"What did he say?" She asks, her voice mousy and barely over a whisper.

"He said the baby is his, and you paid him to keep his mouth shut," I inform her, and her eyes instantly pool with tears, and she shakes her head swiftly.

"Tristan, he's lying. He obviously wants to ruin our wedding." She cries, backing away as I advance toward her.

"Don't fucking lie to me!" I scream, picking up the chair and flinging it across the room. "You're sick in the fucking head, you know that! I knew something didn't add up! I used a condom when we slept together every time. I knew it, I felt it in my gut, but I ignored it and trusted you!" I shout, furious, pacing back and forth. "You almost cost me my fucking life!" I bellow, glaring at her.

"Tristan, I'm so sorry." Sophie cries. "I panicked. I was about to lose you to her. I knew you were breaking up with me to be with her. It was written all over your face. I saw the love in your eyes when you were around her. I was going to get an abortion, but when you got back from Dubai, and you were about to break up with me, I didn't want to lose you, so I just blurted it out. I'm so sorry!"

"Sorry? You're fucking sorry?! Do you have any idea the hell you've put me through? The pain you've caused Shayla?!" I scream at her. "Have you no fucking sense Sophie? How could you try and ponce another man's child on me for your own selfish gains? Do you think I'm fucking stupid and I wouldn't find out that baby wasn't mine eventually? You need some serious mental help! I can't believe I ever fucking loved you. You make me sick!" I utter disgusted and turn to leave, but she grabs hold of my arms, sobbing.

"Tristan, please, I love you so much. Don't leave me. I can make you happy. We can be happy just like we used to be, baby." She pleads. I yank my arm out of her hold and shake my head.

"You wouldn't know love if it slapped you in the fucking face. You can't make me happy, Sophie, you never did, not really. There are only two women who have ever loved me unconditionally. One is my mother, and the other is Shayla. You better pray I catch her in time before she leaves, or you're going to have hell to pay." I snarl and yank the door open and walk out of the room. "The wedding is off," I tell everyone standing there and walk past them and turn to look at Sophie's parents. "Get your daughter some psychological help because she desperately needs it."

"Tristan, sweetheart. What's happened?" My mother asks, following me as I frantically look for my car keys.

"She's been lying to me! The baby isn't mine; it's her ex-fiancés. She's been lying to trap me into marrying her. I'm so fucking stupid. I've lost Shayla too because of her!" I shout, kicking the small wooden table angrily.

"Cole, you can still catch her if you hurry." I look at Josh, who gestures with his head. "Gerald has the car keys. He's outback, go and get your girl, man!" I was furious but so relieved at the same time. That weight I've been carrying around finally disappeared.

Annabelle was right, my body *was* trying to tell me something wasn't right, and I kept ignoring it, thinking it was because I was broken over Shayla. I run out the back of the church. I jump in the car, and Gerald looks at me, waiting for instructions. "Take me to my love, Ger," I tell him, and he smiles brightly, nodding. "Step on it!" I heave a sigh of relief. I can't believe it. It's like I'm waking up from a nightmare. I was so anxious. I couldn't sit still. My hands were shaking, my heart racing like crazy. Please, please let her still be there. I'd fly to Canada and search every city till I find her if I had to. I'm not letting her go. Never. Ever. I'll chase her all around the world because I can't live without her. I don't want to.

While my mind was reeling, I hadn't realised we arrived at her street. I didn't even wait for the car to stop before I dash out and race up to her apartment, taking two steps at a time till I got to the fifth floor. I bang my fist on the door in a flurry, the door opens, and I see Aimee standing there. "Please, tell me she's here?"

Aimee shakes her head, "No, she went to the church to stop you. Didn't you see her?" I shake my head, and a bubble of excitement erupts inside of me. "What are you waiting for idiot, GO!" Aimee shouts, pushing me out the door. I laugh, grab her face, and kiss her forehead with an audible 'mwah' before I run down the stairs again to go back to the church. Aimee sighs, watching me fly down the steps, a smile on her face.

~

GERALD LOOKS at me through the window with a frown as I run toward the car and jump in.

"Sir?"

"Back to the church. Hurry!" Gerald nods and speeds off down the street again, chuckling to himself.

"What's funny?" I ask him, panting, and he shakes his head, trying his best to suppress his laughter.

"The great Tristan Cole Hoult chasing a girl around the city— never thought I'd see the day." He states, and I grin.

"Ger, she's not just *a* girl. She's *the* girl. I'll chase her to the end of the world if I have to." I tell him excitedly, and he nods, smiling as we whiz through the traffic.

"She sure is, sir." He agrees, and we pull up at the Church again ten minutes later. I jump out of the car and race up the steps to the church and look around frantically. "Shayla?!" I call out, and Josh comes over to me, laughing. "Bro, you just missed her. She's gone back to hers to catch you there."

"Fuck!" I shout, placing my hands on my head, panting. I run back out of the church, not even acknowledging the photographers snapping pictures of me as I run around like a lunatic. Can't wait to see that article later. Billionaire architect runs amuck in the city looking for his love. I chuckle as I jump back in the car, and Gerald looks at me with a smirk.

"Miss Harts?" He says, and I nod heaving. I sink back into the seat, trying to catch my breath. This was not how I envisioned our reunification happening, but it definitely fits for Shay and me, that's for sure. I laugh, shaking my head. Only we could royally screw this romantic moment up. I go through in my mind all the things I want to say to her when I finally see her, and I honestly want to scream with joy.

"Sir?" I look over at Gerald, pointing to the black Mini Cooper whizzing past us on the other side of the road. That's her.

I roll my window down. "Shayla?!" I shout, but she's already gone. "Fuck. Turn the car around." I tell Gerald, and he shakes his head and slams his foot on the brake halting the car in the middle of the road. Cars were honking from behind us.

"It will take too long to turn the car around here. If I go all the way around, we'll miss her again. Run!" He tells me, and I get out of the car through the busy street and run toward the church. My lungs were burning, and I was sweating as if I'd just gone ten rounds in a boxing ring.

As I run, I see Shayla in the distance running toward her car. "Shayla?!" I scream as loud as my lungs would allow and watch her as she looks around, searching for me. Her eyes finally find mine, her shoulders slump, and she pushes her car door shut before she runs toward me through the throng of people. I race toward her and catch her as she leaps into my arms. "Oh, baby." I pant, encircling my arms around her tight. I bury my face into her neck and inhale deeply, taking in her scent.

"Oh, my God." Shayla sobs, her arms tight around me, we hold each other like we've been longing too, and my God, have I missed her. This girl's love has shaken me to my very core. Shayla pulls back and looks into my eyes. I smile at her, unable to keep the tears back any longer. I can't believe how close I came to losing her. "Cole, the baby isn't yours. It's Derricks."

I nod, pressing my forehead to hers, panting, "I know, he came and told me everything. She's been fucking lying to me this whole time." I tell her, gazing into her beautiful eyes. "It's over now, baby. Nothing will keep me from you ever again." I assure her, curling my fingers at the nape of her neck, I pull her mouth to mine and kiss her desperately, and she moans, kissing me back just as fervently.

I'm so in love with her; there are simply no words to express how crazy I am about this girl. We pull apart, and I gaze lovingly into her eyes and tell her exactly what was in my heart. "Marry me, Shay, let's go back to where it all began in Vegas, with everyone we love, and marry me again," I express, and she looks at me surprised; her beautiful green eyes fill with tears. "What do you say, baby? Do you want to do this, do you want to be my wife again? For real this time." I ask and watch as she nods.

"More than anything." She whispers, and I beam at her, my heart beating like crazy in my chest. I pull her lips to mine again, and we kiss zestfully for a good couple of minutes in the middle of the bustling street, paparazzi witnessing our whole exchange, but we didn't care. We were both where we belonged. With one another and that's all that mattered. Shayla pulls back and looks at me, smiling. "I love you, you stupid boy." She declares cupping my face in her hands, and I laugh.

"I love you, you silly girl," I reply, and she presses her forehead to mine. "Take me home stud."

"Yes, my mini muffin," I reply, and she throws her head back and laughs cheerfully as I set her down on her feet and we walk to her car together, hand in hand, leaving behind all our woes and heartache. Shayla runs over to Josh, and he hugs her tight. He pulls back, and he fist bumps me before we embrace, all anger and resentment between us forgotten.

"About fucking time, bro." He tells me. I beam at him and pull Shayla into my arms and kiss her forehead. “So, Shay, Aimee’s single, right?” He questions as we all walk together. As much as I wanted to be alone with Shayla, there was plenty of time for that. We went back to hers with Josh. I grin in delight while watching Shayla, and the girls scream, jumping around excitedly at our reconciliation and the news of our decision to get married.

“We’re going out tonight!” Aimee chirps excitedly. “We’re going back to where it all began baby!” We all laugh and clink our glasses of wine. I catch Shayla’s eyes, she smiles at me beautifully, and I grin back, holding her gaze. It’s been really tough, we’ve both got so much healing to do and so much to work through, but I saw everything I needed in her eyes.

The rest of my life.

Chapter Forty-Three

SHAYLA

"YOU'RE DOING WHAT?" Cole's parents utter at the same time. They were staring at us wide-eyed.

Cole and I look at one another as we sit at the dining table at his parents' house a few days later. I press my lips together to stifle the laugh that was bubbling up inside of me at the horrified look on his mother's face.

"We're getting married in Vegas, and we would love it if you could be there with us," Cole tells them evenly, and his mother's eyes almost bulge out of her head.

"Vegas?" She sputters, stunned, and we nod. "Like…in the chapel? With *Elvis*?" I mask my chuckle with a cough, and Cole looks at me, his eyes full of mischief as the corner of his lips twitch.

"Yes, mother. Vegas, the chapel, Elvis, the whole lot." Cole tells her, and she turns her gaze to me.

"Son, just so we can prepare ourselves, how many times exactly are you planning to get married in your life?" Cole's Dad questions, his green eyes twinkling mischievously when Cole chuckles shaking his head, and I giggle.

"This is the very last time." He declares and laces his fingers with mine atop of the table. "To the only woman I can ever see myself being with," I smile, holding his gaze.

"Shayla, sweetheart, do you not want your fairy-tale wedding? With the white gown and the flowers and the beautiful church service? It's every girl's dream, honey." She states, and I shake my head.

"No, it really isn't. I'm sure you've realised this yourself, Elaine, but I'm not like other girls. I don't need the big fancy wedding surrounded by a ton of people that I barely know. A small, cosy, simple ceremony with my nearest and dearest has always been my dream. And Vegas is obviously where our whole journey began, so it holds great meaning for Cole and me, and we would really love our families to be there with us." I explain and bite my lip. "My mother obviously can't be there because she can't leave the house, but it would mean a lot to me to have you there," I tell her earnestly and her eyes soften, and she reaches over and takes my hand into hers.

"Of course, I will be there." She assures me, smiling kindly, and I squeeze her hand a little. "I think it's also time you call me Mum, don't you?" I blink back the tears and nod.

"Thank you…Mum." Elaine smiles, her own eyes watering as she looks at Cole, nodding at her gratefully.

"Now that's out of the way, I must simply insist that you at least wear a white gown." While cutting into her steak, she says, and I chuckle and lay my head on Cole's shoulder when he wraps his arms around my shoulder.

"We can have the reception at the Bellagio after your ceremony at the chapel?" His Dad suggests, and his parents start discussing wedding details.

"You okay?" Cole whispers to me, pressing a kiss to my temple, when he notices the saddened look on my face.

"Yeah, I'm fine," I reply, and he narrows his eyes at me, silently telling me he's not buying it. "I'm just a little sad that my mum won't be at my wedding." I sigh, and he kisses my temple again, his hold tightening around me.

"I'm sure she would love to be there if she could, baby. We can face-time her, or I'll have them set up a video conference, and she can watch the whole thing." Cole suggests thoughtfully, and I smile lovingly up at him.

"That's a great idea, baby. I'd still like for her to be there with my brother and me, but it's better than nothing, I suppose." I say, and he looks at me pensively for a long moment before he nods, and we go back to talking to his parents.

"I can't tell you how relieved I am that my son didn't marry that godawful witch Sophie," Elaine tells me, casting a look at Cole, who was discussing something with his father. "I still can't believe how devious she was, lying to him about the baby."

I nod and sigh, "I know. I'm so thankful the truth came out before it was too late, and he made the mistake of marrying her." I say, looking over at Cole, laughing at something his Dad said.

"I dread to think what kind of life he would have had with her." She sighs and takes my hand in hers, and I turn my gaze to her. "I haven't seen him this happy and content since your divorce, Shayla. You've brought so much love and joy into his life— into all of our lives, and I'm so thankful to you." She states, her eyes showing her sincerity, and I smile gratefully at her.

"I said this before, and I'll say it again, you've raised a wonderful son, and I am truly blessed to be loved by him."

"And him by you, sweetheart." She reassures me, lifting her hand and touching my cheek. "I'm just ever so sorry I treated you so horribly at the beginning." I shrug, shaking my head.

"It's long forgotten." I utter, and she smiles and sits back in her chair with a content smile while watching her boys.

~

As Cole and I had expected, our reconciliation made the headlines once again. Aimee came running into my bedroom the next day with Jo hot on her heels. They threw themselves onto my bed, waking me up from a very peaceful slumber.

"Bish! Wake up! You're all over the fucking internet!" Aimee shrieks bouncing up and down on my bed. I groan and pull the covers over my head, but Jo yanks it back down and flicks my nose.

"Get up, you lazy moo. You have to see this!" Jo chirps excitedly, shoving her tablet in my face. I blink and look at the photo of Cole and I kissing in the middle of the street after I jumped into his arms. I smile when my heart flutters wildly in my chest. There are various other images of me running toward the church and then Cole running out of the church. The headline at the top read:

Nations Sweethearts, Tristan Hoult and Shayla Hart have Reunited!

"Nation's sweethearts?" I utter with a roll of my eyes, and Jo squeals, clapping her hands. Aimee takes the tablet from me and reads the article out loud.

"Listen to this. Tristan and Shayla's whirlwind romance has us all at the edge of our seats. Their surprise marriage and the especially shocking news of a sudden divorce—six months after they got hitched—had us all wondering what had gone wrong between our beloved sweethearts? On the day Tristan was supposed to marry Sophie Turner, Shayla was seen racing toward the church to stop the wedding. It was unlike anything I have ever witnessed in all my years as a journalist. Shayla and Tristan were seen running amuck trying to find one another, only missing each other by mere minutes. When they finally found one another, they raced through the crowd, and Shayla leapt into Tristan's arms, where they declared their love for one another without a care who was watching. *sigh* What a romance. We're all waiting, praying, and anticipating another wedding announcement to follow their reconciliation. Click the video below to witness the moment everyone is going bananas about." Aimee read with a grin, and I cover my face with my hands.

"Oh, Jesus. They filmed the whole thing?" I ask mortified, my voice muffled behind my hand.

Jo pulls my hands back, and they show me the video. "Yes, look. It's better than any rom-com movie I have ever seen, Shayla. People are going crazy over it." She gushes, and I take the tablet and watch the video with a smile. "Hashtag team Cayla baby!" I laugh when they both jump on top of me.

A COUPLE of weeks fly by, and before we knew it, it was three days before our wedding. I giggle and slap Coles wandering hand away from where it was creeping up my thigh under my skirt. "Ow! What was that for?" He asks, rubbing his hand with a playful pout. I give him a pointed look arching a brow at him, and he sighs.

"What did we agree? No sex before the wedding night."

"Yeah, but I don't remember agreeing to no touching or kissing." He grumbles, biting his lip and smirking at me with a naughty glint in his eyes. "Let me fondle you, just a little?" Cole groans, leaning in close, and I look into his eyes and lick my lips alluringly while leaning in also.

"A little?" I whisper, and he nods, looking at my lips ravenously.

"Mhm, a teeny weenie bit." He breathes, ghosting his lips over mine, and I moan.

"Hey!" We jump apart when we hear Aimee shout from behind us, hands on her hips, glaring at us both. "That's not a metre apart." She scolds, and Cole curses, rolling his eyes.

"Jesus! Where is your boyfriend...*Josh*?!" Cole calls out to Josh, who walks out of Aimee's bedroom, buttoning up his shirt.

"What?"

"Can you not keep your girl entertained for more than ten minutes?" He says, widening his eyes. Josh chuckles and shrugs. "There's some major cock blockage going on over here, bro. I had her man. I was so close!"

"You said, ten minutes. Your time is up, bro. I got mine."

I laugh, blushing furiously when Josh looks at me, shaking his head. Aimee gasps and smacks Josh upside the head. "Why you little...we're you distracting me so he could get into her pants?" Josh smiles sheepishly at her.

"Ow, it's his fault. He bribed me with a new car," Josh complains, rubbing his head.

Aimee glares at him, "Listen, you two, I'm just doing my maid of honour duties, no nookie till you get married." She croons, turning around and walking out of my bedroom. "You have three more days. You'll thank me when you have the best orgasm in your lives."

Cole rolls his eyes and looks at me; he stretches his leg out and kicks the door shut. "Cole, she'll only come back."

"Baby, just one kiss... *please* ." He pleads, giving me the most adorable look I've ever seen. I smile as he leans in close, and just as his lips are about to touch mine, I get up, and he falls forward face-first into the mattress. I laugh when he growls and looks at me insatiably.

"Oh, you're playing dirty, Shayla Hart."

"No rule-bending, baby," I tell him with a sugary smile, and he groans, watching me as I walk to the door, his eyes on my bum.

"Fine," He grouses, "But don't complain on the night when I don't last longer than three minutes. You've only got yourself to blame when I'm laying as a happy sally relieved and you're still unsatisfied." I look back at him as I reach for the doorknob, and he smirks at me cheekily.

"You would never," I gasp and quirk a brow as I stroll over to him. I watch as his eyes light up when I lean forward close to his face. "If that instance does occur, you best believe I have many *many* ways of getting mine, baby."

Cole's eyes look over my face, and he bites his lip, "Oh yeah, do tell?"

I lick my lips slowly and lock my gaze with his as I trail my finger down the side of his face. "This may just be a pretty face to most, but it's *my seat*, and you best believe I'll be riding it till I'm crying out your name over and over again," I tell him, and he groans throatily, swallowing hard.

"By all means, hop right on..." He whispers, brushing his nose over mine. "I'm going to ravish you." He growls impatiently while sliding his hands up my thighs under my skirt. "I'm going to fuck you so hard you won't be able to walk straight for days." I pucker up my lips and blow him a kiss as I pull away.

"You better." I purr with a wink as I walk to the door, deliberately swaying my hips while he watches my bum avidly.

"Christ, Shayla." He mumbles as I walk away and falls back on the bed with a frustrated sigh.

Back in the kitchen, the girls and I discussed the bachelor/bachelorette parties, and Aimee suggested we go to a Magic Mike show.

"Oh, Aimes, I dunno. I really don't want anything too crazy." I tell her as I lean against the kitchen counter.

"Shayla, it's your last night as a singleton…*again,"* Jo tells me, leaning over the counter, her honey-coloured orbs wide and pleading. "Let's make it a night we'll remember, and I really, really want to see some hot dancers." I roll my eyes and sigh exasperatedly. "It's okay for you two; you've both got hot boyfriends. I've got no one." She claims with a pout and Aimee, and I pout and hug her.

"Fine, fine, we'll go to the show." I relent, and she grins toothily at me and claps excitedly.

"Yay, I'm so excited. I'm going to Vegas, baby!" Jo exclaims just as Josh and Cole walk into the kitchen.

"What's going on in here?" Cole asks, walking over to me, smiling sexily, those dimples on show.

"Have you guys discussed what you're doing for the bachelor party?" Aimee asks Josh while he lifts her off the stool she's sitting on and pulls her into his lap. They're so cute together. I love it.

"Yeah, we're going to this fancy strip club—" He says and stops suddenly when everyone in the room looks at him, including Cole, who turns his gaze to me slowly. I smile and tilt my head to the side, looking at him expectantly.

"Oh, honey, don't look at me like that. I'm the *groom* I have no say in what goes on. Take your complaints to the best man, please." He tells me, his green eyes wide, feigning innocence.

"That's okay. You can go to your strip club. I don't mind," I assure him, and his brows rise to his hairline.

"Is this one of those times where you women say go, and when we do, you rain all sorts of hell on us when we come back?" Cole asks warily, and I laugh, shaking my head while eating gummy bears.

"Not at all, baby." I smile, feeding him some gummy bears, and he chews while searching my face for any signs of annoyance.

"It's a trap," Josh mutters, looking at Aimee, who grins at him. "There's crazy behind those smiles." I laugh, shaking my head.

"I won't go if you're uncomfortable," Cole tells me earnestly, placing his hands at my hips and I shake my head.

"Don't be silly, go have fun. Besides, the girls are taking me to a Magic Mike show." I grin at him, and his brows go up with surprise.

"Magic Mike? Like those topless men that grind on you with the baby oil…" I nod, smiling up at him, and I see the fire go up in his eyes.

"Yes. I'm rather excited about the pony dance," I say, biting my lip and rocking my hips. Cole's green eyes go wide, and he chuckles a little and looks at Josh, who was also glaring at Aimee. God, these men, honestly.

Cole bites his lips and draws my body against his, "Why don't we stay in a room, and I'll slap on some baby oil and do the pony dance for you?" He drawls, wagging his brows at me suggestively.

I chuckle, "You can do the pony dance? Like Channing?" I ask impishly, and Cole nods with a grin, looking deeply into my eyes. "Can you do the thing where he flips and grinds himself on the floor?" I add breathily, brushing my finger down his well-defined chest.

"I sure can." He whispers, staring into my eyes, and I feel a heat rush straight to my core. Cole leans into my ear, "You want to ride my pony, baby?" He burrs huskily, and I bite down on my lip when my head spun.

"Oh, God, yes." I moan when I feel his erection pressing against my hip, and his lips brush down the side of my neck, making me shudder in his arms.

"I bet if I slide my fingers between your folds, I'll find you dripping for me." He whispers gruffly in my ear, my eyes slid shut, and I release a quivering breath.

"I'll lose that bet." I breathe, unable to mask my need for him any longer. Cole groans in my ear, his thumb stroking the exposed flesh of my hip where my top had ridden up.

"I'm salivating just thinking about tasting you. Spreading your pussy lips apart and wrapping my lips around your throbbing clit, sucking softly, tirelessly, till you come apart for me." He groans privately in my ear, and I was moments away from surrendering myself to him. The deep timbres of his voice and his engorged erection pressed against my belly were enough to drive me absolutely wild for him.

“Uh, guys, I think we’re about to have our very own live sex show over here,” Jo utters wide-eyed watching Cole, and I completely lost in each other.

“Ahem!” Aimee clears her throat, and Josh chuckles, shaking his head watching us while eating gummy bears.

“Ah, it’s too late. She’s under Cole Hoult’s spell now.” He utters, amused, “We don’t exist to them anymore.” Aimee was about to throw a cloth at us to get our attention, but Josh stops her. “Watch how he works his magic.” He whispers, stuffing a handful of gummies into his mouth, grinning.

“God baby, the things I want to do to you,” Cole whispers, his voice dripping in sex while he takes my ear lobe between his teeth and runs his tongue against it teasingly, sending a mass of delicious shivers up and down my spine. I moan quietly when I feel his fingers brush up under my shirt, it was the barest of touches, but it honestly drove me crazy with need. We haven’t had sex since Dubai, and as always, the tension between us was electric, and when you throw forbidden lust to the mix, you’ve got a highly, sexually frustrated couple on your hands. “Look what you’re doing to me.” Cole groans lowly into my ear, pushing his hips into mine so I could feel his hard length.

“Is it bad that I can’t look away,” Aimee whispers, her cheeks turning pink, and Josh snickers, drawing her against him and dropping a kiss on her pulse point.

“Oh my God, I’m single as fuck.” Jo grumbles, stuffing gummies in her mouth while watching Cole and me, “I’m not even embarrassed to admit I’m totally turned on right now.” She sighs and walks out of the kitchen, leaving the two couples alone.

“Why don’t I take you to the bedroom and show you *my* special set of skills,” Josh whispers, nuzzling Aimee’s neck, squeezing her hips. Aimee grins, nodding, and Josh leads her out of the kitchen, leaving us alone.

I moan, tilting my head back when Cole licks up my throat. “Cole,”

“Mm,”

"We should stop," I whisper, snaking my arms around his neck and pulling him closer. "My self-control is waning."

"We will. One more minute." He breathes, brushing his lips along my jaw before he pulls back and cups my face in his hands. I look up at him, and he gazes deeply into my eyes. "You're driving me crazy. Being this close to you and not being able to have you is driving me insane, baby." He tells me, rubbing his nose over mine as he speaks in a low, hoarse tone that makes every hair on my body go up. "I can't wait to marry you. Two days feels like forever to me right now." He burrs, kissing my cheek softly. "I can't wait to go to sleep with you in my arms every night and wake up to your intoxicating scent and this beautiful face every morning." He declares, kissing my chin. "I want you to have my babies." He says, almost pleading, and I sigh contently. "I can't wait to grow old and grey with you."

I smile, looking up into his eyes. "Those better not be your vows."

Cole grins attractively and presses his forehead to mine. "These are my private vows to you." He groans, looking at my lips with heavy desirous eyes. "I want to kiss you so bad."

"So do I, but we can't." I pout like a putout child. "Just keep picturing the moment Elvis says, 'you can now kiss your bride' and how amazing it's going to feel to kiss with all the built-up tension," I explain, looking at his full pink lips and he moans, licking them.

"Let me suck your bottom lip...just a little bit, a gentle nibble." He moans, inching close, staring at my mouth.

I watch him and swallow hard. My heated gaze on his lips. "No, because the moment our lips touch, I won't stop, and neither will you. Kissing leads to touching, and touching leads to..."

"Fucking." He whispers, ghosting his lips over mine, and I bite my lip hard. "Baby, stop looking at my lips like that." He warns frowning a little. "I swear I'm a second away from dragging you to Vegas and marrying you tonight to get it over with." I laugh and cup his face with my hands.

"I do wonder how you spent nine whole months in your mother's womb?" I tease, and his eyes look over my face before he smirks.

"I didn't. I got bored and came out early. Ask her, she'll tell you." He responds, and I laugh, brushing my fingers over his stubble.

"God, I bet our children will be impatient just like you," I tell him pointedly, and his lips curl into a slow smile. "What?" I smile when he stares at me.

"You said *our* children." He intones excitement evident in his tone, and I avert my gaze. I can feel my cheeks go hot, and I know I resembled a tomato at that moment because Cole fully grins.

"You're the one that said you wanted me to have your babies."

He nods, "I do. In fact, I say we get to work on that on our wedding night and throughout our honeymoon because practice makes perfect." I look at him, surprised.

"What? You want to have kids right away? I thought we'd wait a couple of years." I utter, and Cole blinks at me, a sudden disheartened on his gorgeous face.

"A couple of years?" He drones, his shoulders slumping. "I was hoping we could have a baby before I'm thirty, but if you're not ready, then of course, we can wait till you are."

I smile and rub his jaw affectionately, "Honey, of course I want to have a baby, but not right away. I want us to enjoy one another before we start a family, and I still need to get my degree." Cole smiles and nods, kissing my wrist.

"But I want to be a Daddy." He says adorably, and I grin wickedly at him in return, and he pokes up a curious brow.

"You are," I croon sultrily. "You're *my* Daddy." Cole groans, squeezing my hips, any thought of children quickly gone out of his mind.

"Am I now?" He burrs huskily, biting his lip while he drags his thumb over my bottom lip.

"Si Papi," I whisper, and he growls, swallowing hard.

"Don't do that," He hisses, his voice strained. "You know what it does to me when you speak to me in Spanish."

"Te quiero mucho, Papi," I breathe teasingly, telling him I want him in Spanish while brushing my lips along his face. "Estoy loca por ti, mi amor."

"Fuck." He moans, grinding himself against me. "Shayla, baby, please, my dick is about to burst. Either fuck me or behave." He pleads, and I pull back.

"Lo siento, mi amor." I apologise, and Cole shakes his head and walks out of the kitchen, muttering to himself. "Hey, where are you going?" I chuckle.

"To have a wank!" Cole grumbles, joking, and I throw my head back and laugh. I love teasing him so much. He's just so adorable when he's frustrated. I cannot wait to marry him.

Everyone was so happy around us that I was terrified something awful was going to happen. I guess I couldn't believe everything was finally working out for us, and I'm now always on edge just waiting for the other shoe to drop.

"Shayla!" Aimee and Jo call out to me. "We need to talk clothes, get your butt in here, Chica!" I smile and walk out of the kitchen toward Aimee's bedroom. I can hear them clucking away happily about what they should pack. When Cole suddenly grabs my arm, I gasp. He yanks me into the bathroom with him and presses me up against the door.

"Done wanking already?" I question, and he narrows his eyes at me playfully.

"Very funny." He chides sardonically. "So, you were serious before about this Magic Mike show?"

"As serious as you are about the strip club." I retort, peering up at him, and he smirks. "It's not up to me. I'm the bride; I don't get a say in what goes on. I mean, if a hot, muscular, oily stripper wants to grind on me, who am I to say no." I express joyously, fighting the urge to smile as he stares at me blankly. "Aimee says the dancer pulls you up on stage and does all these sexy moves on you, where he picks you up and grinds up against you. I'm actually really excited." I sigh longingly and pat him on his chest. "Have fun at your strip club." I smile and turn to walk out, but Cole cages me in.

"Oh, I will. I'm also looking forward to having a pair of tits rubbed in my face. It's been a while, and the lap dance…" He hisses, staring into my eyes. "The way the stripper rocks her firm arse, rubbing herself against my throbbing cock. As frustrated as I'm feeling, baby, I don't know If I'll be able to control my erection." He claims, goading me while looking into my face. I bite my lip, narrowing my eyes at him.

"You go right ahead and enjoy your lap dance, baby because I know the only pussy you're hungry for is *mine*." I declare, tilting my head up and smiling at him while he grins back at me knowingly.

"Damn fucking right." He murmurs, stroking my jaw lovingly. "You're mine."

"I'm yours," I reassure him, and we stare at one another's lips longingly for a while. "I need to pack, baby," I tell him with a frustrated sigh, and he nods, pressing a kiss to my forehead when I close my eyes.

~

A COUPLE OF HOURS LATER, we pull up at the airstrip, and we board the jet. It was a ten-hour flight to Vegas, the Jet departed at two in the afternoon, and we landed there at midnight UK time and four in the afternoon local time, so it's almost like we went back in time, which was mind-boggling to me.

"Vegas baby!" Aimee and Jo shout as we walk off the plane and jump into the limo waiting for us. I was exhausted with the time difference, but I was so happy to be with all the people I love in a place where it all began for Cole and me.

I push the button to the sunroof opening it. I stand up and pull the girls up with me. We throw our hands up in the air as we drive through the desert, the warm wind blowing through her hair. I close my eyes smiling, turning my face up to the sun. "My best friend is getting married!" Aimee shouts to the people as we drive by them, and they hoot and cheer.

"Oh my God, we're actually in Vegas!" Jo exclaims excitedly, recording us on her phone.

"Shay Shay, where are we?!"

"Vegas baby!"

"Why are we in Vegas?" Aimee asks, giggling.

"To marry my baby!" I croon happily, ducking my head to look at Cole, who was watching me with the biggest smile on his gorgeous face while shaking his head.

After we check into our hotel rooms, Cole and I obviously weren't allowed to share a room till our wedding night; much to his dismay, Cole was sharing a suite with Josh, and I was sharing one with the girls.

My brother was due to arrive later on to join the boys for the bachelor party. I was still so upset that my Mum wasn't going to be with me on my wedding day physically, but she'll be there virtually so she won't miss anything.

Cole and Josh go off together to do the last-minute wedding checks while the girls and I hit the spa for a day of pampering before the bachelorette party in the evening. "Girls, I still can't believe I'm in Vegas and Shay is getting married. It seems so surreal." Jo says, sipping her cucumber and mint water while she snuggles into the lounger she was relaxing on with her green face mask and cucumbers on each eye.

I sigh, closing my eyes while getting my manicure. "I know, I feel like I'm dreaming. I'm anxious something horrible is going to happen and ruin everything." I admit, and Aimee lifts her cucumber and looks at me with one eye.

"Shayla, you've been through so much over the last few months. Of course, you're going to feel uneasy, but don't stress yourself out. Everything is going to be perfect." She assures me. "As your maid of honours, Jo and I will make sure everything will be perfect. Right, Jo?" We look at Jo when we don't hear a word from her. "Jo?" Aimee throws a rolled-up towel at her, and she starts awake, her cucumbers falling off her eyes.

"Huh, what?" She mumbles drowsily, looking between us while Aimee and I crack up laughing.

"How the hell do you just conk out like that? You were awake like two seconds ago." Aimee questions her, absolutely stunned, and Jo shrugs, putting her cucumber slices back on her eyes.

"It's a gift." She mumbles, falling asleep again. To be honest, I was feeling the jetlag myself, but I was too wired to get any sleep. I was absolutely delighted to marry the love of my life in less than thirty-six hours.

After our spa treatments, the girls and I began getting ready for our night out. I was dreading it so much. I hadn't seen Cole all day, he was off with Josh, and it wasn't till we were all ready to leave the hotel that I saw him. I was wearing a backless, white, sequin, bodycon mini dress put together with a pair of red stilettos. The girls curled my hair and hung a 'Bride' sash around me and a veil on my head.

"Is the veil necessary?" I complain, trying to take it off, but they slap my hands away.

"Yes!" They say in unison and look me over.

"You're looking fire, girl. Cole is going to die when he sees you." Jo giggles, smacking my bum, and I shake my head.

"Good, I want him to look at me and remember what he's got to look forward to for the rest of his life," I gush blissfully, applying my red lipstick as the door goes off. Jo rushes off to answer it while I pack a few things into my clutch. I look up when I hear a low whistle and smile when I see Cole standing in the doorway looking drop-dead gorgeous in his black, muscle fit, short sleeve shirt, and black slacks. My mouth waters at the sight of him.

"God damn, baby," He groans, walking over to me, his eyes raking over my body desirously. "You look…" He moans, swallowing hard.

"I look…" I trail off, waiting for him to finish his sentence, but he bites his lip shaking his head.

"Like you should stay in with me and let me do some very naughty things to you." He drawls, placing his hands at my waist and drawing me against him. I grin, wrapping my arms around his neck while gazing up into his stunning green eyes.

"Oh yeah? What kind of naughty things?" I ask alluringly while he watches me, his eyes slightly narrowed.

"Like tying you to the bed and feasting on your pussy all night long, making you come slow and hard till you're a quivering mess." He burrs gruffly while trailing his fingers up between my thighs. I feel an unnatural heat course through me and pool between my legs, making me ache and throb for him.

"I'm definitely down for that," I whisper, closing my eyes as his fingers inch closer to a part of me that was just burning to be touched by him.

"Hey!" Cole and I jump when we hear Aimee once again shouting from behind us. "Tristan Cole Hoult, step away from the bride," Aimee says, wagging her finger at him, and he curses.

"Christ," He rolls his eyes. "How does she do that? She comes in just at the right moment when I'm about to break you." He sighs, frustrated while pressing his forehead to mine. I smile.

"Not long left now, baby, then I'm all yours to do with what you will," I whisper, brushing my fingers along his jaw, and he moans, closing his eyes.

"I honestly can't wait to take you home and start my life with you." He tells me sweetly while wrapping his arms around me.

"Me either." I look up at him lovingly, and he brushes his nose over mine. "Have fun tonight. I'll see you in the morning."

Cole nods and kisses my forehead, "You too, be careful out there, okay. Don't go marrying anyone but me. You hear?" I laugh and nod, pressing my lips to his jaw. "I love you."

"I love you."

"Oh my God, you're going out for the night, you're not going off to war. Come on you." Aimee complains, taking my hand and pulling me away from Cole, who watches me with a pout as I get dragged away from him. I kiss my fingers and press them to my heart, and he does the same with a smile.

We leave the hotel and get into the limo waiting for us outside with bottles of champagne. "Driver, crank up the music!" Aimee shouts, handing me a glass of champagne. "To Shayla and Cole!" She toasts, holding up her glass, I smile, and we all clink glasses.

~

Nights out in Vegas was something else. The atmosphere was just incredible. We walked into the club and were shown to our VIP booth with so much alcohol I honestly wanted to throw up just looking at it. It was going to be a messy night, that's for sure. One too many shots of tequila and sambuca later, I was well and truly drunk. The show was about to start. Aimee and Jo squeal excitedly when the 'Magic Mike' dancers come out on the stage. I literally felt like I was in the movie, it was incredible, and the guys were all hotter than each other.

"We've got some hot men in the U.K, but American boys just hit differently. Damn!" Jo shouts, watching the boys grind on the stage.

"You can say that again. God bless America." Aimee mutters, watching the boys doing backflips with her mouth agape. "If I weren't in a relationship, lord have mercy, I would have sinned all over this bitch." I choke on my drink and laugh at the way she was staring at one of the dancers who winks at her. "Shayla, fucking hell, don't let me drink anymore!" She pleads desperately, and I howl with laughter.

"That's why they call it Sin City, baby." I giggle, and Aimee takes a sip from her drink, her blue eyes avidly following the dancer.

"Oh mama." Aimee groans when the dancer strides over to the side of the stage, takes her hands and runs them over his sweaty abs. Another tall, muscular brunette with dark eyes and a man bun crawls over to me and grins wickedly while he grinds himself on the stage, gazing into my eyes.

Holy shit.

Cole was hotter by miles, but the way he was grinding and staring into my eyes made me flush.

"Lord have mercy." Jo sighs when her dancer leans in closer and takes her face in his hands, and tilts her head back while he brushes his nose up her throat.

"That wasn't considered cheating, right?" Aimee asks me wide-eyed while sipping her drink. "He made me do it. I did nothing but get a little wet." I howl with laughter and shake my head.

"No, you're fine," I reassure her, and she sighs, relieved.

Jo fans herself when her dancer moves away, "I think I just climaxed." She groans, her cheeks pink. Aimee and I laugh hysterically while she sighs, shaking her head. "I wonder when they'll do the pony dance," Jo sighs, sipping her cocktail while watching the dancer on stage thrusting his hips in front of her. "Marry me!" She shouts up at him, and he grins. Aimee and I cackle, watching her trying to claw her way over to him.

"Jo, what are you doing? Get back here." I scold her laughing, and she shrugs, waving me off.

"Ladies and Gentlemen, we have a special show lined up for you next. A little birdie told me we have a bachelorette party here tonight!" the DJ announces, and I look around, my eyes wide while Aimee and Jo start screaming, pointing at me. "Boys, let's get Shayla up on the stage!"

"What the hell did you two do?" I scold the girls, and they shake their heads.

"It wasn't us!" Aimee tells me. I look around, horrified as four dancers come over and pull me up on stage. My heart was hammering in my chest while I look around at all the faces watching me up on stage while cheering.

"Take a seat, Gorgeous." One of the dancers says, guiding me to the seat on the stage. I sit down and look around when everything goes dark, and suddenly the song Pony starts thundering through the speakers. *Oh, God.*

The lights flicker on, and I see two dancers dressed in a white vest top and grey tracksuit bottoms, both wearing red caps. Literally dressed like Mike in the movie. The dancers look up, and I almost faint on stage when I see Channing Tatum walking toward me. The crowd erupts when they see him, and he starts dancing in front of me. I almost died when the second dancer comes up, and I see it's Cole. I watch him utterly stunned, and he winks at me sexily. They rip their vests off. "Oh, my God." I utter, watching them dancing around me. He wasn't kidding when he said he could do that flip thing. He and Channing both do it in front of me and grind against the floor, and I watch avidly as my husband-to-be thrusts his hips up, his hungry eyes on me.

I grin up at him as he saunters over and straddles me, grinding himself against me. Lifting my hands, he runs them over his chest and his rock-hard abs, biting his lip as he stares into my eyes. "Cole? What the hell…"

"Surprise baby." He burrs in my ear, tilting my head back and licking up my throat. I gasp when he lifts me into his arms and lays me on the floor.

I look up at him, my cheeks aflame, and he does the flip and grinds against me. "Oh, my God! You're crazy." I squeal, laughing. My heart was beating so fast I thought it would give out on me. Cole lifts me off the floor and into his arms again, grinning sexily.

"There isn't anything I wouldn't do for you, baby."

"Ladies and Gentlemen, give it up for my boy Cole and his beautiful bride Shayla!" Channing says, and the crowd cheers.

"I can't believe you did this." I laugh, pressing my forehead to his, and he grins, setting me back on my feet.

"I'm going to make every single one of your dreams come true, baby," Cole tells me earnestly while gazing devotedly into my eyes, and I fell in love with him all over again.

Chapter Forty-Four

COLE/SHAYLA

"COLE! Get your arse up and out of that bed!" I leap out of my sleep and groan when my head thumps unpleasantly.

"Ow." I groan, holding my head. "What the fuck." I blink up and see Josh standing over me once my vision clears.

"Bro, Shayla's gone! Get up!" It took a second for his words to reach my brain. I look up at him with a scowl.

"Gone?" I recite my voice hoarse from a night of partying.

"She took off, man! She saw you kissing some girl last night at the club, and she took off." I scowl up at him and dart out of bed. "I tried to stop her, but she just wouldn't listen."

"What?!" I shout, glancing around the room, confused. I don't remember kissing anyone last night. What the fuck! "Who did I kiss? What the fuck happened, man?!" I yell, not even caring about my thumping headache. My heart was racing like mad. Oh God, please, please, don't tell me I've lost her again. I grab my jeans and pull them on back to front in my panic. "When did she leave? Where the fuck did she go?!" I shout, yanking my shoes on— both on the wrong feet and fall over on the floor while trying to run to the door. I stop when I hear Josh laughing hysterically, tears rolling down his face. "Wha—" I realise that he's winding me up and I lean against the door panting, my hand on my heart. "You *rotten* son of a bitch."

"Oh man, that was hilarious." Josh cackles. I glare at him hard.

"Fuck, I have never sobered up so quickly in my life." I sigh, closing my eyes, willing my heart to stop beating so hard. "Don't do that to me, bro! I fucking shit myself thinking I lost her again."

"Nah bro, chill, Shayla is blissfully happy getting ready to walk down that aisle to marry you," Josh reassures me, and I sigh, finally allowing myself to smile and relax. "Shit, what time is it? We have to go to the airport." I say in a panic, and Josh shakes his head.

"I've already been and got her. Everything is on track, don't worry. Let's get you showered and ready. You have less than two hours till we have to leave for the chapel." Josh tells me, and I nod and exhale. I'm so fucking excited; I get to marry the girl of my dreams today. I can't wait to see her beautiful face when she sees the surprise I have planned for her. "Are we doing this, bro? It's not too late to back out?" Josh teases with a smile, and I shake my head slowly.

"Back out?" I intone grinning. "I'm going to skip down that aisle, and no one can stop me," I tell him and walk to the bathroom to shower. "Last night was crazy. I can't believe how drunk we all got."

Josh laughs, massaging his head, "I know, I'm still feeling those jaeger bombs. The highlight of the night, though, Shay's face, when she saw you on stage with Channing was priceless."

I grin while I run the shower. "I know, she was so worked up Aimee had to rip us away from each other. She's real fierce that girlfriend of yours." I tell him and watch as he grins happily.

"That she is," He sighs, biting his lip. "I'm falling hard for her man. It's so fucking fast. It's only been a few weeks."

I laugh, "Welcome to the club, my friend," I state, slapping his back before I close the door and jump in the shower. An hour later, I was dressed and ready to head to the chapel. I look at myself in the mirror in my black tuxedo and readjust my cufflinks. Josh comes and stands beside me, fixing his tie.

"You ready, brother?" He asks, smiling at me. I nod and exhale nervously.

"Like you wouldn't believe." I bite my lip. My stomach was in knots. "I can't wait to see her, I'm so nervous I'm going to faint," I tell him earnestly, and Josh chuckles and squeezes my shoulder.

"You will, when you see her. She looks incredible. She's glowing like an angel." I look at Josh, and I can already feel my emotions bubbling up. I blink back the tears and sigh deeply.

"Let's go do the thing, and we can head to the chapel," I tell him, and he nods. We go to my brother in laws room and knock on the door. Sam opens it and looks at me; he smiles and gestures for me to enter. I walk into the room and smile when I see Shayla's mother sitting on the bed, looking gorgeous in a blue dress. She smiles lovingly when she sees me and stands up, holding her hands out to me. I walk over to her and take her hands in mine, and her eyes well up.

"You look so handsome, darling." She tells me, and I smile.

"And you look beautiful, Sara," I say, and just like her daughter, she blushes and squeezes my hands.

"Cole, I don't know how to thank you. If it weren't for you, I wouldn't have had the courage to be here with my daughter on her wedding day. You've given me my life back, and I will forever be grateful." She expresses, her sincerity radiating in her eyes.

"Sara, I didn't do anything. I only got you the help; you did the hard part and allowed yourself to heal." I assert, rubbing my thumb over her knuckles. "I'm thrilled Annabelle managed to help you face your anxiety and fears."

Sara smiles gratefully at me and nods, tears rolling down her cheeks. "My daughter has chosen herself the perfect life partner. I can see why she has chosen to give her heart to you. You truly are a wonderful man, Cole. All the heartache Shayla has been through and growing up without her father hurt her deeply, but I am so thankful that she's found a man who looks at her the way her father used to look at me." She cries, and I wrap my arms around her.

"Oh Sara, I'm not a man of faith, but I'm thankful first to God himself then to you for bringing such an amazing woman into the world. Your beautiful daughter has changed my life and continues to do so every day, and I honestly can't wait to start my own family with her." I tell her and pull back, and she dries her tears with her tissue.

"I wish her father could have met you," She sighs, reaching up and touching my cheek. "Oh, before I forget." Sara walks over to the table, picks up a little box, and walks over to me again. "The rings." I take the box from her and open it and see the two wedding bands inside. Her and her late husband's rings. "I hope these rings will bring you both as much love and happiness as it did my Richie and me." She smiles tenderly, and Sam walks over to us and pats my shoulder.

"We're giving you the most precious thing to us. Take good care of her, and I have no doubt you will, but make her happy." He says, and I nod, wiping away the tears that roll down my cheek.

"Your sister is my life, Sam. I will take care of her and do everything in my power to make her happy every single day." I reassure him, and he smiles before we hug.

"Good lad."

"Okay, take me to my angel. I'm dying to see her already." Sara claims. I chuckle and nod. We leave her room, and I show her to Shayla's room.

Shayla

"How are you feeling?"

I smile and look at myself in the full-length mirror and look at Aimee and Jo standing on either side of me. "Nervous. My stomach is in knots. But it's a good nervous, I'm anxious to see him already." I say, and they smile and lay their heads on my shoulders.

"You're the most beautiful bride I've ever seen," Jo sighs, her eyes watering.

"No!" Aimee exclaims, waving her hands in my face. "No crying… no crying, we don't have time to do your make up again."

"Can you try to call my mum again?" I utter, glancing around for my phone.

"I did, like two minutes ago. She didn't answer, babe. She might be sleeping still—time difference and all." Aimee tells me, and I sigh, closing my eyes. I hate that she's not here with me.

"Maybe," I whisper, looking at myself again. After trying many wedding dresses, I chose a low back, lace, mermaid gown with a sheer train. It was simple and classy, just how I like it. My hair was up in a voluminous updo with a small stem of white flowers flowing through tastefully.

I vaguely hear a knock at the door as Jo gives me a glass of champagne to calm my nerves. "Shayla?" I turn around when I hear Aimee say my name. The glass slips from my fingers, and Jo catches it before it ruins my dress as I stood stunned, staring at my mother standing right in front of me.

"Mum?" I whisper, and she looks me over and holds her chest, tears flowing.

"Oh my baby, you look so beautiful." She sobs.

"Mum!" I run over and throw myself into her arms. "You're here." I cry when she wraps her arms around me tight.

"Of course I'm here, darling." She cries, pulling back and cupping my face in her hands and looking at me. "I could never miss one of the happiest days of your life."

"But how?" I ask as she wipes away my tears with her fingers.

"Cole." She replies, smiling. "He hired a therapist to help me with my anxiety and fear of leaving the house. He knew how upset you were about not having me here with you, so he's been coming for weeks, standing by me as I tried and failed to leave the house. He picked me up when I broke down again and again tirelessly till I succeeded." I cover my mouth with my hand and sob uncontrollably.

"Oh, my God." I wail and hug her again. "I can't believe you're here."

"Oh, honey, I wish your father could have been here to see you. He would be so proud of you and the beautiful woman you've become." She says, drawing back and kissing my forehead. "You've found yourself a man who loves you deeply, look after him, and love him with not only your heart but your soul."

I sniffle and nod, "I do," I whisper smiling. "I always wished for a love just like you and Dad, and I found it with him." My mother nods and gives me a watery smile.

"Let's get you married."

"Makeup!" Aimee shouts, clapping her hands, and the makeup artist comes rushing over to me. "Let's go, people, let's go!" I laugh when Aimee ushers everyone out of the room and tells them to go down to the cars waiting outside. I couldn't stop crying, and the makeup artist kept telling me off for ruining the eyeliner and mascara she kept reapplying. I was still in shock, seeing my mother here. I was so grateful to Cole, so much, that it took everything in me not to run to the chapel in my gown and throw myself into his arms. He couldn't have given me a more special gift.

Once I finally stopped crying and my makeup was done, Sam, the girls and I all make our way down to the limo waiting to take us to the chapel. "You look beautiful, Sis," Sam tells me, kissing my hand, and I smile, my eyes welling up. "Ow." He hisses when Aimee kicks his shin.

"Don't make her cry again. I swear I will hurt you." She threatens him, and he scowls at her while rubbing his leg. I chuckle and bite my lip.

"Aimes, I'm probably going to burst into tears the moment I see Cole anyway, so it doesn't matter," I assure her with a shrug, and she reapplies her own lip gloss.

"That's different; we don't want you showing up to the chapel looking like a panda." She states, giving Sam a side-glare, and he flips her off and winks at Jo, who flushes and averts her gaze. I look at her, then my brother, and frown. Are they *flirting*? Sammy and Jo? No. No bloody way.

We finally arrive at the chapel, and my stomach flutters nervously as Jo and Aimee fix my dress. I hook my arm with my brothers and smile up at him as the girls walk down the aisle. My parent's song, 'Can't help falling in love,' plays, and I close my eyes for a second, trying to get my emotions in check before we start walking down the aisle. The doors open, and my eyes meet Coles instantly, and the way he was looking at me made my eyes well up. He watches me and whispers, 'Oh my God' before he bites his lip. A tear trails down his cheek while I slowly walk over to him.

Sam kisses my forehead and pats Cole on the back before he steps away. Cole holds out his hand to me. I take it, and we walk to the altar together. "You look stunning." He tells me, and I smile up at him, my eyes swimming with tears.

"So do you," I whisper, squeezing his hand. "Thank you for bringing my mum." I sniffle, and Cole kisses my temple smiling handsomely.

"Of course, baby." We turn to face Elvis, who looks at us and smiles.

"Hey! I remember you two. Didn't I already marry you?" Cole and I look at one another, and everyone in the room starts to laugh. "Second time's the charm. At least you're both sober this time." He teases with a wink, and I grin at Cole. "Let's begin, shall we? Shayla and Cole, turn and face one another, please." I turn and face him, and he takes my hands in his, smiling at me adoringly as Elvis talks about the importance of love.

"Let's get to the vows. Shayla, ladies first."

I exhale and look into Cole's eyes. "Cole, I never believed in fate until I met you. I never knew what it meant to love someone with your soul until you walked into my life. We've been through so much in such a short time, and as much as it hurt, I would do it all again in a heartbeat because you are my fate, you are my heart, and you are my soul. I swear to you here in front of all the people we love that I will love you forever." I vow to him, tears spilling down my cheeks, and he swallows hard, blinking back the tears that gather in his eyes.

He smiles and holds my gaze, "My beautiful Shayla, I'm in awe of you. I don't know how you do it, but you do something that makes me fall deeper in love with you every day. I wish I had met you sooner. I wish I loved you sooner because you are everything beautiful in this world. You were the complete opposite of everything I thought I wanted but turned out to be everything I've always needed. You've changed me in ways that I never knew was possible. You've taught me how selfless love can truly be." He vows, reaching up and wiping away my tears. "And I swear to you here, in front of all our family and friends, that I will make each day we spend together better than the last." I grin up at him and wrap my hands around his wrists. "I'm so in love with you."

"I'm in love with you," I whisper wholeheartedly while gazing into his startling green eyes.

"Oh, my heart, aren't they just the cutest," Elvis utters, shaking his head, wiping a tear from the corner of his eye. "Okay, let's do the rings. Shayla, please take the ring you wish to give Cole."

"Actually. We have new ones." Cole says and takes a box from Josh and turns to face me again. He opens the box, and I look down and frown a little. Cole takes out the larger ring and hands it to me. I look at it and gasp when I realise it's my Dad's wedding ring. I look over at my mum, and she nods, sobbing into her tissue. I look back at Cole, my lips quivering as I struggle to hold back the tears. I look at my Dad's wedding ring and read the engraved message to Cole. "Ever thine, Ever mine, Ever ours." Cole bites his bottom lip as I take his hand and slide my Dad's ring on his finger. Cole lifts my hand and picks up my mother's ring and slides it on mine.

"Ever thine, Ever mine, Ever ours." He declares, staring into my eyes.

"Oh, I have forgotten everything with you two. Shayla, do you take Cole to be your husband?" Elvis asks, and I nod.

"I do."

"Cole, do you take Shayla—"

"I do." Elvis sighs and rolls his eyes chuckling.

"He did this the last time too. I didn't finish the question yet, son." He states, and I laugh at his eagerness along with everyone else in the room. "I'll accept, without further ado by the power vested in me and the state of Nevada, I pronounce you husband and wife." Cole and I grin at one another. "You may kiss your—." Cole doesn't even wait for him to finish his sentence before he pulls me close and draws my lips to his, kissing me slow and deep. I moan and wrap my arms around his neck, kissing him back just as ardently. "Ah heck, there he goes again. Congratulations!" Elvis exclaims, and everyone around us applauds and cheers as we continue to kiss. It was hard not to kiss him for weeks, but it was so worth waiting for this moment. It was perfect, and I couldn't believe we actually did it. He's my husband…*again.*

Cole pulls back, panting, and presses his forehead to mine. "You were right. That was so worth the wait." He whispers, brushing his thumbs along my jaw. "We did it, baby. You're my wife."

I smile, biting my lip, "And you're my husband." Cole grins and kisses me again softly before we turn and face our friends and family, and they all cheer and come up to hug and congratulate us. Cole lifts me into his arms, and just like last time, he carries me out of the chapel, kissing me passionately. After we take photos, we head over to the Bellagio, where the reception was held with Coles relatives and friends.

I pull Cole back just before we walk into the reception hall and look up at him. "Cole, I just wanted to thank you once again for everything you did for my Mum. You have no idea how much it meant to me to have her here." I tell him earnestly, and he smiles and cups my face in his large hands and presses his forehead to mine.

"Baby, I honestly didn't do anything. I just arranged her therapy and supported her. That's it. She did everything else on her own." He states, brushing his thumbs over my jaw.

"I didn't think it was humanly possible to love you more than I already did, but you just keep proving me wrong because every day I fall even deeper in love with you," I proclaim, and he smiles and kisses me softly.

"Me too baby, there are no words to even explain how crazy I am about you. I never want to feel the way I did when I was apart from you ever again." He whispers, sweeping his lips over mine.

"Hey love birds, come on, we're waiting for your first dance!" Aimee chirps, pulling us apart just as Cole was about to deepen the kiss, and she drags us toward the reception hall. Cole groans, shaking his head.

"Aimee, I swear to God I'm going to throw you off the Grand Canyon if you keep interrupting us." Cole scolds her playfully, and Aimee grins toothily back at him.

"You have the rest of your life to kiss her, my dearest brother-in-law, now it's party time!" She tells him, and Cole laughs, shaking his head.

"Ladies and Gentlemen, please put your hands together for the second time, Mr and Mrs Hoult!"

Cole looks down at me, grinning, "You ready Mrs Hoult?"

"Always, Mr Hoult," I reply, and we walk into the reception hall together. Cole pulls me to the dance floor and wraps his arms around me as Amazed by Lonestar starts playing while we dance. I gaze up into his eyes while he sings the lyrics to me, and as happy I was at that moment, I had a sudden flash of all the heartache we both suffered, the breakdowns, the arguments, and how close we came to not being together. Cole brushes the tears away that roll down my cheeks and pulls me closer against him shaking his head at me.

"No more tears, sweetheart." I smile up at him and nod while we continue to sway together. "Baby, I'm amazed by you." Cole sings to me as the song comes to an end.

"Let's party!" Aimee cheers as an upbeat song starts to play, and we all dance together. I pull Cole to me and sing the lyrics to Katy Perrys The One That Got Away to him. "In another life, I would be your girl. We keep all our promises, the us against the world. In another life, I would make you stay, so I don't have to say you were the one that got away, the one that got away." Cole laughs and lifts me into his arms. I grin, cup his face, and kiss him deeply with every little bit of my heart, surrounded by the people we love the most.

The song came to an end, and Josh grabs the microphone grinning like the cat that got the canary. "Ladies and gents, I have a special treat for you all tonight. If you could all turn your attention to the screen behind me. As you all know, Shayla and Cole were previously married, and I happen to have the video of their first marriage. Cole and I look at one another wide-eyed and look at the screen at a very inebriated Cole and I stumbling down the aisle laughing hysterically.

"Evlis, marry me to this gorgeous woman!" Cole slurs slapping Elvis on the back, and he chuckles nodding.

"Does the gorgeous woman want to marry you?" Elvis questions, and I nod, grinning, pulling him to me and kissing him passionately.

"Mhm, I do." I giggle drunkenly when Cole pulls back and winks at me. Elvis nods, and Cole shoves the paperwork at him.

"Make it snappy, would ya." Cole slurs, smiling at me and we repeat the vows Elvis says, giggling the whole time.

"Shayla, do you take Tristan Cole Hoult as your husband?" He asks, and I nod, grinning.

"Yes, I doooo." I coo, stumbling over, and Cole catches me laughing. "Oopsie, I think I just fell for you," I tell him, and Cole presses his forehead to mine before Elvis pulls us apart. He chuckles, shaking his head. "Tristan, do you take Shayla—"

"I do!" He shouts and yanks me into him, grinning widely. "Be mine forever?"

I smile up at him and nod, "Okay." I whisper, and he kisses me passionately before Elvis pulls us apart again, and Cole puts the diamond ring on my finger, and I put his on, and Cole sweeps me into his arms and kisses me again while Elvis declares us husband and wife.

"All hail you, king of rock!" Cole cheers. And after we sign the marriage certificate Cole snatches it from him and looks at me while I dance drunkenly with Elvis, who sings burning love. Cole drags me away from him and pulls me into his arms, "I'm burning for your Honka Honka love baby." He slurs, imitating Elvis himself while he sings. Cole picks me up, carries me bridal style down the aisle, and kicks the door open, walking out of the chapel.

I cover my face with my hands, utterly humiliated while everyone laughs and cheers around us.

"Oh my God, I don't remember any of that!" I utter, looking at Cole, who was howling with laughter, his hands on his knees. I hit his shoulder, giggling, and he pulls me to him, still chuckling. "Josh, you are so dead!" I threaten him, and he laughs, wiping away the tears while holding up his champagne glass to us.

Cole wraps his arms around me, grinning, "Oh baby, I'm still burning for your Honka Honka love." He laughs, kissing me softly, and I blush profusely.

"Shut up. I can see why my mind blocked that out, how embarrassing." I laugh, and Cole kisses my forehead.

"I think it's perfect. It just proves once more that we were crazy about each other even then." I smile, shaking my head while gazing up at him.

"Would you do it all over again if you had the chance?" I ask, and Cole nods.

"Absolutely, every single second without a doubt." I smile and nod, wrapping my arms around his neck. "Shayla?"

"Yes?"

"Be mine forever?"

"Okay."

EPILOGUE

"In the summer of 2019, a handsome boy met the most beautiful girl in a club, they danced, they got drunk and somehow ended up on a plane to Vegas where they got married and thus began their whirlwind love story…" An excited new Dad tells his baby girl as he rocks her back and forth while she's curled up in his arms.

10 months before…

After their beautiful, very untraditional ceremony at the Little Chapel in Vegas and their reception at the stunning Bellagio Hotel, an impatient Cole all but drags a tipsy Shayla up to their suite, where it all began. The newlywed couple make their way out of the elevator, kissing passionately after waiting weeks to make love to one another so their wedding night would be special. Cole carries Shayla to the bedroom and sets her down on her feet. He looks into his wife's beautiful jade eyes while she gazes up at him adoringly. In that very moment, his heart swells with all the love he has for her, and he couldn't help but feel like the luckiest man in the world.

Shayla tilts her head to the side, admiring her husband, a gentle smile on her face. "Make me yours, Cole Hoult." She whispers to him, and he smiles, trailing his fingertips up her bare arms.

"You were *always* mine, Shayla Hoult." Shayla watches him closely as he leans in close, capturing her rosy lips with his and kissing her slow and deliberate, making her moan into his mouth when he brushes his tongue ever so lightly over hers teasingly. Shayla's fingers gingerly unbutton his shirt, exposing the smooth tan skin of his chest. She keeps her eyes on his while she pushes the shirt off his well-defined, broad shoulders. Cole's eyes close, and he swallows hard when she runs her soft hands over his chest while her lips graze along his throat, nipping and sucking gently. Her slender fingers find the belt buckle to his trousers. She undoes it, slowly tugs the belt out of its loops, and hooks it around his neck, drawing his mouth to hers, kissing him vehemently.

Cole wraps his arms around her as they kiss slow and sensual. He drags his fingers down her bare spine, making her quiver in his arms. Shayla pulls away, eliciting a groan of displeasure from Cole, who watches her with hungry eyes as she backs away from him. "Get your sexy butt back here, Mrs Hoult." He drawls, biting his lip and Shayla shakes her head as she slides the straps to her wedding dress down her arms and tugs the zipper down. "You'll have to wait just a teeny bit longer so I can change into something a lot less uncomfortable for you." She tells him sultrily, and Cole shakes his head.

"Baby, I promise you, whatever you put on, I will tear off of you in five seconds flat." He answers while staring at her intently. "I don't have the patience for lingerie right now. I want you *naked* and spread out on top of that bed, ready to be devoured." Shayla bites her lip and nods, and proceeds to unzip her wedding dress.

Cole sucks in a sharp breath as he stood watching as the wedding dress slides off her body and pools around her feet. His eyes leisurely scan her body as she stood in a white lace thong, a garter on her thigh and her heels. "Sweet Jesus…" He moans, soaking up his beautiful wife. Cole eagerly watches as she lets her hair out, and it falls around her shoulders in loose waves.

"I believe you're supposed to take the garter off, honey." She purrs sultrily at him, gesturing to the blue garter around her thigh. Cole smiles and strolls over, and Shayla watches as he kneels in front of her, his green eyes peering up at her as he lifts her leg, kissing his way up to the garter.

Cole bites it and drags it down her smooth leg. Shayla bites her lip, watching him as he tug the lace panties down her shapely legs.

"You're an absolute Goddess baby, I'm going to worship you till my very last breath." He asserts solemnly, and Shayla smiles dotingly at him.

"I'm going to hold you to that promise." She responds breathily, brushing her fingers through his hair, and he kisses her stomach.

"You better." Standing up and lifting her into his arms all in one motion. Cole melds their lips together in a feverish kiss as he carries her to the bed and lays her down on it. Shayla pulls him down and rolls him over onto his back. Straddling him, she rocks herself against the hard length of him, making Cole moan throatily, while he curls his fingers in her hair and kisses her with affection, taking his time feeling out every crevice of her mouth. Shayla pulls away from the kiss and licks her way down his torso, nipping and sucking, leaving her mark all over him. He was hers and only hers. Cole enjoyed every little bit of it as he watches her with hooded eyes while she free's him of his trousers and boxers.

Shayla looks at his member and licks her lips longingly as she settles herself between his legs and wraps her fingers around his length. Cole moans audibly, eyes closed, his mouth hangs open when he feels his wife's hot mouth wrap around him. "Fuck baby, yes…" He shudders as Shayla licks lavishly around the crown, making his hips jerk up.

Cole fists the bed covers while he watches his member slowly disappear into her mouth. "Shayla," He whispers breathily, rocking his hips up, matching her rhythm. "Fuck, baby, you suck so good." Cole hisses, leaning up on one elbow, he gathers her hair in the other hand and watches her sucking him eagerly. When Shayla moans, the vibrations of her vocal cords makes him shiver. Cole bites his lip hard when he feels that familiar stir in the pit of his stomach. As much as he needed to explode in her mouth right then, he pulls her up and kisses her hot and hard while laying her down on her back.

Cole kept good on his promise— and worshiped her, he did. Taking his sweet time kissing every inch of her body, caressing her, sucking, and biting her tight nipples, making her gasp and arch up, pushing her breast up, requesting further contact, silently telling him what she needs, and he obeyed. Cole was paying attention to her every movement, her every sound. Shayla shudders when he licks her mound sluggishly, circling the tip of his tongue; using his fingers, he spreads her cleft, revealing her clit, and circles the tip of his tongue over it lightly. Shayla quakes, curling her fingers in his hair. "Ohhhh baby, I love it when you do that." She moans breathily while rocking her hips slowly. Cole continues to glide his tongue lightly over her clit, loving every second of watching the muscles in her stomach convulse with every flick of his tongue. "Uhhhh yes…" Shayla whimpers when he sucks her hard and slides a finger deep inside her, stroking her g-spot, bringing her close to that sweet release she's begging for.

Shayla opens her eyes and watches him through the mirror on the ceiling as she rocks and grinds herself up against his mouth. Her stomach tightens, and she feels that warmth spread through her and pool at her groin. "Uhh, baby, I'm coming, I'm coming." She whimpers panting, Cole sucks her clit hard and moans when he feels her clit throb and pulse on his tongue. "Uhhh Cole, yes!" She cries out as she explodes, rocking and rubbing herself against his mouth as she rides out every wave and pulse of her orgasm. She collapses on the bed breathless, her body tingling all over with post-orgasm bliss. "Oh my God," She pants opening her eyes and looking up at her husband. "You're incredible, baby." She whispers, pulling him down for a kiss and getting a second-hand taste of herself on his tongue, which drove her wild.

Cole gathers her arms and pins them above her head, lacing his fingers with hers as he slowly pushes himself inside her. "Ohh fuck…" Cole breathes against her lips when his head spun at the tightness of her around him. "I forgot how fucking good you feel." He hisses, pushing himself deep inside her till he's buried to the hilt. Shayla moans, sucking his bottom lip and wrapping her legs around his waist, drawing him as deep as he could go. They lay still for a moment, just kissing, soaking up the feeling of one another until Cole slowly starts thrusting into her with slow, lazy strokes making her mewl and rock up. Cole drags his lips down her throat as he thrusts harder, spreading his legs wider so he could go deeper, angling himself so he could hit her g-spot just how she likes it, and she doesn't disappoint. The harder he thrusts, the louder her moans as she nears her climax.

"You gonna come for me, sweetheart," Cole growls, thrusting hard and deep into her, and she whimpers, biting her lip hard.

"Yes, baby, yes, fuck don't stop. Oh, right there…" She cries, tightening her fingers around his. "Come with me, baby." She whimpers, and Cole presses his forehead to hers while he drives himself hard and deep into her. The bed squeaks louder with every raring thrust, his muscles tighten, and his manhood pulses while he soars toward that earth-shattering, spine-tingling release.

"Oh fuck, come on, baby, take me over." He pleads, panting, and Shayla arches up and grinds her hips against Coles, her pelvic walls clamp down around him as she climaxes, fluttering around him, her body stills in his arms for just a second as she hits the peak of ecstasy, and she quakes, panting his name and takes Cole with her. "Ohhhh fuck, fuck I'm coming baby, ahhhhh Shayla!" Cole growls, pushing deep, and grunts as his cum surges down his shaft, spilling his hot seed deep inside her with a shudder. Shayla kisses him deeply, and he raucously moans as he rocks his hips slower while they cling to the last of the tingling sensations of their orgasm. They lay together, hearts beating frantically, breathing heavily while their bodies calmed. Cole looks down into his wife's flushed face while she peers up at him, smiling lazily.

"That was a hell of a three minutes, Cole Hoult." She whispers teasingly, and he brushes his lips over hers softly with a roguish smile.

"Mmm, baby, you married the wrong man if quick three-minute fucks is what you were after." He burrs, kissing her softly. "Three minutes is simply not long enough to feed the hunger I have for your tight pussy." He moans when she rocks her hips a little firing him up all over again. "Keep doing that, and I'll fuck you all over again, honey."

"Oh, that's cute. You thought we were done?" She grins up at him; her eyes were twinkling mischievously. Cole laughs deeply, burying his face into the crook of her neck.

"No fucking chance. I've got months of sexual frustration to take out on you, baby girl." He groans and rolls onto his back, pulling her on top of him. Shayla straddles him and gasps when he jerks his hips up, thrusting into her hard and ready. "Saddle up and ride that pony baby." He growls throatily, squeezing her hips. "Hey Siri, play pony!" Cole calls out, and a second later, the song starts playing through the speakers in the room. Shayla gapes at him, and he winks at her biting his lip. "Ride it." And ride it she did, until he was singing her name.

The next morning Shayla woke up wrapped up in her husband's arms. She lay still admiring his handsome face and sighs contently. She kisses his soft lips and pulls back a little when he smiles against her lips. Cole moans and pulls her back to kiss him again—which she does—dropping soft little pecks on his lips. "Mm, promise me you'll wake me up like this every morning." Cole whispers, and Shayla smiles fondly.

"I promise, baby." She whispers as Cole pulls her on top of him and looks up into her eyes, his fingers combing through her dark tresses.

"As much as I would love to stay in bed naked with you all day, we've got a honeymoon to get too," Cole tells her, and Shayla smiles.

"You still haven't told me where we're going?"

Cole grins and kisses down her throat. "Cancun." Shayla pulls back and looks down at him wide-eyed.

"Cancun?" She asks, surprised, and Cole nods, smiling up at her. "*Mexico*, Cancun?!"

Cole laughs, amused, "Honey, there's only one Cancun." Shayla rolls her eyes and flicks his forehead before she moves off him. "Ow, hey! Where are you going?" Cole complains. Sitting up in bed, he grabs her around the waist and hauls her back into bed with him. Shayla laughs and squirms against him when he nuzzles her neck, growling. "Ten days, only you, me, white sandy beaches, cocktails, dancing, and a shit load of sex. Oh, I'm going to fuck your brains out all over the place."

Shayla giggles and looks up at him. "Ooh bebé, that sounds like a dream come true." She purrs enticingly, and Cole kisses her deeply but groans in protest when Shayla pulls back. "Before you suck me into your sexual vortex again, we have to go meet everyone for breakfast before we leave." She tells him, and Cole sighs, burying his face in between her breasts.

"I love everyone, I do, but fuck I can't wait to have you all to myself for a while," Cole tells her, and Shayla wraps her arms around his neck and rubs her breasts in his face, and Cole moans with a chuckle. "Oooh, nice."

Shayla laughs and lifts his head to look at him. "We have to go. You'll have me all to yourself soon enough. Come on, Stud-muffin, let's go shower and get ready." Shayla tells him, and Cole rolls off her with an audible sigh.

"Fine, but we're doing it in the shower." He grumbles, lifting her and throwing her over his shoulder before he lands a slap on her butt cheek, and Shayla whimpers.

"Ow! Bebé!" She laughs as he carries her to the bathroom, where they spend a good fifteen minutes having hot shower sex. After they get ready, they head down to the breakfast hall to join their friends and family for breakfast.

"There they are." Aimee chirps when she sees Cole and Shayla stroll over to them. Shayla hugs her mother and kisses her cheek.

"Hi Mama, how are you liking Vegas?" She asks, and Sara nods, smiling lovingly at her daughter.

"It's lovely here. The girls and Sam took me for a walk around the strip this morning. It's sweltering out. Make sure you wear sunscreen." She tells her, and Shayla nods and hugs Coles mother before they sit down with the rest to eat breakfast.

"So…" Aimee drawls, wagging her brows at Shayla. "How was the wedding night?"

Shayla feels her cheeks go hot. She licks her lips and casts a look at her husband, who was talking to Josh.

"She's gone all red look." Jo giggles making Shayla blush even more. "It must have been good."

"Oh my God, shut up." She whispers, chuckling timidly. "It was so damn hot. We barely got any sleep." She gushes, and the girl's squeal excited, and everyone at the table looks at them. "Shhh." Cole looks at Shayla quizzically while she tries to hide her crimson face. "Speaking of sex," Shayla utters, looking at Jo. "How long have you and Sam been going at it?" It was Jo's turn to go red while she looks at Shayla wide-eyed.

"He told you?"

"Hold the fuck up, you're sleeping with *Sam*?" Aimee whispers, stunned, and Jo looks over at Sam, talking with Josh and Cole.

"He didn't tell me anything. I figured it out. How could you not tell me, Jo? We're best friends." Shayla questions with a frown, and Jo sighs, her shoulders slumping.

"I've been dying to talk to you, but you've had so much going on, I didn't want to upset you before your wedding." She explains, chewing on her lip, her eyes cast down. "I really like him."

Shayla looks over at her older brother and sighs. "Jo, I love my brother, but you know Sam isn't the easiest of people to handle. He has a bucket full of issues babe, are you sure you've thought this through?"

Jo nods, "He's different with me, Shay. We've been seeing each other for a couple of months now, and he makes me happy." She explains with a shrug, and Shayla looks at Aimee, who shakes her head with a shrug.

"I mean, if you're sure it won't affect our friendship?" Jo shakes her head and takes Shayla's hand into hers with a smile.

"It won't, I swear." Shayla nods and shrugs, smiling at her friend before she casts a look at her brother.

After breakfast, Shayla and Cole say goodbye to their family and friends to go off on their honeymoon. Shayla was currently sitting in her seat on their private jet on their way to Mexico, watching her husband speaking to someone on the phone. She gets up from her seat and straddles Cole, who looks at her with a smile, placing his hand at her hip, and bites his lip when she kisses down his neck. "Uh-huh," Cole sighs, tilting his head back, giving her more room to continue nipping at his neck. "No, the design was excellent. It's just small adjustments that need to be made. Speak to Jess. She has the details the client has sent over," Cole instructs, snaking his fingers under his wife's shirt and pinching her nipple between his thumb and forefinger, making her moan quietly in his ear. "Mhm, that's great. Listen, I'm on my honeymoon, so my phone will be off. Speak to Jaxson—he's the project manager, he has the authority to make these decisions without me. If not, speak to my father. Okay, great. Thank you." He says and hangs up the phone tossing it aside before he pulls his head back and looks at Shayla, who was looking at him sultrily. "I didn't hear a word he just said to me." Cole informs her, and she shrugs impishly, rocking herself against him.

"You shouldn't have been on your phone while you're on honeymoon then, Mr Hoult." She whispers, pressing her forehead to his while she unbuttons his shirt. Cole groans and slides his hands under her skirt, cupping her shapely behind and squeezing.

"Mm, you're right," He moans, brushing his lips over hers. "I'm a bad, bad man."

Shayla grins, "Yes, you are, and bad men should get punished."

Cole groans and rocks his hips up, rubbing himself against her. "Yes, they should. Punish me, baby." He growls, biting her bottom lip.

Shayla nods and kisses him slow and deep, making him moan before she slips off him and sits in her seat again, leaving Cole in a haze. Cole frowns, looking at her while she smirks at him and spreads her legs, giving him a view of her womanhood. Cole groans, licking his lips before he shifts to kneel in front of her, but Shayla presses her foot to his chest, stopping him. "Ah ah, you can look but no touching." Cole looks at her wide-eyed, and she grins naughtily.

"That's mean." Shayla shifts, spreading her legs wider, and Cole tilts his head, looking at her licking his lips like a man starved. "Don't provoke me, baby. You know how dominant I can be when I'm hungry."

Shayla trails her fingers up her inner thigh while he watches avidly as her fingers inch closer to her mound. "I'm counting on it, baby." She breathily moans while she touches herself.

"Fuck…" Cole hisses, watching her, a dark look in his eyes. Shayla lifts her eyes to his and swipes her tongue slowly along her lips.

"You want it, baby?" She whispers, and Cole nods, staring at her impatiently. "Take it." And he did till she was gasping his name.

One month after honeymoon…

"Honey, where do you want these boxes?" Cole calls out to his wife as he walks through their brand-new home. "Shayla?" Cole frowns, setting the boxes down, and follows the sound of music to their bedroom. He stops when he sees her dancing while she unpacks. Cole smiles, leaning against the door, watching her sway her hips while she folds clothes, completely oblivious to everything around her. Cole walks over, grabs her by the waist spinning her around. He dips her down and kisses her. Shayla smiles, circling her arms around his neck, kissing him back eagerly. Cole pulls her back up and gazes into her eyes. "Can you promise me something?"

"Anything."

Cole smiles, brushing his fingers through her hair. "Don't ever stop dancing around the house like this." Shayla laughs, shaking her head.

"Oh baby, I won't ever stop doing that. I physically can't stop dancing if music is playing. It's in my blood." She assures him, and he beams at her. "I can't wait to gross out our children." Cole chuckles and kisses her forehead.

"Me either." He pulls away from her and frowns when Shayla staggers a little. He holds her waist, steadying her. "You okay?" He questions, concerned, and she shakes her head, laughing a little.

"Yeah, you got me all woozy with that kiss." She tells him, and Cole grins, smacking her bum.

"I'll follow up later, baby." He promises with a wink and leaves the bedroom. Shayla smiles, shaking her head before she goes back to unpacking the boxes.

Two weeks later, they were finally unpacked and settled into their new home. "Hey Shay, what are we doing for mum on her birthday?" Sam questions, and Shayla shakes her head with a shrug.

"I don't know, Sam. I'll figure something out. We still have a couple of weeks to plan it out." She tells him while mixing the guacamole dip. Cole comes over and kisses her cheek, holding a sushi piece for her to eat, but she winces and shakes her head. "Ugh, no, I don't want it, Bebe."

"But it's your favourite?" He utters with a frown, and Shayla shakes her head.

"Not in the mood for Sushi. I'm good with my crackers and dip." She replies with a smile. Cole shrugs and walks back over to Josh and Sam while they pick a film to watch.

"You okay, Shayla? You look really pale?" Jo asks, and Shayla nods.

"Yeah, I'm okay. I think I've got a stomach bug or something. I've been feeling really sick and run down lately." She answers with a shrug, and the girls look at one another and back at Shayla.

"Sore boobs?" Aimee asks, and Shayla blinks at her and nods.

"Actually, yeah, they have been very sensitive this past week, but Cole has been in a friskier mood than usual, and there's been a lot of nipple biting and sucking, so I'm not surprised they're sore."

"Shay, are you sure you're not pregnant?" Jo asks, smiling, and Shayla chuckles, shaking her head.

"God no, I took a test two weeks ago, it was negative. No baby, sorry girls. Grab the popcorn." The girls shrug and follow Shayla to the cinema room, and they all settle in their love chairs with their men. "What are we watching?" She asks, leaning back against Cole, who kisses her neck.

"Scarface," Cole announces proudly, and the girl's all groan. "What, it's a classic?"

Aimee rolls her eyes as she settles herself in Josh's arms. "Yeah, a classic man movie."

"Say 'ello to my little friend." The boys all chant together, and Shayla laughs when Aimee shoves a hand full of popcorn in Josh's mouth, who scowls at her.

Three weeks go by, and Cole was getting ready for another day at the office. "Baby, are you ready?" He calls out and drops his cufflink, which bounces off the bathroom's marble counter and lands in the trash. "Damn it." He kneels and fishes through the rubbish, searching for his cufflink but frowns when his fingers brush against something hard. He pulls out the pregnancy test and looks at it unblinking. Staring at the word 'Pregnant' for over a minute.

"Honey…" Cole gets up and walks out of the bathroom. Shayla looks back at him with a frown till she sees him holding a pregnancy test in his hand. "What is this? Are you pregnant?"

Shayla turns and faces him, her green eyes wide, "Uh, I think so?" She states with a shrug, and Cole looks at her, stunned.

"You think so? This thing says you are?"

"Baby, those tests aren't always accurate." She tells him while putting her earrings in. Cole shakes his head and walks over to her, grabs her hand, and pulls her out of the bedroom. "Cole, where are you taking me?"

"We're going to buy more tests. I need to know right now if you're having my baby or not." He mutters, pulling her toward the car, stuffing her in the passenger seat.

Ten minutes later, they were stood in a drug store looking at the line of pregnancy tests. Shayla looks at each one chewing her lip gingerly while Cole impatiently paces back and forth. “Honey, pick one, would you? You’re killing me here.”

“Cole, I don’t know which one to get; they’re all different.” She scolds him, and he rolls his eyes, walks over to the shelf, and picks up one of each box before he grabs her hand and pulls her to the checkout. “Oooh, pickles!” Shayla moans, staring at the jar of gherkins longingly. Cole looks at her with a frown.

“Really? You’re drooling over a jar of pickles?” He asks sardonically, and Shayla looks up at him with those big green eyes of hers. Cole blinks at her and sighs, picking up two jars of pickles. “Come on, you little weirdo.”

Twenty minutes later, Cole stood in the bathroom, looking down at the line of pregnancy tests while Shayla moans, eating her gherkins. Cole looks over at her while she sucks the gherkin, and he frowns. “I don’t know if I should feel grossed out or turned on right now.” He grumbles, and Shayla shrugs, finishing off her pickle with a little burp.

“Ooh, excuse me.” She giggles, and Cole shakes his head with a grin while she brushes her teeth.

“Why is this taking so long? It says three minutes?!” Cole exclaims, pacing back and forth. “Did you do it right?”

“Baby, it’s only been like a minute,” Shayla mumbles with the toothbrush in her mouth, and Cole sighs. “And it’s not rocket science. It’s pissing on a stick.” She adds, wiping her mouth.

“This feels like the longest three minutes ever.”

“Oh, here we go…” She utters, and they stare down at the line of tests before they look at one another…

THE END

MESSAGE FROM SHAYLA

Dear reader,

thank you so much for purchasing and taking the time to read my book, 'The Accidental Wife' I truly hope you enjoyed reading this book as much as I did writing it.

There are a couple of bonus chapters for you to enjoy below.

If you loved this story, and you want to know more about Shayla and Coles journey, be sure to check out the sequel, Love me Again.

I look forward to hearing your thoughts on the book. If you enjoyed reading Shayla and Cole, please do leave me a review. I'm forever thriving to become a better writer and this helps me tremendously also helps get my book. Out there for other readers to enjoy.

your feedback—good or bad means everything to me.

BONUS CHAPTER

Shayla/Cole

Shayla

Three weeks into arrangement.

I jump out of my skin when a box lands in front of me with a thud. I slowly lift my gaze from my notebook and look up at a beaming Cole standing there with his hands stuffed in his pockets as he rocks back and forth on his heels cheerily. "What is this?" I question, pointing my pen at the wrapped-up box.

Cole grins wickedly, and I already know I'm not going to like what I find in that box. "A gift for you." He tells me, practically giddy. I eye him suspiciously as I unwrap the box, and my eyes go wide when I see what it was.

"Cole, what the *hell* is this?" I ask in a flurry, my neck already heating up. Cole licks his lips and raises his brows till they almost disappeared in his hairline. "Why would you get me.... this?"

"Do I need to remind you of the bet that you lost the other night?" He reminds me gleefully, and I glare at him.

I look around the office and hide the box under my desk, away from prying eyes. "What does the bet have to do with you buying me a pair of..." I look around to make sure no one was listening. "Vibrating panties?"

"The agreement was that you do whatever I wanted." He reminds me airily, and I scowl at him.

"I said within reason. I am *not* sleeping with you." I utter mortified, and he cackles amused and takes a couple of steps closer to me. I cannot believe what I've gotten myself into with this boy. I should never have agreed to move in with him, and I most definitely shouldn't have been making bets with him. We've been living together for almost a month now, and every day is a struggle. The sexual tension between us just keeps growing thicker and thicker. At the best of times, it's almost unbearable. Let me catch you up on this ridiculous bet that Cole and I made. A couple of days ago, we went out to get some food, and they had a challenge of eating thirty of their hottest wings in fifteen minutes. Cole and I took on the challenge and bet that the loser would do what the other wanted for an entire day. And well, the smug bastard beat me by two chicken wings. We spent two days after the challenge taking turns throwing up from the amount of chili we both consumed and messed up our stomachs. As fun as it was, I would not do that again in a rush.

I shudder at the mere thought of that challenge. "Who said anything about having sex?" Cole chuckles, rubbing his jaw as I look up at him and lean back into my chair, regarding him curiously.

"Then why, may I ask, did you buy me the vibrating panties? What's your angle here?" I question curiously, and he presses his lips together, smiling.

"Well, we're going out tonight to watch that movie, remember?" He reminds me and I nod silently, watching him, my eyes narrowed to slits. "You're going to wear those panties to the cinema." I feel my eyes widen as I stare at him unblinking while he grins cheerfully back at me.

"I will do no such thing!" I hiss, sitting forward and hitting him a couple of times with the box in my hand.

Cole laughs, "Ow, hey! Whoa! A bet is a bet. You lost, so now you have to face the consequences." He claims, laughing, and grabs my wrist when I try to hit him again, and he yanks me up against him. "Best part of it is—it's remote-controlled through my phone, so I'll be controlling your pleasure, sweetheart." I feel my face grow hot as he looks down at me, his green eyes twinkling.

"Cole, *please* anything but this." I plead, and he grins and leans forward till our noses touch.

"I'm going to have you singing a different tune later, sweetheart." He burrs throatily as he gazes into my eyes. "Just wait." He adds with a whisper, brushing his nose over mine before he walks around my desk. "Be ready for eight tonight." He throws over his shoulder as he walks into his office. My eyes follow him as he walks over to his desk and sits down, his eyes twinkling with pure joy as he looks back at me.

I bite the side of my cheek with a groan and thump my head on my desk. I jump when I hear the intercom buzz. I push the button. "What?" I groan miserably.

"Stop sleeping on the job. I know you're married to the boss, honey, but you still have to work." He laughs out loud when I flip him off and click the intercom off. I look at him and bite back my smile when I see him laughing, his shoulders shaking as he looks down at his tablet.

Oh, I hate him.

Later that evening, after a long day at work, Cole and I got dressed and ready for our cinema 'date night.' We were going to watch the new Fast and Furious movie that came out. I eye the black lace vibrating panties warily before I put them on. I'm going to kill him one of these days, I swear to God. I can't believe he's making me do this. I mean, it is probably the most risqué thing I have ever done, but that's beside the point. After I got dressed in a faded denim skirt and lace crop top and a denim jacket to match my skirt, I walk out of my bedroom the same time as Cole, our eyes meet, and he knowingly smiles when I avert my gaze and smooth down my skirt. He was wearing a pair of black jeans and a grey Hugo Boss tee matched with a leather jacket. He looked drool-worthy as always.

"Ready?" He asks, his tone light, with just a hint of wickedness. I clear my throat and nod before I turn and walk toward the front door. I gasp and stop in the entryway when the underwear suddenly vibrates, and masses of tingles erupt within me.

"Oh." I moan, closing my eyes and squeezing my legs together. Oh no, this is not good at all. I stiffen when I feel Cole come up behind me, his lips hot on my ear.

"Just checking." He drawls with a deep chuckle. I elbow him in the gut, and he groans, laughing as I open the door and walk out of the apartment toward the elevator avoiding his gaze. I'm not looking forward to this at all. I push the button to the elevator a couple of times, chewing my bottom lip. Cole comes and stands beside me, smirking rather smugly. I look up at him, and he looks back at me, his smile broadening into a full-on dimple bearing grin. He's loving every second of this. The bastard is practically gleaming. We walk into the elevator, and just as the door slide shut, my underwear starts vibrating again...harder.

I gasp and grip the metal bar behind me so tight I think my knuckles were white. I press myself back against the wall, biting my lower lip to stop from moaning out loud. The pleasure the vibrations were bestowing me with was intense. My knees shook as masses of tingles cascades through me and pool between my legs. "Fuck." I moan quietly and open my eyes to find Cole watching me with those mischievous eyes. He steps closer to me and licks his lips slowly.

"Feel good?" Cole asks quietly, his eyes flicker down to my lips before they slowly meet mine again. Yes, it felt too good, and I almost lost the internal battle I had with my own body to not climax. I close my eyes panting.

"Cole please..." I moan inadvertently, biting my lip hard as I feel myself getting closer to orgasm. "Oh God," I pant breathlessly, squeezing the bar tight so I could keep myself upright, and just as I'm about to go over, it all stops, and I groan disgruntled, slumping against the wall.

I open my eyes and look at him. He's watching me heatedly and reaches up, dragging his thumb over my bottom lip. Cole steps closer and tilts my head up so I could look up at him. "Not yet, sweetheart." He teases, brushing his fingers along my jaw before he turns and walks out of the elevator when the doors slide open. I whimper inwardly and begrudgingly follow him to his Ferrari sports car. He tosses the keys to me and smirks, walking to the passenger side.

"You want me to drive?" I sputter wide-eyed, and he simply nods and gets in. I know what he's up to. I've got the right mind to take these stupid knickers off and go commando. I exhale slowly and get into the car and readjust the seat. He's let me drive the car before, but that's not why I was nervous. I was comfortable driving it but not while he's got the control to these panties. I give him a dubious look as I push the button to start the engine, and he smirks at me. Have I mentioned that I hate him?

Cole

I buckle up my seatbelt and watch Shayla as she gives me an 'I know what you're up to' look before she pushes the start button and the engine to my Ferrari roars. I smirk back at her rather smugly, and she rolls her eyes and drives out of the underground car park.

This will probably torture me as much as it is her, but having this control over her is thrilling me in more ways than one. Having the ability to pleasure her without touching her is the most fun I can have without *actually* having her—and by God, did I want her. Shayla makes me feel things I've never felt with any other woman. My attraction to her is off the fucking charts. I reach over and turn the music up while she drives. She keeps glancing at me warily, waiting and wondering when I'm going to turn the vibrator back on. I grin inwardly as the light goes red, and discreetly push the dial on the app up, and I hear Shayla's sharp intake of breath.

I watch in glee as she grips the steering wheel with one hand and the other splays out on her bare thigh. Her eyes close, and her head tilts back against the headrest. "Oh, Chrisssttt." She moans breathily, rocking her hips ever so slightly. I feel the blood rush through my body straight down to my cock, making my jeans that much tighter. The light goes amber and then green, so I turn the dial down, and she sighs, panting.

"Light's green, sweetheart." I smile when she sends me a withering glare, but one filled with desire and burning with need. Did I mention how incredibly sexy the sounds are that she makes when she's turned on? Literally enough to drive any red-blooded man to insanity.

Shayla didn't risk stopping at any more lights. She would put her foot down and zooms past any lights, whether it was green or amber. I chuckle, and she gives me a side glare.

"Remind me again why I put up with you?" She questions as she reverse parks in a bay.

I smirk lazily and shrug, "Because we're married." Shayla rolls her eyes, but I can see the smile pulling at the corner of her lips. "Admit it, come on, you're having the time of your life with me." I tease, poking her sides, and she slaps my hands away.

"I could think of a hundred different things I would rather be doing Hoult, don't give yourself too much credit." She sighs, trying her best to be blasé, but I see the joy in her eyes. I watch her as she opens the door and gets out of the car, her skirt rides up and gives me a nice view of the curve of her shapely behind, and I groan, readjusting myself before I get out of the car myself.

"You're not getting any better at the lying thing, sweetheart. You and I both know you love every second you spend with me." I state, slinging my arm around her shoulder and pulling her toward me.

Shayla snorts in a very unladylike manner and lifts her jade gaze to look at me. "And you get defensive when I call you an egomaniac." She mutters matter-of-factly. I narrow my eyes at her, and she grins back smugly.

"I thought we squashed that little argument weeks ago, or do I have to remind you once again." I express, brushing my lips against her ear and smile when I feel her shiver. "I still have wet dreams about the way you look when you come, baby." I groan in her ear, and Shayla shoves me away from her, her cheeks red hot.

"You know I'm not opposed to kicking you where it hurts, right?" She warns, trying to act all angry, but her eyes give her away. She's loving this as much as I am.

I widen my eyes and look at her, feigning innocence, and she shakes her head, pushing the door open and walking into the cinema complex. We got tickets to one of those VIP cinemas with the double reclining seats. It was a smaller room, cosier with fewer people around. There was no need to queue up for the popcorn and such because it was all served to your seat. "Oh, I like this," Shayla states, reclining back in her seat. I grin and toy with her seat making her recline back and forth, and she laughs, trying to push my hand away. "You're like an errant child. Stop it." She chuckles, trying to nudge my head off her shoulder when I lay on her.

"Oh, I'm loving this." I grin, nuzzling her neck, and she cracks up laughing, attempting to push my head off her. "Mm, you smell so good."

Shayla licks her bottom lip and her eyes close as I continue to nuzzle her pulse point. "Thanks." She sighs and jumps when a waitress pops up, clearing her throat with our order of popcorn and a bottle of wine. I sit up and smile, taking the giant bucket of popcorn while Shayla takes the two glasses for the wine. The waitress sets up our ice bucket with a bottle of wine beside our seats.

"Did you need anything else?" She asks me with a sugary smile, and I shake my head. She gives Shayla an icy look before she smiles at me and saunters off. I glance over at Shayla, who rolls her eyes smiling.

"What?" I ask, and she laughs, pushing popcorn in her mouth and chewing.

"I'm getting really fond of the death glares I get when I'm seen with you. There's really nothing quite like being hated on for absolutely no reason to brighten up your day." She drawls, sardonically sinking back in her seat pretending the watch the adverts.

I reach for her hand before I lace our fingers together and brush a kiss over her knuckles. "There is no one else I would rather spend my time with, sweetheart. I couldn't give a flying fuck about anyone else's opinions." I tell her solemnly, and she turns her gaze to mine as the lights slowly dim around us. Our eyes remain locked on one another for a couple of minutes till the movie starts, and Shayla averts her gaze to the screen. She didn't pull her hand away, so I didn't let go until she did, to pour us some wine.

We watch the movie, and I wait until she's finished her second glass of wine before I turn up the dial to the vibrator catching her off guard while she was engrossed in the movie.

Shayla shifts in her seat, glancing around while biting her lip. She looks over at me pleadingly, and I watch her with a grin. "Cole..." She sighs, her voice quivering.

"Mhm?"

"Come on, someone's going to hear." She whispers, and I look at the screen with cars exploding and look back at her. No one's going to hear anything in this racket.

"That's part of the thrill, sweetheart. You'll have to be quiet." I whisper back as I turn the dial up to the max, and she whimpers, biting her lip hard.

"Oh, god." She breathes, leaning back and squirming in her seat. I recline our seats back, so we're hidden away from any prying eyes. We were sitting at the back in the corner, so no one could see us anyway. The movie was long forgotten. I fully turned my attention to Shayla, trembling, and moaning breathily. I play around with the controls on the app and change the modes to a pulsing one, and Shayla grunts and clutches my arm with a sharp gasp, and she presses her thighs together. "Ohh shit, shit."

"Oh damn," I groan, watching her avidly. This is probably the sexiest thing I've ever witnessed. My mouth goes bone dry while Shayla continues to squirm, and pant, and rock her hips. I know when she's about to come because her back arches up, and she bites her lower lip just before her body stills for a second when she hits that peak, the last moment before she goes over, then she quakes and shudders with soft, breathy moans. That image of her is burned into my memory from the night we spent together in Vegas and what I did to her recently on her bed in her bedroom.

"Cole." She gasps when I switch the mode from pulse to massage. She's fighting it, holding back. I lace my fingers with hers and lean in close to her ear.

"Relax, baby, don't fight it," I whisper, trailing my tongue along with the shell of her ear, and Shayla hisses in response. Her fingers tighten around mine. "Come for me. Come *hard* for me, baby." I moan huskily in her ear and watch in delight as she arches up. There it is.

"Oh my God, Cole..." She shudders, biting her lip hard to keep from screaming, no doubt. She falls back against the seat spent, quivering, flushed.

Fuck me. I want her like a junkie wants his next fix. I was harder than I've been in my life. My dick was throbbing, aching to be buried deep inside her. "You're making me ache in places I didn't know was possible, Shay." I moan, pressing her hand against my crotch. "I'm burning for you, sweetheart." I sigh longingly, pressing my forehead to hers while I trail my fingers up her soft thigh. "Say it.... say you want me." Shayla moans when I brush my lips over hers with the barest of pressure.

She opens her eyes and locks her gaze with mine. "You want me." She whispers, a playful glint in her eyes.

I squeeze her thigh a little and snarl. "I'm going to break you. Mark my words." She holds my gaze and grins waywardly.

"Keep dreaming, Hoult."

"You'll be mine, Hart."

BONUS CHAPTER 2

Shayla

One month into our agreement, and I'm about ready to kill Cole with my bare hands. He seems to be having a grand old time torturing me. It's a Saturday morning, and I'm peacefully wrapped up in my bed, having an incredibly happy dream. That is, of course, until I feel something tickle my nose. I stir in my sleep and moan, snuggling into my pillow, drifting off to sleep again. Not even five seconds later, I feel a tickle on my nose again and lift my hand, thinking it was my hair, to brush it away. I jump awake when I feel something trying to crawl up my nose. I'm deathly scared of spiders, so I open my eyes in a panic and see Cole standing over me, a stupid grin plastered on his ridiculously gorgeous face.

I groan and scowl up at him. "Good morning, Sunshine." He chirps, his eyes sparkling in the morning sun that was beaming into the bedroom.

I blink up at him and sigh, "What do you want?" I moodily grumble when he tweaks my nose. I slap his hand away. "Why do you always wake up at the arse crack of dawn? It's the weekend. Go to sleep!" I pull the covers over my head and snuggle into my pillow again.

I hear Cole chuckle, and the bed dips. I open my eyes when I see him get under the covers on the other side of the bed, looking at me with a playful glint in his green eyes. "Wanna spoon?" I roll my eyes in exasperation, kick his shin with my heel, and he groans. "Ow! Why are you so violent?"

"Why are you so annoying?" I retort, and Cole chortles, which annoys me more. Who is this chirpy first thing in the morning?

"I am no such thing. You said you wanted to go running, remember?" He rests his head in his hand while he looks down into my face, and I whimper in response.

"But it's so early," I whine. Cole smirks and grabs my face between his large hand and squeezes my cheeks like I'm a five-year-old. I pull my face out of his grasp and rub my jaw with a scowl.

"I haven't had my coffee yet. I *will* kill you." I almost growl at him, and he laughs, amused, and ruffles my hair.

"Stop that!" I swat his hand away with a huff. I lift my foot and push him off my bed. He hits the floor with a thud, followed by a groan, which pleases me. I sit up in bed and stretch with an audible moan.

Cole sits up and scowls at me. He grabs the pillow and hits me with it, the force of it throws me back, and I tumble off the bed on the other side with a squeal. Cole throws his head back and laughs. "Oh, you little shit," I grumble, sitting up and grabbing my pillow. We stare at one another on opposite sides of the bed. I crawl up and point at him. "Say your last prayer, Hoult."

Cole smirks smugly and twitches his brows at me. "Bring it, baby." I swing the pillow at his head, but he ducks and hits my midriff. I stumble but catch myself and swing for him again. I successfully managed to hit his head this time and he groans. He lunges for me, and I hit him again, laughing when he tackles me to the bed. "Get over here," Cole mutters with a grin trying to hit me again, but I throw my pillow at him, and he bats it away.

"Cole..." I hysterically laugh as he straddles me, trying to grab my arms, which I kept slapping away. Cole pokes my sides tickling me. "Stop, stop, please!" I giggle, thrashing in his arms.

"Say sorry!" Cole laughs, pinning my arms up over my head with one hand and tickling me mercilessly with the other.

"Never!" I laugh, glaring up at him, and he bites his lip and pokes my sides again. "Cole, please, please stop. I will pee on you, I swear to god...aahhhh!" I was laughing so hard I had tears rolling down my face. I thrust my hips up, which forces him to fall forward. Our heads bump together a little, but not with so much force that it hurt. Our faces were close, *too close*, his forehead pressed to mine, lips a breath apart. Our eyes lock, panting softly. I feel his breath on my lips as I'm sure he could feel mine on his. The smiles we had on our faces slowly fade while we stare into one another's eyes. I swallow hard. Cole has sucked me into a trance again, and I was suddenly very aware of his rigid and robust body pressed against mine.

My attraction to him was growing stronger every passing day. It really doesn't help that he looks the way he does. Cole's eyes flicker to my lips, a look I couldn't quite decipher flashes across his face. The hand's thumb that's holding my arms down strokes my wrist gently, making my pulse jump under his touch. Those magnificent green eyes lift to mine slowly, and he nuzzles his nose over mine. Oh god, I want him to kiss me so badly. I wet my lips instinctively and hear him suck in a quick breath.

"Don't... *do that*," He whispers almost pleadingly, staring intently at my lips, "I'm desperately fighting every urge I have not to kiss you right now." He hisses, and a quivering breath escapes me before I could swallow it. I keep finding myself in situations like these with him. We kissed once already, and it almost led to sex in his kitchen. We can't do this, but neither of us has the strength to pull away. "Shayla..." Cole breathes urgently, his fingers squeeze my wrist while his free hand skims down my side, his gentle touch leaving a trail of fire on my bare skin. "You've given me a taste of you, and now I want more." Cole's soft lips brush mine ever so lightly as he speaks. It makes every hair on my body stand, and goosebumps break out all over me. I was feeling hot, flustered, but that delicious shiver that ran through me causes me to moan quietly.

"Cole," I whisper, closing my eyes. "We agreed to one kiss."

"Christ, Shayla, tell me you're not craving my lips just as desperately as I am yours." Cole groans. His lips were grazing along my jaw. "You're turned on. I can feel the heat of your pussy against my thigh, and it's making me crazy." He growls lustfully, lacing his fingers with mine. "I bet you're soaking—and throbbing, just burning to be fucked—just as I am to be the one that fucks you. *Hard*."

I moan throatily, and my hips rock up against his thigh that he presses against me intimately. "Oh...God." I whimper. Clawing onto the last thread of self-control I have, to not give in and beg him to take me because he was right. I was burning for a taste of him again, to feel him pound into me the way he did that night in Vegas.

"This flaming need I have for you rip-roaring inside of me is making me crazy. I want to lick that pussy until my tongue is saturated in your honey." I close my eyes, my breathing quickens when I feel red-hot desire pool in my belly. Cole nips at my ear while he speaks to me in a deep husky tone. "I want to feed my cock into your hot, dripping wet, insanely tight pussy until I'm balls deep inside of you, and I lose my bearings when you grip me tightly as I stretch you out."

"Fuck." I feel my sex clench tight at the mere thought of it. "Kiss me." I plead under my breath, and his eyes lift to mine for a beat, as if seeking assurance. Cole's eyes flicker down to my mouth before he brushes his lips over mine. I was half expecting a hard, dominating kiss, but he surprised me by coaxing my lips apart with his own, and just as our tongues glide over each other, we hear the front door close.

"Mr Hoult. I'm here!"

Cole's head jerks back, and our eyes open at the same time. His jaw clenched so tightly I could see it throbbing. We hear his housekeeper – Maggie's footsteps as she walks through the apartment.

"Fuck." He utters with a groan and presses his forehead to mine, biting his lip hard. Cole pulls his head back and looks down into my flushed face. "Let's go workout before I punch a hole in the wall." He brushes a kiss to my temple and scrambles off me. He looks down at me longingly, sprawled out on the bed, and rubs the back of his neck, clearly agitated. It's bizarre how we keep getting interrupted in intimate moments. I feel like God himself is trying to tell me something. This boy is bad for me, and I need to get my shit together fast. We're only a month in, and I'm struggling. "I'll let you get ready."

I couldn't tell if I was relieved or more disappointed by the interruption. I muse over that while I brush my teeth, staring at myself in the mirror. My face was still flushed despite my best efforts to cool myself down by splashing cold water on my face. And now, I have to go and watch him work out… all hard and sweaty. Lord, help me and my vagina.

I dress in a pair of black yoga pants and a matching training top. Tying my hair up into a ponytail, I pull a cap on before I walk over to Cole, leant against the wall while scrolling through his phone, scowling. He hadn't noticed me yet, so I take a moment to admire him. He was in grey joggers and a black vest top that showed off his muscular physique. My eyes greedily skim over his luscious bicep, all cut and hard, laced with those sexy throbbing veins that make girls go stupid with lust.

I blink out of my trance when Maggie walks over to me from the kitchen. "Good Morning Mrs Hoult." She greets me warmly as she passes by Cole. She must have caught me staring at him because her lips curl knowingly. She may be older, but she's not blind. She certainly appreciates a fine specimen like Tristan Cole Hoult. God sure did take his sweet time when he was creating him.

I clear my throat and smile at Maggie, "Good Morning, Maggie." I greet her as she walks past me toward Cole's bedroom. Cole looks up from his phone and straightens.

"Are you ready?" I walk past him to the front door, and while he pulls it open for me, he intently watches as I walk past him to the corridor. I can feel those eyes burning into my back as I walk to the elevator, and I push the button, shifting nervously from foot to foot, impatiently waiting for the car to arrive. The tension between us was palpable. My stomach was apprehensively clenching and unclenching, wondering if he will try and kiss me in the elevator. My heart jumps when the bell dings and the doors slide open. I exhale slowly and walk in, pressing my back against the mirror, my hands gripping the bar behind me tightly. I watch Cole as he strolls in after me and presses the button for the lobby, his hot gaze on mine. He looks very intense. I feel my knees wobble a little as he walks closer to me. On the outside, I hoped and prayed I was coming across blasé because inwardly, I was burning.

Cole stands directly in front of me, and I crane my neck to look up at him. He places his hands on either side of my head on the mirror and dips his head so he could see my eyes beneath the cap I was wearing. We stare at one another intently, soundlessly. Cole licks his lips and exhales slowly.

"I'm a very patient and controlled man, Shayla." He speaks slowly, and I resist the urge to gulp. "You are the one and only woman to ever derail me. I don't lose control, ever, but the harder you try to resist me, the more I want you."

I snort and roll my eyes, "Resist you?" I intone sardonically. "I slept with you the very first night we met. You've *had* me." Cole looks down at my lips for a drawn-out moment.

"I can't forget the way you taste." He leans in and whispers in my ear. "The way you sound when you come."

And he says I derail *him*.

I press my hand to his chest and push him back a little, so I can look up at him. "We're sexually frustrated. That's it." I tell him firmly, "If we give in to temptation and sleep together again, things will get messy, and I don't like messy. I don't want to complicate my life more than it already is. We live and work together, Cole. We can never cross over that line. However badly we may want to." I explain, and Cole closes his eyes and nods.

With a groan he pushes off the wall and rubs his jaw, his eyes on me. I could see the frustration in his gaze, and I had the urge to go against my own words and kiss him. He opens his mouth to say something, but the bell rings, interrupting him, and the doors slide open to the lobby. I walk out, leaving him to follow me while I walk to the exit. The doorman greets us cheerily while opening the door for us as we walk out. "Mr and Mrs Hoult. Good Morning."

"Good Morning, Jerry." We greet him together. I stretch my hamstrings and calves, and Cole does the same before we start running. It was still early out, so the streets were mainly clear. We run to a park near the apartment and jog side by side.

"By the way..." Cole pants looking over at me as we jog. "We have a benefit to go to tonight." He tells me, and I frown, watching him speed up and run away.

"What?" I utter with a scowl. "What benefit?!" I chase him, and he laughs when I push him. "You didn't mention anything about a benefit?" I pant catching up to him. Cole shrugs with a roguish grin.

"Because I knew you would downright refuse to go with me." He says coolly, looking ahead, and I glower at him.

"You'd be right. And I'm not going." I declare, shaking my head as we jog. Cole casts me a side glance.

"As per our agreement, you must accompany me to social events as my dear wife." He reminds me, and I growl when he snatches my cap off my head and runs off with it.

"Hey!" I chase him trying to grab my cap from him. The bastard waves it at me, "Give it back." I hiss, shoving him. Cole nudges me away with his shoulder and races off again.

"You're coming!" He laughs, squeezing my side playfully when I catch up to him. I shove him away from me again and run.

"The hell I am!" I argue and run ahead of him. He quickly catches up and lifts me off the ground and throws me over his shoulder. I squeal, hitting his back. "Put me down, Cole!"

Cole shakes his head, laughing heartily. "Not until you agree to come with me."

"You didn't ask me!" I slap his back. "Everyone is looking at us. Put me down right now!"

"I'm asking you now," Cole states, spanking my bum. Women that were jogging by us watch us with grins on their faces whispering to one another. Oh my God, if this ends up on the tabloids, I will kill him.

"No, you're demanding it, you pretentious arsehole!" I grouse angrily, and he chuckles.

"Shayla, save your breath, baby, you're coming. End of discussion." He declares as he puts me down on my feet, and I glare up at him. "You're my wife, you're expected to be there, and we need to keep up appearances." He touches my nose and runs off again, leaving me watching his retreating back dumbfounded. Goddamn, this contract to hell. I shake my head and jog after him. After our run, we hit the gym in our apartment building. I try desperately to keep my eyes on the machine in front of me and not peek glances at Cole, who was in the free weights section. My eyes defy me, and they look up to watch him lifting dumbbells. The muscles in his arms were flexing and bulging with every lift. He was a hot, deliciously sweaty, six-foot-four mess and I wasn't the only one that thought so. Every woman's eyes in that gym were on him, watching him like the eye candy he was. Cole didn't even bat an eyelid, completely oblivious to his effect on the women around him. Or was he aware but good at being blasé about it?

I watch as the women desperately try to catch his attention by stretching in a very prerogative manner. I'm talking arses in the air, bosoms pushed out. I was starting to feel second-hand embarrassment for them. I wince and push the leg press machine for another fifteen reps. I release it with a moan when my legs ache. I open my eyes and see Cole watching me through the mirror while lifting weights over his head and back down again.

I was getting really sick of these girls fawning all over him. It grated me. It grated me more than I would have liked to admit. What the fuck am I getting jealous about? He's not mine. I get off the machine and walk over to Cole, who watches me as I near him. I place my hand on his sweat-damp shoulder and lean over to pick up his water bottle and drink from it while he watches me, a knowing glint in his eyes. Cole puts the weight on the floor, catches my wrist, and pulls me to sit in front of him on the bench, almost causing me to choke on the water I still had in my mouth. I swallow and look back at him through the mirror. His large hands grasp my waist, and he kisses my damp shoulder. "If you want to put on a show to keep the wolves at bay, don't half-arse it, baby," Cole murmurs in my ear.

"I don't know what you're talking about." I clear my throat, and he chuckles wickedly in my ear, the vibrations humming through me.

"Don't insult my intelligence," Cole burrs, squeezing my hips before they travel down to my thighs. "It's a woman's instinct to want to make it known to others what's hers, just as it is a man's to be possessive of what's his." He declares, brushing his lips along my shoulder. Was this his subtle way of telling me I was his? Why did that thrill me? "This is what drives me crazy about you. Most women would have gone into a jealous rage and gone in for the kiss to state her mark, but not you..." He murmurs deeply. "You did it with such poise, in such an elegant and respectable manner. I fucking *love* that."

"I think you're reading too much into it, Cole. I was thirsty and didn't want to walk to the other side of the gym to drink some water." I explain with a sigh when he kisses the base of my neck.

"You're a terrible liar, sweetheart, but let's just pretend for argument's sake that I believe you." He whispers. It was impossible to miss the undertone of amusement in his voice, and that annoyed me.

"Cole, you're not mine to stake a claim over, just as I am not yours." I sigh, trying to get up, but he keeps me against him.

"You will be." Cole exerts possessively. "Mark my words." When his grip loosens, I stand up and turn to face him. He looks up at me, his eyes glittering like jewels. I see the women in the gym still watching us. I place my hands on either side of his face and lean in close, and his eyes go dark with desire.

"Keep dreaming." I moan, ghosting my lips over his before I pull away and walk off, leaving him to the 'wolves' that desperately crave his attention.

Later that day, Cole had arranged for rails and rails of dresses, racks of shoes, and a team of people to help me get ready for this glitzy benefit ball.

I sigh, brushing my fingers through the different materials of the selection of dresses. I find one dress that I liked and pull it off the rack. The make-up artist comes bouncing over to me. "That dress would look fab on you. Tristan did mention he wants you in red. You guys are perfectly in sync with one another. It's totes adorbs." I look at her, and she takes my hand, leading me to the chair in front of the vanity mirror. "We'll keep your hair straight and slicked down at the front. It will look fierce with that dress, and your hair is gorgeous." She chirps, combing her fingers through my hair.

"Sure," I agree with a shrug. I let them get on with whatever they wanted to do. After all, it's important to Cole that we attend this stupid ball together to keep up appearances. I'll do my part and play the dutiful wife as I promised.

Two hours later, I was dressed and ready. The dress was beautiful, fire truck red, a high-low, satin, strapless ball gown. Simple and classy with a diamante belt around the waist. The skirt was full, shorter at the front and longer at the back, so it dragged on the floor a little. I chose a pair of gold, open toe heels to go with the dress and a gold clutch. The girls tried to deck me out in diamonds, but I refused. Too much sparkle would have taken away the attention from the dress.

After the girls left, I spray my perfume and exhale before I step out of the room, making my way to the living room where Cole was waiting, dressed in a tuxedo, fixing his cufflink.

Damn. He looks so good.

Cole looks up when he hears me approaching and looks stunned as though he were mesmerized. His green eyes glide over me, taking me in as he walks over. “Wow.” He utters, lifting my hand and brushing a kiss to my knuckles. “Shayla, you look…sensational.” He declares, gazing into my eyes.

“So do you,” I reply earnestly, and he smiles a little. “You didn’t wear the jewellery I had delivered for you?”

I smile and shake my head. “They were beautiful, but it would have clashed with the dress, and I prefer the subtle look,” I tell him looking down at myself.

“I knew you would say that. My mother chose those.” Cole reaches into his pocket and pulls out another box, and pulls it open. I look at the necklace in the box and smile. It was a diamond heart pendant on a white gold chain. “I thought this would be more you.” He adds. “May I?” I nod, and he takes it out of the box and steps behind me, and brushes my hair over one shoulder before he fastens the necklace around my neck. I touch the pendant, closing my eyes when he kisses my bare shoulder. “You’re breathtaking,” Cole whispers in my ear before he walks around me.

“Thank you for the necklace. It’s gorgeous, and for the compliment.” I declare, hoping my make up hid the blush forming on my cheeks.

“Shall we?” Cole asks, holding his arm out to me with a charming smile. I slide my arm into his, and he leads me out of the apartment, down to the black limo waiting for us. The driver opens the door, and Cole helps me before he walks around getting in from the other side.

He hands me a glass of champagne, and I take it. Our fingers brush, and I feel my insides go all gooey. “Thank you.” I utter, and we clink our glasses before we take a sip. Our eyes meet over the rim of our glasses, and I feel myself blush again. What the hell is wrong with me. I’m a grown arse woman. God damn it. Pull yourself together, Shayla. Fucking hell. It's an arrangement. It's just a game. It's not real.

Cole tells me about the ball we were attending. It was to support and raise money for a Children's hospital for kids who suffer from rare diseases. Cole was the primary benefactor, and they were going to name the wing after his family's name. That made my heart swell fondly. I love that he gives back to those less fortunate.

"Oh Cole, that's so admirable," I say, covering his hand resting on the seat between us with mine. Cole shrugs it off and brushes his thumb over my knuckles.

"What good is having money if you can't help those who need it." He expresses amiably, and I find myself staring at him in awe. He really is perfect.

"You're a good man, Cole Hoult." I declare sincerely, and he smiles at me handsomely, lifting my hand to kiss my palm.

"I try to be." He murmurs against my wrist, his eyes searching mine. He looked as though he wanted to say something, and just as I was about to lose myself in his eyes, the car rolls to a stop, and he looks out the window and then back at me. "You ready?"

I nod and smile. The door opens, and Cole steps out of the limo, and instantly the flashes of cameras go off like crazy. A moment later, he opens my door and holds his hand out to me. I take his offered hand, and he pulls me out of the car. I was so nervous; my entire body was shaking. "Relax, baby, I got you," Cole whispers before he kisses my temple. I slide my arm into Coles, and he leads me toward the hoard of photographers snapping photo after photo of us.

"Tristan, can we get a photo of you and your beautiful wife?" A lady asks, sidling up to Cole, who nods, leading me down the red carpet toward one of those backdrops with the foundation's name. Cole was so calm and collected as he smiles for the photos. It was undeniably attractive. To me, he was just Cole Hoult, but to the world, he was an accomplished, intelligent, irresistibly handsome businessman. I was oddly proud of him, but at the same time, I have never felt so worthless and out of place in my life. I smile for the cameras, and there was one moment where he turns and looks at me. I look up at him, and a magical moment passes through us. It was hard to explain, but the way he was looking at me made my heart soar, which scared the shit out of me.

After the photos, we took our seats, and the event began. Various people got up on stage and gave a speech about what they were planning to achieve by opening the hospital's new wing. They mentioned Coles generous donation of ten million, and he stood, gave a curt nod when everyone applauds him, and gracefully retook his seat. Shortly after, the five-course dinner arrived. Wine and champagne flowed freely, and I was getting lightheaded. “You okay?” Cole considerately asks after we finished our delicious tiramisu dessert.

“Mm, I’m good.” I moan and lick my lips after I set the spoon down on the dish. “Cole chuckles and kisses my jaw. “That was delicious.” I sigh blissfully.

“I love how easily you’re pleased, sweetheart.” He tells me earnestly, and I give him a bashful smile and take a sip of my champagne. Music starts playing, and couples slowly fill the dance floor. “Dance with me?” Cole asks, standing and holding his hand out to me. I look at him a little startled, but nod and take his hand. Cole leads me to the dancefloor, and Ed Sheeran’s ‘Perfect’ starts to play. Cole wraps an arm around my waist and pulls me gently against him. I place my hand on his chest while the other clasps around his. We sway slowly together, gazing intently at one another. I forget to breathe when I look at him. “I’ll never forget the way you look tonight,” Cole confesses sweetly, and I smile up at him. “You take my breath away.”

I wrap my arm around his neck, brushing my fingers at his nape as we dance. “As do you,” I admit with a sigh, while his gorgeous green eyes gaze into mine. “Sometimes I forget that this is your life, and you’re this hot-shot billionaire.” Cole watches me curiously; his eyes narrow a little at whatever he saw written on my face. “When to me, you’re just Cole.”

Cole's lips twitch a little, and I gasp, surprised when he spins me out, pulls me back before he dips me down, his eyes on mine, lips a breath apart. “That’s good because that’s all I ever want to be to you. I only want to be *Cole*.” He tells me intently while I stare up into his eyes, my heart thrashing around wildly in my chest when his eyes slowly drift down to my lips, my eyes close when he starts to lean in...

HOLD ON... THERE'S MORE.

If you enjoyed reading this book, please leave a review. I would love to hear your thoughts and reviews help others find my work!

READ ON FOR TWO CHAPTER PREVIEW OF THE UPCOMING SEQUEL LOVE ME AGAIN.

LOVE ME AGAIN

Cole

"HAPPY BIRTHDAY!"

I look up from my desk and see Shayla standing in the doorway to my home office—naked, a cupcake with a candle in her hand, looking all kinds of gorgeous. I grin and lean back in my chair and admire my wife. Shayla is four months pregnant with my baby, and she's absolutely glowing, literally the most beautiful thing I have ever laid my eyes on. She's got a cute baby bump where she's finally starting to show. "Lord, have mercy. Show me a more desirable birthday gift than you, baby. Get your sexy butt over here, Mrs Hoult." I tell her, and she smiles and saunters over to me.

"Make a wish baby." She purrs, holding out the cupcake with the candle to me. I lift my gaze to hers over the flame and smile.

"What more can I possibly wish for, honey? I have you. We have a baby on the way, and all the success I can ever dream of." I express to her, and she smiles lovingly and bites her lip.

"You forgot the most important thing—health. You can wish for health bebé." I sigh and gaze into her eyes. This is why I love her so damn much.

"You're right. There is nothing more important than our health and the health of our baby." I declare, placing my hand on her stomach where my unborn baby lay. Shayla lays her hand on mine, and I close my eyes and make my birthday wish, which was a lifetime of health and happiness— Oh, and a little girl. Of course, I'll be happy, whatever the gender, but I really want a little princess with Shayla's gorgeous eyes, her smile, her long dark hair, and my dimples. My heart melts at the thought of her running around, shouting Daddy.

"What are you thinking about?" Shayla asks, watching me with a grin on her face. I blow out the candle and grin right back at her.

"I can't tell you, or it won't come true," I tease, pulling her into my lap and kissing her soft lips. Shayla presses her forehead to mine and rubs my jaw.

"Happy birthday, love of my life." She whispers, and I smile, closing my eyes.

"Thank you, light of my life." I cup her face and kiss her deeply. Shayla jumps and pulls back from the kiss, her eyes wide.

"What is it, baby?" I question, concerned, and she shakes her head and looks down at her stomach. Shay lifts my hand and presses it on her tummy, and I frown when I feel something tap against my palm. "Whoa, is that…"

"The baby is kicking." She smiles, nibbling her lip. I rub her stomach and press my forehead to her temple, beaming.

"Shayla, you've given me so much to be thankful for. Your love has honestly changed me and made me a better man." I tell her earnestly, and she smiles, grazing her thumb over my knuckles.

"You were always a good man, Cole. You've always had a good heart. That's all on you, not me." She replies and pulls back to look at me. "Now…" She drawls sexily, picking up the cupcake and licks the frosting with the tip of her tongue, and looks at me sultrily. I lean in, grasping her jaw in my hand, and suck the buttercream off her tongue.

"Mm," I moan and watch as she slips off and walks back a little, her eyes hot on mine.

"What do you say, birthday boy, want to get down and dirty?" She smiles, smearing the frosting of the cupcake all over her breasts. I bite my lip and watch her with hungry eyes.

"Oh, I'm going to devour you, Mrs Hoult," I growl and slap my laptop shut before I get up and walk over to her. Shayla squeals laughing when I haul her up into my arms and carry her to the kitchen, my face buried in her chest, licking and sucking the buttercream off her body, while I lay her down on the marble island in the middle of our kitchen. "Have your breasts gotten bigger, or have my hands shrunk?" I voice when I cup them, and they don't fit in my hands anymore.

Shayla lifts her head laughing. "They're definitely bigger. One of the perks of being pregnant. Enjoy." I look at her breasts wide-eyed and grin like a child in a sweet shop.

"Oh, just try and stop me." I groan, burying my face in between them, and Shayla laughs. I kiss down to her stomach where our baby was growing and kiss it. "Hi baby, Daddy can't wait to meet you." I lift my eyes to Shayla, watching me with a beautiful smile on her face while brushing her fingers through my hair. "Do you think it can hear me?"

Shayla nods, smiling, "The book that I'm reading says the baby starts to hear sounds at sixteen weeks, which I am now. It's the size of an apple at the moment." She replies, pushing out her bottom lip.

"So, you've got a little apple in here." I coo, nestling her stomach, and she grins, nodding.

"Yes, our little apple is blissfully floating around in there." Shayla sighs, content as I rub her stomach. "Mm, that feels nice." I watch Shayla as she closes her eyes while I caress her tummy lovingly. I still find it incredible that a little person is growing inside her right now—a small bundle made of our love combined into a tiny human. I feel so inferior to her or any woman, for that matter. Us men are lesser creatures. "Honey," I lift my gaze to hers, and she smiles dotingly at me. I feel my heart swell. I'm so in love with her.

"Yes, baby?"

"Make me yours." She whispers, and I give her a hundred-watt smile before I push her legs apart and enjoy my birthday treat. By the time we were done, there was buttercream everywhere. We were both covered in colourful frosting as we lay on the kitchen floor panting with satisfied grins on our faces. "I'm sticky in places I definitely shouldn't be," Shayla laughs, and I chuckle.

"Hey, you wanted to get dirty, so dirty we got, baby." I pant, smothering her face with frosting I had on my hand, and she slaps my hand away, snickering. I roll onto my side and look at her. "Let's always do crazy shit like this, okay?" I smile, reaching over and writing my name on her stomach with a heart.

Shayla rolls onto her side, imitating my action, and writes her name on my chest over my heart. "Always." She whispers devotedly, and I pull her to me, kissing her passionately. "We better go shower." She mumbles against my lips, and I nod.

"Mm, let's." I stand up and gently help her up, making sure she doesn't slip on all the buttercream all over the floor. Once we step away from the mess, I scoop Shay into my arms, and we go to the bathroom upstairs. We spend a good twenty-five minutes trying to get all the buttercream off our body, which was more difficult than I imagined it would be.

"You're not going to work in the morning, right?" Shayla asks, running her hands down my back. I shake my head while washing the shampoo out of my hair.

"No. I'm with you all day," I answer, opening my eyes to look at her, and she smiles, nibbling her lip coyly. "Why do I have a feeling you've got something more planned?"

"Because you know me too darn well." She croons, wrapping her arms around my neck, and gazes into my eyes.

"That I do baby. What are we doing?" I probe intrigued while I circle my arms around her waist, and she shrugs impishly and presses me back against the wall.

"Well, first, I'm going to make love to you." She whispers, running her hands over my chest. I groan and watch her excitedly. "And then…" She kisses my jaw softly. "We're going to have breakfast with your parents." She smiles and trails her lips along my jaw. "After that, I'm going to kidnap you, and we're going on a little trip to Amsterdam with Aimee, Jo, Josh, and Sam."

I laugh and kiss her temple. "Boy, I've not been to Dam in an awfully long time. Last time Josh and I went, we got so baked we ended up on the blue light district." I state, and Shayla's eyes go wide, and she laughs.

"No!"

I laugh, nodding, "Luckily, I realised, and I stopped Josh before he did something he would have needed a shit load of therapy for later." Shayla throws her head back and laughs hysterically.

"Well, as bummed as I am that I can't get 'baked' with you guys, I'll be sure to keep you all away from the blue light district." She promises, and I chuckle, shaking my head at the fond memories I had on that trip. This was on Josh's twenty-first birthday, we took a boy's trip with all our friends, and it was certainly a memorable one at that.

AFTER OUR SHOWER, Shayla and I went to bed. The following morning Shay kept her promise and woke me up with soft loving kisses on the lips. We made love before we had to pack for our two-day trip to Amsterdam and meet my parents for breakfast.

"I cannot believe we're going to Dam. I am so excited!" Jo chirps as we walk into the jet. I wrap an arm around my wife and nuzzle her neck lovingly, and she nestles into me. Aimee pops the champagne and pours us all a glass each.

"Sorry Shay, you have apple juice, babe," Aimee says, handing her a glass of apple juice, and she grins. "I'll drink in your place, don't worry." She adds with a cheeky grin.

"Lucky for you bitches, I don't need alcohol to have fun." Shayla shrugs, and I kiss her jaw tenderly while I rub her stomach.

"All right. Toast time." Josh announces, holding up his champagne flute. "To Coles birthday, you may be getting older, but you're still one sexy son of a gun." He toasts. and I laugh, holding up my glass. "Happy birthday Cole!" We all clink our glasses and drink. I'm so incredibly blessed to have such a wonderful life. A great group of friends surrounded me. I have the most beautiful woman in the world by my side, who is having my baby. I was just so happy. The lights in the jet dim, and music starts playing, and we all cheer.

The girls pull Shayla off my lap, and they dance. Josh and Sam start handing out shots of Patron. They were on a mission to get me drunk, that much I knew for sure. "Drink up, bro!" Sam sings, handing me another shot and slapping my back. Aimee pulls Josh to dance with her as Sam walks over to Jo. Shayla looks at me, grinning beautifully. I walk over to her and wrap my arms around her waist, drawing her against me. Shayla wraps her arms around my neck as we sway together to the music. "Your love makes me dizzy, baby." I drawl in her ear, and she giggles.

"That's the tequila, bebé."

I shake my head, smiling down into her upturned face. "No, it's not. I have you, but I still want you desperately. How is that possible." I growl, and she smiles her cheeks flushing.

"That's a good thing because I still want you, and I always will, you sexy beast." She croons and draws my lips to hers and kisses me hot and hard. I moan when she sucks and flicks her tongue over mine.

"Oh gross, I don't want to see that. Oi, get a room you two." Sam grumbles, disgruntled at watching me sucking faces with his baby sister. I flip him off as I continue to kiss her hungrily while we dance together.

WE LANDED in Amsterdam an hour later. Once we settle into our hotel rooms, we hire tandem bikes and cycle through the city together—which wasn't easy to do while tipsy. Sam and Jo fell off twice, and it was rather amusing watching Jo scold him. He's like six feet four and built like a tank, while she's five feet two and petite. Such a miss-match, but she seems to keep him under control. After our bike rides, we walk through the city and visit the Anne Frank museum, where Shayla spent a good forty-minutes sobbing.

"Honey, come on, please stop crying." I urge, wiping her tears away while she sniffles and hiccups adorably.

"It's just so sad." She whimpers, and I wrap my arms around her tighter. "I read the book but seeing it just…" She sobs again. I smile and brush her hair away from her face and kiss her forehead.

"Look, baby, do you want a cinnamon pretzel?" I ask, trying to distract her, and she nods as we walk to the stand. I hand her the pretzel, and she eats it as we walk along the river.

"Dude, what was that?" Josh asks, referring to Shayla's emotional outburst. I smile and shake my head.

"Hormones bro. She's like a bloody yoyo. One minute she's happy, and the next she's crying her eyes out." I explain, glancing at her laughing along with the girls like she wasn't just sobbing seconds ago. "I've noticed she likes to eat, so whenever she gets upset, I give her food, and she's happy again," I add with a shrug, and Josh cracks up laughing.

"Aw, but that's cute, though. How do you feel about the whole baby thing?" He questions, taking a sip of his coffee.

I sigh and bite my lip. "I'm excited man. I felt the baby kick for the first time last night, and it was just the best feeling in the world. Watching the girl, you love, carry, and nurture your baby inside of her is just so magical—despite all the hormones." I tell him, and Josh smiles, nodding.

"I'm thrilled for you, bro. I can't wait to settle down and have a baby." Josh confesses, looking over at Aimee. I follow his gaze and smile fondly.

"How are things with you two?" Josh nods, biting his lip.

"We're beyond happy. Aimee is unlike anyone I've ever met. She's fierce and passionate about everything she does, and I love that about her. She keeps me on my toes, that's for sure." He chuckles, looking over at her. "Do you ever wonder where we would have been right now if that night you met Shayla, you went over to Aimee instead, and I went for Shayla like we were supposed to?"

I frown and try to picture myself with Aimee and shake my head. "Nah. I can't imagine that. I honestly can't imagine my life without Shayla or how I ever lived without knowing her."

Josh chuckles and shakes his head. "I think we both ended up where we were supposed to be. Shayla's like a sister to me now. It's weird to think that I was attracted to her once."

I smirk, "Yeah, let's not open up that can of worms again. I'm just thankful everything worked out for us in the end." I utter with a grimace, and Josh nudges my shoulder, nodding.

I didn't even want to picture my life without Shayla in it. She's my whole world wrapped up in a beautiful five-foot-six package.

CHAPTER 2

Shayla

"OH, HELL YES," I moan as I pick up my caramel latte from the coffee machine. I bring the cup of delicious coffee to my lips, just as I'm about to take a sip, it gets taken out of my hand, "Hey, I was about to drink that," I complain and lift my gaze to my sexy husband who was scowling at me.

"No caffeine while you are pregnant." He scolds me, and I sulk, looking at him.

"But—"

"Ah!" Cole cuts me off, holding up a finger silencing me. "Herbal tea," He says, handing me a hot mug of steaming crap. I look at the tea and back at him.

"What the hell is this?" I question, and Cole smirks.

"Decaffeinated tea. It's camomile, it's relaxing." He expresses and I stare at him blankly.

"Honey, if I wanted to relax, I wouldn't have gotten out of bed. I got the coffee because I need to wake up." I argue, and Cole shrugs. He sips my latte and moans in delight.

"Mm, this is so good." Cole smiles lovingly and leans in close to my face. "Drink your tea." He whispers and kisses my nose.

"Fine, when I fall asleep in the meeting, you've got no one else to blame but yourself," I mutter bitterly and stalk off toward my office while Cole laughs, shaking his head.

"I love you."

"Bite me!" I grunt, sulking.

"Just say where baby!" I hear him call out after me, and I look back at him, sipping my delicious latte, while he watches me with a sexy grin on his face. God, I love him. I take a sip of the tea, and my stomach lurches unpleasantly. I run out of my office toward the bathroom, where I empty the breakfast I had earlier.

"Sweetheart, you okay?" I hear Cole's voice behind the door, and I sigh.

"Yes. The baby and I agree—we hate the tea." I hear him chuckle as I wash my hands and rinse out my mouth. I open the door and see him leaning against the wall. Cole pulls me into his arms and kisses my forehead.

"I'll get them to look into some caffeine-free coffee that's safe to drink while you're pregnant. How's that sound?" I close my eyes and sigh.

"Anything is better than that tea," I mutter with a shudder, and Cole chortles.

"Okay, anything to keep my baby and my little apple happy." He coo's rubbing my stomach. I smile and gaze up into his eyes.

"All we need to be happy is you, baby," I assure him, and he grins before he kisses me softly.

"You've got me forever, sweetheart." He whispers, parting my lips and kissing me slow and deep in the middle of our office while our employees watch us. We pull apart when they all hoot and whistle. I blush furiously and bury my face into Cole's chest, who laughs. "All right, shows over, back to work you lot." He scolds them off before he pulls me toward the conference room for our meeting. We spent over an hour reviewing the in's and out's of this new project with a client who didn't seem to have a clue what he wanted. I had to stop myself from laughing at the expression on Cole's face when the client was explaining what he was looking for.

"All right. I've got all the notes of what you're looking for. I'll work on the design and come back to you in a few weeks?" Cole tells him, and the client nods with a satisfied smile. We shake his hand, and he leaves the conference room. Cole looks at me somewhat bemused, and I giggle.

"You don't have the slightest clue what he was asking for, do you?" I ask, and he shakes his head while scratching his chin.

"Not a clue." He sighs, shaking his head. "He was just fucking waffling the whole time. We will figure something out, though." Cole assures with a shrug, and I smile, nodding.

"That we will, honey." I check the time on my watch and get up. "Oh, I gotta go. I've got a call with my lecturer." I utter and walk out of the conference room back to my office. I was so excited to be back at University to finish my degree. Cole was super supportive and helping me, though he wasn't pleased that I was taking on so much work while pregnant. It was a little tiring, but it's so going to be worth it when I graduate and finally get my degree in a couple of months.

~

A FEW WEEKS GO BY, and it was time for us to find out the sex of our baby. We did discuss letting it be a surprise, but I was too impatient to wait and wanted to find out, and so was Cole.

"How are we feeling, mama?" My midwife asks when I lay down on the bed.

"I'm terrific. Other than my hands and feet swelling, I'm feeling great." I tell her, and she smiles, nodding.

"That's completely normal. Just try and keep your feet elevated and avoid wearing heels." My midwife informed me, and Cole nods, pointing to his ears, indicating that I should listen to her advice. "Are we finding out the sex today?"

"Yes." We both say together, and she grins, pressing the receiver to my stomach. Cole takes my hand and looks at the screen when our baby comes up.

"Okay, I'm just going to do a couple of checks to make sure everything is okay with the baby." I nod and look at Cole, who was staring at the screen in awe. "We're growing nicely. The water looks good. Your baby is now the size of a small banana." I grin, and Cole chuckles, biting his lip. "Okay, let's see if the baby will give us a peek." She says, shaking my stomach a little, and the baby jumps and kicks. "Oh, we got a feisty one."

"Just like it's mother," Cole teases. I slap his arm playfully, and he laughs, kissing my temple.

"Well, guys, say hello to your baby girl."

"Yes!" Cole exclaims excitedly, and the midwife and I jump, startled at his sudden outburst. I look up at Cole, and he kisses me. "I'm so friggin happy."

The midwife laughs, "Well, we can see Daddy is pleased. How about you Mummy?" I nod and look at the screen, my eyes welling up.

"I'm thrilled," I cry, and Cole looks at me with his green eyes wide.

"Oh no, no, not the tears again. Do you have any food?" He asks the midwife, who frowns, looking at him bemused. "It's the only way to stop her from crying." He whispers and hisses when I elbow him in the ribs. "Ow. What? It is."

I scowl up at him. My eyes narrowed, "Is that why you keep feeding me?" I question, affronted, and Cole shrugs sheepishly.

The midwife laughs, shaking her head amused. "You two are adorable. It's completely normal for her to get emotional from time to time; her body is going through many changes every day. You have one job, Daddy, keep the Mummy happy, so baby is happy."

Cole sighs and smiles devotedly at me. "I'll do whatever it takes to keep my girls happy." He whispers, kissing me softly on the lips and wiping away my tears. The midwife gives us a video of the ultrasound and a couple of photos to take with us.

"Have you thought about any names?" Cole asks me as we get into the car. I shrug, pulling my seatbelt on.

"I have a couple ideas. What about you?"

Cole nods, grinning as he backs up out of the parking spot. "I have a few."

"Let's hear it then."

"Well, I like the name, Sienna."

"Sienna Hoult." I nod, grinning but frown suddenly. "Wait, is that a name of an ex or…"

Cole laughs, "No. I just like the name. Let's hear yours."

"Alaia is at the top of my list," I voice, and he grins.

"Alaia Hoult. That's perfect, baby. I love it." He beams, taking my hand and kissing my knuckles.

"You do?" He nods, biting his lip excitedly.

"Yeah, it's such a beautiful name. Alaia."

"Actually, I thought we could give her a middle name. Alaia Mae Hoult." Cole repeats the name, smiling.

"Alaia Mae Hoult, get your butt down here." He says with a frown and then laughs. "I like it. You have to try it out when you're full naming her for when she's in trouble." I laugh and squeeze his cheek.

"You're so cute. All though, I think she's going to have you wrapped around her little finger, my love." I grin, and he nods, licking his lips.

"Damn right she will, especially if she comes out looking like a miniature version of you." He grins, giving me a side stare as he drives. "My beautiful queen and my mini princess."

~

Cole and I went to get something to eat before we went home. I'm currently sprawled out on the sofa, reading a book, while he was on the phone to someone in the Miami office. I can see him pacing back and forth in his office, looking irritated. Twenty minutes later, he came over to me and flops down on the sofa with a heavy sigh. "What's going on, baby?" I ask, putting my book down. Cole opens his eyes and looks at me tiredly.

"I'm leaving for Miami in an hour." He tells me, and I sit up with a frown.

"What? Why?" I question sullenly, and he lifts his head, rubbing my thigh.

"There's a major fuck up with that project for the new airport. The client is fuming and wants to meet tomorrow morning." He explains, brushing his fingers through his tousled hair.

"How long will you be gone for?"

Cole sighs, looking at me. "A couple of days. It shouldn't take much longer than that, baby. Do you want to come with me?" He asks, taking his hand into mine, and I sigh heavily, shaking my head.

"I wish I could, but I have that meeting with the Bryson twins for their swanky new club tomorrow afternoon," I remind him, and he nods with a groan and pulls me to him, so I was straddling him. "Can't you send someone else?"

"No. It's a two-billion-dollar project. I have to go and calm the client down before he pulls the plug on it and gives it someone else." He explains, placing his hands at my hips.

"Well, it's only a couple days, baby. It will give us time to miss each other a little." I say with a teasing smile, and he presses his forehead to mine with a pout.

"Are you sick of me already?"

I cup his face with my hands and look into his eyes. "Sick of you? Are you kidding? It's not possible to be sick of you with all the tricks you can do with that tongue of yours." I tell him with a smirk, and his lips curl into a smug grin while he looks at me,

"Careful now, I might start to think I'm only good for one thing." He murmurs, nuzzling his nose over mine.

"Two things," I whisper, grinning. "You're good with your dick too." I correct him, and he laughs deeply. "Why do you think I married you twice? Good dick is difficult to come by nowadays." I tease him and gasp when he lifts me and lays me down on my back on the sofa while he crawls up over me.

"So is good pussy," He breathes, staring into my eye raveningly. "Looks like we're both privileged in that particular department." He tells me austerely, his emerald green eyes gleaming.

"I believe we are." I kiss him softly while I snake my arms around his neck. "We can use this time apart to do all the fun stuff that we missed out on doing. We skipped the whole dating part of our relationship."

Cole looks at me with a frown. "Elaborate."

I grin and kiss along his jaw, "Well, we can have phone sex…" I whisper in his ear, and he moans. "I can tell you all the things I will do to you when you get back home." Cole squeezes my hips a little and rocks his hips up against me. "I can send you some racy pictures of myself, and you can send me a dick pic."

Cole laughs wholeheartedly, "I have never sent a dick pic to anyone, baby." I bite my lip, smiling impishly.

"Well, here's your chance, stud." Cole chuckles and pulls my mouth to his kissing me ardently. We've not been apart since we got married, so sending him off was hard. I've gotten so used to having him around, and I had this niggling feeling in the pit of my stomach. Cole wraps his arms around me and pulls me against him. "You call me as soon as you get there, okay. I don't care what time it is." I say, peering up at him, and he nods, pressing his forehead to mine.

"I will, I promise." He replies, cupping my face in his hands and kissing me slowly and deliberately as if he was trying to carve every inch of my mouth into his brain. "I love you, baby. I'll see you in a few days. If you need anything while I'm away, you call Josh, understand?"

I nod, "I love you so much. Finish up and hurry back home to me." I wrap my arms around his neck, and he hugs me tightly. "I wish you didn't have to go." I sigh, and he squeezes me and buries his face into my neck.

"Me too, but I'm going to be back home with you and our princess very soon." He assures me, and I nod, pulling back. Cole kneels in front of me; he places his hands on my belly and presses his lips to it, closing his eyes. "Take care of your Mummy for me, okay, princess. Daddy will be back before you know it. I love you, baby girl." I watch him with a pout, and he smiles lovingly at me as he stands and kisses me one last time before he walks out. I sigh and watch him open the car door. Cole looks at me and smiles handsomely; he kisses his fingers and places them over his heart. I smile and do the same back to him, and he winks before he gets into the car, and they drive away.

I close the door and lean against it with a sigh. I look down at my stomach and press my hand against my bump. "Looks like it's just the two of us for a couple of days baby girl." I sigh sullenly and smile when I feel her kick.

I COULDN'T SLEEP the first night without Cole next to me. I missed him terribly, so I hugged his pillow and waited for him to call me. It was a nine-hour flight to Miami; he should have landed by now. It was gone past three in the morning in London. I jump when I hear my phone ring and answer it in a flurry. "Cole?"

"Hi baby." I sigh when I hear his voice. "I just got to the hotel. Please tell me you haven't stayed up all night waiting."

"I couldn't sleep without you," I tell him, and I hear him sigh on the other end. "I got worried when you didn't call."

"I'm sorry, I wanted to call you as soon as I landed, but my phone signal is playing up over here." He explains, shuffling around. "You should get some sleep, honey."

I shake my head. "The house is so empty, and our bed is cold without you," I say, getting all emotional again. "I really miss you."

Cole heaves a sigh. "Oh, baby, I miss you too, so much. Please don't cry. I'm going to be back in two days, okay." I nod, biting my lip. "Let me see that gorgeous face." I pull the phone back when it beeps, alerting me that he was requesting a video call. I accept and wait for it to connect. I smile when I see his handsome face appear on my screen. He grins sexily, "There's my baby."

"Hey stud." I sigh, laying down on the bed. We spoke for a couple of hours—he even let me watch him shower. "Hey, the camera is steaming up. I can't see anything." I giggle as he steps out of the shower, dripping wet, and wipes the lens so I could see clearer.

"Better?" He laughs, running back to the shower again.

"No, better would have been me being in that shower with you,"

"You're telling me. I can't wait to come back home." After his shower, we both lay in bed and spoke until my eyes grew heavy, and I finally fell asleep hugging his pillow. The following day just creeps on and on, especially without him around the office. Every hour that passed by, I missed him more and more and was getting anxious for him to come back home—we facetime at lunch. I fill him in on my meeting with the twins, and he listens to me while eating his salad. I told him I was feeling lonely in that big house by myself, and he suggested I get the girls to stay over till he comes back home the next day.

I called them, and they kindly agreed to keep me company while he was away. "Bish, I haven't the scoobiest idea what I'm doing here, by the way," Aimee says, whisking the batter for the cake we were attempting to make.

I frown, looking at the recipe on the tablet. "Is it creamy?" I ask her, and she shrugs diffidently.

"If by creamy you mean lumpy, then yes, it's creamy." I chuckle and lean over, looking at the lumpy mess she's made of the batter.

"Aimee, you had one job. Cream the butter and sugar. How did you fuck it up?" Jo scolds her while looking into the bowl.

Aimee looks at her with an arched brow. "All right, Betty fucking Crocker, you do it then!" I shake my head, laughing at the two while they bicker. "What are you laughing at?" She chuckles, throwing flour in my face. I cough and sputter waving my hand in front of my face to clear the flour cloud. Aimee and Jo both laugh as I glare at them with a face covered in flour.

"Oh, it's on now." I grab a handful of flour and throw it at them, which then turns into a full-on food fight in the middle of my kitchen. We were all covered in flour, eggs, and batter. I rush over and answer my phone when Cole calls me. The look on his face when he saw the state of me was priceless.

"Jesus, what the hell happened to you?" He chuckles as the girls and I laugh.

"We're baking a cake for you," I tell him, wiping the flour out of my eyes and he laughs out loud.

"Honey, the ingredients go in a bowl, you know that, right?"

"Blame Aimee; she started it by cocking up the batter." I tease, and she throws more flour in my face.

"Here, eat that!" Aimee cackles wickedly.

Cole watches me with a grin while I slap Aimee's bum. "I just wanted to call to say good night, baby. Have fun with the girls. I'll be back home tomorrow afternoon, okay. I love you."

I smile and nod. "I can't wait. I love you, too." He blows me a kiss before he hangs up. I sigh and stare at the phone sadly.

"Bish, you okay?" Jo asks when she notices the gloomy look on my face.

I nod and force myself to smile, "Yeah, I just really miss him." I reply and try to shake off this uneasy feeling that was making my chest feel all tight. After we clean up, the girls and I snuggle up in my bed, and we watch a movie till we fell asleep.

The next day I woke up feeling excited. My baby would be home in a few hours. After breakfast, I had a shower and got dressed, waiting for Cole to come home. I was counting down the minutes.

He didn't come home. It was gone past six in the evening; he was supposed to be home hours ago.

"Shayla, why don't you sit down, babe? You're burning a hole through the floor?" Aimee sighs, watching me pace frantically while redialing Cole's number for the two hundredth time.

"He should have been home by now. Where is he?" I snap irritably as I pace restlessly.

"Shayla, maybe his flight got delayed," Jo suggests, walking over to me and I shake my head.

"Then why hasn't he called me?!" I shout and sigh, closing my eyes. "He knows I would worry. Something's wrong. I can feel it." I whisper. My chest was getting tighter, making it difficult to breathe.

"Shayla, don't say that. He's going to walk through that door any minute, babe." Aimee tries to reassure me, and I shake my head.

"I've had this horrible feeling in the pit of my stomach since he told me he was leaving. It just didn't feel right, and it's getting worse. Something is wrong." I cry, and Aimee wraps her arms around me.

"Shay, calm down, babe, you're pregnant. All this stress isn't good for you or the baby." She tells me, and I gasp when the door-bell rings. I pull away from Aimee's hold and run to the door. I pull it open, hoping to see Cole standing there, but it wasn't—it was Josh. He stood there staring at me, his blue eyes rimmed red, full of despair as he looks at me.

"Shayla..." Josh whispers, his voice breaking, and I shake my head.

"Josh, no."

"I'm so sorry," Josh mutters, taking hold of my upper arms. "Cole's plane has crashed…"

Thank you for reading.

Love Me Again is available on Kindle

ABOUT THE AUTHOR

Shayla Hart is a UK based romance novel writer. She was born and raised in London. Shayla discovered her love for writing late in her 20's when she wrote her first book When Love & Hate Collide which she wrote in 2009. Since then, writing has become a passion and it shows in her work, she's excellent at drawing you into a story and making you feel all the emotions the characters are feeling.

If you love a good romance novel that will give you all the feels, she's the author for you.

Follow her on her social media platforms to get to know Shayla better.

ALSO BY SHAYLA HART

Love Me Again (The Sequel)

An Assassins Oath

Cuffed By Love - Coming Soon

Printed in Great Britain
by Amazon

60365147R00305